SURRENDER
to
DESTINY

SURRENDER
to
DESTINY

THREE ROMANTIC ADVENTURES
FROM THE WAR OF 1812

MaryLu Tyndall

BARBOUR
PUBLISHING

Print ISBN 978-1-62416-756-0

eBook Editions:
Adobe Digital Edition (.epub) 978-1-63058-059-9
Kindle and MobiPocket Edition (.prc) 978-1-63058-060-5

Published by Barbour Publishing, Inc., P.O. Box 719, Uhrichsville, Ohio 44683, www.barbourbooks.com

Our mission is to publish and distribute inspirational products offering exceptional value and biblical encouragement to the masses.

ecpa Member of the
Evangelical Christian
Publishers Association

Printed in the United States of America.

Surrender the Heart

❖ CHAPTER 1 ❖

June 18, 1812
Baltimore, Maryland

I would rather boil in oil than marry Noah Brenin." Marianne tossed the silver brooch onto her vanity.

"Hold your breath and stay still," her friend Rose said from behind her. "Besides, it is only an engagement party, not a wedding."

"But it is one more step to that horrid destination." Marianne sucked in her breath as Rose threaded the laces through the eyelets on her stays. "Why must women wear these contraptions?"

"To look our best for the gentlemen in our lives." Cassandra appeared on Marianne's left, a lacy petticoat flung over one arm. With shimmering auburn hair and eyes the color of emeralds, Marianne's other friend, Cassandra, had no trouble looking her best for anyone.

Marianne huffed. "I don't care what any gentleman thinks of my appearance."

"Which is why you are still unmarried at five and twenty."

"Then what is your excuse at three and twenty?" Marianne arched a brow, to which Cassandra gave a shrug. "I have not yet met a man worthy of me." She grinned.

"Where on earth is your chambermaid?" Rose grunted as she squeezed Marianne's rounded figure into the stays and tied the final lace tight. "Shouldn't she be doing this?"

"I dismissed her." Marianne waved a hand through the air. "I prefer

7

to dress myself." She hoped they didn't hear the slight quaver in her voice. She didn't want her friends to know that her mother had been forced to let the entire staff go and the ones here today were hired just for her betrothal party.

"There." Rose finished fastening the corset and stepped back.

Marianne took the petticoat from Cassandra and slipped it over her head. "Truth is, I do not wish to marry—ever." She squared her shoulders as Cassandra slid behind her and latched the petticoat hooks.

Rose put her hands on her waist. "Noah Brenin is a fine man and a good catch."

Marianne gazed at her friend. She couldn't help but smile at the motherly reprimand burning in her crystal blue eyes. Tall and slender, with honey-blond hair, Rose turned many a head in Baltimore. Just like Cassandra.

Marianne wished she had the same effect on men.

"He is a boor."

"Why so low an opinion of him? Haven't you and he been friends since childhood?" Rose cocked her head and gave Marianne a look of censure.

"I wouldn't call it friendship, more like forced acquaintance. And my knowledge of him is precisely why I know him for the churlish clod he is."

Gathering a cream-colored silk-embroidered gown from Marianne's bed, Rose and Cassandra tossed it over her head, assisting her as she wiggled into it. She adjusted the ruffled lace that bordered her neckline and circled her puffy sleeves. Cassandra handed her a jeweled belt, which Marianne strapped around her high waist and buckled in front. She pressed down the folds of her gown, admiring the pink lace that trailed down the front and trimmed the hemline. After slipping on her white satin slippers, Marianne moved to the full-length looking glass and paused to eye her reflection.

Plain. Despite the shimmering, glamorous dress, *plain* was the first word that came to her mind. That was how she had always been described. Brown hair, brown eyes, average height, a bit plump. Nothing remarkable, nothing to catch an eye.

Simply plain.

Which was precisely why, when the other girls her age were being courted, Marianne had chosen to spend her time caring for her ailing mother and younger sister, particularly after their father died. No whirlwind romances, no soirees, no grand adventures lit up the horizon for her. She had resigned herself to lead an ordinary life. An ordinary life for an ordinary girl.

"Come now, it won't be so bad." Rose brushed a lock of hair from Marianne's forehead and then straightened one of the curls dangling about her neck. "You look as though you were attending your own funeral."

"I daresay I feel as though I am." Tired of staring into the mirror hoping her reflection would transform into that of a beautiful woman, Marianne turned aside, picked up her silk gloves from the vanity, and sauntered toward the window.

"I, for one, cannot wait to get married," Rose said. "To the right man of course. He must be a good, honest, God-fearing man. A man who stays home, not a seaman. And he must be agreeable in all respects."

"What about handsome?" Cassandra asked. Marianne turned to see a blush creep up Rose's neck.

"Well, yes, I suppose I would not be opposed to that." Her blue eyes twinkled.

Facing the window, Marianne slid the white gloves onto her hands and tugged them up her arms. Shouts echoed from the street below, accompanied by the *clip-clop* of horse hooves and the grating of carriage wheels. She brushed aside the curtain to see people running to and fro darting between phaetons and wagons. A warm breeze, heavy with moisture and the smells of the sea, stirred the curtains. A bell rang in the distance, drawing Marianne's attention to the maze of ships' masts that thrust into the sky like iron bars of a prison. A prison that could not constrain the ravenous indigo waters from feeding upon the innocent—an innocent like her father.

Rose and Cassandra joined her at the window as more shouts blasted in with the wind. "What is all the commotion about?" Cassandra drew back the curtains.

"There have been rumors that President Madison will soon declare war on Britain," Marianne said.

"I hope it doesn't come to that." Rose peered over Marianne's shoulder. "War is such horrid business."

"But necessary if the British insist on stealing our men from land and sea and impressing them into their navy." Marianne said. "Not to mention how they rouse the Indians to attack us on the frontier."

"They want their colonies back, I suppose." Afternoon sunlight set Cassandra's red hair aflame in ribbons of liquid fire. "England never was good at losing."

"Well, they can't have them." Marianne's voice rose with a determination she felt building within. Though she'd been born after the Revolution, she had heard the stories of oppression and tyranny enforced upon America by a nation across the seas whose king thought he had the right to dictate laws and taxes without giving the people a voice. But no more. "We won our freedom from them. We are a nation now. A new nation that represents liberty to the entire world."

"I couldn't agree more." Cassandra nodded with a smile. "Perhaps you should run for mayor?"

"A woman in public office?" Marianne chuckled. "That will never happen."

The door creaked open, and Marianne turned to see her mother and younger sister slip inside.

Lizzie's eyes widened and she rushed toward Marianne. "You look so beautiful, Marianne!"

Kneeling, Marianne embraced her sister. She held her tight and took a big whiff of the lavender soap with which their mother always scrubbed the little girl. "Thank you, Lizzie. I can always count on you for a compliment."

"Now, Lizzie, don't wrinkle your sister's dress." Marianne's mother sank into one of the chairs by the fireplace and winced. The slight reminder of her mother's pain caused Marianne's heart to shrink. She squeezed her little sister again—the one beacon of joy in their house these past three years since Father died—and kissed her on the cheek. "You look very beautiful, too."

The little girl clutched her skirt and twirled around. "Do you really think so?" She drew her lips into a pout. "But when can I wear a dress like yours?"

"Come now, Lizzie," Mother said. "You are only six. When you are a grown woman like Marianne, you may wear more elaborate gowns." She gestured toward Rose and Cassandra. "Ladies, would you take Lizzie downstairs for a moment? I need a word with Marianne."

"Of course, Mrs. Denton." Rose took Lizzie's hand. "Come along, little one."

Cassandra followed after them, closing the door when she left.

Marianne sat in the chair beside her mother and gently grasped her hands. She flinched at how cold and moist they were. "How are you feeling, Mama?"

"Very well today, dear." She looked down as if hiding something.

But Marianne didn't need to look in her mother's eyes to know she was lying. The sprinkles of perspiration on her forehead, the paleness of her skin, and the tightening of her lips when the pains hit, spoke more clearly than any words.

Marianne squeezed her mother's hands. "The medicines are not working?"

"They will work. It takes time." Her mother attempted a smile. "But let us not talk of that now. I have something more important to discuss with you." She released a heavy sigh then lifted her gaze to Marianne's. Though illness had stolen the glimmer from her eyes, it could not hide the sweet kindness of her soul. "You don't have to do this, you know."

The truth of her words sliced through Marianne. She stared at the floral pattern woven into the carpet. "You know I do."

"It isn't fair of me to ask this of you." Her mother's voice rang with conviction and deep sorrow.

"You didn't ask, Mama. I want to do this." A truth followed by a lie. Marianne hoped the good canceled out the bad.

"Come now. You cannot fool me." Mama said. "I know this is not the match you would choose."

Releasing her mother's hands, Marianne rose from the chair and moved toward the window. The rustle of her gown joined the sounds of the city filtering in from outside. "In truth, I would choose no match ever." She turned and forced a smile. "So if I must marry, why not this man?"

Her mother gazed at her with such love and sorrow that Marianne felt her heart would burst. Once considered the most beautiful woman in Baltimore, Jane Denton, now withered away with sickness that robbed her of her glow and luster and stole the fat from her bones, leaving her but a frail skeleton of what she once had been. The physicians had no idea what ailed her; they only knew that without the medications they administered, she would die a quicker and more painful death.

Tearing her gaze from the tragic vision, Marianne glanced out the window where it seemed as though the approaching evening only heightened the citizens' agitation over the possibility of impending war. "Marrying Noah Brenin will save us. It will save you."

"But what of saving you?" Her mother's sweet plea caressed Marianne's ears, but she forced down the spark of hope that dared to rise at her mother's question. There was no room for hope now, only necessity.

"You know if we continue as is, all that is left of our fortune will be spent in one year on your prescriptions. Then what will we do? Without my dowry, no man will look my way, since that and our good name is all that has caught this particular fish upon the hook." And without a husband to unlock her inheritance, her father had ensured that the seven thousand dollars would remain as far from her reach as if she did not own it at all.

"Perhaps you will meet another man—someone you love?" her mother said.

"Mama, I am five and twenty." Marianne turned and waved her hands over herself. "And plain to look at." She gave a bitter laugh. "Do you see suitors lining up at our door?"

"You are too beautiful for words, dearest." Her mother's eyes beamed in adoration. "You just don't know it yet."

Shrugging off her mother's compliment, Marianne stiffened her back before she attempted to rekindle an argument long since put to death. "We could take what's left of our money and fund a privateer, Mama." Marianne glanced out the window at a mob that had formed down the street. "War is certain and our fledgling navy will need all the help it can get."

Her mother's nervous huff drew Marianne's gaze. "It is far too much of a gamble. And gambling destroys lives"—a glaze covered her mother's eyes as she turned from the window and stared, unseeing, into the room—"and families."

Marianne grimaced. "This is nothing like what Papa did. I have heard these privateers can make a fortune while helping to defend our country."

A breeze stirred a curled wisp of her mother's hair as she gazed at Marianne with concern.

Marianne twisted the ring on her finger. "Down at the docks, mer-chantmen are already outfitting their ships as privateers. The call for investors goes out daily." If only she could convince her mother, not only would Marianne not have to marry that clod, Noah, but also she could do something to help this great nation of hers.

Her mother's boney hands, perched in her lap, began to tremble. "We could lose everything. And what of Lizzie? I could not bear it."

Shame drummed upon Marianne's hopes. She had upset her mother when the doctor strictly instructed her to keep her calm.

"Perhaps you could take up a trade of some sort?" Mama offered. "I hear that Mrs. Pickersgill makes a decent living sewing ensigns."

A blast of warm wind stirred the gauzy curtains and cooled the perspiration forming on Marianne's neck. "Mama you know I have no skills. I'm not like other ladies. The last gown I attempted to sew fell apart. My cooking would drive the hardiest frontiersman back to the woods, and the pianoforte runs when it sees me coming."

Mother chuckled. "You exaggerate, dearest."

But Marianne could tell by the look in her mother's eyes that despite the humorous delivery, her words rang true. Though a governess and her mother had strived to teach Marianne the skills every proper lady should acquire, she had found them nothing but tedious. She possessed no useful skills, no talents. As her father had so often declared before his death. Marianne had nothing to offer. If her mother would not agree to fund a privateer, Marianne would have to accept her fate in marriage.

"I must ensure you and Lizzie are cared for either by this marriage or by some other means." Mama said with a sigh. "I'm an old woman and will die soon anyway."

Marianne's heart sank at the words. Gathering her skirts, she dashed toward her mother and knelt at her feet. "You must never say such a thing."

"Do not soil your beautiful gown." Her mother smiled and wiped a tear from Marianne's cheek. "Perhaps we should simply trust God with my health and let His will prevail."

Marianne laid her head on her mother's lap like she used to do as a child. She had trusted her father, she had trusted God.

And they had both let her down—her and her mother.

"I will not let you die, Mother. I cannot." Her eyes burned with tears. "As long as I have my inheritance and a man who is willing to marry me, I promise you will be well cared for. And Lizzie, too. That is all that matters now." Marianne lifted her gaze to her mother's, feeling strength surge through her.

"And mark my words, Mama. Nothing will stand in my way. Especially not Noah Brenin."

❖ CHAPTER 2 ❖

Noah Brenin doffed his hat and wiped the sweat from his brow as he made his way down Hanover Street. He adjusted the purple ostrich plume attached to his bicorn. His first mate, Luke Heaton, walked beside him, nodding a greeting to every pretty lady who passed by. Plopping his hat back atop his head, Noah forced his feet to continue. He was late and he should hurry his pace, yet all he wanted to do was turn around and go back to his ship. He had work to do and no time for his father's absurd commitments. Not to mention he had been dreading the announcement of his engagement to Miss Denton ever since he'd agreed to the match several months ago.

Now that the night was upon him, he truly wondered what he'd been thinking. Miss Marianne Denton? Had he gone mad?

"You look more nervous than if we were caught in the sights of a broadside." Luke chuckled, but Noah offered no response. He found nothing humorous about the situation. They turned down Conway Street, trying to avoid the people and carriages crowding the narrow avenue. A blast of muggy June wind struck him as if an oven had been opened. Sweat slid down his back.

A man in top hat and coat stood on the corner handing out pamphlets and shouting, "War is coming. Join the militia!"

Skirting him while holding up a hand to ward off the pamphlet being thrust into his hand, Noah plodded onward.

"It appears war will indeed be upon us," Luke said.

"What is that to me? I don't care unless it interferes with my trade."

"I daresay, where is your patriotism, man?" Luke applied his most pompous tone to a statement devoid of enthusiasm.

An absence of which, Noah shared. "Where yours is. In the lining of my pockets." Noah grinned and halted to allow a horse and rider to pass before he crossed the street. A hot breeze wafted the smell of manure his way as if the city were unhappy with his diminutive allegiance. But who could blame him? England had always been good to Noah. His trade with Great Britain had enabled him to keep his father's merchant business afloat. Why would he wish to go to war against the nation that fed him?

Noah hesitated before a large brick house. Music and laughter bubbled from the windows, grating over his nerves. He steeled himself against another overwhelming desire to turn and bolt for his ship.

Luke studied him, a curious look on his face. "Scads, Noah, Miss Denton cannot be all that bad."

"Humph, you think not? She is a spoiled, silly girl. Let's get this over with. I want to set sail tonight."

"Aye, aye, Captain." Luke grinned as they took the few steps up to a wide front porch and rapped the front door's brass knocker.

A servant answered, took their names along with their hats, and escorted them inside to a parlor brimming with people. The smell of myriad perfumes mixed with the scent of wine tickled Noah's nose. He sneezed then scanned the room, searching for his father so they could proceed as soon as possible. To his left, a large mantel of polished black marble perched proudly against the wall. Around it stood a group of men—none of them his father—involved in a heated argument. From the few words that drifted his way, Noah surmised their conversation centered on the potential war. A serpentine serving table laden with sweet cakes, lemonade, and wine stretched nearly the entire length of the room. Around it hovered several guests, pecking and nibbling at the food like a flock of birds. Walnut wing-backed armchairs, along with two mahogany settees, provided the only seating—all taken by elderly women, their heads leaning together in gossip.

"Mr. Noah Brenin," the butler announced. "And Mr. Luke Heaton."

All eyes turned to the two men, and some of the women whispered to each other behind fans. How Noah hated being on display.

"It is about time." Staring at a pocket watch in his hand, Noah's father's portly frame emerged from a crowd on Noah's right. The scowl on his face made him look much older than his sixty-two years.

Luke murmured a hasty excuse and headed toward the buffet, leaving Noah to deal with his father's foul mood alone. "We were delayed with business aboard the ship," Noah said, hoping to belay the man's usual rebuke.

The frown on his father's face did not falter—a frown Noah had grown accustomed to over the years. His mother sashayed forward, a glass of wine in her hand. "Do not argue please, William. It is our son's engagement." The sting of alcohol from his mother's breath filled the air between them, and Noah cringed, hoping she would not embarrass him tonight.

Then, as if she saw him for the first time, his mother gasped. "What are you wearing? What of the dark silk suit Matton laid out for you in your chamber?" She eyed him up and down and clucked her tongue. "What will everyone think?"

"I haven't a care what they think, Mother." He glanced down at his tan breeches and black waistcoat and saw nothing wrong with his attire. At least he had donned an overcoat and a clean shirt. "I had no time to return home. I have been working all day, preparing the ship to sail. I must leave forthwith."

"Tonight? Why the rush?" His father's forehead wrinkled.

"I must sail my cargo to England as soon as possible before our trade is further restricted. Mr. Glover expects me in South Hampton in six weeks' time or he threatened to purchase his flour, rice, and iron from another merchant." Noah studied his father, searching for some sign of approval of his plan. "With all this talk of war, I dare not delay another day."

"Very well, by all means, leave as soon as you can." His father straightened his coat. "But I do not think it will come to war. We could never hope to win against a nation as powerful as England again. Madison knows that all too well."

"I am not so sure."

"Nonsense." His father chuckled. "What do you know of it, boy?"

At the word *boy*—the only endearment with which his father addressed him—Noah felt as though he were shrinking in size. At six and twenty he was hardly a boy anymore. Hadn't he proved that by now?

His mother sipped her wine and gazed over the crowd as if bored with the conversation.

"It was the American embargo that caused us the most damage." Noah shifted his stance as anger boiled within him at yet another circumstance that threatened his success. "Blasted Jefferson. Now with the threat of war, how do they expect us merchants to survive?"

"Ah, let us not trouble ourselves with it." His father leaned toward him as if sharing a grand secret. "Soon we will not have to worry overmuch." He leaned in and lowered his voice. "Miss Denton's inheritance will assure our merchant business stays afloat until all this trouble with England has blown over." He stretched his shoulders back. "That is, if you don't muck up the opportunity it presents, boy, to make the Brenin name successful and well known. You know your mother and I are depending on you."

Yes, Noah knew that all too well—was reminded of it often. "There is not much I can do if war is declared."

"War, indeed. Bunch of rubbish, if you ask me."

But Noah knew better. He had heard the talk down by the docks. The merchantmen were furious at Britain's impressments of American sailors into their navy, not to mention the trade restrictions. In fact, he knew several merchants who were already refitting their ships to be privateers. But he held his tongue. He had no time nor interest in another argument with his father.

Luke joined them, drink in hand and stuffing a piece of cake into his mouth. "You should try one of these. They are excellent."

Noah's mother finished her wine and gave Luke a lift of her nose. "William, please escort me to refill my glass." She stumbled slightly, and Noah closed his eyes.

"Very well." His father sighed, disappointment reflecting in his blue eyes. "We should make the announcement soon." He gave one last look of disapproval to Noah before he offered his elbow to his wife and led her to the buffet.

Noah took the opportunity to slip into the corner away from the crowds, his first mate following on his heels.

"So where is your beloved fiancée?" Luke surveyed the guests. "And why have you not greeted her?"

Noah gestured with his head toward a cluster of women to the right of the fireplace. "There, in the middle of those three women. And please refrain from calling her my beloved."

Luke's gaze shot in their direction and studied her for a moment.

"The brunette? Hmm. Not so bad, Captain. Certainly not extraordinary, but she seems pleasant enough."

Noah had never thought of Marianne as pleasant. Spoiled, demanding, obnoxious, but never pleasant.

Luke blew out a soft whistle. "But the lady beside her is quite remarkable."

Noah followed his gaze. Fiery red hair framed the delicate features of a near-perfect face. Her emerald green eyes suddenly shot to his and he looked away. He tugged at his cravat. "The redhead? I suppose."

"Who is she?"

"Miss Cassandra Channing, I believe."

"You must introduce me, Captain."

"We haven't time. Besides, word about town is that she is hotheaded and independent."

Luke's blue eyes sparkled. "Ah, but you know how I love a challenge."

Noah chuckled, amazed at his friend's constant infatuation with the weaker gender.

Luke sipped his wine and lifted a brow toward Noah. "You did not answer my question. Why have you not greeted your intended?"

Noah stiffened his jaw. "Because, my good man, it is best I keep my distance from Miss Denton as much as possible." He leaned toward his friend. "For I have every intention of persuading her to break off this absurd engagement."

Luke's eyes widened. "Why would you wish such a thing? Don't you need her dowry?"

"Not if things go well on this next voyage. We stand to make a fortune if I can get to England on time."

"It seems cruel." Luke gazed across the room toward the woman.

Noah shrugged. "Why? Neither of us have affections for the other. I am sure she would welcome a reason to disengage herself from any association with me. And rather than cause her or her reputation any harm, I shall allow her the honor of making the split."

"And how do you plan to do that?"

Noah raised a brow. "Watch and see."

❖

"I daresay, he does present a handsome figure, don't you agree, Marianne?" Cassandra plucked out her fan and fluttered it about her face.

Rose laughed. "Quit drooling, Cassandra. He is not your fiancé."

"Oh, that he were." Marianne sipped her lemonade and studied the man she would marry. Indeed, he had grown up quite nicely from the skinny jackanapes who used to pull her hair when no one was looking. His broad shoulders and thick chest stretched the fabric of his black coat. His light brown hair, streaked with gold by the sun, was combed back in a fashionable style, and not in the usual windblown disarray she'd grown accustomed to seeing among others of his profession. A recent shave revealed a strong jaw that, coupled with his dark eyebrows, gave him the appearance of a man in control of his destiny and determined to get what he wanted.

And Marianne was positive it could not be her. "You may have him, Cassandra. It is settled. I will go tell my mother at once." She took a step forward but Cassandra's strong grasp pulled her back. "You know you cannot do that. He is the only option you have. You must get used to the arrangement."

Marianne stepped back between the two ladies with a sigh and glanced over the gathering of people who were partaking of the cakes, lemonade, and the wine her mother had spent two weeks' of their food allowance on. Some dear friends, some acquaintances, and some she hardly knew but who had been invited because of their positions in society. Edward Johnson, the mayor, Mr. Wilson, the magistrate, two councilmen, and General Stricker. Her father had been an influential man.

Then her eyes met Noah's, and he winced as if he could not bear the sight of her. She lowered her gaze and took a sip of lemonade, wishing she could melt into the cup and disappear. She had not spoken to him in over a year. He was always at sea and when he was in town, he never called on her. Even during the arrangements of their betrothal—a meeting between Marianne's mother and Noah's parents in this very parlor—Noah had slipped out before she'd had a chance to speak to him, leaving her wondering how he felt about the match. But now after looking in his eyes, she had no doubt where his feelings lay.

The chime of silverware on glass filled the parlor, drawing all eyes to Marianne's mother who stood before the fireplace. She gestured for Marianne to join her.

Lizzie appeared out of nowhere, her face beaming. "It's time, Marianne." Her innocent enthusiasm tore at Marianne's heart, making her long to be young again, free from the fetters of adult responsibilities.

Taking a deep breath, she pressed a hand over her roiling stomach and handed Rose her glass. "That is my cue."

Cassandra gave her a little nudge to get her moving as Lizzie tugged on her hand.

"Noah, Noah! Come here this instant." Noah's mother shouted across the room, pointing at Noah with her glass of wine. The dark red fluid sloshed over the rim and slid down the sides. Silence struck all tongues as reproachful glances shot to her and then swept to the corner where Noah stood. His jaw flexed and his face reddened.

Marianne cringed with embarrassment for him. It must be difficult having a mother who overindulged in drink, even though everyone in town knew of Mrs. Brenin's little problem.

Noah strode across the room and approached his mother, took the drink from her hand and set it on a table. "Never fear, Mother, I am here." He took her hand and kissed it before placing it upon his arm for support.

Marianne smiled at the man's kindness toward his mother as Lizzie led her to stand beside her own mother on the opposite end of the mantel. She drew a deep breath to quell her trembling nerves. After her mother greeted her guests, making special mention of those with prominent positions in the city, and thanking everyone for attending, she deferred to Mr. Brenin for the formal announcement.

The formal announcement of Marianne's life sentence—for an engagement was as binding as marriage itself.

Her blood rushed so fast past her ears, she heard little of what Noah's father said, save for the moment when he proudly announced her betrothal to his son.

Lizzie giggled and hugged Marianne. The crowd clapped and all eyes darted to her, causing a blush to rise on her face. She tried to smile, but the agony in her throat prevented her lips from moving. Daring a glance at Noah, she wondered why he had not made a move to stand beside her and take her hand. Instead, he stood as cold and emotionless as the marble mantel behind him. As people swarmed forward to congratulate the couple, Noah's mother pushed her son toward Marianne. "For goodness' sakes, Noah. She doesn't bite." Her shrill laughter blared over the crowd's murmuring. Noah tugged on his cravat as he inched closer to Marianne as if he, indeed, thought she might chomp on his arm.

Fighting back her anger, Marianne accepted the congratulations and well wishes from the guests with as much grace and enthusiasm as she could muster, though both virtues dwindled with Noah's continual disregard. She hoped he would at least pretend he was not marrying her for her dowry alone. Yet, as the crowd moved past, their happy looks transformed into looks of pity, and Marianne fought back the tears filling her eyes.

Soon the throng moved back to their former conversations and Noah faced her, his blue eyes searching hers uncomfortably. He took her hand and raised it to his lips.

Marianne swallowed. "At last you greet me, Mr. Brenin."

"I hope you can forgive me. I often have trouble tearing my thoughts away from business." He flashed a smile, the brevity of which left her wishing for more. "I meant no disrespect." His eyes took her in again. "You look lovely this afternoon, Miss Denton."

A wave of heat flushed through Marianne at his unexpected compliment. "You are too kind." She smiled and he released her hand.

He glanced over his shoulder toward the door. "But I fear I must beg your forgiveness once again, Miss Denton, for I must leave straight away."

Leave? Marianne shook her head. "Whatever do you mean, Mr. Brenin? You only just arrived."

"Yes, I know, but I must set sail immediately or I stand to lose a great deal of money." The look in his eyes did not affirm the veracity of his statement. Rather, he shifted uncomfortably and avoided her gaze.

The lemonade soured in Marianne's stomach. She leaned toward him. "Regardless, you cannot leave our engagement party," she whispered through clenched teeth.

Her mother eased beside her, perhaps sensing her rising anger.

Noah bowed politely in her direction. "Thank you, Mrs. Denton, for such a lovely afternoon."

Marianne's mother eyed him curiously, but she accepted his appreciation with a smile. "You are most welcome, Mr. Brenin. There is more to come."

"Unfortunately, I will not be able to partake of your extended kindness. I am to set sail within the hour." With a nod, he turned and sauntered across the room to join his friend. The two of them exited the parlor. Seconds later, the front door closed with a definitive thud. Once again, everyone looked at Marianne, including Cassandra and Rose, who quickly dashed to her side. Whispers slithered about the room like gossiping snakes and for the second time that night, Marianne wished she could disappear.

"He did not just leave." She heard the spite in her own voice. Not in front of everyone. Not when the party had only begun. Now it would be plain to all that he cared nothing for her or for their marriage.

"I believe he did," Cassandra said.

"Oh dear." Her mother coughed and her face blanched as if she were about to faint. Grabbing her, Marianne led her to a nearby chair. "Rose, get my mother some lemonade, if you please."

Rose skittered away and returned with a glass, which Marianne held to her mother's lips. She took a few sips and then leaned back. "Thank you, dearest. I will be all right."

Marianne set the glass on a table and studied her face as the color returned. Perhaps her mother would recover for now, but blast that scoundrel Noah for upsetting her so.

"I'm so sorry, Marianne," Rose said.

Marianne hung her head, battling a plethora of emotions: embarrassment, shame, sorrow, and finally anger. Clenching her fists, she squared her shoulders. "He's not going to get away with this. Not this time."

❖ CHAPTER 3 ❖

Mr. Brenin, come back here this instant!" Incensed at the man's loathsome behavior, Marianne rushed out the front door after him. Clutching her skirts, she leapt down the stairs and dashed out into the street. "Mr. Brenin!"

Noah halted, shifted his shoulders, and turned to face her. "My apologies, Miss Denton, but I have a ship full of cargo I must get to England as soon as possible."

"You will do no such thing!" Marianne tripped over a stone and stumbled forward. She caught her balance before making a fool of herself and tumbling to the ground. Noah's friend, Mr. Heaton, chuckled as Noah faced forward and continued on his way.

"Go home, Miss Denton." He flung a hand over his shoulder.

"Marianne!" Lizzie's sweet voice filled the air.

"Dearest, come back." Her mother's plea wrapped around her like an invisible rope, halting her, tugging her home to safety and love.

But one slice of her fury severed it in an instant.

"Never fear, Mother, Lizzie, I will return shortly," she shouted as she stomped forward after the two men. Her rage tore away any pride left within her and tossed it to the cobblestones beneath her feet. She knew her behavior only made her shame all the more evident, more humiliating, but she couldn't help her actions. How dare Noah embarrass her in front of everyone, the councilmen, and the mayor? How dare he shame her in such a horrid way? Why, she would be the laughingstock of the whole city. She'd be unable to show her face in any social circle.

One quick glance behind revealed her worst fear. A mob of guests crowded the porch of her home. Some laughed while others looked at her with pity. The latter included her mother, standing alongside her two friends Cassandra and Rose.

But Marianne could not stop. "Mr. Brenin, if you please." She darted before a phaeton. The driver jerked the horse's reins and the animal neighed in protest.

"Watch where you're going!" the coachman shouted. Marianne waved an apology and forged ahead.

"Mr. Brenin!"

Halting, Noah swung about, a look of annoyance twisting his handsome features. Beside him, Mr. Heaton seemed to be having difficulty holding back his laughter. A gust of hot wind tugged at Marianne's curls. Perspiration dotted her neck.

Noah's blue eyes sharpened. "Miss Denton, it is unseemly and most unsafe for you to be chasing me through the city streets."

"Mr. Brenin, it is most rude and incorrigible for you to abandon me at our engagement party."

Noah released a sigh and gazed down the avenue toward the docks, then back at her as if she were an annoying rodent. "I have not abandoned you, miss. I simply have more important—" He halted and flattened his lips. "I have crucial business to attend to. Surely you don't wish to have a sluggard for a husband."

She didn't wish to have a husband at all, if truth be told. Marianne drew a deep breath and composed herself. "What I wish for, sir, is a husband who treats me with respect and doesn't make me an object of mockery before the entire town."

A flicker of sympathy crossed his face before it hardened back to stone. "When I am your husband, you have my word I will never do so."

"How am I to believe you when you so freely disregard me now?"

He smiled, that arrogant half smile that set her blood boiling. "Me? I believe you are the one acting beneath your station, chasing me down the street like a needy little wife."

Marianne contained herself with difficulty. "I am neither needy nor your wife. Can you not spare my dignity with a few hours of your time, sir?"

"Your dignity?" He laughed, his blue eyes sparkling. Removing his hat, he palmed the sweat from his brow. "Is that what this is about? Your dignity? You always did care for the opinions of others."

"Why, you insufferable clod," Marianne spat.

Mr. Heaton chuckled, but was instantly silenced with one look from Noah. The first mate turned toward Marianne, "If I may, Miss Denton, I—"

"You may not, Mr. Heaton." She gave him a scorching look. "Not unless you can convince your captain to return to our engagement party." Marianne eyed Noah's first mate, the man whose daring ways were the talk of the town amongst the ladies. A perfect specimen of manhood save for the tiny scar that sliced through his right earlobe. The twinkle in his eye as he perused her told her he was also a man who had no difficulty drawing female attention.

Yet she felt naught but annoyance at him.

Mr. Heaton shrugged and instead tipped his hat at a lady who passed on his left.

Noah shifted his leather boots impatiently over the cobblestone. "Now if you please, Miss Denton, we must be on our way. I suggest you return home posthaste as the night falls and the crowds appear quite agitated."

"I will do no such thing unless you return with me. How can I face my guests when my own fiancé can't stand the sight of me?"

His eyebrows shot up and he gazed at her curiously, but then he placed his hat atop his head and straightened his coat. "It is not the sight of you that disturbs me, miss, but your attempt to rule over my affairs. Now run along, Miss Denton." He flapped one hand toward her as if to brush her away. "We can discuss this when I return."

Marianne's eyes burned with tears at the man's cruelty, but she willed them away. She would not give him the satisfaction.

Obviously taking her silence as compliance, he swung around and marched down the street, Mr. Heaton by his side. Together, they disappeared into a mob of citizens who were shouting and cursing as one man at the center held up a pamphlet.

"Federalist garbage!" one man yelled.

"I'll not have this treason printed in my town!"

Clutching her skirts, Marianne circled the mob, thankful when they ignored her. Standing on her tiptoes, she peered down Conway

Street, searching for Noah's hat. Since he stood a head taller than most men and wore that pompous purple plume, she should have no trouble spotting him. She knew following a man through the streets would not only besmirch her reputation but put her in harm's way, especially as the sun slipped below the buildings and the shadows crept out from hiding, but she could not let him win again. Not this time. This time he would learn that he could not treat her like a child to be bullied whenever he pleased.

Memories assaulted her of the time when she was five years old and Noah had dropped a frog in her bonnet, only to laugh hysterically when she placed it atop her head and screamed. Or the time he had stolen a pie from Marianne's cook, Maggie, and showered crumbs in Marianne's hair and on her dress to incriminate her for the infraction. She had spent two days alone in her chamber and received no pie for a month as punishment. Memory after memory assailed her, fueling her resolve to forge ahead and bring him back. If she had to marry this unscrupulous rogue, then she had better assert herself from the start. He could set sail as often as he liked, he could do whatever he wanted as long as he cared for her mother and sister, and treated Marianne with respect. Was that too much to ask?

Above the bobbing heads, the imperious flutter of his purple plume marked his location. She dashed between two carriages and followed him as he turned down Light Street. A breeze coming off the harbor whirled around her, bringing with it the smell of the sea, of fish, and crab, and the sting of refuse. Tall ships of all sorts and sizes bobbed in the choppy bay, some docked at the long piers that ran out into the water.

She tripped over a brick, and pain seared up her toe and into her foot. Biting her lip, she continued threading her way through the sailors, merchantmen, footmen, and coaches, as well as ladies and gentleman out for a stroll along the bay.

Noah turned right onto Pratt Street and she followed him.

Workers and slaves hustled over the wharves as they carried last-minute goods to the ships. Baltimore had grown so much since the Revolution that it had become the third largest seaport in America. Though Marianne hated the harbor, she was proud of that fact and proud of her grand city. Ignoring the glances and whistles the sailors cast her way, she dashed through the throng and kept her head down to avoid drawing unnecessary attention.

A pianoforte twanged from one of the taverns lining the street as a cacophony of laughter and song erupted from men taking early to their cups. Marianne shivered, though the night was warm. She hated the inner harbor. Not so much because of the lecherous stares from the seamen or because of the danger, but because of the dark choppy sea that stretched its greedy fingers up the Patapsco River. Didn't the sea claim enough victims upon the open waters? Did it have to invade the land as well?

Continuing onward, she avoided looking at the water licking the pilings of the dock as if smacking its lips in anticipation of a meal. She avoided looking at the ominous spot that loomed up ahead.

The spot where they had found her father facedown in the harbor.

His body bloated and pale from spending days in the water. She swallowed a burst of sorrow and shifted her gaze to the warehouses and taverns tucked across the cobblestone street, all the while silently cursing Noah for forcing her to visit a place she'd successfully avoided for three years.

Noah marched onto one of the piers then dashed across a plank that led to a ship. Mr. Heaton followed, and the air instantly filled with Noah's resounding voice spouting orders to his crew.

Heart stuck in her throat, Marianne inched down the wobbling wharf and halted at the foot of the plank. Her feet went numb. On the ship, Noah and another sailor perused a document. Never once did he look her way. She glanced at the name painted in red letters upon the hull. *Fortune.* Of course. A perfect name for a man who cared for nothing but wealth.

"'Scuse me, miss." A worker hoisting a crate onto his shoulder drew her attention. She stepped aside to allow him to pass.

Other workers loading goods onto the ship passed her by, the plank buckling beneath their weight like a spring. But would that spring snap? Beneath the flimsy plank, claws of foam-encrusted water leapt up in search of unwary victims.

Noah disappeared down one of the hatches, and Marianne knew she hadn't much time. She held her breath and dashed across the plank. The wood shifted beneath her slippers as if it were water itself, but then she felt the firm railing. She looked around, proud of her accomplishment, but not in time to see there were no steps leading down from the ship's railing.

Waving her arms through the air, she tumbled to the deck in a heap of silk and lace. Her skirt flew up, leaving her petticoats fluttering around her.

Chuckles bombarded her from all around, followed by catcalls and whistles. Her face heated.

"Ye ain't supposed to be here, miss." One of the sailors reached out to help her to her feet.

Rising, she released his hand and pressed down her skirts, ignoring the crude comments flung her way.

"Begging your pardon, sir, but I believe I am. I am the captain's fiancée." She thrust out her chin. "And I must speak to him at once."

The sailor, a young man in a checkered shirt, red scarf, and tan breeches, looked her over as if she couldn't possibly be the captain's fiancée. A thick jagged scar ran down his left cheek and disappeared into the scarf tied around his neck. "I expect he went to his cabin, miss."

Marianne turned her gaze away from his disfigurement. "And where might that be?"

But before he could answer, another man grabbed him by the arm and pointed to something above in the yards. The two men climbed aloft, leaving her alone.

Very well. Though she'd never been on a ship before, it didn't appear to be too big. How hard could it be to find the captain's cabin? Marianne sauntered to the hole into which Noah had disappeared and peeked below where a ladder descended into the gloom. Grabbing the rail, she lifted her skirts and carefully lowered herself down the narrow, steep stairs. The smell of aged wood and tar filled her nose. At the foot, she headed down a long corridor, lit by lanterns hooked along the sides. A row of cannons wrapped in thick ropes and sitting on wood carriages lined both sides of the deck. Surely the captain's cabin would not reside next to such dangerous guns.

"All hands aloft!" Feet pounded above her, echoing like drums.

Men passed by her, looks of surprise on their faces. Some tipped their hats, while others stared at her curiously before they sped on their way. The ship seemed to close in on her. Why was everything so cramped down here? How did these men survive in such tight quarters?

"Sir, if you please." Marianne leapt in the path of a sailor. "Can you direct me to the captain's cabin?"

Halting, he eyed her and adjusted his dirt-encrusted neckerchief.

"Come along, Rupert!" a man yelled from above.

The sailor glanced upward and shifted his feet nervously. "It's aft, ma'am," he said before scurrying away.

Aft. Hmm. Marianne wasn't quite sure what this aft meant. Down perhaps? She found another ladder. Surely the captain's cabin was below, away from the noise and clamor where he would have more space and more quiet. A stench that reminded her of rotten eggs assaulted her as she descended farther into the gloom. Holding a hand to her nose, she reached the bottom and continued down another narrow hallway. At the end, a door stood ajar. No lantern lit this room, but the dim light coming in from the hallway revealed nothing but barrels and crates. She was about to shut the door when a tiny meow sounded from the corner. Peering into the darkness, she scanned the room.

"Meow."

"Heave short the anchor!" A man bellowed from above, and the sound of a chain chimed through the ship.

Marianne crept inside the room. "Poor kitty. Down here in the dark all alone." Releasing the door, she felt her way around barrels and chests toward the last place she'd heard the meow. The ship lurched. The door slammed shut. A darkness blacker than she'd ever witnessed closed in on her.

"Meow."

"I'm coming, little one. I'll get you out of here."

A snap that reminded Marianne of the crack of a huge whip crackled the air. The ship jerked again. She took another step forward, feeling the edge of a wooden cask with her gloves. A splinter pierced the silk and into her skin. She winced.

The ship pitched, and she gripped the crate to keep her balance. The sound of wood scraping against wood filled her ears. She inched her way forward. A creak and another scraping noise.

Thump! Twack! The drums and chests came to life around her.

She bumped against something tall beside her. It moved.

"Meow."

"I am here, little one." Marianne reached in the direction of the feline's plea. Warm fur brushed against her glove.

The ship jerked again.

Thunk! Something heavy struck her from above. She crumpled to the floor. The last thing she remembered was the burning pain in her head and the cat licking her face.

❖ CHAPTER 4 ❖

E ase off the topsails, Mr. Heaton," Noah commanded from his position on the quarterdeck. He clasped his hands behind his back and glanced over his shoulder at his helmsman. "Three points to larboard, Mr. Pike."

"Three points to larboard, Captain," Pike answered.

From his position beside Noah, Mr. Heaton shouted orders that sent sailors leaping into the shrouds and scrambling up the ratlines to adjust canvas.

Closing his eyes, Noah allowed the stiff breeze to blast over him and rake through his hair. He shook his head, hoping to rid himself of the memories of home and the agonizing look on Miss Denton's face. He hadn't meant to cause her shame. Confound it all, he should never have agreed to the match. But what else could he do when the Brenin merchant business had suffered so much this past year?

A situation his father blamed entirely on Noah.

Noah clamped his jaw tight. Would anything ever be enough to make up for what had happened eleven years ago? He had done his best: set records in making the fastest crossing to England, made arduous trips during hurricane season to the Caribbean, and worked tirelessly for months on end. And if not for the American embargo five years ago and the British laws prohibiting Americans from trading with France, he would have doubled their income and not been forced to sell one of their two ships to keep the business afloat.

Then his father would not have insisted Noah accept the engagement to Miss Denton. And Noah would not have been forced to behave the cur yesterday. Now he could not rid himself of the vision of Miss Denton's sorrowful brown eyes. Surely her pain sprouted from pride and not from any affection she harbored for him.

Noah gazed across the sea that spread like a dark blue fan to the horizon. The rising sun flung golden jewels upon the waters and capped the waves in foamy white. He stretched back his shoulders. Upon the sea, he was captain of his ship, master of his destiny. Not like back at home where he was simply William Brenin's incompetent son.

"It is good to be back out to sea, eh, Luke?" Noah asked his first mate.

"Indeed." Luke nodded and gripped the railing. "You there, Mr. Simon, haul taut, hoist away topgallants and jib!" he yelled to one of the sailors below on the main deck then released a sigh. "But our liberty at port was rather short this time."

Noah cocked a brow. "Didn't get your fill of drink and women?"

"Is that possible?" Luke grinned as he scratched the stubble on his jaw.

Noah chuckled.

"We could have at least stayed at your engagement party a bit longer," Luke added. "I barely had two sips of wine."

"You know we had no time to spare."

"Persistent girl. I admire her for that." Luke shoved a strand of black hair behind his ear.

"You refer to Miss Denton, of course." The ship rose over a wave, and Noah braced his boots on the deck, annoyed that his friend had brought the woman back into his thoughts. "I daresay she's acquired a bit of spunk in her womanhood."

"She's definitely not a little girl anymore." Luke's eyes carried the salacious twinkle always present whenever he spoke about the fairer sex.

Noah grunted. "I regret running out on her, but it could not be helped."

Luke tipped his hat down against the bright rays of the sun. "From the look on her face, I imagine you won't have too much trouble persuading her to call off your engagement."

"Which is precisely why our need to set sail worked in my favor. Who could forgive such insolent behavior? Why, I imagine at this moment she's already discussing with her mother and my parents the best way to annul the arrangement."

❖

Pain drummed a steady beat in Marianne's head. She willed it away and tried to slip back into the peaceful repose from which she came. But the agony would not abate. In fact, it worsened. A moan escaped her lips. She lifted her hand and dabbed her head. Her fingers touched something moist and sticky that stirred the pain anew.

A deep purring tickled her ears. She opened her eyes to nothing but thick darkness. Confusion scrambled her thoughts. Where was she? Then the creak of wood and oscillating of the floor sent a shock through her. She jolted upright.

Noah's ship.

Her breath caught in her throat. Something furry leapt into her lap, and she screamed. When she tried to push it off, the creature began purring again. Taking a deep breath, Marianne picked it up and drew it to her chest. "Oh, little one. What happened? How long have we been down here?"

The cat's only reply was further purring as it nestled in her arms. Marianne clung to it, fighting the ache in her head and the rising panic that she was out to sea. Fear scrambled through her like a wicked imp, pinching every nerve. *Lord, I know I haven't spoken to You in a while, but please don't let me be out to sea. Please have mercy.*

No answer came save the creaking and groaning of the wooden planks and the faint rustle of water against the hull—all of which made her plea dissipate into the stagnant, moldy air. She struggled to rise, still holding the cat. With one hand she felt her way through the maze of barrels toward the thin strip of light marking the bottom of the doorway. Opening the wooden slab, she made her way down the same hallway she had traversed earlier. Her head grew light, and she gripped the wall to steady herself.

Shouting and laughter sounded from above. She took the first ladder toward the clamor and the ever-brightening sunlight filtering downward. Squinting, she climbed the final stairs and emerged to a burst of wind and a spray of salty water. Above her, white sails snapped in the breeze. Sailors sat upon the yards, adjusting them with ropes. Other men stomped across the deck. Those who saw her stopped to stare. She gazed toward the horizon and trembled. All around the ship spanned an enormous gaping mouth full of salivating azure water.

❖

The sailors, whose normally boisterous voices could always be heard across the deck, grew unusually silent. Ignoring the unease that slithered down his spine, Noah lowered the spyglass and gazed amidships. His heart seized.

A woman in a cream-colored gown with pink trim stood in the center of the deck. He blinked and rubbed his eyes. Had his guilt over the ignoble way he had treated Miss Denton conjured up visions of the woman to taunt him?

"Captain." Luke's voice jarred him, and he opened his eyes to a look of grand amusement on his first mate's face. "I believe you have a guest."

Noah glanced toward the main deck again, praying his eyes had betrayed him. But no, there, in the middle, stood Miss Denton, frozen as if she were a statue.

Anger simmered in his belly as he stormed toward the quarterdeck ladder and leapt down onto the deck. "Miss Denton, what on earth are you. . . ?"

She faced him, a white cat in her arms, terror screaming from her eyes. A red streak crept down her forehead, seeping from a dark, matted blotch in her hair. She said not a word but looked at him as if he were a ghost. She stumbled, and he dashed to her and grabbed her shoulders. "Miss Denton?"

She looked up at him with wide brown eyes. "I am at sea."

"Yes. I find that fact as astounding as you."

"But I cannot be at sea."

Upon closer inspection, the spot of matted hair was a bloody wound. Noah scanned the deck and found his boatswain. "Matthew, call your wife to your quarters, if you please, and have her bring her medical satchel."

"Aye, sir." Matthew disappeared down a hatch.

Marianne lifted a hand to her head. The cat leapt from her embrace. "Forgive me, Mr. Brenin, but I do not feel very well." She fell against him, and he swept her up into his arms.

The sailors began to crowd around. "Who is she, Captain?" Mr. Weller, Noah's gunner asked.

"Put me down, this instant," Miss Denton murmured.

"How did she get on board?" another man asked.

"I have no idea." Noah glanced up at his first mate. A smirk played upon his lips. "Mr. Heaton, you have the helm."

"Yes, Captain."

Leaving his curious crew behind, Noah carefully navigated the ladder and headed down the companionway toward Matthew's quarters. He entered the cabin and laid Miss Denton on the new coverlet that Agnes had just spread on the bed. Matthew stood near the bulkhead, kneading his hat in his hand.

Miss Denton opened her eyes and moaned.

"Oh my, poor dear." Agnes darted to her side. "Who is she?"

"My fiancée." Noah took a step back. "She appears to have hit her head."

"Don't you worry, sir, I'll attend to 'er right away." Agnes's cheeks reddened as she handed a pewter basin to her husband. "Fetch me some water, Mr. Hobbs."

The short, bald man donned his hat and eyed his captain.

Noah nodded his agreement, and the boatswain scurried out the door faster than his stocky frame would seem to allow.

"Noah." Miss Denton tried to lift herself from the bed but fell back onto the coverlet. "I must return home at once."

"I'm afraid that will be impossible."

"I assure you, it is quite possible." Miss Denton's breathing grew ragged. "Help me up, please." She latched onto Agnes's arm and pulled herself to a sitting position.

Noah huffed his annoyance. "You will lie back down this instant, Miss Denton, and allow Mrs. Hobbs to dress your wound. It is a long voyage and I'll not have you growing ill on my ship."

"Voyage?" Her brow wrinkled as if she could not fathom the meaning of the word. Her chest heaved. "I cannot possibly—"

"Inform me if she does not cooperate, Mrs. Hobbs," Noah interrupted, "and I'll have her strapped to the bed." He used his stern captain's voice in an effort to prevent any further defiance.

Agnes swung a look of reprimand his way, and Miss Denton's face pinched. "You wouldn't dare!"

Noah clenched his jaw. "It would be my pleasure." Then turning, he stomped from the room and closed the door.

❖

The rotund woman with the cheery face of an angel dabbed a wet cloth on Marianne's head. Wincing, Marianne gasped at the sting.

"My apologies, dear." The woman smiled. "But ye've got quite a gash on your head and I need t' clean it."

Marianne pushed the woman's hand away and struggled to rise. The white cat, perched at the foot of the bed, opened her sleepy eyes at the interruption. "Oh, there you are, little one. This is all your fault, you know."

"Seafoam?" The woman chuckled and her chubby cheeks jiggled. "That cat always be gettin' in some kind o' trouble."

Lifting a hand, Marianne rubbed her forehead. "I thank you for your kindness, Mrs. . . ."

"Hobbs, but ye can call me Agnes." The woman dipped the cloth into a basin filled with water and wrung it out. "Whatever happened to ye, miss?"

Sinking back onto the lumpy mattress, Marianne closed her eyes against the throbbing as Agnes rubbed the cloth over her wound. "I was searching for No—the captain. I suppose I got lost. I heard a cat meowing and went into a room to investigate. The rest is a bit of a blur."

"Seafoam." Agnes wagged a finger at the cat. "See the trouble you cause." Agnes's laughter bubbled through the room, causing Marianne's nerves to unwind. But only for an instant. For the rush of water against the hull reminded her of where she was.

She gazed curiously at the cheery lady before her. Why would any woman sail the seas of her own volition? "I don't mean to intrude, but whatever are you doing aboard this ship?"

"Me husband is the ship's boatswain. And not wantin' t' be without him, I signed on as cook." She wrung out the bloody cloth in the basin and set it aside. "But I also do laundry and any doctorin' that needs attendin' to." She opened a black satchel and pulled out a bundle of white cloth. "Me, a surgeon." She chuckled. "The Lord has a sense o' humor, I'd say."

The ship careened to the right, and Agnes gripped the bed frame. Marianne guessed her to be around her mother's age, but any further resemblance stopped there. Where Marianne's mother was petite, frail, and peaked, this woman's pink skin, rotund figure, and sparkling green eyes radiated health.

The snap of sails thundered above, followed by the shouts of the crew. Agnes unrolled the white strip of cloth, sliced a portion off with a knife, and gently wrapped it around Marianne's head.

"Being out at sea doesn't frighten you?" Marianne asked as Agnes tied the bandage and sat back to examine her work.

Her face scrunched. "Afraid? Nay. I love the sea. Was born on a ship in the Caribbean." She stuffed her wiry red hair streaked with gray back underneath her mobcap and took Marianne's hand in hers. "Now don't be afraid. Cap'n Brenin be a good cap'n. But you best be stayin' put for a while. You don't want t' find yourself strapped t' the bed." She grinned, revealing two missing teeth on her bottom row.

"Surely he wasn't serious."

Agnes's brow lifted along with her shoulders. "One thing I know 'bout the cap'n. He's not a man given t' jokin'." She coiled the remaining bandage back into a ball and stuffed it in her satchel. "Truth be told, I don't know what's got into 'im. He's usually a perfect gentleman. I ain't never seen him behave so unmannerly towards a lady."

"I have." Marianne pushed aside the resurging memories of his cruelty as a child. "Perhaps he wears a mask of civility for the benefit of his friends."

"Naw. Mr. Hobbs and I have sailed wit' him for five years. He be a good man, you'll see. An' he'll make a fine husband." Her cheeks reddened.

Marianne had her doubts about that as well, but she thought better than to voice them. Obviously Noah had fooled this woman into believing he was something he was not.

Agnes patted Marianne's hand. "Now get some rest. I'll check on you later." Then standing, she ambled from the room.

Rest? Marianne closed her eyes, trying to drown out the rustle of the sea against the hull and the sound of the wind thrumming in the sails. How could she rest when all that stood between her and a watery grave were a few planks of wood?

Seafoam rose, stretched her legs, and sauntered to lie beside Marianne. Turning on her side, Marianne caressed the cat's soft fur. "I thought cats were afraid of water."

Purring rose to Marianne's ears as Seafoam nestled against her.

"Well, if you can be brave, little one, then so can I." Marianne winced at the throbbing in her head even as her eyelids grew heavy. The room began to spin, and she slowly drifted into a chaotic slumber filled with nightmares.

Marianne and her mother and sister were without a boat in the middle of the ocean, thrashing their arms through the foamy waves to keep afloat. A small vessel approached. Marianne's father and Noah sat within it, rowing toward some unknown destination. Pleading desperately for help, Marianne called out to them as they passed. But neither man looked her way. She continued to scream and splash to get their attention. But both men kept their faces forward and their hands to the oars. Soon, they slipped away and faded into the horizon, leaving Marianne and her family to drown.

❖

Noah picked up the lantern and set it beside the chart spread across his desk. Using his divider, protractor, gunner's scale, and Mr. Grainger's best weather prediction, Noah had plotted their fastest route to South Hampton. With clear skies and God's good favor, they'd make port in four weeks. After they reached South Hampton and off-loaded their cargo, Noah had arranged to transport silks and fine china to Nevis in the Caribbean, where he expected the wealthy colonists would pay handsomely for the extravagances lacking in the new world. Then at Nevis, he would fill his hold with coffee and sugar to sell in Baltimore. All in all, he hoped to make a year's wages with this one voyage.

Perhaps then his father would see him as a more-than-qualified merchantman. Perhaps then, that gleam of approval Noah longed to see would appear in his father's eyes. Dare he even hope for an added spark of forgiveness? Reaching into his waistcoat pocket, Noah withdrew a handkerchief—his brother's handkerchief. He unfolded it and laid it across the palm of his hand giving it the reverence of a holy object. To him, it was holy. He traced the deep maroon stains that marred its center and then fingered the lace at the edges. His eyes grew moist. "I'm sorry, Jacob." He stared at it for a moment then gently folded it into a tiny square and slipped it back inside his waistcoat.

Clearing his throat, he forced back all emotion then laid down the scale and walked to a cabinet built into the bulkhead. Opening the door, he grabbed a bottle of port and poured himself a glass, then wove around his desk and gazed out the stern window. A half moon lingered over the horizon. The ebony sea seemed to be reaching up toward it, trying to grab hold of some of its crystalline light for itself.

Noah released a sigh. Everything was going well, everything save one tiny detail.

Rap rap rap.

"Enter." Noah expected Luke with the watch report, but instead of the thud of heavy boots, the swish of silk sounded. He spun around.

"Thank you, Mr. Boone." Miss Denton nodded toward the purser as the sailor's eyes met Noah's uncomfortably before he scrambled down the corridor.

"Such a narrow hallway." She gestured behind her. "How do you endure such cramped quarters?"

"The hallway is called a companionway, Miss Denton."

She nodded and swept the cabin with her gaze. "So this is where your chamber is located." She approached Noah's desk, leaving the door ajar.

"My *cabin*, yes."

"Ah yes, I knew that." A dark red stain marred the white bandage swaddling her head, marking the position of her wound. Brown curls dangled on top of the cloth and crawled from beneath it as if they refused to be restrained. The ship bucked. Her eyes widened as she flung out her arms to keep her balance. Curves rounded the folds of her silk gown that glistened in the candlelight.

Shaking off a sudden wave of heat, Noah averted his gaze. "I believe I told you to rest." He circled his desk, fighting back his annoyance at her presence, and poured himself a second glass of port.

"I did." She glanced across his cabin again, only this time her eyes seemed to soak in every detail before they returned to him. "All day, as a matter of fact, Mr. Brenin."

"I am called *Captain* aboard my ship, Miss Denton."

"Very well, I will call you whatever you want as long as you return me to Baltimore as soon as possible." The lift of her chin and smug look on her face brought him back fifteen years to a time when she was naught but a spoiled girl flaunting her wealth before a poor merchant's son.

"You are in no position to order me about any longer, Miss

Denton...or should I say *princess*?" Noah grinned and sipped his port. The sweet wine slid down his throat, warming him.

Her eyes narrowed for an instant, but then she waved her hand through the air. "You may call me princess if you wish, *waif*."

The word struck him with the same shameful twinge it had when he was a boy.

Her golden-brown eyes snapped his way. "You did naught but tease me as a child."

"And you did naught but belittle me." Noah leaned back on the top of his desk and crossed his boots at the angle.

She bit her lip and began twisting a ring on her right hand.

The look of fear on her face softened the bitter memories of their youth, and Noah released a sigh. "Perhaps we should set aside our childish ways."

"Would that you had decided to do so before you abandoned me in Baltimore." Her sharp tone stabbed him.

"I had no choice. Business before pleasure, you know."

"Pleasure, humph." Marianne leveled a stern gaze upon him. "You looked as if you'd prefer the town stockade to attending your own engagement party."

Noah finished his port and set the glass down. How could he deny it?

A shadow passed over her face, and she looked away. Noah groaned inwardly. He did not wish to hurt her. In fact, it took all his strength to stop from explaining his boorish behavior. Yet perhaps his reasons would hurt her even more. No, the idea to break off the engagement must be hers and hers alone—to spare her reputation, and perhaps her heart.

But what to do with her now? The thought of being forced to endure her company for months made his stomach curdle. Yet perhaps he could use this time to his advantage. Noah ran a hand over the back of his neck and watched her as she struggled to maintain eye contact with him, despite the trembling in her bottom lip. Yes, he would have plenty of time to convince her that he was the obnoxious cad she believed him to be and that life with him would be unbearable.

"Your silence confirms my suspicions." She pressed a hand over her throat and sank into one of his high-backed chairs. "Let us be honest with each other, Noah." She sighed. "You have no intention of marrying me, do you?"

❖

Marianne awaited his answer, but instead he smiled. "You always were rather forthright, Miss Denton."

"While you were never so." She glanced across the cabin again, a much larger room than she would have expected. Yet everything within it—from the three high-backed Chippendale chairs circling a mahogany desk, to the oversized chest with a heavy iron lock, to the fitted racks that held volumes of books and brass trinkets, and finally to the two swords, a pistol, an hourglass, a map, and various instruments that lined his desk—everything was masculine, and well ordered, just like its master.

Her stomach knotted. He had not answered her question. Yet, how could she force this man to marry her when the very thought of it made her own skin crawl?

"I have every intention of following through with my obligation, miss." He folded his arms across his chest and shifted his blue eyes to the massive trunk perched by an archway that led to his sleeping chamber. A breeze blew in from the open door, feathering the hair that touched his collar. The muscles in his jaw twitched, but he would not look at her.

He was lying. She knew it. "Is that what I am, an obligation? How romantic."

He chuckled. "If you want romance, I suggest you search for it somewhere else—in one of those tawdry novels coming out of London, perhaps?" He quirked a dark eyebrow so at odds with his light brown hair. Then grew serious. "While we are being honest, Miss Denton, you know as well as I that it is your dowry that has drawn us together."

Of course she knew that. Then why did his admission cause her heart to ache? Perhaps because it crushed her childhood dreams of someday finding love and romance in the arms of an admirable man. A man nothing like the one standing before her. But then again, why would she expect anything extraordinary to happen to someone ordinary like her? She folded her hands in her lap. "Have no care, Captain. I do not flatter myself to think otherwise. But your desperation must be exceedingly great to force your agreement to such an undesirable match."

Noah adjusted the cuffs of his white shirt then cocked his head toward her. "What has me quite vexed, Miss Denton, is what benefit this match is for you. It is obvious you loathe me."

"Loathe is a strong word." She batted the air, trying to avoid the question. The smell of wine and leather and aged wood filled her nose. She couldn't very well tell Noah that she and her mother were nearly destitute, that without this marriage, they could not touch the inheritance her father left her and purchase the much-needed medicines to keep her mother alive. She wasn't lying to him. He would receive the seven thousand dollars of her dowry the moment they married. But what he didn't know was that he would receive nothing else, no jewelry, or silverware, satin sheets, china, Persian rugs, or any of the luxuries her mother had been forced to sell this past year. Instead he would acquire only Marianne, her sister, and a sick mother-in-law. So, Marianne simply responded, "Our fathers wished it."

He eyed her curiously. "Your father would not wish you unhappy, miss. I assure you I will not make you a good husband."

Marianne gripped the arm of the chair. Her throat went dry. "Why are you trying to dissuade me when you have admitted that you need my money?"

He shrugged and stared out the open door down the corridor. "I see how my presence upsets you. It would no doubt be pure torture for you should we marry."

"What upsets me is your behavior."

"Unfortunately the two cannot be separated."

"That is not true. People can change if they want to. God can change people."

"What has He to do with it?"

Marianne flinched. "God has everything to do with everything."

"If that is so, then He has much to answer for." He frowned and turned to stare out the stern windows.

"You should not say such things, Noah." Marianne's heart saddened. His family had faced tragedy, as had hers. But she had not forsaken God. Or had she? Certainly her trust in Him had waned.

She struggled to her feet. "Enough of this. I cannot sail to England with you. My mother is ill and needs my help."

He faced her. "She has servants who will attend to her, I am sure."

In truth, no. "Only I can see to her properly. And my little sister will be lost without me. I simply cannot be gone for months."

"Then you shouldn't have snuck aboard my ship."

She stomped her foot, the hard wood sending a dull ache through her silk slippers. "Then you shouldn't have run away from me."

He rubbed the back of his neck, and the features of his face grew tight. She wondered if he still had the same nasty temper he had as a boy. "Confound it all, I stand to make a great deal of money on this voyage, Miss Denton. Perhaps even more than your dowry is worth."

More than her dowry? Then he wouldn't need her. Fear clogged in Marianne's throat. She couldn't allow that to happen.

"But time is of the essence," he continued, "And I cannot waste two days returning you home. I'm afraid you are here for the duration of the voyage. There is nothing I can do about it."

The ship pitched, and Marianne shifted her feet to catch her balance. A salt-laden breeze swirled about the room. The candle flickered, and a chill slid down her back. The mad dash of water against the hull mocked her as fear for her mother battled for preeminence against fear of the sea.

"You don't understand. I cannot be aboard this ship." Tears burned behind her eyes, but she would not disclose her fears and provide him with more ammunition with which to badger her.

"But the fact is you are, miss. By your own accord, I might add. And as such, you will be my guest until we return home. Though nothing like the elegance you are accustomed to, I assure you the ship will be quite comfortable."

Marianne felt the blood drain from her face as dizziness threatened to spin her vision. She grabbed the chair for support and closed her eyes.

Noah's boots thumped across the planks. He took both her hands in his. "You have not yet recovered from your wound, Miss Denton. I'll show you to your cabin."

The gentle way he caressed her fingers sent unwanted warmth through her. She opened her eyes.

"What have we here?" He flipped over her hands. Red, crusty calluses stared up at them both. Marianne snatched her hands from his.

"It is nothing. It must have happened when the crate struck me." She took a step back.

He narrowed his blue eyes upon her.

"Very well, Noah." She conceded to allay his suspicion. "Perhaps I do need some rest. You may show me to my room."

He stiffened at her condescending tone, but it couldn't be helped. It was the only way for her to recover from what he had seen on her hands. If he knew she worked as a common servant in her own house, he would no doubt call the wedding off.

Grabbing a lantern from his desk, he gestured toward the door and gave a mock bow. "This way, miss."

Lifting her nose in the air, Marianne followed him down the narrow hallway, lit by intermittent lanterns to another door not far from the captain's. He opened it to a space no bigger than a closet. A box-framed bed attached to the wall filled most of the room, save for a tiny shelf for belongings. A foul, moldy smell swamped over her.

But Marianne didn't care. She'd grown accustomed to sleeping in a chair by her mother's bedside, so truth be told, the stuffed tick on the bed appeared more than inviting.

After placing the lantern on the shelf, Noah leaned on the door-frame and watched her as she eased past him, brushing his arm. "Thank you, Noah."

His eyes widened and he studied her as if she'd said the sea was made of blue pudding.

She pressed down the folds of her gown and shook her head. "What I meant to say was, I suppose it will have to do."

"Yes, it will. Sleep well, Miss Denton." He gave her a sly wink before shutting the door. His boot steps pounded his exit down the hallway.

Marianne sank onto the knotty mattress. She didn't intend to sleep. She had planning to do. Noah must not have any reason to break off their engagement. Her mother's life depended on it. Therefore, she must discover a way to do one of two things: Either make Noah fall madly in love with her or stop him from making his fortune by sabotaging his ship. The former made her sick to her stomach.

The latter brought a smile to her lips.

❖ CHAPTER 5 ❖

Inhaling a deep breath, Marianne trudged up the ladder that led to the main deck. The sound of her stomach gurgling rose even above the crash of waves against the hull. She had hoped to remain below today where she could more easily forget she was in the middle of the ocean. Besides, she had to plan the best way to sabotage the ship, and she wanted to investigate the lower decks. But the biscuit and jam she'd eaten for breakfast were not cooperating. In fact, they rebelled quite vehemently. She poked her head above deck, and a gust of wind tore at the hair she'd managed to pin up in a loose bun despite the bandage wrapped around her head.

Pressing down her skirts to keep them from flying up, Marianne took the final step above. Fear threatened to send her below. She tried to calm her rapid breathing, afraid the heaving of her chest might tear the gown Agnes had lent her—a garment that had obviously belonged to a much thinner woman than Marianne.

Face forward, she inched her trembling feet to the mainmast, grabbed the rough wood, and squeezed her eyes shut, trying to quell the ferocious beating of her heart. Sounds of footsteps, shouts, the gurgle of water, and creak of wood assailed her ears. Hot rays from a sun sitting high in the blue sky scorched her tender skin.

Lord, I need Your help. I need Your strength. Please grant me Your peace and help me find a way to get back home to my mother. The ship canted, and she planted her feet slightly apart to brace herself, realizing how unfamiliar prayer had become to her. *Please watch over her and Lizzie in my absence. And please help me find a way to ensure Noah marries me.* The remains of her biscuit rose in her throat. She swallowed them down. *Or if there's another way to save my mother and Lizzie without marrying that beef-witted clod. . .* She hesitated beneath a spark of guilt. *Forgive me, Lord.* The ship pitched and a salty spray showered over her. *One more thing, Lord. If You don't mind, please keep this ship afloat. Amen.*

She should have felt better—more at peace—like she used to feel after praying, but instead all she felt was the ever-present anxiety that had plagued her since her father died and dragged the entire family fortune with him into the depths of Baltimore harbor. The notes of Papa's funeral dirge had scarce faded when creditors descended on their home like a pack of wolves to collect on his gambling debts. Though he had not been the most affectionate or attentive parent, Marianne had always believed he would care for his family. When he died, she lost more than a father, and more than their fortune, Marianne had lost her trust.

Her trust in man and her trust in God.

"Miss?" A gruff voice startled her, and she snapped her eyes open to see a tall man peering down at her. The same man who had helped her to her feet when she'd first come aboard—or rather fell aboard. Beneath his floppy hat, thick black hair whipped over his shoulders in the wind. "The captain inquires as to your health." Her gaze shot unbidden to a patch of rippled skin that scarred the left side of his face. He seemed to notice the direction of her eyes and frowned. Shoving aside her ill ease at the deformity, Marianne smiled instead and met his eyes directly.

"Oh he does, does he, Mr. . . ."

"Mr. Weller, miss." Intelligent brown eyes examined her from within a face that, despite the scar, appeared young. He nodded at the death grip she had on the mast. "And he insists you go below if you're not feeling well."

Releasing the mast, Marianne cocked her head. "Insists, you say?" She glanced up at the quarterdeck where Noah stood by the wheel glaring down at her, his purple plume bending to the breeze. She could not make out his eyes in the shadow of his hat.

Ever present, his salacious accomplice, Mr. Heaton, stood by his side.

Retrieving a handkerchief from her sleeve, she dabbed the perspiration on her neck and faced Mr. Weller. "And what is your position aboard the ship, sir?"

He stared agape at her as if no one had ever asked the question. "I am the ship's gunner and supercargo, miss."

"What does a supercargo do?" She could well assume what function a gunner served.

"I handle the transfer of all monies, miss, along with carrying out all selling and buying at each port of call."

Marianne smiled. This man could be very useful to her. "Indeed. Do you know much of the workings of the ship?"

"Aye, miss. I suppose." He tugged upon his red scarf, his brows scrunching together beneath the brim of his hat.

Tucking that information away for a more propitious time, Marianne sighed. "Very well, Mr. Weller, would you do me the honor of escorting me up to see the captain? I should like to speak with him, and I am unaccustomed to the shifting deck."

A slow smile lifted his lips. "Why, yes, miss." He extended his arm, but suddenly snapped it back and shoved his hand into his pocket. But not before she saw that only two fingers remained upon it.

He gestured with his other hand toward the ladder and started in that direction. Marianne had no idea what had happened to this man, but she did know how it felt to be less than perfect, to be flawed. Weaving her arm through his, she pulled his hand from his pocket and gave him her best smile.

He eyed her curiously, then led her to the stairs and up onto the quarterdeck just as "A sail, a sail!" bellowed down from the crosstrees.

❖

"Where away?" Noah yelled, trying to ignore Miss Denton, who took a spot beside him.

"Off our larboard quarter."

Cursing under his breath, Noah raised his spyglass and focused on the horizon. Most likely another merchant ship. Nothing to get overwrought about. Certainly less remarkable than the scene he'd just witnessed amidships. Miss Marianne Denton, highbrow extraordinaire, treating scared and deformed Mr. Weller with not only kindness but also compassion. Even from his position above her, Noah had seen the slight cringe on her expression the moment she caught sight of his face. He'd waited for the expected turn of her nose and polite excuse to leave. Shock gripped him at what he beheld instead.

Now, she stood beside him, one hand lifted to cover her eyes as she peered in the direction of his scope, the other hand clutching the railing in such a tight grip, her fingers reddened. The scent of fresh soap wafted over him—no doubt given her by Agnes. The clean lavender smell—a rare one among sailors—tickled his nose and aroused his guilt. Miss Denton should not be at sea. Born to opulence and ease, she was like a duchess among degenerates aboard this ship of rough, crude sailors.

He adjusted the scope until three sails, glutted with wind, came into view. His chest tightened. Not a merchant ship. He handed the glass to Luke.

"What do you make of her?" he asked.

His first mate studied the ship for several seconds before giving Noah a look of concern. "A British warship."

"Yes." Noah took the glass and nodded. "A frigate was my guess."

"She appears to be gaining, sir." Luke scowled.

Miss Denton faced him, her chest heaving and her brown eyes wide. "Will they attack us, Mr. Brenin?"

Noah flexed the muscles in his jaw. "Captain."

She huffed. "Will they attack us, Captain?"

Noah angled his lips and shrugged. "Why would they?"

"They may try an' impress us." Mr. Pike offered from his position at the wheel behind them.

"Balderdash, Mr. Pike. We have no one on board who deserted the British navy." Yet even as he uttered the confident declaration, his glance took in Mr. Weller, who stood at the foot of the quarterdeck ladder. Though the man hadn't directly deserted the Royal Navy, he had allowed them to presume him dead when the brig sloop he served aboard went down in a squall four years ago.

Mr. Weller's gaze met his, and Noah saw raw fear leap in his eyes at the sight of one of His Majesty's ships heading straight toward them.

"Never fear, Mr. Weller," Noah said. "It will not come to that. However, go below and ready the guns in the off chance we need them." Which they wouldn't, of course. Not only because it would be suicide to go up against a British frigate with Noah's small armament, but because all Noah's dealings with the British had proved them an honorable people. Despite the stories he heard on the docks, Noah did not believe the British would steal Americans to serve on their ships. Regardless, he wanted to give his gunner something to do that would help ease his fears.

"Aye, aye, Captain." Weller nodded and jumped down the ladder.

The ship swooped over a roller, flinging creamy spray across the bow. Miss Denton's knuckles whitened on the railing. She seemed to be having trouble breathing.

Fear. He recognized it well. Mind-numbing, debilitating fear. But of what? The frigate? Him? Or was it an act?

Regardless, he had no time for her theatrics. "Make all sail, Mr. Heaton. That should give them the message that we haven't time to stop and chat."

"Haul taut, sheet home, hoist away topgallants and jib!" Luke directed the crew, and men grabbed onto thick lines while others leapt into the shrouds and scrambled above.

Noah watched them clamber with the confidence of monkeys up into the yards. His palms began to sweat, though his feet remained firmly planted on deck. Yes, he knew about fear. He knew about fear very well.

Shaking it off, he raised his spyglass again, trying to determine the frigate's intentions while keeping his mind off Miss Denton beside him and the way her curves filled out her gown. She'd always been a bit plump, while he decidedly preferred ladies of a more slender figure. Why then, did he find his gaze drawn toward her?

"I hear they take no care for a sailor's nationality or whether they ever served in the British navy," she announced with conviction.

"Pure rubbish, Miss Denton." With glass still pressed to his eye, he kept his gaze locked on the frigate. Sailors scampered across her deck and yards, hauling all sails to the wind. Giving chase. Alarm rose within him.

"Have you taken sides with our enemies, Captain?" Accusation stung in her voice.

Sails thundered above him in an ominous boom.

He faced her, making no attempt to hide his frustration. "I take no side, Miss Denton."

Her nose pinked and her eyes narrowed. "It is common knowledge that the British stop and board our ships and impress our sailors without cause. I would think you, of all people, would be angry at such an affront."

Ignoring her, he cuffed a hand over the back of his neck. "Let fall sheet home, hoist away royals and flying jib!" he bellowed across the deck, sending more men to their tasks. Why didn't the blasted woman go below? "They have not attacked me. Consequently, I have no fight with them."

The ship creaked and groaned as it picked up speed. Miss Denton's face whitened. She clung to the railing as if it were her only salvation. When the ship settled again, she righted herself, keeping both hands on the rail. "So it is all about you, then, Mr. Brenin—I mean, Captain? You care not a whit for your country."

Luke gazed at them both, a look of pure enjoyment on his face.

Leveling the scope on the British frigate, Noah welcomed the reprieve from staring into those brown eyes as sharp as spears.

"We have the wind off our quarter, Captain," Luke said. "They are losing ground."

Noah snapped the scope shut and angled a weary glance at Miss Denton. "My country, miss, has done naught but impede my merchant business with their blasted embargoes." He studied the slight tilt of her nose. What would she know of sacrifice and hardship surrounded by luxury in her home? When she had never lifted a finger to work for any of her money.

"You speak as a Federalist and a traitor, sir." She pursed her lips and glanced at the British ship. "If they mean us no harm, then why do they chase us?"

"I have no idea, nor do I intend to find out." Noah's blood boiled at her accusation. "And I am no traitor. I love my country as much as the next man."

The sharp censure in her eyes made him reconsider his words. Did he love his country? Truth be told, he'd been so busy making money, he'd never taken the time to ponder what America stood for nor how she differed from other nations.

Miss Denton clenched her fists as if she intended to punch him. She shifted her gaze to Luke. "What is your opinion, Mr. Heaton? Do you love your country or are you more consumed with how she can help you make money?"

"Nations come and go, Miss Denton." Luke shrugged. "One must look out for oneself in this world."

The ship rose over a wave. The blue water surged onto the main deck before finding its escape through the scuppers back to sea. Miss Denton's chest heaved. From anger or fear, Noah couldn't tell. Still she managed to mumble. "I'm surrounded by Judases."

"That depends on your perspective." Luke gave her a patronizing smile before he glanced off the stern. "They've given up, Captain."

"Very well. Strike the topsails, Mr. Heaton." Noah doffed his hat and ran a hand through his hair. He faced Miss Denton, attempting to curtail his anger, but then he realized his plan was to do the opposite— to prove himself to be a beast.

"Since you know nothing of the merchant business," he began. "Nor of sailing, nor of the British Navy, nor even of work itself, might I suggest you keep your opinions to yourself and keep your person off my quarterdeck."

Her expression fell, and her bottom lip protruded ever so slightly. Though they had the intended effect, Noah immediately regretted his words. But he could see no other way to save them both from this unwanted marriage.

"You have not changed at all, Noah Brenin." The flicker of pain in her brown eyes disappeared, leaving them as hard and cold as polished agates. Swerving around, she moved away from him, gripping the railing all the way to the ladder then with careful movements she descended to the main deck.

"And I thought I was the scoundrel aboard this ship." Luke shook his head, uncharacteristic censure filling his eyes.

Noah's shoulders slumped beneath a press of guilt. "Surely that will convince her of my unworthiness as a husband."

"It convinced me."

❖

"The man is a jingle-brained, bedeviled rogue," Marianne grumbled as she made her way to the captain's chamber. . .cabin, whatever it was called, later that evening for supper. *Why, Lord, do You force me to marry such a man?* Any other man would be better than this one.

Pressing a hand over her stomach, she halted and leaned on the wall. The ship canted to the left, and she stumbled to the other side of the corridor. Swaying lanterns flung eerie shadows over the wooden planks that encased her like a coffin. Indeed, she felt as though she had died and gone to hell—a watery grave ruled by the evil King Noah, a man who was not only malicious but a traitor as well. How could she marry someone who did not share her love of country?

She forced herself to continue. Though she would rather turn down Noah's invitation to dine with him and his officers—knowing it only provided him further opportunity to play his cruel games. She also knew she could not gain any useful information about sabotaging the ship by sitting in her cabin. Which was why she intended to arrive several minutes before the scheduled time for supper. Perhaps she could discover something in the room to aid her cause, and if she got caught snooping around she had an excuse for being there.

Gathering her breath, she peered around the open doorframe. In the midst of the cabin, an oblong table was set with pewter plates and mugs. Candles set in brass holders cast an icy glow over the silverware neatly placed beside each plate. A bowl of fruit and decanters of liquid stood at attention in the center of the table. Beyond it, through the stern windows, the setting sun trailed a red and orange ribbon across the horizon, even as tiny stars poked through the darkening sky above.

She took a step inside and her eyes landed on Noah's desk, pushed off to the side. She headed in that direction when an "Um hum" sounded from the corner. Her heart seized and she spun around to see Mr. Hobbs rising from a chair, a mug in hand.

"Mr. Hobbs, I beg your pardon. I didn't see you there."

"Quite alright, miss." He dragged the hat from his head. "I didn't mean t' startle you."

Oh drat, how could she snoop around with him here? "I must have the time wrong. Am I early for dinner?"

"Aye, just a bit."

"Where is No—the captain?" Marianne glanced out the door, uncomfortable at the thought of being alone with this man.

"He went above for a bit, but he'll be back soon." He waved his hat at her and smiled as if sensing her ill ease. "Don't let me cause you any discomfort, miss."

Marianne studied him. With arms and legs that seemed too muscular for his short body and his bald head gleaming in the candlelight, he appeared like an enormous bulldog. And just as ferocious until she looked in his gray eyes and found only kindness.

"Your wife has been most gracious to me, Mr. Hobbs."

"Aye, she's a good woman."

Marianne could not imagine the pairing. Where Agnes was jolly and friendly, Mr. Hobbs was serious and reserved. Where Agnes was rotund and soft, Mr. Hobbs appeared stiff and hard.

An uncomfortable silence ensued, and Marianne turned to go. "I'll return in a few minutes."

"Nay, miss, if you don't mind. I'm glad we got this chance to talk."

Marianne cocked her head. "What do you wish to speak to me about, Mr. Hobbs?"

"I overheard the captain speakin' t' you earlier. Up on deck."

She lowered her chin beneath a twinge as Noah's callous words shot like arrows through her mind.

"It is not like him, you see. I don't want you thinkin' ill of him. He's like a son t' me."

"Though I appreciate your concern I grow weary of everyone making excuses for his ill behavior."

Mr. Hobbs's lips grew taut. "I don't blame you for thinkin' such. Just don't give up on him yet."

"I have no intention of giving up on him, Mr. Hobbs." Though not for the reasons he thought. Not because somewhere deep beneath Noah's hard crust of cruelty, a speck of kindness survived, but instead because her mother's life depended on it.

Marianne glanced at the captain's desk again. "I wonder, Mr. Hobbs if you would oblige me."

"I'd be happy to, miss."

"Since I am to be imprisoned on this ship for months, I've taken an interest in sailing and navigation. Could you point out the captain's instruments and their function to me?"

"Of course." Mr. Hobbs threw back his shoulders and met her at the captain's desk. "What would ye like to know?"

Marianne pointed in turn at each instrument and asked its function and name, which Mr. Hobbs was more than eager to explain.

"So what would happen if the captain's charts were to be lost?"

"He'd have t' use the stars to guide him, I suppose."

"What about this one." Marianne picked up the odd-looking brass triangle with the curved bottom. "The sextant, was it? What exactly is it used for again?"

"Where's the rum?" Mr. Heaton's deep timbre filled the room, and

Marianne glanced toward the door, quickly setting the sextant back upon the desk. The first mate's dark hair, tied behind him in a queue, matched the black breeches he'd donned. A white shirt, encased in a black waistcoat with gold embroidery completed his ensemble. "Forgive me, Miss Denton. I did not realize you had arrived already." He gave her a roguish grin that he no doubt expected would send her heart fluttering. She squelched any such reaction. She knew his type. He was handsome and he knew it. And he used it to his advantage. Marianne had resigned herself long ago that she would never know how it felt to stir a man's passions by the mere sight of her. And for the most part, she was happy for it.

For the most part.

Noah marched into the room like a captain in command, and her heart quirked a traitorous flutter in her chest. *What is wrong with me?* He tossed his bicorn onto a hook on the wall and eyed his guests. One brow lifted when his eyes landed on her. "Miss Denton, you came?"

"I was invited, was I not?"

"I didn't expect the pleasure of your company."

"I did not wish to deny you of it." She hid her annoyance beneath a sarcastic smirk.

Mr. Heaton grabbed a decanter from the table and poured himself a glass of whatever vile liquor it held.

Noah approached her, pointing at his desk. "What, pray tell, do you find so fascinating among my things?"

"Miss Denton wanted to—" Hobbs began.

"Mr. Hobbs was instructing me on the fine points of navigation, if you must know." Marianne interrupted before the man gave her away.

Noah folded his arms across his brown waistcoat. "I had no idea you had such interests."

"Nor the mind to grasp them?"

He smiled.

Luke dropped into a chair, a grin on his lips.

Mr. Hobbs shifted his stance and gazed between them. "Truth be told, Miss Denton has a keen mind an' a quick understandin'."

Marianne smiled at the elderly man. "Why, you are too kind, Mr. Hobbs."

"Hmm." Noah scratched the stubble on his jaw.

A sailor entered with a tray balanced on his shoulder. Another man followed him, and they both began placing platters of food on the table: biscuits, cheese, a steaming bowl of some sort of soup, and a block of salted meat.

The spicy scent of stew wafted over Marianne. Her mouth watered and her stomach clenched at the same time. Whether it was seasickness or the constant terror of being upon the ocean, Marianne found her appetite had shriveled.

She thanked Mr. Hobbs and moved away from the desk, deciding it would be best to make her exit now before she had to endure any more of Noah's scorching wit.

The ship tilted and one of the sailors stumbled. A glass decanter flew from his tray and crashed to the floor, bursting into a hundred crystalline shards.

"My apologies, Cap'n." The sailor growled as he knelt to pick up the mess.

"No need, Mr. Rupert," Noah said. "Just attend to the mess, if you please."

A red slice appeared on one of Rupert's fingers, and Marianne withdrew her handkerchief from her sleeve and knelt beside him. Taking his hand in hers, she wrapped the bloody appendage. "Be careful, Mr. Rupert." She smiled and his hazel eyes lifted to hers, shock skimming across them. "Let me help you." She began picking up pieces of glass when a hand touched her arm.

"No need, Miss Denton. He can manage."

She looked up to see Noah's brow furrowed as tight as a wound rope.

"Of course." She rose and felt warmth flush through her. What was she thinking? A lady of fortune did not assist servants. Her gaze scanned Mr. Heaton, Mr. Hobbs, the other sailor, and Noah all staring her way.

"If you'll excuse me, gentlemen, my head suddenly aches. I believe I'll forfeit my dinner tonight."

The curious look remained on Noah's face. "Allow me to escort you to your cabin."

She waved a hand through the air. "I know the way. Enjoy your dinner, gentlemen." And with that, she swept out the door.

Making her way down the hallway, she chided herself for her mistake. Noah must never know how destitute she and her mother were.

If he did, it would only fuel his desire to call off the engagement. And that must never happen. Not as long as Marianne had anything to say about it.

She stepped inside her cabin and shoved the door closed then leaned against the hard wood. Her plan was set in place. Now all she had to do was wait for the captain to leave his cabin.

❖ CHAPTER 6 ❖

A rap sounded on her cabin door, and Marianne stopped the pacing she'd taken up for the past several hours as she waited for the sounds of laughter to dissipate from the captain's cabin—which they had done an hour ago. Still she could not get up the courage to do what she had to do. Not until she could be sure Noah was either gone from his cabin or fast asleep.

She opened the door to Agnes carrying a tray laden with cheese, biscuits, a mug, and a basin of water along with her medical satchel.

"Thank you, Agnes. You are too kind." Marianne stepped aside, allowing the elderly woman to enter and set the tray upon the shelf. The sharp smell of cheese drifted on a salty breeze that followed the woman inside, sweeping away the stagnant air that filled the tiny cabin.

"I heard you did not partake of the captain's meal, miss." Agnes's breath came out heavy and fast. "So here's some food fer you an' some water t' clean up wit'."

Shutting the door, Marianne's concern rose at the pale sheen covering Agnes's normally rosy face. "Please sit, Agnes. You look tired."

"I thank you, miss." Agnes moaned as she lowered herself onto the mattress.

"You don't have to serve me, Agnes. I am sure your duties occupy much of your time."

Agnes plucked a handkerchief from her belt to dab her forehead and neck. "Oh, I don't mind. It is nice havin' another woman aboard. Besides, the cap'n ordered me to attend to your every need."

Marianne flinched. "I doubt that."

One gray eyebrow rose nearly to the lace fringing Agnes's mobcap. "For bein' his fiancée, you don't know him very well."

"On the contrary, I grew up with him." Marianne reached for a slice of cheese from the tray and took a bite.

"Pish." Agnes batted the air. "All little boys can be rascals from time t' time."

The cheese soured in Marianne's mouth even as her stomach reached up hungrily to grab it. "He was extraordinarily devilish." She sat beside Agnes. The woman smelled of wood smoke, fish, and spices—not unpleasant odors. In fact, they comforted Marianne.

Agnes chuckled, causing the skin around her neck to jiggle. "It has been my observation that most young boys only tease girls they fancy."

"Don't be ridiculous." Marianne snorted. "I assure you, nothing but disdain spurred him on."

Agnes brushed a lock of Marianne's hair from her face. "Poor dear, you seem so out o' sorts aboard this ship."

Marianne's throat burned at the woman's kindness. She hadn't realized how much she needed a friend, someone whom she could confide in, someone who cared. "I worry about my mother. She is very ill."

Agnes patted her hand. "I am sorry t' hear of it, miss. It is so hard to be away from those we love, especially when they are not well." She clucked her tongue. "How unfortunate you wandered aboard when you did."

"Indeed." Marianne twisted the ring on her finger as a hundred scenes crept out from her childhood memories—scenes of Noah's cruel antics and how he always got the best of her. "Do you have family in America?" she finally asked Agnes.

Agnes's eyes drooped in sorrow. "We did. Mr. Hobbs and I. We had two sons. Both died of the grippe before they reached manhood."

The ship creaked and groaned as it rose over a swell. Marianne's heart shriveled. She couldn't imagine such a horrific loss. "I am so sorry, Agnes."

Agnes cleared her throat, and the momentary moisture disappeared from her eyes. "It was a long time ago. I suppose that's why me and Mr. Hobbs have latched onto Noah. He's like another son to us."

Marianne wondered how such a self-centered boor could make anyone a good son, yet the woman seemed sincere in her approbations. Perhaps the bond between them afforded Agnes some sway over the thickheaded rapscallion—a sway Marianne could use to her advantage. "Would you speak to the captain for me?" she ventured. "Beg him to turn the ship around?"

"Oh no, no, no, dear." Agnes gave an incredulous laugh. "When Noah sets his mind t' make port and sell his goods, there ain't nothing can stand in his way."

Marianne shook her head, her hopes crushed once again. "With men, it seems everything revolves around wealth." Just as it had with her father.

Agnes jerked her head back. "Money? No." Her eyebrows drew together. "That's not the way of it with Noah. It's his father who drives him so hard." She leaned toward Marianne. "If you ask me, I'd say Noah don't care much for the money itself."

"Then why did he leave our engagement party in order to set sail as if the delay would cost him more than he could bear?"

"Did he, now?" Agnes huffed and put an arm around Marianne, drawing her close. "Shame on him. Not like him at all."

Marianne grew weary of everyone's approval of the man. Even though she'd seen little of him these past eleven years, she'd observed nothing about his recent behavior to indicate he'd changed from the churlish imp he had been as a young boy.

"I'm sorry he pained you, miss. Noah lives under a heavy burden these days. Lord knows, I've been praying for him t' let it go."

Marianne bit back a snide remark. What burden could the man possibly have that compared to hers? He worried about pleasing his father, about making money, while she worried about saving her mother's life.

Agnes studied Marianne's expression, obviously mistaking it for one of curiosity. "As his wife, you'll find out soon enough."

The thought brought Marianne no comfort, neither the marrying, nor the discovering of Noah's burden. For now all she needed him to do was turn the ship around and return to Baltimore.

Beads of perspiration lined Agnes's forehead, and she dabbed them away. "He's a good man. I'm sure you'll be very happy."

Marianne swallowed. "I do not seek happiness. Why should anyone expect happiness in this life? Doesn't God's Word portend of trials and troubles and tribulation?" The cheese turned to stone in her stomach, and she pressed a hand over it. In these past years, Marianne had come to believe those verses more than the ones promising joy and peace and abundance.

"Whatever do you mean?" Agnes gave Marianne a motherly look of concern. "Life has its struggles, t' be sure, but there are also many fine moments as well—right fine moments."

"Perhaps, but if I do not look for them, then I shall not be disappointed." Marianne stood, pressing down the folds of her gown. "I am not the sort of person who is destined for greatness. I am an ordinary girl who will live an ordinary life."

"Such a glum outlook, my dear." Agnes took Marianne's hands in hers. "And you are far from ordinary."

Marianne warmed at the affection brimming from her friend's eyes. But then Agnes's face blanched, and she pressed a hand upon her rounded belly.

Marianne grabbed her arm. "Are you ill?"

"Just out o' sorts a bit." Agnes batted the air. "I'll be all right. Now"— she turned and grabbed her satchel—"let me redress your wound and then I'll let you retire."

"Thank you, Agnes, but I haven't been sleeping very well since I boarded."

"The captain neither." Agnes grabbed the bowl of water and plucked a fresh bandage from her bag. "I saw him on deck just a bit ago, staring off into the dark sky as he often does during the night."

Excitement tingled Marianne's veins, and she hardly noticed as Agnes redressed her wound. Hopefully Noah's nighttime stroll would give her plenty of time to slip into his cabin and steal his navigational instruments.

"Thank you, Agnes," Marianne gave her a peck on the cheek as Agnes opened the door to leave.

"I'll leave you to your rest, dear. God bless you."

Marianne watched until the woman faded into the shadows, thinking of what she was about to do. God had not blessed her in many years, and He certainly would not bestow any blessing on her current task. But something had to be done to convince Noah to head the ship back to Baltimore. She was on her own.

Easing into the hallway, she inched her way to the captain's cabin. With a click that seemed to echo like a gong through the corridor, she opened the door and slipped inside. Moonlight poured in through the stern windows in a waterfall of silver that dusted across Noah's desk. The spicy scents of a supper long since consumed swirled around her.

After listening for any sounds coming from the sleeping chamber or the hallway, Marianne made her way to the desk and scanned its contents. Spotting the sextant, protractor, and gunner's scale, she quickly grabbed them and turned to leave. But her eyes latched onto a bottle of ink, and a devilishly naughty idea made her lips curve upward. Setting the instruments back down, she picked up the ink bottle and uncorked it. She studied the map for the best location then slowly turned the bottle over. Thick, black liquid oozed from the lid and spread on the area beside the coast of England into a burgeoning puddle of pitch that covered the sea like lava from a volcano. She smiled and set the bottle on its side, hoping to make it appear as though it tipped over on its own.

Placing her hands on her hips, she studied her artwork with satisfaction.

"Now to find a place to hide you," she whispered to the implements as she picked them back up.

Thud. Thud. Thud. Boot steps echoed in the hallway

Muffled voices and laughter jarred her nerves and strung them tight.

Marianne froze. Her heart thundered in her chest. The mad dash of the sea against the hull seemed to be laughing at her.

Thump. Thump. Thump.

"I daresay, you'll be the death of me, Luke." The captain's voice grew louder.

Marianne's eyes darted around the room. Nowhere to hide. Beneath the desk? No. She whirled around. The sleeping cabin.

Dashing across the room, she dove into the tiny room no bigger than a wardrobe and stubbed her toe on the bed frame. She bit her lip against the groan rising in her throat. The cabin door creaked open and in stomped Noah, and from the sound of the other voice, Mr. Heaton. Lantern light peeked around the corner of the chamber door as if trying to expose her. She folded into the deepest shadows and leaned against the wall. Her chest heaved. Her blood pounded like drums in her ears.

"Confound it all! What's this?" Noah yelled.

Boot steps thundered.

"My chart is ruined!" A foul word spewed from his mouth, stinging Marianne's ears.

"What a mess," Mr. Heaton exclaimed. The rustling of paper filled the room. "How will you chart our course?"

Noah snorted. "I have another one."

Marianne's heart sank. Perspiration trickled down her back.

Drawers opened and scuffling sounded, as no doubt the men sopped up the spilt ink.

"Have a drink with me, Noah. You look as though you could use one." Mr. Heaton said.

The sound of a chair scraping over the wooden planks met Marianne's ears. "Very well. A small glass, if you please."

Chink. Glass rang on glass.

"To a safe voyage," Luke said.

"A safe voyage," Noah replied.

Marianne's heart refused to stop thumping against her ribs. *Oh Lord, please get me out of this.* Silence ensued. After several long minutes, curiosity overcame her fear. Keeping to the shadows, she inched beside the bed and crept into the far corner, which gave her a narrow view of the other room. Noah sat on a chair, his legs stretched out before him. Seafoam sprawled in his lap. He ran his fingers through her fur with one hand while he sipped his drink with the other.

"I believe this long voyage will be far more interesting with Miss Denton aboard." Mr. Heaton leaned back against the top of Noah's desk, drink in hand.

Marianne flung a hand to her mouth. Her mind whirled at the man's remark. Interesting? She had always thought herself rather dull.

Noah eyed his friend. "She has a bit of pluck, doesn't she?"

The cat nestled against his chin. Noah smiled and scratched her head. Marianne shook her head at the tender way he caressed the animal—so at odds with his ruthless character.

Mr. Heaton rubbed the stubble on his jaw. "Very entertaining, indeed. I look forward to your banter with her."

"My torment of her is not for your entertainment. And it pains me to treat her so."

Noah's expression remained stoic. Not a trace of humor could be found either in his voice or on his face. Marianne could make no sense of his statement. If it pained him to insult her, why did he continue?

Mr. Heaton laughed. "And the easy way in which she went to the aid of Rupert. I thought you said she was a highbrow used to a life of ease, surrounded by servants."

Noah shrugged. "It must be a ploy of some kind."

A ploy, indeed. Marianne gritted her teeth.

"Come now, Noah. I know you all too well. The woman enchants you."

"You're drunk."

"She's not at all like Miss Priscilla."

Marianne's ears perked.

"No. She is not." Noah set the cat down, and the feline swept her almond shaped eyes toward Marianne where they remained for several seconds. *The blasted cat knows where I am.* Marianne stiffened, barely allowing a breath to escape her lips. She gave the cat a pleading look that she hoped conveyed in cat language what her heart screamed. *Please, from one woman to another, do not betray me.* Finally, Seafoam lost interest and leapt upon Noah's desk.

"The two women are quite the opposites." Noah stared into space.

"Will you call on her in South Hampton?"

But he's engaged to me! Anger stole Marianne's fear. What a swaggering, lecherous cur!

"Though I would love to, no. It would not be right. I am engaged, after all."

"But if you have your wish, that may not last long."

"Perhaps, but while I am bound thus, I will honor my commitment."

Honor his commitment? Admiration sparked within Marianne. It felt oddly out of place in regard to Noah. Yet the fact that he would even so much as entertain interest in another woman while he was engaged to her doused it immediately.

Noah slapped the remainder of the drink to the back of his throat. "Leave me to my rest, Luke."

Mr. Heaton finished his drink and set his glass down. "Very well." He headed for the door.

Noah stopped him. "Before you retire, check on the watch and ensure the next one will be awakened on time. I will not tolerate further laggardness on this ship."

"Aye, aye, Cap." Luke grinned as he stepped backward through the door and closed it.

Panic turned Marianne's legs to wobbly ropes. This was it. He wasn't leaving his cabin. What would he do to her when he caught her? Remembering the instruments in her hands, she quickly stuffed them beneath his mattress and backed up as far as she could against the wall, awaiting her fate.

Noah shrugged off his coat then began unbuttoning his waistcoat. He tore it off, tossing it to the chair then tugged the cravat from his throat.

Oh no, Lord. Please don't allow him to disrobe. Marianne squeezed her eyes shut, but they refused to close completely, leaving a small slit beneath her lashes. Should she alert him to her presence? No. Perhaps he would still decide to leave for some reason.

Lord, make him remember some command to issue or some ship detail to attend to.

He slipped the shirt over his head then sat down to remove his boots. The sculpted muscles in his chest and arms glistened in the lantern light. Marianne could not tear her eyes from him. She'd never seen a man's chest before, and it both fascinated her and caused an odd feeling in her belly.

He stood and began fumbling with the buttons of his breeches. The ship canted, and Marianne darted into the other corner where she could not see him. Perhaps he would fall into his bed and take no note of her.

"Meow." Something warm and furry rubbed against her leg.

Opening her eyes, she saw Seafoam's white shadow lingering by her feet. Silently, she gestured for the stupid cat to go away, but it continued circling the hem of her skirt. "Meow."

Footsteps stomped. Marianne held her breath.

A half circle of light advanced upon her shoes, then crept up her legs.

"What have we here?"

❖ CHAPTER 7 ❖

A pair of wide brown eyes, streaked with terror, stared up at Noah. He shook his head. The woman amazed him. The last place he would have expected to find Miss Denton was hiding in his sleeping cabin. And for the life of him, he could find no reason for it, save one, which would be an impossibility.

"Pardon me, Noah. I seem to have gotten lost." The fear fled her eyes, replaced by her usual lofty manner as she attempted to brush past him.

"A condition you seem to be making a habit of aboard my ship." He moved to block her. A chuckled erupted from his throat.

She planted her hands on her waist. "I fail to see what is so amusing."

Seafoam jumped onto Noah's bed and plopped down, eyeing them both.

Noah set the lantern down and leaned on the doorframe. A grin overtook his lips as he realized he could have some fun with this awkward situation. "On the contrary, finding you so close to my bed in the middle of the night is quite amusing, or should I say, rather pleasing." He winked.

Her chest heaved. Her gaze flitted about the tiny room, avoiding him entirely. A red hue crept up her neck onto her face like a rising tide.

She lifted a hand as if she were going to push him, but when her eyes met his bare chest, she seemed to think better of it. "If you please, Noah, I need some air."

He stepped aside before she swooned. Then grabbing the lantern, he followed her out into his cabin and placed it atop his desk. He faced her, searching his memory of his conversation with Mr. Heaton for anything the lady should not have overheard.

"Good night, Noah." She kept her head lowered and headed for the door, but he darted in front of her.

"Not just yet, Miss Denton."

She backed away. "I am tired and wish to retire now." The scent of her lavender soap swirled around him

"Then why are you in my cabin?" Noah lowered his head to peer into her face, but she kept her gaze upon the deck.

"If you insist on keeping me here, would you at least do me the honor of donning your shirt?"

He chuckled. That she was an innocent did not surprise him. That his unclad chest affected her, he found oddly pleasing.

"Are you quite sure, Miss Denton?" He quirked a brow.

She raised her chin, her face twisting in disdain as another flood of crimson blossomed over it. "How dare you?"

"Perhaps you cannot wait for our wedding night?"

Her brown eyes simmered. "Why you insufferable cad." She raised her hand to slap him.

He caught it and lifted it to his lips for a kiss, eyeing her with delight.

She studied him then released a sigh. "You tease me, sir." Snatching her hand from his, she stepped back. "But what would I expect from you?"

Moving to the chair he grabbed his shirt and slipped it over his head. His glance fanned over his desk where his chart had been and he spun around. "You. You ruined my chart."

She averted her gaze and began twisting her ring. "Why would I do that?"

Brown curls swayed in disarray around a fresh bandage devoid of blood. Her lips pressed in their usual petulant manner, and her petite nose pinked as it always did when she was distraught.

"To force me to return to Baltimore, perhaps?" He took a step toward her. She retreated.

Then squaring her shoulders, she placed her hands atop her rounded hips. "Who is Priscilla?"

Noah couldn't help but grin. So she *had* heard their conversation.

Shame settled over him, but he shrugged it off. He had done nothing wrong. "A friend."

"How dare you toss your affections to another when you are engaged to me."

"I can assure you, miss. I never toss my affections anywhere."

❖

Marianne studied him. A word of truth at last, for she doubted the man cared for anyone but himself. Then why was she behaving the jealous shrew? His thick chest peeked out from within his open shirt. The sight of it befuddled her mind. How could she think clearly with his firm muscles staring her in the face?

Yet something else caused unease to clamp over her nerves. Why wasn't Noah furious with her for ruining his map? Instead of chastising her and tossing her from his cabin, he seemed to find the incident amusing.

Which only further infuriated her.

He sat back against his desk and released a ragged sigh, then rubbed the back of his neck as if he had the weight of the world sitting upon it. Agnes's words regarding his burden resurfaced in Marianne's thoughts, and she wondered for a moment what was troubling him.

She should leave. She knew she should leave. Especially now that he no longer blocked her way, but perhaps she could garner some useful information.

"Why do you work so hard for your father?"

His eyes widened. Finally he said, "Unlike you, I wasn't born to privilege. I must work to survive."

"I cannot help the situation of my birth." She huffed. "But you can cease holding it against me."

He tilted his head and examined her as if he could not fathom what she said. "Fair enough," he conceded with a semblance of a grin.

Marianne glanced at the closed door and realized how improper it was for her to be alone with him in his cabin. Yet aside from her reputation—which she doubted anyone on board would care to sully with gossip—the only thing in danger was her pride from his continual insults.

The ship rose over a wave, and she raised a hand to the wall to keep from stumbling. "I don't know how you tolerate this constant teetering.

If not for these walls, we would all be thrashed to and fro with each wave."

"Bulkheads."

"Oh, who cares?" She huffed. Releasing the wall, she balanced her way to one of the chairs closest to the door and sat down. "I've seen little of you for eleven years. Your father would visit quite often before my father died, but you were never with him."

"I was at sea."

Marianne nodded, remembering the event that had sent him there. "I was sorry to hear about your brother."

He snapped his gaze away and stood, turning his back to her. "It was a long time ago."

"Unlike you, he was always kind to me."

Noah's back stiffened, and he crossed his arms over his chest. "Yes, Jacob was kind to everyone. Generous, wise, and. . ." He faced her and shrugged. "Well, everything I am not."

Though she could not argue with his statement, Marianne's heart sank at the look of agony on his face. Word around town was that Jacob had died in an accident aboard a ship. Though she longed to know the details of his death, the anger and despair etched on Noah's countenance silenced her.

Her own sorrow at her father's death remained an open wound on her heart. Perhaps they could find some common ground on that alone. "I understand your pain."

His tight expression softened, but the hard look in his eyes remained. "I am sorry for your loss, as well, Miss Denton, but I doubt you understand what I have suffered."

Marianne tugged on a lock of hair, her ire surging with the rise of the ship over another swell. "I understand the loss of someone you love, Noah. Will you credit that to my account or do you hold a monopoly on grief?"

He snorted. "You may suffer as you wish, miss."

"How kind of you," she retorted then chided herself. There was no sense in lowering her behavior to his reprehensible level. Besides, it was obvious he still felt the sting of his brother's death. Until that dreadful day, the Brenin twins had been inseparable. "My mother tells me God brought her the comfort she needed when my father passed. Perhaps you should pray?"

"You may also do the praying, as you wish."

"You don't believe in God?"

"I believe He exists. I simply don't think about Him often. Nor do I think He considers me." The muscles in Noah's neck tightened. "I have discovered it best to keep myself out of the focus of the Almighty's scope, lest I displease Him in some way and suffer the consequences."

Sorrow burned in Marianne's throat. Such a low opinion of God. "Surely you don't believe that. God will bring you comfort, Noah. And hope for the future." She twisted the ring on her finger. Did she believe that? Yes. God had indeed comforted her and her mother. She had felt His presence during their grief. She knew He was real. But in truth, her hope was not in this world. In this life, she had lost all trust that God would work things out for good as He said in His Word. Even so, it broke her heart to see Noah so far from the only One who could help him.

"He can lead you and guide you," she went on. "Grant you wisdom and show you His plan for your life."

"There is no plan, Miss Denton. The sooner you strike that thought from your mind, the sooner you will start to live your own life." He gripped the edge of his desk until his knuckles grew white. "No, a man makes his own plan, his own destiny. As I am making mine."

"And doing so well at it." Marianne straightened her back. "Pray tell, once you have my fortune, will you continue to exhaust yourself year after year, piling up wealth to supply your endless pride?"

"You find me greedy?" He chuckled, his blue eyes sparkling as if he found delight in her insult. But hadn't he always responded to her attempts to inflict pain on him with the same insolent laughter? As if she were of so little importance that she could not possibly affect him at all.

"You don't know me, Miss Denton."

"Then why marry a woman you don't love? To do so only to please your father seems unlike someone who is so"—she paused, searching for the right word, and upon finding none chose the first one that had come to mind—"self-centered."

The lantern flickered, casting golden flecks on the tips of his hair. He scratched his chin, this time not laughing at her barb. "There is much you don't know."

"Pray tell, enlighten me, since I am to be your prisoner for months."

"Prisoner? I am crushed." He laid a hand on his heart even as one side of his lips curved in a mocking grin. "I prefer to call you an unwilling passenger."

"You may prefer all you wish, Captain, but that does not make you correct."

"Your wit has improved with age."

"Yours has not." Marianne remembered Noah and Luke's conversation about her pluck. "But I am happy to entertain you."

"It was Luke who remarked so. Me? I fail to find pleasure in your company, princess." He lowered his gaze but not before she saw a flicker of regret in his eyes. Nevertheless, his words cut deep—deeper than she would have expected. Why was she subjecting herself to his cruelty?

She rose to find her legs unsteady. "It was you who insisted I stay in your cabin."

"To discover the depth of your traitorous activities." His grin had returned, but it lacked its usual luster.

"Since that has been established, I shall relieve you of my company." Marianne swung around.

"Established, you say?" He chuckled. "The only things we have established are that my chart is ruined and that you seem to enjoy lurking about a man's chamber in the middle of the night."

She swerved about. "How dare you! What are you implying?"

One dark eyebrow rose and he gave an innocent shrug. "Nothing. But if you didn't come here to ruin my chart, what am I to think?"

"You insufferable rogue." Marianne narrowed her eyes, then swung about.

"Good night, Miss Denton."

"Good night, Mr. Brenin." She opened the door.

His blaring voice halted her. "And rest assured, I fully intend to keep my cabin locked in the future."

❖

Noah spread his new chart atop his desk. Morning sunlight sprinkled glistening particles of dust across it as he pinned the corners down with the instruments he'd found stuffed beneath his mattress. He chuckled. He had to give the woman credit. She didn't give up and accept her fate as most women would. Persistent and stubborn. Just like when she was a little girl.

Straightening his stance, he threw his arms over his head and stretched. Exhaustion tugged on his eyes. After Miss Denton had left, he'd barely slept an hour. And that hour had been fraught with night-mares—visions of raging seas and black angry skies, of yards high above the deck flung effortlessly to and fro by the screaming wind, of blood on the planks below.

His brother's blood.

He patted the handkerchief in his pocket and shook his head, try-ing to dislodge the tormenting memories. But the pain in his heart felt as raw as it had the day of the tragedy. The day Noah lost his will to live.

Why, when Noah spent so much of his energy keeping his past buried had Miss Denton so carelessly brought it to mind? Yet he also could not shake the pained look in her eyes at his cruel remarks. But he had no choice. Blast it all. He'd truly enjoyed their conversation. The sympathy beaming from those brown eyes had caught him off guard. She *did* understand his pain—perhaps not the depth of it—but her concern had broken down some invisible wall between them. Then all her talk of God, not preachy, but out of true concern for him. He had felt his defenses weaken. And he couldn't allow that to happen. She must be the one to break off their engagement. It was the only way for her to save face and for Noah to appease his father. Then with the added wealth this trip would bring, everyone would be happy. Perhaps he could even consider a courtship with Miss Priscilla in South Hampton.

He pictured the lady in his mind. With curves in all the right places and hair of golden silk, she was the picture of feminine beauty and charm. The daughter of a wealthy solicitor, she carried none of the pretensions and snobbery one would expect of someone of her class. Although Noah had no formal understanding with Miss Priscilla and he'd only spent a few short days with her, he sensed she was as enthralled with him as he was with her. Her father did, however, require that any suitors must be worth at least one thousand pound a year before he would agree to a courtship.

A sum Noah could make no boast of. Not yet.

He rubbed the back of his neck. Then there was his own father—who would disapprove of Miss Priscilla based solely on the fact that Noah chose her. Another disappointment credited to his ledger. A debt that if Noah could not settle soon, would prohibit him from ever being able to make his own decisions. Which was why he desperately needed this voyage to be successful.

Rap rap rap.

"Enter," Noah said. Matthew ambled in, a tray in hand. The sting of rum-laced tea and stale biscuits greeted Noah's nose as the older man set down his load.

"Apologies sent from my missus, Cap'n, but she's a bit indisposed. 'Fraid ye're going t' have t' do with this simple fare this morning."

"Indisposed?" Noah's alarm rose. He circled the desk. Usually a vision of robust health, Agnes rarely took ill.

"A slight fever, is all." Matthew yanked his hat from his bald head. "Miss Denton attends to 'er."

"Miss Denton?" Noah assumed she'd still be tucked in her bed at this early hour.

Grabbing his waistcoat from the back of the chair, Noah thrust his arms through the sleeves, then lifted the mug and took a sip of tea. The taste soured in his mouth. He liked his tea with sugar, but that was a luxury they could ill afford.

Matthew shifted his bare feet over the floor and stared at Noah.

"Thank you, Matthew. Is there something else?"

" 'Bout Miss Denton." Matthew's eyes crinkled at the corners. "If I may speak wit' ye."

Noah puffed out a sigh. Miss Denton again. He had hoped to occupy his mind elsewhere today.

"I 'eard her cryin' last night in her cabin." Accusation fired from his voice.

The sails thundered above as they shifted in the wind, the sound pounding Noah's guilt deep into his heart. He hadn't meant to make her cry. Leaning back on his desk, he sipped his tea, suddenly wishing he could drown himself in it.

"The missus was speakin' t' me 'bout her. Poor girl's mother is ill, an' she's needed at home."

"I realize that, Matthew." Shrugging off his remorse, Noah tightened his lips. "But I have a schedule to keep and cannot alter it for the actions of one foolish girl. I'll take her home in three months. Her mother will not suffer overmuch during that time. In fact, she appeared quite well the day of the engagement party." Noah set down his mug and began strapping on his belt. "Besides, I fear Miss Denton will use any excuse she can to get me to return her home."

"Even so, Cap'n. Her poor mother will be worried sick over what happened t' her."

"Considering that Miss Denton darted down the street after me, I'm sure she will solve the puzzle soon enough." Noah had no time for such nonsense. Blast the woman for weaving her way into Hobbs's sentiments.

Matthew tossed his hat down and eyed Noah with more authority than his position allowed. "What's this all about, Noah? It is not like you t' be so cruel and selfish."

Noah studied the man who had been more of a father to him than his own. "Trust me, Matthew, I am not proud of my behavior. But it serves a higher purpose."

"If yer talkin' about God, I doubt He has much t' do wit' it."

God again. "No. I'm referring to a plan which will free both Miss Denton and me from a marriage neither of us desires."

"So." Matthew folded his beefy arms across his belly. "You're being cruel to her for her own good, eh?"

"Precisely." Noah buttoned his waistcoat and snapped the hair from his face. It was true after all. Along with aiding his plan to break free from his father's control.

A ray of sunlight stroked Matthew's bald head, making him look almost angelic, despite his formidable frame. His dark eyes narrowed into pinpoints of judgment. "I've known you for many years, Noah. And you're a good man deep down in there." He pointed at Noah's chest. " 'Bout time you figure that out for yourself and did the right thing."

❖

Still steaming over Matthew's rebuke, Noah strode toward the man's cabin where Agnes rested. He shouldn't allow his boatswain such liberties with his opinion. Noah was captain after all. But the old man had been there countless times when Noah needed fatherly advice. How could he turn him away simply because his advice was not what Noah wished to hear?

He knocked on the door. A female voice bade him enter, and he opened it to see Agnes lying in bed, her glazed eyes peering at him from within a puffy face, flush with fever. At her feet, Seafoam lay curled in a ball. Beside her, Miss Denton sat dabbing a cloth over her forehead.

Marianne's eyes swept over him before she quickly returned to her ministrations. No greeting? He could hardly blame her after his behavior the night before.

"Noah." Agnes smiled. "What brings you here?"

"To inquire after your health, of course." Noah took a step inside and was assailed with the stale smell of infirmity. "I heard you were not feeling well."

Miss Denton wrung the cloth out in a basin of water.

"Oh, I suppose I'll live." Agnes tried to laugh, but it came out as a cough. She tugged at the lace of her nightdress that appeared to have a stranglehold on her neck. "Just a wee bit hot and me stomach's twistin' and turnin'."

"Is there something I can get you?" Noah wove around the bed and drew a chair on the other side from where Miss Denton sat. Seafoam pried open her sleepy eyes to look his way.

"No thank you, my boy. Marianne has been an angel, takin' care o' me all through the night."

Through the night? Noah gazed at Miss Denton as she laid a cloth over Agnes's forehead.

"I apologize, Noah, for not makin' yer breakfast," Agnes said.

Noah took her hand. "Madam, you think that concerns me? The crew will make do. All that matters is that you get well." Her hand felt warm, but not too warm. He brushed the back of his fingers across her cheek. Hot, but he'd felt worse. His alarm dissipated.

Only then did Miss Denton look at him with the most peculiar stare before she quickly averted her eyes.

The ship pitched and her eyes widened a moment. A sail snapped above.

Rising, Seafoam stretched and made her way to Noah, jumping into his lap. The old cat had been a gift from their father to both Noah and Jacob on their first crossing to England nearly fourteen years ago. A kitten at the time, she had grown up on this ship, knew every crevice and cranny, and had feasted on her fair share of rats. Noah scratched beneath her chin, and Seafoam stretched her neck upward and purred in response. This old cat and the handkerchief in his pocket were the last things Noah had that had belonged to Jacob.

Agnes squeezed his hand, jarring him from his thoughts. "Order Marianne to her cabin to get some rest, Noah. She's been here all night."

"Order her?" Noah chuckled. "I don't believe anyone can order Miss Denton to do anything she doesn't want to do."

Marianne's lips lifted at one corner, and she favored him with a sly glance before facing Agnes. "I am well, Agnes. When you rest, I will rest right here beside you, in case you should need anything."

"You are too good to me, dear." An exchange of affection passed between Agnes and Miss Denton that caused Noah to shift in his seat. For a woman accustomed to ordering servants about to please her every whim, Miss Denton's care for this dear sweet woman was quite baffling.

And Noah didn't like it one bit.

❖

Emerging from the companionway, Marianne slid her shoes tentatively onto the upper deck. She'd been avoiding coming above, loathe to face the endless sea. But after spending two nights and three days in the stagnant, sickly air of Agnes's cabin, she risked confronting her fears in order to get a breath of fresh air. Thankfully, Agnes's fever had abated, and she slept soundly now. She'd be back to her old self soon.

Noah truly cared for Agnes. Marianne had seen it in his eyes as he held her hand. She had heard it in the soft tone with which he addressed her. And Seafoam. Marianne had never seen a man so affectionate with a cat. And a cat so attached to her master. She began to think there was more to this man than she first assumed. Yet that did not change the fact that he did not wish to marry her. Nor that he planned to do so out of obligation to his father. At least she hoped that was still his plan. That he harbored feelings for another woman didn't bode well on that front.

Fatigue hung on her shoulders and weighted down her eyelids.

Squinting against the afternoon sun that sat a handbreadth above the horizon, Marianne made her way to the round object they used to heave the anchor, bracing herself against the surge and roll of the ship as she went. Somehow the vessel's constant sway seemed less dangerous below where if the ship canted and she tumbled out of control, the walls could break her fall. But here above deck, what would stop her from toppling overboard? She gripped the wooden heaving tool and drew in a deep breath of the stiff breeze that swept past her, bringing with it a hint of salt and fish.

Sailors scampered by, tipping their hats in her direction as they passed. Shielding her eyes, she glanced above where men lumbered over the yards with as much ease as if they strolled along Market Street. Another blast of wind rushed over her, cooling the perspiration on her neck. Forcing down her fear, she dared a glance at the vast waters that held the tiny ship captive. Azure blue waves spread to a glowing horizon, each swell capped with golden crystals of sunlight. The ship bucked and a salty spray showered over her. She jerked back, brushing the drops from her arms.

"Miss Denton," a deep voice startled her, and she turned to see Mr. Weller standing beside her. "Good afternoon t' ye."

"Thank you, sir."

"We haven't seen much of you above deck these past few days." He adjusted the red scarf that seemed to be permanently attached to his neck.

"I've been attending Mrs. Hobbs."

"Aye, we ain't got a decent meal in quite some time. I hope she gets well soon." He frowned. "Not that I only care about me food. She's a kindly lady, too."

"Never fear, she's recovering."

He gazed toward the horizon. "The sea is beautiful in the afternoon. If you come t' the foredeck it feels like yer a bird, flyin' across the water." He gestured for her to follow him.

"Oh no, I couldn't, Mr. Weller." She swallowed. "I'm perfectly saf—I mean content here."

He cocked his head and a slow smile spread on his lips. "Yer afraid of water?"

She gave him a sheepish grin, wondering if she should confide in him. Despite his scarred face, nothing but sincerity shone from his brown eyes. And he had always been kind to her. She leaned toward him. "Dreadfully."

The ship bucked and he placed a hand atop hers, "Nothin' to be feared about, miss. This ship is the sturdiest craft as ever I sailed."

"But ships like these do sink, do they not?"

"Aye, from time t' time." He doffed his hat and scratched his thick head of charcoal black hair.

A wonderful idea planted itself in her mind. This man must know a great deal about ships—especially this particular one. "I'll make a bargain with you, Mr. Weller. I'll brave the foredeck if you'll explain just how sound this ship really is."

He extended his arm. "Ye've got a bargain, miss."

❖

Noah sprang onto the deck to the sound of feminine laughter. His eyes soon discovered the source. At the bow of the ship stood Miss Denton and Mr. Weller, of all people. Her, gripping the railing. Him, steadying her with a hand on her back. They held their heads together as if they were old friends.

An uncomfortable feeling skittered across Noah's back. What would Miss Denton and Mr. Weller find in common to discuss so intimately? Why, Mr. Weller rarely spoke to anyone since Noah rescued him from St. Kitts and gave him a job aboard the *Fortune*.

Forcing down his annoyance, Noah took the ladder to his position on the quarterdeck. After greeting Mr. Pike, who was positioned at the helm, he stood at the stanchions with hands clasped behind his back. He attempted to divert his gaze to the sea, but his traitorous eyes made their way back to Miss Denton and Mr. Weller. Where most women would cringe at the man's deformities, she treated him as if he were the Earl of Buckley dropping over for tea.

Wasn't it enough he'd been forced to witness her kindness toward Agnes? Now this? Why, sooner or later he might have to admit he admired the lady. And that would not aid his plans in the least. Not in the least.

❖

Marianne smiled at her new friend. No longer noticing the rippled skin on the left side of his face or his missing fingers. "So there's nothing that can penetrate the ship's hull save a massive rock or a cannon shot?"

"That be correct, miss. Unless"—he winked—"you were to take an ax to it, I suppose."

Which she would never do. The last thing she wanted was to cause the ship to sink. "And what of these ropes?" Releasing her death grip on the railing, Marianne clung to one of the massive lines that stretched taut up to a sail above. But she already knew the answer. Nearly as thick as her wrist and covered with tar, it would take hours to slice through with a knife.

Mr. Weller grinned. A single gold tooth twinkled in the setting sun. "Nay, these lines are fast and hard. Nothin' can break them 'sides a heavy ax or grape shot. Besides, ye'd have to sever more than one o' them to do any damage."

The ship pitched and with it, Marianne's heart. She clutched the railing with both hands again and tried not to look down at the foamy water sliced by the bow of the ship. Without access to the captain's cabin, she must find another way to disable the vessel.

She gazed upward. "And the sails?"

"Sturdy as steel cloth. Nothing but fire or the blast from a ship's gun could penetrate them."

Marianne bit her lip. Neither would suffice without endangering the crew, and she couldn't do that.

"You are a kind lady, miss." Mr. Weller smiled and ran a thumb down the scar on his face. "Most women avoid speakin' t' me." He shrugged and stared at the churning water at the bow. "I suppose my appearance scares 'em."

Marianne's heart shrank. Though she had no disfigurement, how often had she been slighted in favor of more beautiful ladies? She raised a haughty chin. "Then, I daresay, they are missing out on knowing a very knowledgeable, courteous, and chivalrous gentleman."

"Gentleman?" He guffawed. "Ain't never been considered to be such."

She smiled at his easy manner then grew serious. "May I be so bold as to ask what happened to you?"

He tugged his scarf up as if suddenly self-conscious of his scar. A sail above them thundered in an ominous snap. "I was a gunner's mate onboard the British warship, the *Hibernia*, of one hundred and ten guns"—he took a deep breath—"an' durin' a battle wit' a French frigate, our gun exploded. I lost three o' me fingers and a scrap of hot lead struck me face."

Marianne's stomach grew queasy. "How horrible."

"Three other sailors lost their lives, includin' a young powder boy who was no more 'an thirteen."

"Thirteen." Marianne's head began to spin. She could not imagine the horrors of enduring a battle at sea, let alone such a tragedy. The glaze of painful memories clouded Mr. Weller's eyes, and she longed to take his pain away, to say how sorry she was, but words failed her.

"Aye. They say the gun deck is the most dangerous place to be durin' battle."

The ship rose then plunged over a swell. Seawater misted over her. Normally, she would find it refreshing from the heat, but to her, it seemed like spit from the mouth of a monster.

Mr. Weller's hand pressed against her back to steady her. Though she rarely allowed any man such liberties, she appreciated his strong support and felt no threat from his touch.

"So you see, there's naught to be 'fraid of. Unless we end up in a battle with a warship." He chuckled. "Unlikely since we are simple merchantmen."

"Then why does the captain arm the ship?" Marianne gestured behind her toward the three cannons that lined the top deck on each side and the two that perched off the stern.

"Just for defense, miss, I assure ye."

Marianne released a ragged sigh. It sounded as if the only way to prevent Noah from reaching England would be an enemy attack. And even if she could arrange that, it wouldn't bode well for any of them. Her hope dwindling, she gazed out at sea, squinting at the setting sun. Perspiration slid down her back. Out there, beyond the sun, was her precious country, her precious city, her precious home. And every swell they traversed meant they were that much farther away. *Mother, I'm trying to come home.* Fear tightened her chest. Would Lizzie be able to care for Mama without Marianne? Who would do the cooking, the mending? Who would administer Mama's medicines? She faced Mr. Weller and offered a conciliatory half smile.

"Indeed, Mr. Weller, it does sound as though the ship is indestructible."

"Aye, as I've told you. Unless we come under attack or a squall disables the rudder, ain't nothing will stop us from reaching our destination."

"The rudder? How would I. . .I mean how could that happen?"

He leaned on the railing. The sails above cast half of his face in shadows while the sun cast a golden glint on the other half. His brown eyes so full of life found hers. With a strong jaw and cheekbones, he could be considered a handsome man, if one could ignore his scars. Which she found increasingly easy to do. And he was young. She guessed he couldn't be older than thirty years.

"A shot to the rudder would do it." He smiled. "Or running aground during a storm, or by the strain o' a storm on the wheel. Or I suppose someone could chop through the tiller ropes, but I don't see why anyone aboard would do that."

"Why not?" Marianne dared not hope.

"That would leave us unable to steer, save by the sails, and that would be difficult." He glanced above. "O' course that can be repaired right quick."

She bit her lip. "Then it seems as though we are destined for England."

"The captain's a driven man when he's got a cargo full of goods. No, I expect the only thing that would turn 'im around is if he lost his cargo somehow and had nothin' to sell."

Lost his cargo.

Marianne's heart leapt. She smiled. Of course. Why hadn't she thought of that? What reason would Noah have to continue to England if he had no goods to sell?

If his precious cargo met with some unforeseen disaster?

❖ CHAPTER 8 ❖

Marianne ran the back of her sleeve over her moist forehead and stared at the soup bubbling atop the iron stove. She wanted to assist Agnes—still taken to her bed—by preparing the evening meal. But in light of the strange odor wafting up from the gurgling slop in the copper kettle, she was beginning to regret that decision. It wasn't as if she hadn't cooked before. After her mother dismissed most of the servants, Marianne had taken up the duty of preparing the meals. But she'd done so in a well-equipped kitchen, not in a dark, cramped ship's galley with only a smidgen of spices and foods to use in the preparation of her meal.

Ignoring the sweat streaming down her back, she grabbed a cloth and opened the oven door where several whole chickens roasted on spits over the fire. Hot air blasted over her, carrying with it a juicy, spicy fragrance that made her mouth water. At least the chicken would taste good. She silently thanked God that she hadn't been forced to slaughter the poor birds herself. Mr. Weller had gladly assigned that duty to one of the sailors.

Closing the oven door, Marianne took a step back, if only to remove herself from the heat for a second, and bumped into the preparation table. How did Agnes, a much larger woman than Marianne, work in such tight quarters?

She sensed, rather than heard someone watching her and looked up. Mr. Heaton leaned against the doorframe, arms folded over his chest. He smiled. "Smells delicious."

"Thank you, Mr. Heaton." Marianne returned his smile, ignoring the slight quiver of unease at his presence. "I am hoping the taste will agree with the smell." She studied the tall, muscular man. His hair, as dark as a starless night, was so at odds with his clear blue eyes. Eyes that took her in as if she were some strange apparition.

"Can I help you?" she asked. The soothing smell of baked dough swirled about her nose, and she jumped. "Oh no, my biscuits!" Using the cloth still in her hand, she removed the oven tray and turning, dumped the browned biscuits into a large basket. At least she hadn't managed to burn this set. She dropped the tray to the table and began plopping dough onto it for the next batch.

"Is there something you want, Mr. Heaton? I am quite busy at the moment." Though he had given her no cause for alarm and had always been cordial, his reputation among the ladies in Baltimore as a libertine and a rogue made her stomach clench in his presence—especially since she found herself alone with him.

"Just surprised to find you here, miss." His deep voice held no malice. "Noah led me to believe you hadn't done a day's work in your life."

Marianne sighed. That had been true of her once—a lifetime ago, before her father died. "Noah knows very little about me."

He stepped forward and reached to pluck one of the biscuits from the basket. Without thinking, Marianne slapped his wrist, her anger overcoming her reason, for she didn't know whether Mr. Heaton was a man one could slap—even playfully—without repercussions. To add to her discomfiture, the distinct smell of rum filled the air between them. She knew the smell. Knew it quite well, along with the memories it invoked of her father.

Relief came, however, when Mr. Heaton chuckled, his mirth reaching his blue eyes with a twinkle. "Noah knows little about you? I would say that to be true of you, as well, regarding him."

"I've known Noah since I was five and he was six. Can you attest to the same?"

"No, but these past five years I've lived in these quarters with him for months at a time. Can you attest to the same?"

Marianne could see why women's hearts fluttered at his rakish grin that was both sensuous and charming.

"I cannot imagine how you have suffered his company that long." She snorted.

He chuckled and rubbed the scar on his right ear. "Or he mine."

She cocked her head. Though appearing the rake in every way, she sensed something deeper within him—a kindness, a genuineness—that set her at ease. "Do you enjoy life at sea, Mr. Heaton?"

"I do. There's freedom here on these waves, miss. And adventure. You never know what will happen. Take you, for instance. Who would have guessed you'd be sailing with us on the crossing."

"Yes, I quite agree with you on that." Marianne plucked a ladle from its hook and stirred the fish soup. "So you crave freedom and adventure. What else stirs your soul, Mr. Heaton?"

"Wealth." His answer came too quickly. Too resolutely.

Marianne huffed her disappointment. "Indeed? What of charity, kindness, loyalty, honor? Have they no place in your life?"

He shrugged. "They do not fill empty bellies."

"And your belly is all that concerns you?" She looked his way, wondering if her blunt comment would prick his ire. But he only returned a grin.

"At the moment, yes." He eyed the biscuits. "I am quite hungry."

"Then you have come to the right place." Marianne plucked one and handed it to him.

He took it and lifted his brows. "Thank you, miss. I won't tell a soul."

"Do you have family in Baltimore, Mr. Heaton?" she asked.

He swallowed the bite of biscuit in his mouth. The usual cocky expression faded from his face. "My parents are dead."

"I'm sorry." Marianne stepped toward him, the soup dripping from the ladle onto the floor. She knew well the pain of losing a parent.

He lifted his gaze, shifting his eyes between hers—eyes filled with pain and the slight glaze of alcohol, eyes that instantly hardened. "No need. It was a long time ago."

"But that kind of pain can last for years."

He jerked his hair behind him then lowered his chin.

Grabbing a cloth, Marianne knelt to clean up the spilled soup, chiding herself for prying into this man's personal life.

"How is your wound?" he asked.

Rising, Marianne felt the bandage wrapped around her head.

Aside from an occasional itch, she'd all but forgotten it was there. "It gives me no pain."

He chuckled. "I heard it was Seafoam who lured you into your trap below."

"My father always told me my love for animals would cause trouble for me." She smiled then sorrow gripped her at the memory.

She cleared her throat and began spooning biscuit dough onto another tray.

"That cat is a smart one," he said. "I'll warrant she knew exactly what she was doing."

Marianne's hand halted in midair. "What the devil do you mean, sir? I am now a prisoner aboard this ship. How could that be a smart thing to cause?"

Her outburst bore no effect on his insolent grin. "You are good for him."

Lifting the tray, she opened the oven and shoved it inside, slamming the door with a *clank*. "For whom?"

He gave her a devilish smile.

"Noah?" She swung back to the stove to examine the soup. "Absurd. He hates me and I him."

"I doubt that."

"Oh, really? What of Priscilla?"

His eyebrows shot up. "That vain peacock? She's nothing but an empty box wrapped in ribbons and lace."

"So she is beautiful?" Marianne stirred the soup a little too vigorously. Why did she care?

"Very. But she is a bore, if you ask me."

Marianne didn't want to ask him. Didn't want to hear any more about the silly woman.

"Supper will be ready in a few minutes, Mr. Heaton."

"I'll call Mr. Hobbs to gather the messmen, miss." He plopped the rest of the biscuit into his mouth, gave her a wink, and left.

❖

"Dinner is served."

Noah glanced up from his desk to see Luke entering the room with Matthew scrambling in behind him, carrying a tray of steaming food.

"Have you heard of knocking?"

"Not when we bring such delicious fare." Luke kicked the door shut as Matthew set the tray on top of Noah's charts. The savory scent of chicken and the aroma of fresh biscuits filled Noah's nose and he licked his lips. "I thought your wife was still indisposed."

"Aye, that she is." Matthew and Luke exchanged an odd glance.

"Then am I to assume that she prepared this food from her bed?" Noah stood, irritation grinding his nerves at whatever secret the two men shared.

Luke lifted his brows, a mischievous look on his face. "Miss Denton cooked the meal tonight."

Noah allowed the words to needle through his mind, seeking a thread of reason. He dropped his gaze to the plateful of glazed brown chicken and two biscuits. Beside it, a spicy fish scent spiraled upward from a bowl of steaming soup. His mouth watered.

"Quite tasty if you ask me." Matthew licked his lips.

"Miss Denton made this?" Noah eyed them both curiously.

Luke crossed his arms over his chest. "I saw her myself."

Tearing a piece of chicken from the bone, Noah tossed it in his mouth. Tender, moist, and somewhat flavorful. "Astonishing."

"Though not as good as your wife's cooking, Matthew, this is certainly satisfying, especially since I thought I would go hungry tonight." Noah bit into a biscuit, surprised when he found a buttery soft texture within the hard crust.

Seafoam nudged his arm and meowed.

"Even the cat knows good cookin' when she sees it." Matthew laughed.

Noah picked up Seafoam, scratched her head, then set her down on the deck. "Go below and find a rat to gnaw on. This meal is mine."

"Not bad for a woman who never did an ounce of work her entire life." Luke's voice rang with sarcasm.

A vision of blistered hands invaded Noah's thoughts. Who was Miss Denton? Certainly not the spoiled little chit who would go crying to her mama whenever a speck of dirt appeared on her dress. Certainly not the princess who would call a servant over to pick up a handkerchief she had dropped. And then snub her nose at Noah when the maid instantly complied. Either this Miss Denton was not Miss Denton at all, but an imposter, or she deserved a chorus of cheers for such a convincing performance.

❖

Marianne shot up in bed, her heart pounding. Had she overslept? So exhausted after cooking for hours, she'd fallen onto her mattress in the hopes of getting a few hours' sleep before putting her plan into motion. Dashing to the porthole, she searched for any hint of dawn, but the night still hung its dark curtain over the sea. A myriad of stars winked at her as if prodding her onward. She must make her way down to the hold to discover a way to ruin Noah's cargo. Even as the thought sparked her to action, guilt rapped on the door of her conscience. But she would not answer. She couldn't. Her mother's life depended on it. Besides, when she and Noah married, Noah would have all the wealth he needed, and he wouldn't need to work so hard. She was actually doing him a favor.

Striking flint to steel, she lit the lantern on the table, then tucked a knife she'd taken from the kitchen into the pocket of her gown.

She swung the door open, cringed at the loud squeak echoing off the bulkheads, then tiptoed out into the hallway, or companionway, whatever it was called. She listened for any sounds from sailors who might still be about, but nothing but the bone-chilling creaks and groans of the ship and the rush of water against its hull met her ears. From what she had observed, most of the men slept through the night in a section beneath the forecastle by the bow, while the other half kept watch on the top deck, the two groups switching every four hours. Noah's officers slept in separate cabins.

Which meant Marianne could slip into the hold undetected.

Lifting the lantern, she made her way down the steep ladder, and thought to say a prayer for her success, but then decided against it. Though God rarely answered her prayers, she was sure this was a petition He would not only refuse to answer but would frown upon.

The narrow steps creaked and bowed with each footfall. Moisture formed on her neck and arms. At the bottom of the ladder, Marianne scanned the dark hallway to her left and recognized the door of the cursed room that had entrapped her aboard this ship in the first place. The stench of mold, stale water, and something akin to rotten eggs assailed her, and she flung a hand to her nose. Nausea waged a battle in her stomach.

When it passed, she lifted the lantern and scanned the area to her right. Another set of stairs descended to an open lower level stacked to the ceiling with crates, barrels, and huge sacks.

Gathering her courage, she inched down the final ladder. The *pitter-pat* of tiny feet filled the hold, sounding like raindrops on a roof. *Drat.* Marianne froze. Rats. *Oh Lord, maybe I will pray after all. If You are so inclined, Lord, please keep the filthy beasts away from me.* At the bottom, she took a step over the pebbles scattered across the hold floor. The light from her lantern arched before her like a golden shield. Long, furry tails disappeared in the dark gaps between the crates.

She trembled. Resisting the urge to turn around and run to the safety of her cabin, she swallowed her fears and continued onward. She had no choice. *For you, Mama. If you could see me now, you'd be so proud of me.* Unlike Papa who rarely had a kind word for her unless he was well into his cups.

Perspiration slid down her back and dotted her forehead. The sea pounded against the sides of the ship as if it knew what she was about and wanted to stop her. Could it break through the wooden hull and grab her? Mr. Weller had said no.

Several barrels of water and rum sat within easy reach of the bottom of the ladder. But she was not interested in those. Placing one foot in front of the other, she inched her way down an incline to a lower section. Once there, she began examining the crates one by one. As far as she could tell, most were filled with iron tools and fabric. She moved to another section of barrels. Water and rum for the journey no doubt. But it was the sacks that interested her the most. Flour from the mills at Jones's falls in Baltimore and rice from Charleston.

Even if she managed to open the crates, she could not damage iron and besides, the only way to be rid of it would be to haul it up on deck and toss it to the sea—unlikely given her lack of strength and the fact that her deed would not go unnoticed.

But the flour and rice. She smiled. And rum and water. A terrible combination.

From the corner of her eye she glimpsed something too large to be a rat moving. Marianne gasped, and grabbing the lantern tighter, swung in that direction. What other repulsive creatures lived down here? A loud squeak shot through the dank air. Oh my, maybe it was a very large rodent. She gulped.

Then out from the shadows strolled Seafoam, a squirming rat in her mouth. Marianne backed away in horror even as her heart settled to a normal beat. The cat pranced up to her and dropped the rat proudly at her feet. Trouble was, it wasn't dead. Hobbling across the pebbles, the poor beast tried to make its escape. Seafoam leapt in the air and pounced upon it, this time killing it.

Nausea resurging, Marianne pressed a hand to her stomach as Seafoam deposited the lifeless rodent at Marianne's feet, then glanced up at her as if seeking approval.

Despite her queasiness, Marianne couldn't help but smile at the cat's kindness. "For me?" She set the lantern atop a barrel and stooped to pet the cat. Seafoam purred affectionately and circled her, rubbing against her legs.

"You are a brave hunter, little one. But you may have your prey. I've already eaten." Marianne scooped the cat up in her arms and snuggled against her, cheek to cheek. Noah's scent filled her nostrils, sending an odd warmth through her. She remembered the gentle way he had nestled the cat against his chest—in such contrast with his harsh, all-business demeanor.

"I have work to do, little one." She set the cat atop one of the crates, and Seafoam plopped down and began licking her paws and rubbing them on her face.

Marianne pulled the knife from her pocket. "Now, I know you and the captain are good friends, but you must promise me you'll keep silent about this, agreed?"

Seafoam stopped her grooming and yawned before continuing.

"I shall take that as a yes." Then, knife in hand, Marianne swung about and began slashing through the sacks of rice.

❖ CHAPTER 9 ❖

Noah shut his cabin door and trudged down the companionway in as foul a mood on the start of this new day as he'd been for the past three. He ran a hand through his hair and plopped his hat atop his head. Although he'd intentionally avoided Miss Denton during that time, he'd heard enough about her from everyone around him.

"Miss Denton is so kind." "Miss Denton is so generous with her time and strength." "Miss Denton is so witty, smart, capable, honest." Could he not escape the woman? Had she cast a spell on everyone around her? Everyone save him. For he knew the real Marianne Denton. Pompous, spoiled, and self-serving. At least that was the way he remembered her. And the reason he had teased her so as a child.

Weaving around a corner, he nodded at a passing sailor and scaled the ladder to the upper deck in two leaps, ascending to where he hoped to continue evading the woman. For she rarely came on deck. Why she confined herself to the heat and stale air below, he could not fathom. No doubt it was part of her plan, along with her drastic change in character, to invoke his sympathies so he would take her home.

But Noah was no fool.

Sunlight struck him along with a cool ocean breeze, feathering the hair against the collar of his shirt. Agnes's bubbling laughter bounced over him, drawing his gaze to a group of sailors clustered around the mainmast. In their midst, sitting atop a chair, sat Miss Denton with a rope tying her and the chair to the mast. Agnes perched upon a barrel beside her, a huge smile on her chubby face. Noah halted and tried to rub the strange apparition from his eyes.

The sailors chuckled at something Miss Denton said, and she graced them with a smile before returning her attention to a book laid open on her lap.

" 'And the king spake and said to Daniel, O Daniel, servant of the living God, is thy God, whom thou servest continually, able to deliver thee from the lions?'" she quoted.

She reads the Bible to my men. Frustration boiled within Noah. He glanced at Luke who was leaning on the port railing, Matthew beside him, both their gazes riveted upon her.

Noah marched over to them. "What is going on here?"

"I believe your fiancée is reading from the Holy Book." Luke made no attempt to hide his smirk.

"She is not my. . ." Noah flatted his lips. "I can see that. But why?"

"It's the Sabbath," Matthew said as if that should clear any confusion. He shifted his bulky frame. "She marched up here and announced that she'd be performin' Sunday service for those men who'd be interested." He shook his head and chuckled. "An' bless me sailor's soul if most o''em didn't come a runnin'."

Noah gritted his teeth. "Why on earth is she strapped to the mast?"

Matthew raised an eyebrow that was nearly as bald as his head. "Because the poor girl is afraid of the water. You sure don't know much about your own fiancée."

"Confound it all!" Noah ran a hand over the back of his neck as frustration tightened his muscles. "Afraid of the water. Is that what she told you?"

"She didn't have to. It's obvious." Luke shrugged.

"She's merely attempting to get our sympathy."

Matthew's head jerked back as if Noah had struck him. "Are you sayin' she's pretendin'? Now why would she be doin' that?"

"To convince me to return her to Baltimore, of course. She's not the sweet innocent she pretends to be. Beneath that benevolent facade rages a pompous shrew." Noah's harsh tone faded, unable to carry the weight of words he wasn't sure he still believed. "And blast it all, Luke, why are you listening? You don't even believe in God."

"She has a unique way of telling the story of Daniel in the lion's den. Very amusing."

"And that, gentlemen"—her cheerful voice brought Noah's eyes back to her—"is why we must always have faith, even in the midst of hopeless times."

"Amen." Agnes clapped her hands together, her full cheeks rosy once again.

"Me wife surely finds pleasure in 'er company." Matthew spit to the side.

"She's no doubt starved for female companionship." Noah growled. "Enough of this." He stormed amidships.

Miss Denton gently closed the Bible and lifted her gaze to his. Brown eyes, glistening like cinnamon in the sunlight, scoured over him.

"Service is over. Get back to work!" he barked. The men scattered across the deck like rats in daylight.

"Never mind him, dear." Agnes leaned over and untied the rope around Miss Denton's waist then helped her to stand.

Noah rolled his eyes. "Matthew, get that chair stowed below where it belongs."

"Aye, Cap'n." His boatswain ran to the mainmast and hoisted the chair in his arms.

Agnes ambled past Noah, adjusted her apron, and pursed her lips. She didn't have to say anything. Her motherly look of reprimand did its work on Noah's conscience.

"Sail on the horizon. Off the starboard quarter!" Mr. Grainger shouted from above.

Thankful for the interruption, Noah plucked his glass from his belt, moved toward the railing, and lifted it to his eye.

"What has put you in such a foul mood today, Captain?" Miss Denton's voice was soft and assured.

Ignoring her, he gripped the glass tighter and focused on the horizon where the slight shape of a white sail reflected the morning sun. Too far to determine whether she be friend or foe.

He lowered his glass. "It won't work, Miss Denton."

She screened her eyes from the sunlight and gazed up at him with more innocence than seemed possible to feign. "What won't work?"

"Your trying to charm my crew to garner their sympathy."

Her forehead crinkled. "I am doing no such thing. It is Sunday by my best calculation, and the crew deserves a chance to worship." A pink hue colored her nose. "I'm surprised at you for not initiating a proper service while out at sea."

"The sails are gone now, Cap'n," Mr. Grainger reported.

Noah slapped his spyglass shut and faced her. "For one thing, I doubt God notices when people worship Him, and for another thing, Miss Denton, this is a merchant ship, not a chapel, and these men wouldn't be caught dead in church when they are in port." She gazed across the water as if pondering his words, her face pinching. Yet she remained silent. No snide comments, no sharp rebukes, no haughty insults.

Where was the spoiled little goose he'd known as a child? The one he found such pleasure in taunting. He had thought being mean to her would be easy, that he could pick up right where he'd left off eleven years ago. How was he to know the goose had transformed into an angel during those long years, making it all the more harder to follow through with his plan?

Yet he must not falter. For her own good.

"You think my men enjoyed your sermon, Miss Denton? They only attended because it took them away from their duties."

She swept her eyes to his, a moist sheen covering them. Noah hated himself for causing it.

"I'll leave you to your commanding, Captain." Then avoiding his gaze, she teetered over the wobbling deck and disappeared below.

❖

Heavy fog wrapped around the ship. Marianne leaned over the railing and peered through the mist. Below, the sea chopped against the hull so close she could almost reach out and touch it. Claws of foam reached toward her. One touched her hand and she leapt back. Her breath clumped in her throat. Dashing over the deck, she screamed for help, for anyone. But the only answer came in the creaks and groans of the ship—chiding her, berating her.

She was all alone.

She darted to the railing again. Gurgling sounded. She glanced down. Massive bubbles surfaced from below. The sea had risen and was now within her reach. They were sinking! Laughter rode upon the mist and taunted her ears. She peered into the fog. A small boat formed out of the eerie haze

"Hello there!" she yelled. "Help me, I'm sinking."

All eyes in the boat shot to her. Her father, her mother, Lizzie, Noah, Luke, Agnes, and Matthew Hobbs. They smiled and waved at her as if nothing were amiss.

"Help me!" Marianne shouted. "Over here!"

They no longer seemed to hear her or even see her.

A figure appeared near the bow of the small craft—glowing in white light, shining and brilliant. He held up a lantern and faced forward as the boat drifted farther away.

And disappeared into the fog.

Marianne jerked up in bed. Her breath leapt into her throat. She laid a hand on her heart to quell its violent thumping. Tossing her coverlet aside, she swung her feet onto the floor and dropped her head into her hands. *Oh Lord. What does this mean? Will everyone I love abandon me? Even You? Can I trust no one? Why has all this happened to me? Father's death, Mother's illness, our poverty, my forced engagement, and now me upon this ship. Why have You abandoned me?*

"I will never leave you."

Marianne brushed the tears from her face. A spark of hope lit in her heart. Had she heard from God or merely imagined His voice? She looked up. Thunder rumbled in the distance. A mist as thick as the one in her dream slithered into her cabin. She stood, hugging herself against the chill. The rush of water against the hull sounded like a thousand voices taunting her, belittling her. *Trust? You can't trust Him.*

She twirled the ring on her finger. The ring her father had given her. The only thing of value he had ever given her. Before he left her and her mother all alone in this world. Marianne should have sold it when she'd had the chance. The money from the sale would provide a few months of food and medicines. Why hadn't she sold it? The silver felt cold and hard against her fingertips, and she released the band.

You couldn't trust your own father. How can you trust God?

Groping for the tiny table at the foot of her bed, she felt for her flint and steel and with trembling hand, struck it to light her lantern. The glow spread over her cabin, chasing the darkness back into the corners.

"I am the light of the world: he that followeth me shall not walk in darkness, but shall have the light of life." The scripture from John flooded her mind. But her doubts resurrected to do battle with the holy words. Marianne's heart thrashed wildly. She didn't know why. Something evil,

something dark seemed to hover in the room ready to pounce upon her. She donned her dress and shoes, swung open her door, and headed up on deck. Better to face her known fear than to suffer below with her demons.

A cool night breeze fingered the tendrils of her loose hair as she emerged on deck and made her way to the capstan, which she had learned was the name of the drum-shaped heaving tool she liked to cling to. Light from a full moon cast a milky haze over the ship, making it look dreamlike as it floated on the ebony sea.

A watchman up on the quarterdeck tipped his hat in her direction. After settling against the sturdy wooden frame, she dared a glance across the sea. The moon hung over the horizon like a giant pearl, its milky wands setting the waves sparkling in silver light.

"It shall be established for ever as the moon, and as a faithful witness in heaven."

Another scripture from the Psalms floated through Marianne's mind. The moon was God's faithful witness. Was He trying to tell her that He still loved her and was with her? A lump burned in her throat, and she swiped a tear from her cheek.

"Trust Me."

Releasing the capstan, Marianne took a step toward the railing. She grew weary of all the struggles in her life, weary of feeling so incredibly alone, but most of all she was weary of always being afraid. She slid her other shoe across the wooden planks. The ship rose over a swell, and she threw her arms out on either side to steady herself. Another step. *Lord, can I trust You?*

As if in answer to her question, the ship plunged, and she nearly stumbled. Her heart thumped against her ribs. A spray of saltwater stung her face.

No. I can't. She slowly retreated.

Right into a firm hand on her back.

She whirled around to find Noah behind her. She wobbled.

"Steady now." He gripped her shoulders.

Shrugging off his hands, she backed away from him, only to realize she was but inches from the railing. She dashed toward the capstan and gripped its familiar firm wood. Even in the moonlight, she could see the look of confusion on his face.

He proffered his elbow. "Milady, may I escort you to the railing? I believe that's where you were heading before I interrupted?"

Marianne hesitated. Why was he being kind? She could not trust him. Squaring her shoulders, she lifted her chin. "I can make it on my own, thank you, Noah."

"Captain."

Did the man's arrogance never end? "Captain Noah."

"Just Captain will do." He grinned.

Releasing the wood, Marianne started out again for the railing. "What brings you up here in the middle of the night?"

He chuckled. "I could ask you the same. But it's not the middle of the night. Dawn will be upon us in minutes."

Marianne inched her shoes over the planks, forcing down her fear, determined to prove to this man that she was no coward. "Do the floors on this ship ever stop wobbling?"

Noah grinned. "Decks. The floors on a ship are called decks, Miss Denton."

She grimaced. "What does it matter? You know what I mean."

"If you are to spend months aboard, you should know the terminology so you aren't mistaken for a landlubber."

"But I am a landlubber." She huffed. "A landlubber who has no intention of becoming a seaman—or seawoman."

Noah walked beside her all the way to the railing as if he cared whether she fell. Marianne gripped the railing, the perspiration from her hands sliding over the wood. Taking a spot beside her, he inhaled a deep breath as he gazed upon the obsidian sea. He shook his hair behind him. Moonlight washed over him, setting his sun-bronzed skin aglow and dabbing silver atop the light stubble on his jaw. He planted his feet part and clutched the railing, the muscles in his arms flexing beneath his shirt. He seemed to have the weight of the world upon him, and Marianne tore her gaze away before any further sympathetic sentiments took root.

Facing her, he studied her intently.

Marianne stared at the railing, the moon, the fading stars, anywhere but at the liquid black death upon which they floated or the liquid blue death in the eyes of a man who hated her. "Can I help you with something, Captain?"

"It's true then."

"What?"

"You *are* afraid of the sea." He glanced at the tight grip her trembling hands had on the railing.

She hated that it was so obvious. She hated showing this man any weakness. "You need not concern yourself with me, Captain."

"As captain, I must concern myself with everyone on board." His brows lifted. "What has me quite baffled, miss, is in light of this fear, why you would steal the very instruments which will aid us to shore. What were you planning on doing with them? Tossing them overboard?"

A wave of shame heated Marianne's face. She took a deep breath and tried to ignore the sea rushing past them not twenty feet below. "If you must know, yes, that was exactly my plan."

He chuckled. Which further angered her. "I assure you, miss, I've been at sea long enough to know how to navigate without them. Difficult as it would be, it would only delay our reaching the safety of land." He leaned toward her until she could feel his warm breath on her neck. "I would abandon your efforts to turn this ship around, Miss Denton. Mark my words, we will make it to England as well as our other ports of call."

Marianne gave a smug huff. England perhaps, but once he discovered she had ruined his precious cargo, he'd have no choice but to return home to Baltimore. "We shall see, Captain Noah."

"Yet your perseverance and ingenuity are commendable."

"A compliment?" Marianne faced him. "Have a care, Captain, or a crack may form in your heart of stone."

❖

Noah's smile was rewarded by the curve of Marianne's lips. Surprisingly, it warmed him from head to toe. Her brown eyes shimmered in the silver light of the moon now dipping beneath the sea. Why hadn't he ever noticed how beautiful her eyes were? She had removed her bandage, allowing her hair to flow like liquid cinnamon down her back.

Resisting the urge to run his fingers through it, he folded his arms across his chest.

The woman was an enigma. How terrifying the past days must have been for her in light of her fear of the sea. Yet here she was up on deck. Her bravery, her kindness to those she should consider beneath her, her willingness to cook and care for the sick, hammered away at the imperious image he had formed of her as a child. Was she playing him for a fool? Nothing but sincerity burned in her gaze. He wanted to hate her for it. But at the moment, he could find no trace of that emotion in his heart. Quite the opposite, in fact.

She broke the invisible thread between their gazes and glanced away. "What brings you on deck so early?"

"This is my favorite time of day." Even as he said it, a soft glow spread across the eastern horizon, chasing away the dark night. "See there." He pointed. "Dawn arrives. A new day. Fresh beginnings."

Marianne twisted the ring on her finger and eyed him curiously. The light brushed golden highlights over her hair and face, and Noah swallowed down a lump of admiration. Confound it all, what was wrong with him?

The ship bucked, and Noah placed a hand on her back to steady her. Salty mist showered over them and her chest began to heave. "Never fear, Miss Denton, you are quite safe aboard this ship."

She shot him a look of disbelief. "Are you so determined to make your fortune that you cannot spare a few days to return a frightened woman—your fiancée—to her home?"

The muscles in Noah's jaw tightened. "You do not know my father."

"What has he to do with it?"

"This is his ship, his cargo. He and Mother depend on me for their survival."

"A heavy burden to bear alone." Her voice sank with genuine concern.

How quickly she transformed from a woman demanding her way to one who cared for his concerns. He looked away from the sympathy pooling in her eyes and thought of his demanding father, hoping to resurge the anger and guilt that kept him strong. "I must apologize for my mother's behavior at the engagement party. She has taken to an excess in drink as of late." He lowered his chin. "It is an illness with her." Confound it all, why was he telling her this?

She laid a hand upon his, jarring him. "No need to apologize, Noah. Many people who have suffered tragedy find succor in spirits. It is understandable." She offered him a timid smile. "I am sorry."

Noah felt her sorrow—genuine sorrow that began to melt a part of his heart he wasn't ready to let soften. "I do not want your pity," he said in a harsher tone than he intended. He snatched his hand from beneath hers.

She clutched the railing again and flattened her lips in disappointment just as Noah's mother always did when he'd done something wrong. As he always did.

Unlike his father, Noah's mother never chastised him openly. She didn't have to. Noah's failings and weaknesses lurked about their home, hanging from the dark corners of the ceiling like heckling specters. Which was why he preferred to be at sea. He patted the pocket inside his waistcoat. "My mother drinks because I failed her. I failed her and my father. But I will fail them no longer."

Her brows drew together. "Certainly your father understands there are things that affect your fortune that are beyond your control."

"The only thing he understands is success."

A breeze lifted the soft curls of her hair and brought with it the fresh smell of dawn seasoned with a hint of salt. Why was she not angry at him for snapping at her? Why did he battle the strong desire to apologize for all the pain he had caused her?

"Anyone can see you are a more than competent captain."

He cocked a brow. "A compliment? Have a care, Miss Denton. A crack may form in your heart of stone."

They both laughed.

The sun fanned its rays over the sea, brushing golden light over her face.

Unable to resist any further, he took a strand of her hair between his fingers and relished in the silky feel of it. Her sweet feminine scent drifted over him.

Her eyes widened, searching his.

"A sail. A sail!"

Noah slowly tore his gaze from her brown eyes, and for the first time, he felt the pain of their loss. He shifted his attention to the horizon.

"Where away, Mr. Grainger?"

"She's to leeward, sir, about four leagues," the lookout shouted.

❖

Marianne remained frozen beside the railing while Noah marched away, spyglass raised to his eye. Stunned not by the sighting of another ship, but by the tender look on Noah's face as he fingered her hair. What had just happened? She had no idea, but she hadn't time to consider it as the ship exploded in a flurry of activity at the appearance of their new guest. After ordering one of his men below to wake the crew, Noah took a stance on the quarterdeck to study the intruder. Within minutes, sleepy-eyed sailors sprouted from the hatches like gophers from their holes. Luke gave her a wink as he passed and took his place beside his captain.

"Hoist all sail, up topgallants, and courses!" Noah ordered. "Mr. Pike, veer to starboard!"

Mr. Heaton repeated the orders, addressing certain sailors to specific tasks.

Marianne's blood pounded in her ears. Men jumped into the shrouds and scrambled aloft until she could barely see them. They ambled across yards to loosen the sails, dropping them to catch the wind.

"She's British," a man above yelled. "A warship. A frigate."

Following the line of Noah's scope, Marianne spotted the object of excitement. A red-hulled ship, sporting three masts and crowded with sails, stood out stark against the rising sun. White foam leapt upon her bow as she split the dark waters and bore down upon them.

With her heart in her throat, Marianne made her way up onto the quarterdeck and clung to the mast behind the helm. At least from there she could hear what was happening.

Noah slammed the glass shut and slapped it against his palm. Then turning, he spotted one of his sailors. "Run up our colors, Mr. Lothar."

Within minutes the American flag sprung high into the wind on the gaff of their foremast.

"What do they want do you suppose?" Mr. Heaton asked.

"I don't intend to find out." Noah narrowed his eyes upon their pursuer, his face a mask of confidence and command. No hint of fear glinted from behind his sharp blue eyes as he directed his men to their tasks—men who were quick to obey, their expressions displaying trust in their captain. Mr. Weller leapt upon the quarterdeck and stood beside Noah.

"They have the weather advantage," he said.

"I can see that." Noah scratched his chin. "But we are much lighter and swifter. We can outrun them."

"Should I ready the guns, Cap'n?" Mr. Weller clawed nervously at his scarf with his two remaining fingers. "Just in case."

Guns. Marianne swallowed. Surely they wouldn't engage in battle with a British warship?

Noah gave him a curious look. "No need. We will not allow them to get close enough." He looked aloft and then off their bow and the confidence slipped from his face. "Mr. Pike, I told you to bring her to starboard."

The helmsman hefted the massive wheel and grunted. "Cap'n, she ain't respondin'."

Noah marched to his side, gripped two of the spokes and assisted him.

"They're gaining, Cap'n," Mr. Heaton shot over his shoulder.

"The sails are stuffed wit' wind." Mr. Weller scratched his head. "Why haven't we picked up speed?"

Noah released the wheel and rubbed the back of his neck.

The helmsman gazed up at his captain. "It feels like we're draggin' an anchor."

Marianne's heart lurched. She threw a hand to her mouth. "Oh drat."

All eyes shot toward her.

Noah marched toward her. "What have you done, Miss Denton?"

❖ CHAPTER 10 ❖

Marianne watched as Noah emerged from the companionway, his face twisting with rage. His eyes latched upon her like arrows about to fly from their quiver as he made quick work of the ladder to the quarterdeck. His officers followed timidly behind him, their faces reflecting fear. Fear, she assumed, for what he might do to her.

He stormed toward her. Marianne cringed, not daring to release the mast.

"Do you know what you have done?"

"Ruined your rice and flour?" she answered sheepishly.

A cannon blast cracked the peaceful sky with a thunderous *Boom!*

Marianne jumped and stared in that direction, but Noah's eyes never left her.

A splash sounded where the ball dropped into the sea.

"A warning shot, Captain," Mr. Heaton shouted from his spot by the quarterdeck railing. "I believe they want us to heave to."

"Confound it all! More than ruined my cargo, Miss Denton." Noah seemed to be having difficulty speaking. "You have filled my hold with bloated rice and sticky paste and caused the ship to move as if she were a pregnant whale."

"I'm sorry, Noah, I could think of no other way to—" She halted, fear strangling her voice at the crazed look in his eyes.

He backed away and clawed a hand through his hair. "Now we are caught like a fish in a net."

She glanced from him to the frigate and back again. "I thought you said we had nothing to fear from the British." She forced a ring of hopefulness into her voice.

He pointed a sharp finger her way, his face purpling. "Whatever happens is on your head, miss. Mark my words." Then turning, he stormed toward the railing.

Within minutes, the British ship came alongside and kept pace with them. Men scrambled in formation across her deck, some in blue uniforms, others in red—all of them armed. Entangled within the lines above, men in redcoats pointed muskets their way. The charred mouths of fourteen cannons gaped at her from their ports on the main deck.

What had she done, indeed.

❖

Noah eyed the British Naval Ensign flapping at the peak of the frigate's mizzenmast as a man dressed in what looked like a captain's uniform stepped onto the bulwark and held a speaking trumpet to his mouth.

"This is His Britannic Majesty's frigate *Undefeatable*. What ship are you and where are you bound?"

Noah cupped hands around his mouth. "We are an American ship out of Baltimore, the *Fortune*, with a cargo for South Hampton, Noah Brenin commanding." Noah took a deep breath to quell his rising fear. He had traded with the British for years—had friends on English shores. Surely when they discovered the *Fortune's* nationality and their peaceful business, they would leave them be.

The British captain raised the speaking trumpet again. "Heave to at once, Captain, and prepare to receive a boarding party."

Noah shook his head. Surely they would see reason. He raised his hands to his mouth. "We harbor no deserters, sir, and cannot be delayed." He studied the frigate as he awaited a response. Sleek, tight lines and sturdy sails made her swift upon the seas. The barrels of a hundred muskets gaped at him from the tops. Not to mention the fourteen charred muzzles winking at him from her deck. A tremble went through him.

The captain turned to speak to someone beside him. Soon the air resounded with the thunderous fury of a cannon blast. Gray smoke blew back across the British ship, obscuring part of their forecastle.

Once again, the ball heaved harmlessly into the sea just astern of the Noah's ship.

"They be within our range, Cap'n." Mr. Weller's horror-filled eyes bulged as he transfixed them on the British warship. "Let's give 'em a bit o' American 'ospitality, eh?"

Noah shook his head, "We cannot fight a British frigate and hope to win. We would all be killed." Confound the blasted woman! He expelled a deep breath and closed his eyes for a moment then opened them to see the terror etching upon his gunner's face. "Mr. Weller, I will do my best to protect you."

Mr. Weller returned a knowing nod, but the fear never left his eyes.

"Go fetch my pistols and sword, if you please. No, belay that." Noah spotted Mr. Boone on the weather deck and gave him that same order then turned back to Mr. Weller. "Get below and tell the men to arm themselves. Then stay out of sight."

With a salute that gave Mr. Weller's naval experience away, he dashed across the deck. Noah returned his gaze to the frigate. A blast of wind punched him with the sting of gunpowder. He rubbed the sweat from the back of his neck. For the first time in his merchant career, he was trapped—caught in the sights of fourteen guns, eighteen-pounders, from the looks of them. A broadside of which would sink him in minutes. He had no choice but to surrender and hope the captain was a reasonable fellow. Why wouldn't he be? Despite the stories of illegal impressments that had made their way to Baltimore, most British naval officers were men of honor.

If Noah were a praying man, he would have lifted a petition to the Almighty, but he'd given up on God caring about him a long time ago. Noah was on his own now as he had been for years. Straightening his shoulders, he gathered his resolve to preserve his ship and the lives of those upon it.

He eyed his first mate. "Mr. Heaton, heave to."

Luke gave him a wary look and laid a hand on Noah's shoulder in passing as he barked the orders that would lower sails and halt the ship.

No sooner had the ship eased to a slow drift, than a cutter aboard the frigate was swung from its chocks and lowered into the water on their leeward side. From what Noah could make out, a lieutenant, a midshipman, ten marines, and five sailors clambered into the boat and heaved off from the hull.

Mr. Boone returned from below and handed Noah his weapons. After strapping on his sword, Noah turned toward the mast where he'd last seen Miss Denton, expecting to find she had gone below. But there she stood, leaning against the massive wooden pole, terror and remorse burning in her gaze.

"I'm sorry, Noah," she said.

He marched toward her. "No time for apologies, miss. You need to get below."

She shook her head. "I caused this, and I will accept the consequences of my action."

Grabbing her arms, he peeled her from the mast and led her to the ladder. "Do as I say for once, Miss Denton." She ceased struggling and lowered her chin.

Noah halted. "Muster the men amidships, Mr. Heaton," he ordered Luke, who was strapping on his own weapons. His first mate's eyes met his. No fear, only anger seared in his dark gaze, making Noah glad for the first time that he'd chosen such a courageous man for first mate. For never had he needed the man's bravado and stalwart spirit more than he did now.

He urged Marianne down the ladder onto the main deck. She trembled, and his anger diminished. Despite her guilt in causing their present predicament, she must be more terrified than he. "Get below, Miss Denton, and you will be safe." Yet he heard the uncertainty in his voice. "Hide in—"

He was interrupted by a bellow from below. "Drop the manropes!"

He turned to Marianne. "Do as I say." Then he nodded for his men to oblige. Fear rose to join his anger for the lady. He had no idea what type of man this captain was, but he had heard stories of innocent women being captured from merchant ships as well as men.

Seven sailors, followed by ten marines clambered over the bulwarks and landed with resounding authority on the deck of the *Fortune*. A man dressed in white breeches and a blue coat that sported three gold buttons on the cuffs sauntered toward Noah. "Good morning, Captain. I am Lieutenant James Garrick, first lieutenant of His Majesty's ship, *Undefeatable*. This is Mr. Jones, our senior midshipman." He gestured toward a boy no more than twenty, standing beside him as he shifted slitted eyes over Noah's crew.

Noah lengthened his stance, trying to use his height to intimidate the shorter man. "Why has your captain stopped my ship, Lieutenant Garrick? We are but simple merchants. Our countries are not at war."

"War?" The man snickered "We need no war to reclaim what is ours." He glanced over the crew and waved a hand to his men. "Search below and be quick about it." He smiled. "You've got deserters from His Majesty's service in your crew, and by God, I'll have them."

❖

Marianne backed against the break of the foredeck. She hoped to hide behind the swarm of Noah's sailors crowding the deck. She could not go below. Not when this invasion was all her fault. What if Noah or one of his men were to get hurt—or worse, killed? How could she live with herself? If there was any way to prevent bloodshed, she must stay above to offer her hand—or her reason. *Oh Lord, forgive me for putting everyone on this ship in danger. Why have You allowed the British to capture us?* Her thoughts sped to Agnes, and she prayed the woman would remain out of sight. And Mr. Weller as well. Poor Mr. Weller.

Noah stepped forward, the purple plume of his hat waving in the breeze. His blue eyes turned to ice as he glared at the lieutenant. "I am Captain Noah Brenin, and I do not welcome your visit, sir. In fact, I protest this pretence as piracy. I can assure you my crew are all Americans and you, sir, are wasting your time."

Mr. Heaton and Mr. Hobbs took positions on either side of Noah, sentinels guarding their captain.

"Indeed." The lieutenant fingered sideburns that extended down to his pointy chin. "If that is so, we shall be gone before you know it. Now assemble your men in the waist, if you please."

Noah gripped the hilt of his sword. "You have no right, sir."

Marianne held her breath. The wind stopped as if pausing to view the unjust spectacle below. Perspiration slid down her back. Along with her admiration of Noah's courage, rose fear for his safety. *Please, Lord. Do not let them fight.*

"Ah, but we do, Captain." The lieutenant held out his hand. "I'll take that sword and your pistols, too."

Noah scowled and crossed his arms over his chest.

"And your officers as well." The man's glance took in Mr. Heaton and Mr. Hobbs. "And anyone else who has the stupidity to believe they can best His Majesty's Navy," he shouted to the crew.

Mr. Heaton's eyes narrowed. He fisted his hands, and for a moment, Marianne thought he would lunge at the man.

Noah raised his hand, holding him at bay. "If this is a friendly visit, Lieutenant, what need do you have of our weapons?"

"Ah, defiance, but what would I expect from you rebel Americans?" Lieutenant Garrick aimed his pointy finger toward his ship where the muzzles of fourteen cannons, primed and ready to fire, gaped at them from the frigate's deck. "Any resistance will be met with force, Captain."

Even from where she stood, Marianne could see the muscles in Noah's jaw tense. "Would your captain kill his own men to prove a point?" he asked.

"If he had to." Lieutenant Garrick shrugged. "But I assure you. . ." He thumbed toward the line of marines standing in formation behind him. "I would have no trouble quelling any dissension and escaping this"—with lifted nose, his glance took in the deck—"rotted bucket you call a ship before we sink her to the depths." Again, he held out his hand and Noah, his eyes simmering, drew his sword and handed it hilt-end to the infuriating man, nodding for Mr. Heaton and Mr. Hobbs to do the same.

Noah stepped to the center of the deck. "Line up, men!"

Marianne's heart sank. Was there nothing to be done?

The sailors shuffled into tattered lines around the mainmast. Their eyes skittered about as their fearful mumblings drifted to Marianne on the wind.

The royal marines, resplendent in their red jackets and white pants marched forward to face the sailors, their black boots thumping over the deck. The bayonets at the tip of their muskets reflected the sun's rays in blinding brilliance. Lieutenant Garrick, a tall, angular man with a pointy nose to match his chin, took up a pace before the men. He called for any who were British subjects to step forward. When none did, he began addressing each man.

Marianne watched in horror as the British scoundrel questioned the crew regarding their nationality and date of birth. All the while Noah's face grew a deeper shade of purple. "I assure you, lieutenant, these men are no more British than you are an American."

Ignoring him, the lieutenant turned as the soldiers he had sent below leapt onto the deck, dragging Agnes and Mr. Weller with them. Agnes tore from the British sailor's grasp and slapped him on the arm.

"How dare you, you beast!"

The man raised his hand to strike her. Marianne screamed. Mr. Hobbs flew at him, his face mottled with rage. He crashed into the sailor and toppled him to the ground. Noah marched toward the brawl. The British sailors laughed as the two men tumbled over the deck. Agnes threw her hands to her mouth. Marianne dashed to her side and clung to her arm. The older woman trembled as her husband punched the British sailor across the jaw. The man fell to the deck. "You'll not be touchin' me wife, mister." Mr. Hobbs wiped the blood from his cut lip and stood.

The marines turned in unison to aim their muskets directly at him. Noah halted.

Marianne's throat went dry. Surely they wouldn't shoot him. The grin that had taken residence on Lieutenant Garrick's lips during the altercation faded, and he snapped his fingers. "Assist Mr. Cohosh to his feet, and"—he pointed toward Mr. Hobbs—"string that defiant traitor up on the yardarm."

❖

Noah froze. A blast of hot wind struck him. His blood pooled in his fists. No. He would not allow his friend, the man who had been more a father to him than his own, die such a cruel death.

Agnes let out an ear-piercing wail. Marianne clung to her, but she seemed to be having difficulty keeping the woman from falling. Her pleading eyes met his.

Two of the marines grabbed Matthew's arms.

"I protest, sir!" Noah pushed his way over to the lieutenant. "This man was only defending his wife."

"Protest all you like, Captain. This man has struck a sailor in His Majesty's Navy, and he must pay the price."

"This man is not a British citizen, nor in your navy, and therefore does not fall under your twisted justice."

Lieutenant Garrick's eyes flashed. "Nevertheless, it can serve as a warning to you all."

Marianne stormed toward the pompous man. "Lieutenant. You will do no such thing!" she said with an authority that belied her gender.

With raised brow, the lieutenant swerved to face her. Noah tensed. What was the foolish woman doing drawing attention to herself?

She put her hands on her hips and gave the lieutenant one of her

I-know-far-better-than-you looks that always made Noah's blood boil.

"And what have we here?" The man's eyes swept over her. "Ship's cook? Seamstress?"

Noah gestured from behind the British officer for her to stop and say no more.

She glanced at him but continued nonetheless. "I am Miss Marianne Denton, the captain's fiancée."

Noah blew out a sigh and shook his head.

"Ah, even better." The lieutenant grinned, glancing at Noah.

"Please, sir, do not harm this man. I beg you." The limp sails flapped thunderously above them, adding impetus to Marianne's demand.

"And what will you offer me in exchange?"

She narrowed her eyes. "I have nothing to offer you, sir."

Noah stepped forward before Miss Denton dug her own grave and all of theirs as well with her unstoppable mouth. "Ignore the woman, lieutenant. She's mad with fever." He gave her a stern look and pushed her behind him, but not before he saw the fury in her eyes.

"I am not—"

"Now, I insist you leave my ship at once." Noah interrupted her. "You have found no British deserters."

"But I have not finished." Lieutenant Garrick said in an incredulous tone, peering around him at Miss Denton. "Besides, I need to inquire after *your* citizenship, Captain, and your first mate."

"We were both born in Baltimore. I in 1786 and he in 1784."

The lieutenant stared at him for a moment, shifting his eyes onto Luke. Then he shrugged. "I don't believe you. In fact, from today forward you and your first mate can consider yourselves British seamen."

Panic squeezed the blood from Noah's heart. "This is outrageous, sir! We are Americans."

"Americans." The word spit like venom from Lieutenant Garrick's lips. "Nothing but rebellious British colonials." He flung his hand through the air.

Luke charged toward the arrogant man, fists curled and ready to strike. The marines snapped their muskets in his direction. Noah leapt in front of him and forced him back.

The lieutenant laughed. "You will soon learn proper discipline under the strict rule of Captain Milford."

He turned toward Miss Denton. "And I believe I'll take you up on your offer, miss. In exchange for this man's life, you will come with me." He gestured toward Matthew who stood beside his wife, his arm draped over her trembling shoulders.

Miss Denton's eyes grew wide, and she swallowed.

"Leave her be!" Noah barreled toward the man, his only thought to save Marianne, but the point of a bayonet pierced the skin on his chest, halting him. A red spot blossomed on his white shirt, and he took a step back.

Lieutenant Garrick gave him a look of disgust. "No, I will not leave her be. The captain is in need of a new steward. The last one fell overboard during a storm. Quite tragic."

Miss Denton's face paled as white as the sails.

"Yes, I believe she'll do quite nicely." Garrick shifted his gaze to Noah. "That is unless you prefer me to hang this man of yours?" He wrinkled his nose in disdain at Matthew.

Behind the lieutenant, Miss Denton shook her head furiously at Noah. He blinked. She willingly exchanged her life for Matthew's—a man she barely knew?

The lieutenant scanned the crew one more time. The creaking of the ship and flap of canvas filled the silence as each man held their breath and avoided his gaze.

His eyes latched upon Mr. Weller. "You look familiar to me."

"I don't know you, sir." Weller's face remained a stone, save for the sweat glinting on his scarred cheek.

Noah's stomach knotted.

The lieutenant eyed Mr. Weller up and down, his gaze landing on his missing fingers and the scar on his face. "A gunner, perhaps?"

"I never been in your navy." Mr. Weller spat to the side.

"Your accent betrays you, sir." Lieutenant Garrick gestured for his men to grab Mr. Weller as well.

Shock replaced the fear on Weller's face as two marines clutched his arms and dragged him to the railing. Yet he didn't struggle. Instead, his expression turned numb as his lifeless eyes raked over Noah in passing.

A marine grabbed Marianne's arm. He dragged her to the bulwarks. She winced and began to tremble as they approached the railing, but the soldier took no note. Every fiber within Noah itched to charge the man as Luke had done, to fight this incredible injustice, but he knew it would only cause bloodshed.

There was nothing he could do.

"Oh my poor dear," Agnes wailed after Marianne.

Sweat slid into Noah's eyes, stinging them. He glanced one more time over his shoulder at the remainder of his crew, their eyes reflecting both their relief at not being chosen and their fear for him. Matthew took a step forward, Agnes leaning in his arms. At least they had been spared. Matthew nodded his way. A look of understanding passed between them, and Noah knew the man would care for his ship and if possible, find a way to rescue them.

It was the only hope Noah could cling to as he swung over the bulwarks and dropped into the boat that would take him, his men, and Miss Denton to a fate worse than death.

❖ CHAPTER 11 ❖

Sandwiched between two officers—Lieutenant Garrick walking before her and another man behind—Marianne descended a set of wooden steps beneath the quarterdeck and proceeded down a gloomy passageway aboard the *Undefeatable*. Familiar smells burned her nose—moist wood, tar, and the sweat of men, of hundreds of men from what she'd seen above deck.

Each step sent her heart crashing against her chest. A thousand horrifying visions of her future flashed like morbid captions across her mind. Unlike Noah, she did not entertain the notion that any honor existed among these British officers. She had heard the stories of their atrocities inflicted upon American sailors—and she believed them. A shudder overtook her. She stumbled, and the man behind her nudged her forward.

She thought of Noah and Mr. Heaton. What horrors were they presently facing? And Mr. Weller. Poor Mr. Weller. But she hadn't time to contemplate their fate, as hers was about to be revealed. At the end of the passageway, a man dressed in a red coat, white breeches, with musket in hand, guarded a door she assumed to be the captain's. Lieutenant Garrick knocked. A gruff "Enter" followed, and Garrick swept open the door, ducked beneath the frame, and ushered Marianne inside. A massive oak desk faced her and behind it, tearing spectacles from his rugged face, rose a man whose height caused him to lean slightly forward lest he bump his head on the ceiling—or deckhead, whatever they called it. Thick black hair, veined with gray, sprang from the confines of a ribbon at the back of his neck as if unwilling to be restrained. He shifted his broad shoulders beneath his dark blue coat, causing the golden threads of his epaulettes to quiver.

Lieutenant Garrick doffed his hat. "We found three deserters aboard the ship, Captain Milford."

The other officer took a position just inside the door.

Marianne swallowed, searching the captain's eyes for any trace of kindness or decency, but all she found was an intelligence that astounded her and a cruel indifference that frightened her to the core.

He tugged on the sleeves of his coat, the three golden buttons at the cuffs glimmering in the sun's rays that streamed in through the stern windows.

Sensing a hesitancy in the man, Marianne stepped forward. "If I may, sir. They were not deserters, you see—"

"You may not, miss!" the captain barked, forcing the remainder of Marianne's words into a clump in the back of her throat.

"Very good, Mr. Garrick." He shifted gray eyes onto his first lieutenant. "See that they are settled and given their assignments." He rounded the desk, keeping his eyes on Marianne. "And who might this be?"

Lieutenant Garrick lifted his chin. "I thought she would do nicely as your new steward, Captain."

"Indeed?" The captain appraised her as one might a piece of fine furniture or a prize horse. Marianne shifted beneath his impertinent perusal and dared a glance at Lieutenant Garrick behind her.

Gone was the smug facade he'd worn on board the *Fortune*. Instead the man kept his eyes leveled forward and his back straight. "Since we lost Jason in the storm," he added with a tremble in his voice.

The officer's stance of temerity before his captain caused a new gush of fear to rise within Marianne. What sort of man *was* this Captain Milford?

"I'm aware of that, Mr. Garrick. Do you take me for a fool?" The captain snapped, spit flying from his mouth. Then as quickly as his fury had risen, his features softened, and he grabbed a lock of Marianne's hair and rubbed it in between his fingers. He lifted it to his nose. "Has she any training?"

Marianne stiffened. "I would appreciate you not speaking about me as though I were too ignorant to understand you, sir."

The captain's gray eyes chilled, and for a moment she thought he would strike her. But then he broke into a chuckle. Lieutenant Garrick smiled.

The captain speared him with a sharp gaze "That will be all, Mr. Garrick. Attend to the new recruits."

With a salute, Garrick turned and left.

"No, you remain, Mr. Reed." Captain Milford's words halted the other officer.

Marianne's breath grew rapid. Determined not to show her fear, she met the captain's gaze without wavering. Interest flickered in his eyes as he circled her, one hand behind his back. Arrows of sunlight beamed through the stern windows and angled across a cabin much larger than Noah's aboard the *Fortune*. The bright rays skimmed over the desk, the chairs, and a bookcase holding numerous tomes, decanters, and glasses. Two unlit lanterns swung from hooks on the deckhead. A sleeping chamber took up the far left corner. Conspicuously absent, however, were the cannons. Marianne had always heard British captains kept cannons in their cabins, ready for use. Also odd was the row of potted plants that lined the stern window casing.

Captain Milford completed his assessment and stood before her, his gray eyes sharp. "So, miss. Have you?"

"I beg your pardon." Marianne shifted her shoes over the edge of the painted canvas at the room's center.

He gave an exasperated sigh. "Any training as a steward?"

Encouraged by the spark of kindness drifting over his expression, Marianne turned pleading eyes his way. "Captain, I beg you. My name is Marianne Denton, and I am a citizen of Baltimore, Maryland. I am no one's steward, sir. In fact, I wasn't even supposed to be on that merchant ship."

The gold fringe on his epaulettes shook as the wrinkles at the corners of his eyes folded in laughter. "Allow me to enlighten your understanding, Miss Denton. You are no longer a citizen of Baltimore. You are my steward. You will prepare and lay out my clothing, bring me my meals, scrub this cabin, and help keep my affairs in order." His tone rang through the cabin like a death knell. "Is that clear?"

Marianne closed her eyes. *This cannot be happening.* "Captain, if

I may indulge your patience. My mother is very ill. I must get back to her as soon as possible."

"Enough!" He thrust his face toward her. "My mother died while I was at sea. You will soon learn that we all must make sacrifices."

His hot breath, tainted with alcohol, fanned over her skin. Turning, he stormed toward his desk and poured a glass of amber liquid from a glass carafe. He sipped it and took up a pace before the stern windows.

"Many sailors have woeful tales, miss. If I allowed everyone off this ship who had some tragedy ashore, I'd be sailing it myself."

He fingered the leaf of one of the plants. "Isn't that so, my lovely?"

Marianne flinched. Was the captain toying with her? "But I am not a sailor. I am an innocent lady."

He tossed the remainder of his drink to the back of his throat then slammed the glass to his desk. Turning, he brushed invisible dust from his dark blue sleeves. "Do I look presentable, Mr. Reed?"

"As always, Captain." The man's guttural voice drifted from behind her.

"Very well. Very well, indeed." He glanced across the cabin as if trying to remember something, his eyes growing dull and lifeless.

The ship moaned over a swell, and Marianne steadied her shoes against the rising deck.

"Captain?" The officer behind her said. "Your orders?"

He shook his head. "Ah yes. Prepare the ship to get underway, Mr. Reed."

"And the lady?"

"Show her to the steward's quarters."

Marianne took a step forward. "But, Captain, you cannot hold an innocent civilian."

He eyed her and the former sharpness in his gaze returned. "I assure you I can, miss. I can do whatever I wish. I am master of this ship. I can either treat you as my steward or as a prisoner and lock you below. Which would you prefer?"

Marianne pursed her lips and tried to quell both her anger and her fear. She must choose the option that afforded her the most freedom— freedom to help Noah and his crew, and freedom to escape.

❖

Noah lined up with his men on the deck of the *Undefeatable*, awaiting their inspection, and gazed at the *Fortune*—his ship, his father's last ship—as it sailed away over the choppy azure waves. He supposed he should be happy the two nations were not at war for if they were, the British would most certainly have taken his ship and cargo as prize. Though his body had accepted his fate, his mind was cast adrift in a sea of impossibilities, unable to anchor into anything solid, anything real. On his right stood Luke, his hands crimped into permanent fists. On his left, Weller shifted from foot to foot, muttering to himself.

Across the deck, sailors busied themselves with various tasks: scrubbing the deck, tying knots, coiling rope, shining brass, hoisting lines, and unfurling sail as the ship prepared to get underway. Not a square foot of space could be found unoccupied. And weaving among the organized chaos, marched masters' mates, shouting orders as they snapped their stiff rattans against their palm to ward off any dissension.

Lieutenant Garrick popped up from beneath the quarterdeck where he had disappeared moments before with Marianne. *Oh God, please keep her safe.* Noah surprised himself with the first prayer he had uttered in eleven years.

The lieutenant took up a pace before them, placing one hand behind his back. "You three men will be assessed as to your skills and assigned to different watches and positions." He halted and scoured them with a haughty gaze. "A word to the wise. This is a British navy vessel, a disciplined fighting machine, not the unorganized piece of flotsam from which you came."

Noah grimaced, and Luke leveled such a burning gaze upon the man, Noah feared it would sear him clean through.

Garrick didn't seem to notice, so obsessed was he with his commanding performance. "Captain Milford suffers no fools on board, nor does he brook any nonsense. The sooner you accept that, the better things will go for you."

Mr. Weller mumbled something.

Luke gave a defiant grunt, bringing the lieutenant's gaze down on him along with his pointy finger. "I perceive we shall have trouble with you." He cocked his head. "Nothing that a few licks from the cat won't change." He chuckled.

Noah tired of the man's supercilious display.

He nudged Luke with his elbow and shook his head, hoping his volatile first mate would heed the warning. He had heard of men being lashed with the cat-o'-nine who had barely survived. The cruel punishment was inflicted aboard His Majesty's ships for the slightest infractions and was the reason so many of their crew deserted.

Which was what Noah intended to do. And exactly the reason that he and his men had to submit to this man's pompous authority—for the time being.

The sails snapped above. The ship lurched, and Noah ran the sleeve of his shirt across his sweaty brow.

"He won't give you any trouble, Lieutenant. Just show us where to go." Perhaps then he could speak to the captain. Surely a man in command of such an exquisite warship would have the decency and honor to see how great an injustice had been enacted upon them. Any reasonable man could come to no other conclusion save that Noah and his friends were but neutral American merchantmen and not British navy deserters.

Garrick's spiteful gaze shifted to him. "Mr. Simons," he yelled over his shoulder. "Take these men below. Instruct the surgeon to look them over from stem to stern and have them make their mark on the ship's articles. Issue them their slops, mess gear, and hammock, and see to their assignments."

"Yes, sir." A short, squat man with a considerably large bald head approached and led Noah and his crew below deck.

A deep gloom enveloped Noah as he descended the ladder—a darkness and heat that was oppressive, stifling. Perhaps it was the number of sailors crammed into this tiny space. Men seemed to fill every crack and crevice, each one of them busy attending to some task. Down one more deck and they met the surgeon—a pale, thin man with bloodstains on his shirt and sweat layered on his brow. After gazing into their open mouths and squeezing a few muscles, he pronounced them all fit for duty.

Next, Mr. Simons escorted them to the purser's cabin. A thick man with leathery skin leaned on the counter and pointed toward a parchment containing various marks and signatures. "Make yer mark here, if you please."

Noah fingered the quill pen. "And if I don't?"

Mr. Simons laughed, and he and the purser exchanged a glance. "You don't want to be findin' that out, now. The cap'n deals harshly wit' mutineers."

"How can we be mutineers if we aren't in your stinking navy?" Luke grumbled.

Mr. Weller nudged Noah. "We better do it, Cap'n." His voice emerged as a childish whimper.

"Very well." Noah signed the paper and handed it to Luke. "It won't matter anyway."

"Welcome t' His Majesty's Navy." The purser chortled after they had all signed, "Here's yer slops and gear." He tossed each of them a bundle that upon further inspection contained tin cups, plates, a hammock, and clothing that smelled as if it hadn't been washed since the last owner had worn it. After changing and storing their gear in the berth, Noah and his men followed Mr. Simons back up on deck.

As Noah emerged above, he blinked and squinted like some nocturnal animal trapped in the sunlight. "Mr. Simons, can you tell me what became of the lady who was brought on board with us?"

"Don't know nothin' about that. I imagine she's wit' the cap'n."

Noah's throat closed. Surely the captain would do her no harm. Would he?

Mr. Simons drifted past them and pointed at Luke. "You are assigned to larboard watch." He thumbed over his shoulder to a man dressed in trousers too small for his tall frame. "Kane'll show you the ropes."

"I've been sailing ships all my life." Luke huffed his disdain. "I doubt Mr. Kane can show me anything."

"What he'll be showin' you is how to do what you're told an' keep your mouth shut." Mr. Simons's heightened voice held a warning as his baleful eyes narrowed upon Luke. With a shake of his head he continued, "And you." He stopped before Mr. Weller. "Gunner's mate. Since I see you already had a run in wit' a canon," the purser added with a laugh.

The scars on Mr. Weller's face seemed to scream in defiance, yet he simply nodded as a glaze of placid acceptance covered his dark eyes.

"Get below and report to Mr. Ganes."

Mr. Weller slogged off. Noah's gut tensed in defiance.

"And you." Mr. Simons squinted up at Noah. "Weren't you the cap'n aboard that ship?"

"I was."

"Well, now you're a topmastman."

Noah's heart stopped. He glanced up at the towering masts that stretched into the blue sky. "Do you have any other positions?"

Mr. Simons eyed him curiously. "No, but if you're afraid of heights,

I guarantee you'll overcome that right quick." Again he laughed, and Noah had the impression he spent his day laughing at his own jokes.

"Report to Blackthorn there. He'll get you situated."

Noah glanced over at the large, crusty looking fellow standing by the shrouds then back above. Men walked across the yards and footropes as if they were wide city streets.

A vision of his brother, laughing and scrambling up the ratlines and around the lubbers' hole at the mast top, filled Noah's mind.

Gripping the lines, Jacob had glanced down at Noah, a wide grin on his tanned face. "Watch how easy it is, you jellyfish!" he shouted.

Right before. . .

Noah's life had changed forever.

He froze. His body felt as heavy as an anchor. He could never go up there. If he did, he was sure he would die.

❖ CHAPTER 12 ❖

Marianne followed the officer called Reed, a tall, polished man with neatly trimmed coal black hair, out of the captain's cabin and down two doors to a room even smaller than the one she'd been given aboard the *Fortune*.

"The steward's quarters, miss. At the captain's orders, a fresh gown left by one of the sailor's wives has been laid out for you on the bed. I suggest you put it on." His deep voice held the monotonous tone of someone either terribly bored or in complete control of any errant emotions.

She swung to face him. "Mr. Reed, I beg you. Surely you can see I do not belong here." She searched his eyes for a speck of compassion. "I am but an innocent lady, born and raised in Baltimore."

A hint of disdain crossed his gaze. "That you were born in Baltimore, I will not question. That any of you seditious Americans are innocent, I refuse to believe." He lifted a haughty brow and looked above her as if the sight repulsed him.

"We won our freedom from Britain honorably and fairly. Or do you insist that all peoples bow before your great nation?"

"Not all. Only those who owe us the very debt of their existence." The *whomp* of sails thundered above and the ship canted. Marianne gripped the doorframe for support, and Reed gave her a look of annoyance. "Though it appears you are no stranger to servitude, I doubt you are accustomed to the quality of service the captain requires."

"How dare you? You do not know me, sir."

"Guard your tongue, miss. I am an officer and will be addressed with respect." He waved a hand through the air. "I'll send Daniel to instruct you in your duties." And with that, he nudged her inside and closed the door.

Marianne slumped onto the thin, knotty mattress and hung her head. A beam of sunlight struck the ruby in her ring and set it aglow. She twisted it and thought of the day her father had given it to her for her twentieth birthday. He had looked so dapper in his maroon coat and brown trousers with the tips of his styled hair grazing his silk cravat. It was the only time Marianne felt as though he approved of her, if only a little. She could still picture her mother sitting in the chair by the hearth, holding Lizzie against her breast—just a year old at that time. A warm glow, akin to the one within her ruby, swept over Marianne at the memories. They had been a happy family once.

Falling to her knees, she dropped her head onto the mattress. *Why, God, why? I don't understand. What purpose could it have served to take Papa from us?* Tears blurred her vision. *And now this? Captured and enslaved on a British warship. Help me understand.*

The deck tilted, and Marianne's knees shifted over the floorboards. A splinter pierced her gown and into her leg. A pinprick of pain shot up her thigh. Yet no answer came from God. The booming crack of sails above and the crush of water pounding on the hull were answer enough. God had a plan, of that she was sure. However, it was surely a plan that did not consider her or her family's happiness.

"Oh Lord, please take care of Noah and his men. It's my fault they are here," she sobbed. The rough burlap scratched her face, and she lifted her head into her hands. Tears slid down her cheeks and dropped onto the coverlet, forming darkened blotches. "And if You can spare a moment, please look after Mama. I miss her so much. Please do not let her die." The tears flowed freely now, and her body convulsed beneath a flood of them until she had none left.

❖

"Miss! Miss!" A child's voice drifted over Marianne. "Miss!" Someone tugged on her arm. "Miss, wake up!" Marianne searched through the fog in her head, trying to remember where she was.

The British ship!

She snapped her eyes open to a face so sweet and innocent, she thought she might have died and gone to heaven. If not for the ache in her head and the cramps in her legs—and the teetering of the ship beneath her as it sailed through the deadly sea.

"Who are you?" Marianne struggled to sit, then rubbed her eyes.

"I'm Daniel, miss." He glanced out the half-opened door. "Sorry t' disturb you, but the captain will be wantin' his cabin attended to before his noonday meal." With brown hair the color of cocoa and eyes as bright as lanterns in a dark sanctuary, the boy's presence seemed to scatter the forebodings of doom that had consumed her cabin.

"What time is it? How long have I been asleep?" Marianne pushed the hair from her face.

" 'Bout an hour, miss." Daniel smiled, revealing a perfect set of white teeth. "I came by 'efore but figured you needed the rest due to being impressed an' all." He said the words as if this sort of thing happened all the time. Well, perhaps on this ship, it did.

He clipped his thumbs into the waist of his oversized blue breeches. "We best be hurryin', miss."

"Very well." Marianne struggled to stand, then leaned her hand against the wall to steady herself as the ship rolled. She pressed down the folds of the maroon gown she'd donned. A scandalous color, to be sure. But she didn't wish to vex the captain by not accepting his gift. "I suppose you're here to instruct me in my duties."

"Aye." The boy beamed and flung dark hair from his face. Clear brown eyes shone with an invitation for friendship.

An invitation that, despite her circumstances, Marianne couldn't help but accept.

For the next two hours, Daniel instructed Marianne in the fine art of being a captain's steward. The list of duties was exhausting. Not only did Captain Milford want his meals brought from the cook on time, his uniforms delivered to the laundry and returned promptly, and his daily attire laid out each morning, but also the floor of his cabin scrubbed, his rug shook out, his desk and shelves dusted, and the silver on his sword hilts, chalices, and trays polished every day.

"What of these plants?" Marianne asked Daniel as she glanced over the assortment lining the stern window frame. From what she knew of horticulture, one was a strawberry bush, one a lime tree, another a patch of onions. The others she could not name.

"Oh no, miss." Daniel's eyes widened. "You must never touch those. Only the captain cares for his plants."

"A curious thing to see on a ship, is it not?"

"Aye miss. But the cap'n is a curious man, if you ask me."

Yes, she had noticed. "How do you know so much about caring for the captain?"

"I used to help the captain's last steward a bit." Daniel's voice sank. "Before he fell overboard." He shrugged. "An' I guess the captain's partial to me."

"I can see why." Marianne pressed a hand over an ache in her back and glanced out the stern windows. The distant horizon rose and slipped beneath the frame as the ship traversed each ocean swell. Though rays of sunlight brightened the entire cabin, making it almost cheery, they also increased the temperature. Withdrawing a handkerchief from her sleeve, Marianne dabbed at the moisture on her neck and thought of how miserable it must be on deck in the direct sun.

"Have you seen my friends?"

Daniel opened a jar of some type of oil and dribbled some onto a soiled cloth. He nodded.

"Are they well?"

"Aye, miss."

"Can you get a message to them for me? To the tall one with the light brown hair."

Daniel's eyes lit up. "Aye, the cap'n?" The smell of lemons and linseed filled the room.

"Yes." Marianne bit her lip. No doubt Noah would still be so furious that he would not wish to hear a peep from her, but she needed to know how he and the others fared. She'd never forgive herself if something happened to them. "Can you tell him I'm sorry and ask him if there's anything I can do?"

Daniel nodded his understanding as he knelt to scrub the floor.

Marianne plopped beside him and grabbed another rag. "How old are you, Daniel?"

"Eleven." His voice rang with pride.

"What are you doing on board this ship?" She poured oil on the rag and mimicked Daniel's method of polishing the deck. "Is your father aboard?"

He halted for a minute, then continued scrubbing. "I was impressed, same as you."

"Impressed? Stolen?" Her fears began to rise for the boy. "You're an American?" Why hadn't she noticed the absence of the distinct British lilt?

He beamed. "Aye, from Savannah."

The poor lad. Marianne laid a hand on his shoulder. "Where are your parents?"

"Back home, I suppose," he said without looking up from his task.

Marianne stood, her indignation rising with her. "How can the Royal Navy steal little boys away from their parents? Have they no shame?"

"I was on a merchant ship, same as you." He shrugged and gave her a peaceful smile, completely at odds with the alarm she felt. "It is the way of the Royal Navy, miss."

"That does not make it right," she huffed. "What do you do here on board?"

Rising to his feet, he lengthened his stance. "I am a powder boy, miss."

Marianne drew a sleeve over her damp forehead, wincing when she touched her wound. "Powder boy? What does a powder boy do? I thought most gentlemen no longer powder their wigs."

"No, miss." He giggled. "I run the powder to the guns when we're in battle."

Gunpowder? She thought of Mr. Weller. "But isn't that dangerous?"

"Aye." His eyes widened once again as if he were about to tell her a grand secret. "Just a fortnight ago, when we was firing upon a French warship, an enemy shot crashed through the gun deck and my friend William had his face blown clear off."

Marianne threw a hand to her mouth, both at the gruesome event and the casual, unfeeling manner in which Daniel relayed it. The things he must have seen. The horror and bloodshed. How unconscionable for so young a boy. Yet he seemed not to bear the fear one might expect. In fact quite the opposite.

"He's in heaven now." Daniel announced with a calm assurance that reinforced her impression. He stood.

"We must get you off this ship at once." Marianne drew him to her breast.

He pushed her back and gazed up into her eyes. "I know, Miss Marianne. That's what you came for."

"Whatever do you mean?" She brushed the hair from his face.

"Why God sent you."

"Sent me? I don't understand." Had the poor child gone mad in his imprisonment?

Yet the clarity in his brown eyes spoke otherwise. "Yes, miss." He smiled. "God told me there'd be a lady and three men coming to rescue me.

"And here you are."

❖

Heart stuck in his throat, Noah eased his bare feet out onto the foretopsail footropes. The yard he gripped shuddered in the wind, and his sweaty fingers slipped over the rough wood.

"New to the top?" the man called Blackthorn said as he made his way out across the yard ahead of Noah.

"You could say that." Noah barely managed to squeak out the words before a blast of wind tore them away. Instead of the light steady breeze, interrupted by occasional gusts below, the wind here in the tops remained constant and strong like the persistent front line of an enemy attack.

An attack in which Noah believed he would be the first casualty.

"I thought you was the cap'n." Blackthorn said.

"I was. . .I am."

Blackthorn chuckled. "Sink me now, ain't never heard of a captain afraid of heights."

Despite Noah's attempts to hide it, the horror strangling his gut had obviously taken residence on his face.

"Ah now, you'll get used to it. Just don't be lookin' down. Keep a firm grip on the jackstays and beckets and make sure you have a good step before you take it. You'll do fine." He slapped Noah on the back, causing him to grip the yard tighter.

"Sorry," Blackthorn muttered.

As Noah and the other four men spread upon the footropes, waiting orders from below, he ignored Blackthorn's advice not to look down. He hoped to catch a glimpse of Miss Denton, if only to see how she fared. Had the captain harmed her? Had he locked her below? Such a brave lady. If she were as frightened of the water as Noah was of heights, she possessed far more courage than he imagined, for he could not stop the trembling that had gripped him since he leapt up into the shrouds.

His eyes latched onto the captain standing by the binnacle, feet spread apart and hands clasped behind his back. Both the commanding tilt of his nose and the three gold buttons on his cuffs gave away his rank. At least he wasn't below with Miss Denton.

"Strike the foresail!" The order bellowed from below, and the men began to loosen the lines keeping the sail furled.

"What is your opinion of the captain?" Noah asked Blackthorn.

The huge man, who looked more like a bear balancing on a high wire than a sailor accustomed to the topmast, leaned casually against the yard as if he were leaning against a railing below.

"Milford?" He angled toward Noah's ear. "Crazy ole rapscallion, if you ask me. Some say he's been at sea so long he's gone mad. He can be as vicious as a rabid wolf one minute and kinder than Saint Joseph the next." He scratched the hair sprouting from within his shirt. "Trouble is, you never know which one you're gonna get."

Noah loosened the first knot and moved to the next one. The edges of the thick sail began to flap in the wind. He swallowed and tried to steady his hands. "Do you think he would harm a woman?"

"Ah, you're thinkin' of your lady friend." Tearing through a stubborn knot, Blackthorn shook his head. "I don't think so. As long as she does what she's told."

Noah grimaced. The woman never did what she was told!

He studied the captain. The man carried himself with a commanding, capable presence, albeit with an overdone pomposity. But surely that went with the position. Noah could not conceive that a British officer and a gentleman would imprison simple merchantmen against their will, let alone an innocent woman. As one commander to another, Noah intended to reason with him the first chance he got. And if that didn't work, there was always the possibility of escape.

Lieutenant Garrick popped on deck from below, the usual scowl twisting his thin lips.

Blackthorn cursed under his breath. "I'd stay away from that one, if I was you."

Noah inched his way across the ratline. His sweaty feet slipped over the swaying rope, and he gripped the yard. Following Blackthorn's gaze,

Noah snorted as Garrick leapt upon the quarterdeck and took a stance behind his captain. "I believe I've had my fill of Lieutenant Garrick already."

"Ambitious and cruelhearted." Blackthorn grumbled. "If he had 'is way, half the crew'd be keelhauled."

"Let go clewlines and buntlines!" ordered the man below, and the mastmen began lowering the lines that would free the sail to the wind.

Noah pointed toward another man in a lieutenant's uniform who took his post beside Garrick. "What of him?"

"Reed? He's a good egg, for the most part, I suppose." Blackthorn loosened a line and part of the sail dropped, flapping in the wind. "Just a bit full o' hisself, if you ask me. His father's a member of Parliament, they say—which is why he got this commission." The wind whistled through the gaps of two missing teeth on his bottom row. He snapped his mouth shut. Though towering over Noah's six feet and with the muscle to match his height, Blackthorn's easy manner and kindness made him appear less threatening.

"You're not British," Noah said.

"Me? No. Pure American I am. From Savannah, Georgia."

"Impressed, then?"

"Aye, a year ago. I was a waister on a merchant ship. Captain took me an'"—he hesitated and looked down—"me bosun."

"A year?" Noah stared at him aghast. "You haven't tried to escape?"

Blackthorn's dark eyes seemed to lose their luster. "Aye, we did. Or at least we tried. I was flogged, but the cap'n tossed me bosun to the sharks. God save his soul."

"Let fall! Sheet home!" More orders from below.

But all Noah heard was Blackthorn's words *flogged* and *tossed him to the sharks*. And his terror-stricken heart shrank. "But I hear people desert the navy all the time."

Blackthorn gave him the measured look of a man who had traveled a particular road more than once. "They don't ever let their eyes off us Yankees." He released the sail. The canvas lowered further, slapping furiously at the wind's attempt to conquer it. But it fought a losing battle, for air soon filled every inch of the sail with a thunderous roar, stretching it taut and snapping the lines.

"No, you best accept your fate, Mr. Brenin. There ain't no way off this ship."

❖ CHAPTER 13 ❖

Marianne set the tray of pea soup, roast chicken, and tea down on the captain's desk. "Your dinner, Captain."

He grunted and tossed down the documents he studied then eyed her above the spectacles perched on his nose. "You're late."

"The cook extends his apologies, Captain. He is behind on his duties today due to his gout acting up again."

"Addle-brained sluggard." Captain Milford tore off his spectacles and leaned his nose over the food. "Smells like pig droppings."

"I can take it back if you like."

"No no. I'll eat it." He waved her off. "If I waited for a decent meal around here, I'd starve to death. Dismissed."

Relieved to leave his presence, Marianne swerved about.

"Belay that!"

She froze.

"My cabin deck is dirty."

Marianne slowly turned to face him, forcing down her frustration. "Captain, I spent an hour this morning on my knees scrubbing and polishing each plank. I assure you it is as clean as it can possibly get."

He narrowed his eyes and rose to his most ominous height. His chair scraped over the wooden floor, sending a chill down Marianne's spine. Grabbing a bottle from his shelf, he poured himself a drink and took a sip. "Are you telling me that I don't know my own deck?"

A giggle rose in Marianne's throat at the absurd question. She forced it down, fairly certain this man would not find the same humor in the situation. "I was unaware, Captain, that one could become quite so intimate with one's deck." She'd meant to say the words in a light-hearted tone in hopes of bringing levity to the situation, but her voice carried more sarcasm than witticism.

His face mottled in anger, and he marched toward her. Every muscle in Marianne's body tensed. Why couldn't she keep her snide comments to herself? She felt his gaze boring into the top of her head, yet she kept her eyes leveled upon the gold buttons lining his white lapel. His chest heaved beneath them. Would he strike a woman? Would he lock her in the hold? She had no idea what to expect from this capricious man.

Releasing a brandy-laced breath that sent the hair on her forehead fluttering, he stepped back. Then he swung about and stormed back toward his desk. "And my uniform was not laid out properly this morning, miss. . .miss. . ."

"Denton, Captain." Surely he knew her name after a week.

"Yes, Denton." He plopped back into his chair and gripped his side as if it pained him. "My last steward was much better."

Marianne clenched her hands into fists. Her ring pinched her finger, bringing along with the pain familiar feelings of inadequacy. She'd never worked so hard in her life for so little appreciation—as the muscles in her legs and back could well attest. "I am still learning, Captain." Her voice came out as though it were strained through a sieve.

"Nevertheless," he barked, his gray eyes firing. "I do not tolerate slothfulness on my ship."

Slothfulness? Of all the. . .

"And what is that gash on your head?" He leaned back in his chair and sipped his drink.

Shocked by his sudden interest, Marianne dabbed the tender scar. "A crate fell on me aboard the merchant ship. Knocked me unconscious, which is how I came to be—"

"You should have my surgeon look at it." He interrupted with a wave of what could only be construed as disinterest in her tale.

Marianne shuddered. She had seen the man he called the ship's surgeon. "I would prefer that he didn't."

"Preposterous." He frowned. "You will—"

A knock on the door interrupted them, but before the captain could respond, it opened to reveal the object of their discussion. The pale man with a perpetual gleam of sweat on his brow angled his head around the door, reminding Marianne of a snake spiraling from its hole. "Time for your medicine, Captain."

With barely a glance her way, he slithered past her. In fact, since she'd come aboard, not once had the physician acknowledged her presence during his frequent visits to the captain's cabin.

"Good, good," Captain Milford mumbled. "You are dismissed, Miss Denton."

Marianne turned to leave but not before she saw the surgeon pour something from a flask into the captain's drink. A sharp odor, one she was quite familiar with from her mother's medications, bit her nose. *Laudanum.*

Tucking the information away, she slipped down the companion-way, determined to use these precious moments of freedom to go above deck. She'd been stuck below for a week attending the captain's every whim, and she desperately needed to feel the sun on her face. And maybe catch a glimpse of Noah. To see how he fared, and Luke and Mr. Weller as well.

Squinting against the bright sun, she emerged onto the main deck to a gust of chilled wind and the stares of myriad eyes.

"Back to work!" The *crack* of a stiff rope sliced the air, drawing her gaze to one of the petty officers who raised his weapon to strike one of the sailors again. Swallowing her repulsion, she scanned the ship, searching for Noah and his crew, but none of their faces appeared from among the throngs of seaman. Fear crowded her throat. Were they imprisoned below? Above her, at the rail of the foredeck, a line of marines stood at attention, their red and white uniforms crisp and bright, their golden buttons gleaming in the sun.

Threading her way through the bustling crew, Marianne made her way to a spot at the port side railing just beneath the foredeck where no sailor worked. Turning her back to the sea, she swept another gaze across the deck and was rewarded when Luke's coal black hair came into view. It shimmered in the hot sun like a dark sea under a full moon as he—along with a row of men—tugged upon a massive rope.

"Heave!" a sailor shouted.

Moist with sweat, Luke's face reddened. His features twisted with strain as he yanked on the stiff line.

Lieutenant Garrick dropped down from the quarterdeck and headed toward the row of men. "Mr. Kane, what have I told you about being too soft on the crew?" he shouted. "Why, my mother could pull a line harder and faster than these wastrels. This one in particular." He pointed straight at Luke.

Luke, his hands still gripping the line, slowly raised a spite-filled gaze to Lieutenant Garrick. Marianne's breath halted. *Don't say anything, Mr. Heaton. Please don't say anything.* For she had heard how cruel the British could be.

"See the way he looks at me?" Lieutenant Garrick gave an incredulous snort. "An officer in His Majesty's Navy. Strike him, Mr. Kane. Strike him every time he dares look you in the eye." An insidious smile crept over Garrick's lips like an infectious disease.

Luke faced forward again. The muscles in his jaws bulged, but much to Marianne's relief, he said nothing.

Mr. Kane shook his head. "Aye, aye, sir." And proceeded to lash Mr. Heaton across the back with his braided rope. Luke did not flinch, did not move. Not even a wince crossed his stern features.

With a satisfied grin, Lieutenant Garrick sauntered away, head held high.

Marianne swung about and clung to the railing. Better to face the sea than watch that horrible man strut about like a despotic peacock. The sun cast a blanket of azure jewels over the water. Marianne's palms slid over the railing. Her knees wobbled as her fear hit her full force. How could something so beautiful be so deadly?

Her head grew light as a bell rang twice from the forecastle, announcing the passing of time on the watch. One o'clock from what she had learned.

"Aloft there, trim the foretopsail!" a sailor shouted.

Shielding her eyes, Marianne glanced upward. Men lined the yards of the foremast at least eighty feet above her. And right in the middle of them stood Noah, his bare feet balanced precariously over a thin rope. His stained blue jacket and brown trousers flapped in the wind as he clung to the yard in front of him. A large man standing next to him leaned over and said something. Noah's gaze shot to Marianne. Her heart flipped in her chest. Though she could not make out his expression, she sensed no anger emanating from him. In fact, just the opposite. An unexpected bond kept their eyes locked onto one another like an invisible rope, a rope Marianne did not want to sever for the odd comfort it brought her. Odd, indeed. Coming from a man who had more reason to dislike her than ever before, and she, him, for his unwillingness to bring her home and marry her.

The ship plunged over a swell, but despite her fear, she kept her gaze upon him. The smells of salt and fish and wood filled the air and twirled beneath her nose. The dash of the sea against the hull accompanied by creaks of tackle and wood chimed in her ears. Yet, she could not tear her gaze from him. He looked well, unharmed. And she wanted more than anything to talk to him.

"Ease away tack and bowline!" a man shouted from below. And the lock between them broke as Noah swerved his attention to his task, inching over the footrope. Inching slowly over the footrope. Very slowly. While almost hugging the yard. Was he frightened? *Lord, please protect him up there.*

"Quite dangerous in the tops, you know." A familiar voice etched down her spine, and Marianne lowered her gaze to the superior smirk upon Lieutenant Garrick's face.

"Noah is a capable seaman." She replied, taking a step away from him. He followed her as if they danced a cotillion at a soiree.

"You do say?" He glanced up again, his black cocked hat angling toward the sails. "He doesn't seem too steady on his feet, if you ask me."

"I don't believe I did ask you, Lieutenant." She gave him a sweet smile, instantly regretting her unrestrained tongue.

He dropped his gaze, sharp with malice, and eyed her from head to toe.

Marianne shuddered.

"Heave to!" One of the master's mates bellowed. The sharp crack of a rope sounded, and Marianne looked up to see the man whom Garrick had spoken to earlier following out the lieutenant's orders across Luke's back. Mr. Heaton's muscles seemed to vibrate beneath the strike. She cringed.

"Life can be quite difficult aboard a British frigate, Miss Denton," Lieutenant Garrick said, his eyes narrowing into slits.

A gust of hot wind blasted over Marianne. The loose strands of her hair flung wildly about her. She brushed them from her face and stared out to sea, hoping her silence would prompt the annoying cur to leave.

"Especially for a woman."

Perspiration dotted her neck.

He lifted a finger to touch a lock of her hair.

Raising her jaw, she stepped out of his reach. "What would you know of being a woman, Lieutenant?"

"Oh, I know much about what women need." The salacious look in his eyes made her skin crawl. "Sleeping on a lumpy mattress, no proper toilette, clean gowns, or decent food." He clucked his tongue. "Not befitting such a lady."

"Pray don't trouble yourself over it, Lieutenant. I shall survive." *And much more happily if you scurry away to the hole from which you came.*

He leaned toward her, his offensive breath infecting her skin. "Yet you can do so much more than that, miss."

Bile rose in her throat. "And how would I do that?"

He lifted one shoulder and scratched the thick whiskers that angled over his jaw down to his pointy chin. "Kindness, Miss Denton. Kindness to a lonely man like myself."

His words drifted unashamed through her mind, shocking her sense of morality. Did he mean what she thought he meant? Unaccustomed to such vile advances, or any advances at all for that matter, she nearly lifted her hand to slap him, but thought better of it. Instead, she directed her stern eyes upon his. "My Christian kindness I offer to everyone, Lieutenant Garrick. Any further affections will never be yours." *There went her mouth again.*

His gaze snapped to the sea, his jaw twitching in irritation. "I perceive you are unaware to whom you speak, Miss Denton. Perhaps I should enlighten you." He gave her a caustic grin. "My family possesses more land and wealth than you could ever hope to see in your rustic, underdeveloped colonies." He gazed at her expectantly as if waiting for her to swoon with delight.

Marianne fought down her rising nausea. "How lovely for you, sir. But, I fear you waste your time boasting of your fortune to me. Unlike the sophisticated *haut ton* in London, I place more value on honor and dignity than title and money."

"Savage Yankees," he spat, his face reddening. "If we were not on this ship, the strictures of polite society would not allow me to even speak with you, let alone offer you my attentions."

"Then I shall pray we reach port soon so you will be forced to forsake such a silly notion."

"Lieutenant Garrick!" Captain Milford's booming voice stiffened Garrick immediately. "Report aft!"

Garrick frowned. His eyes narrowed and beads of sweat marched down his pointy nose. "We shall see, Miss Denton. A few weeks on board a British frigate might persuade you otherwise. But, mark my words, I am not a patient man." He gripped her chin between his thumb and forefinger until pain shot into her face. Then releasing her with a thrust that sent her face snapping to the side, he marched away.

Another blast of wind tore over her. A sail above cracked in a deafening boom that seemed to seal her fate.

Marianne threw a hand to her throat, trying to check the mad rush of blood. *Lecherous swine.* She stilled her rapid breathing and gripped the railing.

Oh Lord, a mad captain, a ship full of enemies, a lecherous lieutenant. . . And no one to protect me.

❖

Noah slid his aching bones onto a bench and leaned on the mess table. Dangling from two ropes attached to the deckhead, the oak slab swayed beneath his elbows. But he didn't care. Anything was better than swaying to the hard, fast wind up in the yards. Though he had tried to hide it, his legs still wobbled like pudding long after descending the ratlines and jumping to the main deck where he had resisted the urge to bow down and kiss the firm planks beneath his feet.

Luke eased beside him while Mr. Weller took the opposite bench. From amongst a crowd of howling, jabbering men, Blackthorn emerged and slapped a platter filled with salted pork, mashed peas, hard tack, and a bowl of steaming slop into the center of the table before he took a seat beside Luke. Noah sniffed, hoping a whiff of the food would prod an appetite that seemed to have blown away with the wind, but all he smelled was the foul body odor of hundreds of men.

Dinner was the best part of the day, according to the crew, most of whom swarmed the large space below deck that also served as their berth. Now, with hammocks removed and tables lowered from the bulkheads, hundreds of sailors crammed into the room, gathered with their messmates, and stuffed food into their mouths while they shared their day's adventures, told jokes, and relayed embellished tales of the sea.

Noah wanted no part of it. Nor did he ever want to go aloft again.

A week in the tops and his fear had not subsided one bit. He glanced at his first mate and gathered, from the strained look on his face, that he fared no better.

"How goes it?" he asked Luke as he reached up and grabbed the mess pouches from hooks on the bulkhead and flung them on the table. The men opened them and pulled out their utensils.

Grabbing a hardtack from a pile, Luke took a bite and winced—Noah guessed—at the hard-as-stone shell around the biscuit. Luke tossed it down. "Great, if you call spending the day in the blaring sun heaving lines pleasurable."

"Try spending the day spit polishing the guns." Weller moaned.

"You're going t' have to toughen up, lads," Blackthorn said. "This is your life now. The sooner you accept it, the better." He dipped a ladle into a kettle of foul-smelling stew and slopped some into Noah's bowl.

The putrid smell of some type of fish rose with the steam and stung Noah's nose. Perhaps it would suffice to soften his hardtack. Yet when Noah dipped his biscuit into the steaming concoction, it remained as hard as a brick. His stomach pained, and setting the biscuit aside, he tipped the bowl and drained it as quickly as he could. At least it was warm.

Along with the shouts and laughter assailing him from all directions, Noah sensed the piercing gazes of several pairs of eyes. He looked up to see men from the surrounding tables periodically staring at Noah and his friends as they made comments to their companions. Not pleasant comments, he surmised, from the disdain knotting their features.

"Ignore them." Weller grabbed his share of salted pork and plopped it onto his plate. "Some don't take kindly to us bein' Americans."

Luke gave a sordid chuckle. "And here I thought we were British deserters." He downed his stew as Noah had done and wiped his mouth on his sleeve.

"They know exactly who we are." Blackthorn poured liquid from a decanter into tin cups. "An' most o' them lost family in the Revolution." He set a cup before each of them. "One cup o' beer for each of you."

The ship canted to port, sending the lantern above their table swaying like a drunk man. Waves of golden light pulsated over the dreary scene.

Mr. Weller cast a glance around him and mumbled under his breath. Noah eyed his gunner with concern. "I'll get you out of here, Weller,

I promise." Though at the moment, he had no idea how he would accomplish such a feat.

"I place no blame on you, Cap'n." Weller tugged at his scarf. "I knew the risks when I signed on wit' yer crew." He gulped his drink then wiped his mouth on his stained sleeve. "Best not to make promises ye cannot keep."

Noah's stomach shriveled. Is that what he was doing? Promising something beyond his reach, beyond his ability? The permanent etch of disappointment lining his father's face rose to crowd out Weller's visage.

Why can't you be like your brother? Why must you fail at everything?

Noah swallowed and stared into his cup, longing to see his brother in the liquid reflection, rather than his own face staring back at him. What would Jacob do? No doubt something heroic.

Blackthorn scanned the raucous crowd of sailors as if searching for someone. "Like I said, square up, lads, and get used to it. I'm afraid you're here to stay."

Grabbing his cup, Luke downed the beer in two gulps then slammed it down with a thump. "Square up, you say? Any more squaring up and my back will turn to leather."

Noah ground his teeth together. He'd thought he'd seen the petty officer whipping Luke repeatedly. He glanced behind Luke at the red stripes lining his shirt. "What did you do to deserve that?"

"Nothing." Luke stretched his back and winced. "That weasel Garrick ordered me to be lashed every time I looked the master's mate in the eye."

"So don't look him in the eye," Noah said.

A mischievous grin toyed with Luke's lips. "It cannot be helped, I'm afraid."

Noah shook his head and chuckled. "Your insolence will be the death of you yet."

Blackthorn squeezed his cup between his bearlike hands. "Sink me, you'd be smart to stay away from Garrick. Don't look at 'im. Don't speak to 'im. Just do your duty." He lowered his chin. "He'll beat a man senseless for the smallest infraction."

Two tables down from them, the men's voices rose in ribald laughter as if they'd heard his declaration. A look of pained understanding passed between Weller and Blackthorn.

Noah leaned forward and studied the beefy man. "You?"

Blackthorn shifted his dark eyes toward Noah—eyes filled with restrained defiance. He nodded. "These Brits are a cruel breed."

"I'll drink to that." Weller lifted his cup.

Noah remembered seeing Garrick speaking to Marianne earlier that day on deck. The drink soured in his throat. "Lieutenant Garrick, would he hurt a woman?"

Blackthorn gave a cynical snort. "I'd tell your lady to steer clear o' 'im as well."

"Confound it all, we must get out of here." Noah swore under his breath.

A midshipman passed the table, offering them a callous glance. They all grew silent.

"I was like you when I first came here," Blackthorn whispered after the man was out of earshot. "Rebellious, bold, determined to escape." He craned his neck forward and eyed them each in turn. "You best get that thought out of your mind straightaway. They'll either beat the life out o' you so you don't want t' live no more, or they'll kill you." He thrust his spoon at them. "An' that Garrick had it out for me from the beginnin'."

Noah took a bite of pork as he pondered Blackthorn's statement. His jaw ached from trying to chew the tough meat. No doubt the man had suffered much during the year since he'd been impressed. But despite his declaration, Noah had no intention of being a guest on this ship that long.

"Do your best to avoid Lieutenant Garrick's bad side, Luke." If only he could give Miss Denton the same warning. Noah gulped down his beer. The pungent liquid dropped into his belly like a rogue wave. "We'll be off the ship soon enough," he added, hoping to offer the encouragement his men needed to go on, even if he didn't believe it himself.

Blackthorn groaned and shifted wide eyes over the room. "Don't be talkin' like that. We could all be flogged for desertion even at the mention of it."

"Blasted Yankees!" A curse shot their way from the agitated crowd.

Noah eyed Mr. Weller. With his eyes downcast, he had taken up the habit once again of mumbling to himself—the same trait he'd had when Noah found him at Kingston after he'd escaped His Majesty's Navy the first time. Guilt churned in Noah's gut.

Luke downed his stew and tossed the bowl onto the table, adding,

"What did you do before your career in His Majesty's Navy, Blackthorn?"

"Me?" Blackthorn chuckled, revealing his two missing teeth. "As I told yer cap'n here, I was taken from a merchantman out of Savannah." He released a heavy sigh. "Where I left a pretty wife, heavy with child." Again, he surveyed the crowd around them as if looking for someone.

"Indeed?" Luke seemed as surprised as Noah had at the revelation.

"Aye, a good Christian woman—a true saint she be—who redeemed me from"—he cleared his throat—"me prior life."

Luke's eyes lit up. "Ah, a sordid past? I'm intrigued."

"Nothin' I'm proud of, t'be sure." Blackthorn scooped some mashed peas into his mouth. "Some o' the things I did haunt me worst nightmares. But then again, if I'd stayed in that"—he scratched his thick chest hair—"profession, I wouldn't be in me present situation. An' I wouldn't have met me dear, sweet Harriet, either."

The ship tilted. Bowls and cups slid over the sticky table, but no one seemed to care. Noah rubbed the sweat from the back of his neck. Shouts and curses speared toward them from a group of sailors in the distance where a heated argument began.

A young lad wove through the crowd and headed for their table. Blackthorn's eyes latched upon the boy like a lifeline in a storm. His shoulders lowered. "Daniel, where you been?" He mussed the boy's brown hair and urged him to sit opposite him, beside Weller.

"I'm well." The boy's smile took in everyone at the table.

"You weren't at mess for near seven days." A twang of worry spiked Blackthorn's voice.

"I've been taking my supper with Miss Marianne." He gazed proudly up at the burly man.

"Miss Denton?" Noah's heart leapt. He'd been desperate for information regarding her wellbeing but had found no one who could tell him anything.

"Aye." Daniel nodded and grabbed a biscuit. "Helping her learn how to be the cap'n's steward."

A steward? Noah couldn't help but grin. She must be having as tough a time adjusting to servitude as he was to the tops. "How does she fare?"

Daniel bit into the biscuit, crumbs flying from his mouth. "She's well. I like her. She's nice." He said the words with such innocent conviction, it startled Noah.

Nice? Not exactly the way he would describe Miss Denton. Nevertheless, his body tensed as he forced the next question from his lips. "Has the captain... Has she been harmed?"

"No, sir. He works her mighty hard, but no harm will come to her."

Noah released a breath.

"The cap'n ain't like that," Blackthorn added. "He's no abuser of women."

Despite Lieutenant Garrick's behavior, perhaps Noah's belief in the honor of British officers stood true. The realization only reinforced his desire to seek an audience with the man. Surely the captain would see reason to release them once the situation of their impressments was explained to him in detail. But every time the captain had been on deck, Noah had been in the tops, and when he wasn't in the tops, he was forbidden to wander the ship. The only time he was free to slip away was in the middle watch of the night between the hours of midnight and four in the morning, and he dared not disturb the captain's sleep.

Blackthorn scooped some pork and mashed peas onto a plate and shoved it in front of Daniel. The boy grabbed a chunk of meat and took a bite. He shifted in his seat and his gaze suddenly flew toward Noah. "Oh," he said as if just remembering. "I have a message for you from Miss Marianne."

Noah flinched.

"She says she's sorry. And she wants to know if there's anything she can do to help."

Sorry. Was she truly sorry for all the pain she had caused them or was she simply sorry that she endured that pain along with them? Renewed anger coursed through Noah's veins, but he forced it back. Anger over the past would not serve them now. He must focus on the future. Perhaps Miss Denton could help them. She not only had the captain's ear, but she would be privy to his private conversations.

"Tell her to keep her ears open. Will you do that?" he whispered across the table.

"Yes, sir." Daniel's eyes sparkled in the lantern light. "You can trust me."

"Good boy. Report back to me what she tells you. And keep it to yourself."

Weller mumbled as Daniel shifted the mashed peas around his plate.

Blackthorn groaned. "I don't want you puttin' the boy in danger."

"I'm only asking him to tell me what he hears." Noah cupped the back of his own neck. "There's no harm in that."

A fiddle chirped in the distance, the twang keeping cadence with the creak and groan of the ship. Men began to clap and sing to the music.

"I'll be okay, P—Mr. Blackthorn," Daniel said. "These men have come here to help us."

Noah blinked. "What do you mean?"

Daniel straightened in his seat. "God told me in a dream that a lady and three men would come and rescue us from this ship."

Luke chuckled and stared into his empty cup as if in doing so, he could conjure up more beer.

Blackthorn reached across the table and mussed the boy's hair again. "What's got into your fanciful head now, boy?"

Daniel giggled but then shrugged. "I'm just telling you what God told me." He took a sip of his drink. "And then you came." He glanced at Noah with a confidence that inferred he would accept no other explanation for their capture.

"Well, I can assure you being impressed into the navy was not my idea." Noah offered.

"No sir. It was God's."

Noah eyed the boy. If what the boy said was so, then he had even more things to be angry with God about.

"If there is a God, He has abandoned us." Weller muttered loud enough for all to hear. "For I know fer a fact, the Almighty would ne'er set foot on a British warship."

"There is no God, Mr. Weller." Luke's bitter tone startled Noah. "There cannot be. Not in a world as unjust as this one."

Yet his first mate's declaration sparked a memory in Noah's mind. He paused to study his first mate. "I thought your parents were missionaries."

"My parents are dead." Luke scowled and rubbed the scar on his ear.

Blackthorn shook his head. "Sink me, you'd all believe in God if you met me wife. The sweetest spirit I ever came across."

Noah's thoughts took an odd drift to Marianne. "I assure you gentlemen," he plopped a piece of pork into his mouth and instantly regretted it as the unsavory clump hardened in his throat. He forced it down. "There is indeed a God. But I have found Him to be a harsh taskmaster. One who does what He pleases and yet who is impossible to please Himself."

"Sounds like your father." Luke snorted.

Noah slouched back into his seat, allowing the perverse connection to settle into his reason. He opened his mouth to respond when the air filled with blasphemies.

"Blasted Yankees!" a man yelled.

"Ill-bred rebels!" another brayed. Noah looked up to see a mob forming around them. "My pa died in your revolution." A particularly hairy man with pockmarks on his face leaned his hand on the edge of the table.

Luke slowly rose. "And how is that our fault, you callow fool?"

The man spit into Luke's bowl.

Noah stood and held an arm out, restraining his first mate from charging the man.

"That one is uglier than a pig struck with a hot iron." Another man beside the first pointed at Weller. "Don't ye Yankees know how to handle your guns?"

The mob laughed.

Confound it all, now Noah was getting angry. "He lost his fingers on one of your British ships. Therefore, it is your master gunner's incompetence which should be called into question."

The pockmarks on the man's face seemed to deepen. He grabbed the platter of their remaining pork and tossed it against the bulkhead. The chunks of meat fell to the floor with heavy thumps. "You'll see," the man said in a loud voice. "We'll beat you ignorant dawcocks an' send you runnin' to hide behind yer mama's skirts." He clipped his thumbs inside his belt. "Then maybe I'll be the new major o' one of the barbaric outposts ye call a town." He glanced over his friends and they all joined him in laughter. "An' yer mama can clean me shirts."

Luke grabbed the man by the collar and tossed him backward through the mob. He stumbled and crashed into a mess table. Shouts and jeers erupted from the men, none too pleased when their meager stew spilled over the table from the overturned pot. They shoved the man back toward Luke.

The pock-faced man collected himself. Without hesitation, he slammed his fist across Luke's jaw.

Shouts assailed them from neighboring tables as men rose from their meals to witness the brawl. Wide-eyed, Weller struggled to his feet.

Blackthorn grabbed Luke by the arm. "Let it be." His voice held more than a warning. It held terror.

"Please, sir." Daniel headed toward Luke, but Blackthorn pushed the lad behind him.

Noah barreled forward. He must stop this madness before the officers took note.

Luke's dark eyes narrowed into seething points. Jerking from Blackthorn's grip, he raised his fist. Noah shoved himself between Luke and his assailant and grabbed Luke's hand in midair.

"Let me at him, Cap'n." Luke struggled.

Noah shook his head and forced down Luke's arm with difficulty.

"I told ye all Yankees are milksops," the other man chortled and his friends joined in.

"What have we here?" The stout voice of a marine sergeant scattered most of the rats back to their tables. The officer's boots thumped authority over the deck.

"Nothin', sir." Blackthorn stepped forward. "Just a disagreement."

"And as usual, I find you in the middle of it." The man gave a disgruntled moan. "Anxious to meet the cat again, Mr. Blackthorn?"

Blackthorn's jaw stiffened. "No, sir."

"That American insulted our navy, sir." The pock-faced man pointed at Luke. His voice transformed from one of spite to one of humble subservience.

The marine stopped and eyed Luke. "He did, did he?"

"An' we couldn't let it go without speaking up for King George's navy."

In lieu of a hat, he placed his hand over his heart. "Long live the king."

"To the king!" A muffled toast echoed halfheartedly through the room.

Noah clenched his fists. Surely this officer would see reason. "Sir, if you please, this man approached our table and insulted us without provocation."

"I care not what was said." The marine sergeant adjusted his cuffs. "All that concerns me is who struck the first blow?"

"He fisted me first, sir." The pock-faced man gestured again toward Luke. The rest agreed.

"I protest." Noah thrust his face toward the man.

"Regardless." A malicious grin writhed upon the marine's lips. "Perhaps we need to teach you barbaric Americans who is truly in command. "Come with me." He pointed toward Noah and Luke. "The captain will decide your just punishment."

❖ CHAPTER 14 ❖

Marianne pushed the rag over the brass candlestick for the thousandth time. Her fingers ached. Her back ached. And the sharp scent of polish stung her nose. Her only consolation lay in the fact that everyone aboard this ship shared her suffering from overwork. Most of the sailors were young boys far from home or older men torn from their families by impressment gangs back in England. Too illiterate to read the posts sent from loved ones, they carried the missives in their pockets if only to make them feel close to those they left behind.

She stopped to steal a glance out the cabin windows, before which the captain stood, tending his plants. Outside, the lantern perched upon the stern showered a haze of golden light over the captain, highlighting the gray in his hair and making him look almost peaceful—almost.

As if to contradict her thought, he cursed and mumbled something she couldn't make out as he moved from plant to plant with his watering jug.

Then suddenly he swung around. His eyes glazed with the mad look she'd grown accustomed to these past few days. "Odds fish, aren't you done yet?"

Marianne examined the shimmering brass. She thought she'd been done hours ago, but the man saw flaws no human being could ever see. She held the two holders up to him with a questioning look on her face, hoping her annoyance didn't show on her features.

He set down his jug and grabbed the half-full glass of brandy he'd been nursing all night. "I suppose they will do." His voice sounded heavy with defeat and something else. . .a hopelessness that seemed to thicken the air around him.

Rising, Marianne set the brass holders atop his desk and tucked the cloth in the pocket of her skirt. "Captain, if I may ask a favor?"

He grunted.

Marianne had come to interpret that as permission to continue, so she took a step forward. "If you would indulge me, Captain, and if your men would approve, I could read their missives from home to them. I mean, for those who are not schooled in their letters." Though she normally would resist doing anything to help the British, she could not fault these young impressed sailors for being aboard this warship. It was bad enough they'd been forced into naval service, but to not be able to read comforting words from home, or to have to wait for an officer's good humor to read them. . . Tragic. If she must remain imprisoned aboard this ship, perhaps she could at least bring some joy to others in the same position.

Captain Milford sipped his brandy and stared at her as if she'd asked permission to sprout wings. "The midshipmen often read their letters to them. But if you wish. It matters not to me."

"Thank you, Captain." She turned to go.

"Stay. Sit down for a moment." He cocked his head toward a chair, and Marianne groaned inwardly. *Drat.* It had been a long day. Her muscles screamed for rest.

Slipping onto a chair cushion, she stretched her aching back and waited. Only seven days of endless serving and cleaning had passed, yet it seemed like a thousand. And all she saw before her was a multitude of similar days strung together in a muddled line of misery that screamed into eternity. Though she had long ago decided against trying to understand God's purposes—especially when one tragedy after another had struck her family—she found a need growing within her to know the reason for this current madness. She refused to believe the explanation Daniel had given that her that she had been sent to rescue him. Just the fanciful notions of a young boy.

Drink in hand, Captain Milford dropped into a chair in front of his desk. He released a long sigh and stared at the canvas rug beneath his boots. During their forced time together the past few days, Marianne had caught him staring at her more than once, not in a licentious manner, but more as if he wished to converse with her.

As if he were lonely.

"You remind me a bit of my Elizabeth." An awkward smile rose on his lips.

"Indeed?" Marianne wondered if he was paying her a compliment or an insult. Though from the wistful expression on his face she guessed it was the former.

"She was a woman I knew once. Many years ago." He stared off into space as if he were traveling back in time. "Smart, courageous, kind." His eyes snapped to her. "Though you're no beauty like she was."

Marianne lowered her chin. Had he said smart, courageous, and kind? Yet all she heard were the words "no beauty." Why did the flood of pain caused by such insults always drown out the compliments to her character?

"Blast it all, I've hurt your feelings," he growled in a tone that carried no apology. "Women are far too sensitive."

Marianne twisted the ring on her finger until the ruby glowed in the lantern light. "What happened to her?" she managed.

He gulped the last of his drink and slammed the glass down on his desk. Marianne flinched. Rising, he waved a hand through the air then gripped his side. "It matters not."

"I'll warrant you have a family of your own back in England, Captain." She realized her error too late as every line on his face tightened and his eyes flitted about the room as if in search of something.

Finally they settled on her in a cold, hard stare. "And why would you think that?"

Marianne had no response save the nervous gurgling of her stomach.

He stormed toward her. "The Royal Navy is my family, Miss Denton. Been my family all my life. Was my father's family and his father's family before him."

Marianne stared down at his boots and concentrated on the exquisite shine, compliments of her hard work that morning. She didn't want to look up at the intimidating man towering above her. She didn't want to look into those volatile eyes, serene one minute and explosive the next. "I'm sorry."

"Why are you sorry?" he bellowed. Thick hands grabbed her

shoulders and yanked her to her feet.

She stared straight into twitching, gray eyes. The scent of brandy stung her nose. Gathering her bravado, she tugged from his grasp and took a step back. "It seems a rather lonely existence, Captain." She kept her voice steady, despite her quivering belly. "And I would appreciate you keeping your hands to yourself. No gentleman would employ such crude manners."

If he intended to strike her or lock her in irons, she preferred that he simply proceed without delay. For every time she was in the captain's presence, she felt as though she were walking one of those thin ropes in the top yards, waiting to be shoved off to the deck below.

A tiny vein pulsed in his neck just above his black neckerchief. The hungry sea dashed against the hull and tipped the ship slightly to larboard. Marianne braced her feet against the deck and her soul against another onslaught of this man's deranged outbursts.

Instead, he broke into a chuckle and swung about.

"The navy's been good to me," he continued the conversation as if nothing had happened. Perhaps to him, it hadn't. "Why, I've seen exotic places most people never see. I've fought in glorious battles that have changed the course of history." He rounded his desk and caressed one of the leaves of his plants. His rock-hard expression softened. "Tender precious things, aren't they? Grew them from seeds. Just one little seed"—he gestured the size with his thumb and forefinger—"and you can grow a tree that will feed a family."

Marianne released a sigh at the change in his demeanor. He seemed to respect those who took a stand against him, or at the very least, her courage had caused him to shift back to the calm, reasonable captain, not Captain Maniacal, who so often appeared out of nowhere.

"Perhaps you should have been a farmer," she said.

Captain Maniacal returned. His face reddened. "Begone, Miss Denton. I tire of your company."

Before she made it to the door, a knock sounded. The captain growled a curse that made her ears burn, then he shouted for the intruder to enter. A man dressed in a marine sergeant's uniform gave her a cursory glance as he passed. Her heart leapt in her throat as Luke followed on his heels. His brows lifted at the sight of her, and he winked in passing. But it was Noah's blue eyes that latched upon hers that sent her blood racing. She took a step back and leaned on a nearby chair for support. Instead of anger, she saw relief on his face as he perused her. A faint smile lifted his lips.

Behind him, another marine nudged him forward. Lieutenant Reed brought up the rear.

Noah looked well. They both looked well. She silently thanked God.

"What is this about?" Captain Milford grumbled. "Can't a man enjoy his evening without interruptions!"

"Sorry to disturb you, Captain." Lieutenant Reed stepped forward and saluted. "But it appears these Americans have been stirring up trouble with the crew. As well as disrespecting the Royal Navy."

❖

It took all of Noah's strength to stare straight ahead and not turn for another look at Miss Denton. Although she appeared well, and young Daniel had said as much, Noah longed to hear it from her own lips.

"Causing trouble, you say?" The captain's sharp tone brought Noah's focus back on him. A much larger man in person than he appeared from the tops, the captain took a step away from the windows, wobbled, then crossed his arms over his chest.

When the marine had first announced they were to see the captain, Noah's hopes had lifted. At last he would have an audience with the only man who could set them free. Surely, once he explained the altercation during dinner as well as the circumstances of their impressments, this officer, this man of honor, would see reason. But now as Noah stood before the man, the haughty lift of the captain's shoulders and the scowl on his face did not bode well for that notion.

"Well, speak up. What happened?" the captain said.

"Captain, nothing but a—" Noah began.

"Not you, deserter!" Captain Milford barked and spittle landed on his desk.

"Captain," the sergeant said. His voice quavered. "This man started a fight with another crewman and insulted His Majesty's Navy."

Luke skewered him with a glare. "That's a lie and you know it."

"We are not deserters, Captain," Noah said.

"Silence!" the captain shouted. He plopped into his chair as if it took too much strength to keep his bulky frame standing. Black hair, streaked with gray, sprang like the edges of an old broom about his shoulders. He gripped his side then turned to the Lieutenant. "What say you, Lieutenant Reed?"

"I was not present during the altercation, Captain. I have only the marine sergeant's testimony."

"Hmm." Captain Milford's tired, gray eyes focused on Luke. "A fight you say? What was the cause?"

"An insult to the navy, sir," the marine stated.

"Did you hear this insult?"

"No, sir."

Luke grimaced. "I made no such slur, Captain."

The captain rose and adjusted his coat. His angular jaw flexed and gray eyes, alight with cruelty, shifted over the men. Fatigue drew the lines of his tanned face downward.

"Who struck who first?" he demanded.

The sergeant coughed. "I believe it was this man who threw the first blow, sir." He gestured toward Luke.

"Your crewman insulted our country, Captain," Noah said, not wanting the lie to go unchallenged. "And my man here merely gave him a little shove."

"Your country," the captain mumbled. "You have no country but England." He snorted and narrowed his eyes at Noah, then shifted them to Luke. He released a sigh, heavy with boredom, and rubbed the bridge of his nose. "Well, I shall take my marine's word over that of these two deserters."

Noah shook his head as his hope for justice faded completely before this blustering man.

"You both are in violation of Article 22 of the Articles of War which prohibits all fighting, quarreling, and reproachful speech aboard a Royal Navy ship. Since this is your first offense, I'll spare you the cat." The captain waved a hand toward Luke. "Lock him in irons below. No food or drink for two days. Perhaps that shall suffice as a lesson to you, sir, that I do not tolerate brawls on my ship."

Marianne gasped and all eyes shot to her.

"With all due respect, Captain—" Noah stepped forward.

"This is madness," Luke interrupted. "I did nothing wrong."

"Hold your tongues or I'll have you both flogged!" The captain's left eyelid began to twitch. "You are British sailors now, not crude, undisciplined Americans."

"We are *not* British sailors," Luke spit out through clenched teeth.

"Make that three days," the captain said. "Shall we go for four?"

Noah elbowed his friend and shook his head. Luke scowled but remained silent.

"Captain, please!" Marianne's sweet voice flowed over Noah from behind like a refreshing wave. He glanced over his shoulder at her. She stepped forward, her anxious gaze shifted from him to the captain. "Have mercy, I beg you."

The captain cleared his throat and for a moment—a precious, hopeful moment—the harsh glare in his eyes lessened. "I told you to leave, Miss Denton." His steely voice softened as he addressed her. She remained firmly in place. Noah blinked. How had the woman worked her charm on such an ill-tempered beast?

The captain snapped his gaze back to Luke. "Take him," he ordered the marine, who promptly tugged Luke by the elbow and led him toward the door. Noah tried to give his friend a reassuring look before he left, but Luke's gaze remained on the deck.

The marine sergeant smiled, while his companion Lieutenant Reed stared ahead, his lips set in a stiff line.

Captain Milford turned flashing eyes toward Noah. "And this one? What did he do?"

"He, too, was in the midst of the altercation, sir." The marine announced proudly.

"You're the captain of that merchantman we boarded, aren't you?" Captain Milford studied Noah as one would an insignificant organism beneath a microscope.

"Yes, I am, sir." Noah searched the captain's eyes for the honor, the integrity, he had hoped existed in the commander of a British warship. But instead, he found nothing but an apathetic cruelty that set the hairs on his arms standing straight.

"Ah, but you are no longer a captain of anything." Milford circled his desk and planted his thick boots in front of Noah.

"Captain, my men and I are not deserters." Despite the man's obvious derision toward them, Noah had to convince him of their innocence. He leveled a stern gaze upon Milford, captain to captain. "We are American citizens stolen from my ship without cause. Your man Garrick did not even examine our papers."

A slow smile lifted one corner of the captain's mouth. "Tsk tsk. I have no time for woeful tales." He exchanged a glance of amused annoyance with the marine.

"I have friends in South Hampton, Captain," Noah went on, "who can vouch for my character and integrity."

"To the devil with your character and integrity, sir! You and your men are sailors in His Majesty's Navy. You will forget your past. Forget your ship. Forget your country." Milford thrust his rigid face toward Noah. The odor of brandy and sweat filled the air between them. "I run a tough ship, and I'll not stand for insubordination, sir. Do I make myself clear?"

Noah stiffened. The captain swung about and grabbed a glass from his desk, giving Noah a chance to steal a glance at Miss Denton who was behind Lieutenant Reed. Desperation poured from her brown eyes. Desperation for him or for herself, he couldn't tell. Regardless of her culpability in their dire situation, a warship was no place for a lady.

He faced forward. Knowing he might not have another opportunity to speak to the captain in person, he must try to win Miss Denton's freedom. He must risk the captain's temper once again. "Permission to have a word with you, Captain."

Giving a disinterested huff, Captain Milford poured himself a drink and waved him on.

"It's about Miss Denton."

The topic brought the captain's cold gaze back to Noah.

"She's an innocent, captain. She's not a seafaring woman, sir, and found herself on my ship quite by accident."

He glanced at Marianne. Shock filled her misty eyes.

The captain sipped his drink. "Nevertheless, she is here now."

"I appeal to your honor, sir." Noah took a bold step toward him. Surely an officer in the Royal Navy would do no harm to an innocent woman. "She is a civilian. A proper lady with fortune and status in Baltimore. By the laws of civilized warfare, please return her to her home."

"You appeal to my honor, do you?" Captain Milford chuckled. "I have been in enough wars to know, sir, that there is nothing honorable about the men who fight them. You ignorant, savage Americans"—he pointed at Noah with his glass—"ever a source of amusement." He glanced at Reed but the man remained a statue.

The marine sergeant chuckled.

Anger flared in Noah's belly. "Yet I do believe it was we ignorant, savage Americans who defeated Britain's best army and navy and sent you scurrying back to England." He knew he sailed on dangerous seas, but Noah could not allow the insult to his country, to his countrymen, go unchallenged.

The captain's face turned a dark shade of purple. "The presumption, the audacity, sir! I should have you flogged!" He set down his goblet and moved toward Noah.

Marianne gasped.

"Mark my words, young captain"—Milford crammed a finger toward Noah's face—"should our nations meet at war again, we shall squash your American spirit as well as your pathetic military forces and reclaim the land that belongs to us!"

Noah didn't flinch, didn't blink, didn't allow the fury boiling within him to rise to the surface. He had once thought that a country so steeped in traditions of honor and glory, so rich in the history of fighting for their own freedom, would never consider stealing the freedom of others. Now he knew differently. Now he knew better.

Captain Milford's dark brows arched. "For your insolence, sir, you will scrub the weather deck day and night for as long as your slick-tongued friend is locked below."

Noah's breath clogged in his throat.

"And if you are caught sleeping while on the job," the captain leaned toward him, a greasy smile on his lips. "The penalty is death."

❖

After a sleepless night that left her eyelids as heavy as anchors and her head throbbing, Marianne attended her duties with the mind-numbing routine of a longtime servant. She fetched and served the captain his breakfast and then helped him on with his uniform, brushing off specks of invisible dust. Afterward, she ushered him on deck, promising to have his cabin sparkling by the time he returned.

She'd learned to ignore his insulting quips and constant grumbling and placate him with feigned agreements hidden behind an occasional smile. He was British, after all, and who could argue with a man who believed he came from a master race destined to rule the world. Mad or not, when he straightened to his full commanding height and raised his voice to its most vociferous capacity, her insides melted in fear. But she'd learned that not soon after such an incident, his shoulders would sink and his voice lower and he would speak to her as if he hadn't just called her every abominable name he possessed in his vast vocabulary.

Leaning on her knees, Marianne scrubbed the wooden planks of the captain's floor and thought of her mother and Lizzie. Without Marianne's marriage or a certificate proving her death, her mother would never be able to touch Marianne's inheritance. Another year and her beloved family would run out of money to live on. And then what would they do? Marianne's chest grew heavy. If she had not taken matters into her own hands aboard Noah's ship, and ended up a prisoner on a British frigate, Noah would have returned her home after his voyage. Now, because of her lack of faith, none of them would ever see home again.

Lord, I'm sorry I didn't trust You. Yet with the utterance of the words came the realization that she still didn't trust God—that she no longer truly knew how to trust anyone. *Please, God, if You're listening, please help my family.* But her prayer seemed to dissipate into the humid air of the cabin.

The scent of linseed oil and lemons burned her nose. Pain shot into her legs and angled over her back. She grew accustomed to the constant aches, welcomed them, in fact, as punishment for bringing such tragedy upon herself, her family, and her friends. Friends? Could she call Noah, Luke, and Mr. Weller friends? Would they consider her as such? And why, lately, did her thoughts center on the one man who had caused her the most grief—Noah Brenin?

She cringed at the thought that he'd been up all night scrubbing the deck above. And poor Luke, locked in irons below. She must do something to lessen their strict punishments. Yet her attempt to bring up the subject with the captain that morning had resulted in yet another outburst of his fury.

Noah had risked punishment on her behalf. She could not shake the thought, nor could she imagine why he would do such a thing, when she was the one who had put them all in this horrible situation. The door squeaked open and in walked Daniel, wearing his usual bright smile, torn shirt, and breeches. His hands were tucked behind his back as if he were hiding something from her. His eyes sparked with excitement. "Hello, Miss Marianne!"

Sitting back on her haunches, she returned his smile. "Hello, Daniel."

"I brought you something." He swept out his hands and handed her a book.

On closer inspection—a Bible.

Marianne set down the cloth and allowed him to place the holy book on her open palms. She gazed down at it with an affection that surprised her. As a child, she had enjoyed hearing her mother read aloud the wonderful stories it contained. As she grew, she immersed herself in its loving words whenever she needed wisdom or comfort. But, much to her shame, Marianne had not read from the precious book in quite a while—not since her father died. "Is this yours?"

"Yes, miss. But God told me you needed it more than me right now."

"Oh, indeed?" Marianne laughed. "But I really can't accept this."

"You must. Not forever." He shrugged. "Just until you help rescue me."

"Oh, Daniel." Marianne set the book atop one of the padded chairs and began scrubbing again. "I am not so sure you have heard from God. How am I going to help you escape when I can't even help myself or Mr. Heaton and Mr. Brenin?"

Yanking a cloth from a pile, he dabbed some oil on it and began scrubbing beside her. "It don't matter, miss. God'll help you."

"God help me?" Marianne concentrated her scouring over a particularly stubborn patch of dried dirt. "He has better things to do." Much better things or He wouldn't have allowed her father to die, wouldn't have allowed her mother to become ill and wouldn't have allowed their family fortune to blow away in the wind.

Or Marianne to get stuck aboard Noah's ship.

Or her to become a slave to a mad captain.

Halting, she sat back and gazed at the rays of morning sunlight reflecting off Daniel's dark hair and surrounding him with light as if he were precious to God.

While she remained in the shadows.

"I fear you have the wrong lady, Daniel, I'm just a plain, ordinary woman. I am nobody special. And I won't do anything important." She sighed. "I'm terrified of water. I can't take care of my mother and sister properly, and I can't even keep a man's interest long enough so he'll marry me."

Daniel snapped the hair from his face and gazed at her forlornly. "Beggin' your pardon, miss, but there ain't nobody ordinary in God's Kingdom."

Marianne held up the Bible. "I'm not like the people in here: Moses, Abraham, Elijah, Paul, all great men that God used."

"And Daniel." He stopped scrubbing and smiled. "He was a prophet."

"Yes, he was." She wiped a smudge of dirt from his face with her thumb and remembered her Bible lesson to the men on board Noah's ship. Daniel in the lion's den. *And that is why we must always have faith, even in the midst of hopeless times.* She could still hear her voice so full of feigned conviction—a masquerade of the strong woman she longed to be.

"And I am God's prophet, too. He told me so." Daniel's brown eyes sparkled.

Marianne moved to another spot and continued her scrubbing. The boy's childish innocence warmed her heart. Let him have his dreams, his illusions, his hopes. They were probably the only things keeping him alive on this horrid ship.

"What of Esther?" he asked.

Marianne searched her mind for the story her mother had read to her long ago. Ah yes, the queen. "She was beautiful." Not like Marianne.

"Rahab?"

The old stories flooded her mind like rays of sunshine on a cloudy day. Rahab was the harlot who hid the spies of Israel so they could defeat Jericho. Definitely not like Marianne. "She was brave."

"I know what story is like yours." Daniel's eyes widened with delight. "How about Gideon? His clan was the weakest in the tribe of Manasseh, and he was the least in his father's house. Yet God used him to defeat the Midianites with only three hundred men."

Shaking her head, Marianne grabbed the bottle of oil and shifted to a fresh spot on the deck. "I know you mean well, Daniel. And I'm sure God has great plans for you. But my life has been fraught with tragedy. I can never seem to rise above the struggles, to conquer them like others stronger than I." She continued her scrubbing. "I fear God will do what He wills in this world and in my life, and I will always be what I am—a plain, ordinary girl."

She circled the rag over the wooden planks. Round and round like the monotonous circles of her life until her wrists ached and perspiration beaded on her neck. Tears burned behind her eyes. She could not fathom where they came from or why they appeared. Something about Daniel's words, his enthusiasm, his faith, tugged upon a yearning in her heart—a longing, beneath her bitterness, to be something more.

He touched her hand, stopping her. "You don't think God loves you, do you?"

Halting, Marianne drew a deep breath and looked away. She'd never truly considered the question.

Daniel shook his head. Strands of hair hung down his cheek. "Even your name means that God loves you. Marianne, taken from Mary, the mother of our Lord. She was an ordinary girl from an ordinary family. And look how important she was in God's plan."

She gazed at him, astounded by his wisdom. But she could not allow these fanciful notions to take root. For if she did, if she started to believe God truly loved her, if she believed she was special and that He had a plan for her life, then the next disappointment, the next tragedy would rob her of her will to go on.

And then she would end up facedown in the Patapsco River like her father.

"Of course, I know God loves everyone." She shrugged, hoping to shrug away her tears as well, along with the hope that had ignited them.

"You know it up here." Daniel pointed to his head. "But not in here." His hand flew to his heart.

Pouring more oil on her cloth, she leaned over and buffed the wood into a shine. "I believe I'm going to heaven, but I expect nothing else from this life."

"You'll see that you're wrong." Daniel smiled. "When God tells me something it always comes true. He told me a beautiful woman and three men would come on the ship and save me and my da—save me."

Beautiful woman? Marianne chuckled. Now she was certain she was not the woman in Daniel's prophecy. Looking into his hope-filled—no, faith-filled—eyes, she wished with all her heart that she could make his vision come true. But she couldn't. All she could hope to do was to try to alleviate some of Noah and Luke's discomfort during their punishments. A glorious thought occurred to her which might be the solution she sought, but she couldn't do it alone.

She brushed the hair from his face. "Daniel, do you know where Lieutenant Reed is?"

He gave her a perplexed look and glanced out the window. "He may be in the wardroom, miss. He likes to have a cup o' tea about now. What do you want him for?"

Though Lieutenant Reed's stiff, portentous exterior would normally dissuade her from seeking him out, the expression on his face last night and the way he shifted his feet uncomfortably when the captain had unleashed his temper led her to believe there may exist a smidgeon of compassion behind his stuffy facade.

"I want to ask his help to lighten the captain's sentences upon Mr. Brenin and Mr. Heaton."

Daniel's exuberance of only a moment ago faded beneath an anxious look. "I doubt he'll help you, miss. 'Sides, when the captain issues a punishment, it stands. I ain't never seen"—his eyes snapped to hers— "Oh, I forgot to give you Mr. Noah's message."

"Message?" She ignored the tiny leap of her heart. "When did he give it to you?"

"At supper last night before those sailors stirred up trouble. He asked how you were. Seemed real concerned as to your welfare."

The statement uttered in such innocent sincerity sent warmth down to her toes. She shook it off, had to shake it off, but it stubbornly remained in light of Noah's brave appeal to the captain.

Daniel laid his cloth aside and stood. "He wants you to keep your ears open for anything you hear about where the ship is heading or any plans the captain has."

"He wants me to spy?" she whispered, excitement tingling over her skin.

"Aye, miss." He glanced out the door. "An' I can deliver messages back and forth between you."

Marianne's mind whirled with the possibilities.

The ship bucked, nearly spilling her bottle of oil. She grabbed it and steadied her stomach against a wave of nausea.

"I 'ave to be goin' now," Daniel said.

Marianne struggled to her feet. "Thank you for your help, Daniel. And for the Bible."

"My pleasure, miss." Then, after a friendly wave, he disappeared out the door.

Tossing the cloth aside in favor of a more important task, Marianne left the captain's cabin and descended one level for the officer's wardroom. Air, heavy with the smell of tar and damp wood, filled her nose—a not altogether unpleasant scent. Or perhaps she was just growing accustomed to it. Making her way down the companionway, she kept both hands raised, ready to brace herself against the bulkhead should the ship try to knock her from her feet. She couldn't help but smile at her growing knowledge of the names assigned to parts of the ship—names she had not known a month ago.

Rap rap rap. She tapped on the open door of the wardroom and put on her best smile for Lieutenant Reed as he glanced up from a steaming cup of tea. His brow furrowed. "Are you lost, Miss Denton?"

"No, sir. May I have a word with you, please?"

He scanned the room, no doubt checking to see if they were alone. Small cabins that were enclosed by little more than stretched canvas on wooden frames, lined either side of the oblong table at which he sat. Officers' cabins, Marianne surmised. A cupboard at one end held plates, cups, and cutlery as well as a variety of swords, muskets, pistols, and axes.

"Make it quick, miss. You should not be down here." Lieutenant Reed stood, scraping his chair over the deck. He adjusted his black coat, the three gold buttons on each of his cuffs and one button on each collar glimmering in the light of a lantern that swayed overhead.

She clasped her hands together and took a timid step within. "It is about Mr. Heaton and Mr. Brenin."

She detected a flinch on his otherwise staunch demeanor. "And?"

"You know as well as I they do not deserve their punishment."

"It does not matter what I know or don't know." He snorted and plucked his cocked hat from the table. "All that matters on this ship is what the captain says."

Marianne twisted the ring on her finger. "Even if it is unjust and ruthless?"

"You would do well to curb your tongue, miss. The captain is not above issuing the same punishments for a quarrelsome woman."

She studied the stiff man for a moment, gauging him. She knew Noah had risked punishment for her. Could she do less for him? Something deep within Mr. Reed's hazel eyes told her he agreed with her, despite the indifferent shield he attempted to hide behind.

"You know as well as I that the captain is not himself," she whispered.

A flicker of understanding darted across his eyes before they glanced away. "I know no such thing, miss." He tugged on his neckerchief.

"I could report you for such subversive words."

"Then do so, Lieutenant." Marianne no longer cared. If she were to suffer for trying to correct a terrible injustice, then so be it.

Lieutenant Reed shifted his stance. "Order must be maintained on board, miss, or we would be unable to defend our country. There must be a commander aboard this ship just as there must be a king over a country or chaos would ensue."

"Order, yes, but cruelty, no." Marianne gripped the back of one of the chairs. "And permit me to correct you, sir, but chaos ensues when leaders wield their power without impunity. As is happening on this ship."

Lieutenant Reed studied her and for a moment she thought she'd won him to her side. But then he lengthened his stance and settled his bicorn atop his head. "I can do nothing for you."

"Will you at least allow me to bring some food and water to Mr. Heaton?"

Hazel eyes sparked at her from beneath the pointed edge of his hat. "What you do in the middle of the night is of no concern to me." One cultured brow rose slightly before he marched out of the room.

❖ CHAPTER 15 ❖

Noah stretched his stiff shoulders and legs, trying to loosen the tight knots that held his muscles captive. Taking his place in a line of sailors on the main deck, he waited to receive a cup of grog. He'd been scouring the deck for forty-three hours. His head pounded, and his eyelids felt like iron pilings. One glance at his hands told him they were white, wrinkly, and raw from the incessant scrubbing. A flurry of hot wind swirled around him, tugging at his hair and cooling the sweat on his brow and neck. He drew in a deep breath, relishing the smell of the sea. Just another twenty-nine hours. He could do it... He had to do it.

As he slogged forward in line, Noah felt Miss Denton's presence on deck. He had no idea how, but when he glanced over his shoulder, there she was. She seemed to be looking for someone. Their eyes met and for a moment he thought he saw concern flicker within them. For him?

A midshipman, Blake, if Noah remembered, ordered the boatswain to blow his pipe. "For all you men who cannot read, Miss Denton has offered to read your letters from home without cost before you go below for your evening mess."

Read letters? Noah nearly gasped. Why would she do that? She hated the British. A sailor rolled a barrel over for her, and she perched upon it and adjusted her skirts. The setting sun set her hair aflame like glistening cinnamon and cast an ethereal glow over her radiant skin. She smiled at the men forming a circle around her.

Grabbing his ladle of grog, Noah downed it and returned to the foredeck where he'd left off scouring the oak planks. At least they allowed him food and drink. He couldn't say the same for Luke. He cringed at what the man must be enduring chained below in the dark, dank hold.

Picking up the holystone, Noah continued his work while keeping an eye on Miss Denton. Truth be told, he found it difficult to keep his eyes off her. One by one, the men approached her. With a smile, she took each man aside and read the contents of his missive in private. Visibly moved, some of the sailors clutched their letters to their chests as they ambled away while others broke into tears upon hearing what their loved ones had to say. What astounded Noah the most was the kind gestures and gentle way she addressed each man—each British man.

His thoughts drifted to Miss Priscilla. Memories of their brief time together focused more clearly in his mind. Her dismissive, commanding attitude toward the servants in her home, the way she jutted out her chin and looked the other way when they passed the impoverished in the city streets.

Truth be told, in light of Miss Denton, Priscilla's beauty began to fade.

Noah's gaze latched upon Lieutenant Garrick, who stood at the helm of the quarterdeck, his beady eyes riveted upon Miss Denton. What Noah saw in those eyes made his stomach curdle—a look he'd seen in many men's eyes when they sought only one thing from a woman.

A surge of protectiveness rose within Noah that surprised him. But how could he protect her from a man who wielded nearly as much power as the captain himself?

Soon, the group of sailors surrounding Miss Denton dissipated, and a bell rang from the forecastle. Noah counted the chimes as they echoed over the deck. Eight bells. Which meant it was four in the afternoon, the end of one watch and the start of another.

But that made no difference to Noah. He must stay at his task.

Miss Denton rose and started across the deck. She gazed up at Noah ever so briefly—too briefly—when Mr. Weller approached her, holding out a missive he must have had on him when he'd been impressed. Noah frowned. Why hadn't he trusted Noah to read it aboard the *Fortune*?

One of the sailors bumped into Mr. Weller in passing. The same pock-faced man who'd caused trouble with them below. Weller stumbled from the impact, but kept his ground. "Monsters are hatched not birthed. You ain't got no family." He chortled and gazed around him, eliciting the chuckles of other sailors.

Weller glared at the man and curled his fists. The scars running down his face and neck reddened. *Do not strike him, my friend.* Noah silently pleaded. *Or you'll end up like me, or worse.* Leaping to his feet, Noah scurried down the foredeck ladder, shoving men aside in order to save his friend from doing something that would warrant a lashing.

Miss Denton's voice shot across the deck, halting him. "You will take that back this instant, Mr. . . . Mr. . . ."

The sailor froze, studied her for a moment, and dragged off his hat. "Wilcox, miss."

"Do you judge a man by his scars, Mr. Wilcox? Or do you judge a man by his character?" She pointed at Weller. "These scars are evidence of Mr. Weller's great bravery during battle. Have you any to compare?"

The man's spiteful eyes narrowed as Noah made his way toward Miss Denton. Yet despite the fury storming on the man's face and his defiant stance, Miss Denton held her ground. She placed her hands atop her hips. "Apologize at once."

The man hesitated, spit to the side, then spun on his heels and marched away.

Releasing a sigh, Noah approached her. Admiration welled within him, along with the realization that the woman he'd known as a child no longer existed. He wanted to tell her that she should curb that reckless tongue of hers on board this ship. He wanted to tell her that she was the bravest woman he'd ever met.

But the loud shout of a petty officer behind him halted him. "Get back to work, Brenin! Or the cap'n will hear of this!"

Miss Denton gathered her skirts and their eyes met. She smiled at him before she descended the companionway ladder, and Noah's heart soared in the brightness of that smile.

❖

Marianne crept forward, peering through the gloom of the sailor's berth below deck. Her toe struck something sharp, and she bit her lip to keep from crying out. Daniel turned and laid a finger over his mouth then proceeded around a corner and into a large area filled with hammocks that swayed back and forth with each movement of the ship. At well past midnight, Marianne hoped most of the crew would be asleep. Her fears were allayed when nothing but snoring, occasional grunts, and the creaking of the ship combined into a discordant chant. Gesturing for her to wait, Daniel disappeared among the oscillating gray masses. The lantern the young boy held cast eerie shadows over the scene as he wove between the sleeping mounds, making them look like giant cocoons—cocoons out of which woman-eating insects could burst forth at any minute. A chill overcame Marianne at the thought, and she hugged herself. Her nose curled at the stench of sweat and filth that hung in the room like a cloud.

Moments later, Daniel returned and beckoned her onward. On the other side of the room, seated on the hard floor, his legs in irons hooked to the deck, sat Mr. Heaton, his head reclining on his knees. Beyond him, a marine, musket gripped in his hand, slouched against the bulkhead fast asleep.

Kneeling beside Luke, Marianne touched his arm, and he jerked his head up, tugging on his chains. The clanking dissipated amidst the snores and creaks.

He gaped at her, rubbed his eyes, and then blinked. "Miss Denton, what are you doing here?" he whispered.

"Shhh." She glanced at the marine. "I brought you some grog and a biscuit."

He looked over his shoulder, alarm tightening his features. Stubble peppered his jaw, and his black hair hung limp over his shoulders. Even in the dim lantern light, Marianne could make out a purple bruise circling his swollen eye.

"Do you know what they'll do to you if you're caught?" he whispered, then glanced at Daniel keeping watch not three feet away. "And you, too."

"It will be all right." The assurance in the boy's voice gave Marianne an odd sense of comfort.

"Be gone with you, Miss Denton." Luke dropped his head back onto his knees.

Ignoring him, she nudged his chin up and lifted the cup to his lips. "Drink this and be quiet, Mr. Heaton."

She tipped the mug, and he gulped the liquid, releasing a sigh when he had drained the last drop.

"I never thought stale water and rum would taste so good."

"Here." She handed him two biscuits. "Don't leave any crumbs." She smiled.

A snort sounded from one from the hammocks. Another man cried out in his sleep. The guard shifted his weight and scratched his nose.

Marianne froze, her eyes shifting from Mr. Heaton to Daniel.

Taking the biscuit, he gestured for her to leave. She started to get up.

He grabbed her arm. "Thank you," he mouthed.

Her heart pounding, Marianne dashed between the hammocks and followed Daniel up one deck. She held the bundle containing another two biscuits close to her chest.

"Thank you, Daniel." She leaned and kissed him on top of his head. "Now get some sleep."

"Where are you going, miss?" He looked at her with concern.

"I'm going to check on Mr. Brenin."

❖

Noah lifted the collar of his coat to shield his neck from the evening wind that despite the summer month carried the bite of the cold north Atlantic. Though he could tell from the stars and sun that they sailed a southwest course, he had no idea where they were heading or what his plan should be once they got to their destination. Struggling to his feet, he stretched his cramped legs and blew into his hands to try to spark some life back into his stiff fingers.

He scanned the deck. Save for the helmsman, and two lookouts, the rest of the crew was no doubt fast asleep below. Even the poor marine assigned to guard him seemed deep in slumber as he slouched against a railing on the foredeck. Good. That would give Noah a chance to take a respite from his hard labor.

Off their starboard port, a half moon winked at him as waves frolicked in its glistening light as if they hadn't a care in the world. He envied them. He hung his head, fighting back a wave of exhaustion. Sorrow and shame followed close on its wake. He had lost his cargo, lost his father's last ship, and lost all means of providing for his family. Regardless that the fault lay elsewhere, his father would consider it Noah's responsibility and hence, Noah's failure. And a failure he was.

Even if he managed to escape, without his father's merchant business he would be nothing but an impoverished sailor. No doubt Miss

Priscilla would refuse to even see him. Yet it was not her pretty face he found drifting unbidden into his mind of late. It was the face of another woman, not nearly as striking, but a face that shone with its own unique brilliance. Noah stared at the holystones by his feet—the ones he'd been using to scour the deck for the past fifty-two hours. Confound it all, he should be angry at Miss Denton, not dreaming of her like a love-sick schoolboy.

An invisible weight tugged upon his eyelids as he plodded across the deck trying to get the blood pumping in his legs again. How long could a man live without sleep? Another twenty hours to go. He could make it. He had to make it. To fall asleep meant certain death.

Noah spun on his heels and headed in the other direction. A lady dressed in a fiery maroon gown glided over the deck. Her brown hair shimmered. He rubbed his eyes. No doubt the lack of sleep caused him to hallucinate. But then he smelled her sweet scent—Marianne—and he opened his eyes to her creamy face awash in moonlight. "Are you real?" he asked.

"Quite, Mr. Brenin. And I bear gifts." She held out a biscuit to him. Her sweet smile nearly stole his breath away.

Despite her kind intentions, Noah's fear for her safety rose at her foolishness. "You shouldn't be here," he said, ignoring the offer of food despite his growling stomach.

"I shouldn't be many places these days. However, it is on my account you are scrubbing these decks all day and night with no rest in sight." She avoided his gaze. "Thank you, Mr. Brenin, for trying to help me. Though I can't imagine why you did after I put you on this ship in the first place."

After a quick glance across the deck, Noah took her arm and led her to a more secluded spot behind the ship's boats. He ran a hand through his hair. "Despite what you may think, I am still a gentleman, and this is no place for a lady." Is that why he had risked punishment to save her? To appease his gentlemanly duty?

A breeze stirred the tendrils of her hair circling her face. She brushed them back and studied him. "Why aren't you angry with me? I've ruined your life. I've caused you and your friends great harm and loss."

"Who says I'm *not* angry at you?" He folded his arms over his chest. She studied him. "Your eyes."

"Humph. Then I shall have to speak to them about keeping quiet from now on." He couldn't help but smile.

Her nose pinked and she lowered her gaze. "You mock me, sir."

He shook his head and laid a finger beneath her chin, raising her eyes—sparkling brown eyes so full of sincerity and kindness—to his. "I was angry at you, Miss Denton. But what purpose does it serve? You were only trying to get home to your mother." He sighed. "Perhaps I should have returned you to Baltimore at your request. I was so obsessed with getting my goods to England." He rubbed the back of his neck and gazed out to sea. "Now I have no goods and no ship."

"Thanks to me." Her voice sank.

"Egad, but ruining my cargo." He chuckled. "Quite imaginative. I suppose it is fair recompense for all the pranks I pulled on you as a child."

"It was a means to an end." She gave him a sad smile. "I take no pride in the action." She held out the biscuit to him again. He took it this time, allowing his fingers to linger over hers. Why, he didn't know. But her touch had a curious effect upon him, sending tendrils of warmth up his arm. "They are permitting me to eat."

"I know." Her eyes misted with tears. "I thought it would help you stay awake. I brought another one." She held out her bundle, but he pushed it back, shoving the biscuit into his pocket. He had more important matters on his mind than food. "How are you?"

The ship rose over a swell. She stumbled and Noah grabbed her waist to steady her, drawing her near. Her alluring scent filled his nostrils and his body quickened. Confusion hammered through his mind. He wasn't supposed to desire this woman, this woman who had snubbed her nose at him as a child, this woman who was both plain and plump. He was supposed to be convincing her to break off their engagement. Though he wondered if that truly mattered anymore.

He glanced down at her. Her brown eyes shimmered with surprise, and something else. . .ardor? Her skin glowed in the moonlight, her lips parted slightly. And in that moment, he saw nothing plain about her. Even the feel of her rounded curves beneath his hands sent heat into his belly. He released her and backed away.

She averted her gaze.

"How is your head?" He gestured toward the spot where her wound had been, now barely discernable beneath her hair.

She dabbed her fingers over it. "It heals nicely." She gave him a curious glance from the corner of her eye. "If not for this wound, none of us would be on this vile ship."

"Indeed. And you would still be with your mother."

"And you would have made your fortune and be attending soirees with Priscilla and have no need of. . ." She lifted a hand to her nose.

"Have no need of what?"

She waved a hand at him and turned her eyes to the sea.

Noah shifted his bare feet over the deck. Guilt assailed him and he didn't know why. He had done nothing wrong. Was she concerned for her mother? "Is your mother ill as you said?"

She shot fiery eyes his way. "How dare you? I wouldn't lie about such a thing."

He shrugged. "I thought you were exaggerating so I would return you home."

She looked back out to sea.

"I'm truly sorry that you are separated from her." He wanted to erase the pain from her face and see the sparkle return to her eyes.

"She'll die if she doesn't get her medicines. And without me to care for her. . ." She inhaled a sob and lowered her gaze. "I tried to explain to the captain that I can't be here. . ." She rubbed her hands together in frustration, and Noah noticed that they seemed raw, rough.

He took one and flipped it over, examining it in the light of the mainmast lantern. Red blotches marred skin that was streaked with cuts and scrapes. "He works you to death."

"He is particular about the way things are done."

Noah shook his head. In all that she had endured, she never once complained. Without thinking, he placed a light kiss upon the blisters on each hand. She gasped, yet she made no move to take them from his grip. He ran his thumb over her skin. "Does he hurt you?"

She shifted bewildered eyes between his, then shook her head. "The captain is a lonely, bitter man. Truth be told, I think being at sea so long has befuddled his mind."

"He certainly wasn't open to reason the other night." Noah continued caressing her fingers, relishing in the feel of her skin. She gazed across the deck, anguish flickering in her eyes.

Concern for her, for her safety, for her family, flooded Noah like never before. "I will get you off this ship, Miss Denton."

"How?"

"I don't know. But I will find a way." He leaned closer to her. "I promise we will not be here forever."

The wind whipped the curls around her face into wisps of glittering cinnamon.

"Do not promise me anything, Noah. Promises are too easily broken." Sorrow glazed her eyes.

And Noah wanted more than anything to prove her wrong. His thoughts shifted to Lieutenant Garrick and the way he had hovered over Marianne on deck, the way he had looked at her. Noah's muscles tensed. "What does this man Garrick have to say to you?"

Her hands trembled. She pulled them from his grasp and hugged herself. "He is a cad, of course, but he is harmless." Her voice lacked conviction.

"I am not so sure." Noah caught her eyes with his. "Stay away from him."

"I assure you, Mr. Brenin, that is my intention."

The deck tilted again. Marianne reached for his hand. The melodious purl of the sea played against the hull, and Noah had the strangest urge to dance with her across the deck.

"Unless, of course, you plan on charming him as you have the captain?" His tone taunted her. But he meant his words. She possessed a unique charm he could no longer deny.

"Charm?" She huffed. "Surely you jest. I have not charmed a soul in my life."

"I am not so sure." Noah fingered a silky strand of her hair. What was wrong with him? Surely exhaustion had taken over his reason.

She stepped away. Her chest heaved. Then she glanced up into the tops. "They work you hard as well."

Stunned by the concern in her voice, he nodded. "Ah yes, the top yards."

"Is it safe?"

"Safe?" His laugh came out bitter. "It's not safe anywhere on the ship."

She lowered her gaze. Her delicate brows furrowed. "You are frightened of the height?"

Though the man in him wanted to deny any fear, something about her made him willingly admit it. "How can you tell?"

"I am not unfamiliar with fear." She gazed across the molten dark waters and took a deep breath.

"You seem to handle your fears much better than I."

"Don't let me fool you, Mr. Brenin."

"I wouldn't think of it." He smiled.

He glanced aloft, then back down at her eyes—penetrating eyes full of compassion. And something within them bade him to bare his soul. "My brother fell from the t'gallant yard."

Her mouth opened.

"He was teaching me to sail."

She laid a hand on his arm. "Oh, Noah."

He jerked from her, chiding himself for saying anything, for invoking a sympathy he did not want. "It doesn't matter."

❖

Marianne swallowed the lump in her throat even as her eyes burned with tears. "Of course it matters. It wasn't your fault, Noah."

He turned away. "How do you know?"

News of young Jacob's death had spread quickly through Baltimore, but no word followed as to the cause. An accident was all they'd heard. Afterward, Noah never accompanied his father when the man came to visit Marianne's family.

"I know you, Noah."

"Do you?" Agony burned in his eyes. He ground his teeth together. "I caused him to fall." He tore his gaze from her. "I challenged him to race up through the ratlines and around the lubber's hole while I timed him."

Marianne stepped toward him, but he raised a hand to stop her. The ship bucked, blasting them with salty spray.

"It was my idea." His voice cracked. "He was teasing me because of my fear. It made me angry, so I challenged him to best a time only a seasoned topman could match." He hung his head.

A gust of wind whipped over them. Noah's Adam's apple leapt as he swallowed. "I held his bloody head in my hands and watched him die."

Marianne's vision blurred. The horror of it. The agony. She could not comprehend. Her throat burned as she tried to gather her thoughts, but they refused to settle on anything rational, on anything comforting. She laid a hand on his arm. This time, he did not resist.

"You meant him no harm, Noah. It was an accident." Yet her words seemed to fall empty upon the angry waves thrashing against the hull.

"Tell that to my father." Noah frowned. "Jacob the good son, the smart son, the brave son." He shifted moist eyes her way. "He wished it had been me who'd died."

Marianne shook her head, wanting to comfort him, but not finding the words.

"And I've spent a lifetime trying to make it up to him." He gripped the railing and stared out to sea. "But nothing I do will ever be enough."

The weight of his guilt pressed down on Marianne. How could anyone live with this kind of pain, this burden? No wonder Noah was driven to succeed. It wasn't for the money, for the prestige, it was in payment for the death of his brother.

And his father had encouraged it, fostered it. It was, no doubt, why Noah had agreed to marry her—a woman he didn't love.

"I miss him." He rubbed his eyes again then straightened his shoulders. "Forgive me, Miss Denton. It seems exhaustion has loosened my tongue."

"There is no need for apologies." Marianne longed to comfort him but, as in most things, she felt woefully inadequate to the task. She took his hand in hers and squeezed it. "No one can bear the weight of this, Noah. You must let it go." A tear slid down her cheek.

He stared at her curiously. Lifting his hand, he wiped her tear with his thumb then caressed her cheek. His touch sent a wave of heat across her skin that made her thoughts swirl and her body reel.

It meant nothing, she reminded herself. He was beyond exhaustion. He was angry and despondent. Surely any woman with a listening ear and a caring heart would suffice to appease his loneliness. Marianne knew she should leave. She needed to leave, but the look in his eyes held her captive—a look that slowly wandered down to her mouth and hovered over her lips as if only there could he find the sustenance he needed. Marianne's breath halted in her throat.

Then he lowered his lips to hers.

A quiver spread down Marianne's back. Warmth flooded her belly. Noah's lips caressed hers, playing, stroking, hovering. His hot breath feathered over her cheek. She drew it in, filling her lungs with his scent. He caressed her cheek, her neck, and ran his fingers through her loose curls.

Laughter shot through the night air, startling her and jerking Noah back.

"That ought to keep the blasted Yankee awake." One of the watch-man chortled to another man who'd just leapt on deck.

Heat flamed up Marianne's neck. She attempted to regain her breath.

Noah's jaw tightened. "My apologies, Miss Denton." Then avoiding her gaze, he marched away.

Marianne laid a hand on her stomach and stared out to sea. Not exactly the reaction she expected from the first man she allowed to kiss her.

❖ CHAPTER 16 ❖

Marianne fell onto her bed and sobbed. Her first kiss. She should be elated, filled with joy. For she had never thought any man would find her alluring enough to kiss unless it was forced upon him by marriage. Why then did she cry? Sitting up, she wiped the tears from her cheeks and tried to regain her senses, traitorous senses that had danced in a delightful flurry when Noah's lips touched hers. Not simply touched, but caressed as if he truly cherished her.

But that couldn't be. Especially not Noah Brenin.

Noah had not slept in nearly three nights, she reminded herself. The moonlight, the late hour, the slap of the sea against the hull, and Marianne lending a caring ear to his woeful tale, all combined to create an atmosphere, a desire that was, if not imaginary, surely ephemeral. In his weary delirium, Noah had simply given in to the manly desires Marianne's mother had warned her about.

Then why did she care?

This infuriating, reckless boy who had done nothing but make her life miserable as a child, who had shunned her and teased her until she cried herself to sleep at night. This oaf who had abandoned her at their engagement party.

Then why did she wish for something more?

Why did he consume her thoughts day and night? And why did the touch of his lips on hers send a warm flutter through her body?

A kiss. She'd been kissed at last. Marianne smiled and brushed her fingers over her lips. She had no idea it could be so pleasurable.

But in that pleasure she also sensed a power that could rip her heart in two.

❖

Following a line of crewmen, Noah lifted his heavy legs and climbed through the hatch onto the main deck. He rubbed his eyes against the glare of the rising sun that promised a warm day ahead. When the watchman had relieved him of his punishment at four in the morning, he could hardly believe it, for he had begun to think his penalty was more eternal than hell itself. Stumbling below like a drunken man, he had crawled into his hammock. Two hours of sleep. Two hours of precious slumber was all he'd been granted in the wee hours of the morning. But it was the sweetest sleep he'd ever had. In fact, he hadn't even heard the boatswain's cries "All hands ahoy. Up all hammocks ahoy," nor the scrambling of his mates unhooking their bedding around him. Not until Weller and Luke—who had been released at the same time as Noah had—dumped him from his hammock and he fell to the hard deck below did he snap from his deep slumber.

Noah's thoughts sped to the kiss he had shared with Marianne last night. No, it was not last night, but the night before. After she had fled the deck, the rest of that night and all the next day and night had blurred past him in turbulent shades of gray and white and black like a fast-moving storm. Visions of her maroon gown, brown hair, and full lips mingled with holystones and oak planks into a disjointed mirage that had him wondering if he had only dreamed of the kiss.

But no. He could still feel the tingle on his mouth. What madness had possessed him to taste her sweet lips? What madness had possessed her to accept his advance? Whatever the disease, he hoped there was no cure. She had responded with more passion than he would have guessed existed within her. For years, he thought her nothing more than a pretentious prig. When in reality. . . His body warmed at the remembrance. Was it possible she cared for him? Or did she kiss him out of pity or to make amends for what she had done? Since he had not seen her in over a day, he had no way of knowing.

"To your stations!" a boatswain brayed, and the crew scrambled to take their assigned watches across the deck where they would assist with the sailing of the ship or perform necessary maintenance. Normally the crew swept and holystoned the deck each morning, but due to the gleaming shine glaring from the wooden planks—thanks to Noah—he had saved them at least that chore.

One would think they'd thank Noah instead of shower him with grimy looks of contempt.

Flinging himself into the ratlines, Noah followed Blackthorn to the tops, trying to shake the cobwebs from his weary brain even as his old fear rose like bile in his throat. If he could not keep his concentration, he might end up a pile of broken bones and blood splattered on his clean deck—a tragedy after all his scouring.

"Good to 'ave you back," Blackthorn said as they positioned themselves on the footrope.

A gust of salty wind clawed at Noah's grip on the yard. "I'd like to say the same, my friend, but I'd rather be on the deck than up here where only birds and clouds have God's good grace to be." Noah tried to blink away the heaviness weighing down his eyelids.

Blackthorn smiled. The wind whistled through the gaps left by the two missing teeth on his bottom row. "Sink me, I'll look out after you."

Noah nodded his appreciation.

The ship pitched over a wave, and Noah gripped the yard. His feet swayed on the footrope. Every rise and fall and roll of the ship seemed magnified in the tops. His legs quivered, and Blackthorn clutched his arm. Though the morning was young, sweat slid down Noah's back, and he wondered how he would survive the day.

The sharp crack of a rattan split the air, drawing his gaze below to where Luke and his watch mates battled a tangled rope. His first mate winced beneath the strike even as the petty officer glanced at Lieutenant Garrick at the helm. For approval? For direction? Or to plead with the lieutenant for mercy? Noah couldn't tell. Regardless, Garrick nodded at the petty officer then chuckled at his fellow lieutenants lined up at the quarterdeck stanchions like cannons in a battlement. None joined him in his mirth.

Luke swept his gaze up to Noah. Even from the tops, Noah could see the bruises covering his face. Released from his irons around the same time Noah had been sent below, they'd barely managed to grunt at each other before they took to their hammocks.

The ship plunged down the trough of another swell, and Noah

hugged the yard and curled his bare toes over the rope. After his heart settled to a normal beat, he turned to Blackthorn. "What has Luke done to incur such wrath from Lieutenant Garrick?"

"Sink me, who knows with that blackguard?" His friend spit to the side. "He hates everyone, 'specially Yankees. Before they assigned me t' the tops, he used to have me whipped too."

"Reef the topsail!" the order came from below. Men on deck began hauling the tackles. Noah bent over the yard to pull in the reef lines, but he had difficulty keeping his mind on his task. If he didn't get Miss Denton and his men off this ship soon, he doubted any of them would survive.

❖

At six bells before noon, or eleven o'clock, the bosun's shrill pipe halted the men in their work. "All hands on deck!"

Thankful for the temporary reprieve from the harrowing heights, Noah followed his crew down the ratlines to the deck below. Still slower than a fish through molasses, he always landed last on the planks. But he would wager that he was the most grateful for the solid feel of wood beneath his feet.

Captain Milford emerged onto the deck in a burst of pomposity. His crisp, white breeches, stockings, and waistcoat gleamed beneath a dark coat that was lined with buttons shimmering in the bright sun. Black hair, streaked with gray, was pulled taut behind him. Traces of strength remained in the muscles that now seemed to sag with weakness. Climbing the quarterdeck ladder, he took his spot at the railing before the helm and looked down on his crew.

The bosun piped the men to attention and called them to muster in the waist. The marines, fully decked in their red coats and white pants with bayonets gleaming formed a line before the men. The petty officers fell into jagged rows behind them, while the midshipmen and officers assembled in crisp ranks on the quarterdeck, immediately aft of the mainmast.

Captain Milford stepped forward.

Wiping the sweat from his brow with his sleeve, Noah lingered near the back of the mob, anxious for possible news of the ship's destination. But instead of good news, the captain bellowed, "You shall witness a hearing and subsequent punishment of a fellow crewman.

Remain orderly and in your ranks."

Noah bristled beneath the excitement in the captain's voice.

"Master of Arms, bring forth the prisoner," the captain shouted and Noah's throat went dry, hoping it wasn't one of his own men. Relief allayed his fears when the master dragged forward a middle-aged, beefy sailor whose neck seemed to disappear beneath his head. He halted before the railing, his face lowered and the irons around his hands clanking.

Noah's heart went out to him. Luke and Weller pressed in on either side of Noah and gave him a look of trepidation.

"Let us proceed. Read the charges," the captain shouted.

As the master at arms read from a list of offenses, a flash of red caught Noah's eyes. Miss Denton stood by the larboard railing at the break of the quarterdeck, trapped by the conflux of crewmen. Terror screamed from her expression, and Noah wondered if it was the close proximity of the sea or the proceedings that frightened her.

". . .and threatening a shipmate with a knife," the master at arms concluded.

The captain eyed the man with disdain. "What do you say for yourself, Mr. Bowen?"

Mr. Bowen shook his bucket-shaped head and dared to glance at his captain. "No, sir. I only found the knife on deck an' picked it up."

Blackthorn edged beside Noah. "This won't be pretty."

"Sentence has not yet been pronounced," Noah reminded him.

"It will be. And soon. I ne'er seen the captain turn down an opportunity to flog one of 'is men." Blackthorn shifted the muscles across his back. "I got the scars t' prove it."

Noah eyed his back as if he could see beneath his shirt. "For what?"

"Insubordination t' an officer. At least that's what they said."

The captain grumbled and turned to Lieutenant Reed. "Lieutenant Reed, did this man attack his shipmate with a knife or not?"

The lieutenant's jaw twitched. "I cannot say, Captain. I was not present."

The captain turned to his right. "And you, Lieutenant Garrick."

The man licked his lips. "Yes, Captain. I saw it plain as day."

Captain Milford scanned the crew. "Will anyone speak up for this man?"

Though mumbles coursed through the crowd like distant thunder, every sailor kept his gaze lowered and his mouth shut.

"I will not tolerate brawls aboard my ship, Mr. Bowen. Save your fighting for the French, should any of the cowards show their faces out at sea." He withdrew his hat, spurring the same action from his officers and crew. Then in a blaring voice devoid of all sentiment, he read the Articles of War appropriate to the offense. At their conclusion, he turned to the boatswain. "One dozen lashes should do it, Mr. Simons."

The prisoner visibly jerked as if he'd already been lashed. His whole body began to tremble—a tremble that Noah felt down to his own bones.

Three men lifted the main hatch and attached it to the gangway with its bottom fast to the deck. Two marines led Mr. Bowen to the grating, stripped him of his shirt, and tied his hands to the top of the iron frame. Silence consumed the ship. Only the angry thrash of water and the groans of shifting wood screamed their protest of the proceedings.

The sun, high in the sky, lanced the crew with burning rays. Yet no one moved. Sweat slid into Noah's eyes and he blinked. He glanced at Miss Denton. Her hand covered her mouth. Her eyes were wide with horror. *Go below, you foolish woman. No need to see this.* As if she read his thoughts, she turned and shoved her way through the crowd then disappeared below.

Noah wished he could escape as easily. Though he understood the need for discipline aboard ship, he had no stomach for cruel torture.

The captain snapped his hat atop his head. "Do your duty, Mr. Simons."

The bosun's mate took the cat out of a red sack and stepped forward, pushing the crew back to make room for his swing.

He raised his arm and flung the cat across the man's back. A howl that reminded Noah of the cry of a wolf shrieked from the poor soul. Jagged ribbons of red appeared on his back.

Beside Noah, Luke fisted his hands and crossed them over his chest, his face mottled in anger.

Noah surveyed the crew. Weller was nowhere to be seen. Good.

"Is there nothing we can do?" he asked Blackthorn.

Blackthorn shook his head. "It's the way of the navy. If you step in, your fate will be the same."

The cat whistled through the air and landed with a snap upon the man's back once again. The crew remained silent, almost as if they saw their own future flashing before their eyes.

Another strike tore at the man's flesh. The sails thundered above them.

Noah turned around. Fury tore through him. He'd never valued his own country and the justice and freedom for which she stood more than he did at this moment. Why had he so flippantly allied himself with a people who restricted others' freedom, who stole innocent men from their ships and enacted such cruelty without censure?

Mr. Bowen's howls of pain speared the air, sealing the conviction forming within Noah. He would find a way off this ship. He would be free again and when he was, he would spend the rest of his life defending his country against the sharp whip of tyranny.

❖

Marianne fluffed the captain's mattress to remove the lumps and smooth the feathers—just as he liked it—while in truth, she'd rather fill it with large, jagged rocks. She couldn't help but wonder how the man who had been flogged fared. No doubt he would not be lying in his hammock tonight—at least not on his back. Though thankful she'd escaped witnessing the event, she had not been able to escape the man's heart-piercing howls. Howls that infiltrated every wooden plank and beam until the very ship seemed to scream in defiance. Dropping to her knees, she had prayed for him, for that was all she knew to do. It seemed so inadequate.

She stood and placed a hand on her aching back and peeked at the captain sitting at his desk mumbling to himself. It had been a long day. She prayed he would dismiss her shortly and take to his bed. Especially since she doubted she could curtail her anger toward him given his actions today.

A knock sounded on the door. Her hopes dashed when at the captain's bidding, three officers entered, Lieutenant Garrick and Lieutenant Reed among them. They stood at attention before Captain Milford's desk and removed their hats.

"You summoned us, sir."

Leaning on the doorframe of the sleeping cabin, Marianne glanced at the captain. After his evening meal and usual three glasses of brandy, plus the laudanum the surgeon had just poured down his throat, it was a wonder he could sit up. Yet he rose from his chair as alert as if he'd just arisen from a sound night's sleep.

He straightened his white waistcoat. "We shall be arriving in Antigua in seven days, gentlemen, where I expect to receive my orders. At that time. . ."

He continued on with further instructions regarding watches and shore leave, which Marianne shrugged off in light of the first piece of information. Excitement set her head spinning. They would make port soon. Surely that fact would aid Noah in formulating his escape plans.

Turning around, Marianne busied herself laying out the captain's nightshirt and cap while she listened for any further news that might be of use. But there was nothing of note save that very few of the men would be allowed a brief time ashore.

"Now go on. I need my sleep." The captain dismissed them with a wave of his hand. Lieutenant Garrick's brows lifted when he saw her. He gave her a wink that slithered down her spine before he followed his friends out the door.

Marianne approached the captain. "I've laid out your nightshirt, Captain, and fluffed your mattress. Is there anything else I can do for you?" Anger stung her tone, but he gave no indication that he took note of it.

Instead, he sank into his chair, his face twisted with thought. Then he raised hard eyes upon her. "Anything else?" He cursed. "Odds fish, can you tell me why my men rebel against me?" He slammed his fists on his desk. Marianne jumped.

"I don't know what you mean, Captain."

"That blasted Bowen." He reached for his glass, then leaned back and sipped his brandy.

All through the afternoon and evening, he'd been muttering about the flogging earlier that day. Why? Guilt? Marianne doubted it. His anger suggested another conclusion. Perhaps he feared the disrespect of his men. Perhaps he feared losing control of his ship.

Gathering her courage, she took a step forward. "I do not believe he meant to defy you, Captain."

"Defy!" He jumped up and began pacing before the stern windows, rubbing the glass of brandy between his hands. "Mutinous dogs. How dare they conspire against me?"

Marianne tensed. "Sir, I am unaware of any conspiracy."

Before she even finished the words, he circled the desk. His gray eyes flashing, he stormed toward her. The smell of brandy and the fish he'd had for dinner filled her nose. He eyed her up and down. "You are probably a part of it."

The ship canted. Stumbling, Marianne grabbed onto the edge of his desk. The lantern flickered, casting eerie shadows over his face. She swallowed and determined not to flinch, not to show him that her stomach had just dropped to the floor. "You know that's not true, Captain."

His expression loosened like the unwinding of a tight rope. He released a sigh. "You think me harsh, don't you?"

Yes, I think you are a mad, cruel man. She bit her lip to hold back the truth lest she find herself at the end of a cat-o'-nine tails. But it snuck out anyway. "Yes," she said, then braced herself.

The captain let out a loud chuckle. He lifted his glass in her direction, the alcohol sloshing over the sides. "I like you, Miss Denton. Honesty. Quite refreshing."

"If honesty is what you want, Captain, I have plenty of it." She dared to take the opportunity to acquaint him with her opinion of the injustices she'd witnessed.

He walked to the stern window and stared out into the black void of night. A spray of twinkling stars beckoned her from the darkness.

At his silence, she continued, "Mr. Bowen did not receive a fair trial today, and you know it. You never gave him a chance to defend himself. And his punishment was far too cruel."

He swung around. A spray of brandy slid over the lip of his glass. His face scrunched. "What do you know of keeping discipline on a ship this size?"

Marianne stared wide-eyed at him, hoping he wouldn't charge toward her again.

Facing the stern, he snapped the brandy into his mouth. He attempted to set his glass down, but he missed his desk, and it crashed to the floor in a dozen glittering shards. As if unaware of the mess, he turned to examine his plants, brushing his fingers over their leaves.

A lump formed in Marianne's throat. The captain was a harsh man to be sure. But at times like these when he was in one of his dark pensive moods and well into his cups, he seemed more like a little boy than a man. A broken, lonely little boy. Grabbing one of her dusting cloths, she knelt by the desk and began to carefully pick up the shattered pieces.

"You are a good woman, Miss Denton. Not much of a steward, if I do say so." He chuckled. "But kind, quick-witted, completely agreeable.

Your tranquil mannerisms and feminine gestures soothe an old man's soul."

Marianne halted, stunned by his compliments. She was surprised that they affected her so, for she gulped them in like a starving woman long deprived of food. Unbidden tears burned in her eyes. Blinking them back, she continued picking up the glass pieces, afraid to look up into his face. Afraid to discover he only taunted her.

"You are generous and wise and honest," he continued. "Qualities difficult to find among ladies these days."

A tear slid down Marianne's cheek and landed on a glass shard. She picked it up. The sharp edge caught her finger and sliced her skin. Pain shot into her hand. She dabbed the blood with the cloth and picked up the few remaining pieces. In all his years, her father had never once spoken a word of praise to Marianne. He had not been a cruel father—had never raised his voice at her, had never impugned her character. He had simply not been the type of man who freely offered his approval. So she found it ironic that this man who could be so cruel could also speak so highly of her.

Bundling the cloth around the glass, Marianne wiped her face and stood. She had never known her father's opinion of her. She had never known whether he was proud of her. And not until this moment did she realize how desperate she was to hear any approbation at all. She set the cloth down on the desk and raised her gaze to the captain.

He smiled and shifted his eyes away uncomfortably, but she sensed no insincerity in his expression.

He leaned on the window ledge and gripped his side. "I don't feel too well."

Marianne darted to him just in time to catch him before he fell. His weight nearly pushed her to the floor, but slowly she managed to lead him to his sleeping chamber.

"Perhaps some sleep will make you feel better, Captain." She eased him onto his mattress.

"Yes, yes. Quite right. I need to sleep." He plopped his head down on his pillow and lifted a hand to rub his temples.

With difficulty, Marianne managed to swing his massive legs onto the mattress, and then she stared down at the man who, with his eyes closed, looked more like a gentle old grandfather than the captain of a British warship.

Memories assailed her of another time, long ago, and another man. A man very dear to her. As she gazed upon the captain, he slowly transformed into that man—her father, Mr. Henry Denton, home late from a night of drinking and gambling.

Shaking the bad memories away, she removed the captain's boots one by one, unaware of the tears sliding down her cheeks until one plopped onto her neck. How many nights had she done this same thing for her father? How many nights had Marianne cared for him when her mother had been unwilling? How many nights had Marianne gone out with one of the footmen to drag her father from a tavern and bring him home?

Too many.

Until that last night when he didn't come home at all.

The captain mumbled and patted her hand. "That's a good girl. A good girl."

Grabbing the wool blanket, Marianne laid it atop him and tucked it beneath his chin. She batted the moisture from her face. Would she ever stop missing her father? Would she ever forgive him for leaving her?

Resisting the urge to plant a kiss upon the captain's forehead as she'd done with her father, she turned to leave.

"I should have been a farmer, you know," he stuttered, his eyes still closed.

Marianne took his hand. Rough, sea-hardened skin scratched her fingers. His eyelids fluttered and he moaned. A farmer? Yes, she could see him as a farmer. Yet instead of fertile ground to till and tender plants to tend, he plowed His Majesty's ship through tumultuous seas and raised rebellious boys to be officers. No wonder the man was miserable and half-crazed. He had missed his destiny.

"You still can be a farmer, Captain. You still can." But her words fell on deaf ears as the captain started to snore. She released his hand and blew out the lanterns in his cabin, then left him to his sleep.

Pushing her sorrow away, she made her way down the passageway. She must find Daniel and give him the news about Antigua.

She didn't have far to go as she nearly bumped into the young boy when he came barreling down the ladder from the quarterdeck. She ushered him into her room. "I have news to give Noah," she whispered as she lit a lantern and sat upon her bed.

He plopped beside her. "Aye, that's why I was headin' t' see you."

"How did you know?" She eyed him quizzically. He grinned. "Oh, never mind." She leaned close to him. He smelled of brass polish and gunpowder. "Tell Noah that the captain expects to make port in Antigua in seven days, will you do that?"

His white teeth gleamed in the lantern light. "Yes, Miss Marianne, I will. That's good news." He grabbed her hand. "Maybe that is where we are supposed to escape."

"Perhaps. I don't know. I don't see how we can with all these sailors and marines guarding us."

"That's okay, miss. God knows, and He can do anything."

Marianne sighed and brushed Daniel's hair from his face. She wished more than anything that she possessed his faith. "We shall see."

"You don't trust God, do you, Miss Marianne? You don't trust in His love." He leaned his head on her shoulder. "Oh, Miss Marianne, you must. You simply must."

"I'm trying, Daniel." She swung her arm around him and drew him near. "It's just so hard when nothing but bad things happen to me."

"How do you know they're bad?" He pushed away from her.

"What do you mean?"

He shrugged. "You can't know what God's purpose is for the things that have happened until you see the end. It's like the end of a good story, miss. Everything looks real bad until you get to the last chapter."

Marianne couldn't help but laugh at his enthusiasm, but inside, the wisdom of his statement jarred her to her core.

"I best be gettin' back. That Garrick's been keepin' a strict eye on me." With a grin, he slipped out the door, leaving her alone with only the slosh of the sea against the hull for company.

With a huff, she lay back on the bed and tried to calm her nerves. But Daniel's words kept ringing through the dank air of the cabin, refusing to be drowned out by the sounds of the ship.

How do you know?

❖ CHAPTER 17 ❖

Noah leaned his aching back against the hull and propped his elbow on the mess table. With a bit of pork stew and weevil-infested tack in his belly, and the anticipation of a good night's sleep, he wouldn't have expected the angst tightening his nerves. Perhaps it was the vision embedded in his mind of Mr. Bowen's torn flesh and with it, Noah's increased urgency to escape this British prison.

"How do you fare, Luke?" he asked his first mate who'd been too busy shoveling food into his mouth to talk.

Luke released a heavy sigh and stretched his shoulders. "Better than Mr. Bowen."

"I'll say." Weller grunted from his seat beside Luke.

Next to Noah, Blackthorn stared blankly at the bottom of his mug.

Noah pointed toward Luke's empty dish. "Apparently this slop transforms into a king's fare when you haven't eaten for three days." He shoved his own half-eaten meal away. His nose wrinkled as the bitter smell rose to join the stench of hundreds of unwashed men.

"Miss Denton brought me some biscuits." Luke smiled, then winced and dabbed at the purple bruise marring his left cheek.

Noah's brows shot up. "She did?"

"Yes, her and that lad, Daniel."

Blackthorn raised his gaze from his cup.

"Down in the berth, with all those men?" Noah asked. The woman was a source of constant surprise.

"Yes. In the middle of the night. The marine who guarded me was asleep." Luke sipped his beer.

Weller grunted and scratched his head, jarring a few strands of his stiff black hair.

Noah gazed over the mess room, trying to make sense of Luke's words. Sailors hovered over tables, their faces twisted in the dim, flickering lantern light. Shouts, insults, jeers, and chortles shot through the room like grapeshot.

Daniel emerged from the fiendish throng like an angel escaping hell. Blackthorn's stiff features relaxed at the sight of him. "Where have you been, boy? Had me worried about you again."

"Sorry." The boy gave Blackthorn a sheepish grin. "I had to wait for Miss Marianne to leave the captain's cabin."

"How is she?" The enthusiasm in Noah's voice drew the men's gazes his way.

"She's well. She has a message for you." Daniel slid in between Blackthorn and Noah. He grabbed a biscuit from Noah's plate.

"Well, spill it, boy." Blackthorn elbowed the lad. "We are all friends here."

Daniel's eyes lit up. "Antigua. We're to anchor in Antigua in seven days."

The news sang in Noah's ears like a sweet melody. Hope rose within him. He tousled the boy's hair. "Good job, lad."

Blackthorn's coal black eyes skewered Noah. "You ain't thinkin' what I think you're thinkin'."

"Pa, they're here to rescue us," Daniel said.

Noah flinched. "Pa?"

Luke's eyes widened, and Weller lifted his gaze.

Blackthorn huffed and stared back into his mug.

"Sorry, Pa." Daniel lowered his chin.

"Our secret is out, I suppose." Blackthorn growled.

Noah glanced between Blackthorn and Daniel and wondered why he hadn't seen the resemblance before. Same dark hair, same piercing, brown eyes. "Why hide your relationship?"

"So the captain nor Garrick don't use the boy against me." Blackthorn scratched the hair springing from the top of his shirt. The lantern flame set his eyes aglow with fury. . .or was it fear?

Noah's jaw tensed. Would anyone be so cruel as to use a man's son against him? Yet after what he'd witnessed today, he wondered if any honor and kindness existed among these British officers. "Rest assured, we won't tell anyone," Noah said. "Right, men?"

"Aye," Weller muttered.

"Of course." Luke nodded.

Daniel leaned in and shifted eyes alight with glee over the men. The lantern above them squeaked as it swayed in its hook. "You should know my father used to be a pirate."

"Indeed?" Luke's brows lifted and again he winced as if the action pained him. From the look of the swollen puffy skin around his eye, Noah could see why.

"Sink me, ain't nothin' to be proud of, son." Blackthorn leaned back, scanned the table, then shook his head when he noticed all eyes were riveted on him. "Only for a year. Sailed wit' a vile man by the name o' Graves. A fittin' name, to be sure, for he put many people in theirs." He let out a sigh. "Some o' the worst years of me life."

"Unimaginable, man." Luke's tone was incredulous. "Surely you enjoyed the freedom, the adventure?"

Blackthorn blew out a sigh. "At first, mebbe, but it is a lifestyle without honor, and without honor, what does a man possess of any value?"

Luke grunted. "So you quit?"

"Nay, I wasn't strong enough for that." Blackthorn fingered his stubbled chin. "I met Daniel's mother and she reformed me, so t' speak." He smiled. "I was settin' me life straight, tryin' to obey God's commands and make an honest livin'." The lines on his face fell. "But then our merchant ship got captured."

Daniel looked up at his father with such affection it caused a lump to form in Noah's throat and made him wonder what it would be like to have a son of his own someday. Would his son look at him with similar admiration or would he look at Noah with the same disgust with which Noah looked upon his father?

"It ain't your fault, Pa." Daniel glanced at Noah. "Pa thinks this is punishment for his time as a pirate."

"I killed men." Blackthorn hung his head.

A vision of Jacob lying on the deck, blood pooling beneath his head, filled Noah's thoughts. So had he. If there was one thing he understood, it was the weight of such guilt.

"God forgives you, Pa. He told me."

The words pierced Noah's heart as if the boy had directed them at him instead of Blackthorn. Did God forgive Noah as well? And if He did, would that make the guilt go away?

Blackthorn patted the lad's head. "My son fancies himself a prophet."

Weller gave a cynical laugh, then stared at the boy. "Perhaps you can tell us if we'll ever get off this ship."

Daniel sat tall. "I can, mister. And we will. In Antigua."

"Isn't that one of Nelson's dockyards? The main British port in the Caribbean?" Luke frowned.

"Aye." Weller's brown eyes seemed to darken, even as his golden tooth gleamed in the lantern light. "The place is brimming with naval officers and marines. Ain't no way we can escape there. We'd be picked up for sure. Then hung for desertion."

The ship tilted, creaking and groaning. The lantern above them swayed, shifting its light back and forth over the group as if searching for one worthy of its brightness. The bulk of its glow settled on Daniel.

"Not for sure, mister." Daniel's eyes sparkled with youthful exuberance.

Blackthorn sipped his drink. "Though I ain't too sure I believe it anymore, I'd listen to me son, if I were you. He's rarely wrong. In fact, he's a miracle hisself."

"How so?" Noah asked.

Blackthorn rubbed a finger over the gaping holes where two teeth had once stood. "My wife could bear no children, being past the age. We resigned ourselves to being childless. So, I went off to sea. She took a position as governess in the mayor's home. But she never stopped praying for a baby. Then a little more than eight months after I left Daniel came along. The physician called it a miracle." Blackthorn put his arm around the boy and seemed to have difficulty containing his emotions. "He's been the light o' our lives e'er since. Though I'm sure your ma is right furious at me for takin' ye to sea." He swallowed and glanced away. "She must be overwrought with worry o'er what happened to us."

"A miracle child, eh?" Noah elbowed Daniel and the boy grinned.

"My son inherited his strong faith from his ma," Blackthorn gazed with pride upon the lad. "Me? Me feet stand on more solid ground."

The boy's features crumbled. "But God told me Miss Denton and these men would come to free us." He looked up at Noah. "It's what you're supposed to do."

Whether God sent him here or not, Noah knew all too well what he had to do. He had to find a way to get Marianne and his crew off this ship. "It may be our only chance." Noah eyed each man in turn. "What have we got to lose?"

"Our lives," Weller grumbled.

"You call this life?" He paused, looking at each man in turn. "I'd rather be dead." Noah leaned toward Daniel. "Tell Miss Denton that we shall make our escape in Antigua."

❖

Marianne stepped onto the weather deck. The evening breeze, stiff with the scent of brine, swirled around her, cooling her perspiration. Pressing a hand against her back, she tried to stop the ache that had taken residence after yet another day of scrubbing and polishing and buffing and listening to the mindless chatter of the captain. Thankfully he made no mention of her tucking him into bed the night before or of his disclosure of his preference to be a farmer. She hoped he had forgotten, but after his foul mood and gruff mannerism all day, she doubted it, for he exhibited all the signs of a man with wounded pride.

Despite the captain's belligerent behavior, Marianne found her spirits lifted after Daniel gave her Noah's message. Did he have a plan? Could they really escape? She dared not allow her hopes to rise for she didn't think she could survive another disappointment. However, if she did hope just a little, if she did believe they might get off this ship, that meant she would have to put her trust in Noah. She cringed at the thought of trusting anyone again.

The ship rose over a swell, and she balanced her sore feet over the planks, amazed at how accustomed she had become to the sudden roll of the deck. Now, if she could overcome her fear of the fathomless expanse of blue surrounding them, she might enjoy these trips above. Inching her way to the break of the quarterdeck, she gripped the wooden railing and drew a deep breath of the moist air. The sun waved a farewell ribbon resplendent with peach, saffron, and maroon across the horizon.

She surveyed the ship. A few watchmen sauntered about, paying her no mind. Apparently, she had become as normal a feature aboard this ship as any of the sailors. Whether that was a good thing or not, she couldn't say. The clamor of voices, *clank* of plates, and *twang* of a fiddle wafted up from below where most of the crew partook of their dinner, or mess as they called it—an appropriate description based on what she'd seen. The captain and his officers ate much better. And thankfully so did she.

Her thoughts drifted to Noah, and she wondered how he fared. She knew the British sailors treated the Americans poorly, and it saddened her to think he was suffering. Odd, when not two weeks ago, she had wanted to strangle him. What had changed? What had transformed the repugnant brat into a chivalrous gentleman?

She ran the tips of her fingers over her lips and thought of their kiss.

Her belly warmed at the memory.

Truth be told, she wished she could stop thinking about the kiss or about Noah at all. But she could not. And that frightened her more than anything—even more than being trapped aboard this ship. Day and night she wondered about him. How was he faring in the tops? Did they beat him? Did he sleep well? And whenever she came on deck, she searched him out, desperate for a glimpse of him. What was wrong with her? She was behaving like a silly schoolgirl.

She loved him.

The realization stormed through her like a mighty gale. And like a gale, it threatened to tear her to shreds. For Noah had made his desires quite plain. He did not wish to marry her. He had a sweetheart in South Hampton. Marianne was no fool. She knew all too well that any union between her and Noah would only be motivated by his need of her wealth.

But she couldn't allow him to be so miserably matched just to appease his father's guilt-induced mandate.

She loved him too much.

No, if they ever got off this ship and back to Baltimore, she would grant Noah his wish and break off their engagement. She had done him enough damage, caused him enough pain. That way he could silence his father's demands and marry Priscilla—beautiful, cultured Priscilla. Her insides crumpled at the thought.

She would find another way to provide for her mother and sister and purchase the medicine her mother needed. *Oh Lord, please heal my mother. Please take care of her and Lizzie in my absence.* Her heart ached to know how they fared.

"Don't cry, Miss Denton." The slippery voice sent a chill over her. She knew who it was before she turned around.

"Lieutenant Garrick." Marianne batted the moisture from her face. "You frightened me."

The grin on his thin lips turned her stomach sour. "What has you so distraught, my dear?" He slithered beside her at the railing, effectively backing her against the head of the quarterdeck.

Her nerves tightened. She faced the sea. The last traces of the sun slipped below the horizon. "I am concerned for my mother and sister back in Baltimore."

"Ah yes, apart from loved ones. It is the price we pay to serve in His Majesty's Navy." He brushed his coat, drawing attention to the gold stripe and three buttons lining his cuff.

Marianne twisted her ring. Was he trying to impress her? She dared to stare into his narrowed dark eyes. "I am not in His Majesty's Navy." Her sharp tone sent one of his eyebrows into an imperious arch.

"I believe you are mistaken, Miss Denton, for last I heard you are aboard the HMS *Undefeatable* serving as Captain's steward."

"Not by choice."

"Don't be so naive." He ran a thumb down the whiskers outlining his pointed chin. "Most of these men are not here by choice."

"Perhaps if they were, you wouldn't have to strip the flesh off their backs to force their loyalty." She regretted her brazen statement as soon as it left her lips.

A look akin to a demon's scowl came over Lieutenant Garrick's face. Darkness seeped from his eyes.

Marianne's blood turned cold. She glanced across the deck, now murky in the falling shadows. No one was in sight.

He flashed a superior grin. "How could a woman understand the ways of the greatest navy in the world?"

Marianne thought to tell him she hoped never to understand but decided for once to keep her mouth shut.

"It is a lonely career, Miss Denton. Like you, I miss the companionship of family and friends from home." He leaned toward her, his eyes absorbing her from head to toe. The stench of alcohol hung upon his foul breath. "The companionship of a woman."

She backed against the quarterdeck. Her heart thrashed against her chest. The ship plunged down a wave, sending a spray of saltwater over them. Marianne quivered.

"Ah, you shiver, Miss Denton. No need to be afraid. I will protect you." He caressed her cheek.

She jerked away. "And who will protect me from you?"

He grinned. "No one, I suppose. Which is why you should simply give me what I want. It will go much better for you."

Marianne's feet went numb. She dug her nails into the wood behind her. *Lord. Please. Help me.* If she screamed would anyone come to her aid? Would anyone stand up for her against Lieutenant Garrick?

Raising his arm, he pressed his hand against the quarterdeck, blocking her exit. "Ah, I assure you, no one will cross me, Miss Denton. I am second in command and have the captain's favor, and everyone on board this ship knows it."

Her chest heaved for air. She lifted her shoulders. "Then what is it you want, Lieutenant Garrick?"

"I thought you'd never ask." In an instant, he closed the distance between them and crushed his body against hers.

Marianne struggled. She tried to pound her fists against his chest. She tried to kick him. But the weight of his body pinned her to the quarterdeck. His mouth clawed hers. Spit and salt stung her lips. She squeezed her eyes shut and willed herself to wake up. *Just a nightmare. Only a nightmare.* She tried to scream, but only a pathetic squeal groaned from her throat.

Then a deep growl of fury filled the air.

Marianne felt the weight of Lieutenant Garrick's body lift from hers. She struggled for a breath. *Thump!* The sound of something heavy hitting the wooden planks caused her to open her eyes. The lieutenant lay on the deck, one arm hung over the railing, his chest heaving. His sordid features twisted in a mixture of shock and rage.

Before him stood Noah, muscles flexing, fists clenched. His hair hanging around his firm jaw. He turned to her. "Are you all right?"

She nodded, stunned as much by his concern, the fear for her that she saw in those blue eyes as by what he had just done.

"Do you know who I am?" the lieutenant roared. "I'll have you court-martialed and hung for that, Yankee!" He struggled to his feet and straightened his jacket.

The men on watch approached from all sides. Lieutenant Reed's tall, dark form lurked at a distance. Blackthorn headed toward them from across the deck.

Garrick turned and addressed his audience. "You saw it. He struck me!"

"I only pushed you aside to keep you from accosting this woman." Noah ran a hand through his hair. "Or is ravishing women an acceptable pastime allowed officers according to your precious Articles of War?"

Garrick laughed and stormed toward him. "You will die for this, Yankee dog. I hope the trollop is worth your life."

Noah lifted his fist to strike the man.

"No, Noah!" Marianne screamed and grabbed his arm, but he tore it from her grasp.

Blackthorn darted to Noah's side and shoved him back, staying his hand.

Noah struggled against the massive man, but Blackthorn held him in place. "Garrick will have you hanged."

Garrick chuckled. "How noble, Mr. Blackthorn. But I fear your efforts are in vain." He grabbed his hat from the deck and plopped it atop his head. "The man already hit me, and he will pay the penalty. And in case you aren't familiar with our *precious* Articles of War, the penalty for striking an officer is death."

❖ CHAPTER 18 ❖

Noah raised his hands to scratch his face. The iron manacles clanked in protest as they bit into his wrists. Whips of sun lashed the back of his neck as streams of perspiration slid beneath his shirt. Though exhaustion attempted to drag his chin down, he refused to lower his head in defeat. The shrill of the boson's pipe pierced the air. His stomach soured.

Footsteps thundered over the deck as the crew mustered amidships for the trial.

His trial.

The captain glared down at him from the quarterdeck. The supercilious smirk on his face suggested a perverted glee at the punishment of others. To Noah's left, Luke, Weller, and Blackthorn huddled together, lines of fear etched their faces. He hoped the young lad Daniel had gone below out of sight of such horror. He hoped the same for Marianne.

But a flash of maroon linen caught the corner of his eye, dashing his hopes. She stood at the top of the quarterdeck ladder, anguish burning on her features. Confound the woman! He didn't want her to witness his shame, to see him like this, beaten and chained. Nor did he wish to witness the pity, the sympathy now spilling from her lustrous brown eyes.

When he'd seen Garrick's body crushed against hers—heard his lecherous grunts and lewd comments—all reason, all fear had abandoned Noah. The only thing that mattered was protecting her. He was not sorry. He would do it again. He would take whatever punishment their twisted sense of justice meted out to him.

Even death.

Except that would leave Marianne alone with no one to rescue her the next time. Noah grimaced until the muscles in his jaw ached. The hot wind pounded on him, yanking his tangled hair. Above him, the masts creaked under the strain of canvas glutted with the breath of the sea.

Noah barely heard the captain call the inquiry to order or the master at arms read the charge. *Assaulting an officer.* Hushed murmurs of fear rose from the crew. They no doubt knew the fate that awaited him.

"Silence!" the captain shouted. "This is but an inquiry into the charges, Mr. Brenin. If I deem you guilty, you will await a court-martial when we reach port. Now, what do you have to say in your behalf?"

Noah squinted up at him, the captain's silhouette a dark shifting blotch against the brightness of the noon sun. "I did not strike Lieutenant Garrick, Captain. I merely protected the honor of a lady."

Garrick laughed. "I see no lady aboard."

The crew chuckled, drawing a fierce "Order!" from the captain who pounded his fist upon the railing.

"Lieutenant Garrick, what is your side of it?"

The slimy toad, who stood beside Milford, turned to his captain. "I was conversing with Miss Denton, your steward."

"I know she's my steward, blast you!" The captain fumed, sending the lieutenant back a step.

Garrick adjusted his coat and continued, "As I said, I was conversing with Miss Denton when Mr. Brenin charged me and knocked me to the deck. There was no cause for it that I could see other than his vicious Yankee temper."

The captain eyed Garrick with suspicion. No doubt, the man's arrogant belligerence had not missed the captain's notice. "No other cause, you say?"

Garrick shifted his boots over the deck and took a pompous stance. "Isn't it obvious, Captain? He's jealous."

Lieutenant Reed, standing to the captain's left, snorted.

Noah snapped the hair from his face. "Not jealous, sir, but concerned for the lady."

Murmurs sped through the crowd, silenced by one look from Captain Milford.

"Hmm." The captain eyed Noah. "Regardless of the cause, you know, sir, I could have you court-martialed and hanged for striking an officer."

"Lieutenant Garrick is lying." Marianne's bold declaration drew all eyes to her.

❖

Yet she could not allow such atrocious lies to go unchallenged. Nor could she allow Noah to die for her without at least trying to save him.

His blue eyes met hers. The fear and admiration within them gave her the courage to continue.

The captain's jaw stiffened, and his dark brows drew together as if he couldn't believe she had the audacity to speak in front of the entire crew. She knew that look. He was about to unleash his mad fury on her and order her below. She took a step toward him. "I beg you, Captain, hear me out. Lieutenant Garrick assaulted me, and this man came to my rescue. He did not strike the lieutenant but merely pulled him from me." She gazed at Noah and smiled. "To save me, Captain."

Noah's brow furrowed.

"That is pure rubbish, Captain. I—" Garrick began, but with a lift of the captain's hand, he was silenced.

Marianne prayed that reason reigned in the captain's mind this day instead of laudanum-induced hysteria.

Captain Milford scanned the assembled crew. "Were there any other witnesses?"

Midshipman Jones took an unsteady step forward. He dragged his hat from his head, revealing the smooth face of a young man no older than eighteen. "When I came upon them, Captain." His voice quavered. "I saw Lieutenant Garrick on the deck and this man"—he pointed toward Noah—"hovering over the lieutenant, his fists clenched as if he'd struck him."

Garrick smiled.

"Thank you, Mr. Jones." The captain nodded his approval. "Anyone else?"

One crewman separated from the crowd. "That's what I saw, Cap'n, except this one, Blackthorn, was holding Mr. Brenin back from striking the lieutenant again."

The ship pitched over a wave, and Marianne gripped the railing at the head of the ladder. Her chest tightened, but not due to fear of the sea this time. This time, all her fears focused on the future of one man.

One very special man.

The wind whipped the flaps of Captain Milford's coat. "Very well. That will suffice." He faced Marianne with a true look of regret. "The word of three men against yours, Miss Denton. It is admirable that you speak up for your fiancé, but I'm afraid your testimony is of no account."

Marianne's head grew light. She pressed a hand over her chest to steady her heart. What could she say? What could she do to stop this madness? It was bad enough she'd gotten Noah impressed, but she could never live with herself if she got him killed. "They are lying, Captain, I beg you!" Her voice trembled.

Her gaze locked upon Lieutenant Reed, his eyes downcast, red hands clasped tight behind his back. The muscles in his jaw bunched and relaxed as though engaged in battle. He had been there last night. *Why didn't he say something?*

"Lieutenant Reed?" she shouted. He turned guilt-ridden eyes to hers.

"That is enough, Miss Denton!" The captain faced the crew. "Mr. Brenin, you will be confined below until we make port where a proper court-martial can be held." He gave Noah a shrug that fell short of a sympathetic gesture. "Based, however, on this evidence, it's a surety they will condemn you to death."

❖

Death.

Noah allowed the finality of the word to sink into his gut. If it was his time, he expected it to take an uncomfortable residence there, but instead it shot off the deck and bounced over the bulwarks in rebellion until a gnawing ache formed in his belly.

Marianne gasped. He glanced at her. Terror screamed from her face and something else. Pity? Sorrow? He couldn't tell from where he stood. Sweat streamed into his eyes and he shook it away.

Lieutenant Reed turned to his captain. "Captain, if I may speak. I saw the entire altercation, sir."

The captain's features stiffened. "Odds fish, man, why didn't you say something before now?" he barked.

"I had hoped not to speak on behalf of the Americans." Reed nodded toward Marianne. "However, conscience dictates that the truth be known. It is as Miss Denton describes. Lieutenant Garrick attacked her, and Mr. Brenin came to her rescue. As far as I saw, he did not strike the lieutenant."

Noah's breath returned to him. He saw Marianne grab hold of the railing as if she might swoon.

Lieutenant Garrick's face puffed out like a sail at full wind. "What the devil are you saying, sir? The verdict has already been issued."

The captain studied Lieutenant Reed. His gray eyes flashed. "And what of Mr. Blackthorn restraining him?"

"That is true." Reed said. "The lieutenant called Miss Denton a foul name, and it appeared as though Mr. Brenin intended to strike him."

The ship swooped over a wave as if elevated by the truth. Noah steadied his bare feet on the hot deck, too afraid to hope for a different outcome—any outcome beside the one that placed him in a grave.

"This is madness." Garrick gave a nervous chortle.

"Silence!" Captain Milford faced Noah. "Mr. Brenin. What say you? Was that your intent?"

Noah raised his shackled hands to wipe the sweat from his brow. *Clank.* The iron had grown warm in the hot sun and burned his skin. Would the punishment be the same if his intent had been to strike an officer? Would he lose his grip on life once again? Yet he could not lie. "That was my intention, Captain."

The captain adjusted his coat and stared out to sea, weighing Noah's fate on the scales of his madness. The azure water crashed against the hull as if cheering him on.

"Very well." He faced Lieutenant Garrick. "You will restrain your lecherous passions aboard my ship, sir, or, regardless of your connections, it will be you at court-martial next time. I will not tolerate such dishonorable conduct under my command."

The lieutenant's face flushed, and his eyes narrowed.

The captain looked down on Noah. "And you, Mr. Brenin. Strike or attempt to strike an officer again, and you'll wish for death." He waved a hand through the air. "Two dozen lashes."

Though preferable to swinging from a rope, the words lanced across Noah's heart as if he'd already suffered the wrenching blows. Vivid images flashed across his mind—images of what one dozen strikes had done to the last man to suffer such a verdict.

Marianne cried out, and he wondered in his clouded mind whether she shrieked out of horror for his punishment or whether she truly cared for him.

The crew doffed their hats as Captain Milford opened the Articles of War and read the rules regarding Noah's infraction. But he heard none of it.

His mind was numb. Muted sounds of the crew tossing curses his way, of the hatch grating being lashed to the deck, the snap of sails, the thunder of the men's footsteps as they assembled to witness his shame—everything blurred before him. His feet dragged over the deck as they led him to the grating. Splinters pierced his skin. The bosun tore off Noah's shirt. The searing sun struck his bare skin as they removed his irons and bound his hands above his head.

Noah's last thought was of Marianne. He hoped she'd gone below. He hoped the captain would not punish her for speaking out on his behalf.

The pounding of drums sounded.

He closed his eyes.

He heard the cat-o'-nine being pulled from the bosun's mate's bag.

Crack.

Raw pain seared across his back, simmering deep into his flesh.

Snap.

A thousand hot knives sliced through his skin.

Thwack.

He dug his forehead into the iron grating and ground his teeth together.

Blood dripped on the deck by his feet.

Crack.

Sharp bits of the metal cut into his face. His head grew light.

And darkness welcomed him.

❖

Holding a lantern out before her and clutching a bundle to her chest, Marianne crept down the dark passageway. The sway of the ship knocked her against the bulkhead, but she quickly righted herself and continued. Tying the bundle to her belt, she gripped the railing and descended the narrow steps of one of the ship's ladders. Long since faded, the laughter and shouting of the crew had been replaced with snores, grunts, and the ever-present creak of the ship—a sound Marianne had come to believe was nothing but an ominous warning that the hull was about to break apart.

Ignoring that terrifying thought, she descended another level. Rats scattered before her sphere of light, the pitter-patter of their feet echoing through the ship. Swallowing, she shoved aside her fear of the crew, the rats, the sea, knowing she must attend to Noah. She halted at the bottom of the ladder and lifted her lantern. Darkness filled every crack and crevice. Remembering the directions Daniel had given her, she turned left.

Hopefully toward the sick bay where Noah lay recovering.

Apparently his wounds had been so devastating, the surgeon decided to keep him overnight instead of allowing him to return to his hammock.

Rounding a corner, she entered an open space. Wooden bed frames, holding stuffed mattresses, hung from the deckhead and swayed with each movement of the ship. Glass covered cabinets containing bottles of all shapes and sizes stood against the far bulkhead. Medical instruments, including what looked to be a saw and a hatchet, hung from hooks on the opposite wall.

Gathering her courage, she stepped forward. The light from her lantern landed on a man's bare back, ripped and torn like a hunk of meat at the butcher's shop. Noah. She gasped. Her stomach lurched.

She dashed to the wooden table.

His eyes popped open, and he whispered, "Hello, Miss Denton. I hope you'll forgive me for not getting up."

Half-laughing, half-crying, she pulled up a chair beside him and sat down. Setting the lantern atop another table, she took his hand in hers. The metallic smell of blood filled her nose.

His brows lifted then lowered when he saw her tears. "Not to worry, Marianne. The surgeon says I'll be good as new in a few days." Half his face was flattened against the table, making his words slur.

"Noah, I'm so sorry." Marianne could not hold back the tears. "What can I do to help you?" She gripped his arm and shook it in her fury.

He winced. "You can stop doing that for one thing."

"Forgive me." She released his hand. "I've made a mess of things."

"It wasn't your fault that bedeviled rake attacked you."

"No, but it is my fault we are all on this ship in the first place." *And you stood up for me—protected me. Why?* She longed to ask him, but the look in his blue eyes captivated her. Myriad emotions crossed over them: frustration, pain, and one that sent her heart fluttering—regard.

"Why are you here?" he asked.

"Oh." Marianne untied the bundle and opened it on her lap. "I have brought bandages and aloe for your wounds."

"Aloe?" He rose on his forearms, his face contorted in agony.

"It's from the captain's plants. I stole a leaf. It's for healing of the skin." She tried not to stare at the firm muscles rounding in his arms.

"Stole? Confound it, woman. He's not a man to trifle with."

"I can handle him."

Noah released a heavy sigh. The harshness in his gaze faded. "You came down here to attend to my wounds?"

Marianne smiled. "As I have said. Now lie back down and be still."

"Yes, ma'am." He chuckled then winced as he lowered himself to the wooden table.

Marianne spread the milky gel over a strip of cloth and gently laid it across his back. She pressed lightly.

He groaned.

"My apologies." Marianne studied his wounds, searching for the best place to apply the aloe next. The cat had done its work. Streaks of red, torn flesh crisscrossed Noah's back as if he'd encountered a very angry bear with very large claws. She pressed a hand to her stomach at the sight as bile rose in her throat.

"How does it look?"

"Not bad."

"Liar."

She chuckled.

"Did you watch?" he asked.

"No." Marianne shook her head. As soon as the flogging had begun, she'd slipped below. "I am a coward." She spread aloe on another strip of cloth and laid it on his back.

"You are anything but a coward." He winced. "I am glad you didn't witness it."

She finished laying aloe-covered cloths over the worst areas then plopped to the chair. Tears spilled from her eyes.

He reached out a finger and lifted her chin. "Don't cry, Marianne. It will be all right."

He used her Christian name. Twice now. The sound of it on his lips sang like a sweet melody in her ears. "You risked your life to protect me." She swallowed. "Why?"

"I couldn't stand by and watch you get ravished, could I?"

Was there no other reason? "Other men would have."

She brushed a strand of hair from his face. But not him. Not Noah. He'd proven himself to be an honorable man of integrity and courage, even, dare she say, kindness. Not at all like the little boy she remembered.

The ship swayed, groaning and creaking. Lantern light flickered across his prominent chin, strong jaw, and blue eyes—sharp despite the pain he must be feeling.

"Oh, Noah, we are all trapped in this living hell. I fear for you and Mr. Heaton and Mr. Weller and young Daniel."

He wiped a tear from her cheek and allowed his thumb to linger there. "Never fear. We shall escape."

"But how?" She leaned in to his hand and found comfort in its warmth and strength. Memories of their kiss sent her pulse racing. Would she ever feel his lips on hers again? What was she doing? She jerked away from his touch. Fanciful, romantic hopes were not for women like her.

"When we make anchor at Antigua," he answered. "I will figure something out."

She couldn't imagine what plan would succeed with so many officers always watching them, but she smiled nonetheless. Hope would make Noah recover sooner. Hope was what had kept her mother from giving up and dying.

"Don't worry, princess." He reached up and caressed her cheek. "I will get you off this ship."

Princess. Yet the gentle tone in which he offered this spurious title in no way resembled the sarcasm of his youth. Marianne's thoughts jumbled as he brushed the back of his hand over her skin. His masculine scent filled the air between them. And all she wanted was for that moment to never end. For if and when they escaped, she would lose him. Lose him to his merchant business, lose him to Priscilla.

She looked down under his intense perusal. Bloodstains spread across the deck, reminding her that life didn't always end up well. Perhaps she should tell Noah the truth about her fortune. Perhaps she should get it over with before she'd lost so much of her heart, she would never reclaim it. "I must confess something."

"Yes?" He ran a thumb over her chin.

"My mother and I have not been completely forthright regarding our engagement."

❖

Noah could not imagine to what Marianne was referring, nor did he care at the moment. All that concerned him was the look of complete admiration and care beaming from those rich brown eyes.

When had the shrew transformed into an angel? Despite the pain lancing across his back, his heart filled with an affection for her he hadn't thought possible. He could not seem to stop caressing her cheek. So soft. So moist with tears—tears for him.

"My inheritance." She began twisting the ring around her finger.

"It doesn't matter now." Noah surprised himself at the veracity of his statement. For he truly didn't care about the money anymore. Nor about his father's merchant business. All that mattered was this precious creature before him and that he must do everything in his power to protect her.

"I suppose you're right, but I need to tell you anyway." She lifted her lashes. "There is nothing but the seven thousand dollars of my inheritance left." She spat out the words so quickly, their meaning left him stunned.

He stopped caressing her cheek. "But my father informed me the Denton fortune is worth thirty thousand."

Her gaze followed his retreating hand. "It was. Before my father gambled it all away."

Gambled? Noah shifted his back. Pain stretched across his skin like a tight, fiery rope. He remembered spotting Mr. Denton at the card tables now and then, but no more than most men in the city.

"Playing cards and some poor investments," she added.

"He lost everything?" Instead of anger, sympathy rose in Noah's chest.

She nodded and stared at the empty bundle in her lap. "Everything but my inheritance which was locked in a trust until I married."

"The house?"

"Mortgaged."

"The furniture? Silverware? Family heirlooms?"

"All sold."

"And the engagement party?"

"A pretense. A sham. Paid for by weeks of not eating."

Noah eased up on his forearms and stared at the bloodstained wood beneath him. "That's why your hands are blistered. Because you worked."

"When we dismissed our servants, we had no choice." She shifted hopeful eyes to his. "I'm sorry, Noah."

Noah's mind reeled. "So that's why you were eager to announce our engagement."

Marianne swallowed. "It's not what you think. You see, my mother is very ill. We can't afford her medicine without my dowry."

Realization dawned on him. They had used him. Like a pawn in some sordid scheme. Once Marianne married him, releasing her inheritance, she intended to use the money on her mother's medications. Not to support the Brenin merchant business. And who would fault her? Certainly not even Noah's father would choose business over someone's life.

Anger tightened the muscles in Noah's back. They cried out in pain. He had been used, the thought repeated. But how could he fault her when his family had done the same thing? They intended to use the Denton fortune to further their own aspirations. But at least they made no pretense about their motives.

"So you conspired to trap me, eh?" A sudden pain shot from his back into his head, and he gritted his teeth.

Her chest rose and fell rapidly. "I did no such thing. Our fathers wanted us married. My mother and I merely agreed to it."

"Under false pretenses," he growled. "At least I was honest in my reasons for marrying you." Then a second thought struck him—she never truly wished to marry him. Even though her behavior on board the *Fortune* spoke otherwise. Even though the ardor he'd seen in her eyes recently and the way she had kissed him screamed otherwise. She needed him only for his signature on a marriage license and his "I do" at a ceremony. A heavy weight sank to the bottom of his stomach. Noah had been used all his life.

And he was tired of it.

"So now you know." She gathered her things and rose, her chin lifting in that petulant tilt he remembered as a child. "And you have my word that if we ever get off this ship, my first order of business will be to break off our engagement."

MaryLu Tyndall

Noah cringed. Sorrow weighed upon him, forcing his forehead to the table. Wasn't that what he had wanted? Wasn't that what he had tried to prod her into doing on board his ship? Then why didn't her agreement seem like a victory? "Most kind of you." He kept his tone dull, too angry and too proud to let his feelings show.

She turned her back to him and he saw that the hand by her side trembled. When she swung back around, tears pooled in her eyes. "Why did you kiss me the other night?" Despite her obvious effort to appear indifferent, the sorrow in her voice cut into Noah's heart.

He longed to jump from the table and take her in his arms. He longed to tell her that he'd kissed her because he thought she was kind, generous, and beautiful—because he thought he loved her. But she had lied to him. Used him. Like everyone else. "Why did you kiss me back?" he replied without emotion.

Her nose pinked and she drew a trembling breath. "You have your wish, Mr. Brenin. You are free of me. If we ever get off this ship, marry Priscilla, marry whomever you want, but you will never marry me."

❖ CHAPTER 19 ❖

Noah eased over the yard, his sweaty hands clinging to the backstay.

The foreman brayed from below, and Noah and his fellow top-men began hauling in the lower topgallant sail. Beside him, Blackthorn grunted with the exertion as he took up the slack for Noah. Five days had passed, and Noah's back still flamed as though a dozen branding irons lay across his tender skin. Yet the captain had ordered him back to work. Every move of his arms, every shift of his weight, sent searing agony across his torso.

A heavy gust of wind struck him, and he tightened his grip. Though the breeze cooled the sweat on his hands and neck and eased the fire on his back, in his weakened condition, it threatened to shove him to the deck below.

Blackthorn's worried eyes assessed Noah as the crew folded the heavy sailcloth and began tying it. Noah attempted a grin to reassure the man that he was well.

Well—as long as he didn't look down to the deck ninety feet below him. Well—as long as nothing so much as a feather brushed across his back.

He'd not seen Marianne since she'd stomped out on him in sick bay. Why she was angry, he had no idea. She had deceived him, snuck aboard his ship, caused them to be impressed into the navy, and created the circumstances that resulted in his flogging. Yet she dared to raise that smug nose of hers and be cross with him. Him? He would never figure women out. Especially not this particular one. Her moods were as fickle as the captain's.

Just minutes before her anger, nothing but admiration—dare he hope—affection shone in her gaze. But it had all disappeared just as quickly as she had, leaving him alone in the darkness. Though he'd been angry at first at her deception, the more he'd considered it, the more he understood that it blossomed from a love for her mother. She'd had no choice but to agree to the engagement and keep her true inheritance a secret. Her mother's life depended on it. And how could he fault her for such undaunted affection? It was admirable, in fact.

Like most things about Marianne.

Besides, he had behaved the unconscionable cad to her not only in their youth, but on board his ship. Surely he could forgive her, given the circumstances. What bothered him the most was that he wished she'd had an entirely different reason for agreeing to marry him in the first place.

The wind gusted against him as he tied the final knot, tying sail-cloth tight to the yard. The spicy scent of rain bit his nose.

The ship plunged down a rising swell. Bubbling foam swept over the bow. Noah's breath halted as he clung to the yard. He hoped he wouldn't be called upon to strike the upper yards and set the storm sails in these rough seas.

"A storm approaches." Blackthorn pointed to the dark clouds swirling over the eastern horizon.

A storm approached indeed. For tomorrow they arrived at Antigua. And Noah had made up his mind. One way or another, regardless of the danger, regardless of the threat of death, tomorrow they would escape.

❖

Marianne dipped her cloth into the black grease and rubbed it over the captain's boots, buffing as hard as she could in an attempt to achieve the impossible shine he demanded. Normally her hands ached, but if she imagined the boot to be Noah's face, they seemed to soar effortlessly over the leather. Oh, how she wished she could scrub that insolent scowl from his lips as easily.

Lips that had sent a warm quiver through her belly with a simple touch.

How dare he judge her for betraying him when his reasons for marrying her were as self-serving as hers?

She had thought. . . No. If she dared to admit it, she had hoped that after all they'd been through, her inheritance wouldn't matter to him.

"You are a fool, Marianne, the biggest fool of all." She blew a section of hair from her forehead. "A fool for ever thinking that a handsome, honorable man like Noah Brenin would ever love you." The look she'd mistaken for affection in his gaze had been merely gratitude for her ministrations. For how quickly it had transformed into one of fury when he'd discovered her deception.

Yet wasn't that what she had wanted? Wasn't that why she had told him? To invoke his anger at her duplicity so he would stop looking at her like he had been the past few days. Like he cared for her. Like he wanted her.

Like no one had ever looked at her before.

A look she would never see again.

Emptiness invaded her heart at the realization.

The captain marched in, grunted his salutation, and proceeded to the stern windows. Picking up a watering jug, he began tending his plants. From the look of exasperation on his face, Marianne knew better than to engage him in conversation, so she continued her work.

An ear-piercing howl filled the cabin. "What happened to my aloe?"

Marianne's heart clamped. She'd forgotten about the missing leaf, and suddenly wondered why he hadn't noticed until now. He swung around, face fuming, eyes latched upon her.

Midshipman Jones appeared in the doorway.

The captain scowled in his direction. "Burn and blast your bones, what is it now, lad?"

"Lieutenant Garrick's compliments, Captain, but we've spotted a sail."

The captain slammed down his jug, spilling water on the charts laid out across his desk. "Clean this up at once!" he barked at Marianne. Then grabbing his hat, he followed the midshipman aloft.

Thank You, Lord. Marianne breathed a sigh at the temporary reprieve. With any luck, the captain would forget the aloe upon his return. After dabbing up the water, she set the boots aside and went above. They had not spotted a sail since boarding this horrid ship. Were the guests friend or foe? She couldn't keep her hopes from rising.

MaryLu Tyndall

But as soon as she emerged above, those same hopes fell to the hot deck beneath her shoes. Too small to be a French warship, it was most likely a merchant or a privateer, neither of which would take on a British frigate.

The *Undefeatable* pitched over a rounded swell, then swooped down the other side. Balancing over the teetering deck, Marianne inched toward the capstan, not daring to venture to the railing in such rough seas. Bloated, foamy waves billowed all around the ship. The wind clawed at her hair, loosening it from its pins. The scent of salt and rain swirled about her, and she glanced at the dark horizon. She gripped the wood. Her knuckles whitened. *Lord, please don't send a storm our way.* How many horrid tales had made their way back to Baltimore of ships that had sunk to the depths during a squall where not a soul on board was ever seen again?

Unable to stop herself from seeking a glimpse of Noah, she glanced aloft and found him clinging to the third yard above her on the mainmast. Her pulse quickened at the sight of him. With his broad shoulders stretched back and his bare feet gripping the swaying ratline, he seemed more comfortable in the heights than he had been at first. Blackthorn said something to him, and Noah's hearty laughter spilled down upon her like a warm spring shower. She shook off the sensation, not wanting to relish in the new and frightening feelings the man invoked in her.

Especially when nothing would ever come of them.

The crack of a rattan split the air, drawing Marianne's gaze to the petty officer hovering over Luke. Mr. Heaton released the rope and rose to his full height, leveling dark, snapping eyes toward the officer and then at Lieutenant Garrick who stood behind him.

"Again! For your insolence, sir," Garrick commanded, and the petty officer struck Luke once more. Grimacing, Luke bent to pick up the rope and took up his spot in line. His black hair hanging in his face did not hide his fury, and Marianne wondered how much a proud man like Luke could take before he retaliated.

A satisfied smirk on his face, Garrick surveyed the deck, his eyes halting when he saw her. A superior grin crept over his lips. His eyes grew cold, and he started toward her, but Marianne nodded toward the captain at the helm.

Following the direction of her glance, Garrick gave her one last look of scorn, then spun about.

Though she knew her reprieve was temporary, Marianne breathed a sigh of relief. The determined look in Lieutenant Garrick's slitlike eyes told her that he would not be easily swayed from his objective. And for some reason—perhaps because she was the only woman aboard—his objective was her. She must be careful not to be found alone again anywhere on the ship. Perhaps she could appeal to the captain. He displayed some admiration toward Marianne—at least when he had his wits about him. Not to mention she had a feeling that he had lessened Noah's sentence on her behalf. Perhaps if she expressed her terror of Garrick to the captain, he would keep the licentious lieutenant at bay.

Thunder pounded its agreement in the distance as the ship crested a wave and salty spray misted over her.

"Blast her! She's taunting us." The captain's bellow could be heard above the rising howl of the wind. He snapped his scope shut and set his jaw in a firm line. Off their larboard quarter, the unknown ship's sails appeared, then quickly disappeared behind the foamy peak of a surging wave, only to reappear as the vessel crested the roller. Marianne wondered why they weren't chasing the small craft as they'd done with Noah's.

Her answer came quickly from Lieutenant Reed's lips. "She's aweather of us, sir. With the oncoming storm, we'll never catch her."

"I am aware of that, Mr. Reed," the captain spat.

Daniel appeared at Marianne's side, bracing himself so sturdily upon the tilting deck that he had no need to hold on. He smiled up at her, his dark hair tossing to and fro in the wind. "That ship will save you." He nodded toward the ship that dared to tease the HMS *Undefeatable*.

Marianne wrinkled her brow. "I'm sorry, Daniel, but that ship is no match for this one. I fear they are doing nothing but infuriating the captain. Which is never a good thing."

His eyes twinkled as if he knew a grand secret.

Thunder roared again. Thick, black clouds churned in a sooty witches' brew over the horizon, spreading dark fingers up to steal the light of the sun not yet halfway across the sky. A light mist descended upon them. Marianne shivered.

"Take in topgallants and royals!" Lieutenant Reed yelled from his post beside the captain, causing more orders to be shouted across the various stations.

Glancing aloft, Marianne saw Noah inch his way alongside a dozen other men farther up the mainmast. She thought of his brother's tragic death and she shuddered. *Lord, protect him.*

A yellow flash lit up the seas, followed by a jet of gray smoke. The air pounded with the blast of a cannon. Marianne raised a hand to her throat, staring at the audacious vessel who dared fire upon His Majesty's royal frigate. Her hopes for rescue had just begun to rise when the shot fell impotent into the foamy sea several yards away.

A string of vile curses flew from the captain's mouth. He paced the quarterdeck, stopping to stare at the pesky ship though his long glass. Despite the mad rush of wind, she heard bits and pieces of his dialogue. "Show them... How dare they? They don't know who..." He ceased his pacing and took a commanding stance.

"A signal shot." Garrick laughed. "Too far away and too absurd to be a warning."

Captain Milford fumed. "A signal for whom? For what purpose?"

Marianne leaned toward Daniel. "What ship is that?" she asked, but the boy's attention was riveted aloft where excited chatter filtered down from above. She glanced back at the vessel. The gray sails faded against the darkening horizon and soon disappeared.

"That'll teach them!" the captain brayed as if he'd been responsible for the ship's retreat.

"It's a good ship, Miss Marianne." Daniel's voice rose above the wind, and he took her hand in his. "A good ship."

Marianne chuckled. "You are a curious lad, Daniel."

"Is that a good thing?" The mist pooling on his long lashes sparkled.

Giving his hand a squeeze, Marianne smiled. "A most excellent thing."

The mist transformed into raindrops that tapped over the deck and sounded like applause. Applause for what, Marianne didn't know. Perhaps for the ship that had dared to fire upon them, or perhaps for this young boy beside her who seemed more angel than human. As if to confirm her thoughts, Daniel held out a hand to catch the drops of rain, then he closed his eyes and lifted his peace-filled face to the wind, treasuring the moment. Innocent trust and glee in the midst of such chaos. She envied him.

Further commands to lower sail echoed across the ship. Shielding her eyes from the rain, Marianne looked aloft to see Noah descending.

Her heart skipped as the details of his face came into view.

The captain grumbled, handed command of the ship to Lieutenant Reed, and dropped below deck. Marianne should follow him and tend to her duties below or risk his wrath, but the identity of their curious visitor kept her feet in place. Perhaps Noah could offer more information than Daniel's "good ship."

The rain fell harder, and Marianne drew Daniel close, dipping her head against the drops and the buffeting wind. The deck tilted, and she tightened her grip on the capstan. Her legs trembled.

Noah landed on the deck with a thud. He winced and stretched his shoulders beneath his wet shirt. The fabric clung to his corded muscles as red bands appeared across his back. Swinging about, his gaze landed on her and remained. He ran a hand through his wet hair and attempted a smile. Despite the rain, heat rose up her neck at the intense look in his eyes. Not the anger she expected. Quite the opposite, in fact.

Luke joined him, drawing Marianne's attention. She inched her way closer to them, keeping Daniel by her side.

Noah gave his first mate a look as if they shared a grand secret. "Did you see what I saw?" he said to Luke.

Luke smiled and lifted his brows. "I did, indeed."

"What did you see?" Marianne edged between them.

"That ship." Noah gestured to the span of agitated, foamy sea where the gray sails of the vessel had last been seen. "I'd know that ship anywhere."

Marianne shook her head.

"It was my ship, the *Fortune*."

❖ CHAPTER 20 ❖

The ship bucked. Marianne's feet lifted off the deck, and she tumbled against the bulkhead of her tiny cabin. Wind howled. Waves battered the hull with the fury of a jealous lover pounding on the door to his beloved's bedchamber. Dropping to her knees, Marianne gripped the bed frame and leaned her head against the mattress to resume her prayers. The sharp smell of aged burlap filled her nose.

Oh Lord, please do not let us perish in this storm.

The ship rose as if the great sea monster, Leviathan, had picked it up. Marianne clutched the wooden frame. The splinters bit into her skin.

Lightning flashed. An eerie shroud of gray passed through her cabin before plunging the room back into darkness.

Terror sent her mind reeling with visions of herself sinking beneath the violent waves. Gurgling, fuming water filled her mouth, her lungs and stole her last breath. She resumed her prayers. She prayed for her mother and sister back home. It may be the last chance she had to lift them up before God. *Oh Lord, take care of them please. Heal my mother and send someone who will provide for them.*

Thunder cracked a deafening boom in response. The ship trembled, mimicking her own body. The deck careened to the left. She propped herself against the bulkhead. Her thoughts went to the *Fortune* they'd spotted earlier. No doubt Matthew, Agnes, and the crew suffered in the midst of the storm as well. *And protect them, too, Father.*

Yet they had come.

The excitement in Noah's voice at the sight of his ship had been unmistakable. But Marianne dared not join in his optimism. A rescue seemed as impossible as this frigate surviving the ferocious gale that pummeled them.

The ship pitched, then dove. Something thumped to the floor. Groping in the dark, Marianne found the Bible Daniel had lent her. Clutching the Holy Book to her chest, she realized she'd not once opened it since he'd given it to her. "Oh Lord, forgive me. If you save us from this storm, I promise I'll read Your Word."

Yet even those words seemed to fall on empty ears as the ship bolted again. Marianne tumbled into the leg of the table attached to the bulkhead. Her arm throbbed.

Struggling to stand, she supported herself against the door and gazed out the heaving porthole. The sea splashed against the glass, only to be torn away by the howling wind. Lightning shot a white devil's fork across the sky. A chorus of thunder gave a demonic chuckle in its wake.

Marianne hugged herself. She squeezed her eyes against the tears threatening to spill down her cheeks. Her hope that God was indeed the personal God Daniel claimed Him to be faltered beneath a plethora of unanswered prayers and the continual storms that assailed her.

Storms that now seemed to culminate in the ferocious gale lashing the ship.

A strip of light seeped beneath her door, drifting over her shoes.

Pound pound pound. She felt rather than heard someone knocking and moved to answer it. The oak slab began to open, pushing her back.

A burst of light filled the cabin and in walked Noah, lantern in hand.

Without thinking, she fell against him and clung to his shirt. She didn't care that he didn't love her. She didn't care that he didn't want her. She didn't care what propriety dictated. All she cared about was feeling his warm strength surround her. At least she would not die alone.

One thick arm embraced her and drew her close. Marianne buried her face in his shirt drawing a whiff of his scent. He hung the lantern on a hook and wrapped his other arm around her. Muscles as firm as wood encased her in a warm cocoon—a cocoon from which she never wished to break free.

"Never fear, Marianne. It will be all right."

"We shall all die in this storm," she sobbed.

He chuckled, and the rumble in his chest caressed her cheek.

The ship canted. Bracing his boots upon the deck, he gripped her tighter. "No, we will survive, I assure you. This is but a tiny squall."

"A tiny squall?" She lifted her gaze to his. Only a few inches separated them. His blue eyes drifted over her face as if soaking in every detail. They halted at her lips.

Her body warmed, and she pushed off of him. "Forgive me. My fear has relieved me of my senses."

"I made no complaint." A playful glint lit up his eyes.

Her heart leapt. Why wasn't he angry with her? Anger she could deal with. Hatred even. But not the desire, not the ardor she now saw burning in his gaze. The ship bolted, and she thumped against the bulkhead.

He gripped her shoulders. "Why didn't you tie yourself to the bed as you were instructed?" His gaze took in the ropes scattered across the deck.

"And drown in my bed when the ship sinks? I could not bear it."

His chuckle soothed her frayed nerves. He led her to the bed and gently nudged her down on the mattress. She gripped the frame and glanced out the undulating porthole. Surely if he found humor in the situation, the storm could not be as bad as it seemed.

He gathered the wayward ropes. "We will not sink. I've seen far worse than this out at sea."

"Truly?"

He smiled and ran a finger over her cheek. "Truly." Kneeling, he brushed the hair from her face. "Now, may I?" He held up the ropes.

"Tie me up?" She gave him a playful smile. "Wouldn't you enjoy that?"

His deep chuckle filled the cabin as he took her hand in his. "I did tease you quite harshly as a child, didn't I?"

Marianne swallowed, forcing down a lump of traitorous hope at his kindness. "If you call dipping my hair in tar teasing, I suppose. However, I prefer to call it cruelty."

Releasing her hand, he ran his fingers through her loose hair. "And such glorious hair, too."

Her mind whirled. Her breath threatened to burst through her chest. He was toying with her again. That was all. "Mother had to cut so much of it off that I looked like a boy for months."

"I doubt that would be possible."

Her insides dissolved. She must keep her wits about her. She must focus on his bad traits, on his ruthlessness. "And remember when you released a jar full of locusts in my bedchamber?"

He chuckled.

"I see nothing humorous about it." Marianne crossed her arms over her chest and she looked away.

Lightning flashed. The ship swooped over a swell. Noah grabbed her shoulders and drew her near.

Her heart thumped, but not from the storm this time. She lifted her gaze to his. Compassion and strength radiated from his eyes. She pushed back from him. "You've changed."

"Indeed?"

"Pray tell, what transformed the impish waif into a gentleman?" she asked.

His lips curved into a half smile that warmed her from head to toe. "A gentleman, you say?"

She looked away. "Don't let it swell that big head of yours."

With a touch to her chin, he brought her back to face him. "I wouldn't dream of it." He lowered his gaze. The lantern swayed above them, casting shifting shadows across the cabin. "Everything changed after my brother died."

Marianne watched as Noah's shoulders seemed to sink. He shrugged and played with the frayed edges of the ropes still in his hand. "Tragedy has a way of changing one's perspective."

She nodded, her thoughts drifting to how much her life had changed after her father's death.

"As well as reveal one's shortcomings." He sighed. "Then when I was unofficially promoted to captain of my father's ships, I had to grow up in a hurry."

As had Marianne. Forced to carry the burden of care for her ailing mother and younger sister, she found her imperious manner quickly crushed beneath the humbling rock of poverty.

Still kneeling before her, Noah shifted his weight to his other leg, seemingly oblivious to the oscillating deck. "And you, my princess, what transformed you into an angel?" he asked.

Heat burst onto her cheeks. *Angel?* "I was a bit of a highbrow, wasn't I?"

One side of his mouth lifted. "A question I shall refrain from answering."

Thunder bellowed. The sea rumbled against the hull.

"I was, and you know it." Marianne smiled then grew serious. "The same thing that changed you, I suppose. Tragedy." She gazed into his eyes, longing to see what emotions flickered there, but the lantern light swayed back and forth, giving her only glimpses of their deep blue color, taunting her. "I am sorry, Noah, for deceiving you about my inheritance." She swallowed. "There was no excuse for it."

"Yes there was." He took one of her hands again. "You did it for your mother. I understand."

Marianne's vision grew blurry.

He leaned toward her and whispered in her ear. "I'm truly sorry, Marianne, for every cruel joke I played upon you. The antics of a young brat." His hot breath tickled her neck. "Will you forgive me?"

Shock rendered her speechless. She'd never thought she would hear those words from Noah Brenin's lips. No doubt his guilt had gotten the better of him. "I'll consider it." She gave him a playful smile. "But you didn't come here to reminisce about our childhoods, did you?"

"I knew the storm would frighten you."

Sincerity rang in his voice. A lump formed in Marianne's throat, and she looked down.

His finger touched her chin, lifting her gaze to his. "Now will you allow me to tie you to this post so you don't injure yourself?"

She shook her head. That would mean she'd have to rely on him to untie her later on. She would have to trust that he'd remember and that if the ship sank, he'd come for her. "I cannot."

He frowned. "You don't trust me."

"Should I?"

The ship bucked and he balanced his knees on the deck. "Haven't I given you enough reason to?"

Remembering their childhood, she lifted a brow.

"As of late, I mean."

She sobered. "Yes, you have. But trust does not come easy for me, Noah." Thunder roared in the distance. "Everyone in this world has let me down."

Noah frowned and ran a thumb over the lines on her palm. "If you mean your father, I'm sure he never intended to cause you or your mother pain."

Tears burned behind Marianne's eyes. She watched Noah's thick, callused thumb caress her fingers, so small by comparison. His tenderness, his compassion wove its way deep into her soul, coaxing out of hiding a secret she'd never shared with anyone. "There's something you don't know." The words flew off her tongue before she'd had a chance to stop them.

He looked at her.

"My father's death was not an accident." Marianne squeezed her eyes shut. "He killed himself."

❖

Noah's heart shriveled. *Killed himself.* Of all the horrors to endure. . .

"So, you see, he left us of his own free will," Marianne continued. "Abandoned me, my mother and my sister." Though her voice remained composed, even cool, the moisture filling her eyes betrayed her.

"I'm sorry, Marianne." He didn't know what else to say. He'd suffered much rejection in his life but never something like that. "No doubt the shame of losing the family wealth was too much for him." Something Noah could well understand.

"It was his job to take care of us," she went on. "His responsibility to love us. And he let us all down." A tear slid down her cheek. "He and God."

He brushed the tear away with his thumb, his insides crumbling. "You can't blame God for what your father did."

"No? Then why hasn't He answered any of my prayers since? It's like God and my father both abandoned me at the same time."

Noah lowered his gaze. He understood that sentiment, for he had barely spoken to the Almighty since his brother fell to his death.

The ship rose—the pitch not as fierce this time. He squeezed her hand. Thunder rumbled from a distance. He tossed down the ropes, suddenly angry at her father. Angry at the man's cowardice. Angry that any man could leave his family uncared for—unprotected. Angry at what the man had done to this angel sitting before Noah.

The lantern light shimmered over her brown hair, setting select strands aflame in glistening red. He ran his fingers through it again, delighting in the soft curls swaying like waves over the shabby coverlet.

Her brown questioning eyes the color of rich mahogany searched his, yearning. How could he have ever found her plain? How could he have ever wanted her to break their engagement? A man would have to be a fool to let such a treasure escape his grip.

The ship bucked. He drew her close and held her tight. Her sweet breath feathered his jaw. He rubbed a thumb over her cheek and lowered his lips until they were but an inch from hers. Her feminine scent swirled around him, but she did not move, did not jerk away. He pressed his lips upon hers.

Sweet and soft, they met his kiss, caressing, loving. She clung to him, and his body responded. Heat waved through him as he absorbed himself in the taste of her.

His mind reeled with glorious thoughts. If they got off this ship, if she would still marry him, if she would allow him to, he'd vow to take care of her and protect her for the rest of her life.

Thunder bellowed. He withdrew. His heavy breaths matched hers, filling the air between them. Doubts assailed him. Had he truly won her affection or was her ardor born out of her desperate need for him to unlock her inheritance?

He studied her eyes still glazed with passion. No. That was not the kiss of a woman pretending affection.

"What was that for?" she asked softly.

He cupped her chin. "You enchant me, Miss Denton."

Shock sparked in her eyes.

"In fact you always have." Even when she was young and spoiled and full of herself. Something about her had grabbed hold of him. Which was probably why he'd bullied her so much.

A tear formed at the corner of her eye. "I've never enchanted anyone."

He smiled. "I doubt that."

Her nose pinked as it always did when her emotions ran high. He placed a gentle kiss on it.

Shouts filtered up from below. A gray hue swept the darkness from the porthole.

"I must go." Reluctantly releasing her, he stood and grabbed the latch of the door. "A new day dawns, my love. A grand new day." He winked. "For tonight we will escape."

"But how, Noah?" Fear skittered across her gaze.

"Trust me."

❖

Unable to sleep after Noah left, Marianne bound her hair up in a loose bun, dabbed a moist cloth over her face and neck, and went to the galley to fetch the captain's breakfast of oatmeal and a biscuit. Carrying the tray, she nodded toward the marine who stood guard outside the cabin, then entered when the captain screamed her name.

"Where have you been? I've been awake for hours," he grumbled as he flipped his coat tails and took a seat at his desk.

"My apologies, Captain, but it's not yet eight bells, and I had no way of knowing you had risen." She squelched the frustration in her voice and instead kept her tone lighthearted.

This seemed to appease him as he took to his meal with gusto, all the while muttering about making port in Antigua, about meeting Admiral Pellew, and being entertained on the flagship. Marianne listened intently for any valuable information that she might pass on to Noah as she brushed off his dress uniform and polished his boots before laying them out beside his bed. But the only thing of import she gleaned was the captain's mention of receiving orders for his next mission—a mission he seemed most anxious to embark upon.

After he left, Marianne quickly scrubbed and polished the deck, eager to go above as soon as possible. With her eyelids heavy from lack of sleep and her chest still wound tight from last night's frightening storm, she hoped some fresh air would both revive and calm her. She hoped, too, that it might clear her head, still whirling with what had transpired between her and Noah last night.

As she rose above deck, a flurry of morning activity met her gaze. The majority of the crew were on their hands and knees holystoning the decks. Midshipmen sauntered about issuing orders at the petty officers who were armed with rattan canes with which to strike any laggards. A light breeze, fresh and crisp from the storm, wafted over Marianne, and she inhaled a deep lungful as she carefully made her way to the larboard railing. Above her, Captain Milford and his officers stood upon the quarterdeck, like masters of the sea, ruling the ship and the men upon it with an iron scepter.

Shielding her eyes from the rising sun, Marianne dared a glance aloft, seeking the cause of the ceaseless confusion in her mind and the odd feeling in her belly. But Noah's eyes had already locked on hers. A flicker of a smile lifted his lips.

"Land ho!" a cry came from above and all eyes scoured the horizon. A gray mound broke through the endless sea off their larboard bow.

Despite her doubts that Noah could orchestrate their escape, excitement flared in Marianne's chest at the sight of land. She'd been at sea so long, she was beginning to wonder if the earth hadn't been swallowed up by this vast blue ocean.

As the ship grew abuzz with activity, Marianne clung to the railing and did her best to keep out of the way. She did not want to go below and miss seeing the island grow as they drew near.

The sun rose into a clear cerulean sky that held no trace of last night's storm. She wished the same were true of her own heart, for she could not stop thinking about Noah's tenderness toward her—or his kiss. Heat rose up her neck in a wave. Though Marianne had no experience in the matter, she couldn't believe a man would kiss a woman with such passion unless he harbored some affection for her.

"You enchant me." His words bubbled in her heart like a fresh spring, soothing the parched places and dashing the cobwebs from the corners. She longed to embrace them, believe them, and allow her heart to soar with the hope that he truly loved her.

Yet somewhere deep down, fear arose, fear that it was just a dream, a cruel joke. He had made no declaration of affection, no declaration of intent. Perhaps he had simply been trying to allay her fears of the storm.

"Trust me." His last words to her echoed in her heart. And right now, she wanted to trust him more than ever.

❖

Blinking the fatigue from his eyes, Noah focused on wrapping his toes around the footrope as tightly as he could. He elbowed Blackthorn and nodded toward the island that had just been announced as Antigua. Never had a piece of land looked more beautiful. With its sea of green vegetation swaying in the wind and its sparkling blue harbor, the island appeared more Eden than a British outpost. Each minute brought them closer, and soon Noah made out a thicket of masts bobbing in the harbor.

Blackthorn's tepid grin fell short of the enthusiasm Noah longed to see. In fact, the doubt screaming from the man's expression began to stomp on Noah's excitement. Yet he couldn't blame him. The last time Blackthorn had attempted to escape, he'd lost a friend and gained a flogging. But things would be different this time. Noah had made a promise to a certain special lady, after all.

He glanced down to the object of that promise, still clinging to the larboard railing. He loved her. This woman he'd once thought to be a plain, plump, and pompous woman. But she was none of those things to him anymore. When he weighed her on the scales against Miss Priscilla, Miss Priscilla became the common shrew and Marianne the beautiful lady. How could he have been so wrong?

She gazed up at him and smiled. His body reacted to the remembrance of their kisses.

A gusty breeze tore over him, the sweet smell of earth and life riding atop the scent of the sea. Though Noah had long since stopped believing in miracles—especially when it came to his own life—if Daniel had indeed heard from God, then maybe, just maybe the Almighty would grace them with a miracle now. At least for the sake of the boy and his father.

Noah glanced down at the quarterdeck where the captain stood, flanked by his officers. Two quartermaster's mates gripped the huge wheel as they took direction from the sailing master.

"A leadsman in the chains, if you please," the captain bellowed, and one of the sailors dropped the lead-and-line into the water to determine its depths as they approached the harbor.

"Hand the courses!" a command bellowed from below. "Release topsails!"

More hands clambered above to help Noah and the others carry out the captain's orders. The humid Caribbean air swamped around him. Sweat streamed down his back and stung his wounds. Once the courses were taken in, the frigate slowed, and calls from the forechains indicated they had plenty of depth to maneuver.

Noah dared a glance at the burgeoning harbor—a huge, glittering, turquoise bay separated in half by a hilly spit of land. The ship canted to starboard and headed toward the right fork. He squinted against the glare of sun on wave to see the dichotomy of ornately decorated brick buildings standing beside shabby wooden taverns and primitive thatched huts—all three dotting the harbor and extending into the green hills. The clamor of bells along with the squawk of gulls filled the air. An impressive gathering of ships of the line, ensigns flying high, bowed in the water like courtiers before the king.

"Prepare the anchor!"

Men scrambled to remove the lashings from the anchor catted to the starboard bulwark.

The quartermaster hoisted the ship's flags up on the halyard. They snapped in the warm breeze.

Noah climbed down to the deck as the order to back the foretops was given. Luke and several waisters hoisted on the lines to bring the bare yard around. As they passed what Noah assumed was the flag-ship, captain Milford gave the order to fire a salute and the starboard-forward-most gun roared its booming greeting.

Marianne covered her ears, and Noah gave her a gesture she hoped would allay her fears as one after another of the guns fired until six had spent their powder-only loads. Four thunderous booms cracked the sky in response from the flagship.

When the ship had slowed to but a crawl, Captain Milford gave the order to let go the anchor, and with a mighty splash the iron claw dove into the turquoise bay. The captain disappeared below, then emerged moments later in his full dress uniform. He climbed down into a boat that had been lowered in his absence and hoisted off from the frigate with a boatful of sailors at the oars. Excitement crackled in the air as the crew expressed their hope that they would be chosen to go ashore.

Noah's excitement joined with theirs. The others tasted rum and women.

But he tasted freedom.

❖ CHAPTER 21 ❖

Marianne swept through the captain's cabin, busying herself with dusting and making sure the captain's instruments and trinkets were in a line just as he demanded—even though everything had already been set in place. A quick glance out the stern window at the graying sky tinged with pink told her that it would soon be dark. The captain had been gone for hours and by the sound of the thrumming of feet above and the constant harping of an off-key fiddle, she guessed the crew was as anxious as she was to discover their next mission.

She yawned and opened her eyes wide, lest her lids drop like weights to her cheeks. Though she longed to retire for the night, she must remain awake and alert enough to play the spy when the captain returned. Noah and the others depended on her for any information that would tell them the best time to make their escape.

She had already poured the captain's nightly port and laid out his nightshirt. Glancing over the cabin, she searched for something to occupy her time and keep her awake when thumping sounded in the passageway. The door flew open, crashing against the bulkhead. Captain Milford charged in like a drunken bull, stuttering and staggering, and entangling himself in his dark blue coat as he tried to remove it. Lieutenant Garrick and Reed followed after him on a gust of hot wind tainted with sweat and rum.

Garrick gave her a salacious grin. Ignoring him, Marianne moved to the captain's side and helped him ease out of his boat cloak, then she hung it up in the armoire. The captain plopped into one of his stuffed chairs and released a heavy sigh. His officers stood at attention before him.

"What are you worthless toads still doing here?" he barked. "Go inform the crew that we are at war and will set sail as soon as the provisions are brought on board in the morning. And send up the surgeon."

At war? Marianne flinched. *Leaving in the morning?* Drat. Then they would have to escape tonight.

"Very well, Captain," both men said at once and then exchanged looks of disgust. For each other or for their captain, Marianne didn't presume to know. After saluting, they hurried out and closed the door, leaving Marianne alone with the drunken man.

Gathering her resolve, she knelt before him and tugged on his left boot. Though he was capricious, volatile, even cruel at times—not to mention half-mad—she no longer believed he would hurt her. He gazed at her with lifeless, wavering eyes. "You're a kind woman, Miss Denton. Would that I had a daughter like you."

The compliment settled over Marianne like a wet blanket—cold, uncomfortable, and unfamiliar. How she had longed to hear such approbation from her own father. A sudden need to cry burned in her throat.

"Did you enjoy your trip?" She kept her voice nonchalant and her focus on her task. One boot removed. Now for the other.

"The food was to my liking. The company, however, atrocious." He leaned his head back and closed his eyes.

"But surely your time with the admiral was rewarding?" Marianne grabbed his boots and stuffed them into the armoire.

"That blowhard. He doesn't know a great captain when he sees one. Why, I fought beside Nelson at Copenhagen. I captured the French frigate *Vainqueur*. Not many men can make such a boast."

"But you mentioned war, Captain. Is it true?" Marianne inched her way back to him, clasping her hands together.

He gave a maniacal chuckle. "Aye. Your puny nation of rebels—if that is indeed from whence you hail—had the audacity to declare war on Britain a month ago. Can you believe it?"

A surge of pride lifted Marianne's shoulders—pride in her country, in her brave men and leaders. "I can. Since I have recently found myself beneath your unjust rule."

He flashed angry eyes her way and started to rise, and for a moment, Marianne feared she had stepped over the line. Then he sank back into the chair. "Never fear, we shall squash your pathetic rebellion within days." He laughed. "And you will once again be a subject of the crown."

"I am subject to no one, sir."

"And yet it would appear otherwise." He peered at her through half-closed eyes. "I need a drink."

"Perhaps you've had enough." Or perhaps she should allow him his liquor. It might loosen his tongue enough to supply her with further information. Or it might knock him unconscious, which would never do.

Wincing, he pressed a hand on his side. "Where is that blasted surgeon?" His head fell against the back of the chair, eyes closed and mouth open.

Marianne darted to his side. She must think of something to keep him talking. "Captain, captain." She shook his arms. "Tell me what happened to your side that it pains you so."

"Battle wound. Struck by a wooden spike this thick." He lifted his head for a moment and held his hands out to demonstrate the size of a skewer that would have killed him had it struck any part of his body.

"Oh my, Captain. How brave you are."

He drifted off again, and Marianne stomped her foot on the deck. She must discover his orders. Leaning forward, she whispered into his ear, "I'm sure the admiral has sent you on another important mission."

"Important. Balderdash!" His eyes popped open and he tried to stand. Marianne backed away and watched as he swayed like a spindly tree in a storm before falling back into the chair. "I'm to assist the HMS *Guerriére* patrolling the northern colonies and intercept and destroy the American ship USS *Constitution. Assist!*" he hissed, spittle flying from his mouth. "Me, an honored captain!"

Marianne smiled. Resisting the urge to run and find Daniel, she gazed at the man, reeling with drink and despair, before her. The lines on his face seemed especially long, making him look older than his fifty-three years. An ache formed in her heart for him. His bitterness, discontentment, and loneliness kept him locked in a prison that was far more formidable than the ship was to Marianne.

He lifted his head, mumbled something unintelligible, and then dropped it back again. The surgeon could not be relied on to arrive, and she couldn't very well leave him like this.

"Come now, Captain, let me help you to your bed. A good night's sleep and things will look better in the morning, to be sure." She eased her arm beneath his.

"I don't need your help!" He shot to his feet then tumbled to the left. Marianne reached out to catch him before he fell. His weight landed like a huge sack of grain across her shoulder, shooting pain down her back. She stumbled but managed to stay upright. A flood of alcohol-tainted breath stung her nose.

"Well, I suppose I do need help." He chuckled.

The door creaked open, and the surgeon appeared beside her. "Here, I'll take him, miss. You can go on now," he said, wiping sweaty strands of hair from his forehead.

Releasing the teetering man, Marianne spotted Daniel standing at the door awaiting her message, expectation flashing in his eyes. But as she stared at the surgeon's satchel and thought of the laudanum within it, then glanced over the bottles of rum lining the captain's shelves, a glorious thought occurred to her. A wonderful, mischievous thought.

❖

Balancing the makeshift raft on his back, Noah inched his way up the companionway ladder. He peered above deck and scanned for any watchman looking their way. Nothing but a sliver of a moon smiling at him from the horizon and a gentle breeze laden with the scent of tropical flowers greeted him. He gestured for the others to follow and crept across the deck, keeping to the shadows and clutching his only weapon, a jagged piece of wood, close to his chest. One glance behind him told him that Blackthorn, Daniel, Weller, and Luke followed close upon his heels. Not a sound, not a footstep emanated from the group as they inched toward the quarterdeck. Well past midnight, the crew was fast asleep, all save a few watchmen above.

But he would take care of them.

War. The words Daniel conveyed to him earlier still spun in his mind. So President Madison had declared war. A month ago Noah would have been furious at the news. A month ago his main concern would have been the success of his merchant business. But much had happened since then.

America had every right to defend herself against the bullying tactics of Britain. And, by God, Noah would do all he could to aid his country's efforts to shake off their tentacles of tyranny.

Not the least of which was to escape this ship.

A shape formed out of the darkness. Noah threw his hand up and halted as did those behind him.

The sound of deep snoring filtered over him like a soothing balm. The watchman sat on the deck just beneath the quarterdeck ladder, his chin on his chest, fast asleep. Noah eyed the musket in the man's grip and thought better of trying to pry it from him. Instead, he swept a glance across the foredeck where he expected to find another watchman at his post. Instead a dark mound lay crumpled beside the mast. Noah scratched his head. Though only a few men were assigned night watch when anchored at a British port, he had not expected them both to be asleep—a condition that if discovered would mean their certain death.

Perhaps God *was* on his side, after all.

He inched up the quarterdeck ladder and past the helm where another watchman lay curled in a ball by the wheel. Astounding. Shaking his head, he passed him and made out a shape by the mizzenmast. He hoped it was Marianne. After Daniel had delivered the message that they were to set sail in the morning, Noah had sent the boy back to her with the request that she meet them at the larboard stern at four bells of the middle night watch.

As she came into view, his heart leapt. Milky moonlight trickled over her, transforming her hair into chocolate and her skin into rich cream. Instead of the fear he expected to see on her face, a catlike grin played upon her lips as she held up a dark uncorked bottle.

"What's this?" he whispered as the others crowded around. He set down the tiny raft.

"It *was* laudanum," she replied.

"Was?"

Luke chuckled.

Marianne gestured to two empty bottles perched at the foot of the mizzenmast. "The watchmen were quite eager to have an extra ration of grog." She smiled. "A special concoction of rum and laudanum does wonders for a good night's slumber."

Noah brought her hand to his lips. "Clever, brave girl. But how were you able to steal the captain's rum and the laudanum?"

"The captain sleeps soundly." She shrugged. "And I slipped the laudanum from the surgeon's pouch while he put the captain to bed."

Daniel darted to her side and gave her a hug. "I knew you could do it, Miss Marianne," he whispered.

She returned the lad's embrace.

Weller mumbled something and Blackthorn, with a thick rope looped over his shoulder, took up a position at the helm, scouring the deck with his nervous gaze.

Marianne retrieved the two empty bottles, walked to the railing, and tossed them into the water. Their splashes joined the slap of waves against the hull. Facing them, she drew a breath as if trying to gather courage from the humid air around them. "Where is our boat?"

"There is no boat." She inhaled a tiny breath and Noah stepped toward her. A breeze played with a rebellious curl lingering at her neck. He longed to touch it, if only to soften the words he had just spoken.

Even in the shadows, he could see the whites of her eyes widen.

And a tiny wrinkle appear between her brows. "How are we to get to shore?"

Noah took her hand. "We swim."

"But I can't swim." Her hand trembled and she tried to tug it from him, but he fastened his grip and led her back to the mast. Releasing her, he grabbed the tiny raft. "I made this for you. You can float on it. I'll pull you along."

❖

Marianne gazed at the tiny piece of wood—part of a crate, from the looks of it. Every nerve in her body rebelled. "I can't possibly." Terror constricted her throat. She couldn't breathe.

Daniel looked up at her. "It'll be all right, Miss Marianne."

She glanced toward the port town. Nothing but a few blinking lights remained to mark the row of shops, taverns, and warehouses she'd spotted earlier in the day. Miles of water as dark as coal stretched between them and those lights. And in the middle, a maze of British warships barred their passage.

"But how. . .impossible. . .it won't hold me."

Noah shook the crate and then struck it with his hand. "It's sturdy. It will hold you, I promise."

Lowering herself into a small boat would have been difficult enough—something she had spent the day preparing herself to do—but trusting a crate no bigger than a man's chest was beyond the pale. A milky haze eased over the dark waves like an eerie mist. She hugged herself.

"We are all strong swimmers, miss." Luke urged her with his eyes. "We'll help you to shore."

"Aye, miss." Mr. Weller approached, a frown etched across his forehead. "No need to worry. I wouldn't let nothing happen t' you." He fingered the scar on his neck then tugged his scarf up over it.

The sea licked its greedy tongue against the creaking hull of the ship. Marianne's head grew light. Drawing Daniel close, she stepped back into the shadows and leaned against the mizzenmast for support.

Mr. Weller's gaze skittered nervously over the deck. "We must go."

Blackthorn left his post, crept to the railing, and began tying his rope to the gunwale. Weller and Luke joined him.

Noah's eyes reached out to her like a lifeline. "Trust me." He extended his hand.

Marianne swallowed. She wanted to trust him. She wanted to be able to trust someone again. She wanted to get off this ship. But her will was having difficulty forcing her body to comply. She nodded and lifted her hand to take Noah's outstretched one. . .

. . .when a sinister voice blared over them, tinged with sarcasm. "What have we here?"

Clutching Daniel, Marianne slipped into the shadows toward the stern.

Noah froze, his shoulders slumped. Beyond him, Lieutenant Garrick stood hands on his hips and a bestial smirk on his thin lips.

Marianne covered her mouth to suppress a scream. *No, Lord. Not this.* She pushed Daniel behind her and stepped farther back into the darkness where they would not be seen.

Blackthorn, Weller, and Luke faced their enemy, their faces pale.

Noah slowly turned around. He dropped the raft to the deck with a clunk.

"I'll have you all court-martialed and put to death for this." Lieutenant Garrick's chuckle bubbled over the deck, so at odds with his grim statement. "Were you all to fit on that?" He picked up the raft and examined it. Then setting it on the deck, he stomped it with his boot, breaking it in half.

The crunch and snap of the wood skewered any hope left within Marianne.

"Odious cur," Weller mumbled.

"What did you say?" Garrick peered around Noah toward the three men at the railing.

"He said you are an odious cur, sir." Luke grinned, not an ounce of fear on his face.

Garrick's eyes narrowed, and he started toward Luke. Noah stepped in the way and pushed the man back.

The insolence fled the lieutenant's face, replaced by fear. "Guards!" His smirk returned but fell when no footsteps answered his call.

Luke barreled forward. As did Blackthorn and Weller.

Garrick drew his sword and leveled it at Noah's chest. "Not another step or I'll run him through. Guards!"

A red spot blossomed on Noah's shirt beneath the point.

Marianne's stomach collapsed. Daniel gripped her hand from behind. His whispered prayers rose on the wind.

Luke and Blackthorn charged Garrick. Noah ducked and rammed his body into the Lieutenant's torso. Marianne stopped breathing. Garrick toppled to the deck with a thump. His sword flew into the air, struck the binnacle, and toppled to the waist of the ship with a *clank*. His bicorn landed beside him.

Before the man could recover, Noah, his face a mass of rage, lifted Garrick up by the lapels of his dark coat and slugged him across the jaw.

Garrick stumbled backward, terror screaming from his pointy face. "Guards!"

This time, grumbling sounded from the foredeck. The dark mass of the watchman struggled to his feet and peered in their direction.

"Time to go." Luke urged.

"It's certain death now if we don't." Blackthorn peered into the darkness. "Come along, son." Slipping from behind Marianne, Daniel darted toward his father and the two of them started over the railing.

Noah released Garrick and shoved him aside.

"You'll never get away." Garrick straightened his coat, his voice quavering. "I'll have the marines after you in moments."

"Only if you're able to tell them where we are." Noah slammed his fist across the lieutenant's jaw once again. Garrick's head snapped backward, and he fell to the deck in a heap.

Noah turned to Marianne. "Let's go." He grabbed her hand and tugged her to the railing. Luke dove into the water. Blackthorn and Daniel clambered down the rope to the black sea below. Weller straddled the bulwarks and gave Marianne one last look of concern before he held his nose and dropped over the side. *Splash.*

The watchman tumbled down the foredeck ladder and made his way across the main deck.

Noah swung over the gunwale then reached back for Marianne. "Hold on to me. I'll help you down."

Terror clamped her every muscle, nerve, and fiber. "I can't, Noah. There is no raft."

"I'm a strong swimmer. You can hang onto my back." His eyes, brimming with concern, pleaded with her. He nodded as if to reinforce his statement. As if that would somehow dissipate all her fears.

She wished with all her heart that it would.

The watchman's heavy steps sounded on the quarterdeck ladder.

"I can't." She stepped back, knowing all too well the hopeless life she chose. But better to be alive and a prisoner than dead at the bottom of the sea. "Go without me."

Noah's jaw tightened. "No. Come." He held out his hand. "Please trust me, Marianne."

She couldn't. She couldn't trust him. Not him, not anyone, not even God. "The captain's orders are to rendezvous with the HMS *Guerriére* in the north and find and destroy the USS *Constitution*."

"Why are you telling me this now?" Noah huffed. "Come!" He held out his hand.

"It's too late. The marine will see us." She glanced over her shoulder. "Go. I'll divert his attention."

"Who goes there?" the watchman's slurred voice shot over them.

Tears burned in her eyes. She stepped back again. "I'm sorry, Noah."

The watchman's boots thumped upon the quarterdeck. "What's this about?"

Pain, desperation screamed from Noah's eyes. "I'll come back for you." He glanced at the guard then below at the water, then back at her. "Do you hear me? I will come back for you."

But Marianne dared not hope. Promises made were promises broken. She longed to run into his arms, if only to feel his strength surround her one last time. A tear slipped down her cheek.

Then he disappeared over the side.

A splash bellowed hollow and empty.

Swiping her moist cheeks, Marianne turned to face the marine.

"Oh, it's you, Miss Denton. I thought I heard voices." He lowered his musket and swayed on his feet.

"My apologies, Mr. Jameson. I couldn't sleep." Marianne hoped he didn't hear the quaver in her voice nor see Lieutenant Garrick's unconscious form lying in the shadows by the railing.

"Very well." He swung about and stumbled on his way.

Releasing a sigh of relief, Marianne turned and loosened the rope from the bulwarks. The thick hemp dropped to the bay with a hollow swish. She gripped the railing and peered into the thick darkness. Not a trace of the five men, not a shimmer, splash, or flicker marked their passage.

Her legs crumpled like loose ropes and she fell to the deck. They had left her.

Noah had left her.

❖ CHAPTER 22 ❖

Noah dragged his drenched body onto shore and dropped onto the sand. His heart felt as heavy and saturated as his clothes—as empty as his lungs as he gulped to fill them.

He could not shake the look on Marianne's face right before he dropped into the sea—the look of pure terror and desperation. And it had taken every ounce of his strength to leave her.

But he had no choice.

Or did he? During the long, arduous swim ashore, he'd had plenty of time to replay every painful detail in his mind. Should he have grabbed her and forced her to go? But how could he swim with a hysterical woman clawing at him? Both of them would have drowned. Then there was the problem of the approaching watchman. Marianne had been right. They wouldn't have made it very far if he had seen them and alerted the ship. He wondered what had become of Garrick. Had he awoken? He assumed not.

Noah could still hear Marianne's soft voice as she mollified the watchman's suspicions. Protecting them. So they could get away.

While they left her behind.

His gut churned. Waves washed over his legs, trying to drag him back into the sea. Which was what he deserved or worse.

Weller crawled up beside him. Followed by Luke and Blackthorn with Daniel clinging to his back. Their heavy breaths sounded like a flock of birds frightened into flight.

Digging his hands into the sand, Noah lifted himself to his knees. No time to rest. They had chosen a spot far away from the lights of town, but that didn't mean they were safe. "Follow me," he whispered, struggling to his feet.

Trudging through the sand, he made out a clump of shadowy vegetation in the darkness. His gut roiled. If he had stayed with Marianne, he would have been court-martialed and hanged. What good would he be to her dead? Noah was sure Lieutenant Garrick had not seen her in the shadows. Therefore, she could not be implicated in their escape. She would survive.

She must survive.

Self-loathing rose like bile in his throat. What sort of man left the woman he loved in such a dangerous place? *Woman he loved.* The truth struck him like the sharp wind that now blasted over him.

Shivering, he batted away the leaves of a nearby tree and plunged into the jungle. The smell of earth and life saturated his nose. If they could make their way to a less inhabited side of the island, stay hidden, and avoid British authorities, Noah hoped to be able to spot the *Fortune.* He had a feeling Matthew would be searching for them. He knew because that was exactly what Noah would do.

The twigs and leaves of the forest crunched beneath his bare feet, biting into his skin. Noah fisted his hands and tromped through the underbrush, one thought, one purpose driving him forward. Once he got off this island, he would rescue Marianne from that British frigate. Even if he died trying.

❖

Marianne stared at the deckhead above her bed. Since dawn had broken and dared to force its light upon the callous darkness of her cabin, she had occupied her time counting every divot and scratch in the fine oak. What else could she do? Her body, numb from shock and agony, refused to move from the supine position it had assumed upon her mattress after she'd spilled every last tear onto the coverlet. Nor did she want to move. If she were forced to get up and greet the day, she'd be forced to accept that she was all alone, without a friend, without any help, without hope aboard an enemy frigate. And that reality would surely crush her beneath its massive weight.

"Miss Denton!" the captain's growl blared down the passageway and screeched beneath her door. Either he wanted his breakfast or he'd discovered her friends' escape. She supposed she should be frightened that he'd also discovered she'd given rum to the guards, but she could find no fear within the numbness that consumed her. Unless she'd be punished for the offense or hanged, the day loomed before her with endless scrubbing, buffing, polishing, rinsing, and cleaning. Not to mention listening for hours to the captain's rumblings and bracing herself to endure his rapid shifts from madness to complacency.

As far as Marianne could see, an endless, pointless future extended out before her like a dark tunnel that sped to hell but never quite arrived.

Closing her eyes against the pounding in her head, she struggled to sit. Daniel had told her God had a great purpose for everyone. If this was hers, she wondered if she could politely decline.

"Miss Denton!"

Rising, she ran her fingers through her hair—still damp from the thousand tears she'd shed—and tried to pin it up. Then attempting to press the wrinkles from her skirts, she took a deep breath and gathered the resolve she needed to face her bleak future. God had a destiny for her all right. It just wasn't a very pleasant or important one.

Opening her door, she headed toward the captain's cabin. Nodding at the marine guard, she stepped into the lion's den.

Where vile curses curled her ears.

"Where have you been, Miss Denton?" Slouching in one of his chairs, the captain lifted a hand to squeeze the bridge of his nose. "Lieutenant Garrick has disturbed my sleep with some rather unsettling news."

Marianne felt the blood race from her heart. She stepped forward and followed the captain's gaze to see Lieutenant Garrick standing behind the open door.

Instead of the usual smirk on his mouth, a red gash slashed across his swollen bottom lip while a dark purple blotch marred his left jaw and spread upward to cover his bloated cheek.

Marianne suppressed a smile. "What news, Captain?"

Garrick shifted his weight, his eyes fuming. "Do you see that? She smiles."

"Perhaps she finds amusement in your clownish appearance." Captain Milford released a long sigh and rubbed his temples. No doubt he suffered from his overindulgence in drink last night. "How ridiculous you appear, sir. A lieutenant in His Majesty's Navy allowing himself to be assaulted by ignorant Americans—and on board a warship. Absurd!"

Garrick's chest heaved. His face reddened.

"Captain, allow me to fetch your breakfast," Marianne offered. "You don't look well."

"I don't feel well either!" Grunting, he inched to the edge of his chair and rose. "Miss Denton, it appears some of the crew escaped last night."

"Oh?" She forced innocence into her tone despite the angst churning in her gut.

"Lieutenant Garrick believes you were complicit in their plans. . . may have even aided them?" The captain's stern voice held a hint of disbelief as he ambled to the center of the cabin.

Garrick fumbled with the bicorn in his hand. He glared her way.

"Me?" Marianne swallowed. "That's absurd. Who escaped?"

"The men from your merchant ship and a few others of my crew."

Marianne twisted the ring on her finger. "Indeed?" She feigned shortness of breath and clutched a hand to her chest. "They left me." Yet she didn't have to feign the pain burning in her heart.

The captain pressed a hand to his side. "Those loathsome rebels! I'll have them all hanged when I find them!"

Marianne looked down, holding her breath.

"It's the treasonous wench you should hang, Captain." Garrick gestured toward her. "She assisted them."

"Me?" Marianne clutched her throat. "How could I have helped them? I was tucked in my bed all night." She cringed at the lie, but it couldn't be helped.

Garrick's jaw stiffened. "Captain, I implore you. Lock her up at once."

"Preposterous!" Captain Milford gave an incredulous snort. "She's but a silly woman and certainly incapable of such treachery. I'll hear no more of it." He studied Garrick. "But you!" He crooked a thick finger toward the lieutenant. "Allowing ill-bred Yankees to beat you and then escape beneath your nose. Shame on you, sir!"

Lieutenant Garrick looked as though he would explode. Even his red hair seemed aflame atop his head. "Four against one, Captain."

"Fully armed, you couldn't subdue a cow." The captain huffed. "If it weren't for the money your father pays me to keep you here—or should I say to keep you away from home—I'd have tossed you back to Portsmouth long ago."

Marianne blinked at the news, amazed that such arrangements were made. However, it did offer an explanation as to why the captain tolerated a rogue like Lieutenant Garrick.

Garrick's eyes simmered. "But I *am* here, Captain. And you do accept the payment."

"Do not test me, sir." Captain Milford seethed. "Or I may find the extra coins have lost their luster."

A moment of silence passed between them before the captain waved a hand in dismissal. "Send in the watchmen who were on deck last night. Drunk on duty. I'll have them all flogged!"

Marianne's stomach curdled. *Flogged?* Because of her. Because she'd tempted them with rum. Maybe she should confess—tell the captain it was her fault. Perhaps he'd lessen their punishment.

Or perhaps he'd have her flogged right alongside them. Or worse. Perhaps he'd realize her complicity in the escape and have her hanged. She bit her lip. *Lord, please do not let him punish those men.*

Grinding his teeth together, Mr. Garrick turned to leave, then stopped. "What of the deserters, Captain?"

"I have no time to search for them now." Swerving about, the captain stared out the stern windows where the first rays of the sun seemed to hesitate, cowering, outside the panes. "We must get underway. As soon as the supplies arrive, prepare the ship to sail. I'll be on deck shortly. And you, Miss Denton, bring me my blasted tea and biscuit!"

Lieutenant Garrick donned his hat and knuckled a salute before he stormed from the room. Marianne followed him out and shut the door before she realized her error. Halfway down the passageway, the lieutenant turned on her. His eyes boiled like lava. "I know you helped them," he spat out through his swollen lips.

Marianne cleared the tremble from her voice. "You know no such thing, Mr. Garrick."

He snorted and a sultry grin formed on his lips. "Your fiancé left you, eh? No one around to stand up for you anymore." He ran a finger over her cheek and she stepped back.

"I'll find proof that you helped your friends escape and when I do, you'll have to choose between me and the noose."

Marianne shuddered. The noose would win. But she dared not anger him further by telling him so.

With a coarse chuckle, he turned and marched away.

Marianne released the breath that had stuck in her throat. Her future looked bleak. Bleak indeed.

❖

From her position at the stern, Marianne gazed at the island of Antigua as it faded to gray in the distance. Somewhere on that island were Noah, Luke, and the others. At least she hoped they had made it safely to shore.

And weren't locked in some horrid British prison.

A shiver coursed through her, and she gripped her belly. Daniel's sweet face filled her mind, and she chided herself for thinking only of her own poor predicament. Thank God he and his father were finally off this ship. And Weller and Luke. And of course Noah. He had been brutalized aboard this ship because of her. Now he was free. For that she was grateful.

Oh, why hadn't she simply jumped overboard? Wouldn't it have been better to drown than suffer her present fate? She had wanted to. Had desperately wanted to trust Noah.

I am a coward. A coward who trusts no one.

The ship bucked and she braced her feet against the deck. A gust of brine-scented wind whipped her hair and cooled the perspiration on her neck. Above her, the sun inched toward its high command for the day. The captain would be wanting his noon meal soon. His commands blared across the ship from his position on the quarterdeck. No doubt he was still furious about the escape.

She couldn't help but smile. But it quickly faded as a vision of the pleading look on Noah's face crossed her mind. He said he'd come back for her.

But as the island sunk below the horizon and dropped out of sight—just as Noah had done over the railing—she knew that would not be possible. Even if he connected with his merchant ship, even if he could convince his men to pursue the HMS *Undefeatable*, Noah's ship was no match for a British frigate. That much she had learned.

Besides, who would try to defeat a ship named *Undefeatable*?

Especially to free an ordinary woman like her.

No. There would be no rescue party coming to save her. She was destined to serve Captain Milford aboard this ship of horrors for as long as God determined. And from the looks of things, that may be a long time indeed.

Unless, of course, she was hanged for aiding in the men's desertion.

Lieutenant Garrick's threat reignited her fear. She would do her best to avoid being alone with him, but eventually he would trap her. That, too, she must accept.

The captain barked at her and headed down the quarterdeck stairs. Releasing the mast, Marianne turned, all life and hope draining out of her feet onto the deck as she followed him below.

❖

Noah clutched Matthew's hand and swung over the bulwarks. Planting his sandy feet on the deck—his deck, the deck of the *Fortune*—he embraced his friend. "I knew I could count on you."

The man's bald head gleamed in the morning sun nearly as bright as his smile. "Alls we had to do was follow you. I knew ye'd find a way to escape sooner or later."

"How did you find us?" Noah and his men had been hiding in a clump of trees on the southwest side of Antigua, living off coconut milk and crabs for three days.

Luke clambered over the railing, followed by Weller, Blackthorn, and Daniel.

"I figured if you escaped when the ship anchored, you'd be somewhere away from the Brits hiding amongst the trees. All I had to do was sail real slow-like around the island till I spotted your signal fire." He winked.

Noah stretched his back, still raw from the flogging.

Daniel's eyes lit up. "So this is your ship, Mr. Noah?"

"Yes, it is." He tousled the boy's hair and scanned the deck as his crew swamped him with greetings.

"We thought you was gone for sure, Cap'n," Mr. Rupert said.

"Good to have you back, sir," Mr. Pike shouted.

"What's it like on one of them British frigates?" another sailor asked.

"Thank you all." Noah scanned his men. "Not a pleasant experience, I assure you."

Blackthorn eased beside Noah and shook the water from his hair, reminding Noah of a wet bear. "Nice ship, Brenin."

Noah smiled.

"Weller made it back without losing any more of his fingers!" Mr. Rupert said, and they all chuckled.

Agnes emerged from the crowd and absorbed Noah in her fleshy arms, nearly squeezing the life from him. "I was so worried about you, son." She held him back and took a good look at him. Noah felt a blush rising up his neck.

"A bit skinny, but you look well." She slapped his belly then glanced over at Luke and the others. "Where's Miss Denton?"

Noah opened his mouth to tell her, but the words withered on his lips.

"We had to leave her behind." Luke frowned.

"You what?" Her face grew puffy and her eyes sharp. She faced Noah. "You did what?"

"It couldn't be helped, Agnes." The breeze tore his words away as if they bore no weight.

Her eyes filled with tears. "That poor dear. All alone on that enemy ship."

"Don't worry, ma'am." Daniel sidled up to the large woman. "We're going to go rescue her, aren't we, Mr. Noah?"

"That we are." Noah said with as much conviction as he could muster. Problem was, he didn't know how.

"And who might this be?" Agnes drew Daniel into the folds of her skirt.

"My son, Daniel." Blackthorn ran a sleeve over his forehead and stood tall. He exchanged a look with Noah and Luke. "Feels good to be able to claim the lad as my own."

Agnes pushed Daniel's hair from his face. "Why, you sweet boy. What were you doin' on that ship?"

"God's work, ma'am." Daniel smiled up at her.

"An' I'd say he fared better than the rest o' us because of it." Weller tugged at the scarf around his neck and laughed—the first laugh Noah had heard the man utter since they'd been impressed by the British.

"Indeed." Daniel's prophesy of rescue leapt into Noah's mind, and he eyed the boy curiously. Coincidence? Or did the lad truly hear from God? But he didn't have time to ponder it now. Marianne was in trouble.

"Haul in the boat!" he ordered. "We set sail immediately."

Luke began braying orders to the crew, sending them scampering across the deck.

Noah turned to his boatswain. "What is the status of the ship, Matthew?"

Matthew scratched his bald head. "We dumped all the rice and flour that got wet, Cap'n. Still got the cloth we can sell. But as far as sailin' goes, she's fit as a fiddle."

"Good." Noah nodded and glanced at the glistening shores of Antigua a mile off their larboard side then shifted his gaze to the endless turquoise sea. His gut twisted in a knot. Agnes's sorrowful eyes met his, and he knew her thoughts must also be of Marianne.

"Never fear, Agnes, I'll get her back."

She pursed her lips. "I'll hold you to that, Noah." Then with a swipe to rid her face of tears, she gathered Daniel close and led him away. "I bet you're a might starved, too, little man."

Later, in his cabin, with his belly full, Noah leaned back on his desk and faced a line of his men. Luke, Matthew, Mr. Weller, Mr. Pike, Mr. Boone, Blackthorn, and Daniel.

Mr. Pike shuffled his feet. "This is self-destruction, Cap'n." He kneaded the hat in his hands. "The crew ain't sure they want to be a part of it."

Noah shifted his back, glad to be out of the filthy garb the British had given him to wear and back into his own clothes. Rays of morning sun angled in through the stern windows, creating spears of glittering dust through the air.

"We can still make some money with the goods left in the hold." Mr. Boone's voice lifted in enthusiasm. "The trip won't be a complete loss."

Seafoam arched her back and rubbed against Noah's side. He picked her up and scratched her head, surprised that he'd actually missed the cat.

Matthew shook his head. "I like Miss Denton, too, Noah, but chasin' after a British frigate with no plan as to how to rescue the lady, why it be sheer madness."

"You'll get us all killed." Weller scratched the scar on his face and muttered to himself. "Or worse, impressed again."

Blackthorn nodded. "I know I'm not a part of this crew, but I've been on that frigate long enough to know there's no way to get close enough to get Miss Denton off without waking their broadside."

Setting the cat down, Noah folded his hands over his chest, fighting back a wave of frustration. "Yet *we* got off."

"Aye, in a British port." Blackthorn scratched the hair sprouting from the collar of his shirt. "It's the only time the frigate won't be guarded so heavily. Now, that we're at war, we won't be able to get within a stone's throw of a British port should the HMS *Undefeatable* anchor in one again."

Seafoam sauntered over to Daniel.

Noah gripped the edge of his desk until his fingers hurt. Blackthorn was right. They were all right. Then why did everything within him scream in defiance. He gazed at Luke, who stood eyeing them all, unusually silent. The bruises on his face had faded to yellow.

"'Sides," Mr. Boone joined in. "I hear the lady won't go in the water. How are we to rescue her? Sprout wings?"

"Impossible." Blackthorn shook his head and gave Noah a sympathetic look.

Daniel picked up Seafoam and gazed up at his father. "But, Pa, nothing's impossible with God."

"Hush, lad." Blackthorn put a hand atop Daniel's head. "And from what I've seen, Noah, you don't have more than eight guns onboard. Four pounders at that."

Frustration bubbled in Noah's stomach. "What do you say, Mr. Heaton?"

Luke grinned, then shrugged one shoulder. "I say we have a lady to rescue."

"That's the spirit, Mr. Luke!" Daniel cuddled the cat to his chest, and Noah could hear the deep rumble of her purrs from where he sat.

Well, at least Noah had one man and a boy on his side. And a cat.

"Have the both of you gone mad?" Matthew shifted his wide eyes between Noah and Luke.

Noah held up a hand, silencing him. "Gentleman, there is a fully armed British ship of war sailing up the coast of America—the coast of our great nation, *our* coast. She intends to do us harm. She intends to sink our ships, impress our men, and steal from us the freedoms we fought so hard to gain. On that ship is a young American girl held against her will."

Noah took up a pace before the men, examining each one in turn. A surge of strength, of purpose, billowed within him. "We know where this frigate is going. She and her companion hope to engage the USS *Constitution* and sink her to the depths. How can we go about our way and ignore our duty? How can we close our eyes and concern ourselves with money when the very future of our nation hangs in the balance?"

He stopped, blood surging to his fists. "We are Americans. We are a people who stand up for what is right, who do not tolerate injustice, who will do anything for the cause of liberty. Even risk our own lives."

The men remained still, their eyes riveted on him.

"How can we do anything but follow our enemy and do everything we can to thwart her evil plans *and* rescue Miss Denton?"

Matthew's expression twisted. "You've changed, Noah."

"Spend some time on a British warship and see if it doesn't inspire your patriotism." Noah snorted.

A tiny grin played at the corner of Blackthorn's lips. Matthew gave Noah a knowing look while Mr. Boone and Mr. Pike stared out the stern windows.

"But what can we do?" The glee in Mr. Weller's eyes, present since their rescue, had dissipated, and Noah hated himself for it.

"I don't know." He lengthened his stance. "Gentlemen, let us follow this ship the British call the *Undefeatable* and find out if she lives up to her name." He scanned his men, searching their eyes for compliance. "Who's with me?"

"Aye." Luke smiled.

"I am," Mr. Pike and Mr. Boone said simultaneously.

"We are!" Daniel burst out, then tugged on his father's sleeve. "Aren't we, Pa?"

Blackthorn gave a reluctant nod.

Noah glanced at Matthew. The old man shrugged. "You know I'll sail wit' you where'er you go."

"And what is your decision, Mr. Weller?" Noah asked. "I will put ashore all those not wishing to join us. No one would fault you for it."

Weller grunted, then shook his head. "You promised to get me off that British frigate, Cap'n, an' you stuck to your word. Nay, I'm goin' wit' you. Even though I still don't think it's a good idea."

"Thank you, Mr. Weller." Emotion clogged Noah's throat at his men's loyalty, especially since most of them knew the price they would pay if the British caught them again.

"Very well." Noah planted his fists at his waist and cleared his throat. "Luke, inform the rest of the crew of our mission. Those who do not wish to join us will be dropped off at Charleston on the way north."

Ignoring the fear that most of his men would abandon him, Noah dismissed his friends and watched as they slowly marched from the cabin. His friends, indeed. For he doubted he'd find a more loyal bunch.

And he hoped to God he wasn't leading them all to their deaths.

❖ CHAPTER 23 ❖

Marianne set the captain's polished boots beside his bed and examined the black leather gleaming in the lantern light. Perfect. Tucking the rag into the pocket of her skirt, she turned to face the captain, hoping he wouldn't overindulge in drink tonight.

Her hopes faded when she saw him pouring yet another glass of brandy. She studied him as he stood alone with his thoughts, unaware of her censure. Dark circles tugged his eyes downward. The lines on his faced etched a sad tale. He sipped his brandy and stared into the darkness beyond the stern windows as if he wished he were somewhere else. Anywhere else. The light from lanterns swaying overhead sent the buttons lining his lapel shimmering like gold, but their luster fell flat when reflected off his haggard face.

Marianne's heart sank for this man.

It had been two weeks since they'd left Antigua. Two miserably long weeks in which Marianne's agitated emotions had gone from despondency to anger to sorrow and finally to a benumbed acceptance of her fate. If God wanted her to be a slave on board an enemy ship, if He wanted her mother and sister to go uncared for, then so be it. She would accept her destiny. Accept it, yes, but not without feeding a growing anger toward a God who was supposed to care for and love her.

But as John Milton said his poem, "Comus," *"A sable cloud turns forth its silver lining on the night,"* such a silver lining had shone on Marianne's recent storms. For Lieutenant Garrick had not followed through with his threat to prove her involvement in her friends' escape. Nor had he made any advances toward her. In addition, the drunken watchmen made no mention of her actions and had only received a dozen lashes each.

Gazing back at Captain Milford, she cringed in shame at her self-pity, for he was just as much a prisoner as she. Possibly more so. She headed toward his desk to clear off the dishes from his supper and hopefully make a quick exit, but his eyes latched on her as if he just remembered he was not alone.

Marianne picked up the tray. "Is there anything else I can get for you, sir?"

He tossed the remaining brandy into his mouth, then poured himself another glass. "What do you think of your friends leaving you, Miss Denton?" His jaw tightened. "Egad, your fiancé!" He shook his head and stared out the window. "My wealth for a loyal, honorable man. Are there any left in the world, do you suppose?"

Must he remind her? Must he rub salt in the wound when it was still so fresh? Marianne's hands began to shake. The dishes clanked, and she set down the tray. "He really wasn't my fiancé." She hoped the truth of the statement would soothe the ache in her heart, if only a little. It didn't.

The captain let out a "humph," then eyed her, his eyes misty. "Do you think me a monster, Miss Denton, for keeping you on this ship?"

Marianne flinched. She wrung her hands, wondering how to respond so as not to set this volatile man into another one of his tirades. Yet what difference would it make? What could he do to her that could make her situation any worse? Lock her in the hold? She would welcome the change of pace. Hang her from the yardarm? Then she would be free at last. Finally she said, "I think you are a man who has missed his destiny."

One gray eyebrow arched incredulously. "Indeed?" He snorted. "You amaze me, Miss Denton. Pray tell, what destiny have I missed?"

Marianne swallowed against her rising fear. "Though you are a great captain, sir, I don't believe you were meant to be in His Majesty's service. Clearly, you are not happy. You are not fulfilled." Her gaze took in his row of plants on the stern ledge. *No doubt, you should have been a farmer.*

His face grew red and puffy as his eyes skittered over the cabin. "Preposterous!" He shifted his stance then downed his drink. After pouring another, he sauntered to the windows. "What do you know of such things? I have made a distinguished name for myself in the king's navy. While you are nothing but a silly woman."

Marianne hung her head. He was right. What did she know about destiny? If there was such a thing. Either she had missed hers, too, or she was not significant enough to be assigned one. Or worse, *this* was her destiny. "You are correct, Captain. I am nothing but a silly woman." A silly woman to believe in destiny at all. Hers or anyone else's. A silly woman to believe a man like Noah Brenin could ever love her.

He shot a glance at her over his shoulder. "Dash it all, don't cry. I have no tolerance for women's tears."

Marianne drew in a deep breath and pursed her lips. The captain hovered somewhere between Captain Maniacal and Captain Tolerable—a dangerous spot if he continued in his cups. She must urge him to cease drinking and go to bed before he became too morose.

She took a tentative step toward him. "What made you join the navy, Captain?"

Still facing the window, he sipped his brandy and let out a bitter chuckle. "A woman, if you must know."

"Elizabeth?"

He spun about, his eyes snapping to hers. "How do you know of her?"

"You mentioned her before."

He looked perplexed for a moment then sadness shadowed his face. Drink in hand, he circled his desk and fell into a chair.

Marianne eyed the open bottle of brandy on the desk. Perhaps if she put it away. . .

The captain fingered the gold buttons on his waistcoat. "Ah she loved the sea. Loved a man in uniform." He chuckled and sipped his brandy, his eyes alight with happier memories. "And since I had nothing else to recommend me, I joined the navy, promising her I'd make captain and give her a good life."

Marianne corked the bottle and replaced it in the cabinet. "What happened?"

"I married her."

"Indeed?" The news startled her for the captain did not seem the marrying type. She returned to stand before him. The light in his eyes faded to a dull gray.

He waved his glass through the air, sloshing brandy over the side. "But I was never home. I hardly saw her."

Sorrow burned in Marianne's throat, knowing whatever transpired couldn't have been good.

"She was accosted on the streets of Pembroke," he said.

Marianne raised a hand to her mouth.

"A common thief after the coins in her reticule and the gold locket I gave her for our first anniversary. He killed her."

Moving to him, Marianne knelt by his feet and reached for his hand.

He waved her away. "If I had been there, I could have prevented it. She would be with me now."

"You do not know that, sir." Tears pooled in Marianne's eyes. So much pain. So much anguish in the world.

"She never saw me promoted to captain," he added in a nonchalant tone.

She studied him as he stared off into the cabin, his eyes glazed with drink and sorrow. His loss had turned him into a bitter old man. Would Marianne's tragedies do the same to her? Or did she have a choice? "Why do you stay in the navy?"

"I was in line for commander. What was I to do"—he lifted one shoulder—"start over on land with nothing to my name? No one to go home to?" He pressed a hand to his side and winced.

"What a sad tale, Captain." Marianne flattened her lips. "I'm sorry. I'm so sorry."

He shifted moist eyes her way. "Humph. I believe you are, Miss Denton." He leaned his head back and closed his eyes. "Yes, I do believe you are. Sweet, sweet Miss Denton."

"Sweet and silly." Marianne attempted to lighten the conversation.

He laughed. "Perhaps simply sweet."

Marianne smiled at the compliment then eased the glass from his hand and placed it on his desk. "Let me help you to bed."

"Leave me be, Miss Denton." He growled as if suddenly embarrassed of their conversation. "I have no need of a nursemaid."

Since when? But Marianne didn't need to be told twice. Swerving about, she quietly left the room without saying a word and made her way down the passageway. Against her better judgment, she passed her cabin and instead took the few steps to the quarterdeck above. She needed air. She needed to clear her head. The night breeze cooled the tears on her cheeks, and she batted them away. Slipping into the shadows, she leaned against the mizzenmast and gazed off the stern of the ship. A moonless night afforded her no glorious view save that of a dark mass of seething water that extended forever. She fought back the tears that kept filling her eyes. Where did they come from? She had forbidden herself to spend any more time in useless weeping for something that could never be changed.

"You should not be up here alone, Miss Denton." The low voice startled Marianne, and she jumped.

Lieutenant Reed stepped into the light from the stern lantern and faced her, a look of censure on his stiff features.

Marianne's heart returned to its normal pace at the sight of him. "I needed some air."

He glanced over the ship. "It is not safe."

Two bells rang from the foredeck, announcing the passage of a half hour. "Thank you for your concern, Mr. Reed, but am I really safe anywhere aboard this ship?"

"Some places more than others, Miss Denton."

She studied him. His tight expression refused to give her a hint of his emotions. Nor did the stiffness of his spine or the slight tilt of his chin. Yet out of all the officers on board, he had been the most kind to her. Perhaps not all British were cruel beasts, after all. No, she could see now that they were just men like any other men—some bad and some good.

The ship rose over a swell, and Marianne leaned against the mast. A gust tore at Lieutenant Reed's bicorn, and he shoved it down on his head.

Her curiosity rose regarding this officer who seemed to be a conflicting bundle of arrogance and kindness. "Forgive my boldness, Mr. Reed, but why did you join the Royal Navy?"

"I serve because my father procured a commission for me."

"But what of your wishes?"

"The youngest son in my family always serves in the navy." He shifted his feet.

"And your father?"

"He chose Parliament."

A sail snapped above her. The mast behind her vibrated. "Would you have joined the navy if you had no family name to uphold, if your father had not required it of you?"

His face scrunched as if she'd struck him. "Your point is moot, miss. For I do have family expectations to honor. It is my duty."

The lantern light rolled over him with the swaying of the ship. One second she could make out his sour expression, the next it was lost to her in the shadows. "Surely you have your own dreams."

His glance took in the deck before he gazed out to sea. "I had not considered any other endeavor."

Marianne thought of Noah. Even away from the strictures of British hierarchy, Noah's father had enacted the same pressure of familial duty upon him. And both men suffered for it.

Thoughts of Noah scraped across the fresh wound on her heart. A gust of chilled wind swept over her, thankfully drying the tears that formed in her eyes. She must stop thinking of him. She must accept her fate.

Reed cleared his throat and adjusted his neck cloth. "I am sorry your friends deserted you."

Marianne looked down, hoping he wouldn't see the tears fill her eyes.

"If it is any consolation, I've seen the captain release female prisoners before. Two French noblewomen taken off a supply ship." Mr. Reed gazed to the west, in the direction Marianne assumed was her home. Her country. "He set them ashore in France."

"I am no noblewoman, sir, as you can well see for yourself."

"But the captain likes you."

"Indeed?" Marianne chuckled at the absurdity of the statement, though at times she guessed it was true. "Thank you, Mr. Reed, but I'm finding hope to be a fickle friend. I prefer not to consider any other possibility but the station in which I find myself."

"Humph. A coward's declaration." His lips flattened in disdain.

Yet Marianne felt no anger at his insult. He simply did not understand. "No. A realist, sir. I am a realist."

"Even a realist leaves the possibility open for a miracle."

A miracle? Did he mean from God? She wanted to tell him she didn't believe in miracles—not anymore, but she simply gazed out to sea, too numb to argue.

He took a step toward her. "Allow me to escort you to your cabin, miss."

The statement seemed more of an order than a request. "Very well." She followed the tall man across the quarterdeck and down to her cabin where he left her with a nod and a "Good evening."

Closing the door, she leaned against it and peered into the shadows. With the marine stationed at the captain's cabin not ten feet away, this was the safest place on the ship, aside from standing right beside the captain himself.

Inching forward, she knelt before her bed. The ship creaked. The sea rushed against the hull in a continuous thrum as they sped north on their way to sink a ship of the fledgling United States navy.

And there wasn't a thing Marianne could do about it. Nor about her imprisonment, nor about the impending attack.

"I am alone."

"You are never alone."

A voice, loving and soft, heard, yet not heard, rang clear in Marianne's head. She glanced over the cabin, her heart lifting. "Everyone has left me."

"I have never left you."

"Oh Lord." She dropped her head into her hands. "Are You truly there?"

No answer came. Just a sensation of love, of peace, that whirled around her like a warm summer breeze. "Where have You been? Why have You allowed this to happen? Why am I here, Lord?"

A sail snapped above, and the ship canted. Marianne's knees shifted on the hard deck. An ache shot up her thigh. But no answer came.

Had she heard from God at all, or had she simply imagined it?

After several minutes, she crawled atop her bed, plopped down on the hard mattress, and forced her eyes shut. Better to drift asleep into sweet oblivion than to spend another night awake, haunted by her fears.

But sweet oblivion never came. Instead, Marianne wrestled with her coverlet for hours in a semiconscious dream state. Blurred images swept through her mind: Her father's bloated, white face staring up at her, his typical expression of bored despondency present even in death; the sea raging all around her, reaching liquid tentacles up to grab her; her mother, standing on their front porch, calling Marianne's name in despair; Lizzie, gaunt and thin from lack of food; and the agonized look on Noah's face before he leapt over the side of the ship—and abandoned her.

Marianne snapped her eyes open. She sat up, trembling, and wiped the perspiration from her forehead and neck. "Just a dream. Only a dream." She hugged herself.

Light from a late-rising moon entered the window in ghostlike streams of wispy milk, trickling upon her desk, the door, and bulkhead.

She lowered her chin, forcing down her loneliness and fear. Beside her on the bed, a black book glistened, drawing her gaze. A Bible—the Bible Daniel had given her. How had it gotten there? She'd been so mad at God last week, she'd stuffed it into the small trunk at the foot of her bed.

Grabbing it, she flipped it open and moved into the moonlight. She fingered the pages with reverence. The precious Word of God. How often had she read from it with zeal and anticipation? But that was a long time ago. When she believed the words. Before her father died and her world fell apart. "Where have You been?"

"I never left."

That voice again. So soft. So loving. And coming from deep within her. "Perhaps it was I who left You, Lord." She glanced over the room. "But how could I believe Your Word was true after Father died. No. Not died. Left." She wiped a tear spilling down her cheek. "Betrayed us. Abandoned us. If I couldn't trust him, how can I trust You?"

"I never change."

The unassuming statement settled in her mind, joining together abstract events from her past. If that was true, then God had known about—even allowed—all her tragedies. "Why has this happened to me?" Marianne flipped through the pages of the Bible with no destination in mind. The words grew blurry. Her finger brushed over the book of Esther, chapter four. Her mother's favorite book. Marianne could still picture her mother reading the story to her when she was a little girl. The way her face shone with excitement and her voice nearly sang as she relayed the romantic, adventurous story. The kind of adventure Marianne had come to believe only happened to beautiful, talented ladies. Not someone like her.

She skimmed over the tale, refreshing her memory. Esther, a common but beautiful girl, became queen of all Persia. But an evil plot had been hatched to annihilate Esther's people, the Jews. When her uncle begged her to go speak to the king on their behalf, Esther refused. To enter the king's presence without an invitation meant certain death. Marianne read down to her favorite part, Esther's uncle's reply, " 'Who knoweth whether thou art come to the kingdom for such a time as this?'"

The words seemed to fly off the page and circle her cabin, proclaiming their truth and dispelling the shadows. Marianne's eyes burned. She gazed at the words once more. A tear spilled onto the Bible—right in the center of the phrase.

Her throat went dry. "Is this for me, Lord? Is this a message?"

No answer came.

She kept reading, skipping down to Esther's last declaration. She would do as her uncle asked. She would do the right thing. She would approach the king. Marianne read her final words out loud. " 'If I perish, I perish.'"

Such faith. Such trust. She closed the book and laid it aside, wiping the tears from her cheeks. "Esther risked her life, believing You'd be with her, Lord. And she had an opportunity to save an entire race of people. What a destiny."

She lay back down on her mattress and listened to the pounding of the sea against the hull. But she was no queen. She couldn't save a nation. She couldn't even save herself.

❖ CHAPTER 24 ❖

Noah stood before the helm of his ship on the quarterdeck, boots spread apart, arms folded over his chest. A blast of hot summer wind punched him, clawed at his hair, and tried to shove him backward. But he stood his ground. He would surrender neither to the relentless wind nor to the dread churning in his gut.

He rubbed the sweat from the back of his neck, then raked his hair aside. It had grown long during the past month. What would his father think of Noah's shabby appearance? He snorted. Better yet, what would he think of Noah losing half his cargo and sailing his precious ship on its way to engage in a battle they were sure to lose? Noah chuckled as he pictured the expression on his father's face in light of such news, then surprised himself when he realized he no longer cared.

Marianne had changed all that. She had shown him that some things were more precious than wealth, than pleasing his father, than even his own life. In her, Noah had found the heart of an angel encased in a woman he would have shunned. But a heart that made her the most beautiful woman in the world to him. A heart loyal to country and family, an honorable heart, a loving heart—a heart he could only hope he was worthy to possess.

Shaking his head, Noah squinted against the bright sun as it began its trek back down to the sea. Ribbons of sparkling waves reflected a clear blue sky. If the wind continued blowing strong, Noah would make up the time he had lost when he had stopped in Charleston two days ago to send ashore those of his crew with enough sense to escape while they could.

Half his crew, to be exact. Leaving him with only twenty men, only five of whom had prior fighting experience. Mr. Weller, among them. Noah still couldn't believe the man had stayed and risked impressment again—or worse, death.

A gleam struck Noah's eye, and he squinted toward a swivel gun mounted on the foredeck. Cloth in hand, Daniel buffed the brass-capped barrel while Weller and Matthew hovered around the lad, pointing out different sections of the gun. Daniel nodded and listened intently, his expression beaming with eagerness to learn. Noah smiled. The boy added a spirit of innocent hope to the ship. A hope they desperately needed.

Eight guns lined his deck—eight four pounders against the frigate's thirty-two eighteen pounders and four twelve pounders. Not to mention that during battle, the crew of the frigate operated like a war machine, not like his bunch of shoddy, disorganized sailors.

He glanced at Luke who stood beside him. His jaw firm, his black hair blowing in the wind. The scar on his ear stood out in the afternoon sun. Noah had always wondered how Luke got the scar, but he assumed his first mate would tell him if he wanted to. The man had the morals of a rabbit, but the heart of a lion. He had no emotional investment in seeing that Marianne was safe. No loyalty for his country drove him to risk his life. He stood by Noah simply because they were friends.

Luke turned and gave him a knowing look.

"Unfurl the topgallants, Mr. Heaton. Set the stuns'ls. Let's bring her to a swift sail."

With a nod, Luke brayed commands over the ship, sending the men aloft as Daniel and Matthew leapt onto the quarterdeck.

The boy ran up to Noah, his eyes sparkling with excitement. "Mr. Hobbs and Mr. Weller showed me how to load, run out, and prime the gun, Mr. Noah."

Noah smiled at the boy. "Excellent." He may need the lad's help when the time came. Shielding his eyes from the sun, Noah found the boy's father up in the yards, unfurling sail. He, too, had stayed, despite the overwhelming odds against them. Despite the danger to his son.

"And a quick learner he be." Matthew patted Daniel on the back.

"Do you think we'll catch up with them?" Luke's blue eyes stood stark against the fading bruises on his cheeks.

Noah inhaled a deep breath of the sea air. "We have no choice."

"Of course we will." Daniel's voice carried not a shred of doubt as he leaned over the railing and closed his eyes to the wind.

"It's not the catchin' up that bothers me." Matthew doffed his hat and wiped the sweat from his brow. The afternoon sun gleamed off his bald head. "It's what happens when we do find them."

The sails caught the wind in a deafening snap, and the ship canted, picking up speed. The men grew somber, all save Daniel. He clung to the railing and smiled as if he hadn't a care in the world. Perhaps the boy knew something they didn't. If only Noah could know the future. If only he could know whether he led his men to their deaths.

"Daniel." Noah drew the boy's gaze his way. "Have you a word from God on our fate?"

"It doesn't work like that, Mr. Noah." Daniel shoved hair from his eyes and squinted into the sun. "If God has something He wants me to know, He tells me. If not, He don't."

The ship pitched over a wave, sending spray upon the bow. Noah spread his boots on the deck and huffed. "Then how is one supposed to trust Him without any direction?"

Daniel gazed at Noah as if he were the child. "God wants you to trust Him no matter if He tells you things ahead of time or not. Like it says in Romans. 'All things work together for good to them that love God, to them who are the called according to his purpose.'"

Luke snorted and took a step away, as if wanting to get out of ear-shot of the sermon.

Noah wished he could do the same. "Nice words, but I fear they don't apply to me."

Daniel shrugged. "You don't know the end yet."

"What's that, boy?" Luke inched closer, a frown on his face.

Daniel gestured toward Noah. "He doesn't know how the story ends. None of us do. Not until the day we die."

"Which may be sooner than we hope." Matthew chortled.

Daniel tugged up his oversized breeches—the only pair Noah had found onboard to fit the lad. "How do you know everything in your life is going to turn out for good if you're not at the end of everything in your life?"

Matthew's eyes flashed. "The lad makes a good amount o' sense."

"So, I must wait until my death to verify what God says is true?" The sarcasm in Noah's voice surprised even him.

"Or you can just trust Him now and be done with it." Daniel smiled. "Seems to me, He knows a lot more about our lives than we do. 'Sides, He loves us."

Noah flexed his jaw and he steadied himself as the ship bolted again. The faith of a foolish child. A foolish child who knew nothing of life.

Daniel's eyes twinkled. "What if God put together all the things that happened: me and my pa gettin' impressed, then you and your lady friend and crew bein' impressed, the escape, even leaving Miss Marianne behind"—the twinkle faded from his eyes for a moment—"all of it for this moment when a simple merchantman takes on a British warship." He grinned. "It could be your destiny."

"I don't believe in destiny," Noah growled, trying to ignore the lad, trying to ignore the longing buried deep within him—a longing for some meaning to his life.

Daniel frowned and lowered his chin. "It don't matter if you don't believe. You have a destiny just the same. But you have to surrender to God to find it." He shrugged. "An' then you have to do it."

Noah clenched his jaw. He patted his pocket where Jacob's bloody handkerchief lay. He knew the boy meant well, but Noah refused to believe destiny had led his brother to his death. Refused to believe in a God who allowed such a destiny. No, it was far easier to believe there was no such thing. That God was aloof and distant and kept His hand off the affairs of men.

"I feel God telling me that you do have a destiny, Mr. Noah," Daniel said. "Yes, a great purpose."

Noah pressed down upon the boy's shoulder, hoping to silence him. "I'm afraid God takes no note of me or my life."

"God takes note of everyone," Matthew added.

"I'll have no more talk of God or destiny!" Noah barked, instantly regretting his tone. "If the Almighty has been orchestrating my life, then He is nothing but a cruel taskmaster—one I will never be able to please."

"He's not anything like that, Mr. Noah." Daniel's voice weighed heavy with sorrow.

Luke excused himself and leapt onto the main deck. Noah couldn't blame him.

"If I didn't know better," Matthew said to Noah, "I'd think you were describin' your father." He gave Noah a look of disapproval before hobbling away.

Noah flinched. Was he mistaking God for his father? Hadn't Luke told him the same thing back on the frigate? But God had not proven himself to be any different from Noah's father. Both had far too many rules. And all it took was one mistake to invoke their disapproval.

A mistake like Noah's jealousy of his brother—a mistake that had sent Jacob to his death.

He wanted no part of a God like that.

The sun descended farther toward the horizon off the port side. He glanced aloft. Mountains of bloated canvas crowded the masts. Salty mist sprayed over his face as the ship rippled through the sparkling sea on a north by northeast course. If the weather and wind held, they would catch the HMS *Undefeatable* in no time.

"I'm coming, Marianne," he whispered into the wind. "Be strong, princess."

He drew in a deep breath and gripped the railing. Strength and an unusual, if not misplaced, confidence surged through him. Nothing could stop him now.

"A sail! A sail!" someone shouted from above. "Four points off the starboard beam."

Below, on the main deck, Luke darted to the railing and peered at the horizon.

Daniel stood at attention as Noah drew his scope to his eye. A two-masted sloop came into sharp view, the Union Jack flapping from her mainmast. He lowered the glass. Luke scrambled up the stairs and marched toward him.

"It's a British war sloop," Noah stated.

Luke nodded. "And she's bearing down on us fast."

❖

Gripping the broom, Marianne swept the painted canvas that served as a rug in the center of the captain's cabin and gathered the dust into a pile by the door. She had already scrubbed the deck, served the captain two meals, brought his clothes down to the laundry, and polished five lanterns that now hung in various spots on the bulkhead. Her back ached. Her feet hurt. And her stomach growled.

Sweep. Sweep. Dust flew through the air, transforming into tiny pieces of glitter that danced in the afternoon sunlight. Amazing how something so base and dirty could become so beautiful when exposed to the light. She pondered that thought as she watched the thin line of the distant horizon fill the stern windows, then fall out of view, then rise again, then fall. She barely noticed the sway of the ship anymore, barely had any trouble remaining upright. Another month out to sea, and she would forget what it felt like to walk on something that wasn't heaving to and fro.

She continued her sweeping. Ten days had passed since she'd read Esther. Ten days had passed since she thought she'd heard God's voice in her cabin telling her He loved her and was with her.

And nothing had happened.

If she was here for a purpose, other than cleaning and scrubbing and serving, she had no idea what it could be.

She sneezed and dabbed at the perspiration on her neck. It had been a little over three weeks since Noah had dropped over the bulwarks and disappeared into the sea. Since then, each day had slipped by, snatching a bit more of her hope in passing. If Noah had found his ship and intended to come after her, surely he would have arrived by now. She swept more dust into her growing pile. But why would he? What could he and his merchant ship hope to accomplish against such a formidable foe?

She was on her own.

"I am with you, beloved."

She sighed and gazed around the cabin. "Lord, where have You been?" She leaned on the tip of the broom. "I need You. I need to know what You want me to do."

"Trust Me."

Shouts filtered down from above, followed by the pounding of feet on the deckhead. Within minutes the snap of sails thundered, and the captain's booming voice rang through the timbers. Marianne stared above, wondering what caused all the commotion.

The sighting of another ship, perhaps? Her heart froze. The frigate jolted and the purl of the water against the hull grew louder. She listened for any further clues, but only the muffled voices of the crew and the chime of a bell drifted over her ears.

She pondered going aloft to see what was happening when the door swung open, crashing against the bulkhead. Marianne jumped, then moved out of the way as the captain charged into the cabin. Lieutenants Garrick, Reed, and Jones followed on his heels.

The stomp of their boots hefted her pile of dust into the blast of wind that entered behind them, scattering it across the cabin.

She blew out a sigh and laid a hand on her hip. Lieutenant Garrick's gaze slithered over her, and she resisted the urge to swat him with her broom.

Captain Milford circled his desk, dropped his spectacles onto his nose, and leaned over a chart.

The three lieutenants doffed their hats, stuffed them between their right arms and bodies, and lined up before him.

"Here we are." The captain's finger stopped on the chart. "And here is where we spotted her."

Lieutenant Reed leaned on the desk and peered at the chart. "I'd say not more than eight miles northeast of us."

The captain studied Mr. Jones. "Are you sure of what you saw?"

The thin, nervous man nodded. "Yes. American. I'd swear by it, Captain."

American. Marianne's ears perked up.

"If the admiral's information is correct, it must be the USS *Constitution.* We could be upon her tomorrow." Garrick's voice dripped with greed.

"Yes, my thoughts exactly, Mr. Garrick." The captain lengthened his stance and grabbed his chin. "Yet we were told to rendezvous with the *Guerriére* at this location." He pointed at the chart.

"Perhaps they spotted the enemy and took pursuit, Captain," Mr. Jones offered.

The captain's eyes twinkled. "And if so, I believe they would appreciate our help." He rubbed his hands together. Then grabbing four glasses from his cabinet, he lined them on his desk and poured brandy into each one. "We are at war, gentlemen. At war with a bunch of quarrelsome, jingle-headed farmers who have more backbone than brains!" He chuckled and grabbed his glass.

More backbone than brains, indeed. Marianne feigned disinterest as she kept sweeping.

Garrick stiffened his back and grabbed one of the glasses. "There's nothing like the pounding of the guns to get your blood pumping."

"The Americans don't stand a chance, sir." Reed took another glass. "Didn't the admiral say this laughable rebel navy only possessed six frigates, three sloops, and a few smaller vessels?"

Garrick's malicious laugher filled the cabin. "Compared to our six hundred warships, one hundred and twenty ships of the line, and one hundred and twenty frigates. Egad, are they mad?"

Marianne felt his eyes on her, no doubt hoping to gloat her into a reaction, but she kept her gaze on the deck. When he faced forward again, she swept dust onto his boots.

"It will be good to put these rebels in their place." Mr. Reed nodded.

Sweep. Dust showered over Mr. Reed's boots.

"And restore order to the colonies," Captain Milford said. "To the war, gentlemen." He lifted his glass.

Mr. Jones grabbed his.

"To victory!" Garrick said, and all four men raised their glasses together.

A sour taste rose in Marianne's mouth at their pompous display. The sharp scent of brandy filled the room.

"Besides, I hear their land is rich and free for the taking." Mr. Jones sipped his drink.

Marianne ground her teeth together and swept dust onto Mr. Jones's boots.

The captain gazed out the window. "Ah, a nice piece of land to call my own." He seemed to drift to another place as the men stood savoring their drinks.

"Blast it all!" The captain growled so loud even the lieutenants flinched. "Unfortunate that night falls within an hour."

"We shall catch them at first light, Captain," Reed said with confidence.

"If they have not outwitted us." The captain's weary eyes surveyed the chart. "We shall see." He raised a gaze to Garrick. "Maintain our present heading and place extra men in the masthead to keep a weather eye out for her." He slammed his glass down on the desk. "Let us find this American rebel and give her a hearty British welcome."

They all chuckled and tossed the brandy to the back of their throats.

Fire burned in Marianne's belly. Of all the impertinent, bombastic, audacious. . .who did they think they were? Congratulating themselves on a victory not yet won.

The captain grinned. "Who knows if we aren't here for such a time as this?"

Marianne froze. She lifted wide eyes to the captain, fully expecting to see his taunting smile directed toward her. But he paid her no mind and began pouring the men another drink.

"For such a time as this."

Marianne's heart sped to a rapid pace.

What are You trying to tell me, Lord?

"For such a time as this."

Yes, they were chasing an American warship, intent on destroying her. But what could Marianne do? She was a nobody. A prisoner. A servant. Was she supposed to take on an entire ship full of British sailors and soldiers?

She gripped the handle of the broom until her fingers reddened. Yet hadn't she done something similar on Noah's ship? Disabled the entire ship all by herself? She sighed and continued sweeping. There was no cargo to ruin on board this ship. What else could she do? She searched her mind for her conversations with Weller about accidents aboard a ship. What else had he said would disable a ship?

The tiller. Blood rushed to her head.

"Look what you've done, you insufferable woman." Lieutenant Jones stared down aghast at his dusty boots. The other men followed his gaze.

"Egad!" Mr. Reed lifted one foot up to examine the damage as Garrick's curse raked over Marianne's ears.

All eyes shot to her.

She shrugged. "My apologies, gentlemen. How careless of me." Forcing down a smile, she swept the broom over each of their boots, scattering the dust into a cloud.

The captain cleared his throat and gave her a look of reprimand that held a promise of punishment. But that didn't matter anymore. Marianne had a plan. And she knew exactly what she needed to do.

❖ CHAPTER 25 ❖

Noah studied the oncoming sloop. His gut wrenched. From what he could tell, she carried fifteen thirty-two pounders on her main deck, six twelve pounders on her quarterdeck, and two carronades mounted on her forecastle. Twenty-three guns in all and probably more that he couldn't see. He snapped his long glass shut. The *Fortune* pitched over a roller, and Noah gripped the railing. Salty mist stung his eyes. He gazed above where every inch of bloated canvas was set to the gusty breeze.

And still the sloop gained.

"Bring her as close to the wind as you can, Mr. Pike," Noah ordered the helmsman.

"Aye, aye, Cap'n."

The sails snapped. The ship canted to larboard as blue squalls swept over her deck. Noah balanced himself and stared at the oncoming ship. With the confidence of a mighty predator, she dashed after her prey, white spray foaming at her bow.

"What does she want?" Matthew staggered to Noah's side.

"We are at war. She intends to take us as a prize." Noah's voice gave no indication of the fear gnawing at his gut.

Weller mumbled beside him. A glaze of terror covered his eyes as he clutched the two fingers remaining on his right hand. "Not again."

Noah laid a hand on his shoulder, but the comforting words he intended to say withered on his lips.

The *Fortune* crested a wave, creaking and groaning under the strain. "It'll be worse this time." Blackthorn shifted his large frame. "Especially if they discover we escaped from the *Undefeatable*. We'll be hanged or sent to a prison hulk to rot until the war is over."

Noah shook the words from his ears. He would accept neither option. For both prevented him from rescuing Marianne and stopping the *Undefeatable* in its mission against the United States navy. His country's navy.

He surprised himself at the patriotism welling inside him.

"She's gaining, Captain," Luke shouted from the main deck below.

Noah squinted toward the sun, which sat a handbreadth over the horizon. He must stay outside the range of the British sloop's guns until nightfall. It was the only way. "Blackthorn, take Daniel and gather some men. Go below and find anything we can throw overboard, even our food if we have to, and bring it aloft."

Blackthorn nodded, cuffed Daniel on the back of the neck, and dragged him along. The boy laughed at his father's antics. Noah shook his head. Did nothing bother the young lad? Was his faith so strong that it pushed back all fear, even fear of death?

Two hours passed. The slowest two hours of Noah's life. An hour in which Noah's crew proceeded to toss bars of iron, bolts of cloth, sacks of flour, and kegs of water over the side. The *Fortune* picked up speed. But was it enough?

Relieving Mr. Pike at the helm, Noah took the wheel himself. He was desperate to keep busy—do anything besides standing and watching the sloop advance upon them. Weller paced the quarterdeck. Matthew dropped below to douse the fire in the stove and settle Agnes somewhere safe should a battle ensue. Luke stood like a stone sentinel at the stern railing, arms folded over his chest, staring at the oncoming ship.

A blast of salt-tainted wind tore at Noah's hair and shirt, bringing with it a hint of cool evening air. Darkness would be upon them soon.

"Mr. Weller." Noah stopped the man from his nervous pacing. "Gather the men and ready the guns, if you please." Not that the action would matter. The sloop's guns outranged Noah's and could easily hit their target before Noah would have any hope of striking in return.

Beneath the wild black hair lashing about his head, Weller's dark eyes found Noah's and a look of understanding passed between them.

With a nod, he leapt down the quarterdeck ladder. Daniel dashed across the deck to join him, excitement in his every step, making Noah wonder whether the boy's father would want his son assigned to such a dangerous post. But Blackthorn had jumped below again, searching for more things to toss overboard.

"She fired a gun!" Luke bellowed.

The lack of fear in his first mate's voice kept Noah steady on his feet. He'd barely swerved around when a resonant *Boom!* cracked the air. Gray smoke curled up like a charmed snake from the sloop's bow. The ball splashed impotently into the sea twenty yards off their stern.

Twenty yards too close.

"A warning shot." Mr. Pike offered as he approached Noah. "If ye don't mind, Cap'n, can I take back the helm? If I'm goin' t' die, I'd rather die at me post."

A weight seemed to fall on Noah at Mr. Pike's lack of confidence. But how could he blame the man? Noah had never engaged in battle before. He pried his fingers from the wood, not realizing until then how tight his grip had been, then stretched the kinks from his hand.

Luke sauntered toward him. "I believe they want us to stop, Captain."

Noah glanced at the sun barely touching the horizon. It would be at least an hour before the darkness would hide them. A very long hour. He snapped the hair from his face. "To the devil with what they want. Have the men go aloft and trim the sails to the wind again."

Luke gave an approving nod and shouted orders across the ship. Taking a spot at the stern, Noah raised the long glass to his eye but immediately lowered it. The sloop was so close he no longer needed it to make out the details of the ship. At least a hundred men crowded her decks. Crews hovered around the guns, petting and coaxing the iron beasts as they awaited their captain's command to fire. The captain stood on the quarterdeck. The gold buttons on his coat winked at Noah in the setting sun, taunting him to fight, challenging him just like his brother had done when they were younger.

Noah's nerves burned. His blood pounded in his head. "Another hour, Lord. Just give me another hour." He surprised himself with the prayer, but the harrowing situation called for desperate measures. If a miracle did not occur before the day was spent, Noah and his crew would be killed or captured. And Marianne would be doomed.

❖

With her ears tuned to the snoring that emanated from the captain's sleeping chamber, Marianne slid open one of the drawers in the massive oak desk.

It squeaked. The snoring stopped. She froze and listened for any movement. But only the creak of timber and slosh of water met her ears.

The captain resumed his snoring.

Drawing the lantern near, she sifted through the contents of the drawer: a quill pen, a bottle of ink, foolscap, the ship's log, a locket, and. . .there it was. A key. She gripped the cold metal and drew it to her bosom. Not just any key. The key to the cabinet full of weapons in the wardroom.

Where she planned on stealing a knife.

It had been a fairly easy task to draw the location of the key from the captain, especially after several more brandies and a spoonful of laudanum. Assured of his victory tomorrow over the American warship, he had been in a most jovial humor all night long—right up to the moment he'd dropped unconscious onto his bed.

Then she had only to wait a few minutes until his deep breathing confirmed that he was fast asleep.

Clutching the key in one hand and the lantern in the other, Marianne tiptoed out the door, down the passageway, then descended the ladder to the lower deck. Turning a corner, she pressed a hand to her chest to still her frantic heart. The dash of water against the hull joined the pounding of blood in her ears.

The ship groaned.

Footsteps sounded.

Marianne halted and backed against the bulkhead. Perhaps it was just the ship's timbers complaining as usual. She started again, this time more slowly. A light shone from the distance. Another lantern, a candle? But then it went out. Had she imagined it? Whispers curled around her ears. Or was it the purl of the water?

She should go back to her cabin.

But she couldn't. Tomorrow they planned on attacking an American ship—possibly the USS *Constitution*. She couldn't let that happen. Pressing forward, she entered the wardroom. The smell of whale oil and smoke and the dried beef the officers had for dinner whirled about her nose. Lifting her lantern, she scanned the shadows. No movement came from the officer's canvas cabins that lined both sides of the larger room. She prayed they were all fast asleep. The light reflected off the cabinet's glass doors. She squinted. Setting the lantern down on the table, she inserted the key and turned the latch. The door swung open with an aged squeak.

Marianne held her breath. She listened for footsteps, voices, but only the familiar hum of the ship and the snores of the officers met her ears. She perused the knives. Any one of them would do. She plucked a particularly long blade with a sharp point and lifted it toward the light to examine it. The wooden handle felt smooth in her fingers as the steel blade gleamed in the lantern light. Sliding it into her pocket, she closed the cabinet, grabbed the lantern, and dashed out the door.

Now to find the tiller.

She descended another level to the orlop deck. The smell of tar and human sweat burned her nostrils. Her hand trembled, and the lantern clanked. The flame sputtered then steadied. She wished her heart would do the same. With most of the crew asleep, this late hour afforded her the best possibility of completing her mission without drawing unwanted attention. But that didn't mean she wouldn't cross paths with one of them. Her lantern light skimmed over barrels, tackles, spare canvas, and ropes. Nothing that looked like a tiller.

The ship canted, creaking and moaning. She pressed onward. Sweat beaded on the back of her neck. Rats scattered before her arc of light, darting for the cover of the shadows. She shivered at the sight of them then entered a small space that, by her best calculation, should be directly below the wheel. She lifted the lantern to examine the room. Empty save for a stack of crates in the corner and a pile of cordage hanging from a nail in the bulkhead. She started to leave when something above her caught her eye. Two thick hemp ropes dropped down from holes in the deckhead. Strung through iron loops, they extended out along two sweeps of wood.

The tiller!

Reaching up, she brushed her fingers over the itchy, rough hemp. It scraped her skin. The lines were strong and sturdy and at least two inches thick.

But still possible to cut through with a knife.

But not yet. Since the tiller ropes could be repaired within a few days, she must wait until the *Undefeatable* engaged the USS *Constitution* in battle. And not a moment before.

Thank You, Lord. But now, I will need Your help when the time comes. She bit her lip. Would God use her to do this important task? A task that could change the course of history? Or was she only deceiving herself?

Time would tell.

Turning, Marianne hurried back the way she'd come.

And ran straight into Lieutenant Garrick.

❖

Noah spotted a yellow flame burst from the British sloop's hull. "All hands down!" He dove to the hard wood.

Boom! Cannon shot thundered across the sky. Tar and oakum filled his nostrils. He lifted his head. His crew lay scattered across the deck. Water splashed like a geyser not two feet off their starboard quarter.

He leapt to his feet. "Clear the deck! Lay aloft and ease the topgallants!" His gaze met Luke's as his first mate wasted no time in ordering the men to their tasks.

The pursuing sloop crashed through the waves a mile astern. A few more minutes and they'd be within firing range. "Man the guns! Load the chain shot," Noah commanded. At least they'd put up a fight before they'd all be killed. He fisted his hands until they ached. Confound it all. Blasted British.

The remainder of his crew who weren't in the shrouds or at the helm, swarmed the eight guns. With Noah's depleted crew, two men would be forced to do the jobs of three as they took their positions. Daniel and Blackthorn took one cannon at the stern, while Noah joined Weller at the other. A bucket filled with bags of powder sat on the deck along with a pile of shot. Mr. Lothar dashed across the ship, distributing red-hot cotton wicks soaked in lye to each team.

A gust of wind needled over Noah, carrying with it the sting of gunpowder. Off their starboard quarter, the British sloop shouldered the sea, foam cresting her bow. The Union Jack flapped at her mainmast, taunting Noah with the power and audacity of a nation who believed they ruled the seas.

His stomach crumpled. Thoughts of Marianne drifted through his mind. His heart ached. Would he ever see her again or would she be forever doomed to a life of slavery?

Noah gazed across his crew. All good sailors. But they weren't soldiers. Yet despite the terror screaming from their eyes, they manned their posts with bravado. "Good job, men," Noah said. "Steady there. Wait for my order." Noah tried to encourage them with a tone of assurance, yet it sounded flat coming from his lips.

A streak of bloodred sky spread across the horizon as the arc of the sun sank out of sight. A portent of their fate? Noah hoped not. He glanced above. Already the black sky descended, swallowing up any remaining light in its path. "I just need a few more minutes," he whispered again to no one in particular. Deep down he hoped the Almighty would hear and take pity on him. At least for Marianne's sake. And the sake of his crew. Men he was responsible for.

The *Fortune* flew through the sea with everything she could set to the breeze, plunging into the rollers and sending spray back over the deck.

One man at each gun held the burning wick, awaiting Noah's command. He studied their enemy. Not in range yet.

Darkness tumbled upon them. Noah peered toward Daniel and Blackthorn who manned the gun beside him. The red glow of the wick shook in Blackthorn's hands as the giant bear of a man hovered protectively over his son. Daniel stood his ground beside the carronade—the sturdy form of a boy with more courage and faith than Noah had ever seen.

Noah's throat went dry. Though only a shapeless gray mass, he could still make out the sloop as she swept alongside them, a half mile off their beam. The black mouths of ten guns on her larboard side gaped tauntingly at him. His nerves clamped.

They intended to fire a broadside.

"Hard to starboard, Mr. Pike!" Noah shouted. He'd cut them off and try to get close enough to cripple their rigging.

The ship groaned and heaved as the deck canted high in the air. Noah clung to the railing, Weller at his side. "On my order, Mr. Weller."

His gunner nodded.

Yellow flames burst from the British sloop.

"Fire!" Noah yelled. The boom of his guns merged with the simultaneous blasts of the sloop's ten cannons resulting in a thunderous volcano.

Shot whizzed by Noah's ears. He dropped to the deck. The crunch and snap of wood filled the air. A scream of agony. The *Fortune* jolted. Black soot settled on him like a death shroud. He coughed.

The beat of his heart drummed a funeral march in Noah's head. He shook the fog from his brain and struggled to his knees. Agonizing screams and harried shouts fired over the deck. Noah stood. Batting away the smoke, he eyed the sloop, her sails full, her rigging tight. His shots had not met their mark.

And still they came, veering to follow him.

The sound of coughing drew his gaze to Blackthorn and Daniel. They staggered to their feet, but they appeared unharmed.

Luke darted to his side, a bloody gash across his cheek.

"Damage?" Noah asked.

"Grainger is dead. Two others injured. Three of our guns were blown to bits, and they punched a hole in our forward hull. We're taking on water." Luke wiped the blood from his cheek with his sleeve.

Grainger dead. Noah lowered his chin. What had he done? But he couldn't think of it now.

"Put Mr. Lothar and Mr. Boone on the pumps at once. Have Matthew attend to the injured." Noah glanced at the sky, dark enough to see stars flickering back at him, and then at the sloop. Only the foam lining her gray hull gave away her position.

Which meant she could barely see the *Fortune* as well.

Luke brayed orders across the deck then returned to Noah's side.

"Relentless," Noah spat as he watched the sloop tack to starboard, no doubt in an effort to offer him another broadside. "She's like a mad demon."

Luke gripped the railing, his eyes narrowed on their enemy. A slow smile spread over his lips. "Even a demon can't see in the dark."

Noah nodded at his first mate. "Douse all lights. Every light." He directed Luke, then he turned toward Mr. Pike—ever faithful at the helm. "Three points to larboard, Mr. Pike." He faced Luke again. "Have the men lower topsails. Let's alter our position and see if we can't lose them in this darkness."

"Aye, Captain." Luke's approval beamed in his gaze as he turned and left.

Noah stared out upon the choppy waves of the ebony sea. He patted the stained handkerchief in his pocket. "I may be joining you soon, my brother."

With all lanterns snuffed, darkness hungrily consumed the ship, swallowing both sight and sound in every crack, plank, and timber. Only the wash of the sea against the hull and the occasional snap of sail as they tacked to starboard marked their position.

A yellow jet of flame burst in the darkness off their starboard beam, followed by an ominous boom. Noah's spine tightened. Could they see him? Was the *Fortune* outside their range? Seconds ticked by as long as minutes. Visions of his own splintered, crushed body flashed across his mind. But then a splash sounded off their starboard quarter, and he released a ragged sigh.

Matthew joined him. The metallic smell of blood filled the air. "Praise be to God, they can't see us."

"What of the injured?" Noah prepared himself for the answer.

"Mason and Crenshaw? They'll live." Matthew's normally cheery voice sounded as thick as molasses.

Blackthorn slipped beside Noah. "I'll bet on me mother's grave, those Brits'll be there in the morning. Sink me, I've served long enough wit' the likes o' them to know they never give up. They'll follow any spark of light, any sound, and be right on us at first light."

Noah frowned. The tiny thread of hope he'd been clinging to slipped through his fingers at Blackthorn's morbid declaration.

"He's right." Luke sighed.

"At the rate we're taking on water, it won't matter," Noah said. "We'll sink before dawn."

❖

Despite her trembling legs, Marianne squared her shoulders and gave Lieutenant Garrick her most defiant look. It did not, however, wipe the odious grin off his face or make him disappear. Instead, it emboldened him to take a step toward her and finger a strand of her hair. She batted his hand away and tried to skirt around him.

He blocked her exit. "What have we here? Come looking for me, perhaps?"

"Don't be absurd, Mr. Garrick." Marianne tried to shove past him, but he remained as immovable as a brick wall. She pursed her lips and dared a glance into his icy blue eyes. "If you don't mind, I shall be on my way."

"But I do mind, Miss Denton." He scratched the well-groomed

whiskers on his jaw. "Your absence above deck these past weeks has left me pining for a moment alone with you. Then what do I hear in the middle of the night, but you fumbling about the wardroom? Fortunate, indeed."

"Fortune has nothing to do with this." Marianne stepped backward. Her foot thumped against a barrel. A dull ache formed at her ankle.

Mr. Garrick's gaze leeched over her, sucking in every detail. "Whatever are you doing down here, Miss Denton? I perceive you are up to no good."

"I. . .I. . ." Marianne's knees began to quake. "I was searching for the surgeon. I do not feel well." Which was no lie as nausea began to brew in her stomach.

"Hmm. I am sorry to hear it." But his nasally voice indicated more disbelief than concern. "But you are nowhere near sick bay."

"I got lost."

He studied her. The lantern light accentuated the malevolence in his eyes. "Have you given much thought to my offer, Miss Denton?"

Marianne raised her nose. "Not a second's worth, Mr. Garrick."

"Hmm. Most unfortunate." He grinned and leaned toward her. "Most unfortunate for you, that is."

His hot breath, tainted with rum, wrinkled her nose. Marianne slipped her hand into the pocket of her skirt and searched for her knife. The thought of stabbing a man horrified her.

Mr. Garrick loosened the cravat around his neck. "Quite unsafe for a woman to wander around the ship at night."

"Pray don't trouble yourself, Mr. Garrick." She laid a hand on his arm to push him back. "I shall remedy the situation immediately."

Lieutenant Garrick clutched her shoulders.

Jerking from his grasp, Marianne stepped backward. The hard wood of the bulkhead blocked her retreat. "I implore you, sir, to behave with the propriety of an officer and a gentleman in the Royal Navy."

He chuckled. "A gentleman's chivalry extends only to ladies, not rebel wenches."

Indignation stiffened her jaw. "I am no wench, sir. I am a respectable lady."

"Upon my word, Miss Denton, what do you expect me to believe when I find you skulking around a place only meant for officers? No doubt you hoped to awaken me so I would follow you here. Ah, such sweet encouragement."

"I have given you no such encouragement, sir!" Marianne's throat closed. Her sweaty hands slid over the knife handle. She was beginning to think she could indeed stab a man—especially this particular man.

He extended his hand. "Give me the knife, Miss Denton."

So he had seen her. "I'll give you the knife." Marianne's tone held the sarcasm she intended. *Right through your black heart.*

In one swift movement, she tried to draw the knife from her skirts. The handle became entangled in the fabric. Her breath halted in her throat as she struggled to extricate the blade. Finally, she freed it. It slipped from her sweaty grip and clanked to the deck.

"Pathetic display, my dear." Garrick snickered as he kicked the blade out of her reach.

Any hope Marianne had fostered that she would escape this monster smothered beneath a wave of dread. *Lord, please help me.*

Garrick took the lantern from her grip and placed it atop a barrel.

"I'll scream." Her voice quavered.

"No, you won't." He slammed his hand over her mouth.

❖ CHAPTER 26 ❖

E ase her down slowly, Matthew," Noah whispered, not daring to use his normal voice lest the sound alert their enemies. He glanced up into the night sky lightly dusted with stars then over the ebony sea.

Matthew directed the two men holding the tackle ropes on either side of the cockboat. They released the lines inch by inch, and the boat slowly lowered over the side of the ship. As soon as they heard the craft strike water, Luke tossed a rope ladder over the edge. Blackthorn, unlit lantern in hand and rope tied about his thick waist, straddled the bulwarks and nodded toward Noah.

"Are you sure?" Noah asked him once more, barely making out his bulky form in the darkness.

"Aye. You got me off that British frigate. I owe you. 'Sides, I'm the strongest swimmer." He looked over the edge and shrugged. "I'll see you soon." His affectionate gaze took in Daniel before he dropped over the side and eased himself down into the rocking vessel.

"Be careful," Agnes called after him, drawing Daniel close to her.

"Pa can do this. He used to be a pirate," the boy whispered with glee.

Boom! A shot thundered in the distance, cracking through the nighttime silence and drawing each man's attention over their larboard quarter. The remnants of a flame drifted away in a tawny haze. The splash came, crisp and foreboding, just yards off their hull. Like all the other shots the sloop had fired that night.

Noah cringed. One more hit to their hull and they'd sink for sure. His crew had done their best to plug the hole with sailcloth, yet some seawater still seeped in through the canvas barrier.

Mr. Weller tugged at the scarf around his neck. "They ain't givin' up."

"So it would seem." Noah ran a hand over the back of his neck, moist with sweat, though the air was cool. Indeed, it appeared the sloop intended to keep firing their guns all night until they struck their target.

And Noah intended to grant them their wish.

"Mr. Heaton," he said. "Inform Mr. Pike to bring her hard to starboard on my signal. He glanced aloft but could not make out the men he'd stationed in the yards ready to adjust sail. Good. The moon had not yet made an appearance. He hoped it would sleep a little longer.

"Yes, Captain." Luke leapt up to the quarterdeck.

His men removed the tackles and handed Noah the other end of the rope attached to Blackthorn. He tied it to the bulwarks, then glanced over the railing. Too dark to see the boat below although he heard it slap against the hull.

"God be with you, Blackthorn," Noah whispered. He didn't know if the man heard him or not, but the rope grew taut in his hand, and he slowly released it bit by bit over the side.

Matthew took his place beside Agnes and Daniel. Weller leaned on the railing and peered into the darkness. Several minutes passed. The rope tightened with a *twang* and tugged at the knot tied around the bulwarks.

Blackthorn could go no farther. Silence settled on the ship as every crewman gaped into the black bowl surrounding them. A pinprick of light formed in the darkness. It blossomed into a small circle. A circle that wobbled with each passing wave.

Hurry, Blackthorn. The rope slackened then tightened again. A distant splash sounded.

Daniel shot Noah an excited glance. Clutching the rope attached to Blackthorn, Noah began pulling it over the railing, handing portions to Matthew and Weller beside him. Together the men groaned in silence as they heaved on the line.

Minutes passed. Noah listened for the sound of splashing.

A flash of yellow off their stern. *Boom!*

Resisting the urge to hit the deck, Noah hauled the rope. The muscles in his arms screamed. A splash echoed off the waves, not the one he hoped to hear, but one that, from its distance, told him the sloop had taken the bait.

Yet the light remained.

"Ahoy aloft!" Blackthorn's muffled voice rose from the sea.

"Papa!" Daniel peered over the side.

The rope slackened and Blackthorn stumbled over the rail, his chest heaving and his body dripping like a fish.

Noah clapped him on the back.

Daniel embraced him. "I knew you could do it."

Another gun blast thundered. Noah signaled the helm. The ship swerved to starboard, sails snapping in the wind. Noah and his men steadied themselves on the deck as Matthew supported his wife. A spray of white foam spit from their larboard point as the *Fortune* tacked away from the decoy they had planted.

The air went aquiver with the roar of guns. Leaping on the gunwale, Noah grabbed a backstay and stared behind them. The bobbing lantern exploded. Shards of wood and glass shot through the air. Then all went black.

Whispered huzzahs sprang from his crew.

Gesturing for them to be silent, Noah sprang into the ratlines and scrambled above to order his top men to furl sail. The slower the ship sailed, the less noise they would make. A gust of wind tugged at his hair and shirt and flapped his breeches. He'd made it to the lower yard before he noted an absence of fear—at least a fear of falling.

His top crew gathered around him to hear his orders, then went about their tasks. Sliding down the backstay, Noah landed with a thud then stared into the darkness behind him.

Hope caused his breath to quicken. Had they lost their pernicious pursuer in the darkness?

Boom! A yellow jet spiked upward, smoke curling in its wake.

Seconds crept by as Noah and his crew held their breath and waited for the ominous splash, the location of which would tell them if their ploy had worked.

Instead of a distant splash, the eerie whine of speeding shot followed by the snap and crack of wood filled the air around Noah.

❖

Marianne struggled against Lieutenant Garrick's grip. Pinned between the bulkhead and his fleshy body, she gulped for air beneath his sweaty hand.

Her attempts at screaming withered into moans.

Terror turned her blood to ice. She kicked him, clawed at him, but to no avail.

Please, Lord. But even as she said the prayer she knew it would take a miracle to save her. Noah was gone. There was no one on this ship to save her now.

His hands groped over her. He gave a heated groan. Nausea curdled her belly. He fumbled with the hooks on her gown.

"Unhand her at once, Mr. Garrick." The strength of the commanding voice left no room for argument.

Withdrawing from her lips, Garrick froze, his eyes simmering. A spark of fear skittered across them.

"I said unhand her."

Garrick took a step back. Marianne's head grew light, and she leaned against the bulkhead to keep from tumbling to the deck.

Garrick slowly turned to face Lieutenant Reed who stood as prim and proper as ever, a look of abject revulsion on his face.

"This is none of your affair, Reed." Garrick sneered. "Go back to your bed and leave us be."

"The captain ordered you to stay away from Miss Denton, I believe, which makes it every bit my business."

Marianne's breath returned to normal as she studied the two men. They stood sizing each other up like lions battling over prey.

Garrick snorted. "And of course you will run and tell the captain like the bootlicking lackey you are."

Mr. Reed lifted a haughty brow. "Since you are assured of my actions, you must know the outcome does not bode favorable for you."

"That is where you are wrong, sir." Garrick gave a pompous snort. "The captain and I have an arrangement."

"Yes, I know of your arrangement. And it stretches only as far as the captain's patience. Which as we both know is as fickle as an ocean squall."

A spark of fear crossed Garrick's eyes, but he stood his ground.

"And you do know the punishment for ravishing a woman is death, do you not?" Mr. Reed raised his brows.

"Not for me, it won't be." Garrick snorted. "Besides, she's the enemy.

No one would fault me for putting her in her place."

"Enemy or not, you know the captain favors her." Mr. Reed shrugged. "I wouldn't risk it if I were you."

Garrick wiped the spit from his lips and fingered the service sword hanging at his side. "What's to stop me from killing you and throwing your carcass to the sharks?"

"Perhaps the fact that I won the Royal Naval College swordsmanship competition the year I graduated." An arrogant smile danced over Mr. Reed's lips as his hand crept down to the hilt of his sword.

Lieutenant Garrick narrowed his eyes. His breathing grew rapid. "Madness." Casting Marianne a look of disgust, he shoved past Mr. Reed. At the foot of the ladder, he faced them. "You will regret this. Both of you."

"I never regret, Mr. Garrick. Good evening to you." Mr. Reed's calm voice soothed over Marianne. Grumbling under his breath, Garrick leapt up the ladder and disappeared.

"How can I thank you, Mr. Reed?" She released a heavy sigh and took a step toward him.

"What, pray tell, are you doing down here in the middle of the night?" Anger shot from his hazel eyes. "I cannot help you if you put yourself in such compromising positions. Now, come along and I'll escort you to your cabin."

Marianne dropped her gaze to the knife lying on the deck by the barrel. She must retrieve it without Mr. Reed's notice. She must have that knife or all would be lost. If she didn't pick it up now, someone would, no doubt, find it tomorrow. She kicked off one of her shoes.

"Forgive me, I behaved foolishly." She laid a hand over her heart and leaned on the barrel, feigning a loss of breath. She must delay him. "How did you know we were here?"

The harsh look on Mr. Reed's face faded. "I heard Garrick rise from his bed and leave. Something told me to follow him." His brow wrinkled. "I am sorry for your distress."

Marianne gazed up at him. "You are an honorable man for an Englishman."

"We are not all like Mr. Garrick." He chuckled then proffered an elbow. "Shall we?"

Marianne pressed a hand to her back and started to rise, then she glanced at her feet. "Oh, my shoe. Please forgive me, Mr. Reed." She knelt. Fluttering her skirts around her as cover, she grabbed a shoe in one hand and the knife in the other. Slowly, she rose to her feet, tucking the blade within the folds of her skirt while she eased her foot into her shoe. The knife once again became entangled in the fabric. She could feel the tip tugging at the folds. She only prayed it wouldn't tear her gown. Her heart took up a rapid beat as she smiled at Mr. Reed and placed her other hand on his arm.

The curious look on his face made her blood run cold. "Egad, Miss Denton, what is that in your hand?"

❖

Noah gripped the ledge until his knuckles grew red and gazed out the stern windows of his cabin. A streak of orange flame lit the horizon. He froze in the dark, awaiting the explosion. The menacing splash grated over his tight nerves. Close. Too close. This British captain was savvy. Not a single lantern or candle was lit on the *Fortune*, and still he seemed to know where they were. The last strike had taken a chunk out of their capstan. Noah feared much worse the next time they came within range.

The savage dash of water against the hull told him the *Fortune* sailed only as swiftly through the dark seas as the rent in her hull allowed. Not an altogether safe thing to do when they couldn't see two feet off their bow, but Noah had deemed the fate that followed them to be far worse than the risk of striking a reef or another ship.

Confound it all! Noah fisted his hands across his chest and squinted into the darkness. Nothing but black as dark as coal met his gaze. Only the few stars twinkling overhead separated sky from sea. Like Noah, the British commander had extinguished all lights on board his ship. Only the occasional flashes from the sloop's guns gave away their position. A position that seemed to be forever in Noah's wake.

If he could not evade this monster by daybreak, all would be lost.

The anxious gazes and fainthearted groans of his crew had forced Noah below where he could steal a moment alone and try to formulate a plan of escape. But after an hour, none had come to mind. None but pleading with God for their salvation. And that plan offered no more hope than any other.

I have led these men to their deaths. Noah swallowed down the burning in his throat. Just as he had caused his brother's death. Was this to be his legacy? Not only a failure, but also a murderer?

His thoughts swarmed around Marianne, another of his victims. With Noah killed or captured, she was as good as dead. *"I'll come back for you, I promise."* His last words to her chanted a woeful melody in his mind. Another promise he could not keep. And for Marianne, another person she could not trust.

Noah's heart felt as heavy as a thirty-two pounder and just as deadly. Because of him, everyone he cared about was in harm's way. Everyone he cared about would soon be dead. He was nothing but a disappointment, just as his father had always declared.

The man's rage-filled face bloated in Noah's mind. "You'll never live up to your brother. Never," he spat in disgust then wiped his mouth with his sleeve.

And Noah hadn't. Not only had he not lived up to Jacob's legacy, but with this last venture, Noah had far exceeded his own record of shortcomings.

Boom! The thunder of another cannon pounded the air. Noah gazed at the smoke spiraling upward in the distance, no longer bracing himself for the blast. What would it matter? Perhaps it would be better to get it over with.

The splash crackled the air as if laughing at him. Much closer this time.

"I could never please you, Father." Noah leaned back on the edge of his desk and hung his head.

"You please Me."

Noah's heart picked up a beat. He glanced over the dark cabin. The terror of his impending death had no doubt befuddled his mind. Withdrawing the stained handkerchief from his pocket, Noah placed it over his heart. "If I make it to heaven, brother, I hope you won't be angry at me."

If *I make it to heaven*. But why would God let him through those holy gates? He'd been nothing but incompetent his entire life. Even in his death, Noah would fail. God would no doubt raise His voice in indignation, spout a litany of Noah's failures and cast him from His sight.

"I am not like your father."

That voice again, soft, confident, coming from within him. Emotion clogged Noah's throat. He had called both God and his earthly father cruel taskmasters. Was it possible, as both Matthew and Luke had said, that Noah confused the two?

The blast of a cannon roared.

"I love you. I am proud of you."

Proud of me? Noah rose and took up a pace before the windows. Nothing but his warped imagination turned the creak and groan of the ship into words he longed to hear.

Splash. Closer still.

Yet the promise imbedded within that gentle voice was too much to ignore.

"If that's You, God, where have You been?"

"I have never left."

The gentle words floated around Noah, penetrating his heart with their truth. He was the one who had left God. But who could blame him? After God allowed Jacob to fall to his death? After He allowed Noah to carry the guilt for all those years?

"Why, God, why?"

"You do not know the end yet." Daniel's ponderous words echoed through the darkness. Noah pivoted and headed back the other direction. But what happy ending could such a tragedy produce?

"Trust Me."

A cannon thundered. Noah halted his pacing and stared out the window. Yellow smoke dissipated into the darkness just like his faith had done so many years ago. "Trust You with an ending when the beginning has been so horrid?" Noah shook his head and balled the handkerchief in his hand.

No answer came save the moan of the ship and the rush of water. He wanted to trust God. He wanted to believe there was some purpose to this madness. Some reason for the tragedies. Someone who truly loved him.

But would a God who loved him do the things He. . .

"Trust Me."

His brother's smiling face formed out of the darkness. He winked at Noah and flashed a challenge from his blue eyes so full of life and adventure. Guilt pressed heavy on Noah, forcing him to his knees.

"Give Me your guilt, son. I will take it from you."

He squeezed his eyes shut. "I don't know how." A sense welled up in his belly. A strong sense that Jacob's death happened for a reason, that there was nothing Noah could have done to prevent it. Nothing would have changed an outcome predestined from before time.

"But why make me a part of it?"

"Give Me the guilt."

"Please tell Jacob I'm sorry."

"He knows."

A cannon thundered as if affirming the statement.

Noah squeezed the handkerchief to his chest. "God, can you ever forgive me? For turning away from you? For my anger toward you?"

"I already have."

Wiping the moisture from his eyes, Noah shifted his shoulders. He felt as if a massive weight had been torn from his back. He drew in a deep breath and his lungs, his very spirit, filled with such a strong sense of love it threatened to knock him over.

He rose, feeling light as a topsail fluttering in the wind. "I've been such a fool, Lord. My anger kept me separated from You—from this." A love so consuming, so pure, it filled every crack and crevice in his heart. He bowed his head. "My God and my King."

Boom!

He lifted his gaze to the flash in the distance. His predicament had not changed. "Lord, if You could, please save us so we can go save Marianne. But if not, if that is not Your will, please save her and bring her home."

Boom!

Wood snapped. Glass flew through the air in an ear-piercing shatter. The last thing Noah remembered was his face hitting the deck.

❖ CHAPTER 27 ❖

Marianne bit her lip. Her legs wobbled. "To what are you referring, sir?"

Mr. Reed gave her a caustic look. "I am referring to the long knife you are hiding in your skirts, miss."

"Oh, that." Her heart sank. Freeing the blade from the folds of her gown, Marianne lifted it, point forward.

Without warning, the lieutenant grabbed her wrist, plucked the knife from her grasp, and released her hand.

Marianne rubbed the mark he left on her skin.

Mr. Reed studied her. "Where did you get this?"

She glanced at the knife Mr. Reed so casually held in his hand. She must get it back. Without it, she would be helpless to assist her country. But surely this officer would never allow someone who was, for all practicality, a prisoner on board this ship, to have a weapon. Unless. . .

"Mr. Reed, I beg you. Allow me to keep it. I only intended to borrow it for a time. To ward off Lieutenant Garrick. Surely you won't deny an innocent woman the protection she needs against such a lecherous villain." She drew her lips into a pleading pout that she feared made her look ridiculous.

But Mr. Reed did not laugh. Instead, he fingered his chin, his gaze flickering from the knife in his grip to her eyes and back again.

His hesitation gave her hope. "Even if I promise to avoid Mr.

Garrick, you know as well as I there is no guarantee of my safety," she added.

"If you aspire to avoid Mr. Garrick, miss, might I suggest you avoid wandering about the bowels of the ship alone at night." He spit out the last word with sarcasm.

Marianne looked down so he couldn't discern the lie in her eyes. "It couldn't be helped. I was not well and needed the surgeon."

He released a sigh of frustration. "Could it not wait until morning? When you could have the captain summon him for you?"

"I'm afraid not, sir."

"Very well, let me show you the way."

She saw his boots turn and his elbow came into her view. She lifted her gaze and offered him a sweet smile. "No need. It seems I have recovered."

"Just like that."

"I believe Mr. Garrick frightened my illness away."

"Perhaps we should employ him as surgeon instead of first lieutenant. Then he could go about scaring everyone into perfect health." He cocked a brow.

A giggle rose to Marianne's lips, but she held it back. "May I have the knife, Mr. Reed?"

"I could be court-martialed."

"No one need know." Marianne saw the tight muscles in his face loosen. "Please, sir. It is bad enough I am a slave aboard this ship, but must I suffer ravishment as well?"

His hazel eyes darkened. Releasing a sigh, he flipped the knife and handed it to her, handle first. Grabbing it before he changed his mind, Marianne slipped it into her pocket.

He offered her his elbow. "What knife?" His lips curved in a rare smile that made him appear quite handsome.

Taking his arm, Marianne allowed him to lead her back to her cabin. Every step heightened her fear that the lieutenant would come to his senses and take back the blade. Perspiration trickled down her back as they navigated the dark companionway. Finally at her cabin, she opened the door and spun around to thank him, but he had already disappeared into the shadows.

Closing her door, Marianne took a deep breath to steady the thrash of her heart. *Thank You, Lord.* Plucking the knife from her pocket, she held it up to the moonlight, its blade a silver slice in the darkness. *Perhaps You are on my side, after all. Perhaps You do have a task for me to accomplish.* For tomorrow, if they came across the USS *Constitution*, Marianne would be ready.

❖

"Captain, Captain." The word tugged on Noah's consciousness, dragging him back to the living.

"Captain." Arms lifted him from behind. Gunpowder and smoke filled his lungs. He coughed and struggled to rise, struggled for a breath, struggled to open his eyes, yet deep down within him, afraid to struggle for anything.

"Captain, we're hit, and the sloop is fast on our wake." The urgency in Luke's voice slapped Noah like a wall of icy water.

Batting Luke's hands aside, Noah rose to his feet and opened his eyes to what was left of his cabin. Wind blasted in through the broken windows. The scent of the sea joined the smoke and the smell of charred wood. Half his desk was missing, leaving nothing but wooden spikes and burnt shavings. Shards of glass littered the deck, and all that remained of one of his chairs was a pile of splinters. A jagged hole pierced his canvas rug. Leaning over, he peered through it to the deck below. Nothing but darkness. At least the shot had not started a fire.

Matthew flung a strip of cloth around his head and began tying it in place. Only then did Noah notice the blood trickling into his eyes.

Wiping it away, he pushed the men aside and barreled for the door. "Status," he barked to Luke.

"Just the one hit to your cabin, Captain." Luke's voice trailed him. "And we are still taking on water."

"The pumps aren't working?"

"The water is leaking in too quickly."

Noah leapt on deck and then up on the quarterdeck. The nervous whispers of his crew joined the creaks and rush of water. Off their stern, their enemy lurked, cloaked in the invisible shroud of darkness.

"Two points to starboard," Noah whispered to Mr. Pike. "Slow and easy."

Sails snapped in the night breeze. The ship's tilt to starboard was barely discernable.

Noah took up a position at the stern railing, Luke by his side.

Tension stalked the decks like a nefarious demon. But despite their dire predicament, Noah felt no fear. Renewed faith surged through him. He was no longer alone. Almighty God was with him, and He had all things in His hands. Noah bowed his head. *My life is Yours, Lord. Let Thy will be done.*

A jet of bright yellow in the distance followed by a threatening boom seemed to seal their fate.

Yet. . .

The splash landed several yards off their larboard quarter.

Minutes passed. Weller, Blackthorn, and Daniel joined Noah and Luke. All five men formed a staunch line of defense across the stern railing.

Another thunderous blast cracked the silence.

Yet no one spoke.

Not even when the next roar came from even farther away.

No huzzahs. No yells of triumph. Just the silence of men who had let go of hope and who didn't want to cling to its fickleness so soon again.

Noah continued praying silently.

He was still praying an hour later when a thin strip of gray lined the horizon.

With cautious hope, he scanned the sea surrounding the ship. Nothing. Yet still too dark to tell.

Weller coughed.

Daniel began humming a tune.

Minutes passed. The gray strip transformed to saffron and began pushing back the darkness.

Noah swallowed. He gazed over the calm sea, his heart in his throat. Nothing in sight but cobalt blue, furrowed with creamy ribbons. Slowly turning, he took in the entire panorama. Not a hint of sail or mast marred the golden horizon.

"Masthead, what do you see?" Noah yelled to the lookout above.

"I see nothing, Captain. Not a thing!"

The sun peeked over the horizon. Wave crests glittered with golden light.

Huzzahs rang through the ship, pushing the tension overboard to the depths.

Thank You, Lord.

Luke slapped Noah on the back and nodded his approval.

Weller's shoulders lowered, and he released the loudest sigh Noah had ever heard.

"God protected us." Daniel's voice sounded like an angel's. He gazed up at Noah with sparkling brown eyes.

"Yes, He did." Noah drew the boy to himself and gripped his shoulder.

Luke crossed his arms over his chest. "God? Humph."

Blackthorn scratched his head. Morning sunlight turned his tan face to bronze and accentuated his two missing teeth. "Sink me. I'm startin' t' believe that as well."

"I told you, Pa, I told you." Daniel smiled up at his father.

Luke rolled his eyes and turned away. "Where should we point her, Captain?"

"North by northwest. I still intend on overtaking the frigate."

"With a rent in our hold?" A breeze whipped Luke's hair about his head.

Noah furrowed his brow. "Very well, furl sail and send a crew down to patch the hole as best they can and pump out the remaining water. Then we must be on our way."

Every minute they delayed meant another minute Marianne must suffer aboard that British frigate.

"We've lost three guns, Cap'n." Weller gaped at Noah as though Noah's mind had also been a casualty of the battle.

"Aye, but we have five left, do we not?" Noah forced confidence into this tone, but Mr. Weller simply frowned.

Daniel, however, beamed a hearty grin. "That's the way, Mr. Noah!"

Blackthorn gazed out to sea then drew Daniel close. "Ye know my thoughts on the matter. Pure foolery."

Noah chuckled. "And it wasn't pure foolery when we had all eight guns?"

Blackthorn nodded and joined in his laughter.

With a smile, Luke turned and began shouting orders to furl sail.

Noah touched his shoulder. "Wait, let me speak to the men first."

Luke nodded then cupped his hands around his mouth. "Belay that. All hands, assemble amidships!"

Taking a position at the quarterdeck railing, Noah gazed at his measly crew as slowly one by one, his men mustered on the main deck, their curious gazes filtering upward. A surge of pride rose within him at their loyalty and courage.

Taking a deep breath, he said a silent prayer for the right words. Something had changed during the long night, during the fear, during the thunderous blasts, during the heartache. Noah had not only renewed his relationship with God, but the Lord had forgiven him and filled him with such love he'd never known.

And now he knew what he was supposed to do.

"We are no longer a private merchantman." He began, ignoring the quizzical groans. "As of today, we are no longer the *Fortune*." The groans silenced and a sea of wrinkled brows stared back at him. "Today, gentlemen, we are the *Defender*." Noah raised his hand. "I deem this ship a privateer for the United States of America. Let us defend the freedom we have come to love. Let us defend our homes, our families, our cities from the pompous tyranny that is trying to crush us."

The men stared agape at him. Seconds passed. Would they join him? Or would they think him mad?

"But don't we need a letter of marque or somethin'?" Mr. Simon said.

"And more guns?" Mr. Boone chuckled and his fellow sailors joined him.

"Yes, we do." Noah's shout silenced the laughter. "Items I intend to procure next time we make port. But for now, we haven't the time to follow proper procedure. We must help defend the USS *Constitution*."

"An' risk bein' hanged as a pirate?" Mr. Lothar spit to the side.

"Some things are worth the risk, Mr. Lothar." Noah gazed across the grimy faces of his crew. Exhaustion tugged on their haggard skin. "Are you with me?"

The wind blasted over them. A snap sounded from above, and all eyes shot to the American flag flapping on the gaff of their foremast, its red and white stripes waving proudly in the breeze. Each man seemed mesmerized by its beauty.

One by one they dropped their gazes as shouts sprang from their midst.

"For America!"

"We are wit' you, Cap'n!"

"For freedom!"

"For the prize money!" one man yelled, eliciting chuckles from the others.

The men pumped fists into the air.

Luke gave Noah a slanted grin and shook his head. He faced the crew. "Let's be about it, men. Rupert, aloft to furl sail! Mr. Boone, fetch planks and nails to repair the hole!"

The men scattered to their duties.

"Pa, you get to be a pirate again." Daniel snapped hair from his face.

Blackthorn grinned, revealing the black holes of his two missing teeth. "Aye, but not for treasure this time, son. For something far more valuable: honor and country and the life of an innocent woman."

Patting the handkerchief in his pocket, Noah leapt on the gunwale. He grabbed a line and leaned over the churning waters. A crisp morning breeze played with his hair and filled his nostrils with the briny smell of the sea. Blood pumped through his veins, heightening his senses, strengthening his resolve. A sense of purpose filled him. And for the first time in his life, he felt as though he had finally come home.

Perhaps he did have a destiny after all.

Perhaps this had been his destiny all along.

❖

Marianne hefted the sack of laundry in her arms and trudged down the ladder. She blew a breath toward her forehead, sending her hair fluttering and cooling the perspiration on her brow. The smell of rot and sweat and bilge assailed her. Would she ever get used to the foul stench of a ship below deck? Or the heat?

Eight days had passed since she'd hidden the knife in her cabin. Eight days and they'd not come across a single ship, American or otherwise. Eight days in which she'd been forced to endure the captain's furious grumblings as he pored over his charts and snapped at anyone who dared enter his cabin. Marianne was beginning to think she'd risked Mr. Garrick's ravishment to steal a blade she would never need.

Sorrow tightened her throat. Perhaps she had not heard from God. Perhaps she had no destiny at all.

Making her way to the laundry, she lowered the stuffed bag and tossed it beside the others. Griffin, the sailor who cleaned the captain's clothes, looked up from the huge water-filled barrel he stirred and gave her his usual scowl. Black soot blotched his face and his muscled bare arms. Marianne resisted the urge to suggest he dunk himself in the barrel along with the clothes.

Turning, she withdrew her handkerchief and dabbed at the perspiration on her neck and face. The day, like all the others before it, had slogged by with a legion of chores and errands until the ache in her feet matched the one in her back. Possessed by one of his foul moods, the captain had spent the day in his cabin ordering her about and criticizing everything she did. She had not laid his tooth powder and cloth out properly. The water in his basin wasn't warm enough. She'd forgotten his morning sip of brandy. She'd missed a few specks of dust on his boots. After a while Marianne had drowned out his incessant whining and simply nodded and went about her tasks— tasks that had become so routine to her, her mind could be occupied elsewhere with thoughts of distant lands and magical places where she was free and happy and not a prisoner aboard a British warship.

But much to her dismay, Noah always appeared in those distant lands. It had been a little over a month since he'd dropped over the side and left her. Why couldn't she get him out of her mind? Instead of dwelling on what could never be, she'd resorted to praying for him and for Luke, Weller, Blackthorn, and precious Daniel. Praying they were all safe somewhere.

She pressed a hand on her back and started on her way back to the captain's cabin when a burst of muffled thunder echoed through the timbers of the ship. A storm? *Lord, not another storm.* Memories of the last storm she had endured pushed themselves forward in her mind. And there she found Noah again, coming to her cabin to comfort her.

"You enchant me." The memory of his soft words lit a dark place in her heart. She could still see the look of adoration in his blue eyes, so clear and bright against his tawny skin. She could feel his gentle embrace, could sense his warm breath on her neck and his lips on hers. Heat swept over her as she ascended the ladder.

Did he love her? Or was it just the allure of the moment? Regardless, he had not come back for her. He had left her a prisoner both of this ship and of her memories. Memories of being loved and cherished by an honorable man—if only for a moment.

Boot steps pounded on the deck above as she made her way upward. Shouts flew like pistol shot through the air, the captain's authoritative voice chief among them.

Thunder bellowed again in the distance.

All this commotion for a storm?

Curiosity drove Marianne farther above where she halted at the head of the companionway and stared at the flurry of sailors dashing about the deck. A brisk wind wafted around her, playing with the hem of her skirt and fluttering her wayward strands of hair. The captain and his officers stood at the quarterdeck stanchions, taking their posts as masters of the sea, their jaws tight and their eyes focused straight ahead.

The ship bolted. Bracing her feet, Marianne wove through a mob of sailors to the railing. Following the gazes of the officers, she squinted against a setting sun to see the faint tips of masts, crowded with snowy sail, poking above the horizon.

Gray smoke puffed and the thunder bellowed again. That was no storm. It was *cannon fire*. Her heart clamped. Had they found the *Constitution*? Too far away to tell.

And who was firing at whom?

As the frigate sped toward the battling ship, Marianne's gaze distinguished the masts as two sets from two different ships. A cloud of smoke filled the gap between them.

She glanced aloft. With all sails crowding the masts and bursting with wind, the *Undefeatable* flew through the water like an angry demon out for blood. The ship pitched over a rising swell. Salty spray showered over Marianne, threatening to loosen her firm grip on the railing. Her stomach flipped and nausea boiled within. Fear of the sea, fear of death, fear of living out her days on board this ship caused the blood to swell in her head until it throbbed.

Though longing to go below to the false safety of her cabin, Marianne kept her feet in place. At least until she discovered the identity of the ships.

French, British, or American? She shifted her gaze between Captain Milford, his officers, and the ships, knowing one or all of them would soon answer her questions.

Above her, top men scurried across lines to adjust and tighten the canvas to the wind. Thank God Noah was not among them anymore.

Another thunderous boom echoed across the graying sky. "Bear off, haul your braces, ease sheets!" Mr. Garrick shouted.

Minutes passed as the *Undefeatable* plunged through roller after roller, riding the sea high and wide, foam spraying over the deck.

Marianne craned her neck and she squinted toward the ships, but she couldn't make out their ensigns.

"It's the HMS *Guerriére!*" Captain Milford barked, lowering his spyglass.

As the ships closed in on one another, the sky exploded in a barrage of cannon fire and the *pop pop pop* of musket shot. A thick cloud of smoke consumed the two ships. When it cleared, one of the vessels veered toward the setting sun, bringing its flag into full view. The red and white stripes and star-studded blue flapped proudly in the evening breeze.

The USS *Constitution*. And she seemed to be holding her own against the British warship. Marianne's heart swelled with pride, then shrank in fear.

The *Constitution* was no match for *two* British warships.

"Clear for battle!" Lieutenant Garrick bellowed. "Starboard guns stand by!"

The fife and drum played the "Heart of Oak," signaling the call to quarters. A shrill whistle sent sailors scrambling over the deck, removing all obstructions and sprinkling sand across the planks. Some landed on her shoes. Crewmen rigged nets over the deck to protect those below from falling blocks and other tackle. Gun crews mobbed the guns as powder boys leapt above from the hatches carrying the powder bags, wads, and shot. Marianne thought of Daniel and thanked God he wasn't here as well.

But she was. And she had to do something.

Boom boom boom boom boom, the blast of a broadside drew her gaze back to the battling ships, not more than fifty yards away now. When the smoke cleared, the *Guerriére's* main yard hung shattered and lifeless. She resisted the urge to raise a huzzah in the air. Excitement charged through her as the *Constitution* bore around the British ship yet again. The air thundered with another broadside. Marianne held her breath until the sooty smoke cleared. The mizzenmast of the *Guerriére* dragged lifeless in the water. *Thank You, Lord*. The *Constitution* was winning!

Could the ship also beat the *Undefeatable* and rescue Marianne? Dare she hope?

"Run out the guns!" Mr. Reed's deep voice bounced over the deck.

The *Undefeatable* would be upon the ships within minutes. Marianne faced the battling duo again just in time to see the two ships ram into each other and the *Guerriére's* bowsprit become tangled in the *Constitution's* fallen lines. Musket and pistol shot popped through the air. Along with the screams of men.

A gust of wind struck her, bringing with it the sting of gunpowder.

"We've got her now!" Captain Milford shouted.

He was right. Entangled as she was and unable to maneuver, the *Constitution* would have no defense against the *Undefeatable*'s broadside.

Panic iced through Marianne. She must do something. Perhaps this was her time. Perhaps she'd been placed here for such a time as this.

❖ CHAPTER 28 ❖

S ail-ho!" A shout bellowed from the masthead.

"Where away, Mr. Crenshaw?" Noah scanned the surrounding sea.

"Off our starboard bow, Cap'n."

Plucking his scope from his belt, Noah jumped onto the main deck and raised it to his eye. Steadying it against the rise and fall of the ship, he focused on the fading horizon.

"Two sets of sail!" the shout spiraled down from above just as the billowing canvas came into view.

Noah lowered the scope. "Four points to starboard, Mr. Pike," he yelled over his shoulder. "All hands on deck. Let go the topgallants!"

Behind him, Luke repeated orders that sent his meager crew scurrying into the shrouds.

Noah braced his boots over the hard planks as the ship veered to starboard. Wind whipped his hair, tossing it in his face. He snapped it away and raised his glass again.

They'd not spotted a sail since their encounter with the British war sloop. And now two sails appeared near the area Marianne had said the *Undefeatable* was to join the *Guerriére*.

Marianne. His heart jumped at the thought that she was near. *Oh Lord, let it be her.*

Under a full press of canvas, the newly christened *Defender* sped through the choppy seas. But not fast enough. Though his men had plugged the hole with canvas and tar and boarded it up with wood, seawater seeped in to join the waterlogged hold, weighing them down.

Luke appeared beside him, his stubbled jaw stiffening. They shared a knowing glance.

"Make that three sets of sail!" Mr. Crenshaw's excited voice once again showered over them from above.

Noah raised his scope. Three distinct hulls settled on the horizon. And if his eyes weren't playing tricks on him, a cloud of smoke drifted between them.

Cannon shot thundered, confirming his suspicions.

"Seems we're intruding on someone's battle." Luke rubbed the scar on his ear.

"But 'Whose battle?' is the question. Only one interests me."

Scratching his chin, Matthew took a spot on the other side of Noah. Behind them, the setting sun tossed golden spires across the foam-capped waves and reflected on the ships beyond.

Another burst of cannon cracked the air. Noah leapt up the foredeck ladder and dashed to the bow for a better view. He studied the ships through his glass but still could not make out their ensigns.

The *Defender* plunged down a massive swell, and Noah gripped the railing as salty spray stung his face.

More cannon shot exploded.

He focused his scope on the ship closest to him. His heart skipped a beat. He'd know that ship anywhere. The *Undefeatable*. Spinning on his heel, he approached the foredeck railing and spotted Weller and Blackthorn below. "Ready the guns!"

With a shake of his head and a look of disbelief, Weller swerved about and called for the men to assemble. Blackthorn and Daniel scrambled to their positions at one of the stern guns.

Noah patted his pocket, seeking comfort from his brother's handkerchief, but nothing but fabric and air met his touch. It was gone. He'd had it in his hand when the shot crashed into his cabin. Panic seized him. But then he realized something anew—he had another comfort, one that went far deeper than a piece of fabric, a comfort that didn't fade. An odd peace settled on him. He no longer needed the token. His brother was in heaven, and Noah had been forgiven. His guilt was gone. His debt was paid.

Not by a bloody handkerchief, but by the blood of the Son of God.

Noah smiled and turned to Agnes and Matthew who stood arm in arm gazing at the battling ships. The woman's normally ruddy cheeks had turned as white as sea foam.

Even Luke's blue eyes held a hint of foreboding.

Noah swallowed. Was he leading his men to their deaths? *Oh Lord, please be with us.* Turning, he stared at the *Undefeatable.*

Undefeatable, indeed.

Yes, his ship was half its size. Yes, he was taking on water. Yes, he had only twenty crewmen compared to the frigate's two hundred and fifty. Yes, he only had five guns compared to the frigate's thirty-two.

But he had something far more powerful than anything they possessed.

He had God on his side.

❖

Gripping the handle of the knife through the fabric of her skirt, Marianne squeezed past throngs of sailors as they dashed through the companionway. The pounding of her heart joined the pulsing cadence of the crew's boots thumping over the wooden planks as they bumped and shoved her with barely a pardon tossed her way.

She gazed over the harried scene. With most of the bulkheads removed to clear the area for battle, the lower deck had transformed into a large open space that reminded Marianne of a dreary tavern where she'd once found her inebriated father. Only the occasional furniture or crate marked where the walls once stood. The crew's anxious muttering tied her nerves in knots. Though no doubt accustomed to battle, the men's heightened intensity told her that familiarity with war did not lessen their terror. She pressed a hand over her stomach in an attempt to quell her own fear. They intended to do battle against the USS *Constitution*—against her country's ship. And in the *Constitution*'s present situation, entwined with the *Guerriére,* they would win.

But Marianne could not let that happen.

Thankfully, no one noticed her as she slipped down the ladder farther below decks. The mad dash of water against the ship muffled both the shouts above and distant cannon fire, offering a surreal peace—a peace that could be obliterated at any moment with a puncture to the hull.

Allowing the sea's mighty fingers to pour in, grab her, and drag her to the depths.

Marianne trembled. She could not think of that now.

The rotting smell drenched her heaving lungs as she made her way to the tiller. Without a lantern, darkness created ghostly shadows on the bulkhead. Shadows that loomed above her on both sides as though they intended to pounce on her and stop her from completing her mission. Sweat crept down her back and chest, molding the fabric of her gown to her body. The knife slipped from her moist hand. She fumbled for it in her pocket and gained the handle once again.

Voices grew louder. Light poured down the ladder.

Drat. Marianne shrank into a dark corner. Crewmen descended like a waterfall, shouting and cursing. Footsteps tromped over the wooden deck.

Blood raced through Marianne's veins. Her head grew light. She closed her eyes and stiffened against the wood.

Groans screeched through the dank air as if the men lifted something heavy. More footsteps. More cursing. And then they were gone.

Marianne melted against the rough wood. She caught her breath, then inched forward, feeling her way as she went.

The ship pitched. She stumbled to the deck. A splinter pierced her hand. Her knees ached. But she barely felt the pain above the numbing terror that gripped her heart.

If she accomplished this. If she disabled the ship and Captain Milford discovered her treachery, what would he do to her? Did the Royal Navy punish women in the same way they did men? Would she be flogged? Or worse...

Executed?

Her knees transformed to custard. She couldn't find the strength to rise.

Bowing her head, her vision blurred with tears. *Lord, help me. I'm a coward. I need Your courage.*

She sat for a moment, searching for the voice of God amidst the distant gunfire, the creak and groan of the ship, the boot steps pounding like hail above her.

But no voice came.

Yet...

Strength returned to her legs. Bracing herself against the deck, she rose to her feet, and once again grabbed the knife in her pocket.

She took a step forward.

For such a time as this, for such a time as this. Whispery words formed from the water crashing against the hull.

"So be it, Lord," Marianne said. "Whatever comes of this, let it come, but I will obey You. I will fulfill my destiny."

Armed with a courage that was not her own, she entered the tiller room. She withdrew the knife from her pocket then brushed her fingers over the deckhead above her. There. The rough hemp scratched her skin. Gripping the ropes with one hand and the knife in the other, she began sawing through the tight threads.

Minutes that seemed like hours passed. Sweat moistened her face. Blisters formed on her palms. Fear threatened to force her to her knees. But finally, she sliced through the final twine. With a snap and an eerie whine, the ropes split.

Zip. Twang.

Clank! The sound of iron and crashing wood echoed through the hull.

Marianne jumped back. The knife slipped from her hand.

No time to retrieve it. She dashed toward the ladder. Her knee hit a crate. Pain shot into her thigh. Grabbing her skirts, she leapt to the deck above faster than she thought possible.

Joining a line of sailors rushing down the companionway, she followed them up another ladder. Better to be found above than suspiciously hiding in her cabin. She emerged onto the main deck to a wall of smoke-laden wind and a man at the helm shouting, "We've lost steering, Captain."

Curses, followed by commands flew from Captain Milford's mouth. "Send men down to check on the tiller ropes at once, Mr. Reed! Mr. Blake, have the top men adjust sail. We must maintain our course!"

An unavoidable smile toyed upon Marianne's lips as she pressed through the crush of sailors and made her way to the railing. She gazed toward the *Constitution*, still entwined in the *Guerriére*'s lines. Swords drawn, men from both crews scrambled back and forth between the ships. The yellow spark of pistol and musket fire flashed from the top yards.

Wind snapped in the sails above her. The *Undefeatable* yawed widely to starboard.

Away from the battling ships!

A river of foul words spewed from the captain's lips, confirming Marianne's assessment.

"Blast it all!" He pounded a trail across the quarterdeck. "We'll have to come around again."

Lieutenant Reed and a horde of men jumped up from below and approached the captain. Reed caught his breath. "The tiller ropes have been cut through, Captain."

"Cut through?" Red blotches exploded on the captain's face.

"Yes, Captain."

"Who would do such a thing?" Spit flew from the captain's mouth.

Heart clawing at her throat, Marianne swerved around and gazed down at the trail of foam bubbling off the side of the ship. The wind blasted over her, stealing what was left of her breath. Her knuckles whitened on the railing.

She lifted her gaze and saw a two-masted merchantman heading straight for them.

She closed her eyes against the deceptive vision, no doubt a fabrication of her overwrought nerves. Clearly she'd gone mad with fear. As she sought her mind for an ounce of reason, she listened to the sounds surrounding her: the distant crack of gunfire, the rush of water against the hull, the whine of strained wood, the curses and commands of the ship's officers.

Nothing had changed.

"A sail! Bearing fast, Captain, off our stern!" The call from the tops bounced off the deck. She forced her eyes open.

The *Fortune* stormed toward them, foam cresting her bow.

And there perched on the gunwale, gripping a stay and leaning over the edge of the ship, stood Noah, hair flapping in the wind, looking more like a pirate than a merchantman.

❖

Noah's heart soared. Marianne. She stood at the railing, her maroon gown fluttering in the breeze. Wayward strands of her brown hair blew about her face. She was alive. He wished he could see her expression. Wished he knew whether she saw him, and if so, what was she thinking?

"What ails the frigate?" Luke approached the bow railing.

With a frown, Noah's gaze took in the ship once again. At first sight, he'd seen nothing but Marianne. But now he noticed that the frigate veered away from the battle. But why? One glance at her stern and then at her sails brought a chuckle to his lips.

"She's lost steerage."

Luke gave a disbelieving snort. "You don't say?"

Noah dropped from the gunwale to the deck, spouting a string of rapid-fire orders that sent some of his crew up into the shrouds and others to the remaining guns.

"She's lost her steering, my friend," he repeated, slapping a stunned Luke on the back.

Matthew approached, shaking his head. "How?"

"I haven't time to ponder it." Noah could hardly believe it himself. "But let us not miss the opportunity it affords." He found his gunner down on the main deck. "Weller, load the chain shot. We'll go for her masts."

"Aye, aye, Cap'n." The stout man grinned, his single gold tooth twinkling in the setting sun.

"They may not be able to steer, but they've still got their guns." Matthew's voice carried a hint of fear.

Noah gave him a reassuring look. "Then we shall have to stay out of their path, shan't we?"

"What luck," Luke exclaimed with a huff.

"Not luck." Noah's gaze shot beyond the *Undefeatable* to the two warships stuck together in the distance. "Whoever or whatever destroyed the frigate's tiller saved the *Constitution*. Until she frees herself, any enemy that comes along could blast her into splinters within minutes." Noah rubbed the back of his neck. No, not luck at all. *Thank You, Lord.*

A sly grin formed on Luke's lips. "Luck or not, I say we make it so the *Undefeatable* never has that chance."

"Aye, and then we'll go after the *Guerriére*." Blackthorn joined the conversation, rubbing his thick hands together.

Noah flinched. "What, pray tell, has sparked such fervency, Blackthorn? I seem to remember hesitancy on your part in joining this venture."

From his six foot two frame, Blackthorn gazed at Noah, his black hair flailing in the wind. "Sink me, but too much has happened for me to deny that God is with us." He shook his head. "My pretty wife was right all along. About God, about our special son." His gaze took in the ship until he found Daniel at the stern. "An' about God bein' real an' powerful an' active in people's lives."

Despite the chill of the approaching night, Noah felt warmth down to his toes. He grinned and slapped the man on the back. "I couldn't have said it better."

Noah gazed at the *Undefeatable*. He hoped—no, he prayed—that today would be the day the mighty ship would not live up to its name. He needed her to be not only defeatable but also willing to surrender her precious cargo into Noah's hands. Even as his thoughts drifted to Marianne, he could no longer see her on deck.

Good. She'd be out of the line of fire. But Noah still had no idea how to rescue her from the frigate. How did one board a man-of-war, saunter through two hundred armed sailors and fifty marines and beg the captain's pardon while he stole the man's steward? An impossible task, to be sure.

"Nothing is impossible with Me." Noah started beneath the inner voice. "Okay, Lord. Then You're going to have to show me what to do," he whispered. "I'm putting my trust in You."

Crossing the main deck, he leapt to the helm to assist Mr. Pike with the wheel. While Luke handled the sails, Noah gently coaxed the *Defender* to within forty yards of the drifting *Undefeatable*, just off her larboard quarter. So close he could hear the anguish and fury searing in Captain Milford's voice as he stood at the railing, raising his fist in Noah's direction.

The red coats of the marines lining the deck of the *Undefeatable* darkened to maroon in the deepening shadows. Drums thrummed a war song as sailors dashed across her deck. Men crowded the yards, adjusting sail to push the ship in the right direction. Others hovered around guns.

"Steady as she goes," Noah ordered Mr. Pike as he released the wheel and dropped on the main deck.

Luke and Matthew joined him.

"Are you sure they can't hit us?" Matthew's brow lowered beneath fearful gray eyes.

Noah tightened his jaw. "Yes." He hoped. He prayed.

Matthew swallowed hard. He must have sensed Noah's hesitation. He glanced down a nearby hatch, and Noah knew he thought of his wife. If either were hurt, Noah would never forgive himself.

If *any* of his crew were injured, he would never forgive himself.

"Get below, Matthew, and attend to Agnes," he ordered.

With an appreciative nod, the older man rushed away.

Noah snapped the hair from his eyes. "We are out of range of the swivels on their stern, and they can't maneuver their broadside in our direction," he said more to comfort himself than his first mate. At least by his best calculations—the calculations of a man who'd never faced battle before.

As if in defiance of his words, the muzzles of twelve guns thrust through their ports on the main deck. Noah's stomach dropped.

The sky exploded with a thunderous boom.

❖

Marianne paced before the stern windows in the captain's cabin. She wrung her hands together and released a sigh.

Noah had come for her.

The thought swirled around in her mind, making her dizzy, and finding no solid place to land. Her toe banged into the bulkhead. Spinning on her heel, she headed the other direction.

He had come for her. Just as he'd promised. For her? Plain, ordinary Marianne.

Just after Captain Milford spotted the *Fortune*, he'd also spotted her standing at the railing. Immediately, he ordered two marines to escort her below and lock her in his cabin. Why? Did he think she'd jump overboard? If so, he didn't know her too well.

Distant gunfire tapped the gray sky. Boot steps pounded above her. She fisted her hands at her side. She must know what was happening. Was Noah all right?

She glanced at the battle raging outside and realized his predicament. Was he mad?

Single-handedly taking on a British frigate? Albeit, a frigate that had gone on a wayward stroll, but a fully armed and functional frigate, nonetheless.

What was his plan? Did he think he would saunter on deck and steal her away beneath the British officer's blue-blooded noses?

What did it matter? He'd come for her. Her heart swelled.

She'd completed her destiny, and the man she loved had come to her rescue.

She would die happy with that knowledge.

And die she might.

Halting, she leaned her hands on the ledge and plastered her face against the cold, salt-encrusted glass. At the right corner of the window, the edge of the *Fortune*'s stern drifted in the sea just thirty yards away.

Too close.

Weren't they too close?

Her answer came in an enormous roar that jerked the frigate to starboard and sent a quiver through her timbers.

❖

The deafening blasts echoed across the water and pounded in Noah's ears. His crew froze as if time stood still. No doubt they all knew that dropping to the deck would make no difference if one of the shots struck them at this range.

Splash after splash chimed a sweet melody in the sea just off their bow.

"When that cap'n gives a warnin' shot, he gives a warnin' shot." Weller chuckled though his laugh came out tense.

Noah gathered his breath. "Indeed. Aim our guns at their rigging, if you please, Mr. Weller."

"Aye, aye, Cap'n." Weller turned and brayed orders to the gun crew.

Luke's blue eyes, wild with the thrill of battle, flickered over Noah before he leapt into the shrouds to direct the men aloft.

Blackthorn and Daniel hovered around one of the guns on the starboard side. Blackthorn, his stance tight and his dark eyes burning with zeal, stood before Daniel like an iron shield of protection. But as Noah approached, Daniel didn't appear to need protecting. The boy glanced up at him, a mischievous look in his eyes, a grin that reflected no fear, and a lit slow match in his hand.

"I'll allow you the first shot, Blackthorn," Noah said. "I assume you'd want the honors."

A wide grin, devoid of two teeth split the man's face. "Me pleasure, Cap'n."

The honor the title bestowed caused Noah's throat to close. He turned away.

Commotion on the *Undefeatable* drew his gaze to a gun crew preparing one of the swivel guns on their stern.

Luke dropped to the deck with a thud. "The men are ready, Captain."

Noah glanced aloft where his crew awaited orders to unfurl sail.

Mr. Pike, ever vigilant at the helm, gripped the wheel in preparation to bring the ship across the frigate's bow.

Within reach of her swivel guns.

In order so that Noah could rake her and cripple her rigging, then be off in the wind's eye before she could respond.

At least that was the plan.

"On my mark, gentleman!" he bellowed.

Sails flapped and thundered. Then *whoomp*, the canvas caught the wind and billowed above them like bulging muscles. The ship jerked, then veered to starboard, picking up speed.

Bracing his boots on the deck, Noah took his position at one of the guns beside Weller. The *Defender* swept forward, crashing into rollers and sweeping spray onto her deck. Before them, the *Undefeatable* rose like a massive whale emerging from the sea.

"Fire!" Noah yelled.

Weller applied the red-hot end of the wick to the gun's touchhole.

Five guns exploded in a deafening chorus. The ship quivered under the blast, then groaned in protest.

Black smoke slapped Noah in the face.

Coughing, he batted it away, gulping for air. "Hard to larboard!" he shouted.

With straining lines and creaking blocks, the *Defender* lurched and swung away from the *Undefeatable*.

Yellow flames shot through the haze in the distance. The air burst with thunderous *boom* after thunderous boom as the *Undefeatable* gave her reply.

Clutching the railing, Noah shook the salty spray from his face and peered through the dissipating smoke. No eerie whine of speeding shot sped past his ears, no strike jolted the ship, no screams of agony, only the splash of cannon balls sounded as they struck the sea.

But then, in the distance, the ominous snap of a mighty piece of wood crackled the air.

"Move aside! Get out of the way!" followed by various expletives shot toward Noah through the fog.

A thunderous boom echoed. Not the boom of a cannon. But the sound of sweet carnage.

As the last vestiges of sooty mist cleared, Noah's eyes confirmed what his ears had already told him. The top half of the mainmast of the

Undefeatable had toppled to the deck and now hung over the side in a tangle of halyards, cordage, and sailcloth.

Huzzahs filled his ship like bubbles in champagne.

Noah released a breath. His crew swamped him with congratulations.

Without their mainmast, without their steering, the *Undefeatable* was nothing but a crippled hulk.

"Bring us athwart her bow, Mr. Pike. We'll give her another raking." Noah scanned the deck. "Mr. Boone, go below and check for damage. Matthew, retrieve my weapons."

His old friend gave Noah a curious look before disappearing down a hatch.

Off Noah's starboard side, another snapping sound, followed by cheers, drew his gaze. Released from the maze of tangled lines, the *Constitution* eased away from her enemy. Free at last, she appeared in far better condition than the *Guerriére*, whose main- and foremasts toppled to her deck in a snarled heap of lines and canvas. At least now the *Constitution* could defend herself.

Behind the two ships, the last traces of sunlight spilled over the horizon. In minutes, it would be too dark to see anything.

The *Defender* spun around and came in across the drifting *Undefeatable*'s bow. Noah grabbed his spyglass and searched her decks for any sign of Marianne. He saw nothing but the frenzied efforts of the crew as they chopped away the broken mast before it dragged the ship onto her side. Captain Milford stood at the head of the quarterdeck, flanked by his officers, his head bowed and his hands gripping the railing.

Marianne must still be below.

Short of pummeling the *Undefeatable* into surrender with broadside after broadside, and risk injuring Marianne in the process, Noah had no idea how he was going to get her off that ship.

❖ CHAPTER 29 ❖

The pulse of guns throbbed in Marianne's ears. She darted to the cabin door and swung it open. The red blur of a marine uniform jumped in her vision. A musket crossed the doorframe, barring her passage.

"Allow me to pass at once!" She stomped her foot.

The man's face was a mask of control. "My orders are to keep you within, miss."

"Blast your orders, sir. Can you not tell we have been fired upon?"

An ear-piercing snap split the air, followed by an ominous groan, screams and shouts, then a *boom* that shook Marianne straight down to her bones.

A flicker of alarm crossed the marine's stiff features.

Just before the ship jerked to larboard.

Arms flailing, Marianne toppled over the deck and struck the captain's cabinet. Pain flared up her arm and into her shoulder. Shaking the fog from her head, she leaned forward and inched over the tilted deck, back to the open door. Surely the marine would have left his post for more important tasks.

But there he stood, rigid as a wooden soldier.

She slammed the door on him and stumbled to the stern windows. Squeezing onto the ledge, she peered out at the chaotic scene. Turbulent seas churned beneath a smoke-filled darkening sky. Who had struck them? The *Constitution*?

Or, as unimaginable as the thought could be, Noah?

Oh Lord, keep him safe.

Before she finished her prayer, the *Fortune* swung into view, riding high and wide on a valiant steed of foamy white.

Her heart stopped beating as she pressed her forehead to the glass, seeking its captain.

There. On the foredeck, feet spread apart, spyglass to his eye, Noah stood—in defiance of his lack of battle experience—with the confidence of a hardened warrior.

But he wasn't a warrior. He was a merchantman. And by all appearances, a merchantman who had lost his good sense.

"I'm here! I'm here!" Marianne waved her arms in desperation but soon dropped them to her lap. He could not see her.

But she must get his attention.

Why? Even if she did, how could he rescue her? The frigate was disabled, but not the men aboard her. She could hear all two hundred and fifty of them buzzing above her like a swarm of angry bees.

Lord, what do I do?

A undeniable pain lanced her heart as she gazed at the man she loved. He was so close. So very close. So close she could almost see the resolution on his face, could almost hear his deep, courageous voice.

But they might as well be oceans apart.

Withdrawing from the glass, she brushed her frantic fingers over the edges of the window, searching for a latch, a lever, something that might open them. She pounded on the panes. Her palms ached as tears streamed down her cheeks.

She searched again. A latch. There *was* a latch. She unhooked it and shoved open the window. A blast of chilled air shoved her backward. She barreled forward and poked her head through the opening. Wind, stained with gunpowder and smoke, whipped over her face from all sides, tearing her hair from its pins and nearly forcing her to retreat.

She dared to glance below at the foaming, angry waves. Her throat closed, and a shudder ran through her. Tearing her gaze from the sight, she peered toward Noah's ship.

"Noah!" She tried to yell but the heavy breeze stole her words and swept them away.

❖

"There she is!" Noah lowered his scope and handed it to Luke. The *Defender* had tacked around the bow of the *Undefeatable* and now sailed off her larboard quarter. He pointed at the stern of the frigate where two arms waved frantically amidst a wild array of wind-thrashed brown hair.

Luke chuckled. "Quite a woman you have there."

Have? Noah was surprised at the sudden joy that flared within him at his friend's statement. Was Marianne his? Did she forgive him for leaving her? "Sink me, she's broke through the captain's cabin!" Blackthorn's roaring voice ended in a hearty chuckle.

"Miss Marianne, Miss Marianne!" Daniel jumped on the gunwale and flung his arms through the air.

Noah swerved on his heel, forcing the command from his mouth before he allowed reason to strangle it. "Lower the cockboat!"

"Are you daft, Cap'n?" Blackthorn grabbed his arm, stopping him. "You won't get within twenty yards o' that ship before their swivels blast you from the sea."

Noah glanced at the two guns fastened to the *Undefeatable*'s stern railing. Already gun crews hovered busily around them. "Perhaps. But have you any other ideas how to save the lady?"

"We've done our duty, Cap'n." Weller ran the two remaining fingers on his right hand over the scars on his face. "We saved the *Constitution*. But to try and rescue Miss Denton. Why that's sheer foolery."

Noah knew he was right. He also knew he couldn't expect his men to risk their lives any further for him or for Marianne.

Luke gripped Noah's shoulders. "Yet to not try would be even more foolish."

Noah's throat burned at the man's loyalty as Luke cocked a brow, then turned and barked orders to the men to lower the tackles and attach the lines to the boat.

Daniel fed his hand into his father's and gazed up at Noah.

"Do you have a word for me?" Noah hoped to hear something positive from God, anything that would give him a hint that they might succeed.

But the boy lifted clear eyes and shrugged. "Sometimes you just have to trust Him."

With a nod, Noah swung about to watch the narrow vessel dip over the side. Trust was one thing when life was ordinary. But Noah faced impossible odds. He prayed he wouldn't take a shot through his head or a sword through his gut.

Mr. Rupert leapt up from below and approached Noah, a look of concern wrinkling his face. "We're taking in more water."

"How bad is it?"

He shook his head. "We'll probably sink within the hour."

Impossible odds that had just become more impossible.

Noah faced Matthew. "If things go awry, head for the *Constitution.*"

"I won't leave you, Cap'n." The old man's voice brooked no argument.

Mr. Lothar approached, holding out Noah's weapons. Grabbing a pistol, Noah primed it and then stuffed it into his belt and sighed. "Do as I say." Turning, he laid a hand on Matthew's shoulder and gave him a knowing look.

The man snorted in return.

Plucking Noah's sword from Mr. Lothar's grasp, Luke strapped it on his own waist. "I'm going with you."

"And me," Blackthorn said.

Though moved by their loyalty, Noah could not allow it. "This is my fight, gentlemen. I can't ask you to join me. It's too dangerous."

"I didn't hear you ask." Blackthorn kissed his son on the forehead then leapt on the bulwarks.

"There is a good chance we will all be killed." Noah gave Blackthorn and Luke a stern look.

Luke grinned. "Some things are worth dying for."

❖

Yanking her head back into the cabin, Marianne heaved to catch her breath. They'd seen her. A vision of Daniel waving with enthusiasm brought a smile to her lips. And Noah. As soon as he'd spotted her, he fell into deep conversation with Luke and Blackthorn.

About how to rescue her?

But what did it matter? There was nothing they could do to help her.

She twisted the ring on her finger and gazed back out the window. They were lowering a boat. A boat?

No! They'd be blown from the water.

Was Noah mad?

Thrusting her face into the buffeting wind, she waved her arms. "No! No!" But when she retreated, she found her warning had gone unheeded. The boat struck the water, and Luke and Blackthorn flung themselves over the bulwarks and ambled down a rope ladder. Noah dropped into the vessel and took his spot at the bow.

A wave of terror swept through her as they shoved off from the *Fortune* and dipped their oars in the water.

Her heart froze.

Footsteps pounded above her. The eerie squeal and crank of the swivel gun being maneuvered into position sent a shiver down her back.

She must do something.

Dashing to the door, she opened it to the red-coated back of the marine still in position. She slammed it and toured the cabin, seeking anything—anything she could use.

For what purpose, she didn't know.

She slid open drawers, flung open cabinets. Her fingers trembled. *Boom!* The gun fired. The ship quivered.

She raced to the window.

The shot splashed harmlessly into the sea not ten feet from the boat.

Still they came.

Noah, no! What are you doing?

She flung open the armoire doors. Her eyes landed on a coiled rope tucked at the bottom next to the captain's dress boots. Grabbing it, she returned to the window.

She tied one end of the rope to the captain's desk and flung the rest out the window.

If they insisted on coming for her, if by the grace of God they made it to the ship, the least she could do would be to meet them halfway down the stern.

Even though the thought of dangling in midair over the raging sea sent blood pounding in her head.

Even though the thought of sitting in that tiny boat—with only a few planks of wood between her and the sea—made her shake uncontrollably.

Even though she wasn't altogether sure she could even do either of those things.

Still if they intended to kill themselves, maybe God would allow her a few minutes in Noah's arms before they were all blasted to heaven.

She poked her head out the window and glanced down. Claws of angry foam reached up to grab her. She jerked back inside—to the safety of the ship. She grabbed her throat. Her rapid pulse thrummed against her fingers.

Boom! Another shot fired.

She peered again at the darkening sea. The splash sent a frothy geyser into the air just a few feet before the bow of Noah's boat.

Barely flinching, he continued rowing.

She could make out his face now, could even see the firm lines of determination that etched his bronzed skin whenever he'd made up his mind to do something.

Stubborn fool.

Yet. . . She bit her lip. If he could risk his life for her, surely she could face her deepest fears.

Crawling up on the ledge, she clutched the rope and swung one leg over the side. Taking a deep breath, she swung the other leg over.

Close your eyes. Don't look down. Don't look down.

Salty mist struck her face. The wind whipped her skirts. She gripped the rope and slowly lowered herself over the side.

Her feet dangled like bait over the ravenous sea, and she tapped them against the hull until she found a foothold.

Her sweaty hands slipped on the rope.

Boom! Another shot fired above her. The rope quivered like the string of a fiddle.

She opened her eyes to see the shot strike Noah's boat and blow it to pieces.

❖

"Jump!" Noah shouted then dove over the side into the raging sea. Cold water enveloped him. The roar of the blast filled his ears. A liquid wall struck him. Spikes of wood shot through the sea. One pierced his leg. Pain burned up his thigh. The screams of his men, the cannon blasts, the lap of waves, all combined in a muted symphony beneath the gurgling water.

His lungs ached. He righted himself and kicked his feet. His head popped above the surface to see nothing but planks of charred wood where his boat had been. Swirling around, he searched for his friends.

Luke's head bobbed in the distance. Blackthorn appeared beside him.

"Go back!" Noah shouted their way.

"What about you?" Water dripped from Blackthorn's dark hair.

Noah glanced toward his ship. In the encroaching darkness, nothing but a gray shape loomed where he'd left the *Defender*. Even so, he could tell her hull sat lower in the water.

"I order you to go back. Sail to the *Constitution*."

He gazed at the stern of the *Undefeatable* and was shocked to see Marianne hanging onto a rope, dangling midair.

Foolish, brave, *wonderful* girl!

He couldn't leave her. He wouldn't leave her. Even if it meant he became a prisoner of the British navy once again. Even if it meant his death.

"You're mad!" Luke shouted over the waves. He spit out a mouthful of water. Concern shone from his eyes. "Come back with us."

Noah shook his head.

Luke groaned, but finally nodded and turned toward the *Defender*. Blackthorn followed him.

Blue waters transformed to ebony as the last traces of light escaped below the horizon. Gathering a huge breath, Noah dove beneath the murky waters and swam toward the monstrous shadow of the frigate. A monster holding his princess captive.

❖

Marianne listened to the cheers and howls blaring down from above as the men manning the gun congratulated themselves on their good aim.

Holding her breath, she searched the waves. *No, Lord, no.* Her heart felt as though it would explode in her chest. She squinted into the darkness, refusing to tear her gaze away, refusing to admit they were gone. Then slowly, one by one, three heads surfaced, barely discernable in the darkness. She released a heavy breath. They were alive!

But the boat was gone. Obliterated.

Her only way to be rescued swallowed up by the ravenous waves.

Did the crew above see that Noah and his men had survived? She listened for their excited chatter and for the sounds of the gun being reloaded, but only the slosh of the sea against the hull and the pop of distant musket fire swept past her ears.

She leaned her head against the stern. It was cold and wet against her cheek. Her lungs filled with the smell of wood and tar. It was over. Noah had tried.

She would forever be grateful to him for that.

Anguish squeezed every nerve and fiber, threatening to crush her heart. Perhaps getting off this ship was not part of her destiny. *Oh Lord, I don't think I can bear it.* She would miss Noah terribly. And what would become of her mother and sister? Tears barely left her eyes before the breeze batted them away. The cruel wind allowed her no time to mourn.

Yet hadn't she surrendered all to God, no matter His will?

Or was it only when things happened the way she desired that she would give herself freely to Him?

I am sorry, Lord. If I am to stay on this ship, then I will stay.

Her hands burned against the rope's rough fibers.

Bracing her feet on the hull, she slowly pulled herself up. Better to face whatever punishment the captain would wield upon her for breaking his window than drown all alone. That was, if he didn't also discover she'd cut the tiller. Who knew what hideous fate awaited her then.

One final glance over the sea told her Noah and his men must have swum back to the *Fortune*. Good. They were safe.

Then a faint splashing from below caressed her ears. Looking down, she squinted. Tingles ran across her arms. Noah's head popped from beneath the choppy waves. He reached the tip of the lame rudder and gazed up.

"Go back, you fool!" she shouted.

He snapped wet strands of his hair from his face and grinned. "I come to rescue you and you call me a fool?"

Marianne inched down the rope closer to him. "Yes! When that is how you are behaving. What do you think you are doing?"

"I have already told you."

"Are you mad?"

"Definitely." He smiled again.

Marianne huffed. Part of her screamed in fear for Noah's life while another part of her screamed in ecstasy at his chivalrous action.

"Go away before they see you!" She waved him off.

A swell splashed over him and he shook the water from his face. "I'm not leaving without you."

"You have no boat."

"I have my back."

Marianne's fingers grew numb. They slipped on the rope. "Are you daft? I can't come down there."

"Yes you can."

"You know we are both already dead."

"Probably."

His nonchalant tone jarred Marianne. She searched for a glimpse of his expression, to know if he smiled or if fear tightened his features, but the descending shadows stole his visage from her.

"Jump, Marianne. If we are to die, I would rather die in your arms."

Her heart melted as tears filled her eyes. "Don't be such a romantic goose."

A sound came from the captain's cabin. Marianne's mouth went dry. "Leave! I beg you before they discover you." Her voice broke in a sob. "I will not have your death on my hands."

"I will not leave you."

"But I'm asking you to. Please? For me?"

Marianne glanced toward the *Fortune*, but the ship had moved. A nebulous shadow skating on an eerie mist drifted toward them.

"It's time, princess. Jump!"

She shook her head. Her blood turned to ice. "I can't. You know I can't."

"Ah, but you can. You have only to trust me." He clung to the rudder chain with one hand as he held up the other. "I'll catch you, and you can hold onto my back while I swim."

"We'll sink." Pictures of her father's bloated white body swelled in her vision. She gazed down. Below the surface of the murky sea, nothing but cold and dark extended to a bottomless pit.

"We won't sink. I'm a strong swimmer." Noah's confident tone held a hint of panic.

Terror clogged in her throat. She couldn't speak.

"Trust me." He waved her on with his hand. "Come, we haven't much time."

Trust. She'd sworn never to trust anyone again.

"Marianne, I promise I'll catch you." Urgency and conviction fired from his voice.

"Trust Me." The words rose from deep within her, strong and convicting and filled with promise.

"Lord, You want me to jump?" she whispered.

"*Yes. Trust Me, beloved. I'll always be there to catch you.*"

Marianne's eyes burned with tears.

The rope tugged in her hand.

"Ah, here you are." A familiar voice dribbled down upon her.

Marianne slowly raised her gaze to the stern windows where the dark barrel of a pistol hovered over her forehead.

❖ CHAPTER 30 ❖

Lieutenant Reed." All hope fled Marianne, turning her muscles into mush.

He leaned over the window frame, a pistol in one hand, a knife in the other. "Look what I found lying beside the slashed tiller ropes."

Marianne's head grew light. Her fingers slipped on the rough hemp.

"Come up here, Miss Denton at once, or I'll be forced to shoot you."

She studied his face, but it was too dark to see his expression. "Please, Mr. Reed, let us go."

"Lieutenant, I beg you!" Noah shouted from below.

"Beg all you want, Mr. Brenin." Mr. Reed's voice held the pompous ring of the London ton. "But you and this lady are enemies of England. Together you have disabled a British frigate, and you must pay the consequences."

"Take me instead!" Noah yelled.

"No, Noah!" The ship hefted over a swell, sending the rope swinging. Marianne's stomach tightened. Her fingers ached. Pain burned across her palms. Bracing her feet on the stern, she settled the line.

"Let her go and take me," Noah shouted louder this time. "She's a lady and should not be entangled in the wars of men."

"Very heroic, Mr. Brenin." Mr. Reed's voice carried none of the expected sarcasm. "But my life and my career are on the line. I've too much at risk to care about the lives of two Yankee rebels."

A heaviness settled on Marianne. All was lost. With one last glance at Noah, she inched her way up the rope. "Go back, Noah. He can't shoot us both."

"I told you, I'm not leaving you."

Tears spilled down her cheeks, cooled by the night breeze. "Noah, please." She continued climbing. Nearly at the ledge, she halted and glanced up. The knife in Mr. Reed's hand blurred into a silver streak. *The knife.* Of course. "Mr. Reed, if memory serves me well, it was you who allowed me to keep that knife." Threads of strength wove through her trembling voice.

"For protection only."

"But you *did* allow me to keep it."

"Yes."

"And I did slash the tiller ropes with it."

Nothing but the creak of the ship responded.

Marianne gathered her resolve and said a silent prayer. "If I stay on this ship, I will inform the captain of such. And from what little I know of your precious Articles of War, I would say that information will not bode well for your naval career."

The shadow that was Mr. Reed remained frozen in place.

"However, if you grant Noah and me our freedom, Captain Milford need never find out."

Voices barreled down from above. "There's a man on our rudder chain!"

Mr. Reed withdrew the pistol. She heard him sigh. His shadow shifted. Boot steps thundered.

Reed gazed down at her. "Jump and be quick about it."

Marianne glanced at the dark water gurgling beneath her feet.

More boot steps. More voices shouting.

"Do it now!" Mr. Reed hissed, then he disappeared from the window.

"Trust me, Marianne." Noah's voice of assurance wrapped around her from below.

But she couldn't see him in the darkness. Would he catch her?

A light appeared in the captain's cabin, spilling over the ledge like a glittering waterfall.

"*Trust Me.*"

"There's a woman out here!"

Words from the book of Esther drifted through Marianne's mind—

words Esther said after she had decided to follow God and trust Him.

"If I perish, I perish."

Marianne let go of the rope.

❖

If not for Marianne's scream and the shadow of her falling body blocking the light streaming from the stern windows, Noah wouldn't have been ready to catch her.

But catch her, he did.

She barely hit the surface of the sea before he reached out and grabbed her waist. Together they plunged under the water.

Zip zip. Bullets sped by his ears. Grabbing the thrashing woman, Noah dove deeper into the cold, wet void. Darkness surrounded him. The sounds of shouting and the tap of musket fire combined in a muted undersea chorus.

Lord, please save us.

His lungs ached. He dragged a squirming Marianne to the surface.

With effort, he held her face above water. She heaved and spewed up the sea, then screamed.

He covered her mouth and dove again just as the air filled with musket shot.

She writhed in his grasp, kicking her legs. She struck him in the groin. Agony burned down his thighs. He surfaced, biting back a wail of pain. The sea slapped his face. Marianne gasped for air.

One glance over the choppy black waves told him Matthew had not obeyed his last command. The *Defender* slid through the ebony waters just twenty yards away and began to slow.

Too close. The *Undefeatable* could reach his ship with their swivel guns.

"It will be all right, Marianne." He whispered between breaths what he no longer believed then wiped a strand of hair from her eyes. "Hang onto my back and hold your breath."

She nodded. A burst of light came from the *Undefeatable*'s stern, highlighting the terror on her face.

Boom! He pushed her below the surface then dove beside her. The shot struck only a few feet to their right. A wall of water crashed into them, shoving them through the sea.

Noah broke through the waves again. "Hold on." He placed her hands on his shoulders then plunged through the frothing waves. She groped frantically at his shirt, her legs flailing. She clutched his neck. Pain shot through his shoulders. His throat constricted. But she held on.

Tap tap tap. More musket fire sped around them, peppering the sea.

Every muscle in Noah's body screamed in agony. His lungs throbbed. Marianne's weight felt like an anchor on his back, threatening to sink them both.

Lord, help.

Noah's head grew light. He began to sink.

Cold water closed in on him from all around. His mind went numb. It was all over. He had failed.

A strong hand grabbed his arm.

His head popped above the surface. He heaved for air, but Marianne's tight grip on his throat barely allowed a breath to enter his lungs.

"Hold on to me." Blackthorn's voice, thick with effort and concern, sounded like heavenly music in Noah's ears.

Behind him, Marianne gasped. Her hot breath fanned his shoulder.

He felt himself being dragged through the water.

The smell of wood filled his nose. His hand struck the moist hull. His ship.

Blackthorn placed Noah's hand on the rope ladder. "Can you climb?"

Unable to speak, Noah nodded. Grabbing the rope with one hand, he tried to pry Marianne's hands off of his neck with the other.

Her firm grip told him she was alive. But he needed to see her. To make sure she wasn't injured.

Blackthorn assisted him in loosening her grip.

Gulping air, Noah swung around. He couldn't make out her face in the darkness. "Are you all right?"

She leaned on his shoulder, her chest heaving.

Grasping her waist, Noah tightened his grip on the rope and glanced aloft.

"Ahoy up," he commanded as loud as he dared. Groans filtered down as the ladder rose along the side of the hull. Or what remained of the hull still above water.

Matthew clutched Noah's arm and helped him and Marianne over the bulwarks. Blackthorn thumped onto the deck behind them.

Marianne's brown hair hung to her waist in saturated strands. She let out a shuttering sob and started to topple. Noah grabbed her and drew her close. Her cold, wet body trembled against his.

"You came for me," she whispered, her voice raspy and filled with wonder.

Noah embraced her and kissed her forehead as the shadows of his crew surrounded them, muttering congratulations and patting him on the back.

"I can't believe you did that, Cap'n," Mr. Rupert exclaimed.

"Ain't never seen anything like it," another sailor added.

"We thought you was sunk for sure." Mr. Boone chortled.

In the distance, the stern lights of the *Undefeatable* winked at them as the mighty frigate drifted listlessly out of sight.

And out of gun range.

Huzzahs rang from his crew.

Emerging from the shadows, Daniel dashed to Marianne's side. "I told you God had a plan."

"Yes, you did." She pressed the boy close. "Yes, you did."

Noah still clung to Marianne, refusing to release her, too afraid she'd disappear. Her face was just inches from his. Her sweet breath wafted over him. He peered through the darkness for a glimpse into those lustrous brown eyes where he hoped to find appreciation, admiration, and perhaps even—love.

But they were lost to him in the shadows.

Agnes dashed toward Marianne. "Oh, you poor dear."

Reluctantly releasing her to the older woman, Noah gazed in the distance where he could still make out the lights from the *Constitution*.

"All hands aloft! Unfurl all sail!" He faced the helm. "Head for the *Constitution*, Mr. Pike."

"Aye, aye, Cap'n." Yet absent was the usual confidence in the helmsman's voice.

Luke brayed the orders, sending the men aloft, then took his spot beside Noah. He huffed and shifted his stance.

But Noah knew what troubled the man before he opened his mouth. He knew because as the sails filled with wind, the ship barely moved. Hull down, she slogged forward like an anchor dragging over the bottom of the sea.

"We will sink before we reach them. *If* we reach them." Luke's words of defeat landed like grapeshot on Noah's open wounds.

But he could not accept them. Not after all he'd endured.

Noah paced across the deck. "Light every lantern, Mr. Weller. Light every candle, every wick. And load one gun for a signal shot!" He glanced aloft where the American flag flapped from their foremast. Surely, with all lanterns blazing, the *Constitution* would spot the ensign and come to their rescue.

Oh Lord, open their eyes.

They had to see it. He stopped and clenched his fists. He had not risked his life and the lives of his entire crew just to see them all drowned.

❖

Marianne could not stop trembling. And not because her gown was wet. They were sinking. And once again she would be thrust into the merciless sea.

Blackthorn called for Daniel. The lad squeezed her hand then darted to his father.

"Come below, dear. Let's get you into some dry attire." Agnes tugged on her wet sleeve but Marianne remained firm.

"Please, I don't want to go below if we are to sink." Her lips quivered making her words come out harsh.

"No, of course, dear." Despite her calm tone, Agnes trembled when she wrapped an arm around Marianne's shoulder. "What a horrible ordeal you've been through. Just horrible. I prayed for you every night."

Turning, Marianne hugged the woman, taking comfort from her warm embrace. "Thank you, Agnes. God answered your prayers."

Agnes withdrew and stared across the sea. "I hope the Almighty answers the prayer I'm makin' now." She sighed and forced a smile. "Well, the least I can do is get you a blanket. That is, if the water has not reached my cabin yet." She buzzed away and dropped below deck.

Hugging herself, Marianne slipped into the shadows. Her eyes latched on Noah. He marched confidently across the ship issuing orders and encouragements to his men. His brown hair dripped onto his collar. His white shirt clung to a muscled torso still heaving from exertion.

He had come for her.

He had risked his life for her. And now faced with another crisis, he handled himself with such assurance, such wisdom, such bravery.

Marianne swallowed the burning in her throat. Because of her, his ship was sinking. Because of her, he would lose everything. . .possibly even his life.

But God had been faithful thus far.

Lord, I trusted You. I dove into the waters. And You didn't let me drown. Now, please don't allow us to sink.

With lanterns hanging on every mast hook and railing, the ship lit up like a tree at Christmas.

Sails snapped overhead, bursting with wind like bloated specters. Yet the vessel slogged through the water as if pushing through black molasses. Trembling, Marianne inched her way to the railing. If they were going to sink, she would face the waters with the same bravery Noah displayed.

The ravenous waves slapped the hull just a few feet below her. Yet strangely, she felt no fear. She thought of the frightful dream she'd had not long ago where she'd been aboard a sinking ship while all her friends sailed away leaving her alone. Now she realized it was a trick of the enemy to discourage her. She was indeed aboard a sinking ship, but she was not alone. No one had left her, especially not God. She leaned over and examined the waves again. The sea gurgled and spit and carried on like an insolent child. She laughed. Why had she ever been afraid of it? With God's help and Noah's strong back, she had crossed these waters and survived. If she sank in them now, God would bring her home to heaven. The sea would not hold her captive for long. In fact, as she watched the foam-capped ebony waves, she saw them as nothing but slippery fingers always reaching, grabbing, threatening, but ultimately powerless.

The musky scent of Noah surrounded her. Her heart leapt. He stood beside her, his hair and breeches still dripping. Lantern light glimmered in his eyes as they soaked her in from head to toe.

She wanted to throw herself into his arms. To thank him. To tell him she loved him. But before she could, he pressed her head to his chest and covered her other ear with his hand.

The *boom* of a single gun thundered through the ship. Timbers shook and creaked. Marianne felt the reverberations through Noah's strong arms. Strong arms that seemed to filter out the fear. She wished he'd never let go.

The sting of gunpowder burned her nose as smoke enveloped them. Batting it away, Noah released her. She grew cold again.

Both gazed toward the *Constitution*.

The entire crew gazed toward the *Constitution*.

Waiting. . .waiting. . . The sea laughed at them as it broke against their hull.

Had the men aboard heard them? Did they see them? Did they care?

A jet of orange light came in reply, followed by a *boom* that cracked the night sky.

"They've spotted us. We are saved!"

❖ CHAPTER 31 ❖

With Seafoam nestled in her arms, Marianne followed the tall, lithe lieutenant down the passageway. Below deck, the *Constitution* was not much different from the *Undefeatable*. Narrow, dank hallways lit by intermittent lanterns stretched into the murky shadows. Small, cluttered cabins lined the hull, and the smell of bilge and unwashed men permeated every plank and timber.

But there *was* one glorious difference.

The *Constitution* was an American ship, not an enemy. And here, Marianne was a guest, not a prisoner. For she'd been treated with nothing but courtesy since she had boarded last night.

In fact, within minutes of spotting them, the *Constitution* had come alongside and quickly dispatched two boats to deliver Noah and his crew from the sinking ship. But no sooner had Marianne's feet hit the deck than she and Agnes were rushed below to the cabin normally occupied by the ship's master, John Alwyn, who'd been wounded during the battle. There, the two ladies were given hammocks to sleep in, basins of water for washing, and hot tea to soothe their nerves.

Though the hammock was comfortable, Marianne found no sleep during the long night. Her mind kept replaying the harrowing events of the past few days. Stealing the knife, cutting the tiller ropes, crawling out the stern windows, Noah risking his life for her, her dive into the sea, and their ultimate rescue. She thanked the Lord over and over for

His faithfulness until tears of joy streamed down her cheeks onto the coverlet.

God had told her to trust Him. He had told her to jump. And even though everything within her screamed in protest, she had obeyed. And God had saved her—saved her straight into Noah's arms.

Yet she'd not seen Noah since. Or any of his crew. In fact, she'd hardly spoken a word to Noah since she dove into the sea. How she longed to feel his arms around her again, to look into his eyes. . .to find out whether he had come back for her out of a sense of duty, honor, or because of something deeper—something that made her heart leap for joy.

Agnes's heavy footsteps thudded behind her, bringing her back to the present. Marianne glanced over her shoulder. A huge smile broke the elderly woman's face even as her puffy cheeks pinked. She appeared as flustered as Marianne felt. For neither woman knew why they had been summoned to the captain's cabin so early in the morning.

Marianne's stomach tightened around the biscuit she'd eaten for breakfast. She scratched Seafoam beneath her chin. Had something else gone wrong? But when they reached the end of the passageway, deep voices and laughter echoed through the bulkhead, settling her nerves.

Especially since one of the voices was Noah's.

Nodding toward the marine who stood guard outside the captain's cabin, the lieutenant knocked. Upon hearing the captain's "enter," he swung open the door, ducked beneath the frame, and beckoned the ladies forward.

Marianne took a step inside and swept the room with her gaze. A blast of wind swirled around her from the broken stern windows. The scent of scorched wood burned her nose. Black soot and ashes covered the deck and the charred remains of what looked like a cabinet; two chairs and a mahogany desk had been shoved into the corner. Everything else, however, appeared intact. In addition to a few placards, lanterns, and a row of swords, only a single painting of George Washington decorated the bulkheads.

Noah, Luke, and Weller stood at attention before a tall, portly man dressed in white breeches and a dark blue jacket, crowned at the shoulders with gold-fringed epaulets. Matthew, Daniel, and Blackthorn stood behind them while a row of officers lined the aft bulkhead.

Agnes darted to her husband. Wrapping an arm around her, Matthew drew her close.

Seafoam leapt from Marianne's arms and sprang toward Noah.

"Ah, there is the lady of honor." The tall man Marianne assumed to be the captain approached her.

Halting, Marianne watched as he bowed slightly and offered her his elbow.

"Captain," Noah's voice sent a warm tremble through her. "May I present, Miss Marianne Denton. Miss Denton, Captain Isaac Hull."

"Miss Denton." Stylish brown hair curled around his forehead as his dark, intelligent eyes found hers.

"Captain." She smiled, placed her hand in the crook of his elbow, and allowed him to lead her forward.

Luke winked at her as they passed.

"Hi, Miss Marianne." Daniel waved.

She smiled at the lad.

Noah's gaze met hers. A mischievous twinkle flickered across his blue eyes. Aside from a few bruises on his face and the dark circles of exhaustion beneath his eyes, he looked well, commanding—handsome.

"I see your cabin suffered during the battle," Marianne said.

"You see correctly, Miss Denton." The captain released her arm and surveyed the damage. "The *Guerriére*'s bow guns played havoc with my new desk. Alas, but Mr. Hoffmann"—he gestured toward the man who had led her and Agnes here, and who now stood at attention by the door—"saved the day and put out the fire."

The man smiled at Marianne.

"However, Miss Denton." Captain Hull faced her. "It is my understanding that I have you to thank for disabling the HMS *Undefeatable*." He laughed. "*Undefeatable*. I believe they should rename their ship."

One of the officers chuckled.

"I did nothing, really," Marianne said.

"Did you or did you not cut the ship's tiller cables?"

"I did, sir."

"Then you are a heroine."

Marianne flinched. "Me? I believe it was Mr. Brenin who shot out her mast."

Noah smiled, saying, "A feat I was only able to perform due to your action, Miss Denton." Seafoam circled his legs, rubbing against them.

So it was Miss Denton again. Marianne twisted the ring on her finger. "I was happy to do my part, Captain."

"Your part?" He chuckled, sending the golden fringe on his epaulets shaking. "Egad, she is a treasure." He shared a look with Noah. "You disabled a British frigate, miss. A feat many a man has never achieved, yet you are a lone woman. I find your humility refreshing."

Marianne felt a blush rising and lowered her gaze. "God was with me."

"Ah yes. God was with us all." The captain adjusted his coat "Those redcoats would have blasted us from the sea, entangled as we were with that infernal *Guerriére*."

"I love my country, sir. I could do no less." Marianne lifted her gaze to Daniel. "It was my destiny."

Daniel beamed. His father patted him on the back.

"Destiny." The captain cocked his head, then paced before Noah and his crew. "I like the sound of that. I like the sound of that, indeed." He halted and adjusted his white cravat around his fleshy chin. Despite the long pointed nose that reminded Marianne of a cannon, the captain possessed a friendly face that seemed at odds with his commanding position.

He squared his shoulders. "Then it was God's destiny that we are the first American ship to defeat a British man-of-war. And those pompous redcoats thought they ruled the seas. Egad." He fisted his hand in the air. "We taught them a lesson." He took up pacing again.

His officers murmured their agreement from behind Noah and his men.

"Humph. And to think they were saying in Washington and all up and down our coastline that our amateur navy did not stand a chance against the expertise, the experience, and sheer power of the British Royal Navy." He chuckled, his eyes sparkling. He stopped again. "Do you know what this will do?" He asked no one in particular. "This will give great encouragement to our fleet! We have proven that the British navy is not invincible. Not only that, this victory will no doubt prompt Madison to increase our funding for more ships and weaponry. Aye, this is good news. This battle may turn the tide of the war before it has barely begun."

As Marianne listened to the captain's speech, she couldn't help but feel a sense of pride in her part of the battle. If what Captain Hull said was true and this defeat would lead to more victories at sea, then God had used her for something truly important. Little, ordinary Marianne from Baltimore.

Reaching down, Daniel picked up Seafoam and began petting her.

"How many men did you lose, Captain?" Noah asked.

A fresh breeze whirled in through the broken window, stirring flakes of charred wood across the deck. Captain Hull released a sigh, heavy with sorrow. "Seven. One marine, five seamen, and Lieutenant William Bush. All good men." He glanced over his officers who stood at attention in the back of the cabin. "Heroes."

They nodded in agreement.

"You are all heroes," the captain continued, and Marianne got the impression he loved to hear himself talk. "And you." He stopped and pointed at Noah. "You would make a great officer in the U.S. navy. I shall be happy to write a letter of recommendation to Madison and request a commission for you."

An officer in the navy? Marianne eyed Noah. Now that his merchant business had sunk—thanks to her—would he take the man up on his offer?

But he seemed unaffected. "Thank you, Captain. I am honored to have one so distinguished as yourself willing to stand up for me. Allow me some time to consider it."

"Very well. Take your time, Mr. Brenin. I am in your debt."

"And what of you?" The captain narrowed his eyes on Luke.

Luke's lips slanted. "Me? In the navy?" He raised his hand to cover a cough that Marianne could tell was more of a laugh.

Noah smiled.

Weller chuckled.

Luke shifted his stance. "I fear I am not a man who thrives under authority."

Captain Hull studied him. He let out a disgruntled moan. "Regardless, I am in your debt as well."

"If I may call on that debt, Captain," Noah said, drawing the captain's gaze. "My crew and I would be most grateful if you could deliver us to Baltimore at your earliest convenience."

"Can we go see Mother?" Daniel tugged on his father's torn, stained shirt.

Noah glanced at them, then back at the captain. "By way of Savannah, perhaps?"

The captain fingered his chin.

Marianne's heart skipped at the possibility of seeing her mother and sister again soon.

A uniformed man tapped on the doorframe. "Captain, they are signaling from the *Guerriére* that they're ready to bring the remainder of the prisoners aboard."

"Thank you, Lowe." Captain Hull studied Noah, then released a heavy sigh. "Jones's locker be cursed. I think we can manage it. Perhaps"—he chuckled—"God will find it in His destiny to send us another British warship to defeat along the way."

Daniel nestled Seafoam against his cheek and smiled up at his father. The look on Blackthorn's face slowly melted into one of joy. His eyes moistened, and Marianne swallowed the emotion burning in her throat. Finally, after two years, the man would be reunited with his wife.

Agnes kissed her husband's cheek, and Luke and Weller smiled at Noah.

"Excellent." The captain slapped his hands together. "Gentlemen." He glanced over Marianne and Agnes. "Ladies, if you'll excuse me."

And he marched from the cabin.

❖

Marianne stood at the bow of the USS *Constitution*, away from the hustle of the crew, and gazed at the crippled *Guerriére* listing to larboard several yards ahead of them. After their meeting in the captain's cabin, Agnes retired to her cabin with a headache, and Noah and his men darted off to assist Captain Hull in retrieving the remaining British sailors from the defeated ship.

One casual glance and a smile was all Noah had offered Marianne as he left the cabin. Not much to go on. Not much of an indication of where his heart lay. She longed to know what he was thinking. She longed to thank him for risking his life for her, for keeping his word. And deep down, she longed to know if he cared for her as much as she did him.

Shielding her eyes from the afternoon sun, she scanned the horizon. No sign of the HMS *Undefeatable*. No doubt she drifted away during the night at the mercy of wind and tide and would continue to do so until the crew repaired the tiller and the mast. Thoughts of Captain Milford saddened her. She had come to care for the old curmudgeon, who despite his foul moods and maniacal episodes, had been kind to Marianne—even complimentary. She hoped, no she prayed, he would find his way to land and live out his days as a farmer.

A gust of wind danced through her hair and brought with it the smell of gunpowder, the sea, and charred wood. Leaning over the railing, she glanced at the blue waves frolicking against the hull. She chuckled. She was no longer frightened of the water. No longer frightened of anything.

Except spending her life without Noah.

Would they simply return to Baltimore, end their engagement, and go their separate ways? Without a ship, without a merchant business to fund, Noah had no reason to please his father with a forced marriage, especially since he now knew the true state of the Denton fortune. After Noah explained it to his father, the man would no doubt agree to call off the marriage. Then Marianne would have to find another way to care for her sick mother and her sister.

Yet that pain was nothing compared to the gnawing ache of losing Noah.

A light touch on the small of her back caused a flutter in her belly. Noah's warm breath fanned her neck. "Marianne." Shivers tingled down her back.

She turned her head. His blue eyes caressed her face. His lips lingered just inches from hers. She swallowed and faced forward, her heart in her throat.

He slipped beside her, keeping his hand on her back. "You are no longer afraid of the sea?"

His brown hair whipped behind him. She longed to run her fingers over the stubble on his firm jaw.

"No. I believe the Lord has cured me." She gave a little laugh.

"Would that He had done so before you nearly drowned us both." He huffed, his voice ringing with playful annoyance.

Marianne's face grew hot. She pushed his hand away. "Noah Brenin, I was terrified out of my mind. I thought I was drowning. I wasn't myself."

He grinned.

"You taunt me." She lowered her shoulders. "I'm sorry. You are right. I could have drowned us both."

"I shouldn't tease you." He raised her hand to his lips and kissed it.

Her body warmed. "Thank you for coming back for me."

"I said I would."

"You risked everything. Your ship, your men, your life."

"Did you doubt that I would try?" He frowned.

Of course she did. "Few people keep their word under such dire circumstances."

The afternoon sun painted his hair with streaks of gold. He leaned toward her. "It depends on the value of the prize."

Marianne's breath halted. Did he mean her, or saving the *Constitution*? She wished she had more experience with courting. If that was even what this was. She wished her heart didn't twist in a knot whenever Noah was near. She wished she believed that a man like him could love a woman like her. "Yes, Captain Hull seems quite taken with your performance," she said.

"And yours." He frowned again. Shifting his boots over the planks, he gazed at the sparkling azure waves spreading to the horizon. "Destiny. There's something wonderful about knowing you belong to an Almighty God who loves you. A God who has a purpose for your life. Makes the fear of dying fade by comparison."

Marianne could relate. She, too, had found her destiny aboard the *Undefeatable*. But Noah's words stunned her. "Did I hear you correctly, Mr. Brenin? You speak of God and destiny as though you now believe in both."

He smiled. "I was wrong about both. I was wrong about many things." He brushed a strand of hair from her face. "I have discovered God's nothing like my father. I don't have to perform to win His love."

Marianne smiled, her heart bursting with joy. "What of Jacob's death?"

"Part of God's plan." He shrugged. "I may never know His reasons until I die."

"I'm so happy, Noah." She laid a hand on his arm. "I, too, have begun to trust God again." She shook her head. "I am still shocked that He used me, a plain, ordinary woman with no special talents to win a major victory in a war for our country's freedom."

"Plain? Ordinary?" Noah took her hand in his. "Woman, you are the most extraordinary creature I have ever met."

Tears filled her eyes. She gazed out to sea, overcome with emotion. Extraordinary? She flattened her lips. If that were true, why did her father leave her?

"Precious child." God's voice filled her spirit.

And the answer came to her. Her father's problems had nothing to do with her, nor did his death bear any reflection on her value. She twisted the ring on her finger. A ray of sunlight caught the ruby and set it aflame. She had intended to sell it once. For to her, it represented the extent of her father's opinion of her worth. But now she knew her worth. She was a child of God. Precious and beloved. No, she would not sell it. She would cherish this ring as the last memento she had from her earthly father.

She gazed up at Noah and found him looking at her, concern filling his brow.

"You don't believe that I find you extraordinary?" he asked.

"I've never received such flattery."

"Not flattery, my love." He toyed with a strand of her hair, his gaze hovering over her lips.

She laid a hand on her chest to still her beating heart, beating in the hope that the love she saw in his eyes sprang from his heart. "So, it was destiny that brought you back to me?"

"Aye." Wind blasted over them, lifting the hair at his collar. He stared at the *Guerriére*, her masts nothing but shattered twigs, her decks littered with tangled lines and canvas. She listed heavily to larboard, groaning in despair of her ultimate demise. One final cockboat pushed off from her hull and headed back to the *Constitution*. Blackthorn and Daniel waved at them from the stern.

Noah waved back.

"And what does destiny prompt you to do next?" Marianne pressed him. He squared his shoulders. "I believe I shall become a privateer."

Daft man. Ignoring her disappointment, Marianne gave him a coy smile. "Privateering? Why, Noah Brenin, if I didn't know better I'd say you've turned into a patriot."

He gave a jaunty huff. "A few months aboard a British frigate would change even the staunchest renegade." He grew serious. "I've been selfish, thinking only of my father's business, only of our family. . .only of myself. America is a great country. And I sense God leading me to defend her." He faced her, his eyes glittering. "For the first time in my life, I feel as though I have a purpose."

Marianne nodded, admiring his zeal.

"To defend our nation is a privilege worth fighting for—even dying for," he added.

"Dying? I cannot risk losing you again, Noah Brenin." The words came out before Marianne had a chance to check them.

His expression softened, and he ran a thumb over her cheek. "You'll never lose me."

Marianne searched those words for the meaning she longed to hear.

He cupped her chin, and then slowly lowered his lips to hers.

An explosion broke the peaceful afternoon. Jerking away from Noah, Marianne swept her gaze toward the sound. Yellow and orange flames, littered with chunks of wood shot high into the air above the *Guerriére*.

"What happened?" she asked.

"Captain Hull ordered the ship destroyed." Noah gazed solemnly at the scene.

Cheers and howls and huzzahs blared from the crew of the *Constitution,* then all grew quiet as they watched the British ship shudder. Streams of light ran along her hull. The quarterdeck lifted in the air. With an ominous boom, it exploded into fragments that flew in every direction. The hull split in two then reeled and staggered like a drunken man before plunging forward and sinking beneath the sea.

Until nothing but a swirl of foam-capped waves marked the spot where once she stood.

Marianne felt an emptiness in her gut at the sight of the mighty warship sinking to the cold depths—never to sail the majestic seas again.

Yet she supposed that was its destiny.

Noah's jaw tightened as he continued to gaze at the sight.

Had he been about to kiss her? Her heart raced.

He faced her, a mischievous gleam in his eye. "Now, where were we?" He leaned toward her.

Against every urge within her, she held up a hand to stay his advance. "Regardless of what you think, I do not allow just any man to kiss me."

His brow furrowed. "Just any man? Have I been reduced to standing in a line of common suitors vying for your affections?"

Marianne huffed. As if she'd ever had such a line. "Last I heard, Noah Brenin, you had no interest in marrying me."

"And you said you'd never marry me." He gazed at her mouth and began his descent again. "Much has happened since then."

She placed a finger on his lips. They were warm and moist and made her hand tingle. "Enlighten me as to exactly what has happened?"

His eyes lifted to hers, then he backed away, a playful smirk on his face. "For one thing, we have not called off the engagement. Hence, I am still your fiancé and have every right to kiss you." He pressed in again.

Her finger rose. "Then you wish to marry me?"

He straightened his stance. The adoration in his eyes threatened to turn her legs to jelly. His warm fingers pressed on her neck as his thumb caressed her jaw. "Woman, I will die if you don't marry me." He laid his forehead against hers. "I love you with all my heart."

Now Marianne's knees became custard. His words sailed through her, squelching all her insecurities and fears. She clung to him and tilted her head up to receive his kiss.

Warm and hungry, his mouth devoured hers, seeking, caressing, enjoying. He tasted of salt and coffee and. . .Noah. A wave of passion swept through her, tingling her toes.

Whistles and howls from the crew pulled them apart. Marianne's face grew hot.

She smiled. "I love you, too, Noah." She rubbed a finger over his stubbled jaw. "I can't wait to become your wife."

His breathing came hard and rapid. He drew her to his chest. "Me either, princess. Me either."

As commands to get the ship underway shot across the deck, Noah and Marianne stood arm in arm, and stared over the wide expanse of glistening sea that seemed to spread out before them with endless possibilities.

The snap of a sail sounded above them.

The ship jerked forward as the purl of the water played against the bow.

"Do you think God has more for us to do?" Marianne looked up at Noah.

He smiled. "I think God has only just begun."

❖ HISTORICAL NOTE ❖

Captain Issac Hull of the USS *Constitution* was a Connecticut Yankee and the son of a Revolutionary brigadier general. He went to sea at an early age, and by 1798 became a ship master. Known for his quick thinking and natural talent for leadership, he obtained a commission as a lieutenant in the then forming U.S. Navy on board the USS *Constitution*. In May of 1804, he was promoted to master commandant, and he received command of the *Constitution* by the time war broke out on June 19, 1812.

On August 19, 1812, he met HMS *Guerriere*, an enemy frigate. In a battle that lasted nearly four hours, Hull managed to outmaneuver and pound his foe to pieces. (No record is mentioned of the help he received from the privateer, *Defender*, or that a lone woman aboard a nearby enemy frigate saved the day. But we know what really happened—*wink*.)

This battle marked the first time an American ship had ever defeated a British man-of-war. American navy captains gained confidence from this victory and went on to win more victories at sea. There were celebrations in every American city, and Hull was hailed a hero. Congress awarded him a gold medal. Since then, five ships in the U.S. Navy have been named for Commodore Hull.

Across the Atlantic, the British were shocked and dismayed. The *London Times* reported, "The Loss of the *Guerriere* spreads a degree of gloom through the town which it was painful to observe." Later, the newspaper stated: "There is one object to which our most strenuous efforts should be directed—the entire annihilation of the American Navy."

❖ CASUALTIES ❖

The USS *Constitution*
Deaths: Lieutenant William Bush, Six seamen
Wounded: First Lieutenant Charles Morris, Master John C. Alwyn, four seaman and one marine

The HMS *Guerriere*
Killed: 23 sailors including 2nd Lieutenant Henry Ready
Wounded: 56 men, including Captain Dacres himself, 1st Lieutenant Bartholomew Kent, Master Robert Scott, two master's mates, and one midshipmen

SURRENDER THE NIGHT

❖ DEDICATION ❖

To those who have been wounded by life

❖ CHAPTER 1 ❖

August 3, 1814
Baltimore, Maryland

Gong. *Gong. Gong.* The evening air reverberated with warning bells from St. Peter's church. Rose McGuire halted in her trek to the pigsty and gazed across the shadowy farm. Musket fire echoed in the distance. The British were on the move again. Punctuating the unrest crackling through the air, shards of maroon and saffron shot across the western sky, bringing into focus the line of cedar and pine trees that marked the end of civilization and the beginning of the dense forest of Maryland.

Gong. Gong. Gong. The eerie chime scraped a chill down Rose's spine. She glanced back at the brick house in the distance. Though she had yet to spy a redcoat anywhere near her farm, she should go back inside. Swallowing her fear, she emptied the bucket of slops into the pig trough. Grunts and snorts amassed in the putrid air above the enclosure, drawing her attention to her favorite pig, who waddled toward her to receive his evening scratch. Kneeling, she reached her hand in between the fence posts. "Hi, Prinney." His moist, stiff hair bristled against her hand as he lifted his head beneath her caress and nudged against the wooden railings, while the rest of the pigs devoured their kitchen scraps.

"You'll miss your dinner, Prinney. Better get some before it's gone." Rose stood and dabbed her sleeve over the perspiration on her forehead. A light breeze, laden with the smells of hay and honeysuckle, brushed her golden curls across her face. Flicking them aside, she drew in a deep

337

breath, hoping the familiar scents would calm her nerves.

Men and their wars. She hated the war, hated the alarms, hated the violence. But most of all she hated the fear. Two years was far too long to live in constant terror of being overrun by a ruthless enemy.

Picking up her bucket, she hastened to the barn, gazing at her tiny garden as she went. Even in the dim light, she could make out the patches of red and yellow of the nearly ripe tomatoes and the spindly silk atop ripe ears of corn. She smiled. Despite the war, life went on.

Musket shot peppered the air. *Pop. Pop. Pop.* Somewhere close by, soldiers were being shot at or a settler was defending his land—somewhere close by, people were dying. Fear prickled her skin. Just a few more chores and she would go inside. Rose began humming a song her father taught her when she was young. She could still hear his baritone voice as he sang the words—words that always seemed to calm her.

> *Oh fare thee well, my little turtledove,*
> *And fare thee well for awhile;*
> *But though I go I'll surely come again,*
> *If I go ten thousand mile, my dear,*
> *If I go ten thousand mile.*

Setting the bucket down on the dirt floor of the barn, Rose eased beside Liverpool, her milk cow. Why the song allayed her fears she could not say, for it was nothing but a lie. Her father had not even gone ten thousand miles away. Yet he had never returned. Rose shooed a fly from the animal's face and planted a kiss on her nose, eliciting a moo from the friendly cow and a jealous neigh from Valor, Rose's filly in the adjoining stall.

"Don't vex yourself, Valor. I'll take care of you next."

"Rose!" Aunt Muira's voice rang from their home across the small yard.

Rose needed no further encouragement. She would attend to the animals later. "Coming!" she shouted as she made her way through the barn, nearly stumbling over Georgiana, one of her chickens. Squawking, the bird darted across the hay-strewn floor.

Gong. Gong. Gong.

Alarm gripped Rose's stomach. Did the signal mean what she thought? Surely the British would not come this close to Baltimore. Hurrying her steps, she approached the two-story brick house. Light cascaded from the windows like the golden water of Jones Falls in the summer sun, luring her inside to the warmth of the fire and comforts of home. Home. At least she had called it her home for the past five years.

Rose stepped into the kitchen, closing the door behind her. The smells of venison stew and fresh bread wafted around her as she removed her straw hat and hung it on a hook by the door. Cora, the cook, knelt over the massive fireplace, stirring something that bubbled inside the iron pot hanging over the fire.

"There you are, Rose." Aunt Muira, attired in a blue cotton gown with a white sash about her high waist, strutted into the room as if she wore the latest Parisian fashion. "Didn't you hear the alarm? For goodness' sakes, you know you are to come inside when the alarm rings. Oh, look at you dear, covered in dirt again." Her jewel-laden silver earrings—so at odds with her plain attire—twinkled in the lantern light as her sharp green eyes assessed Rose.

Rose glanced down at her gray linen gown and saw not a speck of dirt. But then again, her aunt had a propensity for spotting stains.

"Wash up and take off those muddy shoes, dear. Mr. Drummond awaits his supper." With that, Aunt Muira swung about and swept from the room like a fast-moving storm.

Cora stepped from the fireplace, hand on her back and gave Rose a look of reprimand. "Best do as she says, child." The dark-skinned cook scowled and nodded toward the sink. Black spongy curls peeked from beneath the red scarf wrapped about her head. "You know how the missus can get when her orders aren't carried out."

Slipping off her shoes, Rose skirted the food preparation table and poured water from a pitcher over her hands at the sink. "Do not think poorly of her, Cora. She only wants me to comport myself like a lady."

"Humph." Cora grabbed a cloth, opened the Franklin stove and pulled out a loaf of bread. Setting it beside one that was already cooling on the table, she mumbled, "I don't know nothin' 'bout that, miss. But have you seen Amelia? I could use some help carryin' this food into the dining room."

Rose dried her hands on a towel and smiled. "I have no doubt she will make an appearance when all the work is done."

Cora chuckled and handed her a platter. Together they entered the dining room and placed bowls of steaming stew, fresh corn, and platters of cornmeal cakes on the table.

"Good evening, lass." Rose's uncle, Forbes, smiled from his seat at the table. Short-cropped gray hair sprang from his head in a dozen different directions and framed a ruddy face lined with the trials of a long life. The skin around his eyes crinkled as he squinted at the food-laden table. "Now, what have we here?"

Rose bent and kissed his cheek, then took a seat beside him. "Lose your spectacles again, Uncle?"

He chuckled. "Ah, they'll turn up somewhere, I'm sure."

"Wherever he last placed them, no doubt," Aunt Muira added from her seat next to her husband. "Where is Amelia?"

Cora returned to the kitchen, mumbling under her breath.

Rose shrugged beneath her aunt's questioning gaze. "I saw her this morning. She mentioned heading into town."

"You should discipline that woman, Forbes." Aunt Muira huffed. "She's out of control."

"Come now, dearest," Uncle Forbes said. "She's a grown woman and not our prisoner."

"But we took her into our home to be a lady's maid and companion to Rose. It would certainly be propitious if she would attend to her duties."

"You worry overmuch." Forbes smiled at his wife and took her hand in his.

"And you, dear Forbes, do not worry enough."

Rose shifted her gaze between them as they shared a chuckle. "Amelia has been a great companion to me, for which I thank you both very much. But as a lady's maid"—Rose shrugged—"well, let's just say I have no need of a silly maid anyway."

Uncle Forbes took Rose's hand and gave her a wink. "It pleases me that you two have become such good friends. Now, shall we pray over this grand feast?" Bowing his head, he asked God's blessing on the food, then ladled stew into his and Muira's bowl before passing the pot to Rose.

"You must come inside when you hear the alarm, dear." The candlelight shimmered over Aunt Muira's copper-colored hair streaked with gray. At eight and fifty, Muira retained a beauty and a bearing that gave evidence of her privileged upbringing.

An upbringing similar to that which Rose had experienced, save in her case, all signs of fine breeding had long since dissipated. "But nothing ever comes of them." Rose glanced out the window where darkness had stolen the remaining light, then back at her aunt whose expression had scrunched into a knot.

With a sigh, Aunt Muira rose, circled the table, and wiped Rose's face with her napkin.

Rose gave her a timid smile. "My apologies. I thought I had washed sufficiently."

"I suppose I wouldn't recognize you if you were clean, dear." Her aunt returned to her seat.

Uncle Forbes swallowed the bite in his mouth. "They sound the alarms for a reason, lass. You should heed them as your aunt says."

"But I've yet to see a British soldier anywhere near here." Rose bit into a chunk of meat in her stew, savoring the aromatic flavors. "They wouldn't dare come close to Baltimore. Not after General Smith has gathered such a strong militia."

"I wouldn't put anything past those redcoats." Uncle Forbes spooned corn into his mouth. "Why, they have turned the Chesapeake Bay into nothing but a British pond. A pond from which they emerge like crocodiles to raid upon our poor citizens."

"Leaving hundreds of widows in their wake," Aunt Muira added glumly. "Ruined women and orphans."

A breeze fluttered the calico curtains at the open window and sent the candle flames sputtering.

Ruined women. Rose's stomach soured. She set down her spoon, her appetite gone. "Thank goodness for your charities, Aunt. You and Mrs. Pickersgill are doing much good for those women."

"And you could too, dear. If you accompanied me more often." Aunt Muira gave Rose a look of censure. "They need someone who understands what they have endured."

Uncle Forbes chomped on a piece of venison. "You know, my love, Rose does what she can. We must be patient with her as God has been patient with us."

Aunt Muira smiled at her husband. "I understand." But when his knowing gaze refused to leave her, she huffed. "Well perhaps I'm not patient. It has been five years, after all."

Familiar guilt pinched Rose. "You know I care for the women devastated by this war," she said. "But I'm not as strong as you are, Aunt Muira. I don't have your courage." Though Rose longed to be brave, once had even considered herself brave. But after. . . Well, afterward, her courage had abandoned her like everything else—like every*one* else, including God. "When I look at those women, when I look into their eyes, I see myself." Rose stared down at the cream-colored table cloth. "If only the nightmares would end."

Reaching across the table, Aunt Muira took Rose's hand in hers. "Forgive me, my dear. I simply wish you would learn to trust God."

Trust? Rose grimaced. She had trusted God after her father had been murdered—had kept trusting Him after her mother died. But how could she trust a God who had allowed such a horrific thing to happen to her? "I am trying, Aunt." She winced at her lie.

Aunt Muira drew in a deep breath and shook her shoulders as if to shake off the gloom that had descended on their conversation. She grabbed a johnnycake and placed it on her plate then glanced over the fare. "Oh I do miss having rice. And coffee." She moaned. "And chocolate. It seems years since we've had such luxuries."

Uncle Forbes snorted. "We are fortunate to have food at all with the British blockade."

"More than missing food"—Rose leaned back in her chair and sighed—"I miss peace. I long to feel secure again."

Uncle Forbes grabbed her hand and squeezed it. His brown eyes sparkled with understanding. "You have been through so much in your short life, lass. Peace will come again soon. God will take care of us."

Shrugging off the platitude that had been proven false in her own life, Rose chomped on her corn cake, but the grainy, buttery flavor soured on her tongue.

Uncle Forbes took a swig of cider, dribbling some on his brown waistcoat, and set down his mug. He scratched his thick hair. "Let us pray this war will be over soon, and our lives can return to normal."

"My word, Uncle. Normal only if we win." Rose shook her head. If not. If America once more became a British colony, things would never be normal again.

"Of course we'll win." Aunt Muira nibbled on her corn cake, reminding Rose that true ladies took smaller bites. "It is too much to think otherwise."

"Ever the optimist, dearest." Uncle Forbes gazed lovingly at his wife.

She returned his gaze, then moved her eyes to Rose. "And then perhaps you can finally marry. Goodness, you are all of two and twenty and fast becoming a spinster."

Rose opened her mouth to protest but her aunt continued, "I was eighteen when I married Forbes." The couple exchanged another adoring glance, sending a twinge of jealousy through Rose.

Rose glanced at her food, hoping for a resurgence of her appetite, but it did not come. "I have yet to meet a man who interests me." Or one who didn't sicken her. Truth be told, after rumors of her plight spread through Baltimore, very few suitors had come to call. And even if an honorable man took an interest in her, and she in him, Rose could only hope to have a marriage as good as her aunt and uncle's. If not, she wanted no marriage at all.

"What of Mr. Snyder, the councilman?" Aunt Muira drew a spoonful of stew to her lips. "He's been coming around quite often."

"He is a fat wit."

"Rose, lass." Uncle Forbes squinted toward her. "It isn't kind to say such things."

"I know he doesn't come from an honorable family." Aunt Muira dabbed her mouth with a napkin. "But he has become successful on his own merit."

Rose let out a sigh. "If I do ever marry, it won't be to a man with a dubious character." No, she needed a man she could trust implicitly—someone who would never take advantage of her.

"But dear—" her aunt started to protest when the sound of carriage wheels grated over the gravel in front of their house.

Pound. Pound. Pound. The front door resounded.

The heavy knock at this hour could only mean trouble. Rose's body tightened. Her glance took in the Brown Bess musket perched atop the fireplace.

Pound. Pound. Pound.

"Ah, yes." Uncle Forbes rose from his chair, as he no doubt remembered that Samuel, their footman, was no longer in their employ. "I keep meaning to hire a new man," he mumbled as he disappeared through the dining room door as if he hadn't a care in the world—as if there weren't British soldiers raiding the coast. Rose heard the front door open and anxious words exchanged. The intruding voice sounded like Mr. Markham, Uncle Forbes's assistant from church. Sharing a look of apprehension with her aunt, Rose headed toward the foyer.

A warm summer breeze trailed in through the open door and

swirled about the room. Upon seeing Rose and her aunt, Mr. Markham dragged off his hat. "Sorry to disturb you, Mrs. Drummond, Miss McGuire, but there's trouble down at the church."

"Calm down, man. What sort of trouble?" Uncle Forbes squinted at Mr. Markham and laid a hand on his shoulder.

"Some men in town caught a redcoat, sir. And they're threatening to string 'im up." He fumbled with his hat and cast an anxious gaze out the open door. "He's hurt pretty bad too." He glanced at Rose's aunt.

"Oh my." Lifting her skirts, Aunt Muira headed upstairs only to descend within seconds, medical satchel in one hand and a pair of spectacles in the other. "We should alert Dr. Wilson just in case the man's injuries are beyond my abilities."

Grabbing his overcoat from the hook by the door, Rose's uncle swept it over his shoulders.

"A lynching?" Cora entered the room, fear pinching the features of her face.

"Never you mind, Cora. Keep an eye on Rose and we'll be back soon," Aunt Muira ordered.

"Can't I come with you?" Rose said as the familiar fear clenched her gut once again. "I don't feel safe here without Samuel." She glanced at Cora.

"Don't be blamin' me for him runnin' off." Cora wagged her finger. "He was nothin' but trouble, that one."

"You're safer here than in town," her uncle said. "Mr. Markham will stay with you, won't you, sir?"

The gentleman nodded, seemingly relieved he did not have to return to the mayhem in town. "Indeed, I will."

Uncle Forbes patted his pockets and scanned the room. "My spectacles. Where are my spectacles?"

"I have them, dearest." Aunt Muira handed them to him, then faced Rose. "Promise me you won't leave the house."

Rose swallowed. With the British afoot and the crazed mob in town, her aunt and uncle were venturing straight into danger. "I promise, but please be safe."

Without so much as a glance back, they sped out the door and slammed it behind them. The thud echoed through the lonely house. *Oh God, I cannot lose my family. Not again.*

❖

Alexander Reed trudged through the thick mud. A leafy branch struck his face. Shoving it aside, he continued onward. All around him the chirp of crickets and croak of frogs joined other night sounds in an eerie cacophony. An insect stung his neck, and he slapped the offending pest. Behind him eight men slogged through the woods as silently as the squish of mud would allow, and before him, at their lead, marched Mr. Garrick, first lieutenant of the HMS *Undefeatable*.

The troops of men from various British warships blockading the Chesapeake had barely hauled their cockboats up on the land when darkness had descended. Alex huffed under his breath. This was a job for marines and soldiers, not sailors. Why Admiral Cockburn insisted that naval officers go ashore on these raids eluded Alex. He'd rather be back in the wardroom aboard the HMS *Undefeatable* sipping a glass of port than stomping through the backwoods of this primitive country.

Alex tried to shake the visions of senseless destruction, rape, and murder of civilians ordered by Admiral Cockburn and carried out by his small group that night, but they haunted him with each step. His stomach turned in revulsion. At least he'd been able to slip into the shadows during the worst of it and avoid forever scarring his conscience. Yet he didn't know how much more he could endure. As horrendous as war was, true gentlemen fought with honor and integrity, not by assaulting innocent farmers and their families. When he joined His Majesty's Navy, he had not signed up for this madness. He wanted to make an honorable name in battle and perhaps gain some prize money that would go a long way to erase the stain he'd made upon his family's name. Then maybe his father would welcome him home again.

Home. Alex had been without one for so long, he'd forgotten what it felt like to have a place to call his own. And a family who loved him. Yet these raids brought him anything but honor. To defy orders, however, would bring court-martial upon him and most likely a sentence of death or worse—cashiering, a dishonorable discharge from the navy.

Garrick slowed and slipped beside Alex. Doffing his bicorn, he wiped the sweat from his brow with his bloodstained sleeve. "Easy prey, these ruffians, eh, Reed?"

"They are but farmers. I would not allow your pride to swell overmuch."

"Egad man." Garrick snorted. "You always were a sour pot."

A marine chuckled from behind Alex. "Did you see the look on that woman's face when we burst into her home?"

The purl of rushing water caressed Alex's ears, and he longed for it to drown out the men's malicious commentary.

"This silver tea platter will please my wife back home," another man whispered.

Alex's anger rose. "The silver is not yours, Grayson."

"Aye it is, Mr. Reed. A prize of war."

"Don't mind him lads," Garrick shot over his shoulder. "Reed's always been a stuffed shirt. His father's a viscount. *Lord Cranleigh.*" He mimicked the haughty tone of the London aristocrats then snapped venomous eyes Reed's way. "Perhaps you believe this type of work beneath you, Reed? Don't like to get your hands dirty, eh?"

Ignoring him, Alex trudged forward. Sweat streamed down his back beneath his waistcoat.

Thankfully, a light ahead drew Garrick's attention away from him. "A farmhouse, gentlemen." Excitement heightened his voice.

Reed peered through the darkness. A small house with light streaming from its windows and smoke curling from three chimneys perched in the middle of a patch of cleared land. A barn nearly as big as the house stood off to the right, and a smaller one sat in the shadows to the left.

"Upon my honor, Garrick. It's just one farm. Leave them be," Reed said. "Captain Milford instructed us to strike towns, not single farms."

Garrick gazed up at the black sky, then turned to face Alex. His expression was lost in the darkness but his tone indicated nothing but sinister glee. "It grows late. You take the men and circle around back toward the ship. I'll meet you on board."

Alex released a heavy sigh and watched as Garrick turned, gripped his pistol, leaped over the short fence, and crept toward the unsuspecting farmhouse. If Alex were a praying man, he'd say a prayer for the poor souls within.

But he wasn't a praying man.

❖

Rose hooked the lantern on a nail by Valor's stall. The bells and musket shots had ceased, giving her the courage to venture forth from the protection of the house and finish her chores. Although Amelia had returned, she and Cora had long since retired to their beds. How they could sleep at a time like this baffled Rose. Neither Mr. Markham's snores from the sofa in the parlor nor his meek demeanor when he was awake provided Rose with enough security to risk slumber.

Leaning her cheek against the warm horse's face, Rose drew a breath of the musky scent of horseflesh. "I'm sorry to have forgotten you, precious one." She pulled away and ran her fingers through Valor's mane.

Something moved in the reflection of the horse's eye. Something or someone.

Rose froze.

"Well, I daresay, what do we have here?" The male voice struck her like a sword in the back. Heart in her throat, she jumped and swung about. A man in a British naval uniform, dark blue coat and stained white breeches, glared at her with the eyes of a predator. A slow smile crept over his lips. His dark eyes scoured the barn and then returned to her. He took a step forward. Valor neighed.

Rose's legs wobbled. "I insist you leave at once, sir. This is a civilian home, and my uncle is within shouting distance," she lied, wishing her uncle hadn't left for town.

Wishing she'd kept her promise to stay in the house.

"Indeed?" He cocked a malicious brow and took another step. Blood stains marred his white shirt.

"You are a pretty thing, aren't you?"

"Please sir, I am not at war with you. As is no one in my family." Rose's pulse raced. Her vision blurred.

"Ah, but that is where you are wrong, miss. All Yankee rebels are at war with Britain, the mother country." He grinned and rubbed the whiskers lining his jaw. "And what does a parent do with a rebellious child? Why, he gives the brat a spanking."

Rose's breath crushed against her chest. She darted a quick glance toward the open barn door behind her.

"You will give me what I want," the man continued. "Or"—he sighed and flattened his lips—"I'd hate to see this barn and all your animals go up in flames."

Liverpool mooed in protest.

Rose's head grew light. The barn began to spin around her. She could not endure this. *Not again.* "Please sir, I beg you." Her voice squeaked. "If you have any decency, leave me and my family be."

"Ah, there's the rub, miss. In truth, I have no decency."

Clutching her skirts, Rose made a dash for the door. Meaty hands gripped her shoulders and tossed her to the ground. Pain shot up her arms and onto her back. She screamed. Hay flew into her face. Valor neighed and stomped his foot. The frenzied squawk of chickens filled her ears.

The man shrugged out of his coat and tossed it aside. Never removing his eyes from her, he slowly drew his sword and pistol and laid them on the ground.

Terror seized her. She scrambled on her knees to get away. He grabbed her legs, flipped her over, and fell on top of her. His heavy weight nearly crushed her.

Rose closed her eyes and prayed for a rapid death.

❖ CHAPTER 2 ❖

A woman's scream pierced the air. Alex dashed across the open field. *Blasted Garrick,* he swore under his breath. He halted midway and listened. Barn or house? Another scream, followed by the distraught whinny of a horse. The barn. Alex darted in that direction, glad he'd stayed behind to see what mischief Garrick was about, instead of heading back to the ship with the other men.

Chest heaving, he barreled through the barn's open doors. Squinting in the glare of lantern light, his eyes latched on Lieutenant Garrick lying atop a struggling woman. Fury consumed Alex. He charged toward his superior, laid a muddy boot on his side and kicked him off the lady. Garrick moaned and tumbled over the dirt and hay. He snapped to his knees, raking the barn with his gaze. A pair of searing brown eyes met Alex's. The look of shock on Garrick's face faded beneath an eruption of rage.

"What is the meaning of this, Reed?" He leaped to his feet and brushed the hay from his shirt.

Alex dared a quick glance at the woman. Disheveled golden hair, a muddied gown, and crystal blue eyes that screamed in terror stared back at him.

"The meaning of this, sir"—he swung his gaze back to Garrick—"is that I tire of your cruel treatment of innocent ladies."

"I care not a whit what you tire of." Garrick scowled. "She is rebel trash and therefore no lady."

Alex forced down his anger. He wanted nothing more than to pummel this nincompoop into the ground. "You disguise your licentious appetites behind the shield of war. It is beneath you, sir, as an officer in His Majesty's Navy." Yet even as he said the words, he wondered if anything was beneath a man like Garrick.

"Captain Milford will have you court-martialed for assaulting me." Garrick spit hay from his mouth. "Return to the ship at once." His tone held no possibility of defiance on Alex's part. "Now!" he added with a spiteful gleam in his eye.

Alex remained in place.

A flicker of uncertainty crossed Garrick's expression. "Go now, and I'll forget this moment of insanity." His tone softened.

"Please help me, sir," the woman managed to squeak out, shifting pleading eyes toward Alex.

He drew a deep breath of the muggy, manure-scented air. Seconds passed, affording him a moment of clarity. He could return to the ship and continue with his plan to gain honor and fortune in the navy, or he could defy his superior officer, defend this woman, and lose everything. Why did he care if one more American woman was ravished on a night when dozens had already suffered the same fate?

"Be gone! What is one rebel woman to you?" Garrick chuckled as if reading Alex's thoughts. He wiped the spit from his lips, then leaned over the lady with such lustful disdain it sickened Alex.

Whimpering, she clambered backward.

Alex clenched his fists, silently cursing his infernal conscience. "Upon my honor, I fear I cannot do that."

Garrick flinched and cast an incredulous gaze at Alex. "What did you say?" He lengthened his stance. His narrowed eyes shot to his sword and pistol lying atop his coat on the ground, but then he shook his head and grinned. "Ah, you want the woman, too. By all means, Mr. Reed, you may have her when I'm done." He waved a hand through the air.

"You misunderstand me, sir." Alex forced the anger from his tone. "I'm ordering you to leave the woman alone and return to the ship with me."

"You are ordering?" Garrick's incredulous tone was ripe with spite. Anger flared in his otherwise lifeless eyes. He inched closer to his weapons.

"I would not attempt that if I were you, Garrick."

"No, *you* wouldn't." In one fluid motion, Garrick leaped for his sword, grabbed it, and swept it out before him. "But I would." He grinned. "In fact, there are many things I would do that you would not, which is the great difference between us."

Anguish brewed within Alex as he watched his glorious naval career scuttled. Gripping the hilt of his sword, he slowly drew it from its sheath. "To be different from you, sir, has been my greatest aspiration." Alex gave a mock bow. Why couldn't the libertine relinquish this one lady? Why had he forced Alex's hand? Visions of his own body swinging from a hanging post at Portsmouth flashed before his eyes. But he couldn't think of that now.

"I've been looking forward to gutting you with my blade for a long time, Reed." Garrick sneered.

Alex raised a brow. "Then let us delay your attempt no longer."

❖

Heart cinched in her chest, Rose eyed the two men. When her rescuer knocked the hideous man off of her, terror had given way to hope. But now as the two sailors lunged toward each other, swords in hand, her fears returned in full force.

Clang! Steel struck steel as their blades crossed. The man called Garrick forced her rescuer back beneath the blow. Or was he her rescuer? She could not be sure that this Reed, as Garrick had addressed him, didn't harbor the same plans for her as her assailant. He was British, after all.

Reed shoved Garrick back then narrowed his eyes upon him. He leveled the tip of his sword at Garrick's chest. A confident grin played upon his lips.

Garrick's face reddened and a sweat broke out on his brow. "You'll hang for this, Reed."

"We shall see."

Fear clogged Rose's throat. Her gaze landed on Garrick's pistol lying atop his coat. Pressing her palms against the dirt, she struggled to push herself up, but her legs turned to jelly. She plopped down again and began to hum her father's song in an attempt to calm her nerves and give strength to her limbs.

Sword raised, Reed charged Garrick, and the two parried back and forth. The chime of steel on steel echoed through the barn. Liverpool mooed.

Tears stung Rose's eyes. She gasped for breath as she tried once again to rise.

Garrick dipped to the left and thrust his sword at Reed's side, but the taller man leaped out of reach, then swung about and brandished his blade across Garrick's chest. A line of red blossomed on the man's shirt. Garrick stared at it as if he hadn't realized up to that point that he could bleed.

Valor snorted and stomped her hoof against the wooden rail. Rose struggled to her knees and began to inch toward the pistol.

Garrick's face grew puffy and red. Fear clouded his brow. "Enough of this!" He spat and lunged toward his opponent. Reed jerked backward then veered to the right and brought the hilt of his sword down on Garrick's hand. Garrick's blade flew from his grip and landed in the dirt.

A chicken squawked.

His chest heaving, Garrick gaped at his sword lying in the mud. He raised seething eyes to his opponent.

Reed kicked Garrick's sword aside then lowered his blade. He ran a sleeve across his forehead. His features twisted in a mixture of anger and regret. "Let us put this behind us, Garrick. We are in the midst of war. Tempers are high. Forget the girl, forget this incident, and let's return to the ship."

Yes, indeed, forget about me. Rose shuddered. Almost within her reach, the pistol gleamed in the lantern light, taunting her, daring her to pick it up. To shoot it as she had those many years ago. She could still feel the unyielding wood of the pistol's handle in her grip, could still smell the sting of gunpowder. She had no idea if she could even touch it, but she had to try. Inching forward, her legs became hopelessly tangled in the folds of her gown.

Garrick's vile chuckle bounced off the walls of the barn. "Are those your terms, Reed?" She heard his boots thudding toward her.

She reached for the pistol.

"Fair terms, to be sure, considering I won our little contest." Reed's voice carried a hint of distrust, of hopelessness, which did not bode well for Rose's future.

"Well, stab me, Reed. I didn't take you for such a ninny." Garrick's black boot stepped in her view. He grabbed her wrist and tossed her arm aside. The pistol disappeared.

The cock of a gun sounded. Rose felt the hard press of a barrel against her forehead. She slowly lifted her chin to gaze into Garrick's face, twisted in fury and bloodlust. His eyes sparked like a madman's. Rose's blood grew cold.

"Leave, Reed, or I'll kill your precious rebel," Garrick said.

Reed huffed. "What the deuces, Garrick? Why must you be so difficult?"

For an instant, anger chased Rose's fear away—anger that once again a man had used his superior strength to subdue her. Struggling to her feet, she glared at Garrick as he kept the barrel of his pistol pressed against her forehead. Perhaps she deserved to die at the end of a gun, after all. "Let him kill me, sir. For I prefer that to the alternative."

Garrick blinked then snorted. "Very well, as you wish."

Lord, take me home. Rose's mind went numb as she closed her eyes.

The twang of a sword spinning through the air. The squish of steel into flesh, and the cold barrel left her forehead. Rose pried her eyes open to see Garrick's stunned expression. He glanced from her to Reed, and then down at the blade planted in his gut.

Staggering backward, he gripped the embedded sword with one hand, his pistol still in his other. "To the devil with you," he muttered and leveled his gun at Reed.

The pistol exploded with a loud crack. The shot reverberated in Rose's ears. Smoke filled the air as the smell of gunpowder drifted over her. Dropping the weapon, Garrick crumpled to the ground.

Rose snapped her gaze toward Reed. His eyes met hers. Red burst upon his white breeches. He bent over, clutched his thigh, then stumbled backward. His head struck the wooden post of Liverpool's stall, and he too toppled to the ground.

❖

"Amelia!" Rose nudged the woman, wondering how anyone in the house had slept through the gunshot. "Get up, Amelia."

Amelia batted Rose away with a moan as Rose set the lantern atop a table in her maid's bedchamber. Grabbing a petticoat and gown from a hook on the wall, Rose tossed them at the girl—no, woman. In fact, at two and twenty, Amelia was the same age as Rose. "Get up, Amelia. I need your help. There's a man in the barn."

"A man?" Amelia opened her eyes and struggled to sit.

Rose would laugh at the silly woman's infatuation with the male gender if the situation weren't so harrowing and Rose wasn't still trembling. "Yes, and I need your help."

Rubbing her eyes, Amelia peered in her direction. "A man, miss?"

"As I said. Now get dressed, gather some bandages from my aunt's chamber, and meet me in the barn." Rose's stomach lurched within her. Oh my, what was she to do? Though Garrick was dead, Mr. Reed was very much alive. At least for the moment. But not for long with all the blood pouring from his leg. A wave of dizziness struck her, and she halted and pressed a hand to her chest. Oh why did her aunt and uncle have to be gone on this particular night?

"Whatever is the matter, miss?" Amelia, fully alert now, sprang from the bed. She flung her gown over her head and settled it over her nightdress. She touched Rose's arm. "Miss? Are you ill?"

Rose drew a deep breath. "We need to hurry." She had no time to think about Mr. Garrick's assault. No time to calm herself. "Gather the bandages as I said and Aunt Muira's needle and thread." Grabbing the lantern, Rose headed for the door. She must also get a knife from the kitchen and the aged scotch her uncle kept hidden under the cabinet.

"But, miss—"

"Please do as I say, Amelia. A man's life depends on us."

Rose rushed out the door. A British man's life. The enemy.

Bottle of scotch and knife in hand, Rose stormed into the barn. Mr. Reed's pain-filled groan pierced the air as he struggled to rise. Swallowing her fear, Rose knelt beside him. A circle of maroon mushroomed across his white breeches. The metallic smell of blood filled the air.

"Be careful, sir. You've been shot."

"I am fully aware of that, miss," he said in an unmistakable British lilt that carried a bit of hauteur. He gave up on his attempt to stand and leaned his weight back on his arms. A pair of deep hazel eyes shot a look of curiosity her way. Brown hair the color of rich earth drifted in waves about a strong masculine face, then gathered behind him in a queue.

Rose set down the knife and bottle. A wave of unease crashed over her. Could she trust this man—this *enemy*? Regardless, she should not be alone with him. Despite his injury, he could possibly still do her harm if he so desired. She glanced toward the open door. Oh where was Amelia?

"Would you assist me in rising?" Wincing, he bent his injured leg until the heel of his boot lodged in the dirt.

"I will do no such thing, sir. I'll not have another dead man in my barn."

His glance took in Garrick lying in a heap at the edge of Valor's stall.

"Yes, he's dead." She thought she saw pain cross Mr. Reed's gaze before he closed his eyes.

Amelia burst through the open barn door, her gown sitting lopsided on her shoulders and her long braid of dark hair swaying behind her. "Oh my."

"I need to get back to my ship." Reed moaned.

"You'll bleed to death first, Mr. Reed." Rose examined the wound. Blood seeped from the opening. She knew a little about doctoring from her aunt, and if she didn't extract the slug and stop the bleeding, he may not survive. "We need to get the bullet out and patch you up."

"Bullet out." Beads of sweat broke out on the man's face. His glance took in the barn, Liverpool and Valor, the rafters above, Squeaks, one of Rose's chickens crossing the ground—anywhere but the wound on his leg. He frowned. "But surely you are not a surgeon."

"Lie back, Mr. Reed." Rose gathered some hay to form a pillow. Fortunately, he had fallen near the doorway where fresh hay had been piled to feed Valor, for she doubted she and Amelia could move his large, muscular frame very far. At least the hay would make a soft bed and absorb some of the blood.

"Amelia, the bandages." Rose nudged Mr. Reed's shoulder. Nothing but hard muscle met her touch. He did not budge.

"I insist you lie down, Mr. Reed."

His quizzical gaze took her in as if she were some newly discovered species. "If you'll assist me to my feet, I'll be on my way."

"You will do no such thing." Rose nudged him again.

Reed shook his head as if he were dizzy. "What the deuces, madam. If you please."

Ignoring him, Rose grabbed the knife. "My word, Amelia, the bandages please!" Rose glanced up. Her lady's maid stared at Garrick's body, her face a mask of white.

"Amelia, look at me. I need the needle, thread, and bandages you brought."

The woman shifted wide, frightened eyes to Rose. "What happened, miss?"

"It doesn't matter now." Rose shook her head, trying to scatter the memories.

Reed stared down at his wound as if he had just seen it. He moaned.

"Shouldn't we wake Mr. Markham? Shouldn't we call a physician?" Amelia knelt and handed Rose the bandages and the needle and thread as her gaze took in Mr. Reed's uniform. "He's British, miss."

"I am aware of that." Rose laid them on the cloth she'd spread over the dirt. "Which is why we cannot alert Mr. Markham nor call for the physician. The fewer people who see him, the better." She held up the half-empty bottle of scotch. "Now, Mr. Reed, I suggest you have a sip or two of this." With her other hand, she held up the knife to the lantern. "This may hurt a bit."

Mr. Reed swallowed, and his eyes shifted from the knife down to his wound and back to Rose. "Ladies, if you will but help me to my feet, I will trouble you no further," he said as if he were simply leaving an evening soiree. But then he glanced back at the blood bubbling from his wound. His face grew as white as fresh snow on a crisp winter's morn. His eyes rolled back into his head, and he plopped back onto the hay.

❖ CHAPTER 3 ❖

The sound of squawking rummaged through Alex's ears. *Cluck. Cluck. Cluck.* An infernal noise that defied description. It seemed to peck upon his brain, sending pain shooting down his back. No, down his leg. His left leg. Was it on fire? Was *he* on fire? His throat burned. Sweat tickled his skin as it streamed down his cheeks.

The gurgle of water sounded. A cloth touched his face—its coolness jarred him.

"Oh fare thee well, my little turtledove. And fare thee well for a while." A sweet melody drifted in an angelic song around him. Was he in heaven?

Quite impossible.

"But though I go I'll surely come again. If I go ten thousand mile," the sweet feminine voice continued.

The cloth moved across his forehead as humming replaced lyrics.

"How is he, miss?" another feminine voice asked.

Several moments of silence. "He is feverish. We must pray, Amelia. Pray very hard."

Then the sounds drifted into silence.

❖

Rose dipped the cloth into the bucket of water and wrung it out. Laying it gently atop Mr. Reed's forehead, she sat back with a sigh. On the other side of the naval officer, Amelia gazed at him from her spot perched on a stool. A morning breeze drifted in through the open doors of the barn and rustled the maid's silky black curls.

"Do you suppose we should call for the apothecary?" Concern tightened Amelia's face.

"As I said, we cannot risk it."

"But surely they wouldn't toss an injured man in prison?"

"He's British," Rose snapped, hearing the venom in her own voice. "You heard what they did to that redcoat they caught in town two nights ago." She shook her head. Had it already been two days since that vile man, Garrick, had entered Rose's barn and attacked her? Every moment since then, Rose had been so consumed with keeping Mr. Reed alive, that she'd had no time to sleep let alone recover her nerves from the incident. She gazed at the blisters on her palms—red, puffy, and sore to the touch.

Evidence of the crime committed in her barn—and her duplicity in covering up the murder.

It had taken Rose and Amelia—well, mainly Rose—hours of hard work to gouge out a hole in the soft earth large enough for Mr. Garrick's body. After saying a few words over the man—out of Christian duty—Rose had left his grave unmarked, leaving Garrick in God's hands to face whatever judgment he deserved.

What else could she have done? Should any more British soldiers happen upon their farm and see their fallen comrade, only God knew what they might do to her and her family. She grabbed a piece of hay from the ground and twirled it between her fingers, allowing a bit of strain to seep from her knotted muscles. Yet even so, her head still spun with all that had happened. If not for these blisters and the injured officer lying before her, the entire incident would seem more like one of the many nightmares that so often haunted her slumber.

Amelia pressed down the folds of her violet gown, a puzzled look on her face. "How can you be so kind to this man after what the British did to your family?"

Rose lowered her chin. She gazed at Mr. Reed's pistol and sword lying atop his blue coat by the barn door—reminders that he belonged to the same nation who had murdered her father. And caused her mother's death. "British or not, this man saved my life. If he hadn't, rest assured, I'd have already turned him over to General Smith."

If he hadn't, she'd probably be dead.

Or worse.

"He's quite handsome," Amelia said, a devilish twinkle in her eye.

Rose shook her head. "You are incorrigible, Amelia. You have just as much reason as I to hate the British."

"He is first a man, isn't he?" Amelia quirked a smile that formed a dimple on her cheek. "Besides, it's so romantic the way he dashed to your rescue."

"There was nothing romantic about it." Rose huffed. A chicken approached, cocked her head quizzically at Mr. Reed, then hopped into Rose's lap. Rose stroked Georgiana's feathers as it settled onto her gown.

"You and your chickens, miss." Amelia said as a grunt sounded from the doorway, drawing both ladies' gazes to the pig. Prinney waddled into the barn and made his way toward Rose. "And your pigs." Amelia scrunched her nose. "How do you expect anyone to court you when you smell like a barn?"

Liverpool pressed her nose against the wooden posts of the stall beside them and mooed. The pungent scent of pig droppings drifted on a stiff breeze as if confirming Amelia's words even as Prinney nuzzled up against Rose. Reaching out to pet him, she smiled. "I prefer my barn and my animals to most of the men I've met."

"I simply will never understand you, miss." Amelia flattened her lips. "With your inheritance, you could wear the finest gowns and attend monthly balls at the Fountain Inn"—she leaned toward Rose, a gleam in her eye—"and no doubt catch the eye of a wealthy man."

Memories flooded Rose. Memories of men wealthy in coin but devoid of conscience. Men who thought nothing of stealing a young woman's fortune—and future. "I shall leave the fine gowns and frivolous soirees to you, Amelia." Rose gazed beyond the barn's open doors where the morning sun cast rays over the distant oak trees and lit the wildflowers dotting the field in bright purple and red. The distant rush of the Jones Falls River settled her nerves like a soothing balm. "Besides, I doubt I'll ever find a man I can trust."

Mr. Reed groaned, drawing Amelia's concerned look his way. "Poor man. What are we to do with him? You can't keep him out here forever."

Nudging the chicken from her lap, Rose took the cloth from his forehead and dipped it into the water. Georgiana squawked in protest as she strutted across the hay-strewn ground. "Just until he recovers. Then I'll send him on his way."

Amelia pinched her cheeks, bringing color to the surface, though no man—at least not a conscious one—was in sight. "I do not see how you can keep him from Cora and your aunt and uncle for that long."

Rose wrung out the cloth and placed it back on Mr. Reed's forehead. "I will fetch the eggs and milk Cora needs from the barn. Aunt Muira is in Washington DC assisting at the orphanage for the next few days, and Uncle Forbes spends most of his time at his church. Besides, he keeps his carriage and horse in the stable, so he has no need to come out to the barn." Rose wiped a strand of hair from her face. "I am sure Mr. Reed will be long gone before anyone finds him."

She laid the back of her hand against the man's flushed cheek. Still hot. Two nights ago, after he'd drifted into unconsciousness, Rose had poured scotch over Mr. Reed's wound and dug out the bullet. Then she sewed up the opening with needle and thread. Just like she'd seen her aunt do a dozen times. Rose supposed she should be thankful that Mr. Reed had swooned at the sight of his own blood—as humorous as that was—for at least he had not been awake to see how violently her hands shook. But now she wondered if she had done something wrong, for his fever indicated an infection. And that did not bode well for Mr. Reed.

Rose eased the blanket up to his chin and watched as his eyelids twitched and his breath grew labored.

"Do you suppose he's wealthy?" Amelia asked.

"My word, Amelia. Appearance and wealth. Is that all that matters to you? Why, this man could be part of the very crew who were responsible for your husband's disappearance."

Amelia cocked her head and puckered her lips in that delicate way that seemed to turn most men to mush. "We can't know for sure what happened to Richard."

Rose studied her companion. Each of them had suffered great losses. Two years ago, Amelia's husband had gone missing at sea. A simple seaman aboard a merchant ship that had never been heard from since. Reports filtering back to Baltimore from a fishing boat told a tale of a British frigate's seizure of the merchant sloop. Soon after, Aunt Muira had found Amelia, destitute and starving, scrabbling for scraps of food on the city streets. Of course Rose's benevolent aunt had brought the lady home and given her a position as Rose's companion and maid.

"I cannot bear to think of it." Amelia batted the air aside as easily as she seemed to bat away her husband's memory. But Rose knew better. She'd often heard Amelia's quiet sobs during the long hours of the night.

Mr. Reed moaned and tossed his head. Sweat streamed down his forehead onto the dark hair at his temples. A few days' growth of whiskers shadowed his jaw and chin.

Amelia's forehead suddenly wrinkled. "What would the magistrate, or worse, General Smith think if they found him here?"

"No doubt they'd accuse me of being a traitor. Not just me but my aunt and uncle too."

"And me." Amelia's brown eyes grew wide.

Prinney grunted as if he included himself in the conspiracy.

Rose bit her lip. Amelia had a propensity to gossip with the other ladies in town. "You must tell no one, Amelia. Can you promise me that?"

"Of course, miss." She laid a hand on Rose's arm.

Rose swallowed. She could not put her aunt and uncle at risk. Not after all they'd done for her. Not when they were her only family left— the only ones who cared about her. "We must pray he recovers soon, Amelia. Pray hard."

"If I prayed, miss, I would join you." Amelia shrugged. "But I shall wish really hard."

Rose was about to comment on the woman's lack of faith when a "Hi ho, Miss McGuire!" shot into the barn from outside.

Rose's and Amelia's wide eyes latched upon each other. "My word, it's Councilman Snyder," Rose said. Why hadn't Rose heard his carriage drive up? "Hurry, Amelia, cover Mr. Reed up with hay. I'll delay him."

Amelia gazed at Rose as if she'd lost her mind.

"Just do it, please." Rose scrambled to her feet, stepped over Prinney, and dashed out the door, hearing the crackle of hay behind her.

The summer sun struck her like a hot poker. She squinted against its brightness and nearly bumped into Mr. Snyder, who was strolling toward the barn with tricorn and cane in hand.

His bergamot scent assaulted her. "So nice to see you, Mr. Snyder," she lied. Truth be told, the man made her nerves tighten into hopeless knots, though she could not say why. He had been nothing but kind to her, and he had certainly not hidden his interest in furthering their relationship.

A slick smile that reminded her of a hungry cat curved upon his lips. "Whatever are you always doing in the barn, Miss McGuire?"

"Brushing my horse, milking the cow, feeding the chickens," she waved a hand through the air. *Tending to wounded British sailors.* "The usual chores."

Prinney ambled up behind her as the other pigs grunted from the pigpen.

Plucking a handkerchief from his waistcoat pocket, Mr. Snyder held it to his nose. "You should leave this type of work to a stableboy or farmhand. A lady as lovely as yourself shouldn't be getting her hands dirty." He took her right hand in his and lifted it to his lips, but then halted at the sight of dirt smudged across her knuckles. He lowered her hand with a sigh.

She snatched it from him, restraining a smile. "We don't have a stableboy, Mr. Snyder. Our last groomsman ran off and joined the British army.

"Indeed." He sidestepped her. "What do you expect from a freed slave?" The sunlight shone over his perfectly styled auburn hair cut short to his collar and gleamed over his silk-embroidered waistcoat and spotless cravat. Strong features that could have been considered handsome tightened as he peered toward the barn. "Show me what interests you so much in the barn, miss. I'd like for us to get better acquainted."

Alarm squeezed the breath from Rose's lungs. Though she hated to touch the man—any man—she clutched his arm and swung him around. "You would find it dull, I assure you, Mr. Snyder. I know how you loathe getting dirty."

Halting, he faced her, his blue eyes drifting to her cheek. "Unlike you, I see?" He grinned.

Rose lifted her hand to rub the dirt from her face, but Mr. Snyder grabbed it before she could.

"Is this blood? Are you hurt, Miss McGuire?" His urgent tone filled with concern as he pointed toward dark red stains on her palms. "And these blisters." He pinched his lips. "What have you been doing?"

Pulling from his grip, Rose swallowed a burst of guilt at Mr. Snyder's genuine regard. He had always been kind to her and her family, and she hated the lie that rolled off her tongue. "I. . .I. . .killed a chicken for dinner."

"You?"

Prinney ambled about the hem of Rose's gown and bumped into

Mr. Snyder's leg. Releasing her hand, he leaped backward and swatted the pig away with his handkerchief. "Filthy beast!"

Suppressing a giggle, Rose knelt and scratched Prinney between the ears then leaned down to whisper, "Good pig, Prinney. Now run along."

A moan sounded from the barn. "That sounded like a man." Swinging about, Mr. Snyder headed that way.

"A man?" Rose emitted a nervous chuckle. "What sort of lady do you think I am, sir?" She yanked on his arm, halting him. "Why, that was Liverpool, my cow. Can you not tell a moo from a man's voice?" She offered him a sweet smile as she once again dragged him away from the barn. "Come into the house for some tea, Mr. Snyder. I'm sure you didn't come here to discuss my farm chores."

"Indeed I did not, miss." He dabbed at the perspiration on his brow with his handkerchief. "By the by, you should not be out here alone without at least one male servant to watch over you. Why, there are British soldiers afoot, as well as Indians and various unsavory sorts."

Longing to remove her hand from his arm, Rose grimaced. In truth, she had felt safer before Mr. Snyder imposed his presence upon her. "I agree, sir. My uncle is searching for a new man of work as we speak."

He gazed across the lush field toward the Jones Falls River. The rush of water accompanied the twitter of orioles flittering about the tree tops. "But I do so enjoy a glimpse of such natural beauty."

Rose studied him as he perused the thirty acres of Drummond land that extended to the river on one side and was bordered by a line of trees on the other. The twinkle in his eye bespoke an admiration and longing she had never seen when he looked at her. "Why, Mr. Snyder, if I didn't know better, I'd think you came out here to see my land instead of me." She feigned a grievous tone that ended up sounding giddy. Perhaps because the idea caused her no distress.

"Preposterous!" He snorted then smiled at her and patted her hand that still clutched his elbow. "No land could hold a candle to you, Miss McGuire."

Rose eyed him with suspicion. Despite his charming facade, an insincerity lurked about him—in his mannerisms, his expressions, and even his compliments.

"You know my feelings, Miss McGuire. I would like to ask your uncle's permission to court you." He led her around the corner of the house to the front porch.

"As you have already informed me, Mr. Snyder. And though I am flattered, I must tell you I am not ready to court anyone."

He stopped her at the door, set his tricorn and cane down on a rocking chair and took her hands in his. "It has been seven years since your parents' deaths. Surely you are ready to start your own family." The yearning in his eyes made her stomach fold in on itself. Retrieving her hands, she lowered her gaze. She didn't want to cause him pain— had tried to dissuade his advances, yet still he pursued her. Perhaps she should agree to his courtship. The only other suitors who had come to call had been quickly turned aside by her hoydenish ways and her timidity around men. And with most of the men in town gone off to war—some never to return—Rose's choices were limited. Mr. Snyder was handsome, successful, and kind, and her aunt spoke well of him. *An honorable councilman, my dear. You could do much worse.*

Then why did everything within Rose rebel at the thought of marrying him? "It's the war, Mr. Snyder. I loathe the death and violence and cannot possibly think of courting during a time like this."

He lifted her hand to kiss it then, no doubt remembering the dirt and blood, he released it again. "The war should remind us all of the brevity of life, Miss McGuire. And the need to take advantage of every opportunity." The way he said the word *opportunity*, like a greedy merchant haggling over a purchase, gave her pause. She wished to be more than an opportunity to her would-be husband. In truth, she had a feeling the favorable chance he spoke of had nothing to do with her at all.

And everything to do with her land.

Though her inheritance money had purchased this farm and provided a reasonable living for Rose and her aunt and uncle, when her uncle died—and he was already sixty—Rose would lose the farm unless she married.

And with no other prospects, Rose could not put Mr. Snyder off forever.

Sooner rather than later, she'd have to marry him or risk losing everything and throwing her aunt, Amelia, and Cora out onto the streets.

❖ CHAPTER 4 ❖

*S*plash. *Splash.* A familiar yet strangely unfamiliar sound of moving water drifted through Alex's mind, jarring him awake. The guttural and drawn-out moan of some kind of beast ground over his nerves. A cow, perhaps? Alex shook his head. Searing pain stabbed him and sped down his back. The malodorous smell of manure stung his nose and filled his lungs. A dream. A nightmare. *Cluck. Cluck.* Something pecked his arm. His neck. His cheek.

"What the deuces?" Alex raised his hand with difficulty to bat the offending varmint away. Squawking ensued as he rubbed his eyes in an attempt to pry them open.

The splash halted and footsteps approached. Despite the pounding in his head, he opened his eyes to the sight of an angel—albeit a rather disheveled, dirty angel—leaning over him. Golden curls that caught the sunlight in a glittering halo hung about her face. Blue eyes peered down at him with concern.

"Am I in heaven?" His voice came out cracked and dry.

"No, Mr. Reed. Far from it, I'm afraid." Spreading the folds of her gown, she sat beside him. On the ground. Not on a stool, nor a chair. And he was in no bed. He grabbed a handful of hay with his other hand and felt dirt shove beneath his fingernails.

"Where am I?" Momentary terror struck him. He struggled to rise on his elbows, but he felt weak, as though he were pushing through molasses. And his head. Had it been replaced with a twenty-pound cannonball—a pain-filled cannonball?

"You should rest, Mr. Reed." The angel poured water from a pitcher into a glass. "You've been quite ill."

"Ill." Alex glanced at the bloodstained bandage on his thigh and memories flooded him. Garrick. The sword fight. The firing of a pistol. He raised his eyes to the angel. *The rebel farm girl.*

"Yes, a fever." She lifted the glass to his lips. "Drink this."

Alex's mouth felt like it had been stuffed with cotton. He gulped the water hungrily until it dribbled down his chin. The liquid saturated his tongue and poured down his throat, cooling the parched places and giving him back his voice.

"Easy now." She withdrew the cup and set it down on a small stool beside him.

"Thank you," he managed before his arms began to wobble and he toppled back down onto a bed of hay that he found remarkably soft. The pain in his head dulled only to be replaced by the one in his leg. "My thigh."

"I removed the bullet," the angel said, as if she performed the task on a daily basis. "It is healing nicely."

"You. . .a *woman?*"

"Yes, I assure you, sir, women are quite capable of such complicated procedures." Her tone was caustic.

Caustic and biting—like an enemy. She *was* his enemy. And he was at her mercy. She leaned over him and ran the cloth over his forehead and cheeks. Loose curls sprang from her bun and fell across her delicate shoulders. She smelled of hay and fresh milk. Feminine curves filled out the folds of a plain blue cotton gown. Despite his muddled state, his body warmed at her gentle ministrations. "I meant no offense, miss. . .miss. . ."

"Miss Rose McGuire." She sat back and eyed him quizzically. Her gaze drifted to his chest then quickly snapped away.

Alex glanced down at his open shirt sprinkled with blood. Memories of the sword fight flooded him: Garrick leveling his pistol at this ministering angel before him; her cowering on her knees; Alex's blade protruding from Garrick's gut. Had Alex truly killed him? Or was it all a nightmare conjured up by his feverish mind? "Garrick?"

Pain skittered across her crisp blue eyes. "Your friend is dead."

Remorse fell heavy on Alex. "He was no friend of mine." He tried to rise again but his strength failed him. Should any British soldiers find Garrick's body, there would be an inquiry and a court-martial, followed by a hanging—Alex's hanging. He glanced over the barn. Bales of hay were stacked in a corner, farm tools hung on hooks against the far wall, a ladder led to a loft above, chickens strutted across the floor. No sight of Garrick's body. "What did you do with him?"

"Amelia and I buried him four days ago." Miss McGuire stood and brushed the hay and dirt from her skirt.

"Buried? Four days?" He struggled to lift himself once again. This time he managed to sit. "I must get back to my ship."

Miss McGuire's eyes widened, and she took a step back as if frightened of him. "I assure you, sir, I would love nothing more, but you are in no condition for a long march. Now, I insist you lie down and rest. You need to recover your strength." She gazed at the open doors before facing him again, anger pushing the fear from her face. "The sooner you are out of here the better." With that, she turned around and disappeared into the glaring light as if she had, indeed, come from heaven.

Alex's head spun. Caged in on both sides by wooden railings, he appeared to be lying in some sort of animal stall. The snort of pigs sounded from outside. The stench of manure, aged wood, and horseflesh assailed him; and he fell back onto the hay. Movement caught his eye, and he turned his head to see a pair of giant brown eyes staring down at him from the stall beside his. The cow munched on green twigs and gazed at him with pity. If not for the angel who had just left, Alex would have thought he had died and gone to hell.

Or worse, America.

❖

Rose cradled the bowl in her hands and made her way to the barn, trying not to spill the savory broth. Steam rose from the meaty stew. Her stomach growled. She'd been so anxious to feed Mr. Reed, she'd neglected her own dinner. High in the sky, the hot August sun poured its own steamy rays on her.

"Hello, Prinney." She smiled at the pig as she passed by his sty. He gave her a forlorn snort, but she couldn't stop to let him out now. The redcoat—or bluecoat, she supposed because Mr. Reed was in the navy—had developed quite a voracious appetite since he'd awoken from his fever the day before. Other than bringing him food and checking on his wound, Rose had avoided him as much as possible. She would do only what was necessary to save his life and send him on his way. Anything more would be an insult to the memory of her mother and father. Thankfully, the man seemed even less interested in conversing with her than she did him. Though he spent much of his time in slumber, his eyes were regaining their clarity and his body its strength. A strength that caused Rose to feel increasingly uneasy in his presence—which was why she had elicited Amelia's help today to change his bandage and move him to the icehouse. So far she'd managed to keep his presence from Cora and her aunt and uncle, but it was only a matter of time before one of them ventured to the barn.

Skirting the barn doors, Rose approached him, surprised to see him alert and lying on his back with one arm behind his head. He snapped his hazel eyes her way, giving her a start. A gentle smile curled his lips. "I did not mean to frighten you, Miss McGuire."

"You didn't frighten me." Rose knelt beside him and lifted her chin. "I have brought you some stew."

Gripping the wooden post of Liverpool's empty stall, Mr. Reed lifted himself to a sitting position with minimal effort. Dark wavy hair grazed the collar of his white shirt—a shirt devoid of the waistcoat and cravat that would offer him a modicum of modesty. Instead, the garment hung open over a well-muscled chest. Rose cleared her throat as a heated blush rose up her neck.

"Your color has returned, Mr. Reed." She kept her eyes on the ground as she handed him the steaming bowl.

"Indeed. I feel stronger every day." The sound of his accent grated down her spine. Lifting the dish to his lips, he took a sip, then another and another as he hungrily devoured the stew. "Thank you. I realize that aiding the enemy does not bode well for you or your family."

"No sir, it does not. And the sooner you are gone the better."

"I assure you, I am of the same mind." Dark eyes as deep and mysterious as the swirling water in Jones Falls River remained upon her. "Regardless that our countries are at war, I do not wish you or your family harm."

Rose found no insincerity in his gaze. But that didn't mean she could trust him. She lifted her chin. "Yet when you are well and return to your ship, you will continue to terrorize my friends and neighbors."

Regret clouded his eyes. "I am a part of a war that I did not start nor chose to engage in, miss." He stretched his shoulders, flexing the muscles in his chest.

Averting her gaze, she plucked fresh bandages, a knife, and a satchel from the pocket of her gown. "My aunt returns from Washington tomorrow. If you think you can walk, we should move you to the icehouse where you'll be hidden."

"Sounds rather cold." He gave a mock tremble, followed by a grin.

Ignoring his playful demeanor, Rose pursed her lips. "We have not used it in years, Mr. Reed, but it's down by the river and out of the way. Nobody goes there."

He glanced over the barn, his nose wrinkling in disgust. "And with whom am I to share these chilled quarters? Pigs, chickens, rodents? Or perhaps a sheep or two?" A slight grin toyed upon his lips, but his tone held a hint of hauteur. "Will I at least have a bed?" He grabbed a handful of hay and flung it to the side. "Or do all Americans sleep in the straw?"

Rose grimaced. *Pompous bore.* "No sir. We reserve our barns strictly for odious beasts."

He quirked a brow. Instead of the outrage she expected, amusement settled on his face. "Well, at least I know my place."

"I doubt that, Mr. Reed, since you find yourself in my country instead of your own."

He chuckled. "Indeed." Yet the supercilious grin remained on his lips and something else—a flicker of admiration—crossed his eyes that made Rose's stomach squirm.

She tore her gaze from him. He taunted her. Enjoyed taunting her. Rose glanced over her shoulder out the door. Oh where was Amelia? Rose shouldn't be here alone with this man—this enemy who was twice her size and getting stronger by the minute.

Picking up the knife, she studied the bloodstained bandage wrapped around his leg. The hole she'd been forced to tear in his white breeches offered her a view of a thigh as thick and hard as a tree trunk. She'd never seen a man's bare leg before—barely noticed the muscular tone of it during the harrowing moments when as she'd plucked the bullet out. But now the vision sent an odd sensation through her. Ignoring the feeling, she began to slice through the bandage. Her hand shook.

He touched her arm. She froze and met his gaze, her heart racing.

Releasing her, he shook his head, his eyes searching hers. "Do not fear me. I have no intention of doing you harm, Miss McGuire."

"Yes you do, Mr. Reed. You intend to rob me of my freedom." Rose continued her work, reminding herself that despite his attempt at kindness, Mr. Reed was her enemy. In fact, *because* of his kindness, Rose must never trust him. No doubt finding himself at her mercy, he merely attempted to worm into her graces for his own preservation. When he regained his full strength, she would use her uncle's musket to encourage him to leave. She shuddered at the thought of holding the vile weapon. But she may have no choice.

"I did not mean to sound ungrateful." He rubbed the thick stubble on his chin and eyed her. "Why do you not turn me in to your military?"

"You saved my life, Mr. Reed. How can I do any less for you?"

"War changes the rules of civility, Miss McGuire."

She sliced through the bandage and began to peel it away. "Not for me, it doesn't. Now stay still."

Wishing Mr. Reed would stop talking to her, and in particular stop looking at her, Rose focused her attention on the task of removing the final bandage. She poked at the skin around his wound. No puffiness, no swelling or discoloring to indicate infection. Just firm muscle met her touch.

"Thank you for tending my injury." Despite the British lilt, his deep voice soothed over her, untying her nerves.

"As I said, I was obligated to help you." She forced spite in her tone.

"As I was to prevent Mr. Garrick from ravishing you."

A shiver coursed through her at the memory, and she lifted her eyes to his. "Then we are even, Mr. Reed. And when you are well and are gone from here, we shall owe each other nothing more."

But he didn't seem to be listening to her. Instead his gaze focused on her neck, and a smile played at the corners of his mouth. "You have dirt on your. . ." He pointed toward her upper chest.

Looking down, Rose wiped a muddy smudge from the skin above her neckline then she scoured him with a sharp gaze. "And you are covered in dirt as well, Mr. Reed."

He glanced down the length of his filthy uniform and chuckled. "Indeed."

Amelia floated into the barn on a stiff breeze that fluttered the lacy trim of her lavender gown. She held a sack in one hand. "I've brought the clothes you requested, miss." Her eyes trained on Mr. Reed while a coquettish grin danced over her lips.

Despite the woman's flirtations, Rose released a sigh of relief at her presence. "Mr. Reed, may I present Mrs. Amelia Wilkins, my companion and lady's maid."

"My pleasure, Mrs. Wilkins." Reed nodded toward her. "Forgive me if I do not get up."

Amelia giggled. "No need, Mr. Reed. We are most happy that you did not die."

"I share your enthusiasm." Mr. Reed grinned revealing an unusually straight row of white teeth.

Reaching into her pocket, Rose opened a small pouch and spread saturated leaves over Mr. Reed's wound.

"Poison?" He chuckled.

"Comfrey. To speed the healing process." Giving him a lopsided smile, she wrapped a fresh bandage around his thigh. "So you can leave as soon as possible." She tied it tight, eliciting a wince from him and bringing her a measure of satisfaction, albeit only momentary.

Stretching his leg, he gripped the wooden rail of Liverpool's stall. "Then I will be happy to accommodate you, miss. Do you have a horse I may borrow?"

"Not one I'm willing to forfeit."

"Why not lend him Valor?" Amelia glanced toward the filly's stall where the horse stood watching the proceedings.

Rose gave her a measured look. "Who is to bring her back to me after Mr. Reed boards his ship?"

Amelia took a step toward Mr. Reed. "I will go with him and bring her back."

"Don't be a goose, Amelia. All alone? With British soldiers raiding the countryside?"

Mr. Reed's brow gleamed with sweat as he strained to pull himself up. Leaning upon his good leg, he blinked as if trying to clear his head. "Miss McGuire is right. It isn't safe for a woman alone." He faced Rose. "A carriage perhaps? You could bring your footman for protection."

Rose packed her bandages and salve and slowly stood. "You presume too much, Mr. Reed. Besides, both our carriages are in use."

Mr. Reed's breath came in spurts as he fell against the wooden railing. "I will walk then."

"When you cannot even stand?" Rose took a timid step toward the man who if he were standing to his full height would surely tower over her by at least a foot. The last thing she needed was for him to fall and injure himself further. "It must be miles back to your ship."

"And you're in enemy territory, sir," Amelia offered as she slipped beside Rose. "You'll either open your wound and bleed to death or be caught and hanged."

Mr. Reed peered at them both through half-open lids. Hot wind swirled about the barn, swaying a strand of his hair across his stubbled jaw. "Either way, ladies, I shall not impose on you any further." He glanced down at the hay. "Now where, pray tell, have you placed my coat and weapons?"

Rose grimaced. She wondered when he would ask about them. Thank goodness she'd had Amelia store the heinous things in a trunk in the loft. "They are hidden, Mr. Reed. Out of your reach where you can do no harm with them."

"Do you think me so base as to assault the woman who saved my life?" Incredulous pride saturated his tone. "Or to assault any woman for that matter. I am second lieutenant aboard the HMS *Undefeatable*, miss, an officer in His Majesty's Navy and not without honor."

"I believe your Mr. Garrick gave me a taste of your navy's idea of honor," Rose retorted, tossing her nose in the air.

Amelia fluttered her lashes. "You were so brave to come to Rose's defense."

"I could do no less." His admiring gaze swept to Rose.

Confusion jumbled her thoughts and tore through her contempt. She took a step back.

He frowned. "Very well, I shall leave without my things." Releasing the railing, he took a step forward on his good foot, but started to wobble.

Dashing toward him, Rose shoved her shoulder beneath his arm, gesturing Amelia to do the same on the other side. He smelled of hay and man, and she nearly toppled beneath his weight. Amelia gripped his other side and they managed to assist him out of the barn and across the field.

"Oh my, he's quite heavy, miss." Amelia exclaimed in wonder.

"My apologies, ladies." His murmur came out weak as they led him step by painstaking step to the icehouse and propped him against the front wall.

Rose opened the door and a waft of cool, moist air tainted with mold blasted over her, refreshing her hot skin. She and Amelia assisted Mr. Reed inside and helped him down onto the bed of hay Rose had prepared earlier.

"I am not without compassion." She sighed. "You may stay a few more days until you are well enough to walk."

Mr. Reed propped himself up on his hands and studied the gloomy room.

Amelia handed her the bundle that had been slung across her free arm. "I've brought some of Samuel's old clothes."

Grabbing the sack, Rose tossed it at Mr. Reed's feet. "You may want to change. If someone does find you, it would be better if you weren't dressed like a British naval officer."

"Thank you." Mr. Reed nodded.

Rose glanced at the dreary walls, the empty space, anywhere but into his kind dark eyes. "I shall bring you some food and water later. There's a bucket in the corner where you can relieve yourself."

He wrinkled his nose, and a brief glimmer of repulsion crossed his face before he dipped his head in her direction. "I am completely at your mercy, Miss McGuire."

"So it would seem." Rose started to leave, confusion tumbling within her at his accommodating attitude.

"Why do you hold me with such scorn?" His indignant tone turned her around.

Rose threw back her shoulders. "As I said before, because you are attempting to rob me of my freedom, sir." Sorrow weighed on her heart. "And because your countrymen murdered my family."

His throat moved beneath a swallow, and he opened his mouth as if to say something but then quickly slammed it shut.

"And because of that"—retribution surged through Rose, tightening her voice—"you will keep hidden and behave yourself, Mr. Reed. Or mark my words, I will gladly turn you in to the American military where you will rot in prison until the end of the war."

❖ CHAPTER 5 ❖

Rose adjusted her sprigged muslin gown and fingered the lace trim on her collar. She gazed out the window of the landau as they traveled down Calvert Street. Beside her Amelia pinched her cheeks and chattered incessantly about who she was going to see at church, which couples she had heard were courting, and which privateers might be in town.

Amelia glanced out the coach's small window with a sigh. "Privateering is so romantic."

Aunt Muira exchanged a smile with Rose at the woman's fanciful views of life. Dressed in a plain cotton gown of emerald green, Rose's aunt looked much younger than her fifty-eight years. Perhaps it was the love she shared with Uncle Forbes that kept her so young and vibrant. Rose wondered if she would ever find such happiness with a man.

She turned her gaze back to Amelia and saw her wistful expression. "Privateering is anything but romantic, Amelia." Rose clasped her gloved hands together in her lap, noticing the tremble that went through them. "It is difficult and dangerous work."

"Oh why must you be such a crosspatch, Rose." Amelia closed her eyes as the breeze blowing in through the window sent her dark curls twirling over her neck. "I daresay I hope I am never as frightened as you are of everything."

Rose lowered her chin beneath the affront, yet before her anger had a chance to swell, she remembered her trembling hands. As curt as Amelia was, her maid spoke the truth.

Aunt Muira leaned forward and touched Rose's hands. "How are you faring, dear?" Her dress brought out the deep green in her eyes—eyes full of concern.

"It grows easier each time I travel into town." Rose smiled and her aunt squeezed her hands and leaned back on the leather seat. Though Rose knew her aunt referred to the tragedy that had befallen Rose years ago, it was the recent assault by Garrick that had Rose's nerves twisted in a knot. In fact, despite her trembling hands, she was proud of herself that the incident had not kept her from her Sunday trip into town. A trip she'd only found the courage to take during the past few years. Before that, constant dangers that lurked on the city streets had kept her home frozen in fear. Yet now she was beginning to wonder whether her farm offered her any refuge at all.

Bright morning sun angled across the carriage windows and glittered over Aunt Muira's pearl earrings—a remnant of the lady's former wealth. Her jewelry being the only luxury she had kept from her past.

As they turned down Baltimore Street, Rose adjusted her bonnet and gazed at the brightly colored homes passing by in a rainbow of colors. Mulberry and hackberry trees lined the avenue while pink and red hollyhocks dotted the landscape. Turning, they ascended a small bridge that crossed over Jones Falls River into the east side of the city. The wooden planks creaked and groaned beneath the weight of the carriage. The *clip-clop* of the horses' hooves echoed over the sparkling water that frolicked over boulders and fallen branches toward the sea. On days like this, it was hard to imagine that their country was at war. It was hard to imagine being frightened of anything.

Aunt Muira smiled at Rose—a calm, loving smile that reminded Rose of her mother's. A pang of longing pinched her heart. Oh how she longed to talk with her own mother—to share her fears, her hopes, her disappointments. Though Aunt Muira didn't hide her love for Rose, neither did she harbor much patience for Rose's timid temperament.

The smell of salt from the nearby port mixed with the sweet nectar of flowers blew in through the window, and Rose drew a deep breath. She looked forward to Sundays—a day of rest and worship. Safely surrounded by family, it was a day she could get away from the farm. Away from her problems.

From the British officer hiding in the icehouse.

A twinge of guilt stiffened her. While it was the Christian thing to do, Rose felt like a traitor to her country for helping Mr. Reed. She should hate him. She should want him dead for what his countrymen had stolen from her. But after he returned her insults with courtesy and her threats with graciousness, she could conjure no feelings of contempt toward him. Regardless, she must put him from her mind. His strength was returning and he'd soon be gone. Back to his ship. Back to his nightly raids.

Back to being her enemy.

"You seem lost in your thoughts today, my dear," Aunt Muira said.

"Yes, forgive me." Rose gripped the window frame as the coach jostled over a bump in the road. "How was your trip to Washington?"

Her aunt's lips pursed. "Worthwhile." She shook her head as a breeze sent her red curls dancing. "My heart saddens for those poor little ones. This war has stripped many children of their parents. And of course, Reverend Hargrave takes them all in. Why, the orphanage is bursting at the seams with lost, desperate children." The lines on her face seemed to deepen as she spoke. "And with only dear Edna there to assist him. No one in Washington seems to care. They are far too busy with their politics and their fancy balls."

Amelia tore her gaze from the window. "I see no harm in an occasional ball. It is most agreeable to have a pleasant diversion from the war."

Rose cringed at the impropriety of her maid chastising the lady of the house.

Yet Aunt Muira only smiled. "I quite agree, Amelia." She tugged upon her white gloves. "I myself enjoy a good soiree now and then, yet never at the expense of the comfort of those in need."

Amelia nodded as the landau pulled up in front of Uncle Forbes's small stone church. Mr. Markham leaped down from the driver's perch and assisted them one by one to the cobblestone walkway leading to the front door. A sign by its side read FIRST PRESBYTERIAN CHURCH. REVEREND FORBES DRUMMOND. Pride swelled within Rose for her uncle's accomplishments.

An odd assortment of people ambled through the open front doors, ladies in gowns of calico and pastel muslin, trimmed with ribbons and long colorful scarves. Wide-brimmed bonnets decorated with brightly colored plumes graced their heads. The more fashionable men wore silk breeches and white stockings, cocked hats, lacy cravats, and high-collared coats. Fishermen and seamen dressed in stained cotton shirts and breeches that smelled of fish and brine entered the church right alongside the ladies and gentlemen in their finest and took seats in the back or along the upper balcony.

Rose smiled at the diverse crowd her uncle drew to church as she slipped into their assigned pew near the front. Amelia and Aunt Muira eased in beside her. Cool air swirled around her, enveloping her in the musky aged smell of the church—a smell that always seemed to settle Rose's nerves. As Mr. Smithers, the organist, began to play, a white blur brought Rose's attention to Marianne, her good friend, waving her gloved hand. Her one-year-old son, Jacob, crawled up in her lap as her husband, Noah, eased in beside her and nodded his greeting to Rose.

Rose waved in return. Her heart lifted to see her friend so happy. And also to see that Noah was back in town. Although their relationship had not begun on the best of terms, Marianne and Noah were truly blessed with a great marriage. Rose had no idea how Marianne endured his long absences or the danger he was constantly under as a privateer during wartime. But the sweet woman had a peace about her that Rose envied. Her uncle stepped out from a side door and took his place by the retable. After leading the congregation in several hymns, he began his message. Though his sermons were usually quite thought-provoking, Rose found her mind unable to focus today. Instead, she gazed at her uncle, admiring the man who had once been nothing but an indentured servant.

After the sermon, they stood to sing another hymn before the crowd slowly filtered out of the now stifling church into the stifling summer sun. Rose led Amelia and her aunt to stand in the shade of an elm tree while she peered through the crowd for Marianne. Several young gentlemen and not a few seamen cast admiring glances toward Rose and Amelia. Giggling, Amelia drew her fan out and waved it enticingly about her face.

"Be careful, or you'll signal one of them to come this way." Rose stiffened her jaw. The last thing she needed was to endure some man's amorous dalliance.

"Perhaps that is what I wish." Amelia gave her a playful glance. "At least the rich ones."

"Oh my." Aunt Muira gave a hefty sigh. "What are we to do with you?"

Smiling, Marianne emerged from the crowd, young Jacob in her arms and her sister, Lizzie, by her side. "There you are. I was hoping you hadn't left. We have so much to catch up on." The shorter woman gazed up at Rose just as Jacob grabbed the edge of her bonnet and pulled it down over her eyes. "Oh drat. He's become quite a handful." Marianne nudged her bonnet back up and kissed Jacob on the cheek.

Lizzie cocked her head, sending brown curls bobbing. "Good morning, Miss Rose."

"I can't believe how big you are getting, Lizzie," Rose said.

"I am nine now. Almost ten." The girl announced with a bit of pride.

"Indeed." Rose leaned over. "You have become quite a lovely young lady. Before we know it, you'll be all grown and married like your sister."

Lizzie smiled up at her sister as a blush blossomed on her cheeks.

Aunt Muira brushed her fingers over Jacob's soft skin, a look of longing in her moistening eyes. "He is absolutely precious, Mrs. Brenin."

Rose grabbed her aunt's hand and gave it a squeeze. Why the good Lord had not given children to such wonderful people, Rose would never understand.

Her aunt leaned toward Lizzie. "And my niece is correct. What a young lady you have become, Miss Lizzie. Is that a new dress?"

The little girl beamed and twirled around, sending the flowered calico fluttering in the wind. "Yes, it is."

"It is lovely."

"And I have good news." Marianne's brown eyes glowed. "I am with child again."

"Truly? I am so glad!" Rose's eyes drifted down to Marianne's belly just barely rounding beneath her gown.

Noah appeared by her side and took Jacob from her arms.

"You are looking well, Noah." Rose gazed at his sun-streaked hair and bronzed face. "Privateering agrees with you."

He shared a knowing glance with his wife. "It is my calling, to be sure. My duty to my country. And I won't complain that it is also quite lucrative." He tossed Jacob into the air, eliciting a giggle from the boy. The babe's white lacy gown billowed in the breeze, revealing his chubby legs. "I do, however, long for the day when I can spend more time home with my family."

Marianne's eyes brimmed with love. "You'd be bored silly at home.

As it is, I'm happy with the time we have together."

She faced Rose. "Would you care to spend the afternoon with us, Rose? And Amelia and your aunt and uncle, of course. We plan to have our meal at an inn by the docks then take a stroll down Market Street."

Rose hesitated. The docks meant ships and ships meant sailors. Yet surely with Noah and her uncle along, she would be safe. Ignoring the fear gurgling in her belly, she lifted a questioning brow toward her aunt. Amelia crowded beside her, nearly bursting with excitement.

Aunt Muira tightened her lips and glanced toward the port. "I don't know, dear. I hoped you would accompany me to Mrs. Pickersgill's. She's most anxious to inform us of her new charity for women and children orphaned by the war. You did say you wanted to help, didn't you?"

Rose bit her lip, guilt and longing waging war in her thoughts. Yes, she did. But after what happened with Garrick, the thought of facing women who had suffered as she had caused a lump to form in her throat. "Please forgive me, Aunt, but I. . .I. . .do not think I am up to the task today. Can we go later in the week?" She avoided looking at the frown that must certainly be upon her aunt's lips and focused instead on Noah tickling his son beneath the chin.

"I shall be with them every moment, Mrs. Drummond." Noah came to her rescue. "And I will drive Rose and Amelia home in my carriage before sundown."

"Oh do say they can join us, Mrs. Drummond." Marianne held her bonnet down against a burst of salt-laden wind. "Amelia would be such a help with Lizzie while Rose and I catch up on news."

Aunt Muira glanced at her husband who was still greeting people as they left the church.

"Very well, I suppose so." Aunt Muira withdrew a handkerchief and dabbed at the perspiration on her neck. "But be home in time for supper, my dear. You know how cantankerous Cora gets when we are late."

Rose kissed her aunt on the cheek and watched her join her husband, then she turned toward her friends. "Shall we?" She threaded her arm through Marianne's as they sauntered down the pathway toward Pratt Street and the docks.

"You have come a long way, Rose," Marianne whispered as they neared the water.

Rose glanced over the harbor that was bustling with activity. "Not as far as you think. My nerves are a bundle of knots even as we speak."

Marianne patted her hand. "Well, all the more reason I'm glad you joined us. You are safe with us." She glanced at her husband walking ahead with Jacob in his arms. "My husband can handle the fiercest rogues, I assure you."

Rose admired Noah's strength and confidence as he strolled down the street. She longed for her own protector. But how could she trust any man after what had happened?

As they approached the water, the bare masts of dozens of ships rose like a thicket of bare winter trees. Bells clanged, workers shouted, street vendors hawked their wares, children laughed, and somewhere in the distance music played. The malodorous smells of the harbor mixed with pleasant scents of food as the group hurried to get out of the hot sun and gathered into Chamberlain's tavern. There, they claimed a table on the open patio and enjoyed a refreshing pitcher of lemonade, spiced cake, and fresh crab.

A breeze wafted in from the port, cooling the perspiration on Rose's arms. Lizzie sat beside Amelia, who seemed most pleased to have finally found someone who would listen to her opinionated narrative on the fashion, status, wealth, and courting rituals of those citizens who had the misfortune of passing by the tavern. Noah entertained his son while Marianne and Rose drew their heads together catching up on all that had passed since they'd last visited.

When the sun began its trek toward the western horizon, the group strolled down Market Street. With Jacob in his arms, Noah led the way past an endless succession of one-story brightly colored houses of white, blue, and yellow lining the cobblestone road on both sides, broken up by the occasional quaint entrance of a rich merchant's brick mansion. Locust trees and the rich blooms of honeysuckle, butternut, and Virginia creeper decorated the pathways between the buildings.

Rose leaned toward her friend. "I do believe Noah gets more and more handsome every time I see him."

"I agree." She gave a sultry smile.

"Incredible since, if I recall, you once loathed the very sight of him." Rose chuckled and tugged the brim of her bonnet further down against the setting sun.

"God does work in mysterious ways." Marianne eased her fingers over her belly. "If Noah were in town just a bit more often, my life would be perfect."

"Apparently he's in town quite often enough." Rose giggled and Marianne joined her.

Thinking of a new baby reminded Rose of Marianne's ailing mother. "How does your mother fare?"

"Ah, she is well. Thank you. We have enough money now to hire the best physician in Maryland. Though she requires a great deal of rest, she has flourished under her new medicines."

"I am so pleased to hear it," Rose said as a great throng of gentlemen and ladies dressed in a rich display of brocades and taffetas passed by, flirting, jesting, and enjoying the warm summer air. Ahead, Amelia was thankfully too preoccupied with Lizzie to notice the attention flung her way by some of the passing young men. Rose flattened her lips. With Amelia's comely appearance and coquettish ways, she was bound to draw the wrong kind of attention sooner or later.

The thought had barely drifted through her mind when two handsome gentlemen, attired like London dandies, tipped their hats first toward Amelia and then toward Rose as they passed.

A sudden queasiness gripped Rose, followed by anger.

"You garner quite a bit of attention, Rose." Marianne gave her a sly look.

"I wish I didn't." Rose huffed. She hated the way some men ogled her as if she were a sweetmeat, but at Marianne's frown, she decided to make light of it. "Of course they find me appealing when I am dressed like this. But when they see me petting a pig and my face covered with mud, they simply"—she attempted to mimic the tone of haughty society—*"cannot tolerate such unsophisticated, unladylike behavior."*

Marianne giggled. "A man will come along who finds those things adorable, you'll see."

But Rose was not so sure. Nor was she sure she even wanted a husband anymore. The clip-clop of a horse and carriage bounced over her ears as it passed, laughter spilling from within. "You would hardly know we are at war," Rose said.

"Indeed. But I believe it is important to carry on with our lives as normally as we can even in the midst of war," Marianne said. "Otherwise we will go mad."

Rose played with a curl that dangled over her cheek. "It sickens me to think the British fleet is just miles off our coast."

"Did you hear the pistol shots a week ago?" Marianne placed her hand on Rose's arm. "I heard that British troops were spotted nearby."

Amelia coughed.

"In fact, a poor woman, Mrs. Davison—perhaps you know her?" Marianne asked.

Rose shook her head, afraid to hear any more.

"Why, she was attacked in her own home, and then the brigands burned it down while she watched from her field."

Noah shot a stern glance over his shoulder. "Which is precisely why you and your mother are staying at my father's house while I am away." His commanding voice reminded Rose why he was a captain at sea.

"And I have hired additional footmen for your protection," he added. "Blasted British."

"Were you not impressed upon one of their ships?" Amelia's admiring gaze fixed upon Noah.

He nodded toward his wife. "Both Marianne and I were, yes."

Amelia slipped back beside Marianne, dragging Lizzie by her side. "You were, as well, Mrs. Brenin?"

"Yes." She exchanged an adoring look with her husband. "But we survived."

"Their cruelty is inexcusable," Noah remarked, switching Jacob to his other arm.

Amelia lowered her chin, and Rose knew she thought of her husband.

"Oh look, isn't that Mr. Snyder?" Marianne pointed. "Over there talking to General Smith."

Rose followed her friend's gaze to see the councilman, dressed in his usual lace cravat and double-breasted tailcoat, cane in hand. Her stomach dropped. Could she not escape him? "Let us turn around, shall we?"

She spun Marianne about and headed the other way, but Mr. Snyder's shout slithered down her spine, halting her. "By the by, Miss McGuire."

Rose released a shaky sigh, gave Marianne a look of defeat, and swung back around.

General Smith, with Mr. Snyder on his heels like an obedient puppy, wove between two passing horses and marched toward her as if on a mission. The gold epaulets and brass buttons on his dark military coat glimmered in the sunlight. What could he possibly want with her? Surely he couldn't have discovered her secret. Yet the pointed look on his face made Rose's throat close.

The general halted before her. At least sixty years of age, he carried himself with the authority of a man accustomed to command. Now in charge of the Maryland militia and ordered to fortify Fort McHenry, he had quickly become the most important man in Baltimore. He nodded toward them all. "Miss McGuire, Mrs. Brenin, Mr. Brenin. Good day to you."

Noah and Marianne extended their greetings.

"Good day, General." Rose's smile felt stiff. "Are you enjoying your Sunday?"

"As much as one can during wartime."

Mr. Snyder eased up beside the general, rubbing against his arm as if he hoped the man's authority and wisdom would somehow transfer to himself.

"Miss McGuire." The general directed his gaze toward Rose. "There were several reports of musket and pistol fire near your uncle's land eight days ago."

"Indeed?" Rose forced her breathing to calm.

"Did you hear anything?"

"Me? No." She batted the air. "I sleep quite soundly, sir."

Amelia leaned on a nearby tree, clutching Lizzie to her side.

"Are you all right, Miss Amelia?" Lizzie asked.

Ignoring them, Mr. Snyder shot Rose a look of concern. "Your neighbor, Mr. Franklin, insists he saw British forces on your property." He tapped his cane on the ground.

"Confound it all." Noah's jaw bunched. "I cannot believe the audacity of those redcoats."

Rose lifted a hand to her neck. "My word! On my property?"

Mr. Snyder narrowed his eyes and leaned toward her. "Are you well? You've gone suddenly pale."

Rose drew out her fan and waved it over her face. "It's the thought of British soldiers on my property, sir. Far too distressing to imagine. But certainly I would have seen them."

"I am not implying otherwise." The general cocked his head and stared at her quizzically. "However, for your protection and the protection of Baltimore, I would like to come and ensure all is well."

Noah nodded his approval.

General Smith leaned toward Rose as if he had a grand secret to tell her. "Though this may shock you, miss, there are British sympathizers among us."

Rose's chest felt as though an anvil had landed on it. "Here in Baltimore? I cannot believe it." She feigned a gasp. Wondering if the man was playing with her, if he knew exactly what he would find on her land.

The general huffed in disdain. The lines of his face tightened. "And if I should discover any of them aiding the enemy, I'll have them hanged for treason."

"As well you should, General," Noah added.

The air around Rose grew stagnant and stifling. She gasped for a breath. "Indeed" was all she managed to mutter.

"General, you've upset the ladies." Mr. Snyder furrowed his brows in concern.

"Of course, forgive me." General Smith flipped open his pocket watch. "Nevertheless, I plan to send a few of my men to your farm. Councilman Snyder will accompany them, if that would make you feel more at ease."

"Well, I cannot say." Rose's voice came out shaky, and Marianne took her arm in hers and gave her a curious look. "You should seek my uncle's permission first."

"In wartime, I need no permission, Miss McGuire." General Smith snapped his watch shut and plopped it back into his pocket. "I can have a small band of militia formed within the hour. I assure you, it won't take long. We shall be in and out before your evening repast."

❖ CHAPTER 6 ❖

Alex leaned back against the open doorframe of the icehouse and gazed over the lush green farm. Farm indeed. For it appeared the fields had not been plowed nor planted for quite some time. No doubt the cow and the horse, both of whom now grazed among the grass and weeds, were the only things that kept the forest from reclaiming the land. From the icehouse, which was situated at the edge of the property near the tree line and not far from a river—the mad rush of which had soothed him to sleep the past few nights—Alex possessed a grand view of the property. Smoke curled from the small brick house at the center of the land, evidence that at least one person remained at home. Most likely a servant since Alex had seen Miss McGuire, Amelia, and an older lady leave in a landau hours ago. An elderly gentleman had left on a lone horse at dawn.

The barn where Alex had fought with Garrick and where he'd been tended to by the lovely Miss McGuire stood to the right of the house, while a smaller barn or stable perched on the other side. A quaint manor, to be sure, a rich and fertile land that was well placed beside the river. Yet quite rustic compared to the Reed estate from which Alex hailed. In fact, one might even call this American farm barbaric.

Yet there was something soothing, something peaceful about the scene that eased through Alex like a warm elixir, loosening his coiled nerves and calming his mind. Or perhaps that elixir came in the form of the angel who had tended him so faithfully these past eight days.

An avenging angel, to be sure. Though Miss McGuire appeared angelic on the outside, the fire burning in those blue eyes and her occasional caustic retort spoke otherwise.

She hated Alex. Simply because he was British. He'd never experienced that level of prejudice before. But how could he blame her? Her parents had been murdered by the British. And now his countrymen were attempting to reclaim her country for the Crown.

Alex gripped the knife and continued whittling away at the thick branch he'd found among the trees. Miss McGuire had stolen his pistol and service sword, but she'd not found the knife he kept hidden within one of his boots. He studied his handiwork. Soon he'll have fashioned a crutch that would aid him in his trek back to the Gunpowder River, where he'd first landed. With God's help and a bit of luck, he'd come across a cockboat from one of the ships. God's help. Alex wondered if God had anything to do with any of this. Or if the Almighty took note of Alex's life at all. Lately, it seemed, God had forgotten all about him.

Leaves rustled and a twig snapped. Alex jerked toward the sound, knife before him. A gray squirrel eyed him with bored curiosity before it darted away, pinecone in its mouth. By now, Alex expected Captain Milford to have sent a band of men to search for him and Lieutenant Garrick. It wasn't every day a British frigate lost both its first and second lieutenants. But it had been eight days, and he'd not seen a single British soldier. Either they were otherwise engaged in important battles or Alex suffered from an overinflated view of his own importance. He hoped it was the former. He had spent too many hard years serving His Majesty's Navy to accept such callous dismissal.

He scratched his arm and then his chest—yet again. What pesky varmint inhabited this loathsome clothing the lady had given him to wear? The fabric was course and stiff and the shirt and breeches were far too small. Not to mention the foul smell that permeated his new attire. No doubt the garments had not been properly washed since they were last worn. But he'd had no choice. Miss McGuire had been correct on one point: It would be best if he were not discovered in his uniform.

Alex stretched his leg out over the dirt and winced. It had healed nicely and only pained him when he attempted to stand. Despite being a woman, Miss McGuire had done a good job of extracting the bullet and dressing the wound. In a day or two, Alex should be able to walk the distance he needed back to his ship, back to his people. Oddly, he found no joy in the prospect. He drew in a deep breath of warm air and allowed the scent of honeysuckle and pine to fill his lungs. Though he knew he'd have to go back to his ship eventually, this brief respite from the horrors of war did his soul good. As long as he kept hidden away and did not endanger this rebel family, why should he rush back and risk reopening his wound?

Leaning his head back against the wooden doorframe, he thought of the lovely Miss McGuire. Rebellious curls that refused to be restrained framed her face in a silken web of glittering gold. Her eyes, the turquoise color of the sea he'd once seen in the West Indies—clear and sharp. With a wit to match. So outspoken. So unlike the women he'd known back home. One woman in particular came to mind. Miss Elizabeth Burgess, demure and sweet at least in etiquette and mannerisms. But beneath the outward facade of feminine perfection, a devious vixen raged.

On the contrary, despite Miss McGuire's harsh words and her obvious hatred toward his nationality and uniform her inner kindness overwhelmed him. She had every reason to turn him over to the military authorities. Yet she saved his life, healed his wound, protected him. He'd never been on the receiving end of such true Christian charity.

Slipping his knife inside his boot, he propped the end of the crutch into the dirt and hoisted himself up. The muscles in his back and arms ached and his thigh throbbed, but he felt strength surge through him. Shoving the handle of his crutch beneath his left arm, he tested it with his weight, careful not to place any strain on his injured leg. Perfect. This would do nicely. A gentle breeze wafted over him, cooling his sweat and bringing the smells of the earth, the forest, and life. Sunlight set the field aglow in various shades of green that waved before him like a mossy sea. America was indeed a beautiful land.

But it was Britain's land. And these people were British subjects.

The sooner they faced that, the better. Arrogance and greed had made them forget their homeland—the parent country of their birth. Like rebellious children, they needed to be reminded who was in authority. Hopefully, that reminder would not take the lives of too many people. Or of one lovely lady in particular.

Alex released a sigh of resignation. Regardless of the lady's allure and the peace of this land, he should leave tomorrow night. The longer he stayed, the more danger he placed on her and her family. Alex would rejoin his ship and secure his future as an honored British naval officer. No one need know what had happened with Garrick. Alex had taken the only action available to him in the defense of an innocent woman. It mattered not that she was an American. He had done the honorable thing. And if he continued doing the honorable thing on board the HMS *Undefeatable*, this war would not only bring him the prize money he needed, but the accolades he required to earn the forgiveness of his brother and respect of his father. And maybe even a welcome home.

The clomp of horses' hooves and the grating of carriage wheels filled the air. He glanced toward the road leading to the house. The family returned. But it wasn't the same landau that left that morning. Alex froze. Behind the carriage, a band of horses trotted. He squinted at the sight. Men, armed with muskets and swords, some in blue-and-white uniforms, spread like a stormy wake behind the landau.

So, Miss McGuire had alerted the authorities after all. Alex's heart raced as his mind sped, searching a course of action. There was no way he could outrun them in his condition.

❖

Ignoring Mr. Snyder's outstretched hand, Rose leaped from the carriage, trying to contain her fear behind a polite mask of composure.

"By the by, Miss McGuire," Mr. Snyder said as he assisted Amelia behind her. "You seem flustered." His eyes gleamed as if he knew something.

As if he knew she was about to be accused of treason.

"Not flustered, sir." She offered him a tight smile. "Simply tired after my long day in town and anxious to rest."

"Of course." He nodded, then searched the area—no doubt for a groomsman to take his horse—before he tied the reins to a post with a huff. "Someday I shall be able to afford a coachman." He grumbled under his breath. "And you a footman, perhaps?"

Rose frowned. A ridiculous comment in the midst of wartime.

Amelia brushed past Rose and entered the house, terror screaming from her eyes. The thunder of horse hooves pounded the air and shook the ground as a dozen men, both regular army and militia stormed toward them.

Rose struggled to breathe. In the western sky, the setting sun barely grazed the tops of the trees, sending spindly bright fingers across the farm, poking and prying into every dark corner. Her gaze shot unbidden to the icehouse in the distance. The door was shut. Was Mr. Reed inside or outside? If inside, he'd never be able to leave unnoticed.

Cora came running through the front door, wiping her hands on her apron. "What is happenin', child? Why are these men here?"

"Never fear, Cora." Rose took her arm in hers and led her back inside. The spicy smell of roast rabbit and wood smoke filled her nose. Normally Rose found them to be comforting aromas, but under the circumstances, they only enhanced her fear of losing everything that was dear to her—family, home, and freedom. She faced the cook. "They are here to protect us."

Or arrest us as traitors.

The cook's chubby cheeks quivered as her dark eyes skittered toward the door. "Then why are you shakin', miss?"

Rose snatched her arm back. "I'm just tired." She glanced up the stairs, wondering where Amelia had gone. "Now please run along and finish preparing the meal. Aunt Muira and Uncle Forbes will be here shortly."

With a frown, Cora turned and waddled toward the kitchen, muttering something about soldiers having no business searching the farm.

Taking a deep breath, Rose faced General Smith and Mr. Snyder as they marched through the front door. The general's thick boots thumped over the wood, grinding Rose's nerves to dust. He removed his bicorn and held it by his side. "Miss McGuire, we shall be no bother to you, I am sure."

"No trouble at all." Rose tugged off her gloves if only to keep her hands from shaking. She tossed them onto a table lining the wall of the foyer as she took a mental inventory of any incriminating evidence lying about the farm. Mr. Reed's coat and weapons were in a wooden chest on the top rafters of the barn. Other than that and the freshly dug dirt of Garrick's grave, there should be no sign of any traitorous activities.

Unless the soldiers looked in the icehouse.

If they did, at least her aunt and uncle wouldn't be here to witness Rose's arrest.

Five soldiers entered behind the general, two of whom Rose recognized as men from town who had joined the militia. They wore the same white trousers as the regular army but their dark blue jackets were devoid of the golden stripes and red trim that marked them as military. They both tipped their straw hats in her direction. "Miss McGuire."

"Mr. Cohosh. Mr. Blake." She gave a tremulous smile.

"My men will search your home." General Smith's commanding tone left no room for argument.

Mr. Snyder stood by the door, hat and cane in hand, and a worrisome look on his face.

Rose clenched her jaw. "General, this is pushing matters rather far. Do you think I wouldn't know if British soldiers were in my own house?"

"They are sneaky little devils, Miss McGuire," the general said. "It is for your own protection."

With a huff, Rose gestured toward the stairway. "You are wasting your time, gentlemen. Please be advised that my lady's maid may be in her chamber."

The men scrambled up the stairs, muskets in hand and swords flapping against their breeches.

Rose took a deep breath to steel herself. Then after a moment she turned. "May I offer you some tea, General, Mr. Snyder?" She sauntered toward the parlor, hoping to act nonchalant, but stumbled over the rug.

"No, thank you, miss. I need to direct my men." Swinging about, General Smith plopped his hat atop his head and marched outside as quickly as he had come.

Mr. Snyder hung his hat and cane on a coatrack by the door, then approached her. "I am here, Miss McGuire." He dabbed his fingers on his tongue then raked them through his perfectly styled copper-colored hair. "Nothing will happen to you. I can see these military affairs cause you great distress."

Rose merely stared at the man, hoping he, too, would find an excuse to leave.

"I will accept your offer of tea if you will join me," he said. "Perhaps I can help allay your fears." He gestured toward the parlor and a floral-printed settee that sat in the center of the small room.

Rose's palms grew sweaty. Her stomach bubbled. "Very well." Using the tea as an excuse to leave the man, Rose entered the kitchen, and leaned back on the wall beside the door. Her head grew light, and she raised a hand to rub her forehead.

Cora turned from stirring a pot over the fire. "Are you all right, child?"

"Yes. Would you prepare a tea tray for me and Mr. Snyder?"

The cook frowned and shook her head. "O' course," she sassed. "Along with makin' dinner and cleanin' the house and everythin' else I do around here. Yes, I'll serve tea to you and your gentleman caller." Pulling a tray from a shelf, she set it on the preparation table and eyed a kettle already steaming on the Franklin stove.

Ignoring her, Rose darted to the window above the sink and peered out through the mottled green glass. Blurred figures spread across her field like a swarm of locusts. Several men entered the barn. She could hear Prinney and the other pigs snorting accompanied by the squawk of chickens.

"Search the icehouse!" General Smith's command shot like an arrow through Rose's heart. She swung about and leaned on the sink, nearly collapsing.

Cora's brow wrinkled and unusual concern flitted across her face. "Child?"

Oh Lord, save us. The prayer rose up, unbidden. But when had God ever come through for her? When had He ever answered her pleas? Rose dragged in a breath that stuck in her throat and ignored the numbness that had taken over her body. "I believe Mr. Snyder and I will take that tea now."

Slapping a hand onto her rounded hip, Cora faced the fireplace, muttering under her breath. Her legs trembling, Rose left the kitchen. If she were to be arrested for treason, she would abide it with dignity. She would pay the consequences of her actions. Memories of another equally terrifying event from her past threatened to leech the last of her strength and send her tumbling to the floor. Not all involved in that fateful night had lived to see the dawn. At the time, she had wished to be among those who had not survived. But now, she longed to live. To remain on this farm with her aunt and uncle, and when she was able, to help other women who had suffered the same fate as she had.

She gulped as she made her way to the parlor, trying to dislodge the vision. The soldiers clomped down the narrow stairs, casting smiles her way—*knowing* smiles. The wood creaked in laughter beneath their boots as they stormed toward the kitchen.

Cora burst through the kitchen door, tray in hand, and screeched at the sight of the men. They marched past her, nearly knocking her aside. Tossing a string of choice words over her shoulder, she entered the parlor, slammed the tray down on the rosewood serving table perched before the settee, and left.

"Difficult to procure decent servants these days." Mr. Snyder shook his head.

Taking a cloth, Rose lifted the teapot and attempted to pour a cup of tea for the councilman, but her hands shook, spilling the steaming liquid onto the tray. She set the pot down with a clank and sank onto the settee.

"They are simply soldiers ensuring your safety, miss. I've never seen you so distraught." Mr. Snyder took the opportunity to sit beside her. Her trembling increased. "Why, whatever is the matter, Miss McGuire?" He took her hands in his.

"My apologies, Mr. Snyder." She snatched them back and stood. "I fear I am unwell."

General Smith barged through the front door, two armed soldiers behind him. A fierce look rode on his face.

"Miss McGuire, we have found something most distressing."

❖ CHAPTER 7 ❖

Rose's legs wobbled, and she slumped onto the settee. She lifted her gaze to General Smith and then to the two armed soldiers behind him. The general's face was a cold mask, devoid of emotion. A breeze drifted in from the door and stirred the golden fringe of the epaulets crowning his shoulders. The pinpricks of a thousand needles traveled up her legs, through her stomach and chest, and onto her arms. "You found something, General?" Her voice rasped.

A British naval officer, perhaps?

Dread enveloped her. They had come to arrest her—had probably already bound Mr. Reed and placed him on a horse to escort him to the fort.

Mr. Snyder stood.

The general took a step toward her. His boots pounded like a judge's gavel over the wooden floor.

Rose's heart stopped beating.

"Yes, miss. We discovered this bloody cloth in your icehouse." He flapped the offending scrap through the air before her.

Rose's vision blurred. "In the icehouse?" Her voice cracked. Was he toying with her?

The general studied her. "Are you all right, Miss McGuire?"

"General, if I may." Mr. Snyder waved a palm toward Rose. "Surely you can see the sight of blood frightens the lady."

"Ah, of course. My apologies, miss." General Smith flicked the cloth over his shoulder to one of the men behind him.

Rose laid a hand on her heaving chest and struggled for a breath. "What do you make of it, General?"

Behind him, the kitchen door opened a crack, no doubt so Cora could listen to the proceedings.

"It's obvious," the general said, causing Rose's stomach to clamp again. "A wounded enemy soldier must have taken refuge there. Have you seen or heard anything during the past few weeks?"

Rose searched his hard eyes for any sign of trickery. "No sir." She wrapped her arms around her aching stomach. "We haven't used the icehouse in years. What need would I have to go out there? I can't believe a British soldier was so close. My word." She clutched her throat to stop her nervous babbling.

Mr. Snyder sat down beside her and took her hand. "It's all right, Miss McGuire." True concern burned in his eyes. He faced the general. "You've upset her. Obviously she knows nothing about this."

Rose slid her hand from his.

The general studied the room with censure. "What of your aunt and uncle?"

"I assure you, General," Rose said. "If they spotted an enemy soldier on our land, they would have alerted you immediately."

The general nodded, seemingly satisfied with her answer. "Well, it seems that whoever it was has long since gone. I am sorry to have upset you, miss, but we are at war. And one cannot be too careful."

"Of course. I thank you for your diligence, General." But all Rose heard was "has long since gone." Had Mr. Reed indeed left? Without so much as a by your leave or a thank you for all she'd done for him—all she had risked? She nearly chuckled at her own foolishness. What was she thinking? Mr. Reed had saved her life. He owed her no thanks. She should be happy that he was gone.

"I shall relieve you of my company." The general gave her a short bow, turned, and marched from the room, his men following after him.

Only then did Rose fully release the breath that had jammed in her throat. Only to have her lungs constrict again as Mr. Snyder caressed her bare fingers. Why did the man always have to touch her?

Rose leaped from the settee. "I thank you for coming to my defense, Mr. Snyder."

He shrugged. "It was my pleasure to shield you from the general's harsh demeanor. You know how these military sorts are." He waved a lacy cuff through the air as the last rays of the setting sun glinted off the jewel on his finger.

Shadows blossomed like hovering specters throughout the parlor, adding to her unease. Rose lit a lantern from the embers in the fireplace. When she turned back around, Mr. Snyder stared at her with the most peculiar look. The realization struck her that she was inappropriately alone with him. She could not hear Cora rumbling about in the kitchen. Perhaps the cook had gone out to the privy. And where was Amelia when Rose needed her?

Rising to his feet, Mr. Snyder sauntered toward her, a gentle smile on his lips. "Never fear, you are safe now, Miss McGuire. I shan't allow any harm to come to you."

Then why did Rose feel so uneasy? "We should not be alone without benefit of an escort, sir." She snapped her gaze to the door. "I must ask you to leave."

"You have nothing to fear from me." His forehead wrinkled. "I simply wish to discuss our future."

"I am unaware that we have one." She tried to sidestep him, but he blocked her path. Clenching her fists at her side, she stood her ground. Though the man was annoying, Rose doubted he would do her any real harm. Not with his reputation as city councilman at risk.

"But that is what I wish to discuss, my dear." He loosened his cravat. One golden brow rose above a pair of pleading eyes.

"Mr. Snyder, you overstep your bounds. I am most certainly not your dear." Rose started for the door, but he stepped in front of her yet again. The bergamot cologne he doused himself with stung her nose.

"Rose, I beg you." He took her hand and placed a wet kiss upon it. "Do not deny the affection I see in your eyes. Accept my courtship. I'm sure your uncle would find the match agreeable." He offered her a timid smile. "I cannot bear to live without you."

Tugging her hand from his—yet again—Rose took a step back, a battle of mind and heart waging a war within her. She should accept his offer. He had everything to recommend him and she had nothing, save this piece of land. But something in her heart forbade her—she did not love him. Could barely tolerate his presence. But perhaps she could learn. Couldn't she? To ensure herself a future? "I need more time."

He frowned and lowered his chin.

Rose pursed her lips. "I fear my feelings for you do not go beyond friendship."

He seemed to shrink in stature. "I see. Yet, surely after we are married, your love for me will grow?"

"Perhaps."

"Consider the prestige you will acquire from being a councilman's wife."

"And what will you acquire from the match?"

"A beautiful wife." His mouth remained open as if he intended to say something else.

"And my land." Rose snapped, leveling an incriminating gaze upon him.

His eyes widened, then he shrugged. "I daresay it is not so uncommon to covet such a sweet dowry. Any suitor would feel the same."

Rose knew he was right. Most marriage contracts revolved around money and land. And this man seemed to admire and love her as well. Could she hope for any more? "Mr. Snyder, though I am flattered by your offer, I ask you to wait a little while longer."

Disappointment rolled over his angular face.

"Now, if you please." Rose softened her tone. "For propriety's sake, I must ask you to leave."

He did not move. Fury chased the kindness from his face. "I will not wait forever for you. And I doubt you'll get a better offer."

The truth of his words sliced through her like a hot blade. "Perhaps not. Still, I insist you leave at once."

A cool breeze blew over them. The ominous thud of a boot step.

"I believe the lady asked you to leave." A deep voice that rang with a British lilt floated in on the wind.

Leaning on a crutch, Mr. Reed's body consumed the open space of the doorway. His dark eyes shifted from her to Mr. Snyder.

The councilman spun around at the intrusion. "Of all the. . .who the devil are you?"

"Forgive me, Miss McGuire." Mr. Reed nodded in her direction. "The door was slightly ajar, and I thought it best to ensure you were safe."

Rose tried to form the words "thank you," but nothing came out of her mouth. The kitchen door opened, and Amelia entered, a look of shock pinching her features.

Rose swept her gaze back to Mr. Reed, her mind trying to process what the daft man was doing.

Mr. Snyder stepped toward Mr. Reed. "I asked you to identify yourself, sir."

Mr. Reed's brows lifted as his glance shifted to Rose.

"He's our new man of work, Mr. Snyder." She blurted out the first thing that came to mind.

Mr. Snyder swerved about. "Your man of work? I wasn't aware you'd hired a man." His face grew red and puffy. "He sounds like a British aristocrat!"

Rose's mind reeled. "Yes. . .well. . .his accent. . ."

Amelia halted just inside the foyer.

Mr. Reed hobbled toward the parlor, his boots scraping over the wooden floor. He faced them with the confidence of a man who had nothing to hide. "What Miss McGuire is trying to say is that I spent my formative years in England living with my mother. I suppose I've never quite lost my accent."

"Indeed!" Mr. Snyder's eyes turned to steel. "What happened to your leg, sir?"

"Shot by the enemy."

Amelia slipped beside Rose and squeezed her hand. When Mr. Reed had first announced himself, Rose thought all was lost. But now as she watched him counter Mr. Snyder's insolent questions with grace and bravado, her heartbeat slowed from frantic to flurried.

"Are in you in the army?" Mr. Snyder continued his interrogation.

"Vermont State militia. Wounded at Odelltown, Quebec," Mr. Reed replied with calm assurance.

Rose bit her lip and wondered how he knew such things. But no doubt the British navy kept abreast of recent land battles.

Mr. Snyder's cold eyes swept to Rose. "Your uncle hired a crippled servant? I just saw him today in town, and he failed to mention it."

"What business is it of yours?" Rose shrugged, sharing a glance with Mr. Reed. Even leaning on his staff, he stood tall and bold. Not a hint of fear shadowed his face. He adjusted his makeshift crutch and shifted his broad shoulders as a breeze wafting in the door played with loose strands of his dark hair.

"Yet when I arrived"—Mr. Snyder faced Mr. Reed and fisted a hand on his hip—"you did not come out to take my horse."

"Forgive my negligence, sir. I was mending a fence at the perimeter."

"Ah, such unforgivable behavior." Mr. Snyder's eyes flashed indignant fury. "A good servant hears his master's guests arriving and anticipates their every need." He turned to Rose. "Your uncle needs a lesson in hiring qualified staff." His disdainful glance drifted over Amelia.

"Which is also none of your concern, Mr. Snyder." Rose gestured toward the open door. "Now, if you please."

His gaze shifted from Rose to Mr. Reed, who eyed him with an authority unbefitting a servant. Grabbing his hat and cane from the rack, Mr. Snyder barreled toward the door just as the sound of a carriage crunched over the gravel outside.

"By the by, here are your aunt and uncle now." Mr. Snyder hesitated in the doorway.

Amelia gasped and drew a hand to her mouth.

Rose's heart took up a rapid pace once again. Mr. Snyder was no fool. As soon as her aunt and uncle denied knowing Mr. Reed, he would figure out where he had come from and all would be lost. Releasing Amelia's hand, Rose dashed forward just as her aunt and uncle came through the door. "Uncle Forbes, Aunt Muira, Mr. Snyder was just leaving."

"I can see that. Good evening to you, Mr. Snyder." Uncle Forbes entered the room, his wife on his arm. His glance took in Mr. Reed standing staunchly to the side. "And who, pray tell, are you?"

"As I suspected!" Mr. Snyder swung about and slammed his cane on the floor.

"Uncle." Rose grabbed Uncle Forbes's arm and gestured toward Mr. Reed. "Remember you mentioned to Mr. O'Brien that you were looking to hire a man of work, and he recommended Mr. Reed." Rose lifted her brows and gave him a pleading *please-play-along* look.

Her uncle shifted his gaze between her and Mr. Reed as Aunt Muira released his arm and circled the tall British man.

"And you hired him sight unseen based on his recommendation?" Rose forced sincerity into her tone.

"Pure rubbish." Mr. Snyder took a step inside.

Ignoring him, her uncle scratched his gray beard. "Indeed, the incident grows clearer in my mind."

"Well, this is Mr. Reed." Rose turned her back to Mr. Snyder and mouthed *Please, Uncle*. Out of the corner of her eye, she saw Amelia gripping the stairway post for support.

A curious look claimed Uncle Forbes's face, but deep within his aged brown eyes, Rose spotted a glimmer of understanding. "Mr. Reed, you say?" He glanced over his shoulder.

"At your service." Mr. Reed bowed regally, ever the statue of serenity.

Rose heard the swish of Aunt Muira's skirts as she approached. "Ah, good, Forbes, you finally found someone." She beamed at her husband causing his cheeks to redden.

Uncle Forbes grabbed the lapels of his coat and swung about. "Yes, Mr. Reed, of course. Welcome."

Mr. Snyder huffed his displeasure from the doorway.

"Mr. Reed," Uncle Forbes said. "Can you see to the councilman's equipage?"

Mr. Reed tucked an errant strand of dark hair behind his ear. "I have already prepared Mr. Snyder's horse and carriage for his departure, sir."

Uncle Forbes smiled. "Very good. Very good. See, the man is already fast at work." He faced Mr. Snyder. "Good evening to you then."

Mr. Snyder's face grew as red as his hair. Rose would have laughed if her heart were not still in her throat. Amelia, however, seemed to have no such impediment and let out a merry giggle. The councilman stormed out the door, and Mr. Reed closed it behind him.

Sweeping off her shawl, Aunt Muira handed it to Mr. Reed. "Well, aren't you a fine figure of a man," she exclaimed, looking him over. "I do believe he'll do quite nicely, Forbes. I shall feel very safe with Mr. Reed here protecting the girls."

"I do my best to make you happy, dear." Uncle Forbes handed Mr. Reed his coat, and the poor man gave Rose a quizzical look. She gestured toward the coatrack by the door, and he obligingly hung up the garments.

"Well." Uncle Forbes rubbed his hands together. "I, for one, am famished. What is that delicious smell?"

Only then did Rose once again detect the aroma of roast rabbit and apple dumplings. Withdrawing a handkerchief from her sleeve, she dabbed at her neck and dared a glance at Mr. Reed. Wayward strands of hair the color of cocoa drifted over his collar. Dark stubble lined his jaw and chin, and his deep eyes locked on hers.

He had risked everything to protect her—again. The thought slammed against every opinion she'd ever held of the British. That any man, save her uncle, would risk his life for her caused a storm of confusion to rage within her. It frightened her. It elated her.

It frightened her *because* it elated her.

She shook off the traitorous feelings. He must have something to gain from keeping her safe. But what?

"Mr. Reed, have you been shown to your quarters yet?" her uncle asked.

"No, sir, I have not."

Rose cringed at his British accent.

"I shall show him," Amelia offered excitedly.

Aunt Muira patted her hair and headed toward the stairs. "Do you have any luggage?"

"No, madam."

She turned to Forbes. "Oh dearest, always taking in those in need. So like you." They shared a loving gaze.

During which Rose tried to move her feet to flee to her chamber but found them still frozen to the floor from the shock of all that had transpired.

Uncle Forbes laid his folded hands across his portly belly. "Though normally, Mr. Reed, you'll take your meals in the kitchen with Cora, do join us tonight. We would love to get to know you better."

His eyes widened in shock before a smirk played on the edges of his lips. "I shall be delighted." He leaned on his crutch and the muscles in his forearm bulged beneath the snug cotton shirt.

Rose wondered if Aunt Muira would recognize Samuel's clothing on Mr. Reed's much larger frame. Tearing her gaze from him, she searched her heart for a morsel of anger against his heritage, against him, but found none.

"I'll show you to the groomsman's quarters." Tugging on his arm, Amelia led him toward the front door.

"First, please tend to our landau and horses, Mr. Reed," her uncle ordered.

Mr. Reed's haughty brow rose, but at Rose's insistent nod, he flattened his lips and hobbled outside.

After Aunt Muira excused herself to freshen up for dinner, Uncle Forbes approached Rose, a look of reprimand on his face.

"I'm sorry, uncle. I should not have hired him without your approval." She bit her lip. "But I see he displeases you. I shall relieve him of his duties at once." She hoped he would agree, so there would be no need to explain when Mr. Reed suddenly disappeared. She started toward the door, but her uncle grabbed her arm.

"No, my dear. Your aunt finds favor in him. And he seems well-suited to the task. I trust your judgment." He cocked a brow and for a second, she thought she saw skepticism cross his brown eyes. "Does he come highly recommended?"

Rose smiled at the opportunity to impugn the British man and hence procure his immediate dismissal. "No, not at all. In truth I hardly know him." She leaned toward her uncle and whispered. "He could be a criminal."

"Nonsense, dear." Aunt Muira chuckled as she floated downstairs. "I find him charming. There's a nobility about him that adds elegance to our home."

"I agree." Uncle Forbes straightened his waistcoat. "Let us at least give him a fair chance."

"But—" Rose began, but her uncle lifted a finger, silencing her.

"No arguments," he said.

No arguments. Rose sighed. If only they knew they had just hired a British naval officer to be their man of work, there would be plenty of arguments.

If they knew they had just invited the enemy into their home, they would never forgive Rose.

❖ CHAPTER 8 ❖

Shifting his weight onto his good leg, Alex gripped the back of his chair and waited until Mrs. Drummond, Miss McGuire, and Amelia took their seats. Across the spotless white linen that covered the table, pewter plates, silverware, and glass goblets shone beneath the glimmering light of several candles set in brass holders. A modest display, to be sure, but far more than he expected from these backwoods farmers. Amelia burst into the room, then slowed her pace as she pinched her cheeks and approached the table, offering him a coy glance. She'd exchanged the lavender gown she'd worn earlier that day for one of cream-colored muslin with a pink velvet bow tied about her waist. Alex shifted uncomfortably beneath his drab, stained garb. Never in his life had he attended the evening meal so shabbily dressed. Even aboard the HMS *Undefeatable*, he'd always worn his cleanest uniform.

He glanced at Miss McGuire who slid into her seat across from him. She had not changed for dinner from the simple muslin gown she'd worn all day—a definite breach of proper etiquette. Yet the flowing lines and delicate pattern of the fabric flattered her feminine figure and brought out the glow in her face. He longed for a glimpse of her sea-blue eyes, but she kept them hidden from him and glanced instead at her uncle sitting at the head of the table—the man seemingly oblivious to his lapse of decorum. Both in the fact that he had taken his seat before the ladies and that he had invited Alex, a mere servant, to sup with them. Unheard of!

As soon as the ladies lowered into their seats, Alex moved out his chair and sank onto the hard wood, stretching out his injured leg beneath the table. A plump colored woman whom he assumed was the family slave slapped a steaming bowl and two trays of food in the center. His stomach growled as the spicy smell of gamy meat and butter filled his nose.

"Shall we bless the food?" Mr. Drummond bowed his head, the ladies following suit. As the man prayed, Alex cast a curious glance across the group. It had been years since his own father had prayed before a meal. When had he stopped? He couldn't recall. Yet as Mr. Drummond's voice shook with emotion and his words rang with sincerity, Alex couldn't help the lump that formed in his throat. These people actually believed God had provided this food and would bless it to strengthen their bodies. Yet the fare that sat before him, though it smelled delicious enough, paled in comparison to the nightly feasts Alex had partaken of at the Reed estate back home.

Where thanks had so rarely been given.

Their harmonious "amens" rang over the table, and Miss McGuire handed him a bowl of buttered potatoes. She continued to avoid his gaze as he took the dish from her and spooned a portion onto his plate. No doubt, she was not altogether pleased at his presence at her family's table. But how could he have avoided it? He'd watched the soldiers leave the farm from his spot behind a bush along the tree line. But as he waited, it occurred to him that the foppish gentleman he'd seen enter the house had not left along with them. It was beyond objectionable that the man should be alone with Miss McGuire. Alex intended only to ensure her safety before returning to the icehouse, but when he approached the front door and heard Miss McGuire order the man to leave and saw that he did not oblige, Alex had no choice but to step in.

He handed the bowl to Amelia beside him. The young woman had no trouble keeping her gaze locked on Alex. Creamy skin surrounded by waves of raven hair and sharp brown eyes assessed him with brazen impunity as she flitted her lashes and took the potatoes. Like so many of the ladies he'd known at home, Miss McGuire's companion was a coquettish tease. With the proper attire—and pedigree—she would be the belle of the London season. . .if she weren't such an unsophisticated American.

Ruffians, he huffed to himself. Again, he found it beyond the pale that they would invite a servant to dine at the same table with the masters of the house, but Alex would not complain. The few minutes he'd spent with their cook in the kitchen convinced him he would no doubt suffer from indigestion should he be forced to dine while listening to her incessant grumbling. Besides, being the son of Lord Cranleigh, he had every right and more to sit at any table he chose. *If they only knew.*

Alex stabbed a chunk of some type of meat from a platter that barely held enough for all of them and placed it on his plate.

"Please forgive our meager fare," Mrs. Drummond said as if reading his mind. "I'm afraid that the British blockade of the Chesapeake has restricted our diet and tightened our purse strings. And with no one to hunt game for us, we are forced to purchase what we can from the local trappers."

Alex glanced into her green eyes and was startled at the intelligence he found there. Intelligence and a speck of hauteur that together with her stately bearing could match any of the accomplished, society matrons back home. A sparkle drew his gaze to elegant jewels dangling from her ears—an odd accessory to her plain gown. What a dichotomy. Yet despite the wrinkles lining the corners of her eyes and mouth and the touch of gray that ran through her auburn hair, Mrs. Drummond possessed a refined comeliness Alex had not expected to see among these crude Americans.

"However, we must thank Rose for the potatoes." She gazed lovingly at her niece. "She grows them in her garden, you know."

"And Cora for her delicious apple butter." Mr. Drummond nodded as he snagged a biscuit from the tray. "Best in all of Baltimore." He dipped his spoon into a serving bowl filled with the brown, gooey substance and slathered it over the bread.

"Indeed." Alex smiled at Miss McGuire, but still she would not look his way. "Has the blockade caused you much discomfort?"

Something struck his foot, and he peeked beneath the table, thinking perhaps a dog wandered about seeking scraps of food.

"As you know, Mr. Reed." Mrs. Drummond's tone was edged with pride. "We are a hardy people and have become quite accustomed to living off the fruits of our labors." She sighed. "It is the luxuries we miss. The exotic fruits, sugar, coffee, and rice from the West Indies. The satin, taffetas, and velvets from England and France. Why, I haven't had a new gown in over a year. And the millinery was nearly empty the last time we visited."

"I couldn't agree more." Amelia shook her head, sending her dark curls dancing. "It has been insufferable."

"Come now, my dear ones," Mr. Drummond gently admonished them as he bit into a biscuit, scattering crumbs over his waistcoat. "These are trifling problems compared to the suffering some citizens have endured due to these infernal British raids." His gaze traced to Miss McGuire.

A twinge of guilt struck Alex. Miss McGuire dropped her spoon onto her plate with a clank.

Mrs. Drummond smiled at her husband. "You are right, dearest. Forgive me."

"So, Mr. Reed." Mr. Drummond faced Alex. "I'll warrant my niece has a good explanation for hiring you without my consent, but before I agree to it, tell us a bit about yourself. Where did you meet my niece, and how did you come to be in Baltimore?"

Out of the corner of his eye, Alex saw Miss McGuire stiffen like a mast. "In truth, Mr. Drummond, I was passing by your farm, saw a gentleman enter your house and heard a scream shortly after. Not wishing to pry, but worried for the safety of any ladies within, I crept up to the open door to investigate."

"Such kindness, Mr. Reed." Mrs. Drummond took a sip of her drink.

Amelia sliced her meat and smiled his way. "It's so romantic."

Feeling his throat go dry, Alex poured a glass of the amber-colored liquid from a pitcher and drew it to his lips. Sweet mint filled his mouth. A tea of some kind. Cold but pleasant tasting.

Mr. Drummond drew his brows together and cast a harried glance at Miss McGuire then back at Alex. "Who was the scoundrel, sir?"

"Nobody, uncle." Miss McGuire found her voice, although it sounded as strangled as if she'd swallowed a piece of rope. "The whole event was of no consequence."

Ignoring her, Alex chuckled. "Why, it was none other than your Mr. Snyder. At first glance, I feared his intentions were less than honorable, so I ordered him to leave."

"How gallant you were, Mr. Reed." Amelia took a bite of potatoes.

Mr. Drummond snorted. "I wish I could have seen his face."

Crumbs flew from his mouth onto the table. Alex cringed at the man's lack of manners.

"Now, Forbes. That isn't kind." Mrs. Drummond laid a hand on her husband's arm. "Mr. Snyder is a respectable councilman." She directed her gaze toward Miss McGuire. "And quite taken with you, Rose."

Miss McGuire toyed with the food on her plate but offered no reply nor did she lift her gaze.

"But I'm confused, how did you come to be my new man of work?" Mr. Drummond pointed his fork at Alex—once again showing a lack of good breeding.

Miss McGuire lifted her chin. Wayward strands of honey-drenched hair dangled like glimmering threads about her neck. "Uncle, truth be told—and I'm sorry if this impugns your opinion of Mr. Snyder, Aunt Muira—but the man would not leave at my request. He was being quite obstinate. If not for Mr. Reed's intrusion, I cannot imagine what would have happened."

Mrs. Drummond's features wrinkled. "Surely you do not think he would do you harm, Rose. Preposterous." She chortled as she glanced around the table.

"I didn't think so either, Aunt, but then the infernal man wouldn't leave."

"Our sweet Rose creates a dither out of every little thing." Mr. Drummond tossed the last bite of his biscuit into his mouth.

Miss McGuire's shoulders slumped, and Alex pitied her for her uncle's nonchalant attitude toward her safety. What was the man thinking? Leaving two young ladies at home alone without a man in attendance to protect them?

"You should try this apple butter, Mr. Reed." Mr. Drummond handed the bowl to Amelia, who passed it to Alex. "It is quite delicious."

Amelia slid her fingers over Alex's as he grabbed the dish and set it down on the table. "I think Mr. Snyder left because he was frightened of Mr. Reed."

Ignoring her flirtations, Alex placed a piece of meat into his mouth and was instantly rewarded with a spicy, succulent flavor. Certainly not the hard tack and dried beef he normally received when out to sea. Rabbit, if he remembered the taste, though it had rarely been served at the Reed table.

A breeze swirled in from the open window, sending the candles sputtering, and bringing with it the scent of hay and evening prim-rose. Mrs. Drummond patted her coiffure back in place. "I imagine that Mr. Snyder was indeed frightened. You make quite an imposing figure, Mr. Reed. But do tell us what happened to your leg?"

"Pistol shot," he replied casually. He spooned potatoes into his mouth, finding himself suddenly quite hungry.

Someone kicked his leg beneath the table again. He winced and leveled a gaze at Miss McGuire. She frowned and jerked her head toward the door, no doubt prodding him to excuse himself and leave.

But his stomach resisted the notion.

Mrs. Drummond's green eyes flashed. "Shot! Indeed, from whom, where?"

"In the battle for Odelltown, Quebec, madam. Vermont militia." Alex cringed at the lie once again, but it could not be helped.

"Good heavens." Mr. Drummond set down his spoon, his ruddy face reddening even further. "So you are a soldier?"

Amelia leaned her chin on her hand and gazed at him adoringly.

"He is simply a wanderer, Uncle." Miss McGuire speared Alex with another icy gaze. "With a wounded leg and no particular skills. I only told Mr. Snyder that Mr. Reed was our man of work to get rid of the councilman." She straightened her shoulders and gave him a caustic smile. "So after you've partaken of our hospitality, sir, I assume you'll be on your way."

"Ah, not so quick, my dear." Mrs. Drummond set down her fork. "Your uncle has had a difficult time finding an appropriate replacement for Samuel. I, for one, find Mr. Reed an interesting candidate and wish to hear more about him."

"I quite agree, dearest." Mr. Drummond heaped a second helping of potatoes onto his plate. "Most of the men of Baltimore have either joined the militia defending the fort or have become privateers." He lifted kind brown eyes to Alex. "Or are fighting in Canada as you were, Mr. Reed."

"Yes." Alex spread a dab of apple butter onto his biscuit and took a bite. The creamy flavor of sweet apple exploded on his tongue, but instantly soured beneath his deception.

A smudge of apple butter guarded the corner of Mr. Drummond's lips as they formed a frown. "Were you shot by the British?"

A mixture of fear and anger leaped from Miss McGuire's crisp blue eyes.

"A British naval officer, to be exact," he answered never taking his eyes off Miss McGuire. She kicked him beneath the table. On his bad leg. Pain shot through his thigh. He coughed into his hand to cover up a groan.

Amelia exchanged a harried glance with Miss McGuire.

"Oh my." Mrs. Drummond played with the tiny jewels dangling from her ears. "Thank goodness you survived."

"The wound is healing nicely. I had the best of care." Alex hoped his compliment would assuage the fury pouring from Miss McGuire's face, but it only seemed to agitate her further. Did she think him such a fool that he would divulge his true identity? Upon his honor, he would be gone soon enough.

Amelia took the liberty of refilling his goblet from the pitcher.

"May I ask where your family is from?" Mr. Drummond paused in cutting a piece of meat. "Your accent rings with nobility, sir."

Alex tore his gaze from Miss McGuire's piercing eyes. "Indeed. I am told that quite often. A curse of my upbringing, I fear. But my family is all gone now."

"Oh my." Mrs. Drummond gasped. "Please forgive my husband's impertinence. We did not mean to intrude."

Mr. Drummond plopped his last piece of rabbit into his mouth then directed his gaze at Miss McGuire. "But Rose, lass, I must chastise you. You rid yourself of Mr. Snyder, yet place yourself at the mercy of a complete stranger."

Seconds passed as Miss McGuire pushed a pile of potatoes about her plate. Finally she looked up. "We have met before, Uncle."

"Have you, dear? Pray tell, where?" Mrs. Drummond dabbed her napkin over her lips.

"On the farm a few weeks past."

"I came by looking for work, but your niece turned me away," Alex said.

"I did not think you would approve." Miss McGuire sipped her tea and sat up straight. "In fact, now that you know more about him, I'm sure you'll agree he is not suited for the position."

A smile twitched on Alex's lips at her attempt to be rid of him. The fire sparking in her blue eyes tempted him to goad her further—if only to draw her gaze his way once again.

Mrs. Drummond shook her head. "Oh dear, you shouldn't say such things in front of Mr. Reed. Why, he's a soldier wounded while fighting for our country." She gave him an admiring look. "I for one am in favor of giving you a chance to prove yourself as our new man of work."

Amelia flinched beside him. A loud clank drew Alex's gaze to Miss McGuire. Her goblet lay on its side, the remainder of her tea spilling onto the white tablecloth. "Forgive me." Miss McGuire tossed her napkin over the puddle as her aunt frowned in her direction. "I am sure that Mr. Reed wishes to return to the war." She squeezed the words out through clenched teeth and a tight smile. "Do you not, Mr. Reed?"

"Whatever is amiss with you tonight?" Mrs. Drummond said.

Mr. Drummond brushed the crumbs from his shirt and held up a hand. "Before you accept, Mr. Reed, I should inform you that the position requires you to handle a multitude of duties. As you can see, we are unable to afford many servants. We have Cora, our cook and housekeeper—"

"Then she is not your slave?" Alex had not intended to interrupt, but the way Mr. Drummond had spoken the cook's name inferred that she was more of a family friend than slave.

"Oh goodness no, sir." Disgust shadowed Mr. Drummond's face. "I purchased her ten years ago from a slave trader and offered her freedom and a position in our home should she desire to stay. She's been with us ever since."

An unavoidable admiration for the man blossomed within Alex. Though England's Slave Trade Act forbade British ships from transporting slaves, both Britain and America had not yet removed the scourge of slavery from their colonies. "Commendable, sir. Especially since so many of your fellow countrymen think nothing of keeping slaves."

"My countrymen?" Mr. Drummond's gray brows rose. "Are they not your countrymen as well?"

Amelia coughed. Miss McGuire froze and Alex stiffened at his foolish blunder. "Indeed, I misspoke. It has been a long day."

But Mr. Drummond's smile indicated he took no suspicion of it. "Nevertheless, as I was saying, when Rose came to live with us, we also hired Amelia as her lady's maid and companion. So we are in need of a general man of work to perform the duties of footman, groomsman, and farmhand."

Alex swallowed the meat in his mouth and took a sip of tea to stifle the chortle that longed to emerge from his throat. The son of a viscount hired as a common servant? And by a man with half Alex's intelligence, breeding, and education. It was most comical. "You do indeed have a pleasant piece of land, Mr. Drummond."

"Can I get you another biscuit, Mr. Reed?" Amelia smiled his way, and Miss McGuire glared at her maid.

"No, thank you, miss." Alex withheld a chuckle at the woman's continued flirtation.

"The land." Mr. Drummond waved a hand in the air, "Oh, that's Rose's doing."

"Indeed?" Alex raised brows at Miss McGuire, but she had plucked out her fan and was waving it about her face.

"It does not deserve a mention," she mumbled.

"Of course it does, lass," Mr. Drummond said. "We bought the land with Rose's inheritance."

"And her money provides us with a comfortable living," Mrs. Drummond added. "This home, our carriages and horses, and Cora and Amelia's salaries."

"I am all astonishment." Alex said. And indeed he was. Miss McGuire's eyes chilled. "Is it so unbelievable?"

He grinned.

"You see, Mr. Reed," Mrs. Drummond continued, "Mr. Drummond brings home but a meager salary from his church."

"Your church?"

"Yes. I am the reverend at the First Presbyterian Church in Fells Point."

Alex shook his head. A reverend? Certainly the last profession he would have guessed for this unrefined, bumbling man. "A rewarding position, no doubt."

"It is. And much more than I deserve." The sparkle left Mr. Drummond's eyes. "I came here as an indentured servant—a captured thief from Scotland, and now look what God has done."

Alex cringed. A criminal. His father Lord Cranleigh would choke on his food were he to learn of the depravity of Alex's dinner companions.

Amelia placed an overbold hand on Alex's arm. "Ouch!" She jerked back her hand and speared Miss McGuire with a gaze. Alex smiled. No doubt the poor woman had also fallen victim to the point of Miss McGuire's shoe.

Composing herself, Amelia continued, "Forgive me. I . . ." She took a breath, then went on without explaining her outburst. "Theirs is such a romantic story. Mr. Drummond was an indentured servant in Mrs. Drummond's house."

"I was known then as Miss Muira McGuire, you see." Mrs. Drummond gazed adoringly at her husband. "We fell in love."

"Aye, after I repented of my sins and came to know the Lord." Mr. Drummond cocked his head toward his wife. "Due to your brother's godly influence, I might add."

"Rose's father, Robert. God rest his soul." Sorrow tugged upon Mrs. Drummond's features. "He was a good man."

Alex set down his fork, his stomach suddenly churning.

Mrs. Drummond shrugged. "Of course my father disapproved the match."

"Her family disowned her," Amelia added. "But she ran away with him anyway." She released a wistful sigh.

Left everything? For love? Yet hadn't Alex nearly done the same years ago?

"Is it warm in here?" Miss McGuire huffed as she fluttered her fan over her face and neck.

Mrs. Drummond scooped potatoes onto her plate. "You see, Mr. Reed, my family grew quite wealthy building ships in Norfolk."

"Indeed?" Alex watched as Miss McGuire pushed her uneaten plate of food aside and pleaded with her eyes for him to leave.

"We were poor for many years." Mrs. Drummond took her husband's hand in hers. "Yet so much richer than most."

Alex turned away from the intensity of affection he saw in their eyes—an affection stronger than any he'd witnessed between a man and wife. A strange longing welled up within him to be loved with such passion.

Miss McGuire hurried her fan, sending wisps of golden hair dancing about her neck. "I would never have had such courage to do what you did, Aunt Muira."

Mr. Drummond kissed his wife's hand then faced his niece. "If you would only put your trust in God you could."

"How can I after what He allowed me to endure?" She swallowed, and her gaze flitted over Alex. Could she be speaking of her parents' deaths? Yet the depth of sorrow in her eyes bespoke of something more.

"So you see." Mr. Drummond wiped his mouth with his napkin and tossed it onto the table, though crumbs still speckled his gray beard. "If God redeemed this poor old sinner, how can I not give as much as I'm able into His service?"

Mrs. Drummond leaned back in her chair and folded her hands in her lap. "Our work takes us away from the farm often, Mr. Reed, so we are in desperate need of someone to watch over things."

"You leave the ladies alone? Without protection? In wartime?" Alex found the idea inconceivable. Visions of Lieutenant Garrick's body atop Miss McGuire resurged his anger.

"Only recently. And out of necessity. Samuel our last man of work ran off two weeks ago. Joined the British army. You have no intentions of doing that, do you?" He chuckled.

Amelia clutched her throat, then grabbed her glass and sipped her tea.

Another blow to his leg. Pain speared up his thigh. Alex winced and tightened the muscles in his jaw. "The British army? No sir. That would be my last choice." And indeed it was. He was a navy man through and through.

Alex tapped his napkin over his lips, then sat back in his chair and patted his full stomach. He'd not felt so satisfied and rested in months. If he were back on the ship, he'd have to assume his duties and carry out the commands of his volatile and berating captain. In addition, he'd no doubt be sent out on further raids where he'd witness unspeakable atrocities in the name of war. Or worse, where he might have to perform acts that violated the strictures of decent humanity. No, he was in no rush to return.

He gazed over his dinner companions. Though uncultured at best, the kindness of these simple people eased over his soul like a warm tropical breeze. Besides, he hated the thought of leaving the women alone without protection—of leaving Miss McGuire at the mercy of the next British raid. He shuddered. What harm would it do to stay on and protect them while his leg healed?

Mr. Drummond's eyes twinkled in the candlelight. "Do say you'll stay on as our man of work, Mr. Reed."

❖

Rose thrust her foot once again at the pompous man's leg, no longer caring if she hurt him. Surely he would not agree. But just in case, she wanted him to know her wishes on the matter. Her foot met air, and his smile confirmed that he had retreated his leg to a safer position.

Aunt Muira frowned. "Dear, you've hardly eaten a bite. Are you ill?" She placed the back of her hand against Rose's cheek.

"Now that you mention it, I do believe I'm not feeling well."Turning her face away from her aunt, Rose gave Mr. Reed a venomous look and glanced toward the door.

He grinned.

She'd love to slap that haughty smirk off his lips. He'd done nothing but toy with her through the entire meal! And toy with her aunt and uncle as well. In addition, he had refused to take heed of her numerous hints for him to leave. My word, didn't he understand she had the power to turn him in to the authorities? But of course, he was no fool. Since he had been introduced to Mr. Snyder as the Drummond servant, she could no longer do that without implicating her entire family as traitors.

Mr. Reed nodded toward her uncle but kept his playful eyes upon her. "I'd be happy to accept your offer, Mr. Drummond, but only until you can find a replacement for me. When my wound is fully healed, I must return to my shi—regiment."

What? He couldn't stay! Rose bolted from her chair, tipping it backward. It landed on the floor with a thump. Her uncle gave her a curious look. "Whatever is the matter with you, lass?"

Aunt Muira took her arm. "Perhaps you should retire. You look a bit pale."

Mr. Reed struggled to his feet. "Indeed, Miss McGuire. I fear the events of the day have taken their toll on you."

Rose's jaw hardened until she felt it would snap.

"I commend your loyalty to our cause, Mr. Reed." Uncle Forbes scraped his chair over the wooden planks and stood. He tugged upon his waistcoat. "Such courage and dedication is difficult to find. I accept your offer. In the meantime, I shall make every attempt to procure a replacement for you as soon as possible."

Nausea gripped Rose's stomach. She wrapped her arms around her waist and glared at Mr. Reed. By bringing the enemy into their home, she had endangered all their lives. Why didn't the blasted man return to his ship? He certainly was well enough. What could he possibly want with them?

And then it hit her.

Mr. Reed hobbled to the side and pushed in his chair. Leaping to her feet, Amelia gathered his crutch and handed it to him. He thanked her with a smile as Rose's uncle and aunt crowded around him, welcoming him to the family.

Yes, Rose knew exactly what the man was up to. No doubt, he intended to use his time here to spy for his country—make trips into town, under the guise of running errands, to get a good view of the city's defenses. But he would not succeed, for Rose would do everything in her power to stop him.

❖ CHAPTER 9 ❖

Bucket in one hand, lantern in the other, Rose yawned and plodded through the weeds that surrounded the back of the barn where her uncle kept his horses and carriage. Katydids chirped their nighttime chorus as she peered through the predawn shadows and halted before the door of the servants' quarters attached to the building.

Where Mr. Reed had spent the night.

A chilled breeze coming in from the forest swirled around her with the sweet fragrance of cedar and Virginia creeper. Despite the pleasant aromas, a shudder ran through her as she set down the pail and lantern—a shudder that had nothing to do with the wind. She fingered the handle of the knife she'd stuffed into her leather sash and hoped she'd have no need of the vile weapon. But one could never be careful enough when it came to a man she did not know. Rose had learned that lesson the hard way. She banged on the door.

After a few moments, a loud groan that sounded like an angry bear filtered through the wood. Plucking out the knife, she knocked again.

"What the deuces?" The words, followed by a string of expletives, grated over her ears before the door squeaked open.

Mr. Reed, bare-chested and with loose breeches hanging about his hips, gaped at her through puffy eyes. Hard muscle rounded his chest and arms, and Rose gripped the knife in both hands and held it out before her.

"Miss McGuire." His gaze lowered to the blade trembling in her hands. "Have you disturbed my sleep just to kill me?" More humor than fear filled his voice.

"Only if I have to, Mr. Reed."

"I assure you, I will give you no cause."

"And I assure you, sir, that I will give you no opportunity to give me cause." The words that had made sense in her mind twisted nonsensically in the air between them.

Mr. Reed's brows furrowed. He shook his head. "You are befuddling my mind, miss." He shifted his stance. "What need do you have of a weapon?"

"I do not know you, Mr. Reed. Yet, by circumstance I find myself forced to be alone with you."

"Miss McGuire." He sighed and rubbed his eyes. "If I had wanted to hurt you, I have had ample opportunity." Anguish rolled across his face. "Why are you so frightened of me?"

"I am frightened of many things, Mr. Reed."

He studied her. "As your uncle declared at dinner." He stretched his back, his muscles rippling across his chest.

An odd warmth sped through her. Rose dragged her gaze from him to the dark form of her house in the distance. When she faced him again, she found him staring at her inquisitively. "Why are you looking at me like that?"

"It's just that you don't seem the skittish type, Miss McGuire. You endured the assault of an enemy, went ably toward his gun, removed a bullet from a man's leg, and then nursed him back to health at the risk of your own and your family's safety. Egad, if I recall, you even begged Garrick to shoot you!" He shook his head. "Those are not the actions of a fearful woman."

Rose nearly snickered at his compliment. What Mr. Reed didn't realize was that she had been out of her wits with terror every second of those encounters. "I did what I had to."

"Precisely." One eyebrow lifted and a look of admiration flickered in his hazel eyes.

Against her will, his ardor nestled into a soft spot of her heart. Lowering the blade, Rose stuffed it back into the sash of her gown. "You should know, Mr. Reed, I intend to have this knife on me at all times."

He chuckled. "I consider myself duly warned."

Yet when her eyes drifted once more to his muscled torso, she realized how foolish her statement was. This man would have no trouble overpowering her.

"Please cover yourself, sir," she said, clearing her throat and touching the knife handle again.

Hobbling, he disappeared into the dark room and returned wearing one of Samuel's cotton shirts. "Forgive my state of undress. I did not know it was you at my door."

"Who else would it be, Mr. Reed?" Rose flicked a curl from her face, trying to ignore the heat flushing through her body.

He rubbed his eyes again and gazed over the farm still shrouded in darkness. "Certainly not you at this ungodly hour."

"Enough of this." Rose huffed. "You cannot stay here."

The green flecks in his eyes glinted playfully in the lantern light. "I believe your aunt and uncle have given me their blessing."

Rose clenched her jaw. "You may find your little charade amusing, but I assure you it is anything but."

He leaned on the doorframe and crossed his arms over his chest. "I find you sneaking out here in the middle of the night to see me quite amusing, miss."

Rose's stomach knotted in fury. "I insist you leave at once and go back to your ship."

"Though I would love to oblige you, I fear I am not yet capable." He sighed and glanced down at his leg. "When I saw the soldiers descend upon your farm, I tried to make my escape in the woods. Before too long, I found my strength spent and my pain unbearable."

"Perhaps I should give you some of my aunt's laudanum to assist in your journey."

"Or a horse."

"You know I cannot do that." A light wind played with the hem of her dress and tossed Mr. Reed's loose, dark hair over the top of his shirt. "How long must you keep up this pretense? My aunt and uncle are not imbeciles."

He cocked his head and studied her as if he disagreed with her assessment.

Of all the impertinent. . . A muscle tightened in her neck. Grabbing the lantern, Rose held it up to get a better look at his face. "Can you not see that every minute you spend here puts me and my family at great risk? Any honorable man would leave us be."

"I assure you, I would never harm you or your family, nor do I wish to put any of you in danger."

"Then leave us, I beg you."

His jaw tightened. "In truth, my honor forbids me to leave you and Amelia without protection. Not after what happened with Garrick."

Blood surged to her face. "Oh do not pretend, sir, that you have a care for what happens to us. You are an enemy to everything I hold dear."

The katydids ceased their buzzing. Sorrow passed over Mr. Reed's features before his eyebrows shot up. "Perhaps you forget that it was I who saved you from being ravished a week ago?"

Rose lowered her chin. "I have not forgotten your kindness. Yet I do wonder at your reasons." She gazed up at the man towering over her and gathered both her fury and her resolve. "You have placed yourself in a grand position to spy upon my country, Mr. Reed, and I'm here to inform you I will not allow it." She stomped her foot for effect but the man merely smiled.

"Spy?" Mr. Reed's hearty chuckle tumbled over her, dissolving the power of her accusation. "What could I possibly learn from simple farmers that would aid the British cause?"

The katydids resumed their incessant droning.

Rose's face heated. "Why you pretentious, pompous, overbearing. . ." —the rest of the names popping into her mind should not be uttered by a lady—"We may be farmers but we are not as beef-witted as you assume."

Instead of being insulted at her tirade, he grinned even wider.

Rose sighed. "Besides, you could learn something of import when my uncle sends you into town on errands."

"Miss, unless I were given access to your city's plans of defense, I cannot see how the cost of a pound of flour or whether you wish to purchase beeswax or tallow candles would be of any use to me."

"Is that what you believe to be the extent of our knowledge? How to buy flour and candles?"

He flattened his lips and ran a hand through his loose hair. "I meant no insult, miss. But upon my honor, I am no spy."

"Good. Because I shall see that you have no opportunity to discover any military secrets."

Mr. Reed stretched his shoulders and gazed into the darkness. His features tightened beneath a pensive look. "I realize you hold my countrymen responsible for the death of your parents. I understand your hatred of me."

Rose backed away. "I doubt you understand much about me or my country."

"I assure you that I have no intention of staying but a few days."

"Is that a promise?"

"Unless unforeseen circumstances arise, yes."

"Do you even know how to be a servant?"

He shrugged. A breeze tugged at a loose tendril of his dark hair. "I passed the lieutenant's exam with honors; how hard could it be?"

A giggle rose in her throat. This highbrow had no concept of hard work, at least not the kind required by the only male servant in the house. Perhaps that was how she could get rid of him. She would give him the most vile tasks—tasks that a man of his breeding would consider far beneath him. Tasks so repulsive that his pride—which was obviously enormous—could not suffer the humiliation. Then perhaps he'd leave when he promised. Or better yet, even sooner.

Picking up the pail, Rose held it out to him. "Milk Liverpool."

"Milk who?" Mr. Reed stared at her as if she were an apparition floating outside his door.

"Milk the cow." She gave him a supercilious smile. "Did you think this was merely a social call?"

Mr. Reed gazed past her, confusion wrinkling his face. "What hour is it? Where is the sun?"

"It is five thirty, Mr. Reed, and the sun shall make its appearance soon, I assure you."

"Five thirty." He yawned. "Only thieves and murderers lurk about at this hour, Miss McGuire. Go back to bed and call upon me in a few hours." He started to close the door.

She shoved her foot against the wood and the pail against his chest. "We milk the cow before dawn."

"Need I remind you, I am an officer, not a farmer?"

"Need I remind you that you are under my employ and will do what I say? Or"—she shrugged—"my uncle will discharge you, and you'll have no choice but to return to your ship, Mr. Reed, injured leg or not."

One side of his lips lifted in a smile. "So you plan on driving me away with work?"

She released the bucket. It fell onto his good foot with a thud.

"Ouch." Mr. Reed winced.

"I'll meet you in the barn."

❖

An hour later, Alex found himself sitting on a stool staring at the underbelly of a huge, portly beast. A stench he dared not describe but one that had haunted his dreams while he'd been feverish assailed his senses. Beside him, Miss McGuire lowered herself to another stool and rubbed her hands together.

"Make sure your fingers are warm," she began instructing him, but her words rummaged past his ears unintelligibly. Instead—as a rhythmic *splat, splat* echoed in the bucket—Alex found himself mesmerized by the slight tilt of Miss McGuire's head, the way the lantern light glimmered over her curls, and the moist sheen covering her lips.

"There," she sat back. "Now it is your turn."

Alex shook his head. A rooster crowed in the distance. "My turn?"

"Yes." She faced him with a satisfied smirk. "This will be your job every morning."

Alex stared at the four pink teats with disgust. Yet how hard could it be? "Very well, allow me." He slid onto the stool Miss McGuire vacated. Flexing his fingers, he leaned beneath the beast and grabbed hold of one of the teats. It was warm and slick to his touch.

The cow let out an ear-piercing bellow and swung her enormous face toward him. Alex grabbed his crutch and leaped off the stool in horror.

Miss McGuire giggled. "Afraid of a cow, Mr. Reed?"

"Only when she bares her teeth at me." He regained his composure.

"She won't bite." Miss McGuire placed her hands on her hips. "Try warming your fingers first. I doubt you'd enjoy an icy touch to your. . ." She halted, dropped her arms to her side, and glanced away.

Alex withheld a laugh, enjoying the red blossoming over her fair cheeks. "No, I daresay, I wouldn't."

He took his seat again. Then, after rubbing his fingers together, he placed them on the teat and began to squeeze. The cow let out a long and arduous moo.

Miss McGuire sat on the stool beside him, maintaining some distance between them. "Like this, Mr. Reed." She pressed his fingers onto the top of the teat near the udder then ran them down to the tip. A squirt of milk shot into the pail. "See?" Her eyes met his. Too close. Her fresh feminine scent pushed the malodorous smells of the barn from his nose, and he resisted the temptation to bury his face in her hair. Her lips parted and he stared at them, moving closer.

She jerked her hands back and stood, retreating to the wall of the barn. He grinned, hoping their closeness had a similar effect on her.

But why? When he'd be gone in a few days?

Pushing the unwanted thoughts aside, he returned to his task and attempted to duplicate her action, but the cow stubbornly withheld her milk.

Miss McGuire giggled again.

Alex continued to coax the beast into compliance. "You are enjoying this, aren't you?"

"Immensely." She smiled.

"I am no stranger to hard work, miss, if that is what you are trying to prove. I have served on His Majesty's ships for the past nine years." Finally a squirt of milk shot from the teat.

Onto the dirt.

"Try hitting the pail, Mr. Reed."

He growled his frustration. "Perhaps people were not meant to milk cows. Have you ever considered that? It seems highly unnatural to me."

"Unnatural or not, someone with your education and skills should have no trouble with a simple task that any milkmaid can perform."

Alex shook his head and switched to a different teat. Liverpool let out a guttural groan as dawn painted a luminous glow outside the barn door. Miss McGuire swept past him, her cotton gown rustling.

"Have no fear. I am sure I will master the technique before too long." He glanced up at her. The morning sun formed a golden halo around her head.

"I should hope so, Mr. Reed." The halo faded beneath her biting tone. "You have many more tasks to complete before the day is done."

Alex massaged the teat. Another squirt. This time into the pail. "Now I have it." He shot Miss McGuire a confident glare then squeezed the same teat again. A stream of warm milk shot him in the face. He slammed his eyes shut as the liquid dripped off his chin onto his shirt. Releasing the cow, he swiped the creamy fluid from his cheeks and neck.

"Yes, I'd say you have it now, Mr. Reed." Miss McGuire's feminine laughter bubbled over him. But instead of stirring his indignation, it had the opposite effect.

He smiled up at her. "Quite amusing, I'm sure." They laughed together, and for a moment joy sparkled in her eyes. But then a cold shield lifted over them once again. She pursed her lips. "When you're finished, bring the milk to Cora. Then ask her for the kitchen scraps and return to me in my garden. I'll show you how to feed the pigs."

❖

"You named your pig Prinney?" Shock jarred Alex, followed by a disgust that halted him in midstride.

"I did." Rose knelt to pet the massive beast.

"After the Prince Regent of England?" He still could not believe it.

"He does resemble him, don't you think?" Miss McGuire scratched the pig behind the ears then moved her fingers to do the same beneath his chin. "There you go, Prinney. That's a good boy."

Indignation churned in Alex's belly. How insolent, ungracious, and ill-mannered! He shifted his gaze to the cow in the barn, and he grew more outraged. "Liverpool. You named the cow after our Prime Minister, Lord Liverpool!"

Miss McGuire stood, a grin twisting her luscious lips. A smudge of dirt angled down her neck and despite her blatant disrespect, he longed to wipe it off.

She handed him a shovel. "Time to clean out the pigsty."

Alex gazed up at the sun. Only halfway in its ascent, its hot rays already seared him. Sweat beaded on his neck. "Clean it of what?" He glanced at the clumps of mud and hay and other less desirous nuggets that covered the floor of the enclosure.

"Of the pigs' messes, of course." A sarcastic twinkle shone in her eyes. "You should be good at it by now. Being in *His Majesty's Navy*, don't you often have to shovel Prinney's waste?"

Alex opened his mouth to respond but outrage strangled his voice.

"Afterward, you may clean out the barn as well. And chop the firewood." She pointed toward a pile of thick branches stacked along the side of the barn. Then flashing him a curt smile, she sashayed away.

❖

Rose poured a cup of tea and sat down at the preparation table in the center of the kitchen. Amelia and Cora jostled each other for a position at the window that pointed toward the barn.

"You sure got him working hard, child." Cora returned to her spot at the table and began kneading a lump of dough.

"He's a servant. He's supposed to work hard." Rose took a sip of the tea, bitter like the guilt that soured the back of her throat. She plopped another lump of sugar into the hot liquid and gave it a stir.

"But you never made Samuel do yer chores. I thought you loved carin' for the animals yourself." Cora's tone was tinged with disapproval.

Amelia continued to gaze out the window. "Oh my."

"Amelia, for goodness' sakes, quit drooling."

"He's taken off his shirt," Amelia responded breathlessly.

Rose and Cora both darted to the window, nudging against each other for a better view. Mr. Reed's form came into shape beyond the blurry glass. His shirt hung limp over a fence post as he raised the ax over his head, bringing it crashing down onto a log. Muscles that were anything but limp swelled firm and round on his biceps and chest. Dark hair the color of cocoa loosened from his queue and feathered his broad shoulders gleaming in the sunlight. The sweat indicated he was working hard. But the muscles indicated that he, indeed, was no stranger to work. She should have realized that when she'd seen his bare chest that morning. Perhaps her plan would not succeed after all.

"My, my, my." Cora clicked her tongue. "Ain't seen nothin' like that in quite some time."

A flush of heat waved over Rose. She tried to pull her gaze away but found it riveted on the man. Forcing her eyes closed, she backed away, tugging Amelia with her. "We shouldn't stare at him. It's improper."

But Amelia wouldn't budge.

"Amelia!" Rose dragged the enamored lady from the window and forced her to sit down. "And where have you been all day? It's nearly noon." Rose had long since given up expecting Amelia to assist Rose with her morning toilette.

"I did not feel well, miss. I'm sorry." Amelia poured herself some tea and gave a little pout. "Too much excitement yesterday, I fear."

Cora tugged at the red scarf she always wore tied around her head and picked up the lump of dough. She slapped it back down on the floured table. "What excitement you talkin' 'bout, Amelia? I thought you'd be glad to see a bunch o' handsome soldiers pokin' about here."

MaryLu Tyndall

Rose and Amelia shared a fearful glance.

"I suppose it's just the idea that we could be invaded by the British at any moment." Amelia tossed her raven curls over her shoulder. "And lose everything—this home, this farm, and the family I've come to love."

"Humph." Cora's thick arms flapped as she pressed down on the dough. "You both don't know nothin' about losin' everything. About bein' torn from those you love when you was but five and sold as a slave to strangers."

"I know you have suffered, Cora." Rose laid a hand on the woman's arm, stopping her kneading. "What happened to you was evil of the worst kind."

Dark eyes lifted to hers and a rare glimpse of understanding crossed over them before they hardened again. "I know the both o' you lost your parents too." She looked at Amelia. "But at least you know they're no longer on this earth. I have no idea where mine are. Probably still slaves somewhere, or died in their chains."

"You have us now, Cora. We are your family." Rose dropped two more lumps of sugar into her tea.

"Goodness' sakes, child. You'll use up all our sugar." Cora shook her head and sprinkled flour atop the dough. "Family, humph. I am your cook. I knows my place."

"My word, Cora, you are so much more than that, and you know it." Rose reassured the cook for what felt like the thousandth time.

Amelia smiled. "I certainly don't feel like your servant." Reaching across the table, she squeezed Rose's hand. "You have treated me so kindly, I feel as though we are sisters."

Rose forced back the moisture in her eyes. "I'm so thankful God brought you both into my life."

"Your aunt and uncle have been kind t' me." Cora slapped the dough into a bread pan. "But how can I ever be free while my people are still slaves?" She scratched her curly black hair beneath her scarf and fisted her hands at her waist. "And what has God got to do wit' any of this?"

Rose gazed into the fireplace that took up nearly an entire wall of the kitchen. Iron pots bubbling with the noon meal hung on a crane over the flames. Yet, a chill coursed through her. She understood Cora's attitude more than she cared to admit, for Rose had great difficulty finding God's loving-kindness in any of the events of her life.

Amelia sipped her tea. "God brought you Samuel, Cora. He'd still be here if you hadn't chased him off."

Cora tossed the pan aside, her face deepening to a dark maroon. "That no-good, lazy, sluggard. I'm glad he's gone."

"He loved you, Cora." Amelia shook her head and shifted her shoe over the floor.

Spinning around, Cora grabbed a ladle from a hook on the wall, but not before Rose saw a mist cover her eyes.

"That man don't know how to love no one." Bitterness sharpened her tone as she stirred the pot hanging over the fire.

But Rose wondered. She had always found Samuel to be a hard-working man of honor. A man who had not hid his interest in Cora. But in the end, he took off without a word to Cora or any of them. Rose had heard through gossip in town that he had joined the army—the British army.

Amelia stood and headed toward the window. "I miss my family too."

Rose clutched the woman's hand in passing. "The plague took many of the townspeople. You're fortunate to have survived and to have been married to Richard at the time."

She gave Rose a look of derision. "What did it matter? He is gone now."

Rose released her hand along with a sigh of resignation. Her aunt and uncle had admonished Rose to always trust God, to not complain, and to share her hope with others. But how could she encourage her friends when she held to her own hope with nothing but a thin thread? "We should trust God," was all she could think to say.

Cora gave a cynical chuckle. "If this is God's doin', I want no part o' Him."

Amelia leaned on the window ledge and gazed out. "It seems He has taken everything from me as well."

Rose stared into the amber-colored tea swirling in her cup. No amount of sugar could dissolve the bitterness in her throat. Was it by the hand of God they had all lost so much? She could make no sense of it. If God loved them, then why had He taken their families from them? She knew God existed. She understood that Jesus had come to earth and died and rose again so those who believed and followed Him would go to heaven. Maybe that was enough. Certainly it was more than any of them deserved. Despite what her uncle declared, perhaps their lives here on earth were meant to be lived without God's help. Certainly that made more sense than thinking He purposely allowed His children to suffer so much pain.

❖

Alex thanked Cora for the meal as he opened the door to the kitchen and stepped outside. All he received in return was a grunt from the peevish cook. Her dinner of wild goose and corn bread soaked in buttermilk was far better than her disposition. Closing the door, he gazed at the scorching sun that made one last effort to sear his skin as it dipped below the tree line in the western sky. He'd never experienced such sweltering heat. At least not since he'd sailed to Jamaica three years ago. How did these colonists bear it?

Adjusting the crutch beneath his arm, Alex hobbled over to examine his work. A dozen rows of cut logs sat neatly stacked beside the house. How he had managed to do all that work with one good leg, he could not fathom. Especially in the afternoon's blazing heat. He pressed a hand against his back where an ache had formed hours ago. His wound throbbed, causing him to lean on his good leg, but even that appendage burned with exhaustion.

Turning, he gazed across the farm. He had not seen Miss McGuire since she had turned her pert little nose up at him that morning and sauntered away. Egad, she'd armed herself with a knife. Did she really believe he would hurt her? The thought saddened him.

His glance landed on the pigsty where the stinking beasts grunted and wallowed in the mud. The one named Prinney poked his snout through the wooden posts and looked forlornly toward the barn as if he were waiting for Miss McGuire's appearance.

Infernal woman. Naming a pig after the Prince Regent! Yet Alex couldn't help the smile that played on his lips even as his insides churned with indignation. Truly these colonists were every bit the unrefined, uncultured ruffians he'd been led to believe. And Miss McGuire. He'd never encountered such a woman in all his days. Hair consistently out of place, gowns stained with dirt, consorting with pigs and cows. Yet a healthy, fresh glow brightened her face much more than any powder and rouge he'd seen on the ladies back home, and her eyes—those lustrous eyes as clear and sparkling as the turquoise sea in the West Indies.

He really couldn't blame her for wanting him gone. Despite the pain spiking up his back, he felt his strength returning. Soon enough he would relieve her of his company and head back to the crazy ramblings of Captain Milford and the tight confines of the HMS *Undefeatable*. So unlike the open spaces of this beautiful land. The western sky lit up with splashes of maroon, orange, and gold. He drew a deep breath of air and instantly regretted it. Lowering his chin, he took a whiff of his shirt. He smelled of sour milk, pig droppings, and sweat. If only his father, Lord Cranleigh, could see him now.

Squawks shot from the barn, and Alex hobbled in that direction. Prinney grunted at him as he passed, and Alex made a face at the filthy beast before he swept his gaze to Miss McGuire's garden divided into neat rows of tomatoes, some type of squash, lettuce, potatoes, and corn. Guarding either side of the open barn doors stood two flourishing rosebushes, boasting pink and red blossoms. Yet their sweet scent did nothing to assuage the stench emanating from within. As Alex shuffled inside, he flinched at the sight that met his eyes. Miss McGuire sat in the dirt at the center of the barn, gown spread out around her, with a chicken in her lap. Unaware of his presence, she spoke softly to the bird while she stroked the chicken's feathers. The bird clucked and snuggled against her gown like a cat, and Mr. Reed stood frozen in astonishment. His crutch shifted and struck the wooden doorframe.

She jerked her face up. "Mr. Reed." Her eyes widened. "I thought you were partaking of your supper." Shooing the bird from her lap, she jumped to her feet.

Alex repositioned the crutch and shuffled inside. "I was. Forgive the intrusion, Miss McGuire, but I heard squawking and thought something might be amiss."

"No, I was just. . .just. . ." She lowered her gaze.

"Petting a chicken?" He grinned.

Her eyes narrowed. "Yes, if you must know. They are my pets."

"Indeed? I thought you ate them." He wrinkled his nose at the smell of horse and cow dung that permeated the barn.

"Shhh." She cast a harried gaze around her. "You shouldn't say such things."

If Alex didn't realize she was serious, he would have laughed out loud. As it was, he simply gazed at her, amazed that she always managed to astonish him and bring a chuckle to his lips.

"You have dirt"—he brushed a finger over his own cheek—"there on your face."

She swiped at it, a look of annoyance crinkling her features.

Alex stretched his tight shoulders and took another step toward her. "Did you miss your dinner?"

"Supper. And no, Aunt Muira, Amelia, and I ate earlier in the dining room."

"Ah, I've been reduced to a servant again."

"Not reduced, sir."

"Ah, you are correct, madam." He gave a mock bow to which she pursed her lips and glanced out the door as if planning her escape.

"Where is your uncle?" he asked, longing to extend his conversation with this bewildering, charming lady.

"In town, I assume." She moved toward Liverpool and began to stroke the cow's head. "He does much work ministering at the taverns by the docks."

The cow groaned her approval, then swept her huge brown eyes toward Alex as if to prod him into jealousy at the attention she was receiving. *Fiendish beast.*

"I see you finished the work I gave you." Miss McGuire continued petting the cow.

"As I informed you, miss, I am accustomed to hard labor." He rubbed his sore palms where blisters stung in defiance of his statement.

"I thought perhaps your wound would slow you down." She lifted her gaze to his.

He took a step toward her.

She stepped back, fingering the handle of the knife still wedged in her leather sash. "But I see you are getting stronger."

Alex halted. He hated that she feared him. A breeze blew in, sending the wisps of her hair fluttering about her shoulders even as the last traces of sunlight set them aglow. He shifted his stance uncomfortably and tried to do the same with his gaze. But his eyes refused to let go of their hold upon her as if losing her visage would leave them cold and empty.

Miss McGuire blinked. "Why are you staring at me like that?"

Alex hesitated but the truth spilled unbidden from his lips. "Because you are quite lovely, Miss McGuire."

Shock flashed in her eyes before she swept them down to her soiled gown, then over to Liverpool. She huffed. "You tease me, sir."

"I never tease."

Darkness stole the last shreds of light from the barn, leaving only the light from a single lantern hanging from the post.

"I should be going inside." Miss McGuire headed toward the door. "Please douse the lantern when you leave."

Alex stepped aside to allow her to pass when a *gong, gong, gong* rang through the night air.

She froze and stared wide-eyed at him.

"It's only a bell, miss."

"It's the bell from St. Peters." She glanced out the door, her lip quivering as her chest rose and fell rapidly.

"What does it mean?"

Gong. Gong. Gong.

"It's to warn us." She swallowed. "British raiders have been spotted near town."

A mixture of shame and anger battled within Alex. With his only thought to comfort her, he drew her into his arms. She tightened in his embrace stiffer than a sail at full wind. He nudged her back. "Go into the house. I'll keep you safe."

"No!" She jerked from him, anger darkening her features. "You are one of them."

Alex felt her statement slam into his gut. "I told your uncle I would protect you, and I will."

"You owe me nothing." Grabbing her skirts, she started to leave when Alex clutched her arm.

"I will never allow anyone to hurt you."

"Go join your friends, Mr. Reed." She hissed, then tore from his grasp and dashed out the door just as the crack of a musket shot split the evening sky.

❖ CHAPTER 10 ❖

Gripping the banister in one hand and the folds of her nightdress in the other, Rose crept down the narrow stairway. The aged wood creaked beneath her bare feet and she halted, holding her breath. No sounds met her ears save the slight hiss of wind swirling about the outside of the house. She inched down a few more steps. From the parlor on her right, a single candle sent flickering ribbons of light out the door onto the dark foyer floor. She eased to a spot halfway down the stairs.

Then she saw him. Mr. Reed.

A traitorous wave of relief sped through her, for she had assumed she would not find him at his post. Sinking onto one of the stairs, Rose positioned herself for a better view and drew her knees to her chest. With only a single candle to light the parlor, Mr. Reed stood by the fireplace, one boot atop the base of the hearth, her uncle's Brown Bess stiff in his arms.

Wide awake and guarding them like a protective father...or *husband*.

Despite her angry demands that he join the British raiders, he had ushered her inside the house and once they had gathered Amelia and Aunt Muira, he had assured them that in Uncle Forbes's absence, he would guard them with his life. Amelia nearly swooned in his arms, while Aunt Muira remained the epitome of feminine courage. Rose wondered how brave her aunt would be if she knew it was a British naval officer who offered them his protection.

But when her aunt had handed Mr. Reed the Brown Bess that hung over the fireplace in the dining room, Rose's fear had risen another notch. It was bad enough to have an enemy in their home, but an armed one was beyond the pale. Now he could do with them as he pleased or worse, hail his compatriots wandering about in the forest to come join in the siege.

But no. Rose no longer believed that.

Mr. Reed let out a long sigh, rubbed his eyes, then took up a hobbled pace across the room. Raindrops pattered on the roof as he paused at the corner of a window and lifted a flap of the wooden shutters to peer into the night. Releasing the tab, he resuming his shuffle. Fatigue tugged at his stern features. At well past midnight, the man must have been beyond exhaustion. Especially after all the hard work he'd done that day—work Rose had forced upon him. Guilt pinched her heart. She had expected him to either be gone or fast asleep. Certainly not standing his post as if he were on watch aboard his ship.

With musket propped in one arm, he took a turn about the room. Lines of concern edged his face. Concern for them? Concern for his countrymen? Confusion threatened to crush Rose's disdain for this British man. He moved out of her sight for a moment. His boots thudded over the floorcloth of coarsely woven wool. But then he emerged once again on the other side of the parlor. He stretched his neck and eased back his broad shoulders. Despite his limp, with his head up and stubbled chin jutted forward, he walked with the authority of a man in command. A man who was well equipped to deal with any situation that came his way. She envisioned him in his dark blue navy coat with brass buttons and service sword at his side, and a burst of warmth flooded her—no doubt due to the hot humid night.

Surely as a second lieutenant aboard a British warship, he carried a great deal of authority. The weight of that responsibility seemed to sit heavy on his shoulders tonight. Or perhaps it was the dichotomy of protecting Rose and her family against his own countrymen. She had not considered, until now, the conflict the poor man must be suffering.

Because she had not considered that he would protect them at all.

Reaching the fireplace again, he leaned one arm upon the mantel and released a sigh. He rubbed his tight jaw and gazed across the room. Resolve and deliberation reflected in his hazel eyes. And something else—an anguish that set Rose aback.

Her thoughts drifted to the way he had looked at her in the barn. A look that had sent her belly aquiver. A look as if she was something precious to cherish and protect.

Rose squeezed her eyes shut and shook her head. No. What was wrong with her? He was a British enemy. A spy, most likely. And he would soon be gone.

A sob caught in her throat at the thought. He froze at the sound and glanced her way. Rose's pulse quickened. He approached the door, peering into the darkness. Leaping from her seat, she darted up the stairs into her chamber and quietly pressed the door shut behind her. Her heart crashed against her chest as she leaned back against it. But no creak of stairs sounded. When her breath settled, she grabbed the lit candle on her desk and dropped to the floor beside a trunk at the foot of her bed. Lifting the lid, she rummaged through the contents: a stack of books, an old jewelry box, a deck of cards. A cool musty smell saturated the air. She grabbed the blanket her mother had knitted for her when she was a child and drew it to her nose, but her mother's lilac scent had long since faded. Beneath it, the McGuire family Bible stared up at her. Setting down the candle, she began sifting through crackling pages—pages she hadn't read in years. There, stuffed somewhere in Psalms, was the letter.

The letter she needed to rekindle her hatred of the man downstairs. With tender care, she fingered the broken wax and gazed at her mother's name on the front. Tears filled her eyes as she opened it and read.

My beloved Rossalyn,

The days pass with mindless toil and an empty heart since I left you, and I begin to wonder whether it was a wise choice to join this country's navy and be so often gone from your side. Though the Chesapeake *is a grand ship and I a fair boatswain, the glory of the majestic sea cannot compare to your beauty, my lovely wife. I find Commodore Barron to be a good captain with much battle experience, yet his pride expresses itself in harsh methods one minute followed by neglect the next.*

Tomorrow we hoist our sails for the Mediterranean, and I shall not see you for months. Please know, my darling that you are and always will be my love and my life. My thoughts will ever be

*consumed with you and Rose, and I shall write you daily, though
I know not when the posts will arrive in your hands. Do not be
anxious, my love. I am in God's care now.*

*Please kiss our sweet Rose for me and tell her I shall return to
beat her at whist as soon as I can.*

Yours forever,
Robert McGuire

Even through her tears, a slight giggle choked in Rose's throat at
her father's last sentence. Like warm summer days, countless joyful
memories passed across her mind of the hours she'd spent playing cards
with her father in the sitting room of their home.

But those days were gone forever.

She folded the letter and pressed it to her breast. Tears streamed
down her cheeks as she placed the faded letter within the Bible—the
Bible she hadn't read since her mother died. Then clinging to the holy
book, she lay down on the floor and placed her head on her mother's
blanket.

Sometime later, in the midst of nightmares filled with cannon shots
and British warships, she was awakened by the sound of her uncle's
voice—its comforting cadence nestled around her like a warm blanket
and she drifted into peaceful sleep.

❖

Forcing his leaden eyelids to remain open, Alex circled the quaint but
rustic parlor one more time, if only to keep himself awake by invoking
the pain in his thigh. He knew if he dared to sit on the sofa or one of
the cushioned wooden chairs, he'd be done for and the slumber that
beckoned him would win. With each turn of the room, however, his
anger grew at Mr. Drummond's complete indifference toward his family's safety. During such harrowing times, and especially after warning
bells had been sounded, the man of the house should be home standing
firmly in defense of those he loved. His behavior was reprehensible! But
what did Alex expect from a former thief and indentured servant? Alex
would never tolerate such a lackadaisical attitude on board his ship.
However, it angered him more that he could not order the man to step
up to the task. In fact, as a servant, Alex possessed no power at all.

A first in his life.

A floorboard creaked beneath his boot. His spine stiffened. What was wrong with him? Egad, fatigue must be tying his nerves into knots. As his thoughts had done to his gut. All night long, he'd pondered what he should do if British raiders attacked the house. And he had come up with only one possible course of action—a course that frightened him to the core, for that course was spurred on by a pair of luminous turquoise eyes.

No, he could never allow harm to come to Miss McGuire.

He halted at the fireplace yet again and ran a hand through his hair, tearing strands from his queue. What kind of British officer was he? What sort of man could be swayed from loyalty to his own country by a lady who had nothing to recommend her but a plot of land and a bevy of farm animals?

He chuckled as he pictured Miss McGuire petting the chicken in her lap.

The clomp of horse's hooves jolted Alex to attention. He cocked the musket and lifted the flap of the shutter to see Mr. Drummond's horse enter the stable. Finally.

Minutes later the elderly man burst through the front door, a draft of wind spiced with rain swirling on his heels. Shrugging out of his coat, he ambled into the parlor. "Mr. Reed." His gray eyebrows leaped. "What are you doing in the house at this hour?" He motioned toward the musket in Alex's hand. "And with my Brown Bess."

Alex cleared his throat to stifle his annoyance. "I am protecting *your* family, sir, as you ordered."

Mr. Drummond approached Alex and handed him his coat. "Ah, yes, the warning bells. Very good, Mr. Reed. Very good indeed."

Hot blood surged through Alex's veins as he took the garment. Mr. Drummond should be the one hanging up Alex's coat, not the other way around. If the man knew he entertained the son of a wealthy viscount, he'd no doubt be buzzing around Alex, seeing to his every need.

Or would he?

Something in Mr. Drummond's light brown eyes bespoke of a humility not easily impressed by rank and wealth.

"Have you seen my spectacles, Mr. Reed?" The old man patted his pockets. "It seems I have misplaced them again." He stumbled over the edge of the rug then shook his head with a chortle.

"No sir." Alex's impatience rose at the man's lubberly behavior.

Blowing out a ragged sigh, Mr. Drummond sank into one of the cushioned chairs beside the fireplace and spread his hands over his portly belly.

Tossing the coat onto the back of the settee, Alex circled the sofa, intending to chastise Mr. Drummond for his negligence of duty and family. But he halted when he saw red splotches marring the old man's wrinkled hands. "Is that blood?" he asked.

Mr. Drummond gazed up at him, his tired eyes distant with sorrow. "Yes. But not mine. There was a bit o' trouble down at Gorsuch's Tavern tonight."

Alex flinched. "The British?"

"I wish it had been. That enemy I know how to fight." Mr. Drummond huffed then gestured toward the sofa. "If you intend to stay, have a seat, son. Your leg surely could use the rest."

Son? Alex cringed at the man's familiarity, yet the tender way in which he spoke the word filled Alex with an odd longing. Alex obliged him and lowered himself onto the soft cushions. Immediate relief swept through his tired legs.

"No, my enemy, Mr. Reed, is far more formidable than the British military." Mr. Drummond took a brass-tipped poker and began stirring the lifeless coals in the fireplace.

Alex restrained an insolent chuckle. "Upon my honor, sir, what or who could be more formidable than the British?"

"The powers of darkness." Mr. Drummond's quick and solemn reply startled Alex. "The powers that lure a man to drink too much, to steal, to curse his fellow man, and even to kill." He poked at the dark chunks of coal like a swordsman against an evil foe.

Alex snorted. *Simple-minded Americans.* "You speak of the devil, sir? But I doubt he exists."

Intense brown eyes snapped his way, the candlelight reflecting an intelligence that surprised Alex. "He would love for you to believe that, Mr. Reed. But he exists, I assure you." He turned back to the fireplace. "I have seen his work too often to deny it."

Alex studied the man. Short and bulky of stature with a full head of rebellious gray hair, and a beard to match, he normally exuded a kind, benign demeanor. But tonight as he stared deep in thought at the dark fireplace, he seemed burdened by an enormous weight. Lines folded across a ruddy face that possessed a wide forehead and a stout nose. Perhaps there was more to this man than Alex had first assumed. "What happened tonight?" Alex leaned forward.

Mr. Drummond expelled a long sigh. "Too much drink, too much anxiety about the war, too many opposing sides." His shoulders slumped. "Add to that mix those who have lost friends and family in recent battles. And before I could settle things, someone ended up with a knife in his gut."

Alex's chest constricted. "A friend of yours?"

"Aye, died in my arms." Mr. Drummond stabbed a dark coal in the corner of the fireplace and flung it across the pit. "It fell to me to inform his widow." His voice broke.

Alex shifted uncomfortably, uneasy at the man's display of emotion. "Why you, Mr. Drummond? Why not allow family or friends to tell her? Surely your vocation doesn't require you to perform such agonizing tasks?" At least Alex had not seen the vicars back home do much of anything save attend parties and put people to sleep with their Sunday sermons.

"Oh no, Mr. Reed, a man of God does everything he can to assist and bring comfort to those in need. We who follow in Christ's footsteps are to be an extension of God's love to everyone we come across."

Alex stared into eyes misted with tears yet hard with purpose, and it struck him—the man truly believed what he said. Despite his ineloquent speech and reprehensible manners, wisdom and determination poured from him. Alex searched memories of his childhood for any moments of intimate conversation he and his father had shared, but all he found were visions of a stiff chin bordered in satin and lace and the cold sheen of pomposity that had covered his father's dark eyes.

Then he remembered Mr. Drummond's sordid past, and the man's intentions became clear. "No doubt one must perform many acts of charity to atone for past sins." Something Alex could well understand— exchanging charity and honor for the shameful acts of a rebellious youth. But instead of trying to live up to the impossible rules of a distant God, Alex sought to make restitution by becoming an honorable naval officer.

"Atone?" Mr. Drummond scratched his stiff gray beard and smiled. "All the good deeds in the world wouldn't make up for what I've done. No, I do these things out of love for my Father in heaven."

Father. Emotion clogged in Alex's throat. God as Father? Absurd.

Uncomfortable with the direction of the discussion, Alex struggled to rise, leaning most of his weight on his good leg. "I cannot stay in your employ much longer, Mr. Drummond. I hope you will be able to procure a replacement soon."

Mr. Drummond nodded, but Alex thought he saw a slight smile on the man's lips. "I already have someone in mind, Mr. Reed."

"Very good." Alex said. "I'll leave you to your rest." Turning, he shuffled toward the door.

"Sleep well, son." Mr. Drummond's kind tone threatened to undo the tight bands Alex had formed over his heart.

For never had he heard those words from his own father's lips.

❖ CHAPTER 11 ❖

Standing in front of the house beside her aunt and Amelia, Rose pressed a hand over her churning stomach. The last thing she wanted to do today was take another trip into town. Especially with Mr. Reed escorting them. But she had promised her aunt on Sunday that she would visit Mrs. Pickersgill, and Rose could not go back on her word. Oh why had she made such a vow? What if someone recognized Mr. Reed? What if he came across some valuable military information to take back to his captain?

Rose squeezed her forehead as her thoughts spun a knot of fear and guilt—a knot she saw no way to untangle at the moment.

"For heaven's sake. Where is Mr. Reed?" Aunt Muira clutched her medical satchel and shot a harried gaze toward the stable.

Rose glanced at Amelia. "I imagine he's attempting to harness Douglas to the carriage."

"But he's been in there for over thirty minutes." Aunt Muira bit her lip impatiently. "What sort of servant is he?"

Amelia giggled. "One who isn't skilled with horse and equipage, I imagine."

Aunt Muira cast the maid a curious gaze as Rose headed toward the stable to see if she could assist the poor man. She'd only taken two steps when Mr. Reed appeared, wearing Samuel's used livery and plodding forward on his crutch as he led Douglas and the carriage out from the barn. His black coat and breeches—far too small for his large frame—strained across his chest and thighs, outlining his firm muscles beneath.

Rose averted her gaze and elbowed Amelia to do the same, but the insolent woman gaped at him unabashed.

"Ah, there you are, Mr. Reed." Aunt Muira took Mr. Reed's outstretched hand and climbed into the coach. "We thought you'd become lost."

"Just familiarizing myself with your equipage, madam." He turned a half-cocked smile to Rose and offered her his hand. But when she placed her still-trembling fingers into his firm ones, his look of playfulness faded into one of concern.

Snatching her hand away, she entered the carriage and sat beside her aunt as Amelia's delicate hand lingered far too long on Mr. Reed's before she joined them. Then leaping into the driver's seat, Mr. Reed snapped the reins.

❖

Per Mrs. Drummond's directions, Alex pulled the coach to a stop before a small stone house on the corner of Pratt and Albemarle Streets. He was more than impressed by what he'd seen of the quaint little town on his way here. He'd expected to see nothing but dirt streets lined by dilapidated shops and open-air taverns inhabited by swine, both animal and human. Instead, he'd counted at least five churches, two theaters—albeit rustic theaters—several watchhouses, five inns, two libraries, three markets, two banks, and three newspaper printing offices.

Despite the war, the citizens of Baltimore scurried about their business on foot or in carriages or on horseback. Ladies and gentlemen strolled down the cobblestone streets in finery and frippery that could equal any to be seen among the *haut ton* sauntering down Bond Street—well, almost.

Alex leaped down from the driving seat, set down the step, opened the door, and held his hand out for the ladies. Though the demeaning status grated against his pride, he found being a servant an easy and innocuous occupation—a great respite from the responsibility and hard work of an officer in His Majesty's Navy. He briefly wondered if Captain Milford was searching for him and Garrick or had he assumed them dead or worse—deserters. But what did it matter? The issue would be resolved as soon as Alex returned with his wound as evidence of his tale of being shot in a skirmish and then cared for by a rebel farmer until Alex could make his way back to the ship.

"Wait here," Miss McGuire said. Leaping down, she waved a gloved hand toward him and lifted her pert nose in the air. In fact, since they had begun the journey, her attitude had transformed from a humble farm girl to a pretentious chit that reminded him of certain noble ladies he'd been acquainted with back home. Yet the act was so at odds with her true nature that it appeared more adorable than annoying.

"No, no." The ostrich feathers atop Mrs. Drummond's gold bonnet fluttered in the breeze. "Do come in, Mr. Reed. I would like you to meet Mrs. Pickersgill."

Alex raised a victorious brow in Miss McGuire's direction.

A maid answered the door and ushered them inside to a sitting room, where a short, elderly lady dressed in a plain gown rose from her seat. Gray hair sprang from beneath a white mob cap fringed in lace. She gave them a wide smile as she greeted them warmly. Finally her gaze landed on Alex.

"My, my, who do we have here?" Approaching him, she took his hands. Cold, boney, yet strong fingers gripped his.

Shocked by her familiarity, Alex stiffened.

"This is Mr. Reed, our new man of work," Mrs. Drummond said, pride lifting her tone. "Mr. Reed, Mrs. Mary Pickersgill."

"A pleasure, madam." Alex nodded and kissed her hand.

Mrs. Pickersgill squealed with delight. "My goodness. I haven't heard an accent so regal since I was a little girl in Philadelphia."

Over the elderly lady's shoulder, Alex saw Amelia exchange a fearful glance with Miss McGuire.

"It has been my family's curse." Mr. Reed gave a lopsided grin, to which the elderly lady released his hands and gestured toward a maid standing by the doorway. "Dorothy, please bring everyone some cocoa."

Mrs. Drummond tugged off her gloves and took a seat on a cushioned oval-backed chair. "Mrs. Pickersgill is a flag maker, Mr. Reed."

"Indeed?" But Alex could not take his eyes off Miss McGuire. Her simple walking dress of periwinkle blue brought out the sharp color of her eyes and made her skin glow. She untied the pink satin ribbon of her bonnet and drew it from her head, dislodging a few golden strands.

"She made the enormous flag that flies over Fort McHenry. Have you seen it?" Mrs. Drummond drew his gaze back to her.

Flag, indeed. Alex grumbled silently. These colonies had no need of their own flag for soon the Union Jack would proudly wave once again above their city squares. "I have not had the pleasure."

Mrs. Pickersgill gestured for them to sit, but Alex remained standing.

"I must say I was quite surprised when Major Armistead, General Smith, and Commodore Barney came to call on me that day to commission the ensign." She chuckled. "In their own words, they wanted 'a flag so large that the British would have no difficulty seeing it from a distance'!"

Alex felt the muscles in his neck tighten as the maid brought in a service tray with china cups and a steaming pot of the sweet-smelling drink.

Miss McGuire speared him with a sharp gaze and nodded for him to leave. She tossed her reticule onto a floral-printed sofa, then took her seat beside Amelia. Mrs. Pickersgill slid onto a chair to their left.

The maid poured dark liquid into each cup then scurried from the room.

"I hope you don't mind hot cocoa, ladies. I never did favor tea." Mrs. Pickersgill handed each of them a cup and saucer.

"Not at all." Amelia lifted the cup to her lips. "It is my favorite too."

Mrs. Pickersgill frowned. "Hard to come by with the blockade. I fear my supply is nearly depleted."

Again Alex felt a thread of guilt wind through him.

"Mr. Reed, the flag Mrs. Pickersgill sewed measures thirty feet by forty-two feet." Mrs. Drummond boasted.

"Astonishing," Alex remarked, trying to envision the enormous flag filling the room. "How did you accomplish it?"

"I had help, sir." Mrs. Pickersgill opened a palm toward an empty seat in the corner, but Alex remained rooted in place. Why did these Americans insist on treating their servants as equals?

"My daughter, two nieces, and two servants assisted me, but we had to move the massive cloth to a warehouse nearby just to finish it." She smiled. "I was happy to do it," she waved a hand through the air. "It does present a fine ensign above the fort."

Mrs. Drummond took a sip of hot cocoa. "Perhaps we will take you to see it later, Mr. Reed?"

"Surely a servant has no interest in flags or forts." Miss McGuire shot into the conversation with the force of a cannon. Her cup clattered on the saucer she held, and she set both on the table. Opening the fan hanging on her wrist, she fluttered it about her face. "Perhaps you should check on the horse, Mr. Reed. We will be discussing things which could not possibly interest you."

Mrs. Drummond's eyebrows bent together, and she gave her niece a look of reprimand.

But Mrs. Pickersgill did not seem to notice. "Ah yes, the reason for your visit," she added. "I am most anxious to discuss my idea for a new charity devoted to widowed ladies who have lost their husbands and cannot support themselves."

Alex flinched. To find such generous kindness among these poor colonists. Astonishing. His family and most of his associates back in England possessed far more wealth than these people could ever imagine, yet Alex had not once witnessed such benevolence among them. "Most commendable, Mrs. Pickersgill," he couldn't help but say as he stretched his back against a shirt that seemed to shrink with each passing moment.

"God has blessed me with a skill to make flags, Mr. Reed. Passed down through my mother." Mrs. Pickersgill's expression grew somber as she glanced over the ladies. "But many women do not have the same opportunity to run their own businesses and provide for themselves."

Mrs. Drummond nodded. "And Rose is most interested in helping you, my dear Mary."

At this, Miss McGuire's face brightened. "Yes, indeed I am, Mrs. Pickersgill."

Alex felt his brow wrinkle. Though he sensed Miss McGuire possessed a kind heart, he had not supposed this frightened woman's charity to extend beyond her family and those of her closest acquaintances— people with whom she felt safe. The revelation caused his thoughts to tangle in confusion. And he didn't like being confused. Confusion caused bad decisions. Any emotion caused bad decisions. And one bad decision by a naval officer could cost lives. Distinct lines must be drawn between good and evil, enemy and friend, rebel and patriot. Excusing himself, Alex stepped outside and tested his leg. He must leave tonight. If he didn't, he feared those distinct lines would forever be blurred in his mind, and then all would be lost.

❖

Rose peered at Alex from beneath the brim of her bonnet as they made their way to the brick building behind her uncle's church. He hobbled beside her with difficulty, the hot sun forming beads of sweat on his forehead. Forcing down her traitorous concern for him, she continued walking. She must make his day as a servant such an unbearable prick to his pride that he'd be desperate to return to his ship at nightfall. She must also keep him as far away from Fort McHenry as possible. Oh wouldn't he just love to go see Mrs. Pickersgill's flag. Along with the armament at the fort!

Halting, Rose shrugged out of her spencer and handed it to him. "Aunt Muira, Amelia, do give Mr. Reed your wraps. It is growing far too hot and will only be more oppressive in Uncle's sickroom." She smiled at Mr. Reed as the two ladies complied.

Once they had gone, Mr. Reed's brows arched. "And what am I to do with these, miss?"

"Why, put them in the coach, Mr. Reed." She forced an air of pretension that did not settle well in her stomach. "Or you may carry them until we have need of them again. It matters not to me."

He narrowed his gaze and headed back toward the carriage, wrestling out of his own thick black coat.

"No, no, no, Mr. Reed." Rose called after him. "A footman must always be dressed with the utmost of propriety."

He groaned, and Rose followed her aunt and Amelia into the makeshift hospital before she could make out his curt reply.

Once they stepped inside the dark room, however, all thoughts of annoying Mr. Reed into leaving vanished as the smell of sickness and despair slapped Rose in the face. Shabby cots lined either side of the long narrow room. Lanterns, bloody cloths, mugs, and Bibles covered small side tables wedged between the beds. Two tiny windows perched above allowed barely a breeze and a modicum of sunlight to pass into the dank room. In the distance, Uncle Forbes hovered over one of the beds.

Aunt Muira had already pulled up a chair before the first cot on the left and began to dab a cloth over the man's forehead. Amelia leaned against the side wall, covering her nose. It had been months since Rose had joined her aunt on her weekly visits to this place. Why had she stayed away so long? A wave of guilt swept over her, but she shrugged it off and took a step forward. She was here now. Clutching Amelia's arm, she dragged her down the aisle, promising herself that she would do her best to never again allow fear to keep her from helping others.

❖

Alex stared as Mr. Drummond, two Negro men, and the three women flitted about from cot to cot, caring for the sick. Though sweat streamed down his back and the stench stung his nose, he allowed no complaints to form in his mind in light of the scene of tragedy and despair before him. No doubt Miss McGuire was as hot and uncomfortable as he was, yet she offered caring smiles and gentle ministrations to each patient she visited. Alex tried to picture any of the ladies of his acquaintance back home doing the same, but the vision would not form in his mind. In fact, most of them would not come within a mile of such sickness and misery.

Mr. Drummond greeted his wife with a kiss and then made his way down the aisle. His gaze met Alex's and he slipped beside him.

"Who are these people?" Alex asked.

"These are the outcasts of society, you might say," Mr. Drummond replied with a sigh. "When the main hospital is full, they send those who cannot pay and those who suffer from prolonged drunkenness or who have been injured in tavern brawls to me. Some simply need to sleep off last night's drink and have nowhere else to go. Others need a bit o' loving care and that my wife kindly supplies. While others need the kind of care only God can give."

Alex bristled at the mention of God's care for he had never experienced it in his life, and he wasn't all together sure God was around enough to care for anyone. "What of those who need a doctor's care?"

"A charitable physician from the hospital visits once a week, but in the meantime, my lovely wife does what she can."

Alex watched as Miss McGuire unfolded a letter and began reading it to one of the men. "Does Miss McGuire assist here often?"

"Not as much as she'd like, I'm sure." Mr. Drummond folded his arms across his portly belly and lowered his voice. "She has suffered greatly in her young life. I've never seen a heart so pure and kind, but fear has kept her home. It's the only place she feels safe anymore."

Alex tried to rub the tightness from his jaw. Mr. Garrick's attack certainly hadn't helped her in that regard. "She still suffers from her father's death?"

"Aye, but it is more than that." Mr. Drummond's brow wrinkled for a moment before the gleam returned to his eye. "But she has shown improvement lately, and we hope she'll be able to join my wife on her visits here more often and also when Mrs. Drummond travels to Washington."

"Washington?"

"Aye, my wife assists at an orphanage there, but Rose refuses to travel that far from home."

Alex's gaze followed Miss McGuire around the room, wondering what further tragedies had struck the lady. A hollow ache formed in his gut at the thought of anyone doing her harm.

"Your presence seems to have done her good, Mr. Reed." Mr. Drummond used the end of his stained cravat to wipe the perspiration from his face.

"Me?" Alex stifled a laugh. "I fear you are mistaken, Mr. Drummond."

"Am I?" He scratched his beard, and once again Alex saw a deep, lingering intelligence behind his brown eyes. "I knew it would take someone very special to bring joy again to the lass. Someone we would least expect." He winked at Alex as if they shared a grand secret—as if he knew Alex was British. But how could he?

Besides, joy was the last thing Alex brought Miss McGuire. No point in bringing the error to Mr. Drummond's attention since Alex would be gone soon. "I trust you have been searching for someone to replace me as your man of work, sir?"

Mr. Drummond frowned and patted his waistcoat as if searching for something. "As best I can, Mr. Reed. Meager pickings here in town."

"Regardless, I fear I'll have to be go—"

"Well, I best be getting back to my work." Mr. Drummond slapped his hands together, interrupting Alex. With a nod, he sped off to join his wife.

Alex shook his head and watched as the two of them along with Miss McGuire continued to wander among the cots, holding hands, praying, and conversing with the patients. They received no pay for their trouble, no reward, no public honor—all the things Alex fought so hard to acquire. Things that suddenly seemed as useless as the dust beneath his boots.

Those distinct lines he fought so hard to keep firmly in his mind began to blur even more.

Two hours later, Alex walked behind Amelia and Miss McGuire down Baltimore Street on their way to purchase some fabric for a new dress. He wondered what his father the viscount would say if he could see his son dressed in an ill-fitting footman's livery strolling through a rebel town, ducking into shops filled with ladies' garments and feminine fripperies.

No doubt he'd say what he'd always said.

You'll never amount to anything, boy. Why can't you be more like your brother?

Alex sighed. Perhaps the man was right all along, for if Alex truly admitted it to himself, he was enjoying his time with these humble rebels and dreaded returning to his ship.

Doffing his hat, he dabbed the sweat from his forehead and allowed the breeze blowing in from the bay to thread cool fingers through his hair. The clip-clop of horses' hooves, the grate of carriage wheels, and the chatter of citizens filled the air. Bells rang from the harbor, and somewhere in the distance, a peddler hawked his wares. Pressing forward, Mr. Reed offered his arm to Miss McGuire.

"A footman walks behind his mistress, Mr. Reed, not with her." She snapped at him keeping her eyes straight ahead.

He gave her a crooked smile and drifted back a few steps. "As you wish, miss." He knew he should be angry at her for her condescending treatment, but her ill-fitting cloak of pomposity only endeared her to him more.

They crossed over a wooden bridge, making way for a horse and rider to their left. Beneath them the Jones Falls River slapped its banks and tumbled over rocks as it dashed toward the bay.

As they proceeded, Alex studied the homes that lined the cobblestone street. Square, two-story structures stood back from road with beautiful gardens stretching before them to the street. The sweet fragrance of roses, pinks, sweet williams, larkspurs, and hollyhocks filled the air. Most of the homes boasted a smokehouse off to the side or peeking out from the rear, where no doubt the family cured its bacon and baked biscuits and other varieties of bread and cake. Though nothing like the stately homes in Cranleigh, Alex found the dwellings quite charming—in a rustic sort of way.

He scanned the faces of those they passed. Aside from the occasional grimy slave, tattered beggar, or common worker, most of Baltimore's citizens appeared well groomed and fashionable. Not a few men turned to smile or tip their hats at the ladies.

Miss McGuire ignored them entirely, but Amelia seemed to thrive upon the attention as she pinched her cheeks and returned each greeting with a coquettish smile or a wave of her fan. More than one gentleman seemed intent on answering her call—that was until they saw Alex following close behind.

Farther down the street, Alex became enamored with the signs hanging in front of the shops. Instead of words describing what wares could be found within, pictures and symbols told the passersby what type of shop it was. Alex had never seen anything like it. Were all Americans so unlettered? He passed beneath a sign etched with the picture of a golden fan and umbrella. He peeked in the window to see an assortment of fancy haberdashery. An engraved sundial hung above the watchmaker. The importer of Irish linens depicted his goods with a painting of a spinning wheel, though the store appeared empty when Alex peered within.

A ship's bell drew his gaze toward the east where, in between warehouses and shops, a crowd of bare masts jutted into the afternoon sky, swaying with the gentle movement of the bay. He wondered if any of them belonged to the notorious Baltimore Clipper he'd heard so much about—those swift ships that continually harassed British merchants. He thought to ask Miss McGuire, but knew she'd only accuse him of spying. Instead, Alex drew in a deep breath of the salty air but, oddly, found no longing within him to return to the sea.

After a brief stop at the drapers where, much to Amelia's dismay, she did not find her desired fabric, they turned down Calvert Street to visit, as Miss McGuire informed him, the best millinery in town.

Aside from the aching wound in his thigh and the heat of the day, Alex enjoyed this brief foray into civilization. Having spent months out to sea, any city, even one as primitive as this one, reminded him that life was more than wind and weather, grapeshot and broadsides.

Amelia dashed inside Brekham's Millinery before Alex reached the front of the shop and stopped beneath a sign painted with a large purple hat.

"Stay here, Mr. Reed, if you please." Miss McGuire thrust out her chin and turned to follow her companion.

Alex grabbed her arm, turning her to face him. "I know what you're doing, miss."

Holding her bonnet against a hefty breeze, she tugged from his grasp. "And what is that, Mr. Reed?"

"Trying to humiliate me into leaving." He brushed dust from his coat. "I promised I would return to my ship, and I am a man of my word." He offered her a look of appeasement. "So why don't we spend our brief time together being polite instead of impertinent?"

She seemed to be pondering his suggestion when Amelia burst from the shop.

"There are no hats," the woman grumbled as the bell hanging from the shop's door clanged her disapproval before shutting. Tipping the edge of her bonnet against the sun's bright rays, she gazed down the street. "There is no silk, no satin, no velvet, nothing with which to make an appropriate gown." Her lips drew into a pout. "I tire of this war."

"Amelia." Miss McGuire looped her arm through her friend's. "There also is a shortage of food and medicines, things which are far more important than such fripperies."

Alex grimaced beneath another wave of empathy. What the deuces was happening to him? These Americans deserved discomfort and much worse for their rebellion against England.

"I know." Amelia shrugged. "I know I am spoiled, and I shouldn't say such things. It's just that I heard there will be a ball at the Fountain Inn next week, and I was so hoping to go. I know it won't be like the balls we had before the blockade, but at least we can forget the horrors of war for one night and enjoy the company of the good citizens of Baltimore." Her eyes lit up. "Besides, I think Mr. Braxton intends to ask your uncle if he can escort me."

Miss McGuire smiled, but her eyes were riveted to something in the distance. "Look, there are Marianne and Cassandra."

Alex followed her gaze to a crowd of people across the cobblestone street. A tall muscular man in gray trousers with a double-breasted black waistcoat stood beside a woman in a stylish pink gown. Alex's heart froze.

Noah Brenin.

He'd know that bronzed face and light hair anywhere. He squinted against the sun at the two men who stood by his side. Neither could he mistake the coal-black hair of the one and the brawny frame of the other, nor the smiling face of the lad standing beside his father. Luke Heaton and Blackthorn along with his son, Daniel. All of them had been impressed aboard the HMS *Undefeatable* two years ago—dragged aboard as slaves to the British Crown.

Surely they would recognize Alex as easily as he had recognized them.

"Marianne!" Miss McGuire shouted as she made her way across the street, Amelia on her heels.

Alex turned his face away and scanned the street. People strolled down the avenue, weaving among carriages and horses. He could escape into the crowd, make his way back to the farm to get his uniform, and head to his ship directly.

But that would leave Miss McGuire and Amelia unescorted.

Clenching his fists, he glanced behind him at the millinery shop just as a feminine voice shouted "Rose!" from across the street.

❖ CHAPTER 12 ❖

Grabbing Amelia, Rose darted in between a stream of carriages and made her way to her friends. But instead of the expected smiles and greetings tossed her way; all of them, with the exception of Daniel, stared curiously at the spot she had just vacated.

Glancing over her shoulder, she saw nothing unusual to draw their attention, although she did wonder where Mr. Reed had run off to. Scanning the street, she was about to ask Amelia when Noah spoke up. "I could have sworn I saw Lieutenant Reed."

Mr. Heaton flipped the hair from his face, his dark brows furrowed. "Indeed."

"Impossible, gentlemen." Marianne's skeptical tone belied her words as she turned to Rose with a smile. "What a pleasure to see you in town."

"Mr. Reed?" Rose shook her head. Surely she heard the name incorrectly.

"Aye, Mr. Alexander Reed of the HMS *Undefeatable*," Daniel, whose voice had deepened considerably since Rose had last seen him, announced with a hint of pride.

Rose's knees turned to mush.

"Are you ill, Rose?" Cassandra, her dear friend, gripped her arm and steadied her.

Amelia eased between Rose and Marianne and took her other arm, but from the sound of her maid's ragged breathing and the tremble in her grip, Rose guessed she suffered from the same confusion and terror that consumed Rose.

"I'm quite all right, thank you. Just a bit warm." Rose plucked out her fan and waved it frantically about her face. Anything to keep her wits about her. "My word, what would a British naval officer be doing sauntering about on the streets of Baltimore?" She attempted a laugh that only brought curious gazes her way. "Why, he'd be arrested on the spot."

Amelia's grip on her arm tightened.

Mr. Heaton's jaw knotted. "Or worse, if I ever see him again."

Cassandra placed her hands on her delicate hips. "Come now Mr. Heaton, why are you always so eager to use your fists before your reason?" Ignoring her playful smile, Mr. Heaton huffed and looked away.

Her heart tight in her chest, Rose swept her gaze to the last place she'd seen Mr. Reed. No trace of him remained. But where had he gone? And how did her friends know him? Rose searched her mind, but only one possibility surfaced. Two years ago, Marianne and Noah had returned from the sea with an adventurous tale of capture aboard a British navy ship, of a mad captain, of sabotage, escape, and victory. Rose drew a hand to her head to quell a sudden dizziness. Of all the ships in the royal navy and all the second lieutenants. . .

Mr. Blackthorn, whom Rose had been introduced to three weeks prior as Noah's first mate, continued to stare at the millinery store as if expecting Mr. Reed to reappear. "That man and his cap'n kept me an' my boy prisoner on board his ship for three years."

"Papa, it wasn't his fault," Daniel said. "He was only following orders."

"Mr. Reed was an honorable man." Noah gripped the pommel of his sword, sending Rose's stomach churning. She had no doubt that regardless of his sentiments, he would not hesitate to arrest Mr. Reed and toss him into prison.

"Don't forget, he allowed my precious wife to escape from his ship," Noah continued.

Rose squeezed her eyes shut, trying to wrap her mind around these shocking revelations. A flurry of wind tugged on her bonnet and cooled the perspiration on her neck. The clip-clop of horses' hooves, the prattle of passing citizens, and the occasional bell from the port swirled past her ears. Nothing out of the ordinary.

Mr. Heaton's gruff chortle snapped her eyes open. A breeze stirred his coal-black hair. He narrowed his eyes. "We owe him nothing. He allowed Marianne to escape only to save himself and his career."

"I don't understand. How could letting an enemy go save his career?" Rose asked.

Mr. Heaton crossed his arms over his chest. "He allowed her to keep a weapon on board. That's treason."

A weapon? Rose sped up the fluttering of her fan.

"For my protection," Marianne added. "Against that vile Lieutenant Garrick."

"Oh my word." Rose's knees wobbled and Cassandra steadied her. So Marianne had experienced Mr. Garrick's licentious appetites as well. And once again, Mr. Reed had played the chivalrous hero.

Marianne smiled. "And I threatened to tell his captain if he didn't allow me to escape."

Though the sun had begun its descent in the western sky, its searing rays seemed hotter than ever. Rose ceased her useless fanning.

"God had a plan for Mr. Reed." Daniel nodded with a grin. "To help us escape."

Blackthorn shook his head. "Only you could see God's hand in such a disaster, son."

"God's hand is everywhere." Daniel's gaze shifted to Rose and remained there so long she thought there might be dirt on her face again. "God has a plan for you too, Miss McGuire," the boy said it stoically as if he were speaking directly from another's prompting. "Something important for you to do."

Blackthorn's lips slanted. "Are you sure, Daniel?"

"Yes, father, I'm sure."

Something important to do? Confusion once again jumbled Rose's thoughts. For God? She hadn't exactly been on speaking terms with the Almighty these past years.

Marianne squeezed her arm and smiled. "I would listen to him if I were you."

"My son is a prophet, Miss McGuire." Blackthorn scratched his linen shirt.

A prophet? The explanation did nothing to ease her confusion. Prophets existed only in biblical times. God did not speak to people through prophets anymore. Any fool knew that.

As if to confirm her thoughts, Mr. Heaton let out a skeptical snort.

Blackthorn shrugged and ruffled Daniel's thick brown hair. "He's not often wrong. An' my other son, who's only five, appears t' have the same gift. Got it from me wife, God love her. An' we are now expectin' our third. Mebbe we'll have a whole family of prophets."

Noah slapped his first mate on the back. "Indeed. We could use more prophets in this city."

Pursing her lips, Rose directed her gaze at Daniel. "Well in this case, I fear you are entirely incorrect, Daniel, for I am not destined to perform any great feat." Nor did she want to be. Truth be told, she just wanted to be let alone—to live out her life in peace.

Instead of frowning at Rose's rebuke, Daniel smiled—a knowing smile that sent an odd shudder through her. She glanced toward the millinery. The shadow of a tall man shot back from the window. *So that's where Mr. Reed went.*

Best to be on her way and rescue him from his hiding place.

"We should be going. My aunt will be worried." Rose snatched the fan back from Amelia.

Noah cast a harried glance over the street. "But surely you and Amelia aren't without escort?"

"No. My footman is with us." At his questioning look, she continued, "I sent him to the chandlers to purchase some candles."

"Well, allow us to escort you there," Noah said.

"No need. It is just another block." Rose waved her fan in the air and dragged Amelia away. "Do continue to enjoy your day."

"Very well." Noah touched the tip of his cocked hat. "Good day to you then, ladies."

Cassandra waved. "I hope to see you soon, Rose."

"Yes, soon. Let's get together for tea, shall we?" Rose halted before a passing horse.

"Promise?" Marianne's voice turned Rose around. Her friend slid her arm into Noah's and she smiled.

"Promise." As Rose watched them leave, a myriad of emotions clamored for her attention. The foremost one—fear that her friends would see Mr. Reed and arrest him—was already slipping away.

"What was all that about Mr. Reed, miss?" Amelia exclaimed as they reached the other side of the street. "I had no idea."

"Neither did I." Rose waved one last time at her friends. No sooner had they disappeared from sight than Mr. Reed popped out of the store, brushing imaginary dust from his coat as if being among so many ladies' hats had somehow soiled him.

"Thank goodness. The store owner was about to toss me from the place, accusing me of being some sort of coxcomb."

Rose would have giggled if she wasn't so busy settling her breathing.

"Thank you for not alerting them to my presence." He scanned the street.

"I had no idea you knew my friends."

His eyes met hers. "I had no idea they were your friends, miss. Nor that they hailed from Baltimore."

"Pray tell, how many more of Baltimore's citizens have you impressed on your ship?"

He smiled. "None that I'm aware of."

"Shall we go just in case?" Amelia tugged on Rose's arm, her eyes flashing with fear.

With a nod, Rose slipped her fan into her reticule and headed down the street. Though she hurried her pace, the trip back to the church seemed to drag on forever. All along the street, from every shop and every corner, curious eyes seemed to follow them. But finally, Uncle Forbes's church came into view, and Rose released a shaky breath. That was until General Smith marched from the sick house, Aunt Muira on his heels. Though the General's face was its usual unruffled mask, Aunt Muria's was quivering with distress.

Rose froze, her heart seizing in her chest.

"Thank goodness you've returned," her aunt cried out. "We must go to the Myers' farm immediately."

"Elaine?" Rose's heart clinched. The warning bells of St. Peter's rang fresh through her mind. "What happened? Is she alive?"

The general halted before Mr. Reed and eyed him with a curious gaze. The breath of relief Rose had just released crowded back in her throat.

"It was the British, dear. And yes, she's alive." But the way her aunt said the words caused Rose's hands to tremble.

"And who might you be, sir?" General Smith asked Alex.

Mr. Reed stiffened.

"Why he is our new man of work, General, Mr. Alexander Reed." Her aunt came to the rescue. "Mr. Reed, bring the phaeton around. We must leave immediately."

With a nod, he darted off.

Rose pressed a hand over the veins throbbing in her throat. "What brings you here to our church, General?"

"I heard rumors of wounded British soldiers hiding amongst our own and thought some may have wandered into your uncle's care." The general's hardened gaze followed Mr. Reed as he disappeared behind the church and remained there until he reappeared, leading the horse and phaeton. "And I wanted to inform your aunt and uncle about the attack on the Myers' farm. I know the Myers are friends of your family's."

"Yes, indeed. Rose has known Elaine for years." Aunt Muira gestured for Mr. Reed to hurry.

Rose wobbled, and Amelia slipped her arm through hers.

"Very good. Well, if you'll excuse me. I must be going." General Smith slid his bicorn atop his head. "Ladies." He bowed slightly and after they bid him adieu, he marched away.

Much to Rose's relief.

Numbly, Rose allowed Mr. Reed to assist her into the carriage. She didn't have to ask what had happened to her friend Elaine. She knew. Her thoughts drifted to Elaine's wedding last summer. How happy the couple seemed as they rode off in their open-air carriage after the ceremony, all the guests tossing rose petals at them.

"Tell me they didn't harm James." She asked her aunt after they were all settled on their seats.

"He wasn't home." Rose couldn't remember her aunt's tone holding so much pain. "I need you to be strong, Rose." Leaning forward, she squeezed her hand once again. "For Elaine."

With a shake of her head, Rose tore her hand from her aunt's grasp and lowered her gaze. "I don't know if I can." Yet hadn't she just promised herself to not allow fear to keep her from helping others?

"She's asking for you, Rose. You're the only one who can help her."

Mr. Reed leaped into the driver's seat, jostling the carriage to the right, then snapped the reins and sent them on their way. Amelia stared vacantly out the window as if she couldn't handle any more trouble for one day.

Rose agreed.

No, Lord, please send someone else. Rose stifled a sob. Every ounce of her wanted to help her friend—wanted to help all women who'd suffered as she had, but thick bars of fear kept her locked far from those in need.

MaryLu Tyndall

"I am not strong like you, Aunt." Rose swiped a tear from her cheek. "When I help these women, it's like I'm going through it all over again."

Aunt Muira cupped Rose's face with both her hands and forced her to meet her gaze. "You are your father's daughter. There is strength in you, Rose."

"My father is gone."

"Your father lives on in you. And your heavenly Father is within you as well. Draw upon His strength."

Rose tightened her jaw. God had never helped her before. Why would he now? Yet, Elaine's sweet face drifted through Rose's mind. The way her blue eyes sparkled and dimples formed on her cheeks whenever she smiled. Rose could not turn her back on her friend—as God had done on her—not when Elaine needed Rose the most.

Within a half hour and at the direction of her aunt, Mr. Reed turned the carriage down a dirt road that wound through a valley of tall grass waving in the breeze. A small creek splashed and bubbled nearby accompanied by a chorus of meadowlarks. The happy sounds and beautiful sights were at odds with the despair threatening to sever Rose's heart. Despair for Elaine. Then as if reading her dismal thoughts, a blast of smoke-laden wind blew in through the window and stung her nose. Aunt Muira coughed and drew a silk handkerchief to her mouth. Rose leaned out the window to see a gray mist hovering over a patch of pine trees in the distance. Her stomach tightened. She faced forward again and clamped her hands together in her lap. Aunt Muira touched Rose's arm and offered her a comforting look as the carriage bumped and jostled over the uneven road.

They slowed and Rose thought she heard Mr. Reed groan. Forcing herself to peek out the window again, she saw what was left of a small cottage perched beside a pond. She drew in a gasp. Half of the small house lay in a black charred ruin, the other half, though darkened with soot, remained intact. The coach jostled over something in the road, and Rose's cheek struck the edge of the window. Ignoring both the pain in her face and the one in her heart, she jerked her head back into the carriage and searched for a breath of air. "Where is Elaine?"

"In the house, I believe," her aunt replied.

Amelia gaped out the window. "Oh my."

Mr. Reed brought the carriage to a halt before the scorched building, and Aunt Muira grabbed her satchel, opened the door, and leaped out before he had a chance to hop down and assist her.

Not that he'd intended to aid them, for as Rose took a tentative step down onto the muddy soil after Amelia had debarked, she noted that Mr. Reed remained on his seat.

Staring at what was left of the blackened house.

He glanced her way, a look of horror crossing his face, before he grabbed his crutch and jumped down.

"Come along now." Aunt Muira forged ahead, her tone that of a school matron.

But Rose couldn't seem to move her feet.

A family of ducks—a mother, father, and seven babies—glided happily over the pond to her right as if no tragedy had occurred here. But the wisps of smoke spinning off the charred wood of the cottage spoke otherwise. Movement dragged Rose's gaze to the left of the house where several yards away beneath a massive oak tree, a man halted his digging and looked up. Two fresh mounds of dirt sat amid a scattering of crosses and stones. Rose's throat clamped shut.

Abandoning his crutch against the carriage, Mr. Reed approached her. "What happened here?"

By the guilt lacing his tone, Rose knew he had already guessed. Nevertheless, she could not help but lay the charge at his feet. "Your people happened here, Mr. Reed."

Pain etched across his eyes. He swallowed and offered her his arm. Ignoring it, Rose ventured forward.

Splinters of wood poked out from a large hole in the front door that hung limp on its hinges. Aunt Muira knocked and waited with the patience and composure of a lady making a social call. Within seconds the wooden slab swung wide with a heartrending squeak to reveal James, Elaine's husband. Wild, swollen eyes stared at them from within a red face that was streaked with soot. A torn, stained shirt did nothing to hide the cuts and abrasions across his arms and chest, and a drop of blood oozed from a wound on his head. Without saying a word, he ushered them inside.

Aunt Muira and Amelia disappeared within, but Rose remained at the threshold. The smell of singed wood, sickness, and sorrow threatened to send her back to the carriage. Perspiration dotted her neck. She whispered a portion of her father's song.

Ten thousand mile is very far away
For you to return to me,
You leave me here to lament, and well a day!
My tears you will not see, my love.

Mr. Reed remained by her side but said not a word.

Gathering her resolve, Rose ventured within. Holes in the wall to her left revealed the darkened remains of what had been the kitchen and dining room. Smoke bit her nose and throat, and Rose swallowed. Voices lured her to the back of the house where traitorous sunlight flooded a parlor that—because of what had occurred within—should have been enshrouded in gloom. Aunt Muira drew up a chair before a woman lying on a sofa and leaned over her, hiding the woman's face from Rose. But she knew it was Elaine. And she wasn't ready to face her friend just yet. Amelia knelt beside Aunt Muira and took Elaine's hand in hers, only adding to Rose's guilt at her own inadequacy.

Shards of glass littered the floor below broken windows where torn, singed curtains fluttered on the incoming breeze. The Hepplewhite side cabinet Rose had so adored lay in a pile of sticks by the cold fireplace. No doubt the rain she'd heard last night had put out the fire before it could consume this half of the house. For aside from the shattered windows, and a burn mark on the floorcloth, the parlor appeared undamaged.

Not like the lady lying on the cream-colored sofa.

James approached Rose, arms extended. "She's been asking for you, Rose."

Rose took his hands, and he drew her into an embrace. Startled by his familiarity, she hugged him in return as his body convulsed with sobs.

"I'm so sorry." Rose's voice emerged as a squeak.

He squeezed her tight, then withdrew, wiping the moisture from his face and spreading black soot over his cheek. His gaze swept to the door where a glance told Rose Mr. Reed had followed her into the house.

"And who are you, sir?" James demanded.

"I am the Drummond's servant." Mr. Reed's voice had lost its hauteur.

James's eyes narrowed, and he clenched his fists. "Your accent reeks of British nobility."

Rose stepped between them. "He is a friend." *A friend.* She surprised herself at her quick declaration.

Yet James did not seem so convinced as his lips twisted in a snarl.

Aunt Muira removed medicine and bandages from her satchel and began rubbing something over Elaine's face.

"What happened?" Rose asked James in a low voice.

Anguish darkened his face. "British raiders." His Adam's apple bobbed up and down. "I was in town when the warning sounded. I got here as fast as I could." His jaw tightened. "We caught the bloody wretches in the act before they could burn down the entire house. But not before. . ." He squeezed his eyes shut.

Rose's legs wobbled. Mr. Reed grabbed her elbow and steadied her. The air seemed to retreat from the room. She could hear her aunt whispering words of comfort to Elaine. But Rose knew full well that no kind words, no amount of medicine or herbal tinctures or thoughtful attentiveness, would ever heal the wound Elaine would carry for the rest of her life.

"Thank you, Mr. Reed." She gave him a nod, and he released her arm with a frown.

James stared benumbed at his wife. His jaw trembled. Rose lowered her chin. How could she help this man? How could she help Elaine when she couldn't even help herself? She clasped her hands together and inhaled a shuddering breath.

She must be strong.

"I saw your man digging graves," she said to draw James's mind off his wife for a moment, although even as she said the words she realized the new topic would bring no comfort.

James swiped at his moist cheeks and gazed out the window. "When we fought them off Joseph and Willie were killed."

Rose gasped. James's stableboys were but fifteen and twenty—orphans whom he had taken in to help out around the farm.

"And your wound?" Rose pointed to his bloody forehead.

"They knocked me in the head pretty good." James dabbed at it.

She grasped his hands again. "Allow my aunt to tend to you as soon as she's done with Elaine."

Nodding, he sank into a chair. "They took everything from us. Everything of value." He dropped his head into his hands.

Rose knelt before him. "Thank G—" she started, quickly amending, "but you are alive. You and Elaine." She would not give thanks to God, for there was no sign of Him anywhere.

"Rose." Elaine's weak voice tugged at Rose.

God, if You're there, please give me strength. Rose struggled to rise. Her head grew light, and she lifted a hand to steady herself. Mr. Reed's firm grip on her elbow once again saved her from embarrassment.

She wanted to thank him for his support, for his kindness, but under the circumstances it seemed highly inappropriate. His people had done this. He carried their guilt by association. She must remember that. Tugging from his grip, she made her way to the sofa. Aunt Muira stood and snapped her satchel shut. She gave Rose an encouraging nod and pressed her hand on Rose's arm.

"I've done all I can. Now she needs a friend." Then facing Amelia, Aunt Muira ordered her out of the room. "Mr. Reed," she added as she passed him at the door. "Fetch some water from the pond, if you please. Come, James. Let me tend to that wound."

Rose watched as they ambled out the door, leaving her alone with Elaine.

Lowering herself onto the chair her aunt had vacated, Rose finally glanced down at her friend. Red and purple marks swelled on her cheeks and neck, and her once crisp blue eyes melted in a sea of red, puffy skin. Fresh bandages wrapped around her right arm and forehead. She held out her hand. Rose took it and brought it to her lips.

Nausea churned in her belly.

She brushed the tangled hair from Elaine's face and closed her eyes. She could do this. She must do this.

❖

Thunder bellowed overhead, rumbling across the sky and mimicking Alex's mood. With a snap of the reins, he urged Douglas into a trot and headed back toward the Drummond farm. A horde of emotions battled in his gut. Fury, disgust, and shame appeared to be winning. He knew this kind of thing happened in war. He had seen such atrocities from a distance the night he'd saved Miss McGuire from Lieutenant Garrick. But not until today had he ventured into the broken-down, charred home of a family who'd suffered under war's cruelty and looked into the tortured eyes of its victims. Real people who lived simple, happy lives. Innocents.

The hatred pouring from James's eyes when he'd heard Alex's accent had nearly shoved Alex to the ground. But how could he blame the man?

Worse than that was the loathsome glare Miss McGuire had given him when she'd emerged from the house. With pale face and trembling lips, she had not even taken his proffered hand when she'd climbed into the coach. From his conversation earlier with Mr. Drummond and the way Miss McGuire trembled throughout her meeting with Elaine, Alex surmised that some horrible event haunted her past. Whether it was also at the hands of his countrymen, he couldn't know.

He didn't want to know.

Her rejection stung him like a slap in the face. A slap he deserved and one that woke him up from the dream he'd been living these past ten days. His stomach soured as tiny drops of rain tapped upon his shoulders. Blast his senseless honor. He was a fool—a fool to stay with this rebel family in the hopes of protecting them while he enjoyed a brief reprieve from the rigid life of a British naval officer. He should return to his ship. It was obvious to him now that his presence caused Miss McGuire pain. And that was the last thing he wanted to do.

A gust of wind marched around him, whipping his hair and sending a chill down his back. He wished it would blow away the smell of burnt wood that lingered in his nose, but he had a feeling that the charred scent of death would remain with him for a long while.

Like the look on Miss McGuire's face. She hated him.

The realization made his heart shrink. And if her aunt and uncle knew his true identity, they'd no doubt hate him too. Trouble was, he couldn't blame them. Everything he believed about his country—its honor, might, and superiority—seemed to splatter like the rain landing on his breeches in light of what he'd seen. He didn't know what to believe anymore. Was it right for him to pursue his goals of wealth and honor in a navy that afflicted such horrors upon the innocent? Yet how else was he to erase the stains he'd made upon his family's name and prompt his father to open the doors of their home to Alex once again? He shook his head and watched the raindrops plop onto the muddy road and the breeze thread through the dark leaves of the elm trees lining the pathway.

Lightning spiked across a darkening sky, coating the moist foliage in a sheen of eerie gray. Alex pushed his cocked hat farther down on his head. A gust of wind tainted with the scent of the sea tore over him, flapping the lapels of his coat. He snapped the reins. Thunder pounded the sky like an angry fist. As if Miss McGuire's scorn for him wasn't enough impetus to leave soon, Alex's near encounter with Mr. Brenin, Mr. Heaton, and Blackthorn in town today proved that Alex had no business being here. He didn't wish to endanger Miss McGuire or her family by his presence. Truth be told, he didn't wish to endanger his heart.

❖ CHAPTER 13 ❖

Rose crept over the sandy soil. A thick mist pressed in on her, hovering around her like a multitude of ghosts. She waved her hands through the air to swat it away, but it remained, enclosing her in a white shroud. A light appeared, its glow blossoming through the haze, forcing back the fog. Elaine emerged from the mist. She held a single candle. Her blue eyes were vacant and cold. One bruise remained on her neck. "They're coming." She swept a look over her shoulder then grabbed Rose's hand and dragged her forward. Rose followed her friend. Her heart cinched. But then the cloud swallowed Elaine up, and she disappeared. Rose's hand fell to her side.

"Elaine!" she yelled, her voice echoing through the chilled mist.

Trees formed at the edges of the haze. Rose glanced down at her torn red dress. Something cold and heavy filled her hand. A pistol. Gazing at it curiously, she lifted it. Smoke curled from the barrel. A man lay on the ground before her. Blood swelled on his waistcoat. Lifeless eyes stared up at a dark sky.

Rose dropped the gun. It fell slowly to the ground as if it sank through molasses. Then it landed with a hollow thud. Her hand burned.

She opened her mouth to scream "No!" but she could not hear her voice.

Slumping to the dirt, Rose curled in a ball and squeezed her eyes shut. "No, God, no. Please."

Light flooded all around her as if someone had opened a door. Soothing warmth swept away the chill. Something or someone lifted her chin upward. An ominous figure dressed in glowing white stood before her. The mist retreated before the light, revealing a gentle forest in its wake. Her heart took up a rapid beat. She scrambled to get away from the terrifying man when he opened his mouth and a voice emerged that sounded like the purl of a deep river. "Fear not, beloved one."

Rose halted. *Beloved one.* She gazed up at the man but the glow that emanated from him forbade her to see his face. "Fear not, for you have been chosen by God."

"Chosen? For what?" Rose mouthed, but again she could not hear her voice.

"Fear not."

Rose sprang up in bed, gasping for air. Heart crashing against her ribs, she scanned her chamber. The first rays of dawn filtered through her window, forcing the shadows of her room into the corners. Only a dream. Hadn't she wondered if they would return after she'd visited Elaine?

But what an odd dream. *Fear not, beloved one.* The words danced over her ears. Who was the glowing man? An angel? *You have been chosen.* The statement spoken with such authority and serenity tugged on something deep within Rose, something that brought tears to her eyes. She shook off the sentiment. Nothing but a nightmare—like all the others.

Swinging her legs over her bed, she plucked a handkerchief from her bed stand and dabbed the perspiration beading on her forehead and neck. Her breathing returned to normal, and she hung her head. It had been months since she'd had a nightmare. But she would gladly endure another bout of terrifying visions if she had brought Elaine a mite of comfort yesterday. They had exchanged no words. Rose had simply held her friend in her arms, and they had sobbed together. Perhaps that alone, plus the knowledge that someone understood exactly what Elaine had suffered, was enough for now.

❖

Slipping the halter over Valor's head, Rose tightened the buckle and led the filly from the barn. Though the sun dipped low in the western sky, Rose needed to ride, needed to get away from everything and everyone. After the distressing events of yesterday and the disturbing nightmare that had woken her from her sleep that morning, she'd remained in her chamber most of the day, reading. While successfully avoiding Mr. Reed. For she couldn't be sure how she would react to him. One minute she hated him for what his people had done to her parents, her country—Elaine. The next minute, his kindness, honor, and the favorable words her friends had spoken of him, swung her emotional pendulum back to admiration. And if Rose were honest, a sentiment that went beyond admiration. But she didn't want to be honest.

She tied Valor to a post and eased a brush over the horse's back and down her sides. Despite Rose's treatment of Mr. Reed in town, her ploy to belittle him had backfired. Instead Mr. Reed had been naught but gracious as he sauntered about town—in that worn and tattered and altogether too tight livery—with the hauteur of a nobleman and the confidence of a leader of men. Any fool who looked at him twice could see he was no servant.

Even now, the mere thought of how close Mr. Reed had come to being thrown in jail—not to mention her family tried for treason— sent her chest heaving. Setting down the brush, Rose swung a blanket over Valor's back, then lifted a saddle on top of it and tightened the girth. Douglas, her uncle's steed, looked up from the field where he was grazing.

Mr. Reed had more than proven himself to be an honorable man these past days, and now with the testimony of her friends, Rose could no longer deny that he was also a good man—a kind man.

Grabbing the bridle, she ran her fingers over Valor's cheek and then kissed the filly's nose. The horse leaned against her and snorted. A humid breeze stirred the curls dangling about Rose's neck and brought the woodsy smell of horseflesh to her nose. Overhead, a billowing jumble of clouds darkened the afternoon sky even as the sun spread its golden rays over the farm from its position atop the tree line. At least two hours before sunset. Two hours to run wild through the forest and clear the confusion that kept her mind awhirl.

Clear her mind from thoughts of Mr. Reed. It was for the best. He would be gone soon. Perhaps even tonight.

She couldn't face him. Couldn't say good-bye.

Didn't want to say good-bye.

Which was all part of her confusion.

For if she bade him farewell, she knew he would see right through her facade. And she couldn't bear to let him know how deep her feelings for him ran.

❖

"What are you doing, Miss McGuire?" Alex's voice drew Rose's startled gaze to him. Leaning against the doorframe, he crossed his arms over his chest and eyed her with suspicion. He'd been searching for her all day. After yesterday's events, he had to make sure she was all right before he left. He had to see her one last time, gaze into those turquoise eyes one last time—even if they were filled with hate.

Oddly, her face reddened. She turned away and slipped the bridle over Valor's head and adjusted the bit in the horse's mouth. "As you can plainly see, I am going for a ride."

Alex glanced at the dark clouds overhead as a blast of wind swirled the sting of rain beneath his nose. "Alone?"

Ignoring him, Miss McGuire fastened the bridle under Valor's chin then flung the reins over her neck. "You are no longer my servant or my guardian, Mr. Reed." She stepped onto a stool, put her booted foot in the stirrup, and leaped onto the back of the horse with more finesse than he expected. Straddling the beast like a man, she spread her full skirts out around her legs then grabbed the reins, and lifted her pert nose as if pleased that she shocked him with her unladylike behavior. "Besides, I often ride in the forest alone. It is far safer than town."

Alex lifted one brow. "There may be British afoot."

"Indeed, Mr. Reed, there *are* British afoot." Her pointed gaze made him wince. "Which is why I feel the need to leave." Giving Valor a nudge, she snapped the reins and sped off in a flurry of blue muslin and golden curls.

"What the deuces," Reed cursed then marched to the steed grazing in the field. He hoped he remembered how to ride. It had been several years since he'd ridden his father's horses across their estate. And never without benefit of saddle and reins. But there was no time for that. He glanced toward the web of greenery bordering the farm and caught one final glimpse of Miss McGuire's blue gown as the forest swallowed her up. Foolish woman.

Taking a running start, he leaped onto the horse's back and grabbed a handful of mane to stop himself from slipping off the other side. A shard of pain lanced his thigh. The horse snorted and stomped his foot into the dirt. Thunder grumbled in the distance. "Come on, boy, we've a lady to rescue." With a squeeze of his legs, he urged the beast forward. Nothing. "Forward!" he ordered. The steed shook his head. One large brown eye stared at him as if he were an annoying insect, and Alex fully expected the horse's tail to swat him from his back.

Infernal beast. Fury tightened Alex's jaw. "I said go!" He kicked the horse's sides. Much to his dismay, the horse lurched into a gallop. Catching his balance before he tumbled off the back end, Alex tightened his grip on the mane and leaned forward. Hot wind whipped through his hair, freeing it from its queue. The crazed pound of his heart matched the thump of the horse's hooves over the grassy, moist ground. Alex's body rose and fell against the steed's muscular back. Not until he charged into the forest did the horse slow to a trot. Up ahead, Miss McGuire made her way along a narrow winding trail.

"Miss McGuire!"

She shot a spiteful glance over her shoulder. "Go back to your ship, Mr. Reed. Leave me be."

"I cannot. Your uncle has charged me with your care."

"Well, I discharge you, sir." She urged her horse into a trot.

Ducking beneath a low-hanging branch, Alex followed her into the thick brush, his steed trotting over a soft bed of moss and pine needles. Leaves in every shade of green fluttered in the breeze around him. Tree trunks thrust into the gray sky like ship masts. Insects buzzed. Birds chirped, and Alex drew in a deep breath of earth and life tainted with the fragrance of wildflowers and fresh rain.

Lightning flashed above the canopy, transforming the greens into sparkling silver.

He urged his horse onward. "Miss McGuire, if you please."

"Go away!" she shouted before the foliage swallowed her up once again.

A clearing up ahead afforded Alex a view of her as her horse leaped over a small creek. But after casting one glance over her shoulder, she galloped out of sight.

Coaxing his horse into a sprint, Alex hoped the steed would clear the brook with the same skill. He leaned forward, feeling the beast's muscles tense and stretch beneath him. The horse thrust his hooves into the wind. They flew through the air for one brief, glorious second before they struck the dirt on the opposite bank. The horse bucked. Alex lost his grip. He slid off the steed's back and thumped to the ground. Pain speared up his spine and something sharp struck his head.

"Blast it all," he moaned as he toppled over onto a pile of leaves.

Seconds later, golden curls and glistening blue eyes appeared in his blurry vision. "Mr. Reed, are you all right?" Her fresh feminine scent filled the air between them, luring him from his daze.

Alex shook his head and attempted to rise. Gentle hands gripped his arms and pulled him up.

How mortifying. Shame heated his face, and he closed his eyes.

"Are you injured?" she asked.

"I don't believe so." He glanced over the clearing where their two horses grazed happily on a patch of moss.

"Oh my word." Her eyes sharpened. "You are bleeding." Yanking a handkerchief from her sleeve, she scrambled to the brook and dipped the cloth in the water.

Alex felt a trail of warm fluid slide down his cheek. He raised his hand to wipe it away, but she knelt and dabbed the cloth on his face before he could.

"I told you not to follow me," she scolded.

Pain etched across his forehead. He lifted his hand to his wound again, but she batted it away. "I could not in good conscience allow you to put yourself in further danger, miss."

"Mr. Reed." She sat back. "I know these woods better than you know your ship. I simply wished to be alone." She glanced down.

But not before Alex saw her red nose and puffy eyes. "You've been crying."

Tossing the cloth into his hand, she leaped to her feet and turned her back to him, adding to his confusion.

"I hope I am not the cause of your distress." Alex pressed the cloth to his forehead. Pain burned across his skin.

Dark clouds stole the remaining light of the sun and lured shadows out from hiding.

"You must leave." Her shoulders slumped. "There is no other recourse."

A breeze danced among the loose curls hanging to her waist. Alex shook his head. Was she upset about him leaving? Absurd. "I fear you mistook me. I meant, are you upset because I followed you?"

She swung around, a horrified look on her face. "Of course, I understood you perfectly." She swiped her cheeks and drew a deep breath. "It is this war, meeting my friends in town yesterday, Elaine." She took up a pace across the leaf-strewn ground as thunder growled in the distance.

Alex's eyes followed her as she stormed back and forth across the clearing. The sway of her silky hair, the gentle curve of her cheeks and chin, her delicate nose, her eyes the color of the Caribbean sea, and her moist lips in constant motion as she expounded on the day's events. He swallowed. How lovely she was—this backwoods, rustic farm girl.

He longed to pull her into his arms.

What the deuces was wrong with him?

"And I miss my mother and father more than I can say," she continued, her eyes misting again.

Alex wondered if he should inquire. Would she only hate him more for asking? She ceased her pacing and dropped beside him. Taking the cloth from his hand, she dabbed it over his wound again. "It's just a scratch. You'll live."

"Again you tend to my wounds, Miss McGuire. This could become a habit." He smiled, hoping to lighten her mood, but his words only deepened her frown.

He drew himself up onto a fallen log and pulled her up beside him, glad when she didn't resist him.

Perhaps it had only been thoughts of her mother and father that had prompted the tears he thought were for him. Yet her tenderness toward her parents created an ache in his own heart. Alex had been nothing but a disappointment to his father—to his entire family. But never had they expressed such affection for him or for one another in life as this woman had for her parents in death.

Seconds passed in silence as the warble of birds faded with the encroaching night.

"May I ask what happened to your parents?" He caressed her hand, warm and soft.

She swallowed. Slipping her hand from his, she glanced toward the creek frolicking over rocks and pebbles and sending creamy foam onto the banks. A gust of rain-spiced wind toyed with her golden curls. "My father obtained a commission aboard one of our naval ships, the USS *Chesapeake*. Perhaps you've heard of it?"

Alex flinched as if he'd been struck. The USS *Chesapeake*? He stared down at the mud at his feet. Thunder announced his doom. He felt as though a thousand needles stabbed his heart. "Yes." He didn't want to hear anymore. He knew exactly what she would say.

"Your HMS *Leopard* fired upon her when Captain Barron refused to allow a boarding party to search for British deserters." Though her voice wobbled, it retained the sting of anger.

Alex nodded and lowered her handkerchief. He stared at his own blood staining the white cloth and suddenly felt as though he deserved the wound and so much more.

"Three men were killed that day. Eighteen wounded. One of them my father."

Hope taunted him for a moment. Wounded only? Perhaps he had not been killed by the British after all.

"He died at the Marine Hospital at Washington Point," she continued, crushing his hopes. A few raindrops splattered on the nearby leaves, mimicking the tear that spilled from her lashes. "At least four thousand citizens stood along both sides of Market Square while his coffin was carried in a long procession. Artillery fired minute guns from onshore, and all the American vessels in the harbor displayed their colors at half mast." She sniffed and ran the back of her hand over her moist face.

Alex clasped his hands together if only to keep from holding her as he longed to do. "He must have been quite a gallant officer and well loved." He could think of nothing else to say.

Her jaw tightened. Another tear slid down her cheek. "He was but a simple boatswain, not an officer. But he was well loved. And we were not at war, Mr. Reed. The *Chesapeake* was unprepared to defend herself. Her guns were not primed for action. Why would they be?" She stood and stepped away, as if being close to him disgusted her.

Alex struggled to his feet and moved behind her, longing to take away her pain.

Lightning flashed, glinting everything in gray.

"My mother died a week later of a broken heart." Her voice cracked as she hugged herself. "And I became an orphan at age fifteen."

Alex's heart sank to the dirt. No wonder she hated the British. No wonder she hated him. He placed a hand on her shoulder, but she moved from beneath it.

"Your British navy stole everything from me."

Alex swallowed. "My association causes me great shame."

"You do not know all that I have been through."

Heavy rain drops tapped like war drums on the leaves overhead. "No, I do not." Alex sighed. "But I will listen if you wish to tell me."

❖

At the sound of sincerity in Mr. Reed's voice, Rose turned around. Hazel eyes, as deep and fathomless as the sea he sailed upon, gazed back at her with concern. And something else. . .an affection that sent her heart fluttering. She would prefer hatred, animosity, even excuses. Those she knew how to react to, what to say. But not this.

"You were fifteen." He shoved a wayward strand of his hair behind his ear. "Yet your aunt said you've only been here five years."

The care pouring from his eyes wrapped around her wounded heart and lured her to tell him her sad tale. She tore her gaze away. "Why do you wish to know?"

He rubbed his stubbled jaw and his gaze softened. "Because I care."

Rose narrowed her eyes. The *rap, rap* of rain on the canopy filled the air like steady musket fire. Water misted over her, and she collected her hair over her shoulder. *He cared, indeed.* She would not believe him—could not believe him. She took a step back and lowered her gaze. "If it helps appease your guilt, it was not your countrymen who. . ." Her throat closed. "Who caused me further pain."

His warm finger touched her chin, bringing her gaze back up to his. "My guilt is not the issue here. I only wish to ease the pain I see in your eyes."

Thunder bellowed and Rose turned her back to him and moved farther away—away from his touch that sent an odd tremble through her, not a fearful one, but one that felt like a thousand fireflies swirling in her stomach. "A dear friend of my father's took me in after my parents died. I didn't know of my aunt's and uncle's existence at the time because of their estrangement from the family."

She heard the crunch of pine needles behind her as he moved closer. She gazed at the creek, the sturdy brown tree trunks, the leaves swaying in the wind. Anything to tether her to reality and keep her from spilling her heart to this man. Yet her words poured from her mouth as unstoppable as the water dashing in the brook.

"What I thought was concern for me and love for my father was merely an interest in the fortune left to me by my parents." Out of the corner of her eye, she saw Mr. Reed slip beside her.

"He made me a servant in his home, treated me with indifference and cruelty. All the while he proceeded to spend my inheritance as if it were his own." She glanced at Mr. Reed, but his expression remained stoic as he gazed at the creek.

"Nearly two years later, I was cleaning the desk in his study and came across a letter my mother had written on her deathbed explaining the existence of my aunt and uncle in Baltimore and asking him to ensure that I was placed in their care."

Mr. Reed's jaw bunched.

"I took what was left of my inheritance and ran away. I procured passage on a merchant vessel traveling to Baltimore."

"Alone?" Even now, fear sparked in his eyes.

"I had no choice, Mr. Reed." She would not tell him what happened on that fateful voyage. She could not.

Stooping, she picked up a stick and fingered its rough bark. Her resolve threatened to break beneath the memories filling her mind, but she shoved them back behind the thick door of forbidden thoughts.

Mr. Reed approached, anguish twisting his handsome features. Rain slid down his face. His wet shirt clung to his firm torso, accentuating his muscles beneath. Rose blinked the water from her lashes, realizing for the first time that she was alone with a man in the forest. Where no one would hear her scream. Yet, she found not an ounce of fear within her. Instead, the strangest feeling came over her. She felt safe. Completely and utterly safe. As if nothing could happen to her as long as she was with him. She'd never felt that way before, at least not since she'd been a little girl. The sensation made her giddy and sad at the same time.

He halted before her, peering down at her with such sorrow and longing that Rose nearly melted into him. She wanted him to hold her, wanted him to touch her.

He reached for her and tried to pull her close.

But she couldn't allow that. He was British. He was leaving. It might be already too late for her heart, but she would not endanger herself further. Jerking from his grasp, Rose backed away. "Forgive me, Mr. Reed. I shouldn't have disclosed such personal details."

"No apologies necessary, Miss McGuire." His brow wrinkled. "I'm glad you trusted me with the tale."

"What does it matter?" Rose waved a hand through the air and forced a lighter tone into her voice. "You will be gone soon. Killing more of my countrymen."

"I'm truly sorry our countries are at war."

Lightning flashed. Rain dripped from the tips of his dark hair onto his collar. He shifted his boots in the puddles forming at their feet and cocked his head. Then lifting his hand, he stroked her cheek with his thumb.

Warmth sped through Rose. Her heart thumped against her ribs, and she leaned into his hand. Just for a second. For one glorious second. That was all she would allow herself.

Before she stepped back and forced indifference into her tone. "Leave me be, Mr. Reed. Return to the house."

Disappointment flashed in his eyes. He fisted his hands at his waist and scanned the foliage. "I cannot allow you to wander about without protection. It is too dangerous."

Anger rolled all sentiments away. "I am not a crew member aboard your ship, Mr. Reed, that you can order me about."

He crossed his arms over his chest. "Go then, ride wherever you wish. But I will follow you."

Thunder boomed above them.

"I will simply wait until you fall again." Rose smirked. "Only this time I will not return."

He leaned toward her, a sultry smile on his lips. "Why *did* you come back?"

"I see now it was a mistake." Rose started to leave.

Mr. Reed gripped her arm and turned her to face him. "Your uncle grants you too much liberty."

"We are in America, sir, where freedom is a way of life. Something I wouldn't expect you British to understand."

Mr. Reed smiled. "You have dirt on your face."

Rose grimaced and ran the back of her hand over her cheek. Reaching down, she grabbed a clump of mud and eyed him with mischief, fingering its cool grainy texture. Then before he could grab her hand, she rubbed it on his jaw. "So do you." She grinned.

A look of incredulity overtook his stiff features, as if he couldn't fathom that she would do such a thing. He wiped the dirt and gazed at it as it slid between his fingers. Then one imperious brow lifted, and he spread the mud on her other cheek. "You seem to enjoy it more than I." He grinned.

Rose's blood boiled. Stooping, she gathered a larger blob, then tossed it at him. It splattered over his white shirt. "It suits you as well."

He chuckled and caught the mud before it fell from his shirt. He held it up as if he would throw it at her.

"You wouldn't dare!" Rose backed away.

"Wouldn't I?" And for the first time, a mischievous glint took residence in his otherwise austere eyes.

Rose chuckled and Mr. Reed joined her.

As their laughter faded, the sound of a gun cocking sped through the clearing. Mr. Reed froze and shot a worried gaze her way. Before Rose could react, he dropped the mud, clutched her arm, and dove into a bush.

❖ CHAPTER 14 ❖

Rose curled up against Mr. Reed's firm chest and tried to still her rapid breathing. He reached for his hip as if searching for a sword. But when his hand came up empty, he swallowed her up in his thick arms and motioned her to silence. Leaves tickled her face and a branch jabbed her side, but she remained still. A twig snapped, and the sound of a footfall echoed their doom through the forest. A trapper? But Rose had never come across any trappers this close to town. It had to be a British raiding party. And if one of them recognized Mr. Reed, they would assume he'd deserted his ship and haul him away for trial—or whatever they did in the British navy.

She didn't want to consider what they might do to her.

Rain splattered over the leaves, the soft sound blending in with the increased sound of footfalls heading their way.

A tremble coursed through her. Mr. Reed tightened his embrace. The strength and assurance in his arms eased across her nerves. Their breath intermingled as he pressed her head gently against his chest and held it there, stroking her wet hair.

Rose had not allowed any other man to touch her in years. My word, why did she feel so safe in the arms of this British officer—even in the midst of danger? The scent of wet linen and Mr. Reed filled her nostrils and eased into her lungs like a soothing elixir. She wished more than anything that the world would disappear around them and she could stay in his embrace forever.

But that was not to be.

Another twig snapped, and a pair of brown buckled shoes halted before the bush they hid behind.

Thunder shook the sky. The horses neighed.

The dark gaping eye of a musket plunged through the leaves toward them, pushing aside branches. Rose stiffened.

"Whoever is in there, I demand you toss your weapons on the ground and come out!"

Rose jerked. She'd know that voice anywhere. "Mr. Snyder?" She tried to free herself from Mr. Reed's grasp, but his arms refused to release her.

The musket pushed in farther, spreading the foliage apart until Rose gazed up into the angular face of the councilman. The fear braiding his features fell into a confused frown.

"Egad, what mischief is this?" he barked, his eyes flashing.

Mr. Reed released her, and Rose scrambled to her feet. Swatting leaves and branches aside, she made her way out of the bush. Mr. Reed crawled out behind her and unfolded to his normal towering height.

"No mischief, I assure you, Mr. Snyder." Rose glanced down at her muddy dress and tried to brush off the dirt but only succeeded in smearing it over the blue fabric. With a huff, she lifted her gaze to his.

The muscles in his cheeks bunched and released. His slit-like eyes swept from her to Mr. Reed. He raised his musket toward Alex. "Explain yourself, sir, or I shall be forced to shoot you where you stand."

Mr. Reed's right brow lifted as a smirk played upon his mouth.

"Mr. Snyder." Rose approached him, more angry than frightened. Angry that this buffoon had given them such a scare. Angry most of all that he had interrupted her time with Mr. Reed. "It is not as it appears. What—"

"What it appears, Miss McGuire, would be too scandalous to voice." He gestured with his musket toward Mr. Reed. "Did this man accost you? If so, I'll deal with him here and now."

Rose lifted a hand to her forehead where a headache formed. She gazed up at the canopy. Between the treetops, white lightning flashed across a gray sky. A drop of rain struck her eye, and she blinked.

Mr. Reed folded his arms over his chest as if there were no musket pointed at his heart. Rose stepped toward Mr. Snyder. She must force him to lower the gun trembling in his grip. Just the sight of the vile weapon sent a chill through her. "I assure you, Mr. Snyder, Mr. Reed has done me no harm. We heard your gun cock and thought perhaps the British were afoot given the recent alarms." She raised a quivering hand to the barrel of the musket. Cold, slick steel sent an icy shard through her fingers and up her arm. She forced the weapon down, snapping back her hand as soon as it was lowered. "So, you see, the situation is completely innocent."

Mr. Snyder's lips drew into a tight line. Rain dropped from the trees above and splashed onto his cocked hat before trickling off the sides. "What were you doing out here in the first place alone with this man?"

A tight band stretched across Rose's shoulders at the man's impertinent questions. "He is my servant, sir. In truth, he followed me to ensure my safety."

Mr. Snyder laid the musket across his arms and shifted his stance. "Yet who is to protect you from him?"

Mr. Reed finally spoke, his voice deep and confident. "I would never harm Miss McGuire, and I resent the implication, sir."

"Do you?" Mr. Snyder snapped. "We shall see about that." He faced Rose, his blue eyes stark against the shadows of the forest. "By the by, your aunt and uncle may have a different opinion when they hear of this."

Rose longed to kick mud on the man's pristine trousers, but instead she merely released a sigh.

His face softened. "Are you all right, Miss McGuire? Did he harm you?" He scanned her from head to toe as if he only now noticed her condition. "Scads, you are covered in mud."

Rose clenched her jaw. "Whatever are you doing out here in the woods, Mr. Snyder?"

The rain ceased and a low rumble of thunder bade farewell from the distance.

"Your aunt invited me to dine with you this evening." Eyeing Mr. Reed, My Snyder tossed back his shoulders and stretched out his neck as if he was trying to make himself appear as tall as the British officer.

"And?" Rose planted one hand on her hip.

"When I inquired after you, your lady's maid informed me that she saw you gallop into the forest." He tipped his head toward Mr. Reed. "With this man chasing you."

Rose shook out her gown and swiped wet strands of hair from her forehead. "Well as you can see, I'm perfectly safe."

"Rubbish. You are drenched in rain and have mud from the hair on your head to the hem of your gown. Hardly proper behavior for a lady." He clucked his tongue, then scratched the auburn whiskers lining his jaw.

Mr. Reed cleared his throat. "And sneaking about the forest, pointing muskets at unsuspecting ladies, is hardly proper behavior for a gentleman, sir."

Mr. Snyder's brow darkened. "Rather insolent for a mere servant, Mr. Reed. I'd hold my tongue if I were you." He thrust the barrel end of the musket into the mud as if it were his cane. "Now, make yourself useful and fetch my horse."

Mr. Reed shook the water from his hair, then raked it with his hand. His saturated shirt revealed every knot of muscle, each one tightening by the second. Despite her own wet gown, Rose warmed from head to toe at the sight.

"If I may make a suggestion, Mr. Snyder." Mr. Reed addressed the councilman with the tone of one addressing an inferior. "The next time you take it upon yourself to thrust a musket into a bush, make sure its occupants are unarmed. Only a fool exposes himself to an enemy without knowledge of what weapons he possesses. Upon my honor, I could have shot you where you stood before you knew what hit you." He smiled. "Before I knew it was you, that is."

Mr. Snyder's lips curled in a sneer. "Retrieve my horse at once."

Mr. Reed glanced toward Rose, and she reluctantly nodded. Better to appease the man rather than increase his suspicion.

With a huff, Mr. Reed passed Mr. Snyder, bumping his shoulder. "Forgive me, sir." His voice brimmed with sarcasm.

Hatred burned in Mr. Snyder's eyes. "His insolence is not to be borne," he said to Rose. "He should be dismissed immediately."

"Yet that is not your call to make." Rose hugged herself against a sudden chill.

Leaning his musket against a tree, the councilman shrugged out of his overcoat and flung it over her shoulders. "You are nearly soaked through, Miss McGuire."

Not wishing to accept the man's garment, but not wanting to anger him further, she drew it around her. "How kind of you." Though the rain had ceased, water still fell from the leaves all around them, echoing drip-drops through the darkening shadows.

Mr. Snyder leaned toward her. "Forgive my outburst, miss, but I am only concerned for you."

She gave him a tight smile in reply as Mr. Reed tossed the reins of Mr. Snyder's chestnut gelding to him before proceeding across the muddy clearing to retrieve Valor and Douglas. Unable to resist, Rose gazed after him, studying his strong jaw, peppered with evening stubble, his deep eyes, and confident gait. A longing gripped her to be alone with him again, to feel the safety of his arms around her.

After assisting Rose onto her horse, and mounting his own, Mr. Snyder rode by her side. When they arrived at the house, Mr. Reed led all three horses to the barn while Mr. Snyder, taking Rose's arm with one hand and his cane in the other, ushered her toward the front door, babbling on about city politics, and offending her nose with his moldy bergamot scent. Her nerves tightened at his touch, creating a whirl-wind of confusion in her mind. How could she feel so safe in the arms of a British navy officer and so troubled upon the arm of an American councilman? She glanced over her shoulder, hoping for one last look at Mr. Reed.

But he had already disappeared into the barn.

Something had happened between them that afternoon in the for-est. A wall had been broken down—dare she even say, an affection had sprouted? But what was she thinking? She faced forward and silently chastised herself as Mr. Snyder opened the door. Mr. Reed had prom-ised that he would leave soon, and he was too honorable a man to break that promise.

❖

Alex circled the table and poured persimmon beer into the pewter mugs of each seated guest. First Mr. and Mrs. Drummond, then Amelia, who never failed to give him a coquettish smile, and now the lovely Miss McGuire. He moved behind her chair, hoping for a glance into those turquoise eyes. Not a speck of dirt marred her lovely complexion or the creamy white gown trimmed in pink ribbon she'd donned for sup-per. The lace bordering her neckline rose and fell with her heightened breath. Did his presence invoke the reaction? Or was she merely ner-vous that Mr. Snyder would find him out?

The sad story she had told him of her parents' deaths and the family friend who had stolen her wealth fired through his mind like grapeshot, igniting his fury. How could anyone have abused the trust of a young girl who had so recently lost her parents? And what tragedy had befallen her on her trip to Baltimore? Though Alex could guess, he hoped with everything in him that he was wrong. Regardless, his heart soared that Rose had entrusted him with such intimacies.

Alex had loved only one woman in his life—a woman who was now his brother's wife. A woman whom he'd thought returned his love. But he had been terribly mistaken—brought on by his foolish emotions. Perhaps he was equally in error now. Yet the moments he and Miss McGuire—Rose—had shared in the forest, as the rain misted down upon them, caused his heart to swell as it never had before. He could still feel her quivering body against his, the way she molded into him as if they were made for each other, and the way her trembling ceased when she leaned against his chest. Alex shook his head. What the deuces was he thinking? He could never entertain thoughts of such a connection. He and Miss McGuire were worlds apart. Enemies. He poured her drink and avoided looking at her further.

Making his way around the edge of the table to Mr. Snyder, Alex gazed out the open window where a cool breeze ruffled the calico curtains. The rain had ceased, and stars blinked against a coal black sky.

He wove around the table, silently cursing himself for allowing his feelings for Miss McGuire to rise and for staying among these rebels as long as he had. Pure foolishness. For the longer he stayed, the harder it was for him to go.

He tipped the decanter of beer over Mr. Snyder's mug—smiling at the devious idea that struck him—and filled it to the brim.

The councilman turned from something he was saying and stared at the glass. "You daft loon, how am I expected to sip this without spilling it?"

"My apologies." Alex bowed slightly and gave Miss McGuire a coy glance. Finally she met his gaze. A smile danced across her eyes.

Mr. Snyder gave a frustrated sigh as Alex made his way to the kitchen to help Cora carry in the platters of food. As soon as he entered the bright room, smells of turkey, pastry, and warm bread enveloped him, prompting a growl from his belly and making him wonder why he never remembered such comforting scents in the Cranleigh estate back home.

"Well, it be about time." Cora huffed his way. "This food's gettin' cold."

Alex grabbed the first platter that held two large meat pies, amazed that even the cantankerous cook warmed his heart. "You are ever a delight, Miss Cora." He winked.

With a shake of her head, she flattened her lips, but then she smiled and batted the air with a cloth before dropping it onto the table. "Now, you go on, Mr. Reed. Your charm don't work on this old gal." Picking up a platter of biscuits in one hand and a bowl of fried greens in the other, she followed him into the dining room where they placed the food in the center of the table. Cora left while Alex stood against the wall as he'd seen the footmen do in his father's estate during meals. He chose the wall opposite Miss McGuire, which afforded him a clear view of her.

"Shall we ask God's blessing on this glorious feast?" Mr. Drummond said.

Glorious feast? Alex shook his head. Surely his father would not think so of the meager meal.

"We thank You, Father, for the abundance You have provided and for Your continued protection over us during such tremulous times. May Your will be done on earth as it is in heaven. Amen"

"Amens" sounded around the table, and Alex was once again struck with not only the simplicity and genuineness of the prayer but with the way Mr. Drummond addressed Almighty God as Father.

Mrs. Drummond passed the plate of biscuits to Miss McGuire. "Dear, Mr. Snyder brought us a pound of sugar today. He knows how you enjoy it in your tea."

Miss McGuire nodded toward the councilman, but her smile faltered on her lips. "You are too kind, sir."

"Anything for you, Miss McGuire." His gaze remained overlong upon her before he rubbed his hands together. "As I was saying, General Smith was all up in arms this afternoon at the fort."

"Indeed. Whatever for?" Mrs. Drummond asked. "We saw him earlier and he seemed only concerned with finding British spies and, of course, with the Myers' tragedy."

A look of sorrow passed between Rose and her aunt.

Alex swallowed.

"Indeed, I hadn't heard." Mr. Snyder addressed Rose. "What happened?"

Rose shook her head. "I do not wish to discuss it."

With a shrug, Mr. Snyder resumed his tale. "It appeared the entire British fleet was heading for Baltimore!" He grabbed a biscuit from a passing plate. "That's twice now those loathsome British have turned their ships toward our harbor only to retreat when they've sufficiently terrorized the town."

"What do you make of it, Mr. Reed?" Mr. Drummond asked, his voice carrying an odd hint of amusement.

Shocked at being addressed during the meal, Mr. Reed shook his head. "Me? What would I know of it?"

A breeze swirled about the table, sending the candle flames flickering. Amelia dropped her fork onto her plate with a clank.

"Forgive my impertinence, Mr. Drummond, but why do you address a servant during supper?" Mr. Snyder glanced around the table for affirmation. "Highly irregular."

"Because, my dear fellow, out of all of us present, only Mr. Reed has actually fought in this war." Mr. Drummond's voice held more frustration than Alex expected from the kind man.

Rose coughed and grabbed her throat.

Mrs. Drummond studied Alex. "What happened to your head, Mr. Reed?"

Alex reached up and touched the small cut on his forehead. "I fell from a horse, madam. It is nothing."

Amelia giggled and Mrs. Drummond resumed her eating.

Mr. Drummond took a huge helping of meat pie. "Do regale us with your opinion, Mr. Reed."

Alex cleared his throat, then looked to Rose for permission. She nodded and he finally said, "In truth, I suspect the British fleet enjoys toying with your city, sir. They wish to test your response and keep you wondering when the next attack will be. Their hope is that you will ignore them when the real one comes."

Mr. Snyder chuckled. "Foolishness, Mr. Reed. You are a soldier, not a sailor. What would you know of the mindset of the British fleet?" He shoved a spoonful of turkey pie into his mouth.

Amelia shared a smile with Rose.

Mr. Drummond chomped on a biscuit, sending crumbs flying. "Makes perfect sense to me. I just wonder what they are waiting for. They've already burned Georgetown, Fredericktown, and Frenchtown and attacked Norfolk and several other cities along the Chesapeake."

Mrs. Drummond shook her head, her ruby earrings glimmering in the candlelight. "And now that dastardly Napoleon has been defeated, we shall have to contend with the entire British imperial sea force."

"As you know, I, for one, am against this war." Mr. Snyder thrust out his chin. "How can we expect to win against such overwhelming odds? Why, to continue fighting is nothing but a reckless and wanton hazard of life and property."

"Would you have us bow down like lame puppies and hand over our freedoms?" Mr. Drummond's ruddy face darkened.

Mr. Snyder flinched. His right hand twitched slightly as he sliced his biscuit. "I don't see that we have a choice."

"Some things are worth dying for, Mr. Snyder." Rose sipped her drink and offered him a tight smile.

He raised his shoulders. "Our Canadian campaign has been disastrous, and we have lost several ships to the Royal Navy, the USS *Chesapeake*, the frigate *Essex*, the *Wasp*, the *Vixen*." He sighed and took a bite of his biscuit.

Rose gripped the handle of her fork until her knuckles whitened. "But you neglect to mention the victories we've had at sea, sir. The USS *United States'* defeat of HMS *Macedonian*, the capture of HMS *Frolic* and *Penguin*, the sinking of HMS *Peacock* and *Reindeer*. Not to mention the many victories of our privateers."

"And the *Constitution's* defeat of *Guerriere*," Alex chimed in as the memories of witnessing that battle from his impotent ship tumbled through him. Oddly, with no accompanying resentment.

Mr. Snyder batted a lace-covered hand over his shoulder toward Mr. Reed as if dismissing the comment as frivolous.

Mr. Drummond's gray brows rose. "Indeed, Mr. Reed." He lowered his gaze to Mr. Snyder. "Sir, I perceive you to be outnumbered in your antiwar sentiments in this house."

Mrs. Drummond laid a hand on her husband's arm. "Do not be so hard on Mr. Snyder, dearest. It is a noble quality to be so concerned for the loss of life."

Mr. Snyder smiled in her direction, but his shoulders lowered nonetheless. "Thank you, madam. That is my only concern. I am a patriot at heart. Besides, since the blockade, not many of our privateers have been successful."

"I beg to differ with you, sir." Rose lowered her spoon, ignoring her aunt's pointed gaze. "I am friends with several privateers, and they still do quite well harassing British shipping. They bring their prizes to dock in New York or Virginia, sell them there, then travel overland back to Baltimore." Suddenly her eyes widened, and she snapped her gaze to Alex as if she just realized she had divulged a grand secret that he could well take back to his British commanders.

Though the British navy was well aware of the practice of Baltimore privateers, Alex gave her a teasing smile nonetheless.

She pursed her lips and exchanged a nervous glance with Amelia before directing her gaze back to him.

Mr. Drummond took a sip of his beer, shifting his glance between them. A drop slid into his thick beard.

"Why do you keep staring at your servant, Miss McGuire?" Mr. Snyder shifted his gaze between them. Nothing but malicious suspicion exuded from the man. But Alex ignored him. The councilman was a gnat. What harm could he do? Yet when he glanced at Miss McGuire, he could see the fear in her eyes.

❖

Rose gave a slight shake of her head toward Mr. Reed in the hopes of dissuading him from further goading Mr. Snyder. The councilman was a prig, but he also was not without power. And with the right information, the power to ruin them all. Oh why did her aunt continue to invite the man to dinner? Couldn't she see how Rose despised him?

Mr. Snyder dabbed the napkin over his mouth and proceeded to regale them with details of the city council's recent decisions regarding funding and new buildings and preparations for war.

As he babbled on, Mr. Snyder grabbed his glass and drew it in haste to his lips. Beer spilled over the sides and splattered onto his trousers.

Curses shot from his mouth as he leaped to his feet. "This is your doing, Mr. Reed!"

"Your language, sir." Mr. Drummond reprimanded the man as he wiped crumbs from his shirt.

Amelia giggled, but Aunt Muira quieted her with a stern look and excused herself to the kitchen. Covering her smile, Rose pretended to gasp in horror while Mr. Reed dabbed an extra napkin over Mr. Snyder's trousers. "No doubt you forgot your full glass, sir."

Mr. Snyder swatted Mr. Reed's hand away just as Aunt Muira returned and handed him a dry cloth. "Please accept our apologies, Mr. Snyder." She glared at Mr. Reed who gave her an apologetic look before backing up against the wall.

When Mr. Snyder had calmed himself, the group resumed their meal, but Rose found her appetite had fled into the night. She didn't know whether to laugh or cry. Amelia must have sensed Rose's discomfiture for she clutched her hand beneath the table. Rose returned her maid's comforting grasp. She could no longer deny that Mr. Reed's presence had a stimulating effect upon her or that her heart would be in danger should he tarry among them. Though she tried to keep her eyes off of him, they wandered unbidden his way nonetheless . . .over his black coat, white cravat, and slick dark hair pulled tight behind him. She remembered the way wet strands had dangled over his cheek in the forest, rain dripping from their tips. Now, he stood against the wall as regal as any nobleman. Perhaps he was a nobleman. The son of a baron or an earl. Suddenly, she longed to know more about him— everything about him. Doubt budded within her as she wondered what he could possibly find appealing about her and her common family.

Still clutching Rose's hand, Amelia lifted a spoonful of greens to her mouth. "We met Mr. Brenin and Mr. Heaton in town today."

"Indeed?" Relief filled Aunt Muira's voice, no doubt at the change in topic. "And Mr. Brenin's dear wife, I assume?"

"Yes and Miss Cassandra as well, along with Mr. Brenin's first mate and his son, an adorable young lad."

"Daniel, I believe his name is." Rose's uncle helped himself to more turkey pie. "A fitting name for him."

Amelia nodded. "You are right, Mr. Drummond, for the boy uttered a prophecy over Rose."

Rose squeezed her hand, urging Amelia with a look to speak no more if it. The boy's words, though spoken with sincerity, were but silly notions of an adventurous mind, and Rose didn't want to arm her uncle with any further ammunition to prompt her to do something she was not yet ready to do.

Mr. Snyder dabbed honey over his biscuit. "That Mr. Heaton is quite the rogue, I hear. Untrustworthy sot."

Rose's uncle gave Mr. Snyder a quizzical look before turning to Amelia. "Pray tell, what did Daniel say?"

"He said that God had something important for Rose to do."

Rose huffed and glanced at Mr. Reed. His hazel eyes twinkled playfully in the candlelight.

"You don't say?" Rose's aunt sipped her drink.

"Very interesting. Interesting indeed." Uncle Forbes seemed deep in thought.

"The ravings of a childish mind." Mr. Snyder sipped his beer—more carefully this time.

Rose held her churning stomach.

Uncle Forbes tossed his napkin onto the table and leaned back in his chair. "I have no doubt that my niece is destined for something great."

Emotion burned in Rose's throat at her uncle's compliment. She smiled at him then turned away before anyone saw her eyes moisten.

After dinner, Rose's aunt and uncle bade her to join them in the parlor for tea with Mr. Snyder, though she tried to beg off with an excuse of a headache. Must she endure more time with the annoying man? And without Mr. Reed present, there was nothing at all to interest her. Even Amelia stole away, offering Rose a look of sympathy over her shoulder.

She sipped her tea and glanced out the parlor windows where the open shutters gave her a view of the trees in the distance standing like prickly dark sentinels guarding the farm. Yet they hadn't guarded her against Garrick's attack. Mr. Reed had done that. Risked his career to save her. After supper, Uncle Forbes had dismissed Mr. Reed from further duties. Now that he could walk without a crutch, there was nothing to keep him here. Would he leave without saying good-bye? An emptiness gnawed at her belly. She had wanted to give him his uniform and weapons and take out his stitches before he traveled so far. But perhaps the surgeon on board his ship would do a better job. If Mr. Reed's captain believed his story. *Lord, please let him believe him.* Everything within her longed to dash outside and bid Mr. Reed good-bye, wish him Godspeed, and feel his arms around her one more time.

But it was better this way.

❖

Mr. Snyder stood by the fireplace, one arm draped across the mantel, wondering how to bring up the sensitive topic of Mr. Reed with

Miss McGuire's family. He decided on the direct approach. "Mr. Drummond," he addressed Rose's uncle who sat beside his wife on the sofa. "Now that your servant has left the room, I feel it is my obligation to inform you that I found him and your niece frolicking about in the woods, covered in mud and in a rather"—he cleared his throat—"provocative embrace."

Mrs. Drummond gasped and fingered a coil of her red hair. "Good heavens, Rose. Is this true, dear?"

Oddly, the statement brought a smile to Mr. Drummond's lips.

Rose pursed her lips, her cheeks growing red. "Not entirely, Aunt. For one thing, we were not frolicking"—she skewered Snyder with a pointed gaze—"and we were only covered in mud and huddling together in a bush because we feared Mr. Snyder was part of a British raiding party."

Her uncle chuckled and folded his hands over his portly belly.

"As I told you before, Mr. Snyder," Rose said. "My close proximity to Mr. Reed was, in short, due to your intrusion upon our afternoon ride."

Snyder stomped his shoe on the hearth and huffed. He certainly hadn't expected his accusation to sit well with the lady, but he hoped she would see the necessity of bringing the event to her family's attention in light of their future together. Couldn't she see that he was only concerned with her safety and her reputation? *Ungrateful girl.*

"There you are, Mr. Snyder." Mr. Drummond pressed down a patch of gray hair that had spiraled out of control atop his head. "Surely that explains things to your satisfaction. I assure you, our Rose is a lady of utmost propriety."

Snyder bit his lip. This was not going as planned. He had expected Rose's uncle to scold her vehemently and to forbid her to spend time alone with Mr. Reed without her maid present. But the old man remained his usual imbecilic self. "It was not my intention to indicate otherwise."

Rose stood and meandered toward the window.

Mrs. Drummond fingered the rubies hanging from her ears. "Of course not, Mr. Snyder. I thank you for looking out for our dear Rose."

Mr. Snyder gave the lady a nod of appreciation. At least someone in this house saw reason. He skirted the high-backed chair and lowered himself onto its soft cushion. Dabbing his fingers on his tongue, he pressed back the hair at his temples and leaned toward Mr. Drummond. "Surely, sir, you agree that this sort of behavior is most unseemly, regardless of the cause."

"I do." Mr. Drummond scratched his beard. "But it appears no harm came of it." A serene peace that Snyder had always taken as ignorance blossomed in the old man's brown eyes. Snyder squirmed on his seat and glanced at Rose who still stared out the window. Starlight shimmered over her, setting her hair aglow as a breeze ruffled the loose strands dangling at her neck. He swallowed down a lump of desire. Why did she shun his every advance while at the same time granting favor to a servant? He had not missed the amorous glances she lavished upon Mr. Reed during supper, nor that the infuriating man had returned them. What did the obnoxious servant possess that he did not? His heart shrank. Wasn't it enough that he lived with the shame of his family's sordid past? Did he now have to endure the rejection of a woman who preferred the company of a common servant over his?

"Forgive my impertinence, Mr. Drummond." Snyder attempted a different approach. "But perhaps if you hired another servant? Mr. Reed seems a bit. . .how shall I say"—*insidious, insolent, and far too handsome*—"unsuitable to be placed in charge of Miss McGuire."

Mr. Drummond's lips slanted. "I fear you overstep your bounds, sir." His stern tone turned Rose around and brought a smile to her lips.

Mrs. Drummond set down her tea and laid a hand on her husband's knee. "Oh Forbes, dearest, I find Mr. Snyder's concern admirable, don't you, Rose?"

But the look on Miss McGuire's face exuded anything but admiration. In fact, it bordered on disgust.

Snyder lowered his chin, his gut constricting. He would not allow this toad, this mere servant, to steal the woman he planned to marry.

Mr. Drummond glanced down at a brown stain on his waistcoat as if he had no idea how it had gotten there. "Nevertheless, Mr. Snyder, you may rest assured that our Rose is in no danger with Mr. Reed. Besides, his stay here is only temporary. You have nothing to fear from him."

"Fear, sir?" Snyder gave a hearty chuckle that sounded more spurious than he intended. "I do not fear the man. My thoughts are toward Rose's safety and reputation."

"I assure you, there is no need." Kindness returned to Mr. Drummond's tone. "It is Mr. Reed's job to protect Rose, particularly on days when we cannot be home."

"Ah yes." Mrs. Drummond took a cloth and lifted the teapot. "I fear I am not here as much as I'd like. I'm often drawn away with my charities."

"Oh do say you'll be here tomorrow, Aunt Muira," Miss McGuire said.

"I'm afraid not, dear. I must go to Washington tomorrow." She moved the teapot over Snyder's cup.

Rejecting Mrs. Drummond's offer of tea, Snyder stood. "Which brings me to my point for accepting your kind invitation tonight. There is a ball at the Fountain Inn next week, and I would like your permission to escort Rose."

"Oh, how kind of you, Mr. Snyder." Mrs. Drummond nearly leaped from her seat. Thin lines crinkled at the corners of her green eyes. "Isn't it, Rose, dear?"

Miss McGuire's gaze skittered about the room. She clasped her hands together and stared at her uncle as if seeking assistance with the answer, but his gaze was riveted to the carpet.

"Forgive me, Mr. Snyder, I am not feeling well," she finally said. "Can we discuss this at another time?" Then clutching the folds of her gown, she dashed from the room and ran up the stairs, leaving Mr. Snyder stunned in her wake.

Containing his frustration, Mr. Snyder thanked the Drummonds for a lovely evening and then saw himself out. He barreled down the steps of the front porch, hoping the fresh evening air would cool his humors. It didn't. *Ill-mannered hoyden.* How dare she treat him with such disrespect? He stormed forward, muttering to himself, and nearly ran into Mr. Reed, who stood ready with his horse.

He snatched the reins from the invidious man. "I know what is going on here, Mr. Reed, and I won't stand for it."

The servant smiled. "You do say?"

"Your behavior toward Miss McGuire is most inappropriate."

Mr. Reed chuckled and tossed the hair from his face. *He chuckled!* "And yet, since you are neither her relation nor her suitor, Miss McGuire is none of your affair."

"Neither is she yours, sir. At least not beyond your duties."

"Indeed." Finally, a frown scattered the man's insolent grin.

"Mrs. Drummond approves of me," Snyder continued, taking

advantage of the small victory. "She has informed me that she intends to encourage Rose to accept not only my courtship but my future proposal of marriage."

The servant raised a brow. "And Mr. Drummond. . . ?"

"I am close to winning his blessing as well." The gelding snorted as if even the horse knew Snyder lied.

"Then, I congratulate you, sir." Mr. Reed bowed slightly. "But shouldn't it be up to the lady?"

"Silly girls do not know their own minds." Snyder tossed the reins back to Mr. Reed. Pulling his leather gloves from the saddle pack, he began to tug them on his fingers. "Rose will see the sense of our match. I can give her a good name, the prestige of my office, and a decent living."

"How could any woman resist such an offer?" Mr. Reed's annoying grin returned.

Snyder gazed into the impudent servant's face, half in shadow, half lit by a lantern hanging from a nearby post. "Indeed." He spat through a clenched jaw.

Reed tilted his head. "And you, of course, will receive her land."

Snyder stiffened. He had underestimated this bumpkin. "Why shouldn't I desire this land? It is the last available parcel that borders the Jones Falls River. And with the proper placement of a flour mill, in a few years it will be worth a fortune."

The corners of Mr. Reed's mouth tightened, and he gazed into the night. "Perhaps the lady would prefer to be desired for herself rather than for her land."

Snyder tugged on his other glove. "I assure you there is no lack of affection for her on my part. But pretty ladies are in abundance in Baltimore."

"But not pretty ladies who will inherit land such as this." Mr. Reed winked at him.

Snyder eyed him. "I see we are of the same mind, Mr. Reed."

But the servant huffed in disdain. "I am nothing like you."

Mr. Snyder frowned, his ire rising. "I advise you to forsake your pursuit of her. You know I will win."

"I have my doubts."

Snyder snatched the reins again, longing to slap them across Mr. Reed's face. "Do not cross me, sir."

"Or what?" Again, that infuriating grin.

"I suspect there is more to that despicable British accent than you admit, Mr. Reed." Shoving his shoe into the stirrup, Snyder swung onto his horse and tugged the reins. The horse neighed and stomped his front hooves. "Whatever you are hiding, I will find out your secret, Mr. Reed. Mark my words."

❖ CHAPTER 15 ❖

Alex loosened his clenched fists at his side and watched until the darkness swallowed up the last trace of Mr. Snyder. Turning, he leaned against the fence post and gazed at the Drummond home. Through the parlor window he could see Mrs. Drummond sitting on the sofa beside her husband, his arm flung over her shoulders. They leaned their heads together in deep conversation, interrupted by bouts of joyful laughter. Alex had never seen his parents enjoy each other's company. He never thought such an intimate relationship was even possible. Mr. Drummond kissed his wife on the cheek then stood and assisted her to her feet. He grabbed the lantern and then, arm in arm, the couple left the parlor and headed upstairs. Alex shifted his gaze away. It landed on light spilling from a second-story window he knew to be Miss McGuire's bedchamber. Not the sort of man who spied into ladies' boudoirs, he was glad for the thick curtains, which forbade him an unintentional peek within. His eyes moved to the final wisps of smoke curling from the chimney above the kitchen where the light from a lantern faded. No doubt Miss Cora retired for the evening.

A lump formed in Alex's throat.

Home. This quaint, rustic farmhouse exemplified the meaning of the word. Home wasn't a large estate with cathedral ceilings and marble floors, where oil paintings of the masters, exquisite tapestries, and gold-gilded mirrors decorated the walls, where drafty halls extended outward like a maze, and opulently decorated rooms stood cold and empty. No, home was a place where people loved each other and shared their lives. It was something Alex had yearned for all his life and would probably never know, aside from these few glorious days.

Blast Mr. Snyder for trying to destroy this home. Alex's hot, angry breath mingled with the humid air swirling around him. He would have loved nothing better than to flatten the man where he stood, but that would only cause more trouble for this precious family.

❖

As soon as Rose heard her aunt and uncle's chamber door click shut, she leaped from her bed, pressed out the folds of her gown and inched toward the door. No sounds save her aunt's and uncle's quiet murmurs filtered to her ears. Opening her door and cringing at the tiny squeak, she crept down the hallway and headed downstairs. In the foyer, she grabbed a pair of scissors, some bandages, and comfrey salve from her aunt's medical satchel, which sat atop a side table, before she exited the front door. Fresh air perfumed with wildflowers swirled around her as she clomped through the mud toward the barn. After briefly greeting Liverpool, Rose climbed the loft and retrieved Mr. Reed's torn uniform and sword from a trunk. The mere sight of his pistol made her chest tighten. Unable to touch the heinous weapon, she left it there and made her way around the other side of the house to the back of the stable. Prinney, whom she'd let loose from his pen earlier, waddled after her, grunting for her attention.

"I haven't time now, Prinney."

Mr. Reed opened the door to her knock and stared at her in utter shock. He had removed his overcoat and waistcoat, leaving only a tight linen shirt across his firmly lined chest. Prinney grunted and nudged her leg.

Rose swallowed and gazed past Mr. Reed into the gloomy room.

"Miss McGuire."

"Mr. Reed." She forced her chin forward. "I have come to remove your stitches before you leave." She pushed past him, ignoring the way the light breeze frolicked among the loose strands of his dark hair.

"Why, I. . .Hmm." He shoved a large rock in place to prop the door open.

His act of propriety at keeping the door ajar only endeared him to her more. Prinney ambled in after her as Rose took a deep breath of the humid air that smelled of mold, hay, and Mr. Reed. A cot holding a crumpled wool blanket guarded the right corner. His waistcoat, coat, and an extra shirt and pair of breeches left by Samuel hung on hooks lining the back wall. A cold potbellied stove perched in the left corner. On a table in the center of the room, sat a single lantern and a vase holding two pink roses. *Pink roses?* She stomped over the dirt floor toward his bed. Hay crunched beneath her slippers. "I am not without a heart, Mr. Reed." She tossed his uniform and service sword onto the blanket.

He hobbled toward her. "That is one fact that has not escaped my attention."

She dared a glance into his eyes and found only sincerity—and something else. . .ardor, affection perhaps—within them. She looked away, trying to conjure up anger, hatred, anything to douse the affection burning within her. "How dare you pick my roses?" She jerked her head toward the vase. "I didn't grow them for your enjoyment."

He blinked. "Indeed? Well I have enjoyed them anyway."

Rose narrowed her eyes.

He chuckled and held up a hand of truce. "In truth, I did not pick them. One of your beasties must have trodden your bush for I found these two flowers barely hanging on and about to fall to the ground." Moving to the table, he touched one of the petals and bent over, taking a whiff. "They do brighten the place, don't you agree?"

Rose shook her head as she watched Mr. Reed's thick, rough hands stroke the delicate petals. And the way he enjoyed the flower's sweet scent. It was the last thing she expected him to do—any man to do, let alone a British officer. She threw back her shoulders. "Please take a seat, Mr. Reed."

Prinney grunted in agreement and pressed his snout against Rose's leg.

Mr. Reed sank into the chair. "Am I to assume the pig is your protector?"

At his sarcastic tone, Rose tightened her lips. "This pig is Prinney, as you are well aware. And he has been a better friend to me than most people I know." She lowered her gaze to the bandages, scissors, and salve in her hands. "And if you misbehave, I do have my scissors, sir." She cocked a brow and put on her most formidable look, but it faltered when a giggle rose to her lips at the absurdity of her statement.

Mr. Reed joined her. "In that case, I shall comport myself as a perfect gentleman."

Rose gazed out the door into the darkness. He had never behaved otherwise. She must remember what his people had done to Elaine. She must avoid gazing into those caring hazel eyes. She must avoid pondering why her heart leaped at the sight of him instead of tightened as it did with most men. She kneeled by his feet. "I need to cut through your breeches."

"Cut through?"

"It is either that or have you remove them."

A red hue crept up his face, and for some reason, it brought a smile to Rose's lips to see that a man could blush so easily. Rose took the scissors and began to cut through the black linen. "You won't be needing them anymore."

❖

Alex's heart sank at her words. In truth, he wasn't ready to go. He longed for a few more days' reprieve from the harsh British navy—a few more days feeling as though he belonged to a family. A few more days with this precious lady. He studied the way the lantern light made her hair shimmer like fine gold. Her delicate fingers worked so gently to cut the fabric of his breeches without disturbing his wound.

She finished slicing through his breeches, then moved the lantern closer to get a good look at his thigh. "What, no complaints, Mr. Reed? No excuses why you should impose upon my family's hospitality further?"

Alex longed for a glimpse into her lustrous eyes—eyes that could not hide her true feelings—but she kept her chin lowered.

He sighed. "No. I am a man of my word. I am well enough to leave. And leave I shall."

A visible shudder ran through her. Sniffing, she gazed into the empty space of the room.

A spot of dirt marred her graceful neck, bringing a smile to Alex's lips. "You were very brave yesterday at your friend's house." He didn't exactly know why she'd been so frightened, but he'd fought in enough battles to know courage when he saw it. Her tender care in light of what she must be feeling toward him—toward all British—caused his throat to clog with emotion. He wanted to tell her how sorry he was for what his fellow countrymen had done. But he couldn't find the right words. More than likely, she would not believe him anyway.

She chuckled. "Me, brave?" Shaking her head, she snipped one edge of the stitches. The scissor blade was cold against his thigh. She tugged at the thread and a slight twinge of pain made Alex wince. "You don't know me, Mr. Reed."

Alex rubbed the stubble on his jaw. "It pains me that I will not have the chance."

She gazed up at him, her eyes misty pools of turquoise. "You speak foolishness, Mr. Reed. Are all British filled with such inane flattery?"

Alex lifted an eyebrow.

Prinney snorted, then meandered over to sift through the hay by the door.

Miss McGuire tugged on the thread again, and Alex watched it slip though his flesh. Queasiness rolled across his gut.

Her cheeks glowed like sweet cream in the lantern light, and Alex longed to brush his fingers over them. While her eyes were downcast, he leaned over and drew in a deep breath of her fresh scent if only to implant it upon his memory.

She finished pulling the remainder of the stitches, then plucked some salve from a small jar. She spread the paste over his wound—a wound that was now nothing but scarred, pink flesh. Afterward, she cut a stream of bandage from a roll, placed it over the wound and wrapped it around her thigh. Every touch of her fingers to his skin set him aflame.

"That should suffice until you see your ship's surgeon." She stood and avoided his gaze.

Alex let out a humph. The ship's surgeon was a ninny. He'd trade that man's ministrations for this lovely creature's any day.

She picked up her things and headed toward the door. But Alex wasn't ready to say good-bye. He stood and plucked a rose from the vase. "Allow me to escort you back to the house, Miss McGuire. It is dark."

She stopped but did not turn around. "Your job of protecting me is over, Mr. Reed."

Alex slipped beside her. "Well then, I thank you, Miss McGuire, for tending my wound and saving my life."

"And I thank you, Mr. Reed, for rescuing me from your comrade." A breeze wafted in through the open door, fluttering her curls. Prinney ambled outside as if bored with the conversation.

"We shall call it even then." He took her hand in his and felt her tremble. Raising it to his lips, he placed a kiss upon it.

At last she lifted her gaze to his. Eyes sparkling with tears searched his face. Tears for what?

"Forgive me. I have upset you." Alex frowned, longing to see her smile again. He held out the rose to her.

She eyed him quizzically but did not take it. Instead, she tugged her hand from his.

"A token of our time together?" He attempted a smile that did not reflect the agony in his heart. "The color reminds me of your lips."

She snatched the flower from his hand and stepped out into the darkness. "Godspeed, Mr. Reed. I pray we do not meet again." Then turning, she fled into the night.

❖

Hoisting a burlap sack stuffed with his uniform over his back, Alex made his way to the barn—Miss McGuire's barn. Somehow being in the place she held so dear, the place where he had first seen her, made him feel close to her. And he needed one last dose of her presence before he left her forever. Mr. Snyder's threats rang fresh in Alex's mind. He must leave tonight. Should the councilman discover Alex's true identity, the entire family would be tried for treason.

And Alex could not let that happen.

He stomped forward, his boots squishing through the weeds and mud. His service sword stuffed in his belt, slapped against his thigh. But how could he leave Miss McGuire at the mercy of Mr. Snyder? With no other prospects, the Drummonds would no doubt force her to marry the nincompoop. A nightingale took up a harried call from a tree by the barn. A warning? Yes, that was what he must do. Before Alex left, he must warn Mr. Drummond of the councilman's true intentions. But how? Mr. and Mrs. Drummond had already retired to their bedchamber.

Halting, Alex gazed back at the house. A sliver of a moon peeked from above the dark treetops in the distance as if God were smiling down upon him. He sighed. When had he started thinking of God that way? If God was real and He did answer prayers, Alex could sure use some help. Pausing, he decided to give it a try. He'd never prayed before, not really. But seeing the Drummonds' faith lived out daily stirred a deep part of him, made him want to talk to God like a friend. Closing his eyes, he took a deep breath and began, "God, if You're there, I need to speak to Mr. Drummond tonight." A breeze heavy with moisture and the scent of cedar stole his whispered words away. He nearly laughed out loud at his pathetic appeal.

Shaking his head, he ventured into the shadowy barn, struck flint to steel, and lit a lantern hanging on a center post. Removing his sword, he leaned it against a post and set his sack beside it. Liverpool let out a low groan and a chicken crossed his path, scolding him as it made its way to the chicken roost against the far wall. The smell of hay and manure and leather swirled around him. He chuckled, realizing he no longer found the scents offensive. Surely the woman had bewitched him. He moved to Valor's stall and eased his fingers over the horse's face.

"What do you think, mighty Valor?" The animal nodded her head up and down, then gazed at Alex with brown, intelligent eyes that reminded him of Mr. Drummond's. Alex chuckled. "I believe you are far wiser than you allow me to believe. Much like the man of the house."

"What's that you say?" Mr. Drummond's cracked voice turned Valor's ears in the direction of the door.

Alex jerked around to see Rose's uncle approaching him, lantern in hand. Stunned, he could only stare wide-eyed at the older man. During the time Alex had been here, he'd never once seen Mr. Drummond come out to the barn. A tremble jolted him. Had God answered his prayer? Impossible.

"Talking to a horse, Mr. Reed?" Mr. Drummond's eyes twinkled.

Alex chuckled. "I seem to have more success conversing with horses than people."

Mr. Drummond set his lantern down atop a post and gave Valor a pat on the side. "Oh I doubt that, Mr. Reed, although you did stir Mr. Snyder into a dither this evening."

Alex shot a glance at his sword and pack, but thankfully, they were hidden in the shadows. "I beg your forgiveness, sir. I fear the man brings out the worst in me."

"Think nothing of it, Mr. Reed. I quite enjoyed the exchange."

Alex blinked. He'd expected a proper scolding from a man who lived his life by God's law. "Indeed? I was under the impression Mr. Snyder was a friend of yours."

Mr. Drummond swatted at a fly buzzing about his head and pressed a hand on his back. "I am quite delighted to say that I do not count him among my friends, though I do pray for his soul." Pulling up a milking stool, he sat down with a moan. "Old age, Mr. Reed. I do not recommend it." He chuckled. "No, it is my dear Muira who favors a match between the councilman and Rose, though I have been unable to ascertain her reasons."

Alex studied the elderly man. Everything he said and did slammed headfirst into Alex's long-held opinions of how clergymen should behave. But Mr. Drummond had opened a door, and Alex decided to step through it. "If I may, sir, I believe Mr. Snyder's interest lies more in Miss McGuire's land than in the lady herself."

Mr. Drummond nodded as a look of sorrow deepened his eyes. "As the good Lord has told me."

The odd words struck Alex like a wave of icy water. "God speaks to you?"

"Aye, quite often."

Valor snorted and bobbed her face up and down again.

Alex ran a hand through his hair and scratched the back of his head, hoping to ignite some insight into the man's way of thinking. "Is this an American invention? For I cannot fathom it, sir."

"American? No. I'll wager God even speaks to Englishmen from time to time." Mr. Drummond chuckled.

Alex doubted it. None of the bishops he'd met back home claimed such an intimacy with God. In truth, they seemed more interested in politics than faith. "So, your government has no say in the dictates of religion?" Alex asked.

"Indeed. We are free to worship and believe as we please."

Liverpool groaned as if uttering her approval. And Alex had to agree with the beast. At least these Americans had it right on one account for he had seen how government used the cover of religion as an excuse for all manner of hatred and ill treatment. But God speaking directly to man? "I beg your pardon, sir, but perhaps you only *think* you hear from God."

Mr. Drummond patted his waistcoat pockets. "He speaks to all his children, but many never hear Him because they are not listening or they do not believe God speaks at all."

Again, the man shocked Alex. Doubts pecked at his rising faith like vultures on a wounded beast. "Pray, tell me how He speaks to you, sir. In a burning bush, or perchance an angel appears to give you the message?" Alex snorted.

Mr. Drummond smiled and pointed toward his chest. "In here. A still, small voice, a knowing that always brings peace."

Pushing away from the stall, Alex took a step back, suddenly wondering if the man was mad. "I have never heard such a thing."

"Perhaps because you do not believe you can." Mr. Drummond's gray brows rose.

"You are a reverend, sir. If God does still speak to man—and I'm not saying He does—hearing His voice is no doubt a privilege of your profession." Alex nodded, content with his explanation.

Mr. Drummond's brown eyes flooded with wisdom and something else—a love so intense it caused Alex to avert his gaze. He shifted his boots over the dirt.

"It is a privilege of all He calls His children," Mr. Drummond said.

Children. Was Alex God's child? He didn't want to be anyone's child ever again. Children were commodities to be used or tossed aside at the whim of an uncaring parent. "You speak of God as if He were, indeed, your father."

Mr. Drummond nodded.

Alex gave the man a caustic look. "A bit disrespectful, wouldn't you say, calling the Creator of the world by so familiar a name?"

"He is the Father of all, my son." A gust of hot wind tore through the barn and Mr. Drummond coughed. "When we believe in His Son, Jesus, we are adopted into God's family and are privileged to call Him Abba, Father."

Son. Mr. Drummond had called him son again. And with more affection than Alex's own father had ever spoken his name. Family. Home. Love. All the thoughts that had recently brought such warmth to Alex now rose like a whirling tempest within him.

Mr. Drummond fingered his beard. "I believe God has brought you to us for a reason. He has told me you have an important task to complete."

"Absurd." Alex tugged on his tight waistcoat. "It only proves that no one truly hears from God, for I assure you, sir, I will never do anything of import. At least not that you would consider so." Alex frowned. No, the feats he hoped to accomplish in His Majesty's Navy were the only things important to Alex. And they would only further his own family name and wealth and hopefully gain him entrance to his home again.

Though he was beginning to wonder why he sought so hard after that goal.

Mr. Drummond folded his hands over his portly belly. "There's only one way to find out. Ask God to show you His will and then submit to His direction."

"Humph." Alex crossed his arms over his chest.

A smile—not an insolent, pretentious, or taunting smile—but a smile that bespoke a knowledge that Alex did not possess settled on Mr. Drummond's lips.

Alex rubbed a hand over the back of his neck and glanced out the barn doors. Nothing but darkness met his gaze. Thick darkness—the kind of darkness a man could get lost in and never return. Which was what Alex intended to do. He snapped his gaze back to Mr. Drummond. Golden light from two lanterns spilled over the man, surrounding him in an ethereal glow. Something in the confidence and peace in his tone, on his face, sparked hope within Alex.

But what did it matter? He must leave this place, leave this man, and leave Rose. "Mr. Drummond, I beg you to protect Miss McGuire from Mr. Snyder. I believe a match between them would cause her great unhappiness."

"Oh, you do?" The knowing smile on the man's face curved into a taunting one.

"And it is not because of any affections I may have for her."

"I made no mention of any affections." Laughter sparkled in Mr. Drummond's eyes. He cocked his head. "Is there something you wish to ask me, Mr. Reed?"

Alex studied the odd man. "No, sir," he said carefully. He couldn't afford to reveal his growing affection and then leave. It wouldn't be fair to Rose.

"Hmm. Very well."

Alex huffed. "I must leave. Go back to my sh—regiment."

Mr. Drummond lowered his chin. "As I feared."

Upon his honor, Alex could not figure the man out. "Surely you do not wish me to stay here because of my exemplary skills as a servant?"

Mr. Drummond laughed. "No, but you are good for Rose."

"I fear you are mistaken."

"Am I? I have not seen her so lively, so vibrant in years."

Alex looked away. He didn't want to hear it. It hurt too much to know that he could bring her joy only to have to break her heart. "I assure you it is not my doing."

"Hmm."

"Nevertheless, I must leave you tonight." Alex forced determination into both his tone and his resolve. "I cannot thank you enough for your kindness in offering me a position in your home."

"Tonight?" The elderly man struggled to rise. "You cannot possibly leave tonight."

❖ CHAPTER 16 ❖

Crying. A woman's crying echoed through Rose's ears, bouncing off the walls of her mind, jarring her awake. She turned on her side and drew her quilt over her head. The sobbing continued. Did it come from within her? Had the sorrow that had weighed so heavily upon her when she retired that night followed her into her dreams? Sitting up, she swiped her cheeks. No. Not her tears.

Whimpering drifted through the walls. *Amelia.* Leaping from her bed, Rose swung a robe over her shoulders and crept through the dark hallway into Amelia's chamber next door. The poor woman lay curled in a ball on her coverlet. Misty fingers of moonlight streamed in through the window, caressing her, even as her long black tresses fanned over the coverlet like silken threads. Amelia's chest convulsed. Rose inched to her side and laid a hand on her arm.

Amelia shot up, her eyes wide. "Oh miss, it's you." She gasped for air and looked down. "Forgive me, I woke you again."

Rose sat beside her and enfolded her in a tight embrace. The aged bed frame creaked. "Has something else distressed you or is it. . ." Rose hated to even mention his name lest the woman break into sobs anew.

Which Amelia did anyway at just the hint of him—Richard, her husband.

"I miss him so much, Rose." She inhaled a sob, then leaned her head on Rose's shoulder.

"I know." Rose stroked her back. "I know." Tears burned behind Rose's eyes. It had been two years since Richard disappeared at sea, yet still his young wife mourned him as if he'd left only yesterday. "Your love was one of a kind."

Amelia pushed back from her. Glassy brown eyes brimming with pain gazed at Rose. "It was, wasn't it?"

Rose nodded and wiped a moist strand of Amelia's hair from her cheek. Though she knew no man was perfect, the way Amelia described Richard as an honorable, kind, and brave man who loved Amelia deeply made Rose long to be loved by such a man. Oddly, a certain British officer filled her vision—an officer who was gone forever just like Richard. Her heart grew heavy. And for the first time, Rose felt the weight of her maid's ongoing agony. "You were blessed to have had Richard for as long as you did. Most women will never be loved so passionately."

Amelia nodded, then fell into Rose's embrace again. "Why am I not getting better? Why do I still think of him every moment of the day and dream of him during the long night?"

"Because he will always be with you, Amelia. And you, with him." Rose grabbed a handkerchief from the table and handed it to her maid. She blew her nose and gave Rose a tiny smile. "Thank you, miss." Then dropping her hands into her lap, she gazed out the window. Starlight drifted over her, transforming her skin into porcelain and her tears into silver. "Even when I play the coquette and attract all manner of attention from men, the pain does not subside."

Rose grasped her hands. They trembled.

"I am beginning to believe that no man can ever take Richard's place," Amelia said.

Rose swallowed. She wouldn't have agreed with her maid a week ago. A week ago, she would have told her to give up her romantic, fanciful notions. She would have told her that one man was as good as the next, as long as he was honorable and hard-working. But Mr. Reed had changed everything. Rose had never met anyone like him. And she doubted she ever would again. Suddenly a hint of Amelia's pain filled her own heart, and tears blurred her vision.

Amelia lowered her chin. "I need to find a husband. I've burdened your aunt and uncle long enough."

Rose gripped her shoulders and resisted the urge to shake her. "Don't be such a silly goose, Amelia. You are family now. Surely you know that." She wiped a wet strand of hair from Amelia's face.

"Well I suppose if that weren't true, they would have dismissed me long ago." Amelia's laugh came out as a sob, and Rose drew her into a tight embrace and held her until her sobs subsided and they both drifted off to sleep.

❖

Alex hoisted the ax above his head. His muscles burned. Sweat streamed down his bare back. He thrust the blade into the wood, then repeated the process again and again until finally the log separated into two. A sound that reminded him of a ship's mast snapping shot through the air. Halting, he settled his breath as James Myers strode up to him, a bucket of water in hand, and scooped him a ladleful. Alex set down the ax and poured the cool liquid into his mouth until it dribbled down his chin. After handing the ladle back to James, he ran a hand through his sweat-moistened hair. "Thank you."

Dropping the ladle into the bucket, James scanned the scene. "It is I who should thank you, Mr. Reed." His Adam's apple bobbed up and down, and Alex followed his gaze to the house, or what was left of it.

"It would please me if you would call me Alex."

James chuckled. "It would please you? Now, aren't you the gentleman? With that accent, you could almost be mistaken for some elegant British nobleman."

Alex coughed into his hand. "God forbid."

From across the field, Mr. Drummond strolled up to them. "And just what does God forbid?" He tugged off his hat and ran his sleeve over his forehead.

James scooped some water for the elderly man. "God forbid that Mr. Reed...I mean Alex would be a British nobleman."

A sparkle lit Mr. Drummond's brown eyes as he snapped them to Alex. "A travesty, indeed."

Unsettled by the man's keen perusal, Alex gazed back at the house. With all the burnt rubble cleared away, the structure appeared sound. Shards of darkened wood poked out from the remainder of what had been the kitchen, but the foundation was intact. Two young men from town, Mr. Anders and Mr. Braxton stood atop the roof joining the new frame to the existing one. A week or so of hard work should make the humble home as good as new. Not that Alex knew anything about carpentry, but he'd overheard as much from Mr. Drummond.

Alex stretched his shoulders, wincing at the ache that spread down his back. Though he'd been forced to lift heavy objects and perform various laborious tasks in the navy, he couldn't recall ever wielding so large an ax or working so hard and long in such sweltering heat—not even when he'd chopped wood for Miss McGuire. Oddly, Alex embraced his discomfort. For the first time in his life, his hard work served a noble purpose. Shading his eyes, he glanced up at the sun slinging fiery rays upon him as if the glowing orb were angry at some offense. *Which one?* Alex wondered.

Hot wind whipped around him, and he closed his eyes, allowing it to cool his chest and arms. He drew in a deep breath of air tainted with a hint of salt and sweet summer flowers.

James clapped him on the back. "Well, I thank you again, Alex." True appreciation beamed in the man's eyes. "Now I best get this water over to Harold and Jarvis and then get back to my own work." He tipped his hat and headed toward the house.

Mr. Drummond's gaze remained on Alex. "Not done much carpentry work before, eh?"

Alex chuckled and picked up his ax. "Is it that obvious?"

"Just a bit. But you're doing a great job, son. Thank you for staying. We'll have this house up in no time."

"It's the least I could do." Alex said the words before he realized their implication.

Mr. Drummond scratched his gray whiskers, and a hint of a smile flickered over his lips. "Now why would you say something like that?"

Alex gripped the ax handle so tight a splinter of wood pierced his skin. If the man only knew. "I meant after all this family has suffered." When Mr. Drummond had asked Alex to help rebuild this poor farmer's home, Alex had seen it as a way to offer penance for the crimes of his countrymen. He hated that he'd had to break his promise that he would leave last night, but how could he refuse the opportunity?

"You are a kind soul, indeed, son." Mr. Drummond's look of approval nearly forced Alex to take a step back. Then, smiling, the man turned and walked away.

Alex watched him as he left: the slight hobble in his gait as if one of his legs pained him, his gray hair poking out in all directions from beneath a wide-brimmed hat, the humble yet confident lift of his shoulders. And a longing welled within Alex, a longing to have a father like Mr. Drummond. Alex's own father had never paid him a single compliment, nor even a kind word or encouragement.

Mr. Drummond took up his spot leaning over a log, shaping and cutting the ends with a long knife while James perched atop a ladder giving water to his friends. He must have said something funny as the men atop the roof joined him in laughter. Alex shook his head. These people found joy even in the midst of tragedy, even with their country at war and the enemy surrounding them. These Americans might be a rustic breed, but they were hardy and they cared for one another. They helped one another. Alex had seen nothing like it in his life. Men willing to give up a day's or a week's worth of hard work for someone else. And receive nothing in return. Astonishing. Shame drew his gaze to the grass surrounding his boots—shame at his own reason for offering his assistance. Penance. A purely selfish reason that had nothing to do with kindness.

Hoisting the ax onto his shoulder, Alex moved to the next felled trunk and dug the blade deep into the wood, angry at himself, angry at his father, angry at his countrymen. And even angry at Miss McGuire for being so charming and wonderful.

And for stealing his heart.

❖

Rose clucked her tongue and nudged Valor forward. After both her and Amelia's difficult night last night, Rose thought it best that they find something productive to do today. If only to keep their minds off their sorrows. So when Cora had informed her that Uncle Forbes was over at the Myers' farm helping to rebuild James and Elaine's house, Rose decided to bring him lunch, along with enough food for any other men helping out. And perhaps speak to Elaine again.

"Oh I do hope Mr. Braxton will be there. I know he's a friend of Mr. Myers." Amelia's excited chatter drifted over Rose's shoulder even as the woman's grip on Rose's waist tightened. "Maybe he'll ask me to the ball."

Rose let out a huff, amazed that Amelia could recover so quickly from a night of such anguish. But then again, Rose knew the woman's flirtatious ways were the only thing that gave her the strength and impetus to survive another day without Richard.

She patted Amelia's hand. "Maybe he will."

Pushing up the brim of her straw hat, Rose gazed at the archway of thick elm branches overhead. Trumpet vines spun upward around their trunks and curled around branches before dangling over the dirt path like the green tresses of a forest maiden. Rose swatted one away and drew a deep breath of the fresh mossy air, trying to allay the ache in her heart.

"There they are." Amelia's arm speared out on Rose's right side.

Two men stood atop what was left of the roof, her uncle and James leaned over a massive log perched above the ground on two wooden trestles, and out in the field stood another man, ax raised over his head, dark hair blowing in the breeze.

Bare-chested.

Rose's stomach clamped tight. Her heart raced. Removing one hand from the reins, she rubbed her eyes and refocused them on the man.

"It's Mr. Reed," Amelia said with merely a hint of surprise in her voice. "What is he doing here?"

Rose 's thoughts spun in a chaotic jumble. "I have no idea."

"Oh my, look at him."

"I'd rather not."

"Why not? He's absolute perfection."

"My word, Amelia, shame on you. You shouldn't stare at him." But even as she said it, Rose's eyes shot his way again as if they had a mind of their own. He plunged the ax into a log, then yanked it free and lifted it over his head once more. Muscles as firm as the wood he chopped rippled through his chest and arms beneath skin glistening in the noon sun. She swallowed and urged Valor through the open gate and up the path to the house, where she pulled the horse to a stop. Her uncle looked up from his work and smiled. "There you are, lass."

James dug his ax deep into the wood and rushed over to assist Rose from her horse. After her feet hit the ground, she turned and took the basket of food from Amelia before James assisted her down as well.

"We brought you lunch." Rose held the basket out to James.

James leaned forward and took a whiff. "Very kind of you, Miss Rose."

The two men on the roof descended the ladder and dropped to the ground, heading their way.

Amelia pinched her cheeks then turned to face them. "Good day,

Mr. Braxton." She gave the young man a coy glance.

Doffing his hat, he ran a hand through his blond hair and nodded in her direction. "Good day, Mrs. Wilkins. A pleasure to see you again."

Out of the corner of her eye, Rose saw Mr. Reed toss a shirt over his head and start toward them. "Is Elaine home, James?" she said. "I'd love to see her."

"No, I'm afraid not." James placed the basket atop a table covered with carpentry tools. "She went to stay with the Brandons in town until I can get the house repaired."

"How is she doing?"

"As well as you might expect, Miss Rose. She'll be sorry she missed you." Anguish burned in James's blue eyes before a gentle smile stole it away.

Mr. Reed's tall figure filled the corner of Rose's eyes. Part of her was furious that he had not left, the other part elated. In truth, she had no idea which part to embrace. She decided on anger. It was the safer choice. "We should be going." She could not question him now in front of these men. Turning, she tugged on Amelia's sleeve, but the woman continued talking with Mr. Braxton.

Uncle Forbes approached Rose, a smile on his face. "So soon? I'll not hear of it, lass."

"It's far too hot this time of day, Uncle." Rose batted the muggy air around her neck. "You can bring the basket home with you later."

"Come, come, my dear." He proffered his elbow. "I'll grab my lunch, and we can sit under the tree by the pond."

Mr. Reed approached James and peered into the basket. His hazel eyes latched upon Rose. Regret flickered across them along with a burning affection that caused her skin to flush.

Turning away from him, Rose took her uncle's arm. "Very well." At least she would be away from Mr. Reed. Away from his effect on her. From the way one look from him could dismantle her anger and turn her insides to mush.

The warmth and strength emanating from Uncle Forbes's arm helped ease Rose's taut nerves as they made their way to the huge oak tree. Lowering onto the soft grass, Rose spread out her skirts as her uncle excused himself to get his lunch. Untying the ribbon beneath her chin, she drew off her hat and gazed at the leaves fluttering in the breeze, the red and yellow marigolds in Elaine's garden, the ducks gliding over the pond. Yet voices drew her gaze back toward the house where her uncle stood in deep conversation with Mr. Reed. Grabbing one of the lunch bundles, Mr. Reed headed her way.

Her way?

Too late to jump to her feet and run away.

Tightening her jaw, she returned her gaze to the pond, trying to erect barriers around her heart. His shadow fell across her. He cleared his throat.

She glanced up.

"Your uncle said you wished to speak to me." A breeze twirled among the dark strands of his hair.

With a frown, Rose searched for her uncle and found him sitting with James and Mr. Anders, eating his food. Why would he say such a thing?

"Miss McGuire?" The deep timbre of Mr. Reed's voice caressed her ears.

She forced a stoic expression. "I fear he was mistaken, Mr. Reed."

"Then forgive the intrusion, miss." He nodded and turned to leave.

"Why are you still here?" she called after him.

He swung about, a puzzled look on his face. "You are angry?"

"No." Rose fingered a blade of grass. "Yes. . .I don't know. It's just that I prepared myself for you leaving."

One dark brow rose. "Prepared?" A spark of hope glimmered in his hazel eyes.

"Oh, never mind." She waved at him. "Do sit down, Mr. Reed, and eat your lunch."

He hesitated, glanced over his shoulder, then finally dropped to the ground beside her. He propped his boots on the dirt and leaned his arms across his knees. "When your uncle asked me to help today, I thought it my duty to stay and assist in cleaning up the mess my countrymen made. I hope you understand."

Understand? That he was an honorable, kind man. Yes, she did. But she wished she didn't. She wished he were a selfish, arrogant brute who would just leave.

"Rest assured, I intend to leave tonight." He raked his moist hair back from his face.

"I do not believe you." She smiled.

He chuckled and unwrapped the cloth bundle in his lap. Pulling out a chunk of yellow cheese, he offered it to her. She broke off a piece and popped it in her mouth. The sharp taste matched the angst brewing in her stomach.

Tearing off a clump of bread, he took a bite and stared at the pond glistening silver in the bright sun. Unable to stop herself, Rose gazed at him, memorizing every detail, the angular cut of his jaw, the black stubble on his chin, the way his dark hair grazed his open collar. Even sitting on the grass, he exuded strength and confidence. The wind flapped his loose shirt, giving her a peek of his chest. She turned away. Her eyes misted. She would miss him—this British naval officer.

Images of her father beckoned to her from deep within her soul. Sudden guilt followed the usual sorrow flooding her, and she lowered her gaze. Surely her feelings for this British man betrayed her father's memory. And she hated herself for it.

Amelia's giddy laughter echoed over the field, and Alex glanced in the maid's direction. The poor woman stood far too close to Mr. Braxton, clinging to his arm and waving her fan about flirtatiously.

"Your companion plays a dangerous game."

"Why do you say that?" Though Rose could imagine, she wondered at Mr. Reed's concern.

"She throws herself at every passing man." He took a bite of dried pork. "She's a sweet woman, to be sure, but one of these men will take advantage of her."

"Yes, I fear that as well." Rose handed him back the cheese, her churning stomach unable to accept another bite.

"Perhaps your uncle can curtail her behavior." Mr. Reed's tone carried no condemnation, only concern.

"No, I fear my uncle is too often gone." Rose plucked a dandelion weed. "Do not think badly of her, Mr. Reed. She is not as wanton as she may seem. Her coquettish ways cover a deep wound."

"Indeed?" Mr. Reed swallowed his meat and looked her way.

Should Rose tell him the tale? What would it matter if she did? He'd be gone soon anyway. "Her husband was lost at sea two years ago."

Mr. Reed glanced back at Amelia, but said nothing.

"She believes him dead, but it's possible that he was impressed by your navy." Rose allowed anger to seep into her voice.

Sharp eyes snapped her way. "What is his name?"

"Richard Wilkins."

Something sparked in Alex's eyes before he looked away.

Rose laid a hand on his arm, her pulse quickening. "You know him?"

He shook his head. "I don't think so. . .perhaps. The navy impresses many men."

"Indeed you do." A welcome disdain ignited in Rose's belly, and she did all she could to fan its flames. Better to be angry with this man than allow her sentiments to grow for him. "You steal them from their families, never to be seen or heard from again."

Mr. Reed's jaw bunched and he released a labored sigh. "It is an inexcusable practice, Miss McGuire, one which I have never approved of. But rest assured"—he gave her a measured look—"your American navy is not without equal blame. They hold our sailors hostage as well."

"Perhaps. But I thank you for reminding me of something."

"What is that?"

"That you are British through and through and always will be." Grabbing her skirts, Rose struggled to stand as modestly as she could. She started to leave. "Good day, Mr. Reed."

He grabbed her hand, turning her gaze back to him. "I am first and foremost a man, Miss McGuire. Neither British nor American."

She feigned a tug on his grip, not wanting him to release her. Something deep within his eyes—longing and pain—kept her in place.

He squeezed her hand. "Much to my chagrin, I have discovered that my opinion of you Americans was quite erroneous at best. Perhaps you would offer me the same courtesy?"

Warmth spread from his hand up her arm and down her back, causing her to shudder. "How can I when I know so little of you?"

With a sigh, he glanced toward the pond then back at her, still not releasing her hand. "Very well. If you'll sit back down, I'll do my best to regale you with the horrid tale of my childhood."

❖

Snyder eased his gelding to a walk as he approached the Drummond farm. White smoke drifted from the kitchen chimney where their Negro cook no doubt prepared the evening meal. If he was correct in his assessment, she should be the only person home at the moment. Last night, Snyder had overheard that Mrs. Drummond intended to travel to Washington today and Mr. Drummond would be at the Myers' farm helping to rebuild their damaged house. Snyder had just seen Rose and Amelia ride off on horseback. And since Mr. Reed was not with them, he must be already at the Myers', assisting Mr. Drummond.

Snyder smiled at his own ability to accurately assess any situation.

Heading toward the stable, he loosened his cravat. Sweat broke out on his neck, and he dabbed it with the folds of silk. Blast this infernal heat. Rarely did he venture outside when the sun was at its zenith, but he would gladly endure all the discomfort in the world, if he accomplished his mission. Slipping off his horse, he tied the reins to the post outside the stable. With one glance toward the house, he circled the building, found the door leading to Mr. Reed's quarters and sneaked inside. The musty smell of mold and hay accosted him. Sunlight filtered through the single dirty window, twirling dust through the air as he scanned the room, looking for something, anything that would prove Mr. Reed's true identity. He took off his hat, grateful for the cooler air, as his eyes grew accustomed to the shadows. A glimmer drew his gaze to something underneath a cot in the corner. Making his way toward it, he knelt, pulled out a sack and peered behind it. Malevolent delight surged within him, for there lying in the dirt was the silver hilt of a British service sword.

❖ CHAPTER 17 ❖

Alex rubbed his stiff jaw and gazed at the ducks skimming over the glassy waters of the pond. A mother and seven ducklings. A family. Happy and carefree. He envied them. Rose sat patiently beside him. With the folds of her gown spread like creamy wings over the grass and her golden hair framing her face like a halo, she looked like an angel. She *was* an angel to him. An angel whose blue eyes gazed at him expectantly making him hesitate to divulge the shame of his youth, hesitate to watch disapproval curve those beautiful lips into a frown, for his story would do nothing to engender her good opinion of him or of his countrymen.

"Mr. Reed?" Her questioning tone snapped him from his daze.

He shook his head. "There isn't much to tell, Miss McGuire. I simply did not want to see you run off so angry."

"Well, now that I've sat down again, I would like to know more about you." She glanced toward the trees lining the other side of the pond and sorrow rolled over her face. "Even if I am never to see you again."

"Very well." Alex tied the edges of the cloth sack containing his lunch and set it aside. "My father's name is Franklin Reed, Viscount Cranleigh, or just Lord Cranleigh to his friends." He chuckled. "Among his many achievements, he is also a member of Parliament."

The corners of her lips tightened, and she lowered her chin as if the news upset her, but then she gave him a timid smile. "Then should we be addressing you as Lord Cranleigh?"

"No." Alex returned her smile, happy to see his status did not intimidate her as it often did those of common birth. "The sons of viscounts receive no title." He plucked a piece of grass and tossed it aside.

Rose's forehead wrinkled. "Was your father cruel?"

Alex leaned back against the tree trunk, amazed at her discernment. "He was not a father at all." He shrugged. "But I suppose I was not much of a son either."

"I cannot imagine that."

Her compliment settled on his shoulders like the warmth of the sun filtering through the leaves above them. "I was the prodigal son, Miss McGuire. Got into all sorts of trouble in town. Drank to excess, harassed the watch, caused great embarrassment for my family." He wouldn't tell her the rest—consorting with questionable ladies, gambling, and the two nights in prison he'd spent before his father had come to bail him out.

"Why would you do such things?" She stared at him as if she couldn't conceive of anyone defying their family in such a way.

"I was an angry young man."

"Angry at what?"

"My father, my elder brother, life. . .I don't know." Visions of his boyhood antics strolled through his mind like a nightmarish parade, showering him with remorse, yet reminding him of the inward fury and emptiness that had haunted him day and night.

"But you had everything—wealth, prestige, family."

Alex snorted. "Wealth and prestige, yes. But not family. Not the kind of family you're thinking of." Alex glanced toward Mr. Drummond who was laughing with James. "My father was a very stern man. He favored my elder brother, Frederick, and found me lacking in every way." Alex huffed as he pictured his brilliant, gifted brother sauntering into the family sitting room with the flourish and elegance of a London dandy—and how his father's eyes would brighten at the sight of him. "Where Frederick was skilled in learning and quick with books, I resisted instruction and bumbled my numbers. Where he was an accomplished horseman, well." Alex chuckled. "You saw my skill on a horse."

Rose smiled and clasped her hands in her lap, yet sorrow lingered in her eyes.

Alex stretched his back. "So, my dear father, Lord Cranleigh, sent me away to the navy. Obtained a commission for me as a midshipman aboard the HMS *Aquilon*."

"You didn't wish to go?" Rose's forehead puckered.

Alex shook his head. "I had no aspirations to fight silly sea battles across the globe."

Rose shifted her gaze to the pond where the mother duck swam into a patch of lily pads and gathered her young around her. "I'm sorry."

"It was good for me." Wind blew a strand of his hair into his face, and Alex flipped it aside. "The discipline, the hard work. I came home to visit my family for a few weeks during the summer of '06 and became quite taken with a certain lady."

"Oh." Her tone was one of dismay. Rose glanced at the hands in her lap.

"There was but one small impediment. She was my brother's fiancée." Alex studied her, gauging her reaction.

"My word." Rose gasped, but still she would not look at him.

Certainly the story was no credit to Alex's character, but the sad tale was a huge part of what had formed him into the man he was today—a huge part of what had driven him to this point. And for some reason, now that he had begun, he wanted Rose to know all of it, to understand him. If she didn't, if she turned her nose up at him in disdain, he would no doubt grieve, but it would be far easier for him to leave her forever.

"And worse, the lady encouraged my affections," he continued. "Toyed with the infatuation of a young man. I was beside myself with love." He shook his head and chuckled. "Or so I thought."

Finally Rose lifted her gaze to his. Nothing but compassion swam in her eyes. "Do not be so hard on yourself. You were but eighteen."

Alex glanced down at the grass fluttering in the breeze and swallowed the burning in his throat. "Yes, I was young, and she but a vixen in disguise. At a dinner party at our house, she lured me into the library and showered me with kisses—quite passionate kisses, I might add."

A red hue flooded Rose's cheeks, making her even more adorable.

"I proposed to her on the spot—asked her to break off her engagement with my brother and run away to Guernsey with me to get married."

Rose drew a hand to her mouth.

"Never fear, Miss McGuire." Alex gave her a sad smile. "As it turns out, the woman had some sense after all. She laughed at me. Not just a slight giggle, but a rather unladylike chortle."

Rose put her hand on his arm. Pain burned in her eyes, but she said nothing.

Alex stared at the dirt by his boots. "My brother inherited the bulk of the family fortune, you see. And marrying a seaman was beneath her."

Rose squeezed his arm. "I'm so sorry."

Alex tore from her grasp and stood. He stepped toward the pond, turning away from her, not wanting her to see the pain moistening his eyes. He no longer loved the vixen. Hardly ever thought of her. Then why did her rejection still grieve him so?

He heard Rose get up and felt her presence behind him.

"She informed my entire family of my silly proposal." Alex could hear the bitter sarcasm in his own voice. "I dare say, I was on the receiving end of everyone's jokes for days to come. And oh"—he glanced at her over his shoulder—"my dear brother called me out to a duel."

Rose eased beside him. "What did you do?"

"I nearly killed him." Alex fisted his hands across his chest. "I begged him not to fight, but his blasted honor"—Alex hung his head—"his blasted honor..." Sorrow choked him, forbidding him to speak.

Several seconds passed. "What happened?" Rose finally asked.

Alex dared a glance at her. "I disfigured him. Not intentionally of course, but my sword etched a thick scar upon his face and neck." He drew a line across his own face, indicating the extent of the wound while shame soured in his belly. "Last I heard, he'd become addicted to laudanum, and he suffers daily from severe melancholy."

A wisp of Rose's hair blew across her cheek. Though she uttered not a word, the air between them billowed with her disapproval.

"After the incident, my father ushered me back to the navy in the middle of the night with the admonition that I was no longer welcome at the Reed estate. He said I was worthless, not his son. I returned to my ship a different man, Miss McGuire." Alex ran a hand through his hair and gazed at the family of ducks. "I am determined to restore the honor I stole from my family, gain their forgiveness, and perhaps earn the right to return home."

Alex swallowed the burning in his throat and drew a deep breath of fresh air, hoping to clear away the memories. He reluctantly faced Rose, expecting to see disapproval in her eyes—pity. But what he saw instead made him want to take her in his arms, deny his country, his heritage, and stay with her forever. Instead, he clenched his fists and took a step back. No. He had promised himself that he would never again make a decision based on flighty emotions. He had learned the hard way that silly sentiments befuddled his mind and led him down a path to destruction. He must always rely on his mind and his good sense. And at the moment both were warning him to run as far away from this precious lady as possible.

❖

Pain darkened Mr. Reed's features, and Rose's heart grew heavy. She wanted to embrace him, to tell him that, despite his youthful indiscretions, he was the most honorable, capable, kind man she'd ever met. Not until this moment did she realize that not everyone had fathers like the wonderful one she had experienced. "Thank you for sharing such intimacies with me, Mr. Reed." Rose knew it had not been easy to tell her of his shame. "And I no longer believe all British are evil." She waited until he met her gaze. "Knowing you has convinced me otherwise."

At first shock skittered across his eyes, then sorrow, before he lowered his chin.

A gentle breeze swirled around them, tossing Mr. Reed's loose hair and cooling the perspiration on Rose's neck. "You are not worthless, Mr. Reed. I hope you know that now."

"Perhaps, perhaps not." The lines on his brow deepened. "I'm not sure what I know anymore."

At the risk of losing her own heart, Rose stepped toward him. Instead of a commanding naval officer, he seemed more like a lost, little boy. "I'm sorry for what happened to your brother, but he is the one who challenged you. You can hardly blame yourself."

He grimaced. "I could have run away and not met him that morning."

"Perhaps." Rose brushed a curl from her face. "We all make mistakes when we are young and impetuous." She cringed as memories of her own stupidity rose to taunt her. "My uncle says that God forgives all our sins if we are truly repentant."

Alex snorted. "Ruining someone's life is unforgivable, especially when that someone is your brother."

"Your brother was left scarred. He did not lose a leg or an arm or receive some other debilitating injury. It seems to me that his own vanity ruined his life, not you."

Alex flinched but then a smile broke upon his lips.

Rose blinked. "Why are you grinning at me?"

"Do you never fail to speak what is on your mind?"

"Why should I?"

His hazel eyes shifted between hers. "You have me quite befuddled, Miss McGuire." He lifted his hand and caressed her cheek as if her skin were made of porcelain and he feared to break her.

Rose's heart fluttered wildly. Tossing her reservations aside, she leaned into his hand and closed her eyes, imagining what it would be like to be loved by such a man. He rubbed his thumb over her cheek and released a sigh, his hot breath filling the air between them.

A soft moan escaped Rose's lips as her dreams took a turn into possibility.

But he had said he wanted to restore his family honor and make his father proud. Rose was but a common farm girl. An enemy. She would only bring him shame and worse—further rejection from his family.

Opening her eyes, she stepped away and turned her back to him.

They had no future together.

"Good-bye, Mr. Reed. I insist you leave tonight. Go back to your ship and leave me and my family alone. You don't belong here. I don't want you here." Then grabbing her skirts, she marched away before he saw the tears spilling down her cheeks.

❖

Alex kicked a boot full of hay into the air and took up a pace across the dirt floor of his servant's quarters. More like a horse's stall for all its comforts. Then again, the workers in his father's house had far better sleeping quarters than what he'd seen of the Drummond family's chambers. He huffed. It was not the dirt floor or hay-stuffed mattress or the meager furnishings that caused Alex's stomach to fold in on itself. No, it was the look of ardor burning in Rose's crisp blue eyes earlier that day and the way she'd leaned into his caress and moaned softly.

As if she cared for him.

As if her affections for him went beyond mere friendship. Even the anger in her voice as she stormed away and told him she didn't want him to stay, bespoke of opposite feelings within.

Alex reached the log wall and spun about. He passed by the lantern flickering on the table and glanced out the window to see only darkness beyond.

He should be gone already.

As soon as he and Mr. Drummond had returned, Alex had begged off from supper and any additional duties with an excuse of utter exhaustion. The elderly man had not questioned the statement, but he had gripped Alex's shoulders in a hearty embrace and thanked him for his toil. And something else. . .he had said he would pray for Alex.

Too tired to ask why and unsure he wished to hear the answer, Alex had simply nodded and walked off—away from the rustic American preacher who used to be a thief—and the man who had been more of a father to Alex these past few weeks than his own had been in the many years he'd lived at home.

Intending to grab his sack and sword and slip out into the night, Alex, instead, found himself an hour later clearing a trail of pounded dirt across the hay-strewn ground of his quarters. His gut contorted, his heart constricted, and he struggled to release each breath. He should leave. He must leave.

Yet the thought of going back to his ship and being forced to fight against these Americans, these people whom he'd come to admire—and some even love—caused bile to rise in his throat. He shook off a sudden chill that shuddered over him and scanned the room, seeking the source. Yet he found no holes in the walls nor open window or door that would allow a breeze to enter. The hot, humid air swamped back over him, and he ran his sleeve over his forehead and swerved around to trek across the room again.

If Rose returned his affections. If she could overcome his nationality, his heritage, then maybe. . .maybe Alex could become one of these backwoods Americans. And once accepted as such, his presence would no longer endanger this precious family.

He clenched his fists until his nails bit into his flesh. He was either a fool or completely mad for even entertaining such a thought.

Perhaps both.

He stopped pacing and fell into the chair beside the table. Leaning forward, he dropped his head into his hands and squeezed his eyes shut.

"What do you want, Alex?"

The whisper rang ominous and clear, and yet it came from nowhere. Alex lifted his head. Perhaps he had gone mad, indeed. But the question remained. What did he want? Honor, position, power, fortune like his father possessed? Was his father happy? Alex searched his memories and found no moment of joy in his childhood home, no smiles upon his parents' lips, no gentle touches or embraces. Then why, when he had been so miserable as a child, did he seek after the same things? Alex shook his head.

"I love you, son."

Tears burned behind Alex's eyes as the silent words drifted over him. *Son.* Such an endearing yet powerful term, implying an affection and a bond that could never be broken. He remembered what Mr. Drummond had said about how God spoke to him—from deep within him.

Exactly where this voice seemed to originate.

Alex's breath halted in his throat. "God?" he spoke into the still air, then felt foolish and lowered his chin. Why would God bother with him? Yet hadn't God answered his prayer last night asking for the chance to speak to Mr. Drummond?

A cold chill enveloped Alex, jarring his senses. No, nothing but a coincidence. Yet hope sparked a tiny flame within him that God would actually speak to him. That he *did* care for Alex like a father cared for a son.

"Lord, if You are listening, tell me what to do. If I stay, I'll lose everything I've ever worked for and bring further disgrace to my family. If I go. . ." Alex hesitated.

"You'll lose all that I have to offer you."

Offer me? God had something for him? Alex stood and took up a pace again to settle his nerves. His mind played tricks on him. The voice surely rose from his scrambled imaginings. He threw back his shoulders, wincing at the ache that stretched across them like a tightrope. The pain of his sore muscles seemed to jar him back to reality. Back to the honor and duty of a British naval officer and the son of a viscount. He had to leave, and he had to do it now or he feared he never would.

❖ CHAPTER 18 ❖

Rose scratched Liverpool behind the ears, eliciting an affectionate moo from the cow then moved to Valor's stall. The horse lifted her head over the railing. One large brown eye assessed Rose as she approached—an eye so full of sorrow and compassion it nearly crumbled the wall of tears behind Rose's eyes.

"Oh Valor." She leaned her cheek against the horse's face, inhaling the musky, sweet scent of horseflesh. "I can always rely on you. You'll never leave me, will you?"

Valor blew out a snort in response and stomped her hoof.

Though Rose had snuffed her candle and crawled early into bed nearly an hour ago, slumber had escaped her.

Just like Mr. Reed. He was no doubt on his way back to his ship by now. *Lord, keep him safe.*

Rose kissed Valor and took up a pace across the hay-strewn ground. It was better that he left. Better for them both. Better for their countries. Then why did she feel as though her heart would dissolve beneath the pain? She swerved around and headed the other way. "Oh Lord, of all the men in the world, why did You allow me to fall in love with a British officer?" Tears escaped the corners of her eyes and spilled onto her cheeks. She didn't understand God's reasoning. But then again, she didn't understand why God had allowed any of the tragedies in her life.

The light thud of a footfall jarred her heart into a frenzied beat.

Memories of Lieutenant Garrick's attack bombarded her. She swerved toward the open door.

Mr. Reed stood at the entrance to the barn—an apparition of her grieved mind. A gust of wind tousled a strand of his hair that had broken free from its tie. Still donned in the stained livery of a footman, his white shirt stretched across his thick chest like a milky band in the moonlight.

She rubbed her eyes and took a step back.

He held up a hand. "It's only me, Miss McGuire." His deep voice sent her heart into a different kind of frenzy.

Rose swallowed. Every inch of her wanted to throw herself into his arms. A seed of hope began to sprout within her that perhaps he wouldn't leave at all. Perhaps he had come to tell her he intended to switch sides, to become an American. "What do you want?"

"Forgive me. I. . .I. . ." He shifted uncomfortably. "I didn't mean to intrude. I was looking for my uniform and sword."

"I gave them to you."

He blinked as a puzzled look tightened his features. "I hid them under my bed, but when I went to retrieve them, I found them gone. I thought. . . . I thought. . . ."

"You thought I took them? Why would I when I want you to leave?" The lie made her cringe. His statement dried up her hope. A breeze blew through the barn, bringing a chill with it. She hugged herself.

His puzzlement turned to concern as he approached her. "You've been crying." The timbre of his British accent eased through her like warm tea on a winter's night.

Rose looked away. Sorrow constricted her chest.

Touching her chin with his finger, he moved her gaze back to his. Lantern light angled over his sharp jaw and flickered in his hazel eyes now brimming with affection. "Rose, surely you are aware of my feelings for you."

Rose's breath halted in her throat.

"The pain of never seeing you again overwhelms me." His warm hands enveloped hers and he looked down.

Rose's breath returned and gusted out of her mouth. A sob emerged behind it.

Which he must have taken as shock, or worse, disapproval. "My apologies for being so bold." He gazed down at their hands and released his grip. "But situation and time deny me the luxury of proper etiquette."

Rose finally found her voice. "Why do you tell me this when you are leaving?"

"Because I want you to know. I want you to remember me. To know that you affected me deeply—changed me."

Hope sparked in Rose's heart. "Then why not stay? Become an American."

He shook his head and stared at the ground. Dark strands of hair hung around his face, hiding his expression.

A tear slid down her cheek. He looked up.

"I've made you cry." He started to turn away, but Rose grabbed his hand. His warm fingers wrapped around hers as if he'd never let go. "You are the first man I've allowed to touch me—the first man I've felt safe with in years."

"That pleases me more than I can say." He gathered both her hands in his once again. His manly smell surrounded her like a shield. A look of complete and unfettered concern beamed from his eyes. "Rose, tell me what happened to you."

❖

Alex watched as Rose turned and made her way to the barn door, leaning against its frame. He followed her. A breeze swirled around them, fluttering the hem of her gown and dancing among the golden curls that hung to her waist. Moonlight encased her in a protective glow as if she were too beautiful, too pure to touch.

"Remember when I told you about the so-called friend of my father's who took me in after my mother died and made me a servant?" Her voice quavered.

Alex nodded.

"I didn't tell you everything that happened to me after I ran away from him." She shifted her gaze away.

"You bartered passage aboard a merchant ship, if memory serves me."

She swallowed hard and opened and closed her mouth several times as if trying to say something.

"There is no need to tell me."

Blue eyes shot to his, cold with pain. "I want to. I want you to know."

She turned away from him and gazed out upon the farm. "At first the captain and crew were kind to me. They gave me my own quarters and fed me well."

The muscles in Alex's chest tightened. The tone of her voice, the defeated pain, said it all. Somehow he knew what was coming, and he didn't want to hear it. Didn't want to know that anyone had hurt this precious lady.

"But one night, two sailors crept into my cabin. One of them assaulted me—" Her voice cracked.

Blood pulsed hot in Alex's veins.

"During the struggle, I grabbed the pistol of the man attacking me. And I shot him." Her delicate jaw grew taut. "The captain burst into the room before the other man could react. But he was too late. The sailor was dead and I was. . ."

Alex stepped toward her.

She shuffled away. "The captain put me ashore, stating he wanted no more trouble aboard his ship."

The anguish in her tone sent a lance through Alex's heart.

"I traveled on foot, keeping to the trees that lined the coach trails, not daring to trust anyone again. Finally, two weeks later, I arrived at my aunt and uncle's house in town, starved and beaten." Drawing in a deep breath, she faced him, her features tight and a distant look in her eyes.

Alex tightened his jaw. Her sad tale had not surprised him. He had suspected as much. But now that he knew for sure, he could understand why she was frightened of everything. Why she feared even going into town. What this poor girl had endured at so young an age—just seventeen. It took all his strength to contain the rage bubbling up inside him at the sailors who had accosted Rose. But his anger would do her no good right now. Now, she needed understanding. She needed love and acceptance.

Her shoulders began to quiver beneath a sob. "I killed a man." She shook her head. "And the worst of it is I'm not sorry for it."

Alex reached out for her, but she backed away.

"I'm a murderer," she said. "The Bible says 'thou shalt not kill.'"

"I'm told by a very reliable source that God forgives." Alex grinned, hoping to lighten her mood.

"Does He forgive when I'm not sorry?"

Alex had no idea. He suddenly wished for Mr. Drummond's wise counsel, anything to help ease Rose's torment. "Is that why you abhor guns?"

"Yes." She tilted her head upward, allowing the moonlight to soften the hard lines of anguish. "What that sailor did to me was done. I am defiled. But because of that pistol, I now live with the guilt of his murder."

"You were defending yourself. No more than I or any military man does in war." Slipping in front of her, Alex took her in his arms. After a second, her stiff body relaxed, and she began to sob. He kissed her forehead and caressed the back of her head. He continued to stroke her hair and allowed her to cry even as fury tore through him. What he wouldn't give to find the remaining sailor and bring him to justice.

When her sobs were spent, Alex drew away from her and cupped her face in his hands, forcing her to look at him. Her red nose and tear-streaked cheeks glistened in the moonlight. "You are not defiled to me. You are the most precious thing I have ever encountered." He eased a lock of her hair from her face. "I truly do adore you."

"Then stay with me." The look of pleading in her moist eyes threatened to crack his resolve. No, to blast it into fragments. But what of his country, his family honor, his brother, his recompense? Would he be making another rash decision based on the passion of the moment that would only cause him further pain? Yet now as her lips parted and her eyes lovingly caressed his face, all those things seemed to drift away in the night breeze.

He lowered his mouth to hers.

❖

Rose closed her eyes and felt Alex's lips touch hers. Moist and warm. Pressing her against him, he planted soft kisses over her mouth. His body stiffened and warmed. His kiss deepened. A surge of heat flooded her, swirling in her belly and sending pinpricks over her skin. She melted into his arms and lost herself in his scent, the feel of him, the taste of him. Her mind careened into an abyss of pleasure and love—a place she never wanted to leave.

An evening breeze wafted over them, bringing with it the scent of summer hyacinth. Silver light surrounded them. Leaves fluttered on trees as though they were laughing with delight. Rose never wanted this moment to end.

He withdrew and caressed her cheek with his fingers.

Rose was afraid to open her eyes. "I'm dreaming."

"After that kiss, I assure you, you are not." His voice was deep and sensuous.

Rose fell into him, and he swallowed her up in his arms.

"So this is the way of things?" a voice dripping in spite shouted from the darkness.

Jerking back from Alex, Rose spun to see Mr. Snyder approaching the barn, one hand on his cane, the other fisted at his waist.

"What are you doing here?" Rose's mind reeled at the interruption.

Alex groaned. Valor neighed and retreated into her stall as if the sight of the councilman sickened her.

"The question should be, what are you doing, Miss McGuire, compromising yourself with a family servant? Beyond unscrupulous." He huffed and jutted out his chin.

Alex moved in front of Rose, easing her behind him as the councilman entered the barn. "One more insult to Miss McGuire, and I shall demand satisfaction."

The spark of confidence in Mr. Snyder's eyes did not fade beneath Alex's threat, and that alone sent a sliver of dread down Rose's back.

"Fraternizing with the enemy, my dear?" Mr. Snyder twirled his cane in the air and moved toward Alex, a malicious smirk on his thin lips.

Rose's heart stopped beating, or so it seemed. The barn began to spin.

"Whatever are you babbling about, Mr. Snyder?" Alex's tone remained confident and demanding, but she could tell from the way he fisted his hands at his waist that Mr. Snyder's words had struck their mark.

The smile fell from Snyder's lips, and a hateful frown took its place. "I'm talking about your being a British naval officer, Mr. Reed."

Rose's legs nearly gave out, and she stumbled. Alex turned just in time to catch her before she fell. Wrapping an arm around her waist, he drew her to his side.

"Now isn't that sweet?" Snyder planted the tip of his cane in the dirt and leaned both hands upon it.

"You're mad, Snyder," Alex spat. "Where is your proof?"

One cultured brow lifted. "I have in my possession a certain service sword."

Rose felt a tremble jolt through Alex.

"I see from your stunned expression that you know the sword. It has an engraving, I believe." He tapped his chin. "Let me see if I can recall it. Ah, yes. Alexander M. Reed, HMS *Undefeatable*." He grinned like a cougar about to devour his prey. "An award perhaps for some courageous action?"

Rose gasped, and Alex tightened his grip around her waist. She glared at Snyder, surprised by the hatred burning in her soul for this man. "What are you going to do?" she asked.

He puckered his slimy lips and widened his eyes. "Well, nothing actually." Then he grinned. "As long as you both do what I say." Despite his assured stance, a bead of sweat forged a trail down his cheek.

"Pray tell, what is that?" Defeat and sorrow deepened Alex's tone.

"It's quite simple really. You, Mr. Reed, will scurry back to your ship or wherever you came from." He gestured with his hands as one would usher a mouse to a hole. "And you, Miss McGuire, will agree to marry me."

Nausea leaped into Rose's throat. The air thinned around her.

Rose felt Alex's body stiffen, heard the grunt of disbelief at the man's nerve.

"No doubt you know what will happen if you do not comply," Snyder pushed. "If I turn you in to authorities. . ." The rat paused for effect. "Miss McGuire and her family will be arrested for harboring the enemy." Then he waited, a malicious smirk on his face. Rose wanted to wipe it off, wanted to tell him to take a flying leap.

Finally Alex sighed. "I'll go back to my ship, Snyder, but leave Miss McGuire and her family out of this. They've done no wrong."

"Perhaps." Snyder sauntered toward Liverpool. The cow swung her head over the stall and snorted at him, halting him in his tracks. He wrinkled his nose, then turned to face them.

"Not very smart, are you, Mr. Reed?" Snyder cocked his head. "I'll still have your sword. And unless you have forgotten your unfortunate meeting with General Smith in town,"—he grinned—"ah, yes, I know about that. Well, let's just say, I'm sure he'll remember you were employed as the Drummond servant."

"We will deny that we knew his true identity." Though she tried to sound authoritative, Rose's voice cracked.

"No one will believe you, my sweet Rose." Snyder's lips slanted. "Not with the evidence I have gathered from Mr. Reed's quarters, and the fact that the British were seen on your property the night Mr. Reed suddenly appeared. Egad, the man's own regal accent betrays him."

Rose's legs trembled. He was right. General Smith was no fool.

Mr. Snyder brushed a speck of dirt from his coat, and Rose thought she saw a flicker of pain cross his face. "I am not a cruel man. I had hoped my fears of a dalliance between you and Mr. Reed were but a figment of my overimaginative mind. If so, there would be no need to resort to such measures."

The spark of hope that had ignited within her earlier, now extinguished, leaving her soul empty and dark.

Alex shifted his stance. "And if the lady refuses to marry you?"

"That would be most unwise." Snyder pointed his cane at them and chuckled. "For I can assure you that Miss McGuire and her aunt, uncle, most likely her maid and cook too will be tried for treason and executed."

❖ CHAPTER 19 ❖

Alex stormed into the servants' quarters. The wooden door slammed against the wall, raining dust upon him from the rafters. Fury blazed a hot trail down Alex's back, legs, arms, until he felt he would burst unless he struck something—or someone. He lifted a boot to the lone table and kicked it. It flew through the air and crashed against the far wall then fell, in shatters, onto the dirt floor.

Alex heard Rose's soft footsteps enter behind him. He ran a hand through his hair, tearing strands from his queue, and tried to collect his rage. But no sooner had his anger dwindled than an overwhelming sorrow threatened to crush him. He shook it off. Anger was better. It kept him focused, determined. It kept him from sinking into despair.

But a sob filtering from behind him proved to be his undoing. He turned around. Moonlight cast Rose's dark silhouette in a silver aura. He opened his arms, and she dashed toward him. The soft curves of her body melded against his chest, and he tightened his arms around her as if doing so would always keep her with him, always by his side. He stroked her hair. She trembled beneath another sob. Releasing her, he cupped her face and lifted her gaze to his. Tears streamed down her cheeks. He wiped them gently with his thumb.

"What are we to do, Alex?" Her face was etched in sorrow.

He hated to see her in such pain. Hated to feel it himself. Hated to be the cause of it. To the devil with Mr. Snyder! Alex had met scoundrels in his life. Many in fact during his time in His Majesty's Navy. One of them, Garrick, lay in a shallow grave not too far from where they stood. But the councilman surpassed them all.

He kissed Rose's forehead, then pressed her against him.

"I will die if I marry him," she cried.

Alex agreed for he felt as though he would die as well if she married that buffoon. Silently, he cursed himself for his selfishness, for staying too long, endangering this family and this precious woman.

Alex pushed away from her. Tears pooled on her lashes, and a red hue colored her nose and cheeks. Golden curls tumbled over her shoulders like spun silk. He took her hands in his. "I will not allow that to happen." Releasing her, he took up a pace across the room, not wanting her to see the moisture filling his eyes, not wanting her to see his inner conflict that surely must be evident on his face.

A sob moaned in her throat. "You could stay, switch sides, then it wouldn't matter that Snyder has your sword?"

"I can't." Alex halted and gazed at the dirt. He couldn't let his family down yet again. Couldn't make another bad decision based on foolish sentiments.

"So you would have me marry that fiend?"

"No." The thought made Alex's stomach churn and brought a sour taste to his mouth. "I will not allow that to happen."

"I don't see how you can prevent it." She turned her back to him and her shoulders lowered.

"Trust me, Rose." Alex reached up to touch her but thought better of it. Truth be told, a plan had formed in his mind even before Mr. Snyder had galloped away.

When she faced him again, her face was dry, and her eyes held the distant look of surrender. She had accepted her fate. He knew she would eventually. He knew because she was wise and strong—not a woman given to flighty, romantic notions. It was one of the things he loved about her. And a quality he wished he possessed more of, for at this moment, if she would but beg him to stay one more time, he doubted he could resist her.

"I shall pray for you, Alex. I'll pray that you can someday return to your home in England." Her voice threatened to crack.

"And I shall pray the same for you as well." He stepped toward her and fingered a strand of silky hair. "I will never forget you, Rose."

He studied her creamy face, memorizing every detail, the tiny wrinkle on her forehead that told him she was upset, her thin brown eyebrows drawn together in a frown, her high cheeks flushed with emotion, her moist lips. One last kiss. Could he steal one last kiss? He lowered his lips to hers. They tasted of tears and trembled at his touch.

Before she tore away from him and fled into the night.

Alex dashed to the door. Rose's white skirts billowed in the breeze and seemed to be floating over the ground like an angel as she receded into the darkness.

Then she was gone.

He rubbed his burning eyes. The sooner he left the better. He searched the room for his belongings and remembered Mr. Snyder had stolen them all. He had nothing but the clothes on his back. And those weren't even his. Blowing out the lantern, he stood at the door and took one last look at the room that had been his private chamber this past week. No four-poster oak bed topped with a silk embroidered coverlet, no mahogany writing desk, or rich velvet curtains, no Persian rug or marble-framed fireplace, but this small dirty room had brought him far more comfort than his elegant bedchamber at home. He closed the door, passed the house— forcing himself not to look at it—then headed toward the dirt road.

Anger simmered within him until it seared his vision and branded his thoughts with purpose. A dark cloud drifted over the moon, stealing the light and casting the dirt road into even deeper shadows. No matter. Alex knew where he was going. Well, almost.

Mr. Snyder may think he has the upper hand in this dangerous game, but Alex would be a pirate's lackey before he'd allow that snake to marry Rose. A hint of a plan had taken root in his mind even before the slimy toad had finished his threats. It was the exact carrying out of that plan that eluded Alex at the moment.

Despite his promise to himself, he cast one last glance over his shoulder at the Drummond home. Golden light cascaded from the windows, beckoning him back to the only place that had ever felt like home—to the people he'd grown to love. A shadow crossed the upstairs casement. Rose? He swallowed and fisted his hands.

"Good-bye, my love," he whispered into the wind.

The clomp of horse's hooves drew him about to see a lone rider heading his way. Before he had a chance to even consider where he could hide, the man closed in on him, Alex recognized the familiar form of Mr. Drummond. The older man pulled his horse to a stop and peered down at Alex.

"Is that you, Mr. Reed?"

"Yes sir."

"Sink me, what are you doing out here in the dark?" His horse pranced over the dirt. "Hop on and I'll give you a ride back home."

Home. "I can't go back, Mr. Drummond. Ever." He owed this man the truth and welcomed the opportunity to thank him for his kindness.

The old man gave him a curious look, then flipped his leg over the saddle and slipped from the horse with more agility than Alex would have expected. "What's that you say? Of course you can go back."

Alex shook his head, squinting to see the man's face in the darkness. A face that had always brought comfort to Alex. But the shadows forbade him a view. "Mr. Drummond, you have been very kind to me, and I thank you for taking me into your home and into your employ. And for gracing me with your friendship."

"What happened, son?" Mr. Drummond's voice grew solemn.

Alex shifted his stance, unsure of how much to disclose. "Let's just say that if I stay, I will endanger your entire family."

"I'd say you've had quite the opposite effect, particularly on Rose." The dark cloud slipped aside, allowing the moon's light to seek out Mr. Drummond and bathe him in its creamy glow.

"Believe me, sir, for your own safety and for Rose's, I must leave." Alex bowed his head and avoided looking into Mr. Drummond's brown, caring eyes. "Please extend my thanks and appreciation to your wife." He turned to leave.

Mr. Drummond grabbed his arm. "Has this anything to do with you being a British naval officer?"

A sudden breeze stole the words away before Alex's mind could grasp them. He blinked and scratched his head. "You knew?"

"Aye." Mr. Drummond chuckled.

Alex would have laughed if he weren't so filled with sorrow. This man he'd once considered to be nothing but a bumbling fool turned out wiser than them all. "How?"

"Ah, shame on me, Mr. Reed, if I don't know what's happening beneath my own roof."

"Why didn't you have me arrested? Or at least tossed out of your house?"

Mr. Drummond folded his hands over his prominent belly. "You are good for Rose. I've never seen her so happy."

The reminder opened a fresh wound on Alex's heart. "But I am her enemy—your enemy."

"Your country, yes. But not you, Mr. Reed. I count myself a good judge of character, and I could tell the first time I met you that you are an honorable man with a kind heart." He sighed and rubbed the back of his neck. "I don't much care for this war, Mr. Reed. But I also don't judge a man by color, status, money, or nationality." He tapped a finger on Alex's chest. "God judges by the heart, and I try to do that as well."

The man's words defied everything Alex had been taught his entire life. He stared at the man in wonder. "I am all astonishment, sir."

Mr. Drummond grinned. "Besides, God told me you and Rose are a good match."

"I wish that were true." Alex winced beneath another jab to his heart.

"Why not stay and find out?"

"Upon my honor, I cannot, sir. I have obligations in England to attend to. But, I fear my identity has been discovered and your family threatened."

"Mr. Snyder, eh?"

Again the man amazed Alex. "He has my service sword with my name engraved upon it."

Mr. Drummond groaned.

"He threatened to turn in your family as traitors. He forces Rose to marry him," Alex snapped, his anger rising once again.

"Well, we can't let that happen, can we?"

Alex shook his head at the man's confident tone. "She will do it to save you and your wife from the traitor's noose."

The elderly man scratched his bearded jaw. Anticipation rose as Alex waited, hoping he would offer an alternative plan. But no wise answer spilled from his lips.

Alex released a heavy sigh and gazed into the dark forest lining the path. Why torture himself? There *was* no other alternative. Yet even as his thoughts took a dive into despair, the idea planted earlier in his mind sprouted a promising leaf. "Are you acquainted with a Mr. Noah Brenin?"

"That I am."

"Would you do me the kindness of showing me where he lives?"

Mr. Drummond's eyes twinkled. "Would I be correct in perceiving, Mr. Reed, that you've got some trickery up your sleeve?"

"Aye, that I do, sir, a plan that will keep Rose from being forced to marry that callow nodcock."

"God always finds a way, Mr. Reed." Mr. Drummond grabbed his horse's reins, clipped a buckled shoe into the stirrup, and swung onto her back. "Hop on, Mr. Reed. I'll take you to Mr. Brenin myself."

❖

Alex followed Mr. Drummond up the porch stairs of a modest two-story home, capped with a hipped roof. Golden light, along with a child's laughter and a discordant melody streamed through the open green shudders, barely glazing the tips of a multitude of flowers that must have been brilliant in the daylight.

Mr. Drummond knocked on the door. Each rap tightened the band around Alex's nerves. Was he mad? Asking help of man he had impressed and enslaved aboard his ship? If Mr. Drummond had not insisted he join Alex on his mission, Alex couldn't be sure that Noah wouldn't strike him across the jaw and have him arrested on the spot. How could he blame him?

Clearing his throat, Mr. Drummond rapped again as a light breeze laden with salt and fish blew in from the harbor only a mile away. Even at this distance, Alex could see the bare masts of a multitude of ships spear into the night like white, ghostly claws above waters churning with anxiety. A sense of unrest and dread settled over the city. Alex could feel it in the air, see it in the faces of those they passed. All due to his countrymen.

The door swung open to a tall, sallow-skinned man whose lips puckered as if he'd just drunk a mug of sour milk. Folds of skin fell over a lavender neckcloth that appeared far too tight but held the only color in an otherwise drab black suit.

"Mr. Drummond and Mr. Reed to see Mr. Brenin, if you please." Mr. Drummond brushed past the man without an invitation, and the butler's face soured even further.

"Wait here." He walked down the hall and entered a parlor on their left, where open double doors flooded the otherwise dim hallway with light and gaiety.

Moments later, the laughter and music fell silent, and the grim man returned. "Follow me."

When Alex stepped into the room, the joyous sparkle in the eyes of those present faded as each gaze latched upon him. Marianne, Noah's wife, who sat at the pianoforte, leaped to her feet and covered her mouth with her hand. A glass slipped from Noah's grip and shattered on the floor, spraying the contents over the wooden planks. A child let out a startled cry, and an elderly woman took the baby in her arms and rose from a floral-printed settee, her worried gaze shifting from Alex to Noah.

Noah stepped over the broken glass, his face tight and his skin flushed. "What are you doing here, Reed?"

Mr. Drummond's gray eyebrows arched at Alex. "I wasn't aware you were acquainted with the Brenins."

Alex cleared his throat. He hadn't wanted to tell Mr. Drummond for fear he wouldn't bring him to their home. "Yes, they had the misfortune of being impressed on my ship."

"Then you know who this man is?" Noah proceeded toward a cabinet against the far wall, flung it open and grabbed a pistol.

"Indeed I do." Mr. Drummond said. "But before you go shooting him, he is here as a friend to Rose, not an enemy."

"A friend to. . ." Noah spun around, pistol in hand.

Marianne stepped out from the pianoforte. "Then we did see you in town the other day?"

Alex nodded in her direction. "Good evening, Miss Denton. I mean Mrs. Brenin, the last time I saw you you were hanging off the stern of my ship."

"Indeed." Marianne said with a slight smile.

Noah methodically poured gun powder into the barrel, then rammed the bullet inside with a ramrod. "Mr. Drummond, surely you know that bringing him here endangers my entire family."

The elderly woman gasped, stumbled and lowered herself and the child back onto the settee.

Mr. Drummond scratched his beard. "That will not happen, I assure you. We only need a moment of your time. Please I beg of you to trust me. Rose's future is at stake."

Noah cocked the gun with an ominous click then pointed it at Alex. Though his insides began to clench, Alex forced a stoic look upon his face. Surely the man wouldn't shoot him here in front of his family?

Marianne wove around the shattered glass and slid beside her husband. "Mr. Reed was always kind to us, Noah. Hear him out, for Rose's sake."

The young boy, who could be no more than one grabbed a wooden doll from the elderly woman's hand and stuffed the arm in his mouth.

Mr. Drummond faced the woman on the settee. "Mrs. Denton, always a pleasure. You appear in fine health these days," he said as if there weren't a gun pointed at Alex.

"Indeed, Reverend Drummond." The woman, whom Alex assumed to be Marianne's mother, clutched the child tighter. Veins lined her thin, frail hands, yet her eyes were clear and her voice strong. "There is nothing like a grandchild to keep an old lady around past her time."

Lowering his pistol, Noah flattened his lips. "What is it you want?"

"May we speak to you alone, Noah?" Mr. Drummond asked. "It is a matter of grave importance."

Noah's eyes narrowed. He glanced at his wife who nodded her approval. "Very well." Still gripping the pistol, he led the men across the hall to another room, closing the doors behind them. Tobacco and wood smoke combined to form the masculine scent of a man's library. Bookshelves lined the right wall from floor to ceiling. A cold fireplace stood on Alex's left. Candle sconces hanging intermittently on the fore and aft walls sent flickering light across the sturdy wood furniture. A walnut desk guarded the far wall while various cushioned Windsor chairs were scattered throughout. Whitewashed walls decorated with oil paintings of ships and the sea sat above a wooden chair rail that circled the room like a ship's bulwark.

Placing his pistol atop his desk, Noah crossed his arms over his chest. "Now, what is this about?"

Mr. Drummond took a seat and deferred the question to Alex, who after taking a deep breath, spent the next few minutes explaining how he had come to be on the Drummond farm and the ultimatum Mr. Snyder had issued to him and Rose earlier in the evening.

Gripping the edge of his desk, Noah stared at the cross-stitched rug by his boots. "Egad man, what were you thinking staying with the Drummonds so long?"

Alex walked to the fireplace, placed his boot atop the marble hearth and gazed at dark coals. "I should have left as soon as I could walk. I intended to leave last night, but—"

"I enlisted his help to rebuild the Myers' house." Mr. Drummond coughed.

Noah glanced up. "You don't say? Unheard of. A British officer cleaning up the mess he made." Sarcasm stung in his voice.

Alex grimaced. "I felt obliged." Then he snapped his eyes to Mr. Drummond as the realization struck him. "As you knew I would."

Mr. Drummond shrugged. "I had to think of some way to keep you here."

"To keep him here?" Noah's face scrunched. "Are you daft, Reverend?"

"Perhaps." Mr. Drummond smiled and patted the pockets of his waistcoat as if searching for something. "He's good for Rose."

Alex turned his back to the mantel and crossed his arms over his chest. "In truth, I was having difficulty leaving anyway." Would he sound foolish if he shared his feelings for Rose with Noah?

Noah's blue eyes turned to ice. "I would think you'd be anxious to return to your ship and continue terrorizing innocent farmers."

Alex flinched beneath the blow. "If you must know, I have no desire to do either."

"Why not stay, become an American?" Noah asked. "Then Snyder's threats would be empty."

Alex hung his head. Oh how he wanted to. With everything in him. But he couldn't. Hadn't he already made enough mistakes by following the leading of his heart? "I can't."

Noah snorted.

Mr. Drummond quit his unsuccessful search and stood. His gaze shifted between Alex and Noah, finally landing on Noah. "Mr. Reed only wishes to help Rose."

Moving to the fireplace, Noah eyed Alex. A wood-encased clock perched upon the mantel marked Alex's future with an eerie *tick-tock, tick-tock*. "You love her?"

Alex said nothing.

"Yet you'll leave her." Noah's voice spiked with disdain. "For what? Title, fortune? Ah, don't want to step down off your British pedestal, become a common American, eh?"

Alex met his gaze. "That's not the reason."

Mr. Drummond stepped toward Noah. "Will you help us, Mr. Brenin?"

"What else can you do now but leave?" Noah said. "Haven't you done enough damage?"

Alex shook his head. "I can't. Not until I make things right. Not until I fix it so Rose will not be forced to marry that insolent ninny on my account."

"I don't see how you can prevent it." Noah huffed.

Alex lengthened his stance, feeling his resolve strengthen." He leaned toward Noah. "I have a plan, but I need your help."

Noah lifted one brow. "A plan?"

"Yes. To break into Snyder's home and steal back my sword."

❖ CHAPTER 20 ❖

Rose pried open her swollen eyelids to see nothing but the scratchy underside of her quilt. Sunlight filtering through the fabric twisted the threads into chaotic patterns. She traced them with her eyes until dizziness overtook her. From the top, the quilt's multicolored strands formed a beautiful pattern. But underneath they appeared disorderly and without purpose—just like her life. Birds outside her window chirped a traitorous, joyful melody. How could any creature be happy when Rose was steeped in such overwhelming sorrow?

Alex was gone.

Forever.

Why hadn't the world stopped spinning? Why did the sun keep rising? Something besides her broken heart should mark the passage of such an honorable man.

Her chamber door squeaked open. "Rose, dear." Aunt Muira's tone sounded heavy, muffled. Smells of fresh biscuits and coffee from downstairs penetrated Rose's quilt and caused her stomach to rumble. She pressed a hand to her belly—as traitorous as the birds and the sun.

"Rose, dear." Her aunt repeated as she sat on one side of the mattress. "I know you're under there."

"I don't feel well." Rose squeaked out, her nose curling at her own sour breath.

The quilt slipped from her face, and Rose squeezed her eyes against the bright light.

She felt her aunt's hand on her face, her neck. "You've been in bed for two days now, dear." She sighed. "You have no fever, and I can find nothing at all wrong with you."

Rose opened her eyes and blinked at the fuzzy image until her aunt's comely visage came into focus. *Nothing wrong with her?* If only her aunt knew. Rose had the worst kind of sickness. One that would never heal.

Aunt Muira brushed tangled curls from Rose's face. "Tell me what is bothering you, dear." A ray of sunlight caught one of her pearl earrings and set it aglow.

Rose swallowed. Her mouth felt as though it were stuffed with hay. "May I sleep a bit more, Aunt Muira? I'm so tired."

Her aunt's lips tightened into a thin line, and she sprang from the bed. "Absolutely not. I insist you join us for breakfast. You didn't eat all day yesterday." She swung around and the folds of her lilac gown swirled in the air making a swooshing sound. Gathering undergarments from Rose's dresser and a gown of lavender muslin from her armoire, she laid them across the foot of the bed. "Some food and fresh air will do you good." She planted her hands on her hips. "Perhaps then you will tell me what ails you." She gave Rose a sweet but determined smile before she swept from the room and closed the door behind her.

With a groan, Rose sat and punched her mattress, sending a spray of dust sparkling in the sunlight. Dizziness threatened to send her back onto her pillow. She drew a deep breath and swung her legs over the side of the bed. She had no choice. Sooner or later she had to get up and face life, no matter how empty her future seemed. Today was as good as any.

Minutes later, she entered the kitchen to find Amelia, her aunt, and Cora sitting around a table laden with platters of biscuits, fresh jam, eggs, and blocks of yellow cheese. A plethora of fragrant smells—butter, sweet cream, spice, and coffee—sent Rose's stomach lurching. Sounding like one of Rose's chickens, Amelia babbled excitedly about the ball in three days at the Fountain Inn. Apparently, Mr. Braxton had finally asked Uncle Forbes if he could escort Amelia.

"There you are, dear." Aunt Muira said.

Amelia's eyebrows slanted together. "You look horrible, Rose."

Rose slid into the wooden seat beside her aunt as Cora poured her a cup of coffee.

"You shouldn't be sayin' such things, Miss Amelia. Your mistress's been ill." Cora set the tin pot down in the center of the table and moved to the open fireplace.

"She's not ill, Cora. Rose's just upset about. . ."

Rose's glare halted her maid in midsentence. Not only did she not want Cora and her aunt to know what had happened, she didn't want to hear *his* name out loud. Not yet.

"Thank you, Amelia, for caring for my animals while I was indisposed." Rose attempted to change the topic of conversation.

It didn't work.

"Upset about what?" Aunt Muira took a delicate bite of toast smothered in strawberry jam.

Taking the silver tongs, Rose plopped a cube of sugar into her coffee. Then another.

Aunt Muira's hand stopped her from plucking yet another one from the china bowl. "Careful, dear. Those are all we have until the war ends."

Setting down the tongs, Rose stirred her coffee and took a sip, hoping the savory liquid wouldn't rebel in her stomach. The rich flavor that reminded Rose of cocoa eased down her throat and helped settle her nerves. But it needed more sugar.

Cora returned from the fireplace and placed two pieces of toast before Rose.

"Thank you, Cora, but I fear I'm unable to eat anything."

"Of course you are, dear." Aunt Muira leaned over and spread butter and jam over Rose's toast before shoving the plate closer to her. "Now, do tell us what has you so distraught. I've never seen you keep to your bed for two days. Not since. . ."

Her voice trailed off, but Rose knew what she intended to say. Not since Rose had turned up on their doorstep starving and beaten five years ago.

Cora circled the table and laid one hand on her hip. "If you ask me, I'd say it has somethin' to do with Mr. Reed leavin'."

His name shot like an arrow through the room and pierced straight into Rose's heart.

"Wherever did he run off to, Rose?" Aunt Muira dabbed her napkin over her lips. "Forbes won't say a word except that Mr. Reed has gone back to join the war."

Amelia shared a quizzical glance with Rose.

Rose took another sip of coffee and warmed her hands around the cup. But her vision blurred with tears.

Cora tugged at her red scarf. Amelia set down the piece of cheese she'd been nibbling on. Aunt Muira's gaze flitted from Cora, to Amelia, to Rose. She placed a hand on Rose's back. "Oh dear, tell me your affections did not lean toward Mr. Reed."

The china cup cradled in Rose's trembling hands clattered on the saucer.

"Oh my." Aunt Muira laid a hand on her heart. "How could I have missed it? You poor dear. And now he's gone."

"I knows just how you feel, child." Cora sank into a chair and shook her head. "I felt like my heart would never recover after my Samuel left."

Amelia gave the cook a tender look. "Why did you allow him to leave?"

"I didn't *let* 'im go. He took off hisself."

"He left because you scolded him to death." Amelia offered.

"Now, now, Amelia, that isn't kind." Aunt Muira said.

"No, she's right." Cora sighed. "I didn't mean to. Just mad at the world, I guess." She fingered a folded white napkin. "If I had to do it all over again, I'd never let him go. I sees now it was my unforgiveness that drove him away."

Aunt Muira stretched her hand across the table to the cook. Cora gripped it briefly then released it as if she was uncomfortable with the display of affection from her mistress.

Amelia frowned. "But you weren't unforgiving of anything Samuel had done. How can that drive anyone away?"

Cora tossed down the napkin and stood. "Bitterness made me too afraid to love—to risk losin' that love." She gazed out the window. "An' now he's gone."

Unforgiveness and fear, yet again. Two topics that kept flashing across Rose's path like garish actors across a stage. Pushing out her chair, she stood, skirted the table and kissed Cora on her cheek. Cora's big brown eyes met Rose's, and she saw the brokenness in their depths.

"Must every woman in this house fall in love with our servants?" Aunt Muira's exasperated voice scattered the gloomy spirit that had descended upon the kitchen.

"Not me!" Amelia waved her hand through the air, sending her raven curls bouncing. "I intend to marry a man of fortune."

"Speaking of eligible men, Rose." Aunt Muira sipped her tea and set the cup down with a clank. She gave Rose one of those motherly smiles that said she knew what was best for Rose even if Rose did not. "I've invited Mr. Snyder to supper tonight. Perhaps he can pull you out of your dour mood and make you forget all about Mr. Reed."

❖

A nauseous brew of disgust and agony churned in Rose's stomach, threatening to erupt with fury on the odious snake of a man sitting across from her. Maybe then he would leave and stop smiling at her with that salacious grin of victory. Dinner had been unbearable, but now sitting in the stuffy parlor with him might prove to be her undoing. At least she was not alone. Amelia sat next to her on the settee, sipping her tea, while Rose's aunt and uncle sat side by side on the sofa. Mr. Snyder occupied the high-backed chair and pretended to listen to her uncle's discourse on the war.

"I hear word of British ship movements along the coast of the upper Chesapeake," her uncle was saying.

Mr. Snyder set his cup on the table and adjusted his silk cravat. "No doubt more idle threats intending to frighten us into submission." Candlelight reflected devilish flames in Mr. Snyder's eyes.

"I beg to differ with you, Mr. Snyder," her uncle said in a tone that lacked its normal solicitude. In fact, her uncle had seemed unusually ill at ease during their evening meal, making curt remarks toward their guest and offering up a chorus of groans and sighs, mimicking the silent ones grinding through Rose.

Aunt Muira had attempted to make up for his behavior by engaging Mr. Snyder in a discussion of the city militia's readiness to fight and the council's recent decision to keep pigs from running rampant through the city streets.

Which gave Mr. Snyder the center stage he so often sought and relished in. But which had further squelched Rose's appetite for the broiled cod, potatoes, and fresh greens that stared up at her from her plate, uneaten.

"Our lookouts have spotted a new British fleet, commanded, some say, by Sir Alexander Cochrane," Uncle Forbes continued. "A formidable force of four ships of the line, twenty frigates and sloops, and twenty troop transports." He stretched his shoulders and leaned back on the sofa. "Since the British have already successfully blockaded the Chesapeake, it worries me."

"Yes." Rose's aunt folded her hands in her lap and swept green eyes filled with concern over them all. "It would seem the defeat of Napoleon in France has emboldened the British to pursue victory here as soon as possible."

For the first time since she'd met her, Rose detected a slight glimmer of fear cross her aunt's eyes. Which only set Rose's own nerves further on edge.

Uncle Forbes laid a hand atop his wife's. "Never fear, dearest. God is in control. We must continue to pray for our victory."

"Pray, humph." Mr. Snyder dabbed his fingers over his tongue then slicked back the red hair on either side of his temples. A vision of the slithering tongue of a snake formed in Rose's mind.

"We must act. We must take up arms and force these devilish British off our shores." He speared Rose with a devious, determined gaze. She knew he spoke of Alex. She averted her eyes to the open window where thick darkness seemed to pour into the room from outside like black molasses. Not even a wisp of a breeze entered behind it to relieve the dank, oppressive air that always seemed to hover around Mr. Snyder.

"All this talk of war." Amelia pouted. "Can we talk of brighter things, perhaps?" She scooted to the edge of her seat. "Like the ball at the Fountain Inn?"

"Is that all you think about, Amelia?" Rose instantly regretted her tone as her maid swallowed and stared down at the hands in her lap.

"Forgive me." Rose set down her cup and grasped Amelia's hand. "I fear I am not myself lately."

"As much as I love a good soiree"—Uncle Forbes fingered a stain on his cravat—"shouldn't we be preparing for a possible invasion instead of dancing the night away?"

"It is good for morale, dearest." Candlelight shimmered over Aunt Muira's burgundy-colored hair, streaking it crimson. "The citizens of Baltimore need to escape the constant threat of attack, if only for one night."

If only Rose could escape the constant threat of the man sitting across from her. She flattened her lips and found Uncle Forbes's tender gaze still on her. Did her uncle know of the councilman's insidious plan? But how could he? Rose had thought it best to keep the man's threats from her family. There was no need to cause alarm over something that could not be changed.

As if Mr. Snyder's presence wasn't disconcerting enough, her uncle's odd behavior only increased the turmoil clawing at her insides. Plucking out her fan, she waved it over her heated skin.

"By the by, speaking of the Fountain Inn." Mr. Snyder's nasally voice shot through the room like a quiver of arrows. Rose resisted the urge to duck to avoid being pierced by one.

"If I may, Miss McGuire, it would be my honor to escort you to the ball."

She should have ducked.

Her stomach gurgled and a sour taste rose to her mouth. Why was he putting on such airs? He knew she could not refuse him. She could refuse him nothing as long as he threatened her family. Yet. . .she bit her lip. Perhaps he would release her from the obligation of attending this silly ball. She pasted on a smile. "You are too kind, Mr. Snyder, but I have not been well lately and wish to remain home."

"Indeed? But it is three days away. Surely you will regain your strength by then." One cultured brow rose above eyes that hardened at her denial.

"Rose, dear." Aunt Muira patted her hair in place. "A night of fun and dancing will do you good. And I can think of no better escort than Mr. Snyder."

Uncle Forbes coughed and slammed down his teacup.

"Do say yes, Rose." Amelia jumped in her seat, bouncing Rose on the settee. "Think of the fun we could have together."

Rose smiled at her maid, urging her with her eyes to remain silent and wishing she had confided in Amelia about what Mr. Snyder had done. But Rose had hardly been able to think about his threats, let alone speak them out loud.

"Yes, I insist." Mr. Snyder's tone held no room for argument.

She directed a chilled gaze his way. Was there no end to the man's petitions? Wasn't it bad enough that he had threatened her family? That he now forced her to marry him? Despondency tugged her shoulders down as she envisioned a future consisting of Mr. Snyder's iron rods of demands erected one by one around her until she was a prisoner to his every whim.

Her foot twitched. She wanted to kick him. She wanted to toss her hot tea in his face. Instead she smiled sweetly. "A gentleman never insists, sir."

"More tea?" Aunt Muira took the china pot and poured more of the amber liquid into Mr. Snyder's cup in an effort, Rose assumed, to alleviate the tension rising in the room.

He thanked her aunt with a tight smile.

"With Mr. Reed gone, who else will ask you?" Amelia gripped Rose's hands.

Rose glared at her maid.

"Aye, perhaps you should go, Rose." Uncle Forbes folded his hands over his rounded belly. "I am of the opinion that you'll be glad you did."

Rose swept a confused gaze toward him as perspiration formed on her neck. Her uncle had always seemed unimpressed by Mr. Snyder and had never encouraged a courtship between them. Was he now against Rose as well? Was everyone against her?

"It's settled then." The snake set down his cup. The clank echoed Rose's doom through the parlor. He stood and brushed invisible dust from the sleeves of his coat. "The hour is late. I shall relieve you of my company."

Relieve, indeed. Rose smiled.

An uncharacteristic alarm rolled across her uncle's face. "So soon, Mr. Snyder? Why you've barely been here a few hours."

Rose clenched her jaw. *Please let him go, Uncle.*

"Indeed, but I have some urgent business which requires my attention." Mr. Snyder bowed. "I thank you for the lovely supper, Mrs. Drummond, Mr. Drummond. Mrs. Wilkins, always a pleasure." He turned to Rose. "Would you do me the honor of seeing me out, Miss McGuire? I wish to speak to you."

Uncle Forbes struggled to his feet with a groan. "Are you sure I cannot interest you in some pudding?" He glanced toward the kitchen. "Cora!"

"Dearest, what is wrong with you?" Aunt Muira rose and took her husband's arm. "We have no pudding prepared, and Cora has retired."

Mr. Snyder's nose wrinkled. "I am quite all right, I assure you. Perhaps some other time."

Yes, like when the oceans turn to mud. Rose followed him into the foyer.

"Perhaps a sip of brandy then?" Uncle Forbes asked.

"No, thank you, sir." Mr. Snyder turned toward Rose and gestured toward the door. "Shall we?"

"I really shouldn't go outside in the night air." She feigned a cough.

"Nonsense, dear, it's only a few steps," Aunt Muira scolded. "We'll keep the door open for propriety." She nudged Rose forward.

Retrieving his hat and cane from the coatrack, Mr. Snyder turned toward her uncle. "You really should hire another footman, sir."

"I have every intention of doing so." There was no mistaking the aversion in her uncle's voice. Then why did he suggest she accompany Mr. Snyder to the ball?

Aunt Muira opened the door, and Mr. Snyder proffered his arm toward Rose. Ignoring him, she stepped onto the porch and swatted at a bug hovering around the lantern atop a post.

She wished she could swat Mr. Snyder away as easily. Instead she followed him down the path, feeling as though it was her heart crunching beneath his shoes instead of the gravel.

Halting at his horse, he leaned toward her. "You shouldn't treat your future husband with such contempt. It may cause suspicion, my dear."

"What do you expect, Mr. Snyder?"

"I expect you to comport yourself as a lady."

The smell of the bergamot he splashed on his hair threatened to choke her. Withdrawing a handkerchief from her sleeve she pressed it over her moist neck and gazed above. A dark cloud drifted over the sliver of a moon, stealing away its light. Just as Mr. Snyder had drifted into her life, stealing away her future. *Why God?* Rose lifted up her first prayer since Alex had left. Even now her anger forbade her to pray more.

Mr. Snyder untied the reins and faced her, sorrow clouding his features. "I hate to be so disagreeable, but you force my hand. You must attend the ball with me—to show our friends and family our devoted attachment before our engagement is announced."

"And if I don't?"

His eyes hardened, but the sorrow remained. "I think we both know what will happen."

Rose sighed. "But if you expose my association with Mr. Reed and send me and my family to prison, then you will never marry me or get your hands on my property. Why risk it for a silly ball?"

He gazed at her as if for the first time he realized she actually possessed a mind underneath her golden tresses. "Indeed. Why risk it for a silly ball, Miss McGuire?" He tugged on his riding gloves then slid his cane though a loop on his saddle.

She narrowed her eyes. "So I am to attend the ball and play the part of your devoted admirer, is that it?"

"Precisely." He brushed his fingers over her cheek, and she stepped back, her stomach tightening.

"And what do I get in return?" Rose asked.

Agony pierced the hard sheen covering his eyes. "I know you are angry with me, Rose. But in time I hope you will forgive me. I can make you happy if you'll but give me a chance." He lifted his hand toward her again, but she stepped out of his reach. Frowning, he donned his hat and swung onto his horse. "And maybe someday you will come to love me."

Instead of answering, Rose gazed, benumbed, into the darkness that extended into an unforeseen oblivion.

"Until the ball, my dear." Mr. Snyder kicked the horse and sped off down the trail.

Dust showered over Rose, but she couldn't move. She hugged herself, willing her tears back behind her eyes. Young Daniel had said she had a destiny.

What he hadn't said was that her destiny was a fate worse than death.

❖ CHAPTER 21 ❖

Alex followed Noah down the streets of Baltimore. The last rays of sun slipped over the western horizon, luring shadows from the alley-ways and darkened corners. A bawdy tune wafted on the breeze from the docks as lanterns atop posts lining the avenue remained as dark as the encroaching night. No need to give the British fleet a glowing target. A wise decision on the part of General Smith.

Behind Alex, Mr. Heaton's boots thudded over the sandy lane. The men said not a word to one another. A bell rang in the distance, accompanied by the lap of waves coming from the harbor a mile away. They passed a row of shops all closed for the day: cobbler, chandler, millinery, iron-works, and a bakery. Their engraved wooden signs swung in the breeze from iron hooks above their doors. A carriage rumbled by, its occupants chattering happily. Down the street, a man shouted for his son to come inside. A night watchman, armed with musket and sword, strode by them and tipped his hat. "Good evening, Mr. Brenin. Mr. Heaton." His eyes grazed over Alex in passing as Noah returned the greeting.

They turned the corner onto Howard Street. The smell of horse manure, salt, and tar from a distant shipyard stung Alex's nose. Tension pricked the air and clawed down his back.

"Just another block," Noah shot over his shoulder.

Alex thanked God for this man's help—and for Luke's. He'd been surprised they both had agreed to accompany him on his nefarious deed. Surprised and also ashamed to accept their kindness in light of Alex's complicity in the suffering they'd endured aboard the HMS *Undefeatable*. So many conflicting emotions roiled in his gut, he didn't know what to feel.

Except at the moment fear seemed to dominate the others. Alex had spent the past two days holed up in Noah's home, pacing the floor, agonizing over the mess he had caused. Now, ever since Mr. Drummond had informed Alex he had managed to lure Mr. Snyder from his house for the evening, Alex had begun to wonder if he hadn't lost what was left of his reason.

He was a British officer in the middle of a rebel city on a mission to steal back his sword from a member of the city council. Absurd!

Considering the way his countrymen had terrorized these citizens of late, if he were caught he'd be no doubt strung up on the nearest tree. And what of Mr. Heaton and Mr. Brenin? They risked the same by helping him.

No, not for him, to help their friend Rose. Which spoke volumes as to her character. Something he could well attest to, for he would do anything to ensure her happiness.

Even if her future wasn't with him.

Alex clenched his fists. He hoped Mr. Drummond had not invited Snyder to the farm. The thought of the depraved councilman being anywhere near Rose caused Alex's stomach to fold in on itself. But there was nothing to be done about it.

At least not yet.

Rows of houses stood at attention on either side of the street. Slivers of light peeked from behind closed shutters and curtains, but otherwise the homes remained shrouded in darkness. Noah stopped before a modest, single-story cottage at the end of the street. The simple home gave no indication that a councilman lived within. A garden that boasted of more weeds than flowers filled the small front yard, while an iron gate that hung loose on its hinges did a pathetic job of barring entrance. No wonder the man sought after Rose's property.

"I would have expected Mr. Snyder to live in a more stately home." Alex stopped beside Noah.

Luke laughed. "Indeed, the man has an uncanny ability to play the part of royalty when, in truth, he lives like a pauper."

A group of gentlemen emerged from a house across the street, and

Noah nudged Alex and Luke into the shadow of a tree beside the fence. "Truth be told, Mr. Reed," Noah whispered, "Mr. Snyder cannot claim a very noble pedigree. In fact"—he scratched his jaw and watched as the group of men sauntered down the street and out of sight—"his father was hung for horse thievery and his grandfather for piracy."

Alex flinched and gazed back at the house. "Upon my honor."

"Honor has nothing to do with it." Luke snorted and flipped the hair from his face.

"This was his father's house." Noah studied a passing horse. "The only thing left him after he paid his family's debts."

"How did he become a councilman?" Alex asked. No man so dishonored could ever hold such a prestigious office in England.

Noah shrugged. "He's intelligent and has a way with words. And Americans don't tend to hold a person's parentage against them." He gazed toward the harbor. "I suppose because so many of our ancestors came here to escape their pasts."

Alex ran a hand through his hair. So unlike his homeland where bloodline and title were everything. Yet one more quality to admire about these Americans.

After scanning the street one last time, Noah pushed open the broken gate. The loud squeak of rusty hinges frayed Alex's already pinched nerves as Noah led them down the dirt path to the front porch.

"How are we to get past the servants?" Alex whispered.

"There's only one—a middle-aged spinster who runs the house." Noah stepped over a fallen branch.

"And?" Mr. Reed raised his brows.

"Why do you think I brought Mr. Heaton?" Noah halted at the porch steps then dipped his head to the left. "This way, Mr. Reed."

Luke winked at Alex as he proceeded up the steps. A *rap, rap, rap* echoed through the air even before Alex rounded the corner of the house.

"Mr. Heaton," a female voice exclaimed. "I'm sorry, but Mr. Snyder is not home."

Alex followed Noah through a sea of tall grass and weeds to a darkened window at the back. Balancing on a pile of firewood stacked along the wall, Noah pressed on the wooden frame of the window. The bottom half slipped upward.

"Ah, God is good to us, Mr. Reed. We don't have to break the glass."

Hoisting himself up on the window frame, Noah squeezed headfirst through the opening. A thump sounded from the room, and Noah's hand appeared in the window. "Hurry, the two of us can search much faster together."

The opening proved a more difficult obstacle for Alex's larger frame, but with Noah's assistance, he soon landed on the wooden floor of what he assumed to be Mr. Snyder's bedchamber.

"You are looking more lovely than ever, Miss Addington." Luke's deep flirtatious tone filtered beneath the door.

A woman's giggle was the only reply.

Noah fumbled among the objects sitting atop a desk in the corner then struck flint to steel and lit two candles. He handed one to Alex "Hurry. We don't have much time before Mrs. Addington sees the light beneath the door."

Alex scanned the room, which was filled with a shabby bed and an assortment of chipped furniture. Unexpected pity welled inside him for the humble way in which the man, who put on such haughty pretensions, actually lived. How difficult it must be to keep up such airs.

"Oh, you shouldn't say such things, Mr. Heaton." The giddy female voice echoed down the hall. "You make an old woman blush."

Alex scanned the room as Noah flung open the drawers of a pine dresser and sifted through the contents.

"What makes you think he's hidden my sword in here?" Alex searched behind the volumes of books lining shelves on the far wall.

"I know this man," Noah said. "It's far too important for him to keep anywhere else."

Easing open the drawers of the small oak desk perched in the corner, Alex examined the contents: foolscap, quill pens, a pocket watch, ink, a pistol, and a key.

Noah swung open the doors of a cabinet, sending an eerie creak through the room. They both halted. The tap of steps padded across the floor outside the chamber.

"Don't you run away from me, Miss Addington." Luke's deep voice halted the footfalls. "If you would honor me with your charming company, I would be happy to await Mr. Snyder's return."

Noah rubbed the back of his neck and lifted the candle over the contents of the cabinet. Only breeches, shirts, hats, stockings, and cravats stared back at him. He swung about. The candle flickered the frustration in his eyes. "Confound it all, where could he have put it?"

Alex ran a sleeve over his moist forehead, not willing to give up. His sword had to be here or all was lost.

Dropping to his knees, Noah peered beneath the bed.

"Oh no, Mrs. Addington. Please give me another moment of your time." Luke's sultry voice slithered through the door cracks.

"Mr. Heaton, you do make an old woman feel young again."

The scraping sound of wood on wood jarred the silence, and Alex turned to see Noah pulling a small trunk from beneath Mr. Snyder's bed. He yanked on the lid. "It's locked."

The key. Pulling open the desk drawer, Alex retrieved the key, knelt beside Noah, and inserted it into the lock. A click sounded and the latch loosened.

Luke laughed and Mrs. Addington joined him.

"God is good." Noah smiled.

Alex lifted the lid, wondering at the way the man always gave credit to the Almighty.

A glint of gold reflected the candlelight. Alex's sword. Beneath it laid his tattered uniform. He grabbed the hilt in a firm grip as if it were an old friend and stood, swinging it through the air.

"Oh, here you are Mr. Snyder. Mr. Heaton has come to call on you, sir." Mrs. Addington's voice lost its coquettish tone.

Alex's heart slammed into his chest. Noah's eyes widened. He plucked up Alex's uniform, closed the lid, locked it, then shoved it back under the bed. Alex took the key from him, slipped it into his pocket, and blew out his candle.

"What is it, Mr. Heaton? I have neither the time nor the inclination to talk with you at the moment." Mr. Snyder's squeaky voice ground against Alex's nerves.

"I daresay, Mr. Snyder, if you could spare a minute, I'd like to discuss the city's plans for a water aqueduct from the spring," Luke said.

"At this hour?" Snyder's tone stung with annoyance. "Go away, Mr. Heaton."

Tucking the uniform under his arm, Noah squeezed out the window and dropped to the ground with a thud.

Alex tossed the sword to him then flung one leg over the window ledge. Bending his body, he attempted to shove it through the small opening.

But the creak of a door sounded behind him.

❖

Entering her uncle's makeshift hospital, Rose lifted a hand to her nose at the putrid stench. Amelia drew out her handkerchief and flapped it in the air as if she could bat away the smell. Looking up from one of his patients, Uncle Forbes squeezed the man's arm, then stood and approached them. His brow furrowed at Amelia's discomfiture. Handing her a bucket, he sent her out for fresh water.

He faced Rose. "Thank you for coming today, lass."

Rose removed her hat and gloves and hung them on a peg. "My pleasure, Uncle. I'll do what I can." Anything to keep her mind off a certain British officer. Grabbing a stained apron from a hook, she wrapped it around her waist and tied it in the back. Her uncle's brown eyes shifted over her as if he could read her mind.

She wished he could. She wished she had someone to talk to about Alex, someone to confide in about Mr. Snyder's nefarious plans. But her uncle didn't know Alex was a British naval officer. And, for his own safety, it was better that way.

"Just encourage those that are awake, lass. And see if they need anything. Dr. Wilson already tended to their wounds yesterday." He patted his pockets and plucked out his spectacles. "Ah, there they are." He grinned.

An hour later, Rose drew up a stool at the last man's cot. He was asleep, though his eyelids fluttered. A nightmare perhaps. She knew all about nightmares. Across the aisle from her, Amelia read the Bible to an aged man, whom Rose's uncle had found begging on the street, his feet eaten up with gout. Though the comforting words from the Psalms should have eased Rose's nerves, they seemed to have the opposite effect.

Uncle Forbes pulled up a stool on the other side of Rose's patient. "Good. He's asleep for now. Doc said he had an infected bullet wound, but looks like his fever finally broke. Brave man, this one. He got shot protecting a settler he didn't even know."

Brave. It seemed an unattainable trait to Rose.

"Lass, before I forget, your aunt and I will be traveling to Washington after the ball at the Fountain Inn."

Fear coiled around Rose's heart, confirming her prior assessment. "Why must you go as well?"

"Your aunt has a wagon full of supplies to deliver and can't manage them herself. Besides, it's been awhile since I've had a chance to visit with Reverend Hargrave." He cocked his head. "Never fear, Mr. Markham has offered to stay at the house."

Rose shook her head. "Why am I always afraid, uncle?"

From behind his spectacles, his brown eyes warmed. "Fear is not God's plan for us, lass. In fact, His Word says 'There is no fear in love; but perfect love casteth out fear: because fear hath torment.'"

Torment. That was exactly how Rose would describe her constant fear—tormenting. But how could she rid herself of it? After all she had endured, what normal woman wouldn't be overcome with fear? And what did love have to do with fear? Her love for Alex had only caused more fear. "But I cannot seem to help it. Bad things keep happening to me."

He reached across the cotton coverlet and gripped her hand. "You have been through many frightening things for one so young."

His hand felt hard and scratchy like the bark of a tree.

"Others have as well," Rose said. "You and Aunt Muira have suffered much. Yet you both have such courage and strength."

He chuckled, and the lines at the corners of his mouth scrunched together, lifting his beard. "Courage? I wouldn't call it that. I prefer to call it faith."

Faith and courage. Love and fear. Confusion once again scrambled Rose's thoughts. "It seems the more I love, the more afraid I become." Rose withdrew her hand and twisted her finger around a loose curl at her neck. "When you love someone, doesn't it make you terrified to lose them?"

"That's not the love God is speaking of, lass." He smiled.

"What other kind of love is there?"

"God's love. Only His love is perfect."

Rose rubbed her temples where a sudden ache began to form. "What does that have to do with fear?"

Uncle Forbes's spectacles slid down his nose. "You don't believe God loves you, do you?" His tone held a drop of sorrow.

Rose gazed at the sleeping man. His lips twitched. His eyelids flitted. So agitated even in slumber. Just like her. "The Bible says He loves me."

Her uncle tapped his chest. "But you don't know His love in here."

Rose huffed. "I don't understand."

"When you truly believe God loves you and have experienced it in your heart, there's nothing to fear. Don't you see?" He removed his spectacles and placed them on the side table, then leaned over the man to take her hand once again. "The Bible says that if God is for us, who can be against us? 'He that spared not his own Son, but delivered him up for us all, how shall he not with him also freely give us all things?'" He squeezed her hand. "You see, when you're God's child, there's nothing to fear."

Rose frowned. "But that's where you're wrong, uncle. There is much to fear in this life. Bad things happen to God's children. What of me? What of Elaine and James Myers?"

"Aye, but you mistake me, lass. I didn't say bad things would never happen. I said regardless of what happens, there's nothing to fear. Because God loves you, everything has a purpose. Everything will work out for good in the end. That's a promise."

Rose wished she could believe that, desperately wanted the peace that believing those words would bring. If she could, then she needn't worry about her future. She needn't worry about being forced to marry Mr. Snyder and never seeing Alex again. Somehow things would work out for the best, and God would see her through.

"You must first let go of your bitterness and unforgiveness, child." Her uncle's brown eyes held such wisdom, such peace. "Perhaps that is what is keeping you from truly receiving God's love in your heart."

Withdrawing her hands, Rose clasped them in her lap and lowered her gaze. "I don't know how to let go."

"Then those who have done you harm will always have a hold on you. They will always dictate your happiness. Do you want to give them that power?"

Rose shook her head. She hadn't thought of it that way. "But if I forgive them, doesn't that mean they have escaped without punishment?"

"Escaped?" Her uncle snorted and pressed down a strand of his unruly gray hair. "No, lass. If they don't repent, they will have to answer to God on judgment day. And if you don't forgive them, you will as well."

❖ CHAPTER 22 ❖

Rose gazed out the window of Mr. Snyder's hired coach and tried to drown out his incessant babbling. Beside her, Amelia, dressed in a beautiful gown of creamy satin embroidered in glistening emerald, pinched her cheeks with excitement. Next to Amelia, light from the lantern perched outside the carriage transformed Aunt Muira's satin burgundy gown into shimmering red. Across from the ladies sat three gentlemen, Uncle Forbes, Mr. Braxton, and Mr. Snyder, who had insisted he provide their group with a plush hackney to convey them to the ball. And who now regaled them with the tale of how he had convinced the council to adopt a provision for another theater to be built in town that would "greatly enhance the city's reputation as a bastion of civilization."

Or so he declared.

Rose pressed down the folds of her own gown of royal blue silk trimmed in white satin netting—a gown drawn from the collection her aunt had kept from her youth and altered to fit Rose's smaller frame. She tugged at the white sash around her waist. A matching ribbon adorned her hair, which had been pinned up in a cascade of curls and decorated further with jeweled pins and a spray of tiny wildflowers. A gold necklace, embedded with rubies and pearls—also her aunt's—hung over a neckline that was a bit low for Rose's taste. Nevertheless, the elegant attire made her feel like a princess. At least until Mr. Snyder had appeared at the house, with black top hat in one hand and his ever-present cane in the other, wearing a grin that reminded Rose of Prinney's pink snout after a fine meal of kitchen slops. And suddenly, instead of a princess, Rose felt like the icing on a cake about to be eaten by the devil himself.

Wind gusted through the coach's window, and she closed her eyes, imagining she was on board a ship with Alex, sailing to an exotic port where it didn't matter from whence they hailed: America or Britain, France, or even the moon. She wondered where he was at that moment. What he was doing. Was he safe? Had his captain accepted him back on board without repercussions?

Was he thinking of her?

Rose shook her head, trying to scatter the thoughts away. They served no purpose other than to feed an ever-growing depression that hovered over her like a dark, icy fog.

Amelia slipped her hand into Rose's, and she felt the woman's tremble of excitement even through her gloves. Rose smiled her way and then dared a glance at Mr. Braxton, whose gaze had not left Amelia since he had entered the carriage. Perhaps her maid would find true love again after all.

As Rose had found. If only for a few days.

But now that she had experienced it, nothing else would do—especially not the man sitting across from her. She felt his eyes upon her, but she refused to honor his sordid stare with a glance of her own.

Instead, she studied her uncle sitting across from his wife. She'd never seen him looking so dapper in his black overcoat, embroidered satin silver waistcoat, and breeches. He tipped his hat toward her, drawing a smile from Rose, yet something in the curve of his lips, the depth of his gaze, gave her pause. It was as if he knew some grand secret. Returning her gaze to the window, she released a sigh. Fairy tales and dreams were for little girls. Not for women like Rose, who had seen too much of the cruel world to no longer believe in happy endings.

Mr. Snyder tapped his cane on the floor. "I daresay, it promises to be a glorious evening. I am quite looking forward to it."

Uncle Forbes lifted his hand to his mouth to cover what sounded like a chuckle but ended as a cough.

Aunt Muira frowned at her husband before responding, "Indeed, I do agree, Mr. Snyder. This ball is just what this city needs to take our mind off the war."

"And what is your opinion, Miss McGuire?" Mr. Snyder addressed Rose in a tone that dared her to speak her true heart.

She flashed a caustic smile his way and tugged upon her long white gloves. "I fear I do not share your enthusiasm, Mr. Snyder."

Amelia looped her arm through Rose's. "Oh I do pray you will cheer up. We shall have so much fun." The woman's lavender perfume swirled around Rose, mingling with the rose oil she had dabbed on her own neck.

"I agree." Aunt Muira's tone was scolding. "Count your blessings, dear, or they shall be taken away from you and given to someone more appreciative."

Uncle Forbes coughed again, and Rose swept a gaze his way again. Was he ill? But no. A smile creased the corners of his mouth.

Blessings, indeed. Rose tapped a gloved finger over the window frame in an attempt to count out those blessings. But the few she recollected were instantly shadowed by the disastrous future looming before her.

Soon the hackney turned down Light Street, which was aptly named this evening for the many streetlights setting the block aglow—the ban on city lights apparently lifted for this gala event. A parade of ladies in flowing gowns, escorted by gentlemen in top hats and coats, drifted down the avenue toward the Fountain Inn. Coaches, curricles, and chaises, along with gentlemen atop horses swarmed the cobblestone street. The *clip-clop* of horses' hooves, the rattle of carriage wheels, and the laughter and chatter of the crowd rose in a chorus of gaiety that thumbed its nose at the British troops blockading the port.

The driver pulled the coach to a halt before the Fountain Inn, an elaborate structure that rose several stories into the night sky. Light shone from the upper windows onto iron-grated balconies before spilling down upon the crush of people swarming to enter the front doors. The gentlemen leaped from the carriage, the footman lowered the step, and Mr. Snyder's bony hand appeared in the doorway. The audacious jewel on his middle finger winked at Rose in the lantern light. She drew a deep breath. She could do this. She could endure one night with this hideous man. Just one night at a time—although he insisted on many more. But she could not think of that now, or she feared she would lose all desire to live.

Avoiding Mr. Snyder's outstretched hand, she clutched her gown and descended the steps, searching the crowd for any sign of Marianne or Cassandra. She could use a friend tonight. The ladies' coiffures adorned with ribbons, flowers, and plumes bobbed alongside waves of black hats that swept through the front door like seawater pouring through a crack into the hold of a ship. With her hand all but hovering over Mr. Snyder's arm, she allowed him to lead her through that crack, wondering all along if she would drown in the agony of her heart.

Once inside, Mr. Snyder ushered her through the main courtyard of the inn, where a large trickling fountain was the centerpiece in a flower garden set aglow by flickering lantern light. Rose gazed up at the inn's chambers perched upon levels of terraces that circled the gardens. Several couples stood near the fountain or sat on the iron benches in deep conversation. She glanced over her shoulder to see Amelia hanging on Mr. Braxton's arm, her eyes sparkling with excitement as they scanned the surroundings. From behind Amelia, Aunt Muira offered Rose a gentle smile. Rose knew her aunt meant well. And by all accounts, Mr. Snyder was a perfect match for any young lady. Until he revealed the devil buried beneath his polished facade.

Following the swarm of chattering guests, Mr. Snyder, with his head held high, led Rose through another set of doors to their left. A few heads turned their way as they moved into the brightly lit ballroom. The elegant tones of a minuet began at the far end of the hall where musicians sat on a raised stage. Two massive crystalline chandeliers hung from an arched stucco ceiling that was etched with flowers and gilded in gold. Mirrors on either side of the room reflected the light from dozens of candles. The smell of sweet punch, beeswax, and a myriad of perfumes tickled Rose's nose and made her long for fresh air.

After their names were announced, Rose scanned the ladies who stood at the edge of the dancing couples, gossiping behind fluttering fans like a gaggle of geese flapping their wings. No sign of her friends anywhere. Rose's heart sank even lower. She turned to ask Amelia if she had seen Marianne, but Mr. Braxton had already swept her out onto the dance floor.

Aunt Muira and Uncle Forbes soon followed, gazing into each other's eyes as if they were the only ones in the room.

Rose swallowed a lump of sorrow. Her aunt and uncle shared an intimate, eternal love Rose had but tasted, but would never know in full.

"Would you care to join them?" Mr. Snyder's blue eyes studied her, and Rose searched her mind for an excuse.

It came in the form of her dear friend, Marianne, who hurried to join her from across the room in a flurry of pink satin. She grabbed Rose's arm. "I was so glad when I heard you were attending."

"How did you hear?" Rose turned from Mr. Snyder and gave her friend a questioning look, glad for the excuse to avoid his question. She had only just agreed to attend three days prior and had not spoken to anyone since.

"Oh, never mind." Marianne smiled and nodded toward Mr. Snyder. "Good evening, Councilman."

He scrunched his lips together as if tasting something sour. The music stopped and those who remained on the floor lined up in two rows as others joined them, men along one side and women on the other. "Mrs. Brenin." Mr. Snyder said. "If you'll excuse us, Miss McGuire and I were about to partake of the country dance."

He grabbed Rose's arm to drag her onto the floor when Noah wove his way through the crowd to stand before him. "Mr. Snyder, I have a matter of great importance to discuss with you, sir. Would you join me in the other room for a glass of port?" He flashed a smile toward his wife. "I'm sure the ladies can entertain themselves in our absence."

"Importance, you say?" The councilman's chest seemed to expand beneath his velvet waistcoat. "Can't it wait?"

"Not unless you wish to keep the mayor waiting."

Snyder peered around Noah toward the side doors. "Mayor Johnson wishes to speak to me?"

"Indeed. He asked for you directly." Noah's tone was serious, but his blue eyes held a twinkle of mischief.

"Of course. No doubt he seeks my wise council on a matter of urgency." Mr. Snyder jutted out his chin. Releasing Rose's arm, he faced her. "I shall return shortly to claim that dance, my dear."

Rose shot a pointed gaze at his back as he left. She breathed a sigh of relief as music filled the room once again.

Cassandra, decked in a shimmering gown of emerald, appeared out of nowhere and sidled up beside Rose. She made a face at Mr. Snyder as he exited the room with Noah.

"You shouldn't behave so, Cassandra." Rose covered her mouth to hide her unavoidable smile.

"Why not? He deserves it." Cassandra fingered the lace on her glove and gave Rose a coy glance.

Marianne's eyes sparkled. She clutched Rose's arm again and seemed ready to jump out of her shoes. If Rose didn't know her friend better, she'd think it was the ball that thrilled her so. But she *did* know her friend. And Marianne had never been overfond of such social functions. Rose's gaze shifted to Cassandra, who wore an unusually sly look, even for her.

Rose lifted a brow. "What's going on with you two? Did Noah purposely steal Mr. Snyder away for some delightfully foul purpose?" Not that she would object. But what confused her was how her friends would know to aid her in such a manner. She'd never spoken to them of her aversion to Mr. Snyder or of his recent threats.

Cassandra batted the air with her white glove. "What does it matter? He's gone." Her green eyes scanned the crowd as if looking for someone. They locked on something in the distance, and Rose followed her gaze to see Mr. Heaton standing by himself across the room, drink in hand. His normally unruly black hair was slicked and tied at the back of his neck as he stood tall and handsome in a well-tailored suit of black lute string with velvet trim. His dark eyes focused on Cassandra as if there were no one else in the room worth looking at. He raised his glass toward her with a nod.

"My word." Rose leaned toward Cassandra. "Mr. Heaton presents quite the handsome figure tonight."

Marianne smiled. "And it would appear he only has eyes for you, Cassandra."

Cassandra tore her gaze from him. "Don't be absurd. Mr. Heaton has eyes for anything in a skirt." Her giggle faltered on her lips.

Rose glanced back at Mr. Heaton and found his gaze still directed their way before he turned and slipped through a side door.

"Doesn't he captain your ship, *Destiny*?" Rose asked Cassandra.

"Yes. And he's already made quite a fortune in prizes." Marianne's delicate brows lifted.

"He's a rogue and not to be trusted." Cassandra spat. "I have begun to regret investing in his privateer." She pressed down the folds of her emerald gown.

Several gentlemen approached the three ladies, requesting dances with both Rose and Cassandra. Rose politely refused each one, forbidding them to even sign her dance card. Cassandra, however, at least allowed them that small encouragement, although, in truth, she appeared more than aloof.

Rose hadn't danced since her father had twirled her around their parlor when she was a little girl. The thought of a man touching her, even briefly, in such a seductive dalliance made her heart cinch. That was, any man but Alex. And with him gone, she'd never have the opportunity. Even the cheerful music rasped in her ears like a contentious chime. Truth be told, she'd rather go home and bury her head beneath her pillow.

Rose fingered the heavy jewels around her neck, as out of place on her skin as she was at this ball. Her glance took in the dancers floating over the marble floor like swans on a crystalline pond. She spotted Amelia as she executed the steps of the quadrille with perfection—steps the young maid had practiced with Rose and her aunt in the parlor all week. Amelia's face glowed with delight, and Rose smiled, happy for her companion, despite the agony weighing down her own heart.

Two more gentlemen approached. Rose politely declined the taller man's offer to dance while Cassandra batted the other one away.

"Why not dance with the gentleman, Rose?" Marianne gripped her arm and swept her gaze over the room as if looking for someone. "It may help to lift your humors."

"I agree." Cassandra waved her silk printed fan about her face. "You shouldn't be so glum at so gay an event. Who knows when we'll have another evening such as this one with this war going on?"

"Then why aren't you dancing?" Rose asked Cassandra.

"Because I have become, shall we say, more selective regarding whom I choose to pair up with on the dance floor."

Marianne leaned close with a smile. "Which means she's waiting for a particular gentleman to ask her."

Cassandra huffed, but a grin played with the corners of her lips.

Rose would have giggled if her insides didn't feel like they'd been run over by a carriage. "Please go enjoy yourselves. I'm afraid I'm not good company tonight."

"Rubbish." Marianne said. "Why don't we go get some punch before the two of you break every gentleman's heart in the room?" She tugged on Rose's arm and led the way toward one of the side doors.

A billowing crowd of chattering people packed the refreshment parlor, helping themselves to the libations on a buffet lining the far wall.

Men circled gaming tables perched about the room, playing whist or faro. The smoke of a dozen cigars hovered over them like storm clouds. Rose drew a hand to her nose.

"Oh no, there is Mr. Snyder." Marianne dragged Rose to the side. "Perhaps we can get a drink without him seeing us."

"He knows I'm here, Marianne." Rose gave a cynical snort. "Besides, he appears to be quite in his element."

Standing beside Noah, Mayor Johnson, General Smith, and two other councilmen, Mr. Snyder held a drink in one hand and his cane in the other. His voice—which sounded much like the squeaking of a rusty hinge—rose above the crowd and ground against Rose's ears. By the bored expressions on the faces of his audience, he no doubt regaled them with his grand vision for the city. Noah stood at his side. Mr. Heaton suddenly appeared and handed Noah a glass of red liquid, which, after relieving Mr. Snyder of his empty one, Noah placed in the councilman's hand.

Craning to see between the undulating crowd, Rose eyed them with curiosity. Neither Noah nor Mr. Heaton were the type to flatter someone in power, nor had they ever expressed an interest in Mr. Snyder's affairs or politics in general.

She leaned toward Marianne. "I must thank Noah later for keeping Mr. Snyder occupied. But I don't wish to keep your husband from you all evening."

"Oh think nothing of it." Marianne eased her toward an oblong table laden with cold tea, punch, and spiced wine. Rose selected a glass of punch and had barely taken a sip when Mr. Snyder, Noah, and Mr. Heaton descended upon them.

Mr. Snyder's eyes carried a distant glaze that seemed at odds with the man's normal intense focus. He extended his arm. "A dance, my dear?"

"I do not feel—" she began to protest.

"Nonsense." He dragged her through the clamorous mob and out onto the dance floor where they joined a row of couples lining up for a reel. One glance to her side told her that Marianne, Noah, Luke, and Cassandra had followed. Oddly, their presence brought her some comfort.

The music began, and Rose bowed toward Mr. Snyder, whose gaze skittered about the room like a bird who'd lost his flock. They stepped toward each other. "Are you all right, Mr. Snyder?"

"Yes, of course." Yet his voice wobbled slightly. He coughed and stepped back. They circled around and met again. When he moved toward the lady beside Rose, his face grew flushed, and he stumbled.

They stepped together. Rose placed her hand upon his upraised one and they floated down the middle of the rows, with the ladies on one side, the men on the other. "Did the mayor say something to upset you?" Rose asked.

"No, of course not. Naturally, he wanted my opinion on the defenses of the city."

Naturally. Rose strung her lips tight as they made their way down the line of dancers. Marianne and Noah grinned at her in passing.

"You are marrying an important man, Miss McGuire," he added, though his tone lacked its usual rigid pomposity.

He stepped away, then back again. "Perhaps now you won't find the idea so disagreeable?" His grin broke into an odd giggle.

Heads turned their way.

Beads of sweat sprang upon his forehead.

Rose took his arm and swung beside him. "Mr. Snyder. I fear you are unwell. Would you care to sit down?"

He shook his head as if to rid himself of whatever ailed him. His breath became labored, and he nodded. "Perhaps I should."

Rose led him to one of the velvet stuffed chairs that lined the walls, but he refused to sit. Instead he began to pace, placing a hand over his heart. The dance ended, the music stopped, and the room instantly filled with chatter.

Noah led Marianne from the floor, and Mr. Heaton did the same with Cassandra. They headed toward Rose who was helping a pale Snyder walk without stumbling. People began to stare.

"It would appear your Mr. Snyder has partaken of too much spirits." Cassandra cocked her head, a devilish smile on her lips.

Rose stared at the councilman. So unlike him.

"Pure madness! I had but two glasses of wine." Mr. Snyder hissed and tugged upon his cravat.

A few ladies at the outskirts of the crowd moved away.

Luke crossed his arms over his chest and grinned.

Rose resisted the urge to chuckle. At least she wouldn't have to dance with him again. Perhaps if the man drank himself unconscious, she could convince her aunt and uncle to leave early.

Mr. Snyder halted his pace, drew a deep breath as if he were choking, and then sank into a chair.

The chattering subsided as if a predator had entered the forest.

Heads swerved toward the door. Fans began to flutter. Gentlemen and ladies leaned toward one another in whispers.

The announcer's voice rang through the room. "Mr. Alexander Reed."

❖ CHAPTER 23 ❖

Mr. Alexander Reed."

The name drifted through the air like sweet music, a glorious tune from Rose's past. Until it sharpened and shot straight through her heart.

Was this some cruel joke? Rose shifted her gaze between the grins on Marianne's and Cassandra's lips.

Mr. Snyder muttered something then dropped his head into his hands.

Rose stood on her tiptoes and peered over the crowd.

Then she saw him. Standing at the entranceway, a head above most of the other men. A gold satin waistcoat, trimmed in black velvet, peeked out from beneath his dark coat. A pair of black pantaloons were tucked into Hessian boots. His hair was tied behind him, revealing the strong set of his jaw. Hazel eyes as rich as the velvet of his coat locked upon hers.

Rose's breath shot into her throat. Her head spun. She stumbled. Marianne and Cassandra gripped her arms, steadying her.

"Alex is here? How. . . Why. . .?" Alarm tightened the skin on her hands, her arms, her neck until they tingled. "He shouldn't be. . ."

"Go to him." Marianne gave her a gentle nudge.

Rose gaped at her friend. "You knew?" She swept her gaze to Cassandra on her other side. "You too?"

They both smiled.

A thud sounded behind her, and she swerved to see Mr. Snyder slumped onto the floor. "My word." She headed toward him, but Noah and Luke hoisted him up between them.

"He'll be all right, Miss Rose." Luke winked. "He just needs to sleep it off now."

Sleep *what* off? The crowd parted amid a flurry of gasps and condemning glances as Noah and Luke dragged the councilman away.

Rose faced forward, her mind reeling with confusion. The throng split again. This time for Alex, who glided toward her with the authority and ease of a ship parting the sea. Her heart raced.

He gave her a sultry smile, then bowed and took her hand. "Miss McGuire, you look lovely tonight."

Rose wanted to laugh, to cry, to fall into his arms. "Why, thank you, Mr. Reed."

Music began and laughter and conversation joined in a chorus around them as the party resumed. Rose opened her mouth to ask the thousand questions rolling on her tongue, but nothing coherent emerged.

"Would you care to dance?" His deep eyes drank her in as he gestured toward the dance floor.

The haze in her mind refused to form a logical thought. Rose nodded as she kept her eyes fastened upon him, expecting him to disappear at any moment. Alex couldn't be here. He'd be caught—locked up as a prisoner of war. Strong fingers curled around hers, and a jolt of heat coursed up her arm and into her head, adding to her dizziness.

Either she was dreaming or she had gone completely mad. She'd gladly accept either option as long as she never woke up or regained her sanity.

Alex led her onto the floor and entered the parade of couples moving in a country dance. The music, the candlelight, the jewels, plumes, and colorful sashes all swirled around Rose in a blur as she gazed at the man she loved.

They stepped toward each other.

"I don't understand," she whispered.

He arched a questioning brow.

"Why? How?" Rose asked.

"Does my presence displease you?" He swung her around, leading her across the floor with the skill and grace evident of his nobility.

"Quite the contrary." Rose dipped and swung around the gentleman to her left.

Alex took her hand once again. "Then let us enjoy the moment." A speck of sorrow stained his otherwise jovial tone.

Rose did her best to silence the questions, the fears, and embrace the seconds of pure bliss as Alex moved her around the floor. Dare she hope he had decided to stay? She gazed up at the firm cut of his jaw, his regal nose, and dark brows above eyes that scanned the throng for possible enemies. Always ready. Always alert. His masculine scent filled the air between them. The brief moments of contact with him heated her skin, leaving it cold when he moved away, only to be warmed once again by his presence, his touch, the adoring look in his eyes. If this was a dream, it was a dream that brought all her senses to life.

He spun her around another couple and then allowed his gaze to travel over her face as if he was memorizing every inch of her. As they passed the edge of the crowd, dozens of curious eyes followed them. Jeweled heads leaned together behind fans in heated whispers, no doubt trying to guess the identity of this dark, handsome stranger, all the while wondering what he was doing with an unsophisticated girl like her.

The music stopped. Alex released her, and the room suddenly chilled. He proffered his elbow. "Would the lady care for a stroll in the gardens?"

Rose laid her hand on his arm. "The lady would."

Ignoring the stares of the crowd, they sauntered from the floor as if they were king and queen. Rose searched for her friends, but they had conveniently disappeared. Instead, at the far end of the hall, her uncle smiled her way before ushering Aunt Muira into the next room. Was he part of this scheme as well? So many questions. But they would have to wait. All that mattered now was Alex.

He wove his way through the crowd with ease toward the door. General Smith and two officers stood to the side of the entrance. Rose stiffened, but then remembered Alex had been introduced to the general as their footman. Though Alex's presence with her would be considered unusual, it would not raise undue suspicion.

Fresh evening air swept over her, cooling her skin and fluttering the lace at her neckline. A crush of people filled the garden. Laying his hand over hers, Alex led her through the back opening into additional gardens behind the inn where only a few couples lingered in secret assignations.

He stopped beneath an arbor of climbing roses and slowly turned to face her. The light from a nearby lantern reflected a mixture of agony and admiration in his eyes. He brushed his fingers over her cheek, and Rose closed her eyes, hoping, wishing to keep him with her forever.

The sweet scent of roses, honeysuckle, and Alex wafted about her. "I hope I never wake up."

Alex said nothing, though a tiny smile graced his lips.

Alarm snapped Rose from her dream. She glanced over her shoulder. "If Mr. Snyder sees you. . ."

"He won't. Your friends have seen to that."

Tears filled her eyes. "I had no idea they even knew about Snyder or my feelings toward you."

Threading his fingers through hers, he kissed her glove, all the while keeping his eyes on her. "I thought I would never see you again." His voice deepened in sorrow.

"I fear for you, Alex. I do not know who Mr. Snyder may have told." She gripped his hand. "Why have you come back?"

Whispers from a couple sitting on a bench across the way drew his gaze. He scanned the surroundings, then turned to her and smiled. "I have something to show you."

"What could be so important that you risk your life?" She fell against him. Strong arms engulfed her. His strength washed over Rose like an elixir that soothed away all her fears. If only she could bottle it and save it forever. "I could not bear to see you imprisoned. . . or worse."

He kissed her forehead and took a step back, then lifted the flap of his coat. A flicker of gold glimmered in the lantern light. The hilt of a sword. Why had she not seen it before? He drew it from its scabbard.

His service sword. A giggle bubbled in her throat but never released. "How did you get this?"

He slid the blade back into place. "I stole it." His eyes sparkled mischievously.

"From Mr. Snyder?"

"I had some help."

Rose threw a hand to her throat as realization struck her. "Noah and Luke?"

"Indeed." Alex nodded.

"And they didn't turn you over to General Smith?"

"Your uncle convinced them to help me in order to save you from Snyder."

Rose drew in a breath. "They risked being arrested for me."

Alex nodded and brushed a thumb over her cheek. "And they allowed me this one last chance to see you, to tell you in person that you don't have to marry that beast."

Pain stabbed her heart. "Before you leave."

"Yes. They are allowing me to go back to my ship, and for that I am grateful." Alex rubbed the back of his neck. "I know they could all be arrested for treason should anyone find out."

"And my uncle too. What a dear man." The air around Rose grew warm as she began to understand what her friends had risked for her. Tugging off her gloves, she gazed up at Alex and stroked his firm jaw, memorizing the scratchy feel of it.

He placed his hand atop hers. "I could not leave knowing you would be forced to marry that vile man because of me."

A tear slid down Rose's cheek. He gazed at her for a moment then leaned toward her. His warm breath tickled her throat and sent a quiver through her. Then his lips found hers. Lost in his taste, Rose melted into him, fighting back the tears that threatened to spill once again from her eyes.

"He's here. I know I saw him!" Mr. Snyder's slurred voice shot into the garden. Rose jumped from Alex. Her wide eyes met his. A chill enveloped her.

"I assure you, sir, the Drummond servant left their employ last week." Noah's urgent tone sped past them. One glance over her shoulder told Rose, the councilman headed toward them, Noah and Luke on his heels.

Alex pulled Rose into the shadows.

"Go!" she whispered, her tears flowing freely now. She pushed him away. "Go." Agony rent her heart in two.

Gently clutching her face in his hands, he kissed her once more. Then releasing her, he turned and ran into the night.

❖

Alex plodded down the weed-infested trail, his heart so low in his chest it felt as trodden as the pebbles beneath his feet. The rhythmic stomp of boots and beat of war drums reminded him that he was back among his people. Brushing aside a vine, he gazed through the thick forest toward the west where the setting sun wove bands of auburn and gold through the trees and across the path. He stepped through one of the glittering rays but felt none of its light and beauty. In fact, he'd begun to wonder whether he would ever feel joy again.

Two days had passed since he had left Rose at the Fountain Inn. After he'd slipped into the shadows, he'd turned for one last look at her as she stood, tears spilling down her cheeks, staring into the darkness. He'd nearly shed his own tears at the anguish on her pretty face—at the pain in his own heart. But naval officers did not cry. Especially not British naval officers.

Which was what he was once again.

At least that's what he kept telling himself. For as he marched through the Maryland countryside alongside British soldiers, he felt none of the patriotism, pride, or loyalty toward his country that had been inbred in him since his youth.

Truth be told, he felt more like a traitor now than he ever did when he lived with the Drummonds.

Sweat dripped down his back beneath the dark coat of his uniform. Save for the shade of a few trees, the sun had pummeled the men mercilessly as they marched all day with barely a respite. Forbidden to shed the outer coats of their uniforms, many had fallen by the wayside, too exhausted from the heat to continue. Alex pressed onward, embracing the scorching heat, the blisters on his feet, the ache throbbing in his thigh, hoping the discomfort would dull the pain in his heart. He shifted his musket into his other hand and shook out the cramp that had formed in his arm. The smell of unwashed bodies along with the occasional groans filled the air around him.

He tried to shake off his ill feelings. He must forge ahead. He must do his duty. He must not allow foolish sentiments to lead him astray. Yet something deep within him had changed. Something at the core of his being. His very beliefs and values had been turned upside down, and he doubted he'd ever be able to set them aright again.

Nor did he want to.

No, he was no longer the same man. It was as if he had been blind his entire life only now to be given sight. Doffing his hat, he dabbed at the sweat on his forehead as orders ricocheted through the trees, sending the band of men turning to the right.

He must keep his focus. He had his family's honor to think of.

Yet the word *family* in connection to his childhood home seemed blasphemous when compared to what he'd come to know of the true meaning of the word with Rose and the Drummonds.

At least after Alex had left Baltimore and traveled all night, he had no trouble finding a boat to row him back to the HMS *Undefeatable*. He supposed he should thank God that Captain Milford accepted his woeful tale of being shot and cared for by a Loyalist farmer for nearly three weeks until Alex had been able to walk on his own. The captain posed no question as to the whereabouts of Lieutenant Garrick. No doubt most of the men on board, including the captain, were not sorry to see the first lieutenant gone. Alex felt a pang of sorrow for the man who had inspired not an ounce of mourning for his loss.

Yet, no sooner had Alex settled into his berth than he'd been ordered to join a group of marines and seamen who were to rendezvous with a band of troops under the command of General Ross at Marlboro. Their orders were to drag one six-pounder and two three-pounder cannons over the asperous terrain to an undisclosed battlefield. Unable to convince the captain he had not regained his full strength, Alex now found himself, once again, trudging across American soil. Something he had promised Noah and Luke he would do all in his power to avoid.

Last night when they'd camped at Marlboro, the British soldiers had helped themselves to the American settlers' homes and food. They'd stolen sheep and horses and stripped crops and fruit trees like a swarm of locusts. At least they had not murdered or ravished any of the farmers' wives in the process. For that, Alex was grateful. And surprised. Since Admiral Cockburn had joined General Ross, Alex had expected far worse, for the admiral's insatiable lust for American blood had claimed many lives along the Chesapeake.

Alex's agony increased with each step he took. Perhaps if he prayed, God would hear him. Yes, he would pray to Mr. Drummond's God. Not the God Alex had grown up with in the Church of England. No, Alex had come to see that the true God was a God who loved unconditionally and who heard and answered prayers. Bowing his head, Alex could think of no appropriate words to start the dialogue. Yet, oddly a powerful presence encompassed him as if a good friend had stepped into the ranks beside him. A voice spoke, an internal, soothing voice that Alex realized must be the voice of God, repeating the same words over and over again.

"Trust me, trust me."

No matter what happened, Alex determined to do just that. Yet he also prayed that part of his destiny did not entail firing upon the American people he'd come to admire as if they were his own countrymen.

His own countrymen. The words rang so loud and clear within him that he nearly shouted them out loud. Not only did the revelation burst in his heart, but it settled in his reason as if it were pure wisdom.

God, are you telling me to become an American? Excitement heightened his steps.

What of his family? What of gaining their favor once again? A flurry of letters filled his vision—letters he had sent back home begging his brother and his father for forgiveness.

All of them unanswered.

"There is One more whom you must ask."

Alex swallowed and stared down at his muddied boots as he marched onward. He had never asked God to forgive him. In fact, Alex had never forgiven himself. "I'm sorry, God. I'm sorry for what I did to my brother," he whispered.

A weight seemed to roll across his shoulders and fall to the dirt beside him. He stretched his back and gazed upward into the blue sky. Unexpected joy filled him. His skin buzzed with excitement. God had forgiven him. God had forgiven him! How could Alex not forgive himself?

He bowed his head. *Thank You for Your forgiveness, God. I forgive myself. Please help me never to do something so foolish again.*

He cringed and raised his gaze. Yet wasn't staying with Rose just another foolhardy, irrational move?

No. It wasn't just a frivolous sentiment. Though Alex's heart was elated, becoming an American also rang true in his mind and in his spirit—the spirit that now was connected to God Almighty.

Alex chuckled out loud, drawing the gaze of a few of the soldiers. Perhaps he was the half-wit his father had so often called him. Here was the proof. What son of a wealthy viscount would turn his back on his family, his inheritance—egad, even his country—for a farm girl who spoke to pigs and cuddled chickens? A woman who feared everything and yet saved the life of an enemy whose people had killed her father.

A woman who loved without measure.

The lure of home, family, love, and a pair of luminous turquoise eyes made all the things he had sought for his entire life seem suddenly unimportant—trite. He would give up all the fortune and titles in the world, even the throne of England itself, to make Rose his wife.

Later that night Alex squeezed between two seamen and lowered himself to a rock before the blazing fire—one of many that dotted the landscape. The boldness of his countrymen! Setting up camp so brazenly in the middle of their enemy's land. As if the Americans hadn't the wit or the bravado to attack them. Quite astonishing. Yet hadn't Alex been a willing participant in that enormous British ego most of his life?

The seamen and marines under Alex's command greeted him as they dipped bread into the stew filling their tin plates. The scent of beef and unwashed men swirled about his nose, and he grabbed his own plate, hoping his appetite had returned. But the sounds of the men slopping their grub reminded him of Prinney, and sorrow clamped over his heart once again. He set the plate down.

He wanted to leave. Find his way back to Rose's farm. Tell her he loved her. Become an American. But he must be careful. The countryside was flooded with British soldiers on high alert. If he were caught, he'd be put in irons and sent back to his ship. If the Americans caught him before he could explain, they'd shoot him on the spot. He couldn't risk it. The best strategy would be to wait until they spotted the American army. Then he could slip away in the night, white flag in hand, and report to their commanding officer. But so far, they'd not spotted a single American troop.

He gazed across the dark night to a field dotted with white canvas tents that reminded him of a fleet of ships at sea. But where was General Ross leading this fleet? Alex had sent one of his own men, Mr. Glasson, to loiter about Ross's quarters and glean what information he could about the general's objective.

And there Mr. Glasson came now, emerging from the crowd of

soldiers milling about the camp as he rushed to their small group. He knelt beside them, his eyes twinkling in the firelight. "I found out what you asked, Mr. Reed. I ran into Lieutenant Scott, one of Admiral Cochrane's men."

"So, where are we heading?" One of the men asked before he took a swig of water.

"Tomorrow we march into Washington." Mr. Glasson smiled and rubbed his hands together. "To burn her to the ground."

❖ CHAPTER 24 ❖

Rose knelt beside the pigsty and eased her hand through the wooden posts. Prinney waddled toward her, snorting and grunting in glee. Memories drifted across her mind, of Alex's face twisting in indignation when he'd discovered whom she'd named her favorite pig after. A traitorous smile lifted her lips. The first in days. Three days, in fact, since she'd last seen Alex in the gardens of the Fountain Inn. That entire evening seemed like a dream to her now. Like one of those mystical childhood fairy tales where the prince arrives at the ball and sweeps the princess off her feet. Only to be separated later by some evil wizard.

Which was a perfect description of Mr. Snyder.

Thank goodness the laudanum Noah had slipped into his drink had befogged his faculties enough to give her and Alex time to say good-bye one last time. That Alex had risked so much to see her softened the blow of his leaving. He loved her. Then why did he have to leave at all? Perhaps, he just didn't love her enough.

She ran her fingers over Prinney's rough hide. The pig nuzzled against her hand. "At least I still have you, Prinney."

He grunted in return, encouraging his fellow pigs to join in the chorus.

Rose stood, pressed a hand on her back and glanced over the farm. The noon sun capped the field in a bright bowl of glistening light, transforming ordinary green into emerald, browns into copper, and yellows into saffron. Even her ripe tomatoes sparkled like rubies. A light breeze, plump with the scent of cedar, hay, and horseflesh, stirred the tall grass into swirling eddies of green and gold. Chickens crowded around the hem of her gown. Grabbing a handful of dried corn from the bucket, she scattered it across the dirt. The birds clucked and flapped and strutted back and forth, snatching up the tiny seeds.

Picking up the bucket, Rose headed toward the barn. Even the beauty of this place could not penetrate the fortress of gloom around her heart. She already missed Alex so much, she had no idea how she would endure the rest of her life without him.

Wind whipped through the barn doors, tossing loose strands of her hair into her eyes and blinding her for a moment. Groping her way to Liverpool's stall, she brushed the curls from her face.

And ran straight into a man.

Rose screamed and leaped back. Mr. Snyder stood before her, cane planted in the dirt, and a look of deviant fury warping his face.

Terror gripped her. Her aunt and uncle had left for Washington DC the day before. Cora and Amelia had gone to town on errands, and Mr. Markham was no doubt asleep in the parlor. "What are you doing here?"

A caustic smile twisted his lips. "To inform you, my dear, that I know what you and your friends did. Malicious and traitorous gnats. I should have you all arrested."

Annoyance swept her fear aside. "Why don't you then?"

He shook his head and stepped toward her. "You think you have won, Miss McGuire, but you have not." He grinned. "You will still marry me"—he clipped her chin between his thumb and forefinger—"or I will inform General Smith that you harbored a British naval officer in your home for weeks." His bergamot cologne stung her nose.

"I beg you to do so, sir." Rose snatched her chin from his fingers and thrust her nose into the air. "You have no proof and Alex. . .Mr. Reed is gone."

"Ah yes, gone back to join the troops who attack us daily. Why, in fact, your beloved naval officer may be at this very moment marching into a trap."

Rose stiffened. "What do you mean?"

Victory flashed across Mr. Snyder's contemptuous gaze. "I heard from General Smith that a band of British troops are headed toward

Washington." He brushed dust from his coat. "As if they could occupy our capital. Bah!" He chuckled then studied her. "Oh, I see fear on your pretty face. Now, don't fret about the lives of your fellow Americans, my love, I'm sure the regular army and Maryland militia will give the British quite a welcome. Hopefully one which obliterates every last one of them."

A dozen thoughts spun in Rose's head until it grew light. Her aunt and uncle were in Washington. Did they know about the attack? Were there enough American soldiers to protect them? And what of Alex?

She took a deep breath and gripped the edge of Valor's stall. "Mr. Reed is no doubt back on his ship."

Mr. Snyder cocked his head and smiled. "Ah yes. One would think so, but I also heard there are several naval officers among the British horde. *Tsk tsk*. It would be a shame to see him killed. And by one of our own."

Rose's legs wobbled.

"Which brings me back to why you will still marry me," he continued, twirling his cane in the air. "Who do you suppose General Smith will believe, a prominent councilman or a British doxy?"

Rose longed to wipe the supercilious smirk from his lips. "A rather inebriated councilman, from all appearances at the ball. Perhaps he'll believe me, over you, sir."

"Humph." Mr. Snyder tugged on his cravat, then pressed his fingers through the red hair at his temples. "You are nothing but a British strumpet, a sullied orphan girl."

Rose tried to ignore the insult, but it slipped into her heart anyway. "I insist you leave at once, Mr. Snyder. You are no longer welcome here."

A spark of fury seared in his gaze. It grew larger and larger until it seemed to consume his eyes like a wildfire. Rose swallowed and took a step back.

"I will take down your entire family." Lifting his cane, he slammed it over the post. The ominous snap of wood shot through the barn like musket fire.

Liverpool let out a long mournful groan as the chickens scattered in a frenzy.

A wave of acid flooded Rose's belly. She hadn't thought Mr. Snyder capable of violence, but suddenly she was not so sure.

Mr. Snyder tossed the broken stick to the ground, then clutched Rose by the throat.

Clawing at his hands, she gasped for air.

He thrust his face into hers until she could smell the sausage he'd had for breakfast. "I will have this land and you as my wife if it's the last thing I do."

Valor let out a thunderous bray and kicked her stall.

Rose scratched at his hands, her lungs screaming. Visions of another man's harsh grip upon her throat blasted through her mind. *Oh God, no!* Panic set in, first clenching her heart then weaving its way through every muscle and tissue. Just when she thought she might lose consciousness from lack of air, Mr. Snyder released her, shoving her back against Valor's stall.

Lifting a hand to her throat, Rose coughed and gulped in air, shifting her gaze between the open barn door and Mr. Snyder, lest he come at her again. Instead he stood there, his chest heaving, his expression one of shock and self-loathing. "Forgive me." Then suddenly, spinning on his heel, he marched from the barn.

A minute later, Rose heard his horse gallop away. She wanted to succumb to her trembling legs and crumple to the ground. She wanted to cry. She wanted to run and lock herself in her chamber.

But she couldn't. Her aunt and uncle were in the center of a city about to be attacked by the British. She couldn't count on the military evacuating them. Despite what Mr. Snyder declared, Rose's aunt had informed her that Washington was often left largely unprotected because most of the army stationed there was called out to battle in other locations. No one in their wildest dreams considered an attack on Washington DC possible.

And perhaps it still wasn't.

But how could she be sure?

Daniel's words of destiny rang in her ears. *God has something important for you to do.* She hadn't believed him. Not until this moment. Now she feared the destiny he had spoken of was fast approaching.

She must go to Washington to warn her family.

Climbing to the barn loft, she retrieved Alex's pistol from a trunk. She hated bringing the heinous thing but it might come in handy. Thoughts of Alex caused her heart to shrink. Was he indeed marching on Washington? If so, he'd be forced to shoot Americans. Which made him her enemy once again. Not to mention put him in grave danger. And the worst of it was, if he died, she would never know. She didn't know whether to pray for him or her countrymen. Perhaps both. After climbing down the ladder, she prepared Valor to ride, stuffed the pistol in the saddle pack, and led the horse out of the barn.

No sooner had she reached the open field than her legs went as limp as blades of grass, her chest felt as though Liverpool were sitting on it, and her head spun around a pounding ache.

She could not go to Washington!

Alone.

What was she thinking?

She gazed over the grassy field beyond. Her home. Her sanctuary. Would it remain that way? Over the treetops the afternoon sun sped toward the horizon as if frightened of the coming night. Distant thunder rumbled from slate gray clouds looming in the east.

Oh Lord, please protect my aunt and uncle.

Even at a gallop, the trip would take her at least four hours. She might already be too late.

She sank to the ground and dropped her head into her hands. "I cannot go. Lord, what if I'm attacked again?"

"I love you."

God? Rose glanced around her but heard only the rustle of the wind dancing through the tall grass. "What if I don't make it in time?"

"I love you."

Did God love her? Memories of the dream she had a few weeks ago filled her thoughts. The man in white had said she had something important to do for God, just like Daniel had proclaimed. Rose wiped her sweaty palms over her gown.

"Go." The inner voice again. Gentle, yet not demanding.

"Me? Lord. I'm nothing but a frightened little mouse." A heavy wind swept over her, twirling the dirt beside her into a whirlwind. She hugged herself. "I don't know if I can do this."

"Trust me."

Trust. Indignation forced her to her feet. She fisted her hands at her sides. "Trust!" She shouted into the sky. "Where were You when I was attacked? Where were You when I was ravished?" Her voice cracked.

"Right beside you."

"Lord." she sobbed.

"Precious daughter, forgive them."

Rose closed her eyes. Light and shadow battled across her eyelids. The warmth of the sun embraced her as the wind caressed her hair and cooled her moist cheeks. Forgive. She didn't feel like forgiving the sailors who had assaulted her, the family friend who had used her. But maybe it wasn't about feelings. Mr. Snyder had asked for her forgiveness before he'd stomped out of the barn. Could she forgive him as well?

Rose clenched her fists. "I forgive them, Lord. I forgive them all."

Love such as she'd never known before instantly fell upon her, cloaking her, filling her. More than the love of her earthly father, this love was like a fire, consuming all fear in its path.

She opened her eyes. And suddenly she knew. It didn't matter what happened to her. She belonged to God. The Almighty Creator of the universe was her father. He would always be with her—even through the bad times. There was a plan.

A purpose behind the agony.

Half-giggling half-sobbing, she lifted her arms out to her sides, thirsting for more of this love, wanting to soak it in, to bask in it. She twirled around like a child frolicking among a field of wildflowers until she nearly stumbled with dizziness. So this was what Uncle Forbes meant when he said, *"Perfect love casts out all fear."*

"Thank You, Father."

Thunder groaned in the distance again, reminding her she hadn't much time.

Wiping her face, she drew a deep breath and swung onto Valor's back. She clutched the reins and faced southwest. Fear still lingered within her. She felt its tormenting claws grinding over the fortress of love that held it at bay, clamoring to be released, but with God's help, she would not allow it. Not ever again.

❖

Snyder urged his gelding down the trail leading back to the Drummond home. No sooner had he reached Madison Street than he regretted his harsh treatment of Rose. He hadn't intended to be so vile. In fact, quite the opposite. But the smug look of victory on her face had unleashed the devil within him. How dare she toss him from her farm like so much refuse? The audacity! Never in Snyder's life had he been treated with such brazen impudence. Especially not from an orphaned farm girl.

Snyder's own inferior birth and dubious heritage rose to sneer at him, but he shoved the unsavory thoughts aside. He had risen above the legacy left him by his father and grandfather. And he would rise further still.

For he had every intention of marrying Miss McGuire, despite this temporary setback.

With Mr. Reed gone, the lady had no other worthwhile prospects. Certainly none as advantageous as himself. His housekeeper, Miss Addington, had reminded him of that fact last evening as he stormed about his parlor, shoving vases and trays to the floor in his fury. "Easier to catch bees with sweet nectar than with tar," she had said. He wished he'd taken her advice instead of behaving the ignoble beast. But who could blame him after all she and Mr. Reed had done? Nevertheless, he determined to make amends immediately, before her anger festered. He would swallow his pride and apologize for his behavior. Sooner or later, she was bound to see him in a favorable light and forgive his past indiscretions.

Adjusting the bouquet of wildflowers he'd picked along the side of the road, he snapped the reins and smiled at the assurance of his success. He was handsome, accomplished, and had much to offer the lady. Now all he needed was a bit of charm and a barrel of patience, and soon this prime land would be his.

A band of sooty clouds lined the eastern horizon, but the afternoon sun still beat down on him. Withdrawing a handkerchief, he mopped the sweat from his brow as he led his horse through the farm's open gate and glanced toward the barn where he expected to find Miss McGuire. His eyes were rewarded with the sight of her standing beside her horse.

Urging his gelding into a trot, he headed her way when, much to his surprise, she leaped upon her filly, kicked the beast's sides, and galloped across the field, disappearing into the forest.

By herself! Did she know there were British afoot?

Snyder stared after her as a gust of wind swept away the cloud of dust kicked up by her horse. Of course she knew there were British afoot. Perhaps that was why she'd left in such a hurry—to rendezvous with a particular British naval officer.

Snyder ground his teeth together. *The tramp.* Tossing the flowers into the dirt, he flicked the reins and sped across the field after her.

❖ CHAPTER 25 ❖

Alex had barely slept ten minutes before a bugle blared and drums pounded through the camp, waking the troops to a new day.

A day his countrymen intended to march into the American capital and crush the heart of this fledgling nation.

Struggling to rise from the hard ground outside the tent, he stretched the ache in his back and rubbed his eyes, trying to shake the fog from his brain.

Soon men in red coats emerged from tents like fiery wasps from their nests as officers stormed by on horseback shouting orders. After a cold breakfast of dried pork and water, the men tore down the tents, packed the supplies, and lined up in formation. Cool morning air, whispering the promise of a reprieve from the summer heat, drifted over the tired soldiers as they marched double-file into an immense forest where thick branches and a plethora of leaves in all shapes and sizes formed an archway of green overhead that shielded them from the sun. Behind Alex, the seamen in his charge heaved on thick ropes attached to the ship's guns. It would have been much easier to pull the iron cannons in a wagon but due to a shortage of horses, none had been provided. They were good men, brave and loyal, some barely sprouting whiskers on their chins. The guilt of Alex's treason ground hard against his soul. He bowed his head. *Lord, please allow no deaths this day. Please save this wonderful nation and her capital.*

He felt a stirring in his soul. A mission. The American capital must not fall.

He didn't know why. But he felt God telling him, assuring him that these rebel Americans would remain a free nation.

That they must remain a free nation.

His eyes locked on the service sword swinging at his side and the brass buttons lining his blue naval uniform. They seemed out of place on his body—as if they belonged to someone else. He raised his gaze and shifted his shoulders beneath an oddly pleasing sensation. He no longer felt like an Englishman. Instead he felt like an American. Longed to be part of this nation that stood for freedom and liberty and a man's right to pursue his own path to happiness—a nation that did not honor a man simply because of his pedigree.

Soon the cool air of morning dissipated, ushering in a blanket of muggy heat. A groan rose in Alex's throat, and he tipped up his bicorn and wiped the sweat off his brow. The task before him seemed insurmountable. Not only did he have to do his best to avoid battling the Americans, but he had to slip away from the British undetected, and make his way to the American troops without being shot by either side. The more he pondered it, the more impossible the task seemed. And the more dangerous.

After another hour the British troops emerged from the forest into an open field. Though the sun stood only halfway to its zenith, heat struck Alex with such ferocity, he felt as though he'd walked straight into an oven. Dust from the hundreds of boots that had preceded him rose to clog the air. Alex coughed and gasped for breath. His eyes stung. Not a wisp of wind stirred to clear the air or cool his skin.

On their right, they passed bundles of straw and the smoking ashes of campfires strewn across a field, evidence that a large body of men had camped there the night before. Farther ahead, the fresh imprints of hooves and boots sent a tremble down Alex.

The American troops were close. Alex's heart leaped. Perhaps he could escape before the fighting began.

Yet the unrelenting heat punished them without mercy. Seasoned soldiers fell by the wayside, too exhausted and dehydrated to continue. Alex took a position beside his men and aided them in pulling one of the cannons. Sweat soaked his coat, shirt, and breeches and dripped from the tips of his hair. His breath heaved and every muscle ached as he followed the ranks onto a huge field dotted with thick groves. An eerie silence fell. Everyone seemed to hold their breath, waiting for the signal to form a square for battle.

Alex loosened his cravat and wiped the back of his neck. In the distance, a heavy dust cloud appeared. Drums beat the forward advance, and the troops continued down another road, passing a small plantation on their right before climbing a grassy knoll.

Ignoring the blisters on his hands and the burning in his thighs, Alex tugged on the thick rope. The soldiers who marched before him slowed. Their bodies stiffened like masts. The air twanged with tension. The clomp of horses' hooves joined the shouts of commanding officers. Releasing the rope to another seaman, Alex darted up the hill and pressed through the throng of sweaty men.

Across a field of tall grass, not half a mile away, stood line after line of American soldiers, some in uniform, others not. All well armed. And beyond them in the distance, Alex could barely make out what must be the buildings of Washington DC rising into the afternoon sun.

Alex's muscles tightened. He gripped the musket on his shoulder. The battle would begin in seconds.

❖

Rose galloped into Washington DC and headed down Maryland Street toward the Capitol. Reining Valor to a trot, she scanned the city. Unlike Baltimore, which boasted cobblestone streets through the main part of town, this road and all the ones that spanned from it were nothing but patches of mud and dust. Brick buildings rose on each side and a ditch filled with sewage and stagnant water lined the avenue. The stench curled Rose's nose even as the sight shocked her.

This was the capital of their grand country?

Clucking drew Rose's gaze to a group of chickens prancing off the side of the road. A massive pig snuffled through a pile of garbage to her left. The only signs of life in the otherwise vacant city. After the long ride, the familiar sight of animals loosened her tight nerves if only a bit before she turned right toward Delaware Street where she knew her aunt's orphanage was located. Up ahead a black man ducked in between two buildings. Rose called to him, but he did not reappear.

Despite the heat of the day, a cold chill slithered down her spine. Where was everyone? Then it occurred to her. She'd ridden unhindered into the capital. No one had stopped or questioned her. Not only that, but she'd not spotted a single soldier, American or British. Had Mr. Snyder been misinformed?

Rose scanned the buildings framing Delaware Street. Up ahead, a two-story, whitewashed home drew her gaze, and she slowed before it. The words SUFFER THE LITTLE CHILDREN TO COME UNTO ME stood out in black letters on a sign that hung on a post just inside a tattered fence. Taking a deep breath to calm her thundering heart, Rose dismounted, tied the reins to a hitching post, and grabbed the pistol from the sack. The front door stood ajar. No light or sound emerged from within. Creeping forward, she gripped the handle of the gun and nearly laughed at her own hypocrisy. She could never use the vile weapon even if her life depended on it. Never again.

She stopped before the door and listened. Only the mad rush of blood through her head pounded in her ears. She pushed the door open wider, sending an eerie creak chiming through the house.

"Aunt Muira! Uncle Forbes!" She stepped inside the shadowy foyer. Open books, toys, and children's clothes littered the wooden floor as if the inhabitants had fled in a hurry. The sweet scent of children and innocence and aged wood drifted past her nose.

Footfalls sounded from the back of a long hall. Rose's heart pinched. "Aunt Muira?"

"She's not here." The gentle voice of a man preceded his appearance around a corner. Smiling, he approached Rose. Short-cropped gray hair matched a cultured beard that ran the length of his jaw. Caring brown eyes assessed her. "You must be Rose."

Rose lowered the weapon. "Reverend Hargrave?"

"Yes." He examined the gun and his brows scrunched together. "Why have you come here? It's not safe."

"I heard the British intended to attack Washington, and I feared for my aunt's and uncle's safety." Rose stuffed the pistol into her sash and clasped her hands together to keep them from trembling.

"Oh dear girl, how kind of you." He released a sigh. "Indeed. We heard the same horrendous news. But they've all left. Your aunt and uncle and Miss Edna. They took the children in our wagon and fled the city not two hours ago."

Rose glanced out the door, then back at the reverend, her mind and heart spinning. "Where did they go?"

"I have no idea, my dear. I'm so sorry." He laid a hand on her arm. "But never fear, they are safe."

Relief eased through Rose, and she sighed. Moving to the door, she gazed over the deserted street. "Where is the army, the militia? Why aren't they defending the city?"

"They marched out hours ago." The reverend's footsteps rang hollow over the floor. "Although I do believe there are still some troops down at the naval yard."

Rose swerved around. Though she'd rather hop on Valor and head straight home, certainly God had sent her here for a reason. Perhaps that reason lay at the naval yard. "Where is the yard?"

"Down Virginia Avenue beside the east branch of the Potomac, miss." Concern tightened his features. "But you needn't worry about them." His tone turned urgent. "I beg you to return to Baltimore where you'll be safe."

Rose stepped toward him. "What if the British make it past our troops? What about you?"

He stooped to pick a book off the floor, then smiled. "One of the children is sick and couldn't travel. Besides, they won't trouble a man of the cloth."

Rose did not share his confidence. Yet the peace that surrounded this man put her fears to shame. "God be with you, Reverend."

"And with you." He gave her a reassuring nod.

Turning, Rose fled out the door, dashed toward Valor, and swung onto the saddle. Shielding her eyes from the setting sun, she urged the horse into a trot and headed east.

Past the Capitol building that centered the town. Though not yet completed, its tall white columns stretched to the sky like unrelenting monuments of freedom. The Hall of Representatives stood on the right side—a massive oval surrounded by Corinthian pillars. A wide wooden boardwalk connected its two wings, where they no doubt planned to build an enclosed walkway. Rose galloped past. No time to admire the majestic buildings.

"Oh Lord, please help me," she whispered, but the wind slamming over her face tore her words away along with the pins from her hair.

Flinging strands from her face, Rose raced onward. She tightened her grip on the reins. Her fingers ached. Her heart crashed against her ribs. Fear beckoned to her, begging for release. But something had changed. Rose now knew that God loved her and would never leave her. She may feel fear, but it no longer enslaved her.

She galloped down the street toward the white brick wall that enclosed the navy yard and was surprised once again to find the outside gate abandoned. In fact, no one manned the guard house at all as she led Valor onto the sun-bleached yard. Tall brick buildings framed the inner courtyard. Beyond them loomed the massive arched buildings where the ships were made. Cannons, their muzzles pointed through the battlements of a long stone wall, guarded the yard from seafaring invaders. In the distance, bare ship masts stretched like spires into the sky, stark white against the black clouds lining the horizon.

Rose slid off Valor and headed toward what appeared to be the main headquarters when a thin, bald-headed man with tufts of hair sprouting like brown thickets above his ears emerged and nearly ran her down.

"Miss! What are you doing here?" He placed his cocked hat atop his head, his blue eyes flashing.

Rose threw a hand to her chest. "Sir, are the British marching on Washington?"

He gave her a skeptical look and chuckled. "Where have you been? Why haven't you left town?" He glanced over his shoulder. "You need to leave immediately, miss."

A dozen men emerged from the same building and flooded the yard, some giving her a cursory glance as they passed. Their arms were laden with weapons and cans of some kind of powder.

Rose frowned and gave the man a venomous look. "Who are you, sir, and what are you doing to defend this city?"

He snorted and narrowed his eyes. "I am Commodore Thomas Tingey, miss. And who, pray tell, are you?"

"Rose McGuire from Baltimore." The smell of tar and gunpowder stung her nose. "Where is the militia? Where are the troops defending Washington?"

He gave a sardonic chuckle. "Troops defending Washington?" His bitter tone sent a chill through Rose. "What troops we had marched off to cut off the British advance yesterday." He swallowed and gazed into the distance, sorrow claiming his dusty features. "I have just received word that they have been defeated at Bladensburg."

"Defeated?" Rose's knees wobbled.

"I'm afraid so, miss." He touched her elbow to steady her. "The British could be here any minute."

Valor neighed, and Rose sent a harried gaze over the barren yard where evening shadows began to creep out from hiding. "Aren't you going to do something?"

"Miss, I have but a handful of sailors. I've been ordered to fire the yard at the first sign of the enemy."

"Fire the yard?" Rose glanced to the grassy fields that extended to the Potomac River.

"Aye, we've already set up explosives. Our last task is to lay trails of gunpowder, so we can ignite the blast when the time comes."

Rose glanced at the bare masts of several ships at dock and a few being built on land. "What of the ships?"

Tingey scratched the stubble on his chin. "A shame indeed, miss." His gaze shifted to the docks. "I won't mourn the old frigates, *Boston* and *General Greene,* but the sloop *Argus* and the new frigate *Columbia.* Now, those will be hard losses." He eyed her. "But would you prefer they end up in British hands, along with our naval stores and ammunition?" He brushed past her, shouting orders to the men, then flung a glance back her way. "Now, miss, I urge you to leave the city immediately." His stern tone and the commanding look in his eyes brooked no argument.

Rose nodded, defeat settling like an anchor in her gut. "I will, sir. Is there anyone else in town I can assist in evacuating?"

Commodore Tingey pursed his lips. "I understand the first lady stubbornly resists leaving. I have orders to gather her up on our way out of town."

"Mrs. Madison?" Rose heard the excitement in her own voice. "Can you direct me toward her house?"

Commodore Tingey gestured with his hand. "Past the Capitol, on Pennsylvania Avenue. You can't miss it. Good luck. She's a stubborn one." He tipped his hat at her and marched off shouting "Godspeed to you, Miss McGuire" over his shoulder.

"God help us all." Rose swallowed, then mounted Valor and rode out of the yard, feeling suddenly small and useless. "Why have You sent me here, Lord?" The wind whipped over her, swirling taunting voices in her ears. *You have no destiny. Foolish girl. There is nothing important for you to do here.*

Fear, her old familiar friend, surged through her like a prisoner suddenly released, giddy with delight. Pulling Valor to a halt, she stared at the deserted streets of her nation's capital. The setting sun cast a rainbow of orange and gold over the homes and government buildings. She blinked and rubbed her eyes as if she'd just awoken from a dream. What was she doing here? So far from home. With no one to protect her.

"Oh Lord," she sobbed. "What can I do against an entire British army?" She nudged Valor into a slow walk. Hope spilled from her with each tear that slid down her cheek. The British would take Washington.

And there was nothing she could do about it.

Boom. A distant cannon sounded. Rose clutched the reins. The leather bit through her gloves into her skin.

Their glorious country would fall, and its people would once more be subject to the tyranny of a king who lived across the sea. How could that happen?

"Trust me."

That voice again. So sure and strong, resounding from within her. Created out of her own desperate need to be valued, loved, and cared for? Or truly the voice of God?

She turned down Pennsylvania Avenue, fear threatening to rise and choke the breath from her lungs, her throat. The sun dipped below the horizon, stealing more of the daylight. She should go home. Now, before the troops arrived. Before the soldiers found her—a woman all alone, vulnerable.

And she suffered the same hideous fate all over again.

She would rather die.

A beautiful white mansion rose among the smaller homes along the street, its front door wide open. No doubt the president's home. A carriage with two horses and a footman waited out by the street. It appeared Mrs. Madison was in no need of assistance. Rose kicked Valor to pass the house and head out of town when a woman's scream blared from one of the windows.

❖ CHAPTER 26 ❖

Alex knelt beside the lifeless body of Mr. Kennedy, a seaman under his charge. Blood oozing from several bullet holes in his chest marched like a maroon death squad over his brown shirt. Though not a bruise or cut marred his young face, his vacant eyes stared at the blue sky above—serene, yet empty. Alex brushed his fingers over them, closing them forever. Somewhere back in England, a mother had lost a son. And she was not even aware of the tragedy. Nor would she be aware of it for months.

Ignoring his throbbing thigh and the ache spanning his back, Alex rose and scanned the scene. Exhausted from the stifling heat and the harrowing battle, soldiers had dropped to the ground wherever their weary legs had deposited them. A group of men cleared the British dead from the field while another band picked greedily through the pockets of the dead Americans. From what Alex could tell, more British than Americans had been killed, although neither total reached one hundred.

Plucking his keg from his haversack, Alex uncorked it and poured tepid water down his throat. Despite the temperature, the liquid cooled his parched mouth and filled his empty belly. He lifted his arm to wipe his lips and jolted at the sight of blood splattered over his sleeve. Not his blood, thank God. But someone's blood. Perhaps Mr. Kennedy's or another unfortunate soldier who had slipped from earth into eternity. He prayed they'd gone in the right direction.

To his left, a pair of hollow blue eyes stared at him from within a face blackened by soot. Seaman Miller sat among a group of sailors and offered Alex a sad smile. Despite the horrific chaos raging around him, he had remained at his post by the six-pounder Alex had ordered him to command. Not once had he hesitated in his duty. Alex nodded his approval toward the man of a job well done.

A shout of orders drew Alex's gaze to a large group of captured Americans being led by a colonel who pranced before them in the pomp of victory. He hoped they would be treated humanely but knew they'd probably be either impressed into the Royal Navy or transferred to prison hulks for the remainder of the war.

Tugging off his stained cravat, Alex mopped the sweat from his neck and brow and glanced at the sun halfway on its descent in the sky. He guessed it to be about four in the afternoon, which meant the battle had lasted three hours. Three hours that had seemed like mere seconds—terrifying, agonizing seconds. Though Alex had been in many battles at sea, there was something different, something far more grue-some about fighting on land. Everything moved slowly and methodi-cally upon the sea; on land, everything occurred with such intolerable rapidity and chaos. At sea, as the ships maneuvered for the next broad-side, the men had time to clear off the wounded and catch their breath, even say a prayer. But on land, the bullets had never stopped whizzing past Alex's ears, the cannons never stopped firing, the explosions never stopped blasting.

And the men never stopped screaming.

Two soldiers lifted a wounded man off the dirt and placed him on a stretcher. He groaned in agony. Nausea bubbled in Alex's belly, nearly forcing it to spew the water he'd just consumed. He corked his keg and placed it back into his haversack. Bowing his head, he thanked God that he'd not been forced to fight face-to-face with any of the Americans, for he doubted he could have looked straight into the fire of freedom burning in their eyes and willingly extinguished it.

In the end, it must have been the British Congreve rockets that had sent the enemy fleeing. The rocket's shrill screech still rang in Alex's ears. Despite their ominous sound, they were grossly inaccu-rate, and Alex doubted any of the rockets had met their mark. But the bone-chilling howl—a roar that Alex imagined sounded like a legion of demons escaping from hell—was sufficient to invoke terror in the staunchest soldier.

Certainly terrifying enough to send the untrained, undisciplined American militia into a panic. Even so, their rapid, chaotic retreat surprised Alex. And disappointed him. He had hoped for more bravado from these Americans he had come to know as both courageous and determined. Of course slipping away and joining them in the heat of battle had not been an option. He'd have been shot on the spot. And now the Americans were gone again. Alex was beginning to think that he wouldn't be able to desert the British until the entire war was over. At least it seemed that way until a minute ago when Admiral Cockburn had stormed up to Alex and selected him to join the march into Washington.

❖

Rose dashed through the open door of the White House and halted, listening. Another scream blared from the right. Clutching her skirts in one hand and plucking her pistol from her sash with the other, she sped up the stairs, slowing when she reached the top.

"I order you to leave my house at once, sir!" A lofty female voice, tainted with a slight quaver, drew Rose down the hall to the right.

"Not a step farther, sir. Do you know who I am?" the woman shouted.

"Yes, madam, the mistress of this rebellious squalor of a country." The man's strong British lilt coupled with his invidious tone sent a wave of dread over Rose.

Ducking beneath lit sconces and framed paintings, she inched over the ornately woven rug toward an open door at the end of the hallway. Her legs shook like branches in a storm.

"How dare you?" the woman's superior tone resounded through the hall.

Lord, help me. Rose stopped at the side of the open door and dared a peek inside. A soldier in a red coat and white breeches stood with his back to her, leveling a sword at an elegantly attired lady wearing a feathered turban. From what Rose had heard about the president's wife, the lady had to be Mrs. Madison.

Mrs. Madison took a step backward and nearly bumped into one of the high-backed chairs surrounding a long dining table at the center of the room. A flick of her eyes told Rose the woman had seen her. Ducking back beside the doorframe, Rose leaned against the wall to quell her sudden dizziness. She had the advantage of surprise.

And a gun. She should shoot him.

But she couldn't.

Not again. But she could hit him with it. Knock him out. Her hands shook. The pistol slipped in her sweaty palms. She tightened her grip, gulping for air that seemed to have retreated with the rest of Washington's inhabitants. If she failed to rescue Mrs. Madison, the soldier would no doubt turn on Rose and then kill the president's wife anyway. Closing her eyes, she silently hummed her father's song, hoping to find solace in the words.

> *O can't you see yon little turtledove*
> *Sitting under the mulberry tree?*
> *See how that she doth mourn for her true love*

Rose shook her head. It wasn't working. Terror kept her frozen in place. Yet hadn't she just declared herself to be free of fear's bondage?

"I hate to inform you, madam, that we have taken your capital and that you are now a prisoner of war." The man chuckled. "Or should I say, prize of war."

"I am no one's prize, sir."

"We shall see, madam."

Rose closed her eyes. *Why has my fear returned, Lord? Where are You?*

"Trust me."

I can't.

"I love you. I will never leave you."

Rose drew a deep breath. She wasn't alone against this British soldier. The Creator of the universe was with her. Pretty good odds, she'd say.

If she believed it.

Rose lifted her chin. *I do believe it. I do believe You, Lord.*

Clutching the barrel of the pistol with both hands, she held it above her head and charged through the door. Before the soldier could turn around, she slammed the handle of the weapon on his head. He dropped to the floor in a heap. A red puddle blossomed like a rose on his blond hair.

The gun slipped from Rose's hands. It fell onto the wooden floor beside him with a *clank*. She raised her gaze to Mrs. Madison.

The lady's wide eyes softened, and a smile grazed her painted lips. "Why, thank you, my dear. The buffoon was becoming quite annoying." Opening her arms, she gestured for Rose to enter as if welcoming her to an evening dinner party.

As if there weren't an unconscious British corporal lying on the floor.

Rose stepped over him. Her legs shook and she stumbled. Mrs. Madison clutched her arm to steady her. "There, there, dear. It is all over now."

Rose glanced at the soldier, then back at Mrs. Madison. "It appears the British have already arrived in the city. You should leave at once."

Releasing Rose's arm, Mrs. Madison flapped a gloved hand over the man as if to brush him away. "Just a scout of some sort." She sighed. "Now, pray tell, who are you, and how did you come to be in my home?" The woman smiled, lifting the circles of red rouge painted on her cheeks. Candlelight sparkled in her eyes and glimmered off the gold jewelry around her neck.

Rose glanced at the long, elegant dining table behind Mrs. Madison. Exquisitely painted china plates framed a white linen cloth that held candlesticks, pitchers, crystal glasses, and platters upon platters of food. Candlelight reflecting off the silverware and brass brightened the entire room. Only then did the scent of beef pudding, wild goose, cornmeal, and sweet pickles reach her nose. Rose shook her head at the odd sight.

"I am Rose McGuire from Baltimore, Mrs. Madison. I was riding past your house when I heard your scream." Rose's heart refused to settle, and she pressed a hand over it. "I beg your pardon for entering uninvited, but the door was open."

"You beg my pardon?" Mrs. Madison's laughter bounced over the room with a friendship and gaiety at odds with the situation. "My dear Miss McGuire, your boldness saved my life." She studied Rose from head to toe. "And such a slip of a girl too. But so full of bravery."

Brave? Rose found the compliment difficult to swallow.

Mrs. Madison glanced at the open door. "I do wonder where Jean ran off to, as well as Mr. Jennings. If they had been here, this wouldn't have happened."

Plucking a telescope from the table, she glided toward an open window. The swish of what Rose assumed to be a silk Parisian gown—for she'd never seen anything so exquisite—drifted through the dining hall.

"I haven't seen my husband all day." Mrs. Madison lifted the glass to her eye and peered out the window into the darkness beyond. A night breeze ruffled the red plume atop her embroidered turban and fluttered the rich damask curtains. "He left early this morning to meet with his Cabinet at the navy yard. Pray don't think poorly of him." She glanced at Rose over her shoulder before lifting the scope to her eye again. "Mr. Madison did leave a troop of men to guard me, but they ran off to Bladensburg. Who knows what happened to them? God, be with them." She lowered the telescope and released a sigh. "All day long, I've been watching with unwearied anxiety, hoping to discover the approach of my dear husband and his friends, but alas, I can descry only groups of military wandering in all directions, as if there is a lack of arms or of spirit to fight for their own firesides."

"Mrs. Madison." Rose moved to stand beside her. "I hesitate to relay such bad news, but I've heard our troops were defeated at Bladensburg."

She waved a gloved hand through the air. "Yes, so I heard, though I can hardly believe it. Major Blake has come twice to warn me of the danger, but how can I leave my own house?" She faced Rose and shrugged. But then her jaw tightened and fury rolled across her face. "Ah, would that I had a cannon to thrust through every window and blast those redcoats back to England."

Rose couldn't help but smile. What a charming, courageous woman. She lowered her chin. "Mrs. Madison, how can you be so brave when you are all alone, defenseless against the British troops that are surely heading your way?"

Mrs. Madison smiled and grasped one of Rose's hands. "Please call me Dolly. And I am not alone, Miss McGuire. God is always with me."

Her statement jarred Rose while at the same time bolstering her own convictions. Hadn't God said the same thing to her only minutes before?

A shuffle at the door sounded, and Mrs. Madison released Rose's hand. "Jean, there you are."

A tall, wiry man with short-cropped brown hair stared down an aquiline nose at the British soldier on the floor.

"Yes, remove him, if you please, Jean. Tie him up and set him on a sofa somewhere."

"What happened, madame?" The man's French accent was unmistakable.

Mrs. Madison turned toward Rose. "Miss McGuire, may I introduce Jean Sioussa, my doorman. Jean, this is Miss Rose McGuire out of Baltimore. She saved my life when this"—she pinched her lips together—"man tried to accost me in my own dining room."

"Mon Dieu." Jean's curious gaze drifted from the soldier to Rose, and finally landed on Mrs. Madison. "I am sorry I was not here."

"It is nothing, Jean."

"Madame, I have loaded everything onto the carriage: the trunk of cabinet papers, documents from the president's desk, the large chest of silver, velvet curtains, clocks, and the books we packed earlier."

"Thank you, Jean."

Shaking his head, he knelt, grabbed the soldier beneath the arms and hoisted him up. The injured man emitted a low groan, and a wave of relief spread over Rose. In the melee, she hadn't thought to check if she'd killed him.

"I'll attend to this man and be back for you, madame," he said before dragging the soldier off down the hall.

Mrs. Madison set the telescope on the table and glanced over the elaborate meal. "I serve dinner promptly at three o'clock, you know." Sorrow stung in her eyes. "Though Mr. Madison often complains, I always invite as many distinguished guests as I can." She ran her finger over the carved mahogany of one of the chairs. "But no one came today."

Rose laid a hand on Mrs. Madison's silk sleeve. "I'm sorry."

"But I did manage to save the portrait of dear George Washington. It used to be displayed there." She pointed to the wall where a magnificent gilded frame hung empty like a vacant eye. "Jean managed to extricate it intact on its inner frame." Mrs. Madison's eyes regained their sparkle. "We gave it to some reliable friends who promised to take it away to safety. God knows what the British would do to it."

The pounding of horses' hooves drummed outside, and Mrs. Madison darted to the window. Rose followed and peered below to see a Negro man waving his black hat through the air.

"Clear out! Clear out! General Armstrong has ordered a retreat," he shouted, his voice heightened in fear.

"Why, that's James Smith." Mrs. Madison gripped the window frame. "He accompanied my husband to Bladensburg."

The man dismounted and rushed toward the house. Mrs. Madison swung around just as he barreled into the room and handed her a note. Breaking the seal, she unfolded it and began reading. Her face paled. Even the heavy rouge on her cheeks seemed to fade. "Mr. Madison orders me to flee." She swallowed and glanced over the room. "So that's the end of it. I must leave my home in the hands of those implacable British oafs."

She turned to Rose. "Please come with us, Miss McGuire. I promise you'll be safe."

Rose grasped her gloved hands. "Thank you, Mrs. Madison, but I have a horse outside. I promise I'll leave for Baltimore posthaste."

"Very well. Godspeed to you, dear." She squeezed Rose's hands. Her eyes glazed with tears. "Pray for our country. This is a dark day indeed. But our God is bigger than any force on earth, even the British." She lifted one cultured eyebrow and drew a deep breath.

Releasing Rose's hands, she swept past the dining table, snatching as much silverware as she could hold along the way and stuffing it into her reticule. Jean followed her out the door, leaving Rose all alone.

Hugging herself, Rose moved to the window. Mrs. Madison leaped into the waiting carriage with a servant girl in tow. The driver snapped the reins, and Rose watched as the vehicle dashed down the street until darkness stole it from her view. Thunder roared from the east. A chill struck her.

She had saved the president's wife!

That must have been the important thing Daniel had said she would do—her destiny. Despite the fear, the terror, she had pressed through and done what God had asked of her. *Thank You, Lord.*

And yet it appeared her country was about to fall under tyranny once again.

Turning, she gazed at the fine fare set on the table. A shame it would all go to waste. Releasing a ragged sigh, Rose headed toward the door. She must leave the city and head back to Baltimore before the British arrived in full force. Head down, pondering her best escape route, she rounded the doorframe.

And ran straight into a British soldier.

The same soldier she had knocked unconscious. He tossed the remnants of ropes from his wrists to the floor and lifted a hand to touch the wound on his head. Dark eyebrows bent above eyes that smoldered with hatred.

❖

Shifting his weight, Alex winced at the pain from the blisters on his feet. His glance took in the band of two thousand troops, mostly red-coats, milling about among lit torches on the east lawn of the Capitol building. *In the heart of Washington DC.* Doffing his hat, he ran a bloody sleeve over the sweat on his brow and gazed up at the nearly full moon that drifted in between masses of dark clouds. Thunder bellowed. Or was it cannon fire? He couldn't be sure. His ears rang constantly with blasts of guns from earlier that day. Would the pounding ever cease? Or would it always drum in his ears as a reminder of the day he'd helped to defeat freedom?

As quickly as he wiped it away, sweat beaded once again on his brow. Though the sun had long since set, its oppressive heat remained. Only a slight evening breeze offered any relief. He supposed he should at least be thankful for that. Unavoidable anger swelled inside him. Anger that the British had won. Anger that they now intended to strip this great nation of its freedoms. And anger that he was being forced to partake in such a travesty.

Tugging off his cravat, he ran it over the back of his neck as he listened to the excited chatter of the men around him. Voices, once stinging with fear, now buzzed with the excitement of victory.

They'd entered the capital city of America without opposition, save for a volley of fire from a house when they'd first marched down Second Street. A house Admiral Cockburn had immediately torched, much to the dismay of anyone who had remained within. Now, as they waited before the seat of American power for someone—anyone—in authority to come out and discuss the terms of surrender, Alex began to wonder if a single soul remained in the city at all.

Boom! An enormous blast lit the eastern sky. The soldiers snapped to attention, gripped their muskets, and stared aghast at the yellow and red flames flinging into the darkness at the end of Virginia Avenue. Fear silenced every tongue as they waited to be attacked. But no bullets whizzed past them, no cannon blasts thundered. Finally, a scout galloped off on horseback to investigate. No doubt, the Americans had destroyed something they didn't want the British to confiscate. Which meant the city, indeed, belonged to the British.

Several minutes after the scout returned, Admiral Cockburn leaped on his horse and ordered the men to storm the Capitol building. As Alex filed in behind the troops, sharpshooters at the front of the line fired a volley through the windows of Congress. Admiral Cockburn thrust his sword into the air. "Storm the rebel bastion!" And the troops dashed forward in a chaotic wave of hatred and greed, breaking windows and bursting through the front door of the House of Representatives. With a heavy heart, Alex followed them inside. His defiance of the order would be too obvious.

The Senate chamber was a stark contrast to the rustic appearance of the city streets. Velvet-curtained balconies circled the room above a marble trim on which some words had been etched. Rows of rich wooden desks and chairs lined a red and gold embroidered carpet. Ornate white columns guarded the main floor that opened to a painted oval ceiling above.

While the troops scoured the building for objects of value, Alex took a spot just inside the chamber doors and watched as Admiral Cockburn sauntered through the impressive room, his face a mask of shock. "Indeed," he turned to the officers following him. "I am all astonishment. This American senate chamber is a much more imposing spectacle than our own House of Lords." He gave a sordid chuckle, straightened his coat, and mounted a platform. He sank into an elaborate wooden chair from which, Alex assumed, either the president or some other important government official conducted business.

The admiral banged the gavel for attention. "Shall this harbor of Yankee democracy be burned? All for it, say aye."

"Ayes!" rang through the room like gongs of doom.

General Ross marched into the chamber and halted. Frowning, he folded his arms across his chest, and Alex got the impression he was not at all pleased at the way Cockburn conducted himself. Yet after a few minutes, the general slipped out, doing nothing to stop the insolent mayhem.

As the men began gathering furniture to burn, Alex's gaze landed on a large black book atop a curved mahogany desk at the front of the room. It seemed to beckon to him, and before he knew it, he had eased from his spot by the door and inched closer, trying to avoid attracting the attention of Admiral Cockburn still sitting in the elevated chair. The closer Alex got to the book, the faster his heart beat. A Bible. And beside it on a placard, were painted the words, "In God we trust." He raised his eyes once again to the unfinished engraving on the marble trim lining the room. "In God. . ." it began.

Alex retreated to his spot by the door and scratched his head. Mr. Drummond had told him that the government in America prided itself on staying out of religion. Alex had assumed that meant that the government had nothing to do with religion and faith. But from the presence of the Bible in their Senate chamber and the words engraved on the placard and started on the trim above the room, the truth of the matter appeared to be quite the opposite. Americans deemed that government should stay out of religion, but they in no way wanted religion to stay out of government. In fact, this government appeared to embrace faith in God.

Vile laughter shook him from his thoughts as the men flung burning lanterns on top of a massive pile of desks, tables, and chairs in the center of the room. Alex's throat went dry. He fingered the hilt of his sword. He must stop this madness. But how? He was one against thousands.

Cockburn marched from the room, laughing.

Alex resisted the urge to plunge his sword into the admiral's heart and instead, ground his teeth together as the flames began to lick the wooden legs and arms of the furniture. A swarm of troops fled the room behind the admiral, flinging obscenities in their wake. Soon, the whole chamber blazed with a heat so intense the glass of the lights began to melt. Alex darted out the door and stepped outside for some air only to see more flames leaping from the Senate chamber's windows. The temporary wooden bridge that separated the two wings also burned, as well as a few nearby homes and the Library of Congress across the way. In truth, the whole city seemed ablaze as red and orange flames reached their flickering fingers up to God pleading for mercy.

Blood rushed to Alex's head as a wave of nausea struck him. He stumbled to his knees beneath a tree and tried to collect himself. Tears burned in his eyes. This honorable, God-fearing, free nation had seen its last days. It didn't seem right.

Cockburn and Ross mounted their horses, and Alex gleaned from the excited chatter around him that their next target was the American president's home. Was nothing sacred? Alex gazed toward the distant forest, longing to return to the Drummond farm—to beg their forgiveness and forget that he once knew a nation of proud, free people.

But he couldn't. Tensions were too high. He'd never make it alive.

Instead, he struggled to his feet, rubbed his eyes, and fell in behind the raucous crowd. The city that only moments ago had been shrouded in darkness now lit up as bright as day. Waves of heat from the flames swamped Alex as he dragged his feet over the sandy street. He hung his head, wanting to pray but not finding the words.

Clearly God had deserted them all.

❖ CHAPTER 27 ❖

Clutching her throat, Rose backed away from the British soldier. Though he was not much taller than she, the broad expanse of his shoulders beneath his red coat spoke of great strength. A white baldric crossed his chest and disappeared beneath the red sash tied about his waist. The bloodstains on his red coat and gray trousers were the only marks on his otherwise pristine uniform.

She opened her mouth to ask him what he wanted, but her words emerged in a pathetic squeak. It didn't matter. She could tell from the hatred and fury storming in his blue eyes that he wanted to kill her. Once again, he dabbed the blood-encrusted patch of hair atop his head. "You churlish American chit!" He reached for a sword that no longer hung at his side then glanced down at his belt for what she assumed were his pistols.

Also gone. *Thanks be to God.*

Rose drew a breath. "I'm sorry I had to hit you so hard, sir, but I could hardly have allowed you to murder my first lady."

He grunted and surveyed the room.

"If you're looking for Mrs. Madison, she has left." Rose lifted her chin and met his gaze with defiance, though she felt none of the bravery that Mrs. Madison had attributed to her. Instead, her legs quivered like wet noodles.

"Dashed off like a coward, no doubt." He sneered. "Like all the cowards in this city."

Rose gripped the back of a chair to keep from crumbling to the ground. "What do you expect, corporal? We are but innocent women and children."

His gaze wandered over the food-laden table, and he licked his lips. "None of you rebels are innocent."

He took a step toward her, staggered, then shook his head. A spark lit his eyes, and he bent over and plucked up a knife tucked within his boot. Twisting it in his hand, he grinned with delight. Rose cast a harried gaze over the floor for her pistol. There it was, by the door where she'd dropped it. Out of her reach.

She would die soon. An odd peace settled upon her at the realization. She had fulfilled her destiny, and now God would take her home. It was for the best. Without Alex, and with the prospects of forever living under Mr. Snyder's threats, she had no reason to go on. She prayed only that her passing would not be too painful.

The corporal advanced. This time there was no wobble in his step.

Rose squeezed the back of the chair until her fingers hurt. "I could have killed you, sir."

He tugged at his white collar and grinned. "You should have."

Reaching behind her, Rose groped across the table, seeking anything with which to defend herself. Her fingers latched onto a fork.

The corporal took another step toward her. The candlelight glinted off his knife.

Lord, help me. Rose clutched the fork and started to swing it forward when the sharp cock of a gun behind the corporal cracked the air. The soldier halted.

"Ah, just as I suspected." The male voice bore no British lilt. But its familiar cadence caused Rose's heart to collapse nonetheless. She peered around the soldier.

Mr. Snyder's stylish figure filled the doorframe. His pistol swerved between Rose and the British soldier.

The corporal's eyes narrowed, more with disdain than fear. Tucking the knife beneath his coat, he turned to face this new threat, slowly raising his hands in the air.

Rose stared aghast at the councilman. She blinked, thinking her eyes must surely be playing tricks on her. "What are you doing here, Mr. Snyder?"

His brows rose above icy blue eyes. "Why, I followed you, Miss McGuire."

"Followed. . .my word." Rose's head spun. She dropped the fork onto the table. "Thank God you arrived in time. As you can see, this soldier—"

"What I see, Miss McGuire"—Mr. Snyder seethed between clenched teeth—"is that you are consorting with the enemy."

The British man moved, and Snyder snapped the pistol toward his chest. "Ah, ah, no you don't, you odious redcoat. I'd have no qualms about shooting you where you stand."

Rose's thoughts whirled in shock and confusion. "Consorting with. . .are you daft?" Anger tossed her fear aside, and she fisted her hands on her waist.

The corporal lowered his gaze to the floor.

"Quite the opposite, I assure you. Wasn't it bad enough you fraternized with one of them on your own farm? Now, I find you here in Washington"—he gave an incredulous snort—"in the White House of all places, delivering vital information to this officer."

"Deliver. . ." Rose slammed her mouth shut to cool her temper and collect her chaotic thoughts. "I came here to warn the president of an impending attack, you buffoon. And this man was about to kill me."

"Yet, I see no weapons in his hand. Or on his person, for that matter." Mr. Snyder smirked. "No, my dear, this time, I have caught you in the act. And if justice is served, you will be tried as a traitor to your country. Even I cannot overlook such bold treason."

The soldier lifted his gaze. A bold, malicious look flashed in his eyes.

Ignoring the shiver that ran down her back, Rose stepped toward Mr. Snyder. "Don't be absurd. Now, if you please, let's bind up this man and be on our way. I fear the British are marching into the city as we speak."

"No thanks to you, I'm sure." Mr. Snyder eyed her with disgust. "I daresay, I am quite disappointed to discover that you are, indeed, a traitor, my dear. I was willing to lower my standards in order to gain your land, but I could never endanger my career as councilman by marrying a British spy." He sighed. "More's the pity. Now I shall have to find someone else to marry."

Frustration bubbled in Rose's gut.

An explosion thundered in the distance. The floor quivered. Mr. Snyder's wide eyes flew toward the window, and the corporal darted toward the door and stooped to the ground. Rose's gaze followed the reach of his hand, but before she could react, he grabbed the pistol Rose had dropped earlier. In one fluid motion, he leveled it at Mr. Snyder and fired.

Rose screamed.

Shock rolled over Mr. Snyder's face. The pistol shook in his hand. He fell backward through the open door and the corporal leaped toward him. Mr. Snyder's weapon discharged. The soldier halted in midstride, let out a shriek, and clutched his chest. Crumpling, he toppled to the ground. Mr. Snyder stumbled backward. Red blossomed on his silk waistcoat.

Dashing past the soldier, Rose grasped Mr. Snyder's arm to steady him. He glanced down at the blood bubbling from his chest. His breath rasped in his throat. His legs gave out, and Rose eased him to sit on the floor.

"My word." She scanned the room for anything to stop the bleeding. Dashing to the dining table, she grabbed a bundle of napkins and ran back to Mr. Snyder. He slumped to the wooden floor. Placing the cloths over his wound, she pressed as hard as she could. "We have to stop the bleeding."

Mr. Snyder moaned.

"Never fear, Mr. Snyder. It's just a bullet wound. I've dealt with them before." Her mind drifted to Alex and the wound in his thigh. Beneath her fingers, the maroon circle advanced on the cloth like an unrelenting army. Her stomach knotted. This was a much more serious wound. *Dear Lord, please help him.*

Shouts blared in through the window from outside. British voices. Jubilant voices accompanied by the bray of horses and the ominous thud of many boots.

Mr. Snyder's wide eyes locked on Rose's as he whispered, "The British are here."

❖

Amassed in a crush of exultant soldiers, Alex entered the American president's house. Each step of invasion into the private home of the great leader forced his shoulders lower in shame. His comrades were not of the same mind. In fact, Admiral Cockburn, who had sauntered in ahead of Alex, seemed quite giddy as he declared to the poor young American bookdealer he'd corralled for a guide, "Ah, Jemmy's palace at last!" He tipped up the front of his cocked hat. "Do give me a tour, lad. I wish to collect souvenirs that I may presently give to the flames." He faced the troops standing in the foyer and waved a hand through the air. "Men, at your pleasure." His release sent the soldiers scattering like ants from an anthill in search of treasure.

Alex wanted no part of it. Instead, he ambled behind the twelve officers who followed the admiral upstairs. Best to keep his eye on Cockburn and salvage anything of import during the mayhem, for Alex could think of no other reason God had allowed him to partake in this madness. If simply to witness the cruelty of his nation, he'd already seen enough. What other purpose could there be for his presence here besides to save some important document or national artifact from the angry flames?

The band of imperious men sauntered down a long hall to an open door from which spilled bright, flickering candlelight. The scent of beef and goose along with the metallic smell of blood and stench of sweat formed a malodorous blend that made Alex cringe. Thunder bellowed outside, mimicking the fury storming within him. As they approached the door, a dark shadow halted the admiral. A dead British soldier lay crumpled in the corner. Alex made his way through the crowd. No, not dead. A faint lift of the man's chest and flutter of his eyes gave evidence of a lingering, yet dwindling life. A large crimson stain darkened his red coat. Kneeling, the admiral gazed at the man. "Crenshaw, go fetch the surgeon." One of the men dispatched from the group and darted down the hallway.

"You." Cockburn stood and pointed at Alex. "What is your name, lieutenant?"

"Reed, Alexander Reed, sir."

"Stay with this man until the doctor arrives."

"Aye, aye, sir."

As the men filtered through the open door, Alex knelt beside the poor fellow. His ashen face, blue lips, and the gurgling sound in his throat, did not bode well for his surviving the night. Leaning back on his haunches, Alex peered into the large room, which from all appearances must have been the president's formal dining room.

Cockburn surveyed the table with a hearty laugh. "Egad, how thoughtful of Jemmy! Up until now, I had considered him to be nothing but a fatwitted ruffian." He took a seat at the head of the table and gestured for his officers to join him. As each man sat around the elegant spread, Admiral Cockburn snapped his fingers for the bookseller. "Pour me a drink, good fellow." The thin, timid man filled the admiral's cup from a pitcher of ale on the table.

He raised it in the air. "To Jemmy's health."

"To Jemmy's health," the men repeated before they all burst into a bout of devilish laughter.

Alex tore his gaze from the scene and closed his eyes. Such insolent lack of respect. The sounds of glass breaking, wood splitting, and raucous laughter drifted down the hall as the soldiers ransacked the mansion from cellar to garret. The clank of silverware and the moist slap of lips from the dining room told Alex the men now brazenly partook of the president's meal.

The soldier mumbled, and Alex opened his eyes to find the wounded man staring at him. The intense look on the man's face nearly sent Alex backward. He opened his mouth and seemed to be trying to speak. Leaning forward, Alex brought his ear near the soldier's mouth. "Rebels in the house. I shot one. The other's a lady," he managed to squeak out between strangled breaths.

Alex nodded and squeezed the man's hands. "Hold fast. The doctor is on the way."

The corporal shook his head. "They couldn't have gotten out."

"Another toast to Jemmy, gentlemen." Admiral Cockburn's insidious voice slithered over Alex from the dining room. "For being such a good fellow as to leave us such a capital supper."

"Here, here," the men chanted as another bout of pretentious laugher ensued.

Alex's stomach churned.

The wounded corporal's hand went slack in Alex's and fell to the floor by his side. He released one final ragged breath, and Alex brushed his fingers over the man's vacant eyes. Then bowing his head, he prayed for the violence to end. For this night to end.

Alex had seen enough death for one day.

Rising to his feet, he peered at the admiral and his officers shoving food into their mouths and drinks down their throats as they regaled each other with bombastic anecdotes.

Rebels in the house? Alex headed down the hall. Perhaps that was why God had sent him here. If there were injured rebels in the house, Alex had better find them before the British soldiers did.

❖

With one hand, Rose dabbed her handkerchief over Mr. Snyder's slick brow and cheeks while she kept the other pressed over his wound. He moaned, and Rose adjusted the pillow she'd made from his overcoat. The hollow thud of boots and the bone-chilling screech of laughter echoed through the thin walls of the small unfinished chamber Rose had discovered at the other end of the house. Intended to be servants' quarters or perhaps a storage area, the room was barren of furniture—save for the velvet-upholstered sofa she and Mr. Snyder hid behind. No rugs covered the wooden floors, no desks or chairs stood about, nothing hung on the walls, and no curtains framed the two large windows. The dark, empty chamber seemed to accentuate the noises around her: ominous footfalls, glass shattering, drunken laughter, crashes and thumps that kept her heart tangled in fear.

It had taken every ounce of her strength to haul Mr. Snyder to his feet and then—with him draped over her shoulder—assist him down the long hall in search of a hiding place. She had lugged him toward the back of the house and then up another flight of stairs before she could go no farther.

"Rose," he whispered, his voice as ragged as his breathing.

"Shhh, Mr. Snyder. I'm right here." She dabbed his forehead and looked at his blue eyes in the shadows—eyes that had lost the sting of arrogance and determination. Though she pressed as hard as she could on the wound, Mr. Snyder's once gold waistcoat had transformed into a brown pond. Too much blood.

He was losing far too much blood.

Boots thumped nearby, and a door slammed in the distance. Rose swallowed a lump of terror. If any of the soldiers entered the room, she prayed the obvious lack of valuables would force them to leave. Unless, of course, they took the time to walk over and peek behind the sofa. If they did, perhaps the Lord would make her and Mr. Snyder invisible. Why not? Surely the Creator of the universe could perform such a simple task.

Despite the mad thumping of her heart and the sweat trickling down her back, Rose felt an inner peace. Whether God saw her through this harrowing night or took her home, she was content that His will would be done. And that it would be for the best. What a wonderful change God had worked in her heart from just a few days ago! Yes, some of her fear remained, but God's peace had removed the sting from it, rendering it impotent.

"I'm sorry, Rose." Mr. Snyder coughed. A trickle of blood spilled from the corner of his mouth.

Rose flattened her lips and stared at the man who had threatened her family, who had sent her beloved Alex away, forever destroying Rose's chance at true love and happiness. She searched her heart for any animosity and strangely found none, as if his life-threatening injury or perhaps God Himself had swept it all away.

A flash of lightning lit his face, and Rose nearly gasped at the gray pallor of his skin. Beneath her hand, his heart still beat, though its pulse had weakened. A tear slid down her cheek. She bit her lip. *No, Lord. No. Please do not let him die.*

Yet. . .a shameful thought skipped across Rose's mind. If Mr. Snyder died, Rose and her family would be safe from his threats. She sighed and wiped the blood from Mr. Snyder's lips. Even still, she did not wish him dead.

Withdrawing her right hand from his wound, Rose placed her other one upon it, then shook out the cramp in her palm. Not that holding the wound was doing any good. This amount of blood indicated a major organ or artery had been penetrated. If only her aunt or Dr. Wilson were here. Then again, what could any of them do in the middle of an enemy-occupied city?

"I have been a beast, Rose." Mr. Snyder's voice cracked. "I wanted your land. And I wanted you." He attempted to smile.

"It doesn't matter now."

"But it does. I want you to understand." His voice rasped like the scraping of wood on wood. "I longed to be a man of importance, of prominence. I wanted recognition, status, I wanted to be admired." He coughed and another stream of blood spilled from his lips. "And someday, maybe even loved." His sorrowful eyes met hers.

Thunder pounded on the walls of the house. Rose's heart collapsed in anguish for Mr. Synder's pain. "A man's true value is not measured in his wealth or status, but in his honor and charity," she said.

Understanding flashed in Mr. Snyder's dull eyes. "Yes, I see that now."

Somewhere a window shattered. Hideous laughter ensued.

"You must leave, Rose." Mr. Snyder's tone grew urgent. "Before they find you. I am done for."

Rose gripped his hand. "I won't leave you."

His forehead wrinkled. "After all I've done?"

The patter of rain sounded on the roof like the march of a thousand soldiers.

She squeezed his hand.

His eyes misted. "Forgive me, Rose?"

Rose dabbed at the sweat beading in the red whiskers that lined his jaw—the ones he always kept so expertly trimmed. "Yes, of course." A sudden fear gripped her as she watched his life ebb away—fear for his eternal destination. "But it's God's forgiveness you need to seek."

He nodded, coughing. Sprinkles of blood flew from his mouth.

Rose smiled and wiped the tears spilling down her cheeks.

He coughed again, then expelled a deep breath.

And went completely still.

A flash of lightning revealed eyes devoid of life.

Releasing the pressure on his chest, Rose curled up into a ball on the floor beside him and began to sob.

Thunder cracked the sky with a loud boom.

The door squeaked open. Swallowing a sob, Rose peered beneath the sofa. A breeze wafted around her with the scent of rain and sweat and smoke. Boots, immersed in a circle of light, thudded over the wooden floor. Black Hessian boots. Rose held her breath.

Oh Lord, make him go away.

Inching to the edge of the sofa, Rose dared a peek around the corner. She gasped.

Alexander Reed stood in the center of the room.

❖ CHAPTER 28 ❖

Too shocked to move, Alex stared at the woman he loved. He shook his head. He'd gone mad. There was no other explanation, for Rose would not have traveled this far from home. Holding up the lantern, he took a step toward her. Rain tapped an eerie cadence on the roof. Lightning flashed outside the window, coating her in silver. Alex blinked and rubbed his eyes, trying to settle his heart. Only a vision. Just a vision conjured up by his despair.

Thunder rumbled through the walls. He snapped his eyes open.

The vision moved. It gripped the sofa and slowly stood. Wide, lustrous blue eyes gaped at him.

He inched toward her. "Rose?"

She flew into his arms. He wrapped one arm around her and dropped his face into her hair. The smell of hay and honeysuckle confirmed what the warmth flooding his body told him.

She was real.

She began to sob. "I thought I'd never see you again."

Withdrawing, he set the lantern on the floor, then gripped her shoulders and glanced over her, looking for any injuries, as sudden fear dashed away his joy. "What the deuces are you doing here?"

Sadistic laughter barreled down the hallway.

Rose wiped the tears from her face and fell into him again. "My aunt and uncle were at the orphanage. I came to warn them."

Alex bundled her in his arms and kissed the top of her head. "You foolish, wonderful lady."

Lantern light flickered over her face as her eyes, bounding with love, sought his. He stroked her cheeks and lowered his lips to hers. They tasted of salty tears and Rose. She moaned, and he pressed her against him and ran his fingers through her hair. "I love you, Rose."

"You love me?"

"Yes." He brushed the hair from her face. "And I want to stay with you. Become an American."

She blinked and took a step back. "Then what are you doing here?"

"Trying to find your military so I can desert mine, trying to stop the destruction." Alex ran a hand through his hair. "I'm not sure anymore."

"I can't believe you want to become an American." Rose approached and cradled his face in her hands. "Is it true?"

"Truer than anything I've ever known." Alex smiled and leaned his forehead against hers.

A loud blast from inside the house jolted him back to reality. Releasing Rose, he gripped the hilt of his sword, stepped to the door and peered out. Fear tightened his gut. "Your aunt and uncle?"

"They were already gone when I got here."

"Then what are you doing in this house?"

"I came in to warn the president's wife." Tears streamed down her cheeks, and she raised a hand to cover her mouth. "Mr. . .Mr. . ." Her voice quaked. "Mr. Snyder."

Alex turned to give her a questioning look. "What of Mr. Snyder?"

"He followed me." Her eyes snapped to the only piece of furniture in the room. Thunder growled outside. "He's dead." Rose shuddered and stared at the sofa.

Picking up the lantern, Alex skirted the velvet couch. Blank eyes stared up at him above a blood-soaked cravat and waistcoat. He tore his gaze away and looked at Rose. "How?"

"A British soldier shot him."

Alex swallowed as realization settled. Yes. The soldier who had died by Alex's side. More footsteps pounded outside the room, joining the tap of raindrops atop the roof. Alex grasped Rose's hand once again. This time he noticed how cold and moist her skin was. Terror like he'd never felt before consumed him. He must keep Rose safe.

"We have to get you out of here. Soldiers are searching the entire mansion. They will find you."

The ominous clap of a footfall sounded behind him. Alex spun around.

The dark figure of a British soldier stepped inside the room. "Ah, I see you've found a sweet American tart, my friend. Care to share?"

❖

The soldier sauntered into the room, pistol in one hand, a bottle of liquor in the other. All hope fled Rose before an advancing onslaught of fear. Her pulse roared in her ears. No matter what happened, she would never forget these final minutes God had allowed her with the man she loved.

Alex moved in front of her as if he could shield her from this man. From the world. She wished he could. *Oh Lord, please protect him. Please don't let him do anything foolish.* She glanced over the room, searching for anything she could use as a weapon, but found none. Mr. Snyder's pistol was in the dining room where he'd dropped it beside his ever-present cane.

Alex's hand flew to the hilt of his service sword. "The woman is my prisoner."

"Egad, man. She's a rebel wench." The soldier, a sergeant, evidenced by the three strips on his red coat, peered around Alex. "And a comely one at that." Desire burned in his dark eyes. Rose's stomach soured.

"Besides." The man wobbled past Alex. "Admiral Cockburn has given us his leave to take whatever we find in the house." The smell of alcohol emanating from the brute burned Rose's nose.

Alex moved in front of her again. His muscles seemed to ripple beneath his dark navy coat. But then his shoulders relaxed, and he let out a sigh of compliance. "Very well. I suppose I'll oblige you, sergeant." He gave a chuckle that would have convinced Rose of his sincerity if she didn't know him better. He pointed toward the soldier's pistol. "No need for that, is there? We are on the same side, after all."

The sergeant glanced at the weapon in his hand as if he'd not realized he held it. Stuffing it in its holster, he hefted the bottle to his lips and took a big draught. He wiped his mouth and handed it to Alex.

Alex took a sip then gestured toward the hallway. "Do get the door, sergeant, while I get the wench ready. We don't want to be disturbed, do we?"

Lightning flickered outside, flashing an eerie gray over the sergeant's angular face. His wide grin reminded Rose of a row of dead bones standing at attention. "Aye, I like the way you think, sir." Removing the tall black shako from his head, he set it on the sofa, scouring Rose with a salacious gaze before he turned and started toward the door.

Alex didn't hesitate. Drawing his sword, he struck the man's head with the hilt. With a moan, the sergeant folded to the ground like a used piece of foolscap.

Rose gasped and stared at Alex.

Thunder roared, rattling the windows.

Alex flashed a smile her way, then knelt by the man and began unbuttoning the brass buttons on his coat. "Quick. Take off your clothes."

"What?" Rose shook her head as if Alex's words had somehow become jumbled.

"Your clothes, Rose." His voice was urgent. "I'll turn my head."

Slipping into the shadows, Rose hesitated for a moment until she realized what he intended to do. She wanted to protest the mad idea, but her voice once again would not cooperate. Instead, she clutched her gown and lifted it over her head.

Alex made quick work of the man's brass buttons and tore off his coat, then began fidgeting with his fatigue jacket beneath. "Your petticoat, Rose. I need your petticoat." His voice was gentle, but commanding, brooking no argument—just as Rose assumed he sounded when he shouted orders aboard his ship.

Lifting off her petticoat, she tossed it to him. It landed by his side as he removed the man's linen shirt. Shouts and laughter echoed through the house. Rose's fingers shook as she attempted to unhook her stays. Without success.

Rain pattered on the roof, matching the frenzied beat of her heart. Smoke filtered into the room. An off-key ballad chimed from somewhere in the house. She cleared her throat. "I need. . . I need help with my stays." Too embarrassed to face him, she turned around and stared at the cracks in the dark wall.

She heard his boots clap over the floor, felt his warmth at her back, his breath on her neck, and his fingers groping at the laces. "Upon my honor, how do you wear these infernal things?"

Rose suppressed a giggle, felt her stays loosen, her breath release, and heard him depart. She swerved about to see him with his back to her again. Such a gentleman. He removed the man's shoes then began tugging down his trousers as Rose shrugged out of her stays. They fell to the floor, leaving only a thin chemise between her and the world. Between her and this man. A chill struck her and she hugged herself and receded farther into the shadows. Two months ago, she would have been horrified to be so scantily clad in a man's presence. But she trusted Alex more than she'd ever trusted anyone. And despite their terrifying circumstances, she found an odd comfort in that realization.

Alex gathered the man's clothing in a pile and pushed them toward her. "Put these on."

Rose stooped to pick them up. "Surely they won't fit."

"We'll make them fit. It's the only way."

The shrill tear of fabric echoed through the room from Alex's direction. Rose donned the trousers, then slipped on the linen shirt, fatigue jacket, coat and shoes. Her feet swam in the buckled black boots, and the coat hung nearly to her knees. She had to hold the trousers up to keep them from falling. How would she ever pass for a British soldier?

Using the strips of torn petticoat, Alex bound the man's feet and hands, then stuffed a gag in his mouth. He stood. "That should hold him until we get away."

"I'm dressed." Rose said, her voice emerging as a squeak.

Alex spun around, grabbed the man's tall shako from the sofa and handed it to her. "Do your best to stuff your hair into this."

Rose placed it atop her head and began forcing her thick tresses inside it while Alex tightened her belt around her waist and buttoned the coat buttons. Even with her hair stuffed beneath it, the silly hat kept slipping down her forehead.

Alex stepped back, shook his head and chuckled. "We must keep to the shadows and pray most of the men are well into their cups." Lantern light twinkled in his eyes and gleamed off the brass buttons lining his coat. "For I doubt any man with half his wits about him would think you are anything but an alluring female."

Amazed at his nonchalant attitude, Rose searched her heart for even a speck of courage to match his. Instead, fear knotted in her throat. "Are you sure this will work?"

Alex grabbed her hand and pulled her to the door. "No."

Not the answer she wanted to hear.

Stopping, he faced her. "Stay behind me. Say nothing and keep your head low."

Rose nodded. Air seized in her throat. "Lord, help us."

"Yes, indeed." He gave her a half smile, cupped her chin, and kissed her. "It will be all right." Then he lengthened his stance, threw back his shoulders, and marched from the room as if he owned the night.

Rose followed him down a long hallway to a flight of stairs. He led her down them as the sounds of mayhem and madness assailed her from all directions: crashes, thumps, and the crackle of fire. Smoke stung her nose. Thunder bellowed and drunken laughter grated on her nerves. A mob of soldiers passed on their left, torches in their hands. The smell of alcohol wafted over her. Rose's knees quaked. But the men seemed more intent on setting fire to the house than on paying her and Alex any mind.

Rose's teeth began to chatter. Perspiration slid down her back beneath the heavy coat. She tried to keep her eyes on Alex's back, to gain courage from the commanding cut of his uniform, from his confident gait. He led her down another hall to the main set of stairs. Down below, the front entrance of the house beckoned to her. *Freedom. Escape.* But it might as well be as far away as Baltimore, for a crush of sailors and soldiers mobbed the foyer.

Yet Alex didn't miss a step. No hesitation. No fear.

Heat swamped Rose, and she turned to see flames bursting from the dining room. A lump formed in her throat. She fought back tears. There would be time to mourn for her country later. They started down the stairs. Two sailors brushed past them, laughing. A band of marines huddled near the front door.

They reached the foot of the stairs. They were almost there. Almost free.

Alex nodded at the marines by the door and exited the house. Rose lowered her chin, raised her shoulders, and stepped out behind him. Not until they reached the outer gate did she feel the rain pelting down on her or the breath returning to her lungs. One glance around her told her that Valor was no longer tied to the post. Sweet Valor. She hoped some British redcoat had not confiscated the poor horse. *Please take care of Valor, Lord.* A gust of wind whipped over her, and she pressed a hand upon her hat and followed Alex down Pennsylvania Avenue.

Hurrying her steps, she eased beside him. The clomp of her over-sized shoes echoed her betrayal. Rain misted on her, cooling her skin. Bright lights plucked at her curiosity, yet she kept her face down, hidden. When they had walked at least two blocks and the cacophony of destruction had lessened, she dared to lift her chin and scan the surroundings. Fires raged across the city. Unaffected by the rain, flames leaped out of windows and shot from roofs toward heaven. Smoke rose like prayers into the night sky, obscuring the stars and moon.

Rose's heart collapsed. Her throat burned, and a shiver overtook her despite the heat of the night and the fires. "Dear God, how could this happen?"

Alex started to take her hand, then pulled it away. "I'm sorry, Rose." Light from the flames flickered determination in his eyes. His jaw tightened. "I'm ashamed of what my countrymen have done."

Musket shots peppered the sky. An explosion shook the ground.

Alex cast a worried gaze across the scene. "Follow me." Turning down Thirteenth Street, he plodded forward, head down.

The drum of boots and the clomp of horses tightened Rose's nerves. She dared a peek at a band of troops heading their way, led by two officers on horseback.

A pig crossed the path in front of them. It stopped, stared at them for a moment before grunting and ambling away.

"Friend of yours?" Alex teased.

Rose flattened her lips. "How can you joke at a time like this?"

"It relieves stress."

"It's not working." Rose glanced down at the oversized attire and her massive footwear that clomped over the sand so loudly—they'd no doubt betray them to the passing troops. She wanted to laugh, wanted to cry. Instead she softened her step, lowered her chin, and kept her mouth shut. The soldiers passed.

A gust of wind blasted over them. Before she could stop it, Rose's shako flew from her head. It clunked to the ground, releasing her long golden tresses down her back. She shrieked.

"You there, halt!" A voice blared over them from behind.

Without so much as a glance over his shoulder, Alex grabbed her arm with one hand, withdrew his sword with the other and dashed down the street. Rose ran as fast as her legs and enormous boots would allow. Horse hooves followed them like war drums. Shouts and hollers of jocularity filled the night as if the men were engaged in a fox chase on the English countryside.

Alex ducked in between two brick buildings, batting shrubbery aside with his sword. His breath came hard and heavy. The mad crunch of pebbles beneath their feet sounded like gunshot. His tight grip on her hand was the only thing that kept her going—that gave her hope. One glance over her shoulder revealed flaming torches bobbing atop an incoming wave of soldiers.

"There they are!" one of the men shouted.

Rose's feet burned. Her heart crashed against her ribs. One of her boots slipped off. Then the other. Sharp rocks tore the skin on her feet. She cried out in pain.

Halting, Alex glanced at her feet then swept her into his arms and continued to barrel down the alleyway out onto a narrow dirt street. His steps were heavy and thick and their pace slowed even as his breath increased. The shouts of their pursuers grew louder.

He set her down and cupped her face gently, lifting her gaze to his. His heavy breath filled the air between them. "Go, hide in that house." He gestured over her shoulder to a small one-story brick structure. "I'll draw them away from you."

"No, I want to stay with you!" Rose tugged on his arm, unable to fathom losing him again.

A sea of torches turned the corner at the end of the street and rumbled toward them like a tidal wave. "They will find us, Rose. There's no time. Do as I say!" he barked.

Tears filled her eyes and Alex's figure blurred before her. "Please Alex, don't leave me."

Leaning over, Alex kissed the tears flowing down her cheeks then brushed his lips over hers. "I'll find you. I promise. Now go!"

Turning, Rose forced her feet to run to the house. Opening the door, she slid inside and ran to peer out one of the broken windows. Glass cut her foot and she squelched a cry of pain—pain that she felt both outside and inside as Alex's dark shape disappeared down the street. A second later, a horde of angry men who appeared more like fire-breathing dragons flew after him.

Leaning back against the inner wall, Rose threw a hand to her chest to slow the frantic beating of her heart. The cold brick of the walls seeped through her gown. "Oh Lord. Please protect him."

❖

Alex waited long enough to see that Rose had followed his orders, but perhaps he delayed too long. One glance over his shoulder told him the mob of soldiers was only yards behind. Sprinting with all his strength, he forged into the darkness, thankful that this part of town had not yet been set to fire. He heard the stomp of a dozen boots behind him, the diabolical laughter and devilish chuckles of his own countrymen. Men he had supped with, trained with, and marched beside. How quickly things had changed.

One more glance told him that none had separated from the group. They had not seen Rose slip away. Thank God.

Alex dashed between what appeared to be two shops. His thigh cried out in pain. His lungs slammed against this chest.

"There they go!" a belligerent voice trumpeted behind him.

He glanced once more over his shoulder to see a myriad of bobbing torches like lit cannons on the wobbling deck of a ship. Lit to fire at him. Too close. Far too close.

Lord, please don't let them catch me. For Rose's sake.

Alex swung his gaze back forward, tripped over a rock, stumbled past a bush whose sharp branches tore at his coat. He righted himself. A pop of a pistol rang through the air and the shot zipped past his ear.

He burst from the alleyway onto the street and turned right, not hesitating to choose which way. He chose the wrong way. The dark gaping hole of the barrel of a musket nearly impaled him. He stopped just in time before it did.

"One more move and I'll shoot," the soldier ordered.

Alex raised his hands in the air as he struggled to regain his breath. In moments he was surrounded by the torch-wielding mob. Sweat streamed down his forehead into his eyes, stinging them. He scanned the faces, twisting and undulating in the flickering torchlight, like sinister demons released from hell.

One man approached him and spit at his feet. "Where is the woman?"

"What woman?"

The man struck Alex across the jaw, sending him reeling to the side. The pain spiked into his mouth and down into his neck.

"Never mind. We shall find her." The lieutenant snapped his fingers. "Bind him. We'll see what Cockburn has to say about this traitor."

❖ CHAPTER 29 ❖

The distant pop of a gun startled Rose as she stood inside the small house. Turning, she glanced out the window once again. A different band of soldiers sauntered by. Others separated into smaller groups and wandered among the buildings across the street. Was the shot directed at Alex? *Oh Lord, please protect him.* As her eyes became accustomed to the darkness, shapes began to form: a settee, oak tables, a pianoforte, and a rocking chair.

Groping her way among them, Rose made her way toward the back of the house. With all the British running around, she had best find a place to hide. Even though everything within her wanted to run out and find Alex, rescue him as he had rescued her. A tear slid down her cheek, but she brushed it away. No time to be frightened. No time to be weak. She was not alone. And neither was Alex.

"Yes, I will never leave my children."

The voice within her confirmed her convictions, bringing forth another tear from her eye. But this time, a tear of joy.

Laughter and more shots tore in through the window from outside.

She ran her fingers over the wallpaper lining the hallway and bumped into various sconces and pictures hanging there. Finally, she entered a room in the back that appeared to be a storage room filled with bulky sacks, crates, and shelves lined with jars. A table in the center had been pushed aside. Rose squinted into the shadows, searching for somewhere to hide, when her eyes landed on a dark square beneath the table. Kneeling, she discovered it was a hole that led to a cellar beneath the house. The trapdoor lay pushed aside, along with a crumpled rug that no doubt was used to conceal the opening.

Footsteps thundered outside. Closer. Closer. Shouts. The neigh of a horse.

Rose's muscles tensed. Then the sounds faded.

"Is anyone there?" Rose whispered into the dark cavity. "I am a friend." But no answer came. Grabbing the rug, she hugged it to her chest, imagining that the family who lived here must have hidden down below from the British. She wondered what had happened to them.

She didn't have time to consider it. The front door blasted open and heinous laughter filled the front parlor.

❖

Alex tugged from the pinching grips of the men on either side of him and met the imperious gaze of Admiral Cockburn. The man before him, though powerful on earth, had proven himself to be a cruel and heartless man who used his God-given power to abuse and subjugate those beneath him. Alex did not fear him. God was with Alex. Truth was with Alex. And no matter what this man did to him, truth and love would win in the end.

At last, Alex understood how Mr. Drummond's eyes could be so filled with peace in the midst of the storms.

Cockburn eyed him up and down as if he were but another bug to squash. "What have we here, Lieutenant?"

The man to Alex's right threw back his shoulders. "A traitor, Admiral. At least that's what he seems to be. We found him running through the streets of Washington with a woman dressed in a sergeant's uniform."

The admiral chuckled and the smell of alcohol spilled over Alex. Which did not bode well for his sentencing. Often during the long day, Alex had witnessed the fiendish effect drink had on the admiral's sensibilities.

"Indeed, and where is the rebel wench?" The admiral slapped the telescope he was holding against his other palm.

The lieutenant looked down. "Got away sir. But we'll find her."

"That you will, Lieutenant, or I fear you'll meet the same fate as this poor man."

Alex could hear the lieutenant gulp.

Admiral Cockburn raised his chin and looked down his nose at Alex. "Mr. Reed, did you say? What have you to say for yourself?"

Lengthening his stance, Alex gazed behind the admiral where flames still devoured the Capitol building. Though they stood yards away, he could feel the heat, and it only sufficed to fuel his anger. How dare they destroy these symbols of freedom? He met the admiral's gaze. "I was only protecting an innocent woman from being ravaged, Admiral. There's no crime in that."

"No crime you say? Ha." The admiral glanced over his men. "No crime save leaving her untouched, I'd say."

Some of the men chuckled.

From the left of the group, a soldier aided another man to the center—a sergeant dressed in nothing but his underclothes. He rubbed his head and his eyes nearly fired from their sockets when they landed on Alex. "Aye, that's the man. He struck me over the head."

Alex shrugged. "He was going to ravish the woman."

Cockburn leaned toward Alex. "It's what the rebel wench deserved. So you let her go?"

"I did."

Cockburn's jaw twitched. He nodded toward the lieutenant on Alex's right, who hauled his arm back and slugged Alex across the jaw once again. At least it was on the other side this time. Renewed pain tore across his cheek.

"She could have possessed valuable information, Mr. Reed." Cockburn continued while Alex rubbed his jaw. "Why else was she still in Washington? Egad. The incompetence! Such insubordination for a second lieutenant in the Royal Navy." Cockburn shifted his stance, the fringe on his epaulets quivered. "Wait until the Admiralty Board hears of this. You'll not only be cashiered my friend, but hung as well."

Alex allowed the words to enter his mind and then slither down into his gut. Not a pleasant way to die. But as he thought back on the events of these past weeks, he wouldn't have changed a thing.

Alex's silence evoked rage from the admiral, who immediately growled. "Tie him up and stand watch over him while we finish destroying the city. Tomorrow, we'll escort him back to the flagship. I'll wager we can gather up enough captains to host a court-martial right here in the Chesapeake. Then before we even set sail, we can hang you from the yardarms."

❖

Rose dove into the cellar, nearly stumbling down the ladder. Reaching up, she placed the rug atop the trapdoor, and then from below, she eased it over the hole, cringing when it snapped into place. Lowering her shaky legs rung by rung, her feet finally found the cool hard dirt of the cellar floor. Pain etched across her soles. She winced. Chilled air tingled over her neck. The smell of sweet herbs and mold whirled about her.

The hollow thump of at least a dozen boots thundered overhead and shook the trapdoor. Dust rained over her. Covering her mouth and nose, she suppressed a cough as a plethora of male voices trumpeted through the rooms above. Thunder growled in agreement of her dire predicament even as footfalls continued to pound above her. The squeal of a rat somewhere in the cellar sent a shiver down her back.

Furniture legs scraped over the wood. The sound of cloth flapped like sails in the wind. A pair of shoes tromped over the trapdoor again and halted. The boards creaked and wobbled. With her hand still pressed over her mouth, she closed her eyes.

"What a night, eh?" one man said.

"Cowardly rebels!" Another man chortled. "Leavin' their capital for us t' plunder."

"Aye, wait till my lady sees the silverware I'm bringin' home—" his voice heightened with scornful insolence—"compliments of the citizens of Washington DC."

The man moved off the trapdoor and sauntered about the room. He must have shifted the rug aside for a sliver of lantern light spilled through a tiny crack in the boards.

"I ne'er seen such an easy conquest. Why, we should be able t' take the rest of these despicable colonies within a fortnight and be home before Christmastide."

Insidious chuckles pummeled Rose like hail.

"An' tomorrow," another soldier piped in. "Admiral Cockburn says we can finish burnin' the rest o' the city."

Footfalls rumbled over the floor again, but this time, their hollow thuds receded.

"This looks like a fair place to hole up for the night," one man declared, his voice fading as he walked into another room.

"Milford, did ye bring the bottles of brandy we found?"

"Aye, I said I did."

Insolent rogues. Rose didn't know whether to be terrified or furious. As long as the soldiers stayed, she was trapped and couldn't go in search of Alex.

Alex. He had come for her! Saved her once again! Rose pictured him as he marched into the empty room in the president's mansion in his dark naval uniform with long coattails, brass buttons, and service sword glittering at his side. He wanted to stay with her! Her heart should indeed be soaring. If it weren't so twisted with fear. And fury. She must find Alex. But how, with all those soldiers sleeping above her?

Blinking she strained her eyes and gazed over the dank cellar. Soon objects began to form out of the darkness: barrels, crates of what appeared to be potatoes or apples, sacks of grain. Above her, bundles of herbs hung from the rafters like sleeping bats.

Kneeling, Rose felt her way over the dirt floor and sat, leaning her back against the support wall. She drew her knees to her chest and laid her weary head upon them. "Lord, help me."

Hours later, above her in the front parlor, the men's drunken revelry quieted.

Even the thunder and lightning fell silent, and the rain ceased its march across the roof. A deceptive peace descended on the house as if the abominations of the night had not only drained the city but the earth and sky of all their energy.

Including Rose. All the stress of the evening, the fear, the horrors, spilled from her. Her eyes grew heavy. Cool, dank air crept over her. She shuddered. Then a sudden warmth enveloped her—a strange supernatural warmth—and she closed her eyes and fell into its embrace.

❖

Alex shifted his back against the rough bark of the huge tree he sat beneath. He gazed upward. A hickory tree, he thought, though it was hard to tell in the darkness. He twisted the thick ropes binding his hands together. Pain spiraled up his arms. Though he'd been tugging against the bindings for hours, the only thing he'd accomplished were patches of raw bleeding skin around his wrists. From his spot, sitting atop a grassy knoll just outside the city limits, he had an excellent view of Washington. To his right a group of soldiers hovered around a campfire. They played cards, laughed, drank, and told off-color jokes, all the while over their shoulders the bastion of freedom burned to the ground. The flames that rose over Washington would have been a beautiful sight with all their brilliant oranges, reds, and yellows dancing in the night like some garish ballet.

If it wasn't such a horrendous scar on the history of mankind.

Alex's thigh throbbed, his hands were a bloody mess, and his back ached, but the largest pain of all came from his heart. He had promised Rose he'd come back for her. And now, he doubted he could keep that promise. Thoughts of her hiding somewhere in that burning city, frightened and alone, waiting for him, gnawed at his gut like some satiated predator intent on giving him a slow death.

No, Alex couldn't help Rose. But God could. Bowing his head, Alex spent the next several hours in prayer. For Rose, for her family, and for America to survive this devastating night. Somewhere amid the crackle of fire and the fading shouts of men, Alex succumbed to his exhaustion and fell asleep.

A slap across the face jarred him awake, and he peered up into the smirk of one of the soldiers who had been guarding him. "Wake up, traitor. You should witness us finishin' off your precious rebel city." The sting on Alex's face was nothing compared to the pain etching across his soul at the man's words. He shifted his gaze to the city, now bathed in dawn's glow and to the smoke rising from the buildings like incense to heaven. He prayed the scent made it all the way to the throne of God.

The soldier spit to the side of Alex, gathered his things, and along with several of the other men, left Alex tied to the tree with only a single soldier to guard him. It might as well have been a thousand for as tight as the ropes were about Alex's waist and hands. Even if he made it through the ones binding his wrists, his entire body was tied to the trunk of the tree.

He watched the solders descend the hill laughing and slapping each other on the back in anticipation of another day of plundering and destruction.

Scanning the city, Alex tried to find the house where he had left

Rose, but the smoke and remaining flames obscured his view. "Lord, watch over her. Please get her home safely."

"Pray for a storm."

The silent words couldn't have been clearer within Alex. He shook his head. Was he destined to go mad along with everything else?

"Pray for a storm."

Alex glanced over the city. Sunlight shot bright arrows down between puffy gray clouds. They'd had a small storm last night, but today the sky appeared to be clearing. "A storm, Lord?"

"Yes."

Emitting a sigh of submission, Alex bowed his head. "Very well. Father." He nearly choked with emotion at the title with which he now addressed God. He finally had a Father who loved him—who would never close His home to Alex. And if Alex should indeed hang from Admiral Cockburn's yardarm, God would welcome him home forever. "Please bring a storm upon this land, this city," he continued, feeling his zeal rising. "One that will send these British back to their ships and back to their country!" He laughed at his own foolishness then leaned back against the bark.

If God didn't intervene soon, Alex didn't want to contemplate what would happen to Rose. "Thy will be done."

❖

The thud of shoes and the crackle of morning voices permeated Rose's slumber. The men's voices grew louder, and she stirred, rubbing her face. When reality forced itself into her dreams, she bolted upright and opened her eyes. Shouts and curses flew through the air above them. Footfalls pounded. A door slammed and then all grew silent. Above her, a sliver of sunlight speared down into the cellar, indicating that a new day had dawned. Struggling to her feet, she shook off the last vestiges of slumber, chastening herself for falling asleep under such dire circumstances. Yet she remembered nestling into the peace of a warm hug. A dream? Or her Father in heaven? She smiled and tilted her ear to the ceiling. No sounds. The soldiers had gone. Why hadn't Alex come to get her? Renewed fears leaped up to grab her heart.

There was only one explanation. Alex must have gotten caught. She clenched her fists and gazed upward. She had to rescue him. But how? Terror gripped her at the thought, but she forced it back. "I am not alone. I am not alone."

Slowly creeping up the ladder, Rose lifted the trapdoor, holding it slightly ajar. No movement. No sounds. Placing both hands against the wood, she moved it from the hole, sliding it to the side. The bitter smell of brandy and sweat bit her nose as she emerged from the cellar into the storage room then inched to the door and peered down the hall. No movement, no voices. Nothing to alert her. Making her way down the hall she entered the front parlor. What had appeared last night to be a neat and nicely furnished room now resembled more of a tavern after a violent brawl. Broken furniture, crumpled rugs, and empty bottles of brandy and rum that lay on their sides, mouths open, as if they too were intoxicated.

Shoving down her disgust, Rose dared a peek out the front window. Redcoats filled the streets, some marching in formation, others crowding in groups laughing and no doubt regaling each other of their conquests the night before. Some still carried torches.

Rose ducked back to the side of the window and felt like crying. She wasn't going anywhere. At least not for a while. "Haven't they done enough, Lord? Oh please make them stop." She dropped her face into her hands and sobbed.

"Pray." A strange sensation overcame Rose—a presence so strong it seemed the room could not contain it.

"Pray for a storm." The voice resounded within her, sweet, yet strong, like a harmonious chord from a violin.

A storm? Rose didn't understand. What could a storm do against the entire British army?

"All right, Lord." Lowering herself to her knees, Rose clasped her hands together and prayed. First she thanked God for His love, His mercy, and for allowing her to see Alex one last time. Then she prayed for rescue for them both, for America to survive, and lastly, for a storm to strike the city.

Rising to her feet, she took up a pace across the parlor floor, keeping an eye on the soldiers outside, and wishing she had more faith to believe God would perform the things she had just prayed for.

❖

BOOM! An enormous explosion thundered in the distance. The ground shook. The hickory tree shook, jarring Alex from his prayers. The soldier, who guarded him, dashed to the edge of the hill, musket ready. Beyond him, a massive plume of smoke rose in the air from the area of town Alex remembered as Greenleaf Point where the city's arsenals had been kept. Tortured screams etched across the sky and sent a chill down Alex's back. Pieces of rocks, shells, and bricks shot through the air like grapeshot leveling some of the men as they dashed away from the blast. When the smoke cleared, even from this distance, Alex could see bodies—and what used to be bodies—scattered over the ground.

The Americans had no doubt left the British a surprise. War made devils out of men. Alex shifted his gaze away and closed his eyes. "Lord, please help them." He didn't know what else to pray for, save that this hideous war would end. His prayers for a storm all morning had gone unanswered. Perhaps he hadn't heard from God at all. Yet, despite the unanswered petition, a peace surrounded Alex as if God was somehow pleased that Alex had been obedient. The approval of a Father who loved him. Alex savored the foreign sensation. Yes, indeed, he could get used to having God as his Father.

No sooner had the wounded been carried off to the hospital that General Ross had set up near the Capitol building, than the *tap tap* of a light rain drummed on the leaves above Alex. Distant thunder accompanied the continued shouts and stomp of troops through the city streets.

The tapping increased in both tempo and speed. Water dripped on Alex's face. Shaking it off, he gazed into a sky that had darkened to near black in a matter of minutes. Angry clouds boiled in fury above him, marching across the city. Soon thick blades of rain fell upon them as if a giant armory had been opened in heaven. The solder guarding Alex ducked beneath the tree alongside him. He drew the edges of his coat together and held down his hat, sharing a wary gaze with Alex, as the torrent of wind and water increased.

The fierce gusts grew and grew until Alex could no longer keep his eyes open. Tucking his head between his upraised knees, the realization struck him that his prayer had been answered. Awe swept through him while at the same time the wind threatened to carry him away. Lightning crackled the air around him, painting his eyelids silver and buzzing over his skin. He smelled the electricity and something else—burnt flesh. Not his. At least he hoped not. Thunder pounded. The ground shook as if God Himself walked through the capital of America.

Screams and shouts assailed Alex, but still he could not open his eyes. In fact, he could barely move. The wind tore at his coat, at his breeches. The ropes on his hands loosened. He felt rather than saw large objects flinging through the air around him. Something struck his tree. The trunk trembled against Alex's back.

Still the wind howled. Rain pelted him like the sharp tips of a cat-o-nine tails. The massive truck of the tree groaned and began to sway. The wind lifted Alex off the ground. The ropes around his waist tightened until he felt they would cut him in two. If they broke or if the tree fell, Alex knew he would surely die.

❖ CHAPTER 30 ❖

The tiny house shook beneath a blast of wind. Rose peered once again out the window to see pieces of wood, buckets, and sand flying through the air. Soldiers, bent at the waist, struggled to walk, bracing their shoulders to the wind. Some crawled over the ground like spiders.

A storm! Just like she had prayed for. Above her, an eerie crack sounded. A plank loosened from the roof and flapped up and down, banging out a warning. It flew away and wind tore through the parlor.

Rose should get below. Making her way to the back room, she lowered herself into the cellar and replaced the trapdoor.

Thunder cracked and roared and fumed. What little light that drifted down into the cellar instantly blackened. Torrents of rain fell from the sky as if the very gates of heaven had been flung open to release God's wrath. Backing into the shadows, Rose gazed upward, waiting for the floor to cave in. Thunder growled again. Louder and louder it grew, as if a million-man army galloped toward her.

Turning, Rose groped her way through the darkness and dove behind a stack of crates. Hugging herself, she trembled and prayed. Something massive struck the house. Rose screamed. The walls shook.

Raindrops that surely were as thick as hail struck the house from every direction. Eerie sounds like a thousand voices screaming and the crash of mighty waves whipped the small building. Rose couldn't think. Couldn't breathe. All she could do was huddle in the darkness and pray.

WHAM! An ominous crash blasted over Rose's ears. The trapdoor flew open. It slammed shut. Then it opened again. Over and over, it opened and shut like a giant mouth that dared to scold the storm for disturbing its rest. Air whipped into the cellar, spinning in a chaotic whirlwind. The crates in front of Rose performed a deranged dance. Potatoes and apples flew through the air. One struck the back of her neck. Pain shot into her head.

The door slammed shut, and something heavy landed on it, silencing it.

Rose's ears grew numb to the deafening sounds around her.

Minutes that seemed like hours went by.

Finally the winds abated. The rain lessened and the thunder retreated.

Light peered through the cracks in the trapdoor as if seeking survivors. Water dripped around its edges.

Still trying to calm her thrashing heart, Rose stood on shaky legs, and made her way up the ladder. The trapdoor wouldn't budge. She had to get out of here. She had to find Alex. Groaning, she hefted her back against it and pushed with all her might. Finally the wooden slab moved, and she shoved it aside. Closing hers eyes against the light, she ascended one more rung of the ladder. A gust of wind and rain slapped her face.

Which meant the house was no longer standing. Preparing herself for the inevitable scene, she opened her eyes. Nothing but shards of wood and broken glass remained of the structure that had sheltered her. Or of the buildings beside it or the ones across the street. A cannon sat where the foyer had once been—a testament to the power of the wind. The red coats of slain soldiers dotted the gray landscape. In the distance, the setting sun cast an orange glow over the round dome of the Capitol and the sidewalls of the president's mansion. Both still standing. Other than that, nothing but complete devastation met Rose's eyes, as if the city had been blasted with enemy cannons for days. But this was no enemy.

This was the hand of Almighty God.

❖

Alex opened his eyes to a sight that he had never expected to see and one that would be forever imprinted in his mind. Scattered across what was left of Washington were the red and blue coats of slain soldiers, dead horses, pigs, and the towering remnants of government buildings that had not fully succumbed to the fiery flames.

He raised his hand to find ropes no longer binding them, then tugged at those around his waist. After a few short pulls, they too fell to the ground. He stood, wobbled beneath a wave of dizziness, then leaned a hand on the tree for support. The hickory tree. He studied the trunk, nearly stripped of its bark. "Thank you, my friend." He patted it. For if he had not been tied to it, he would have surely been swept away with the other men. What he had thought had been a prison, God had used to save his life. *Thank You, Father.*

A bird flew overhead, and somewhere a horse neighed. Drums beat a march of retreat in the distance. The British were leaving. Alex scanned the devastation again. Most of the homes and buildings were flattened or gone. *Rose.* His heart shriveled. *Oh my sweet Rose.* Alex barreled down the hill, weaving his way through debris and death with one purpose in mind. He must find her.

❖

Amid praises to God for her deliverance and gasps in horror at the death and desolation around her, Rose made her way toward the Capitol. Her feet ached and bled, but it didn't matter now. She must find Alex. "Oh God," she cried, forcing back thoughts that he was a prisoner of the British—or worse, dead. "Please help me find him."

Yes, Rose finally believed God loved her. She could still feel His presence all around her. And bad circumstances didn't mean she would lose His love. She drew in a deep breath. If Alex had not survived, she would still not give up on God. She now believed that God had a plan, and she must trust Him no matter what. She only prayed His plan involved Alex being alive and well.

Halting, she wiped her moist face then held up her arm to shield the sun while she glanced over the broken city. Her eyes locked on a figure moving toward her in the distance. It blurred beneath the steam rising from the puddles. Friend or foe? She swallowed and continued, but made her way toward a broken wall to her right—a place she could hide behind should the person turn out to be her enemy.

Yet there was something about the man, the lift of his shoulders, his confident stride that kept Rose's eyes on him. A dark blue navy coat formed out of the dull gray around him. *British navy.* Alex? Rose shook her head. What were the chances? She'd better hide. Yet when she tried to move her feet they wouldn't budge. An invisible band seemed to have been strung between her and the mysterious man, keeping her in place.

Still he continued marching toward her. Dark hair the color of cocoa blew against his collar.

Her heart jumped.

He stopped. "Rose!" That marvelous deep British lilt released her feet from bondage, and clutching her oversized pants by the belt, she dashed toward him, ignoring the pain spiking up her legs. "Alex!"

He ran to greet her. Rose flew into his arms, laughing and sobbing all at the same time. He flung her around, showering her with kisses, then lowered her to her feet and held her face in his warm hands. "Thank God."

Rose took his hands and kissed them, smiling up at him. "I love you, Alex."

His arms swallowed her up again, and he lowered his lips to hers. "I love you so much, Rose." He kissed her, at first gently caressing her lips, before claiming her mouth as his own.

Rose forgot about the war, forgot about the destruction, the death, just for one glorious moment. All that mattered was Alex. And that he was alive. And that he loved her.

Releasing her, Alex planted a kiss on her nose and drew back, rubbing his thumb over her cheek. "Are you unharmed?"

Rose nodded. "You?"

He kissed her forehead then swung an arm over her shoulder and turned to survey the city.

"What now, Alex?" Rose asked.

"Let's go home."

❖

Five hours later, Alex halted the horse at the edge of the Drummond farm. Rose leaned back against his chest and drew in a deep breath. She'd never remembered such a beautiful sight. Coated in moonlight, the fields, the barn, and the house glinted in sparkled silver as if the place had been dropped on earth from a better world somewhere far away.

"Home at last." Alex's warm breath eased down her neck.

It had been a long journey. And the longest two days of her life. If not for the incessant ringing in her ears, Rose would have thought she'd only imagined the storm that had set them free.

Had set her nation's capital free.

But visions of death and destruction kept popping unbidden in her mind.

After finding a pair of mismatched shoes along the side of the road for Rose, Alex had led her through the vacated streets of Washington in search of some means by which to travel home. Averting her eyes from the death around her, Rose had kept her gaze on Alex's back and her thoughts on God. Finally, they found three fully saddled and harnessed horses grazing in an open field across from the Capitol. No doubt spooked by the storm, the animals must have returned to the city only to find their masters gone. Alex managed to catch one, while the other two galloped away.

They passed the first few hours of their journey in silence, too numb, too in awe, to speak. But eventually Alex began singing an old church hymn, and Rose joined him. They spent the next hours thanking God for sparing them and for bringing them together. A few somber moments passed when they spoke of Mr. Snyder's tragic death. Neither of them had wished the councilman any harm. The man had simply chosen the wrong path.

Just like all choices in life. One path led to greater light while the other led deeper into darkness.

During the last hour of the journey, Rose had leaned back against Alex's chest and thought about the paths God had laid before them. Daniel had been right. She and Alex each had something important to do. God had used them mightily—had used her mightily. Rose found the feeling both overwhelming and humbling.

"I wonder if God would have sent the storm without our prayers," Alex said as if reading her thoughts. "It baffles me that the Almighty needs the petitions of mere man to do anything."

Rose gazed at the light spilling from the parlor window of her home. No doubt her aunt and uncle were awake worrying about her. "Uncle Forbes says that our prayers are powerful and effective and rise like incense before the throne of God." She stretched her legs and winced at the ache that spread through them from riding so long. "The prayers of God's people have stopped rain from falling, closed the mouths of lions, and raised the dead. Though I don't suppose God needs our prayers,

I do believe He uses them to do His will."

The horse snorted and pawed the dirt, and Alex gripped the reins. "I am in awe that He used someone like me to help save this great nation."

"And me as well, little terrified me." She laughed. "Yet now without my fear, I feel God's gentle nudge to help women who had suffered as I have—to help them past the shame and let them know God loves them."

Alex wrapped her arms around her. "I'm so proud of you."

Rose stared at the farm she'd grown to love. "I wonder what else God has for us to do?"

Alex nudged the horse forward. "Let's go find out."

❖

Sliding from the horse, Alex tied the reins to the post and turned to reach up for Rose, but she had already dismounted. Dragging her oversized trousers in the mud, she limped past him. With her mismatched shoes clomping a discordant tune over the ground, her red coat hanging nearly to her knees and her golden tresses brushing against her waist like silken threads, she was, by far, the most adorable foot soldier he'd ever seen.

They mounted the steps to the front porch, and Alex swept open the door.

"Rose!" Mrs. Drummond flew toward her and swallowed her up in her arms. Amelia emerged from the parlor, her face pale, and dashed toward Rose's other side.

"Dear, where have you been? Your uncle and I have been so worried." Mrs. Drummond glanced over Rose's attire and her brow furrowed. "My goodness, what, pray tell, are you wearing?"

Mr. Drummond appeared behind them, hands folded over his portly belly and a knowing smile on his lips. "Perhaps she joined the British army, dearest." He winked at Alex.

Amelia giggled, and Mrs. Drummond swung a stern gaze his way. "Oh you do enjoy teasing me, Forbes." She faced Alex. "And you, sir. A British naval uniform? Has the world gone mad?"

Alex opened his mouth to respond, but Mrs. Drummond continued her frantic speech. "We only just arrived home last evening, but the storm kept us from searching for you."

"Where are the children?" Rose asked.

"They are well." Mrs. Drummond exchanged a glance with her husband. "We left them in Lewisville with friends of Reverend Hargrave. But we were worried you would panic when you heard the British were marching on Washington, so we came home immediately."

"Then when we found you gone, lass," Mr. Drummond added, "I'm afraid we were quite distressed. We intended to head out at first light."

"We were in Washington." Rose said.

Amelia gripped her arm. "We heard the British set fire to the city!"

Rose exchanged a sorrowful look with Alex. "Indeed they did."

"Oh my." Amelia covered her mouth.

Mrs. Drummond withdrew a handkerchief. "Oh the shame of it." She dabbed her eyes. "Mr. Markham informed us he could see the flames from Federal Hill. But, dear, you overcame your fear and went to find us?"

Rose clasped her aunt's hand. "What else could I do?"

Mrs. Drummond's eyes glistened. "Oh you poor dear. You must have been terrified."

The kitchen door flew open, and Cora sped into the room, halting as her eyes settled on Rose. "There you are, child." She ambled forward and stood by Mr. Drummond.

Rose smiled. "Good to see you, Cora."

Alex winked at the cook and the woman rolled her eyes.

"But do tell us what happened?" Mrs. Drummond waved her handkerchief through the air. "How did you come to wear this hideous uniform?"

"It's a long story, Mrs. Drummond." Alex took Rose's hand and glanced at Uncle Forbes. "God rescued us and the entire city."

"Indeed?" Mr. Drummond cocked his head, then moved beside his wife. "Come, let us sit down in the parlor. I cannot wait to hear it. Cora, bring some tea and biscuits."

Alex squeezed Rose's hand. "First, there is a matter that cannot wait."

One gray eyebrow rose on Mr. Drummond's face.

Casting a glance at Rose, Alex cleared his throat, suddenly feeling more nervous than he had during all the terrifying events of the past week. What if the man said no? For the first time in his life, Alex had nothing to recommend himself—no land, no money, no prospects. In fact, why on earth would Mr. Drummond accept his proposal? Sweat blossomed on Alex's forehead and neck. "Sir, if I may." He glanced at Rose who prodded him on with her eyes. "If I may."

"If you may what, Mr. Reed?" Mr. Drummond smiled.

"With your permission." Alex blew out a sigh. Better to get it over with. "May I have your niece's hand in marriage?"

Mr. Drummond grinned and slapped Alex on the back. "Yes, indeed, you may! I thought you'd never ask."

"Marriage? Oh my." Aunt Muira shook her head and gripped Amelia for support.

Cora chuckled. "Heaven be praised."

Amelia squealed in delight and hugged Rose.

Alex faced Rose and found her looking at him with so much love and admiration, he nearly fell backward. Mr. Drummond, Mrs. Drummond, Amelia, and even Cora crowded around the couple, offering words of love and congratulations as they welcomed them home.

Home. Alex smiled as warmth spread through him.

He was home at last.

❖ HISTORICAL NOTE ❖

In the early evening hours on August 24, 1814, after defeating the Americans in battle at Bladensburg, British Major General Robert Ross and Rear Admiral Cockburn led some fifteen hundred British soldiers and sailors, unhindered, down the streets of Washington DC. The troops halted in an open field east of the Capitol building and waited for someone in authority to emerge and discuss surrender terms and prize money. But no one came. After the Americans blew up the naval yard, Admiral Cockburn led a party of men into the Capitol building. Thus began a night of revenge, drunken mayhem, and devilish destruction as British troops went on a rampage through the capital city, stealing valuables left behind by its citizens, and setting fire to every government building they could find. Among the buildings destroyed were the Capitol, the Library of Congress (housing 3,000 volumes along with many maps and charts), a home owned by George Washington, the president's house, the War and Treasury building, and the office of the *National Intelligencer* newspaper (which had slandered Admiral Cockburn).

Dolly Madison, the president's wife, barely escaped her home before the troops arrived, carrying as many paintings, documents, and artifacts she could hold. (Although, there is no record of a British soldier or lady from Baltimore in her house on that day, the possibility exists!) Admiral

Cockburn, in a raucous display of vengeful arrogance, did indeed partake of the dinner Mrs. Madison had laid out for her husband's men, as well as offer a multitude of insulting toasts to the president whom he referred to as "Old Jemmy."

Early in the morning of August 25, the British aroused themselves with the intent to set fire to any remaining buildings and wreak as much additional havoc as possible. But this new day would not afford them success. At two in the afternoon, a detachment of two hundred redcoats marched to Greenleaf Point to finish off the arsenal and destroy any remaining buildings left by the Americans. However, before leaving, the Americans had concealed a large quantity of kegged powder in a dry well near the barracks. One of the British artillerymen accidentally dropped a lighted portfire into the well. The resulting explosion rocked the city, unroofed houses, and shot pieces of brick, stone, and earth into the air. Twelve British died and thirty were wounded.

Soon after the explosion, a terrifying storm struck the city. One eyewitness commented, "Of the prodigious force of the wind, it is impossible for you to form any conception. Roofs of houses were torn off by it, and whisked into the air like sheets of paper. . . . The darkness was as great as if the sun had long set. . .occasionally relieved by flashes of vivid lightning streaming through it, which together with the noise of the wind and the thunder, the crash of falling buildings and the tearing of roofs as they were stript from the walls, produced the most appalling affect I ever have or shall witness. . . . Our column was completely dispersed as if it had received a total defeat."

The two-hour storm not only doused the remaining flames, but killed thirty British soldiers, scattering the rest over the landscape. The British gathered their survivors and quietly withdrew from Washington.

Surrender the Dawn

❖ DEDICATION ❖

To anyone who has ever felt like a failure.

"I am the Light of the world,
he who follows Me will not walk in the darkness,
but will have the Light of life."
JOHN 8:12 NASB

❖ CHAPTER 1 ❖

March 26, 1814
Merchants Coffee House, Baltimore, Maryland

M iss Channing, no privateer in his right mind would accept money from a woman investor. It is simply bad luck."

Raucous laughter—all male—shot through the tiny coffee shop that smelled more like ale and sweat than coffee.

Wrinkling her nose beneath the odor and bracing her heart against the mounting impediment to her well-laid plans, Cassandra rose from her seat. "That is merely a foolish superstition, Mr. McCulloch. I assure you, my money is as good as any man's."

Snickers and grins interspersed with the occasional salacious glance continued to fire her way. But Cassandra brushed them off. After an hour of sitting in the muggy, male-dominated room, listening to various merchants selling shares for the equipping of their vessels into privateers, she had grown numb to the attention.

When the customs agent had finally announced eight shares offered at two hundred dollars each to be invested in the *Contradiction*—a one-hundred-and-three-ton schooner out of Dorchester, housing one long nine gun, ten men, and captained by Peter Pascal—Cassandra had raised her hand. With her one thousand dollars, she could purchase over half the shares rather than be one of many investors in a larger, better-equipped ship. Owning more of a privateer meant higher returns. And she definitely was in dire need of higher returns.

Mr. McCulloch shoved his thumbs into the pockets of his trousers and shot Cassandra the same patronizing look her mother often gave her younger sisters when they failed to comprehend what she was saying. "Aye, your money is good, Miss Channing. It's the mind behind the coin that begs concern."

"How dare you, sir! Why, you are no more. . ." Cassandra clutched her reticule close to her chest and spat out, "My money and my mind are equal to any man's here."

Again laughter pulsated through the room.

"It's the comely exterior of that mind that I'm partial to," one man yelled from the back, prompting yet another chorus of chuckles.

Cassandra narrowed her eyes and scanned the mob. Did these men honestly believe they were amusing? Most of them—with the exception of a few unsavory types loitering around the fringes of the assembly—were hardworking merchants, bankers, shop owners, mill workers, and farmers. Men who often tipped their hat at her on the street. Her gaze locked with the wife of the coffeehouse proprietor, scrubbing a counter in the right corner. Sympathy poured from her eyes.

Mr. McCulloch scratched his head and gave a sigh of frustration. "A share in any privateer gives you a voice in its affairs. A business voice, miss. A voice that needs to be schooled in matters of financial investments and risk assessment."

The men nodded and grunted in approval like a band of mindless lackeys.

Cassandra tapped her shoe on the wooden floor, the hollow echo thrumming her disdain through the room. "A mind like Mr. Nash's here, I presume." She gestured toward the gentleman standing to her right. "No offense, sir"—she offered him a conciliatory smile—"I'm sure you have acquired a plethora of financial wisdom while shoeing horses all day."

The low rumble of laughter that ensued was quickly squelched by a scowl from Mr. McCulloch.

"And Mr. Ackers." She nodded toward the stout man sitting at the table next to hers. "Surely you have become a master of investment while out tilling your field?"

The proprietor's wife emitted an unladylike chortle that drew all gazes her way. Her face reddening, she disappeared through a side door.

"Besides," Cassandra huffed. "What business decisions need be made for a privateer already armed, captained, and ready to set sail?"

No reply came—save the look of complete annoyance shadowing the customs agent's face.

Cassandra pursed her lips. "Let me make this very easy for you, sir. You need investors, I have money to invest." She clutched the silk reticule until her fingers ached. "I am not without good sense, and I assure you I will seek out advice from those more experienced should the need arise."

"We cannot trust that you will do so."

"That is absurd!"

"Trouble is, miss, there's not a man among us who'd be willing to partner with you."

Nods of affirmation bobbed through a sea of heads.

Cassandra scanned the crowd, making eye contact with as many of the men as she could. "Is there no man here brave enough to stand with me?"

The hiss of coals in the fireplace was her only reply.

Mr. McCulloch sifted through the stack of papers before him. "Perhaps we could allow you to invest a much smaller percentage in a privateer if you promise to forsake your voice in any decisions and if the other shareholders would agree to it." His beady eyes swept over the mob, but not a single gentleman spoke up.

Cassandra batted her gloved hand through the air. "I will not accept a smaller percentage, sir."

"Then I fear we are at an impasse." Mr. McCulloch plucked out a pocket watch, flipped it open, and stared at it as if it contained the answer to ridding himself of her company. His gaze lifted to hers. "Miss, your father was a good man. I am sorry for your loss. But not even *he* would risk the bad luck that would surely come from aligning with a woman in any seafaring venture."

Tears burned in Cassandra's eyes, but she shoved them behind a shield of determination.

Mr. Parnell, a worker at the flour mill, gave her a sympathetic smile.

"Perhaps you should marry, Miss Channing," Mr. Kendrick, the young banker assisting Mr. McCulloch, said. "A woman your age should not be unattached." A wave of interested eyes engulfed her. "Then with your husband's signature, you may invest in whatever you wish."

Cassandra's blood boiled. She wouldn't tell them that she had no intention of marrying any time soon, and certainly not for the sole purpose of investing in a privateer. "Any man I marry will allow me to do with my money as I see fit, sir."

Again, a quiver of laughter assailed her.

Withdrawing a handkerchief from within his waistcoat, Mr. McCulloch dabbed at the sweat on his bald head. "If you don't mind, Miss Channing, we have serious business to discuss."

An angry flush heated Cassandra's face, her neck, and moved down her arms as a hundred unladylike retorts flirted with her tongue. Tightening her lips, she grabbed her cloak, turned, and shoved her way through the crowd as the man began once again taking bids for the *Contradiction*.

Contradiction, indeed. This whole meeting was a contradiction of good sense.

After turning down several gentlemen's offers to walk her home, Cassandra stepped from the shop into a gust of March wind that tore her bonnet from her hand. Too numb to chase after it, she watched as it tumbled down South Street as if all her dreams blew away with it. Perhaps they had. Perhaps her dreams had been overtaken by the nightmare of this past year.

Yes, only a nightmare. And soon she would wake up and be comfortable and carefree as she once had been. And her country would not be at war. And her father would still be with her.

But as she watched the sun drag its last vestiges of light from the brick buildings, elm trees, and the dirt street, her dreamlike state vanished. It would soon be dark, and she had a mile to traverse to reach her home.

Through a rather unsavory section of town.

Swinging her fur-lined cloak over her shoulders, she shoved her reticule tightly between her arm and body, pressed a wayward curl into her loosely pinned bun, and started down the street, nodding her greeting toward a passing couple, a single gentleman, and a group of militiamen as she went. The snap of reins, the clomp of horse hooves, and the rattle of carriage wheels filled her ears as she wove between passing phaetons and horses. An icy breeze tore at her hair and fluttered the lace of her blue muslin gown. She drew her cloak tighter around her neck. A bell rang in the distance. A baby cried. Sordid chuckles, much like the type she'd just endured in the coffeehouse, blared from a tavern along Pratt Street. Was the entire town mocking her?

Up ahead, the bare masts of countless ships swayed into the darkening sky like thickets in a winter wind. Most were abandoned merchant ships. Some, however, were privateers, while others were merchantmen that had been issued Letters of Marque to board and confiscate enemy vessels—both forbidden investments to her.

Simply because she was a woman.

The briny scent of fish and salt curled her nose as she turned down Pratt Street. Dark water caressed the hulls of the ships like a lover luring them out to sea. Where they could damage British commerce and put an end to this horrendous war. But the blockade kept many of Baltimore's finest vessels imprisoned in the harbor. Only the fastest privateers could slip past the fortress of British ships capping the mouth of the Chesapeake and only then, during inclement weather. The rest remained at sea, hauling their prizes to ports along the Eastern Seaboard where they sold them, along with the goods in their holds, for considerable sums of money.

Which was precisely why Cassandra needed to invest the money left to her by her father and brothers in a privateer. She patted the reticule containing the banknote for a thousand dollars—all the wealth her family had left in the world. Now what was she to do? Cassandra swallowed down a rising fear. Investing in a privateer had been her last hope. How else could a single woman with no skills provide for a family? Cassandra's mother and sisters depended on her, and she had let them down.

❖

Luke Heaton trudged up the companionway ladder and emerged onto the main deck of the ship—his ship. Or his heap of rot and rust, to be more precise. Setting his hammer atop the capstan with a thud, he shuddered against the crisp air coming off the bay.

Biron looked up from the brass binnacle he was polishing. "Did someone die?"

Luke gave a sardonic chuckle and grabbed the open bottle of rum from the top of a barrel. Plopping down on the bulwarks, he took a swig and wiped his mouth with his sleeve. "Yes, this ship. All she's good for is a watery grave."

Biron continued his polishing. "At least she stays afloat."

"But not for long. She's got two gaping holes in her hull."

"They can be fixed." Biron shrugged, but the encroaching shadows stole his expression. Setting his bottle down, Luke struck flint to steel and lit the lantern hanging from the main mast.

"What of the rotten spars, rusty tackles, and frayed sheets?" Luke ran a hand through his hair.

A twinkle lit Biron's brown eyes. Or was it merely the lantern's reflection? "All repairable."

The ship teetered over an incoming wavelet, and Luke stretched the ache from his back. An ache formed from working all day belowdecks trying to transform this heap into a swift sailing vessel. "Repairable yes, but with what, is the question." Luke took another sip of rum. "How did I ever end up with this old bucket?"

"You won it in a game of cards, if I recall."

Yes, the hazy memory returned. Along with another more disturbing one—another card game the following night when he'd lost all the money he intended to use to repair and equip his new acquisition.

The *Agitation* was indeed living up to her name.

Luke huffed out a sigh and fingered the rim of the dark bottle. A gull squawked overhead, taunting him, while the waters of Baltimore Harbor slapped the hull in laughter. The smell of rum along with his own sweat combined with the scents of wood, tar, and salt. He loved the sea. Had wanted nothing more than to return to her after his captain and best friend, Noah, had cast him from his ship.

Luke shifted on his seat as the memory stung him. The year he'd spent as Noah's first mate on his privateer, *Defender,* had been the best year of Luke's life. But he'd gone and ruined his first opportunity to make an honorable living, as he had done to everything else he touched. Even so, the experience hadn't been a complete loss, for privateering had left Luke with a love of the sea, a love for his country, and a yearning for the riches he could make in the trade. But now with no money and a broken-down hull of a ship, that dream began to sink beneath the murky waters of the bay.

"I should sell her."

Biron's gray-lined hair shimmered in the lantern light. "What? And give up?"

"Don't be a fool, old man." Luke stood and began to pace. "Where am I going to get the money to fix and arm her as a privateer?"

"Perhaps God will provide."

"Humph. God, indeed." Luke would expect no help from the Almighty—even if He did exist.

Ceasing his scrubbing, Biron looked at Luke with understanding. "I know your responsibilities weigh heavy on you, Cap'n."

Responsibilities. Luke gazed at the sliver of a moon smiling at him in the eastern sky. Was that what he would call John? Perhaps. Yet, he was so much more than that. A responsibility Luke would never forsake. And one he hoped with everything in him, he was worthy of.

Biron spit on his rag and began rubbing the binnacle again. "It is a good thing you have someone dependin' on you, or you'd while away your time in taverns, wastin' your money on wenches, wine, and whist."

"At least I find I am good at those."

Biron chuckled and shook his head. "My guess is that you are good at many things, Cap'n. If you'd just believe in yourself—and in God."

"I'm not your captain yet." Luke eyed his friend. Sturdy as a ship's mast and just as weathered, Biron had been at sea his entire life. Tufts of gray floated across his dark hair like clouds across a night sky. "Why do you stay with me, old man?"

Biron scratched his whiskers. "You promised work for this aged seaman, and I'm holding you to it, Cap'n." He smiled.

Luke took another swig. "I wouldn't place your bet on me. I'll no doubt disappoint you."

Biron set down his cloth and stood, stretching his back. "Ah, I wouldn't be too sure about that, Cap'n." He winked, tugged at his red neckerchief, and made his way over to Luke. "It grows late, my friend. I'll see you in the morning." With a moan, he hefted himself onto the dock and gazed up at the night sky. "You never know what tomorrow will bring." He turned around and winked at Luke. "Or even tonight."

❖

A sudden chill struck Cassandra. She hugged herself. In her musings, nighttime had spread a cloak of darkness over the city. With the exception of a sailor sitting on the deck of his ship by the dock, an old man ambling down the street, and a couple disappearing in the distance, no one was in sight. Facing forward, she hurried along.

Footsteps sounded behind her.

Her chest tightened. She quickened her pace.

More shuffling. The crunch of gravel. A man coughed.

She glanced over her shoulder. Two bulky shadows followed her.

Air seized in her throat. She hurried her pace and nearly tripped on the uneven pavement. The footfalls grew louder. Grabbing her skirts, she started to run. Where were the night watchmen? Why, oh why, had she been foolish enough to bring all of her money with her? *Lord, please. . .* her prayer fell limp from her lips. God had never answered her petitions before. Why would He now?

She crossed Light Street. A cat meowed.

A man jumped out of an alleyway in front of her.

Cassandra screamed and spun around. The two men approached her. Shadows swirled over their faces, masking their features. "What do you want?" Her voice came out as a squeak.

"We wants what's in yer purse there, miss."

❖

Luke took another swig of rum and squinted into the shadows where Biron had disappeared. Across the street, a lady walked alone. Two, maybe three men crept behind her. Foolish girl. From her attire, he could tell she wasn't one of the tavern wenches. What was she doing wandering about the docks so late? Luke flipped the hair from his face and slowly set his bottle down. The ship eased over a ripple and the bottle shifted, scraping over the oak planks. The men continued their pursuit. Luke shook his head. The last thing he needed was more trouble. He shouldn't get involved. He should stay on his ship. But the rum soured in his stomach. *Oh, lud.* With that, Luke shot to his feet. Searching the deck for his sword, he sheathed it and leaped onto the dock. The woman started to run. Another man leapt out in front of her. They had her surrounded.

❖

Cassandra's pulse roared in her ears. Her legs wobbled. She would not allow these ruffians to steal all that kept her and her family from starvation. Her terror quickly turned to anger. She jutted out her chin. "Well, you cannot have it, sir!"

"If you give us the purse, there'll be no trouble."

"Oh, I assure you gentlemen, if you do not leave this instant, there'll be more trouble than you can handle."

The men exchanged mirthful glances then broke into fits of laughter.

Cassandra ground her teeth together. She grew tired of being laughed at. Tired of being told what she could and couldn't do.

One of the men, a short, greasy-looking fellow, approached, hand extended. She recognized him as one of the men at the coffeehouse. "Give it up, miss."

"You'll have to pry it out of my dead hands."

The slimy man grabbed her arm. Pain shot into her shoulder. "If ye insist."

❖ CHAPTER 2 ❖

Cassandra struggled against the man's grip. "How dare you!" She pounded her reticule atop his head. Tossing up his other arm to fend off her blows, he ducked and spewed obscenities, while his companions held their stomachs in laughter.

Fury pinched every nerve into action. She would not lose this money. She could not lose this money. Her life and the lives of her family depended on it.

The man's grip tightened. Pain spiked through her arm and into her fingers. They grew cold and numb. Raising her leg, she thrust her shoe into his groin. He released her and doubled over with a groan. The other men stopped laughing. Thick fingers grabbed her arms on both sides. She screeched in pain.

"That's enough out o' you, miss. Now hand over that purse!" The man to her right—who looked more like a toad than a man—shouted, sending a spray of spittle and foul breath over her. Strands of hair hung in his bloated face as his venomous eyes stabbed her with hatred. He reached for her reticule.

Cassandra thrashed her legs. Her thrusts met nothing but air. The men on either side of her tightened their grips. She cried out in pain. Her palms grew moist. Toad-man released her and yanked the purse from her hands.

Somewhere a bell rang, chiming her doom.

"Give that back to me at once!" Cassandra grasped for her reticule, but the man jumped out of her reach and gave her a yellowed grin in return.

All hope spilled from Cassandra, leaving her numb. This couldn't be happening. "Please," she begged. "It's all I have."

"Not anymore." The bald man on her left lifted his beak-like nose and chortled.

She kicked him in the shin. He cursed and leaned over, pinching her arm even tighter and dragging her down with him.

The toad chuckled.

When Cassandra righted herself, she saw the tip of a cutlass slice through the darkness, cutting off toad-man's laughter at his neck. The sharp point pierced his skin. A trickle of blood dripped onto his grimy shirt. He froze. His eyes widened. Cassandra's gaze traced the length of the blade to a tall, dark-haired man at the hilt end, his face hidden in the shadows. "Return the lady's reticule, if you please, sir," a deep, yet oddly familiar voice demanded.

Cassandra released her breath. Her thrashing heart slowed its pace. Dare she hope for rescue?

"And you." The dark man nodded toward the beak-nosed ruffian still clutching her left arm. "Release her and back away, or your friend will forfeit his head."

A salty breeze swirled around them like a tempest, as if some unknown force were examining the proceedings. Despite the chill of the evening, a trickle of sweat slid down the toad's forehead. Beak-nose released her arm. Cassandra rubbed it, feeling her blood return.

The third man, whom Cassandra had kicked, slowly rose from the ground and slid a hand inside his coat.

Cassandra opened her mouth to warn her rescuer, but with lightning speed, he plucked a pistol from his coat, cocked it, and pointed it at the villain. "I wouldn't do that if I were you."

The third man raised his hands in the air.

Her rescuer turned back to Toad-man. "I *said* return the lady's reticule." He pressed the tip further into the man's skin. He yelped. More blood spilled.

"Whatever you say. Whatever you say." With a trembling arm, he held Cassandra's purse out to her. Snatching it, she pressed it against her bosom and took a step back, her heart slowing its pace.

"What are you doin', George?" Beak-nose whined. "There's three o' us and only one o' him."

"Ye aren't the one wit' a sword in yer neck, are ye, now?"

Her rescuer faced Beak-nose. A sheen of moonlight drifted over his face, over his firm stubbled jaw, strong nose, high forehead, and raven hair. Cassandra's mouth fell open. *Luke Heaton*. Her friend Noah Brenin's roguish first mate—the man he had tossed from his privateer for drunkenness and cheating at cards.

"I told you to unhand her," he demanded.

Beak-nose gave a cynical laugh that sent a tremble of fear through Cassandra. "As you wish." In one fluid motion, he released her arm and drew a sword from his belt, leveling it upon Mr. Heaton.

"What. . .ye goin' to do. . .now, hero?" Toad-man's voice came out broken beneath the tip of Luke's sword.

Beak-nose thrust his sword at Mr. Heaton. Leaping back, Luke blocked the slash with his blade. The chime of steel on steel vibrated a chill down Cassandra's back. The toad rubbed his neck and gazed at the blood on his hand as if he could not conceive from whence it had come.

With his gun still cocked and pointed at the third man, Luke met each thrust of Beak-nose's sword blow for blow. The chime of their blades rang through the night like the warning bells of Christ's Church. Cassandra gripped her throat. She should take her money and run. No man could fight such odds and win.

But how could she leave? Rogue or not, Mr. Heaton risked his life for her. She must do something to help. Frantic, Cassandra scanned the surroundings. A stack of bricks lay on the side of the building, no doubt for repairs. She grabbed one. The rough stone snagged her silk gloves as she crept toward Toad-man.

Beak-nose brought his blade down once again on Mr. Heaton. Moonlight glinted off the metal as grunts filled the air. Leaping out of its path, Heaton swung about and drove the man back with a rapid parry. The *whoosh whoosh whoosh* of his blade filled the air. His last swipe sent Beak-nose's sword clanging to the ground. He quickly snatched it up. But before he could recover, Mr. Heaton lunged toward him with a ferocious assault that sent the man reeling.

Taking advantage of the moment, the toad drew his sword. Cassandra gasped. She raised her hands to strike him with the brick. He swung around, growling, and shoved her aside. Arms failing, she dropped the brick and tumbled to the dirt. Pain shot up her back.

With blade extended, Toad-man advanced toward Luke. Still holding his pistol in one hand, Mr. Heaton fired at him. He missed. The crack pierced the night air as the smell of gunpowder bit Cassandra's nose. The toad emitted a vile chuckle. Tossing the weapon down, Mr. Heaton swung his cutlass in his direction. He ducked beneath Toad-man's clumsy slash then met his advance with such force, it spun the man around. Sweeping his sword back to the left, Mr. Heaton countered Beak-nose's next attack.

Cassandra's head grew light. She glanced down the street for anyone who could help. No one was in sight. Yet Mr. Heaton seemed more than capable of handling these two men. But not capable of keeping his eye on the third man, who finally managed to extract his pistol from his coat and aim it at Mr. Heaton.

Grabbing her skirts, she jumped to her feet and retrieved the brick. Raising it above her head, she closed her eyes and brought it down on the man's head. A sharp crack made her wince. Followed by a moan. She peered through her lashes to see him topple to the ground in a heap. Her gaze locked upon Mr. Heaton's. A slight grin crossed his lips before he turned to meet Toad-man's next charge.

In fact, Mr. Heaton continued to fight both men off with more skill and finesse than Cassandra had ever witnessed. Where the ruffians groaned and heaved and dripped in sweat, Mr. Heaton carried himself with a calm, urbane confidence. Finally his blade met the toad's left shoulder, eliciting a scream from the man that quite resembled a woman's. Clutching his arm, the villain sped into the night, leaving his partner gaping at Luke, his chest heaving. He backed away, dropped his blade, and uttered, "It's not worth this," before bolting down the street.

Sheathing his sword, Mr. Heaton collected his pistol from the ground, slid it inside his coat, and slapped his hands together as if this sort of thing happened every day. He started toward Cassandra. Her heart vaulted into her throat. Perhaps she was no safer with him than she had been with the scoundrels who'd assaulted her. He was the town rogue, after all. A drunkard and a ruffian. He halted, towering over her by at least a foot, and she resisted the urge to take a step back. He smelled of wood and rum. Recognition flickered in his eyes and something else—pleasant surprise? "Are you harmed, Miss Channing?"

"No, Mr. Heaton." She gripped her reticule. "I thank you, sir, for coming to my aid."

He glanced at the man lying in a heap in the dirt. "I've never seen a woman defend herself with a brick." His lopsided grin sent an odd jolt through her heart.

"It does not always require a man's strength to defeat a foe."

"Indeed." He chuckled. "Then perhaps I should have left you to your own devices. No doubt you could have pummeled them all unconscious."

Cassandra narrowed her gaze. "Perhaps I could have."

"Nevertheless, miss, you shouldn't walk about town at night without benefit of an escort."

"Lately, there are many things I'm told I should not do."

He swayed slightly on his feet and the smell of rum once again stung her nose. "Indeed. I suffer from the same malady."

"I doubt our situations are comparable." She glanced at the dark frame of a schooner tied at the dock. "How did you come to my rescue so suddenly? I did not see anyone else about."

"I was working on my ship when I spotted you across the street."

His ship. But she'd heard no one would hire him as a captain. "A privateer?"

Mr. Heaton gazed at the vessel bobbing in the harbor and sighed. "Alas, she could be one day." He gestured toward her reticule. "What is it you have in your reticule that would lure such rats from their holes?"

She eyed him suspiciously, wishing she could see the details of his face more clearly. "Nothing of import." She gripped it tighter. "I had business at the Merchants Coffee House." A chill prickled her skin. Surely this man wouldn't attempt to rob her after he'd defended her so admirably. She took a step back. "I thank you again, Mr. Heaton, but I really must be on my way."

"Allow me to escort you home." Closing the distance between them once again, he proffered his elbow. His massive chest spanned her vision even as his body heat cloaked her in warmth. Her breath quickened.

"There is no need." Turning, she waved him off. "I'm sure there are no more ruffians afoot." *Except you, perhaps.*

Mr. Heaton fell in step beside her. "Nevertheless, I would never forgive myself should any harm come to you, especially carrying such a fortune."

Shock halted her. "What did you say?"

One dark brow rose. "They wouldn't accept your money, would they?"

Cassandra flattened her lips.

Mr. Heaton scratched the stubble on his chin. "I was aware of the proceedings at the coffee shop tonight, miss. I would have been there myself looking for investors if I'd thought anyone in town would take a chance on me as captain." Sorrow weighed his voice.

Cassandra took in this news and allowed it to stir excitement within her. If only for a moment. But no. Even if he would take her money, Mr. Heaton was not a man to be trusted. She clutched her reticule closer and started on her way.

Clearing his throat, he walked beside her. "You have nothing to fear from me, Miss Channing. I am no thief. A gambler, perhaps, even a libertine, but no thief." He stumbled but quickly leveled his steps.

Cassandra shook her head. How on earth had he managed to wield his sword so skillfully in his condition? She stopped and faced him. "You are drunk, sir."

"Ah, yes." He gave her a rakish grin. "How could I forget? Apparently, I'm also a sot."

Cassandra searched for a glimpse of his eyes in the darkness, but the shadows denied her. How could he joke about such a disgusting habit?

"Wondering how I managed to fend off three men?"

"Two." She lifted her chin. "I took care of one of them."

He chuckled and reached up as if to touch the loose strands of her hair.

She began walking again. "Please leave me be, Mr. Heaton. I thank you for your assistance. Good night."

"You should see my swordplay when I'm sober, miss," he shouted after her.

"I'd rather not see you at all, Mr. Heaton."

She heard his footsteps behind her. Turning right onto Howard Street, she quickened her pace. Without the street lights—kept in darkness due to the war—she could barely make out the gravel road. The crunch of her shoes on the pebbles echoed against the brick warehouses on her right. One glance over her shoulder told her that Mr. Heaton still followed her, though he remained at a distance. If his reputation wasn't so besmirched, she might find his actions quite chivalrous. Instead, suspicion rankled her mind.

Down Eutaw Street, Cassandra halted before her small yard—the shadow of a two-story brick house loomed behind a garden of red roses and goldenrods. She swung about to say good night and nearly bumped into Mr. Heaton.

"Oh, forgive me, Miss Channing." Yet he didn't step back as propriety demanded. Turning, she headed up the stone path to the door.

"If you're seeking a ship to invest in, Miss Channing, mine is quite available." His boot steps followed her.

She faced him. "I am seeking a reputable ship, Mr. Heaton. With a reputable captain." She feigned a smile. The lantern light perched outside her door reflected a devilish gleam in his eyes—blue eyes. She could see them now, mere inches from her own face. Her heart took up a traitorous thump. "Preferably a sober one."

"I've been at sea my whole life. Sober or not, I'll make a good captain and bring you a fortune in prizes. Ask your friend, Noah."

"I have," she said, lifting a brow. "He warned me to stay away from you."

Mr. Heaton chuckled and tugged on his right earlobe. "He did, did he?" His eyes scoured over her as if assessing her for some nefarious purpose. "Good advice, I'd say." A sad smile tugged on his lips. "Well then, I bid you good night, Miss Channing." He bowed slightly and turned to leave.

Slipping inside her door, Cassandra closed and bolted it, then she leaned back against the sturdy wood. No matter if his was the last privateer in the city, she would never align herself with Mr. Luke Heaton.

❖ CHAPTER 3 ❖

The sound of Mr. Heaton's boots crunching over the gravel as he departed drifted in through the window to Cassandra's right, while her mind whirled with the events of the evening. A muddle of emotions knotted in her gut: from anger to terror back to anger again and finally settling on an odd feeling that heated her face and tightened her belly—a feeling she could not name.

A jumble of wheat-colored curls flew from the library door, followed by a screech that burned Cassandra's ears. Darlene barreled down the hallway with Mr. Dayle fast on her heels. Or as fast as the young footman could be with four-year-old Hannah clinging to his leg like a barnacle to the hull of a ship. Dexter, their sheepdog, flopped in after them, barking.

A groan sounded from within the closed parlor to Cassandra's left.

"Cassie, you're home!" Darlene shouted, but before Cassandra could wrap her arms around her sister, the child slipped behind her, hiding in the folds of her gown.

Shuffling over the wooden floor like a sailor with a peg leg, Mr. Dayle halted before Cassandra. Dexter sat by his side and stared up at them—though Cassandra couldn't be entirely sure the dog could see anything through the curtain of fur covering his eyes. His tongue hung from his mouth. Giggles drifted up Cassandra's back and over her shoulders to bounce off Mr. Dayle's rather bedraggled, yet comely face. Light from the chandelier spilled on his blond hair, thick mustache, and fair eyebrows, making him appear to glow. "My apologies for not meeting you at the door, miss, but there appears to be something wrong with my leg."

"Indeed?" Cassandra forced her brows together. "I hope it isn't serious." She gazed down at Hannah, wrapped around his trousers, her thumb in her mouth and a smile flickering across her blue eyes.

"Hmm." Cassandra leaned over. "Appears to be an anchor of some sort—a red-haired anchor."

Mr. Dayle glanced down. "Egad, what is this that has grown upon my foot?"

Dexter chomped on a fold of Hannah's gown and began tugging her away from Mr. Dayle, growling.

Hannah inched her thumb from her mouth just enough to emit a giggle before she thrust it back inside.

"You wouldn't happen to know where Miss Darlene ran off to?" Mr. Dayle brushed dust from his gray coat. "She made quite a mess in the library, and when I insisted she clean it up, she disappeared."

Cassandra tapped her chin. "Young girl about six years old with light hair and green eyes?"

"Yes, that's the one."

Both girls giggled. Darlene poked her face out from between the folds of Cassandra's skirt.

Dexter released Hannah's gown and barked.

Mr. Dayle hunched over like a monster. "Ah, there you are." Grabbing Darlene, he swung her into his arms, her lacy petticoat fluttering through the air.

Hannah leapt to her feet. "Me too! Me too!"

Cassandra laughed. There were some things worth coming home for.

"Cassandra, is that you?" Her mother's sharp voice sliced a hole in the happy moment.

And there were some things not worth coming home for.

Mr. Dayle released the girls and set them down on the floor.

"Thank you for being so good to them, Mr. Dayle." Cassandra drew her sisters close. "I know they can be"—she glanced down and brushed curls from both girls' foreheads—"rather difficult to handle."

Dexter forced his way in between the two girls and lifted his paw up on Cassandra's skirt. She patted him on the head. "And you too, Dexter."

"My pleasure, miss." Mr. Dayle bowed slightly then winked at the girls, eliciting further giggles. "Your mother was not feeling well tonight, and Margaret and Mrs. Northrop were otherwise engaged."

"And I'm sure you have your own duties—"

Darlene whispered something in her younger sister's ear, and the two started toward the stairs. Cassandra grabbed Darlene's arm. "Oh no, you don't. You both stay here with me." She faced Mr. Dayle again. "I'm sure you have more than enough to attend to without playing nursemaid to my sisters." Since Cassandra had been forced to let most of the staff go last month, poor Mr. Dayle held many roles at the Channing home: gardener, footman, butler, steward, and apparently nanny when the occasion called for it. But the tall man in his thirties never once complained.

Mr. Dayle smiled. "I'm happy to help."

"Cassandra!" Her mother's voice sounded like a bugle stuffed with a wet rag.

"She's in the parlor." Mr. Dayle gave her a sympathetic look before he clutched Dexter's collar and led the dog down the hallway. "I'll put him outside, miss."

Kneeling, Cassandra wrapped her arms around her sisters.

"Cassie, Cassie." Hannah climbed into Cassandra's lap while Darlene kissed her on the cheek.

"Come on, girls, let's go see Mama, shall we?" Cassandra attempted to straighten Darlene's gown but it remained hopelessly wrinkled. "And your hair, Dar. It's a tangled mess."

"I'm sorry, Cassie." Darlene pouted, but a devilish twinkle shone in her green eyes.

Cassandra ushered the girls down the hall and through wide doors to their left. The smell of tallow mixed with her mother's jasmine perfume assailed Cassandra as she led her sisters to the floral sofa across from their mother. Cassandra gave them her sternest "stay where you are" look.

"Where have you been, Cassandra?" Sitting like a stiff washboard on her velvet upholstered settee, her mother threw a hand to her chest. "I was so worried, my palpitations returned."

"Forgive me, Mother." Cassandra kissed her cheek and took her seat in a chair beside the fireplace. No sooner had she set her reticule down on the table, than Hannah tore from the sofa and crawled up in her lap. Spreading the girl's gown over her dangling feet, Cassandra embraced her youngest sister, inhaling her scent of lavender soap, fresh biscuits, and a pinch of mischief. Light from numerous candles perched on the tables and across the mantle set the room aglow, bringing out the rich colors in the mahogany furniture, and the exquisite burgundy and gold tones of the oriental rug that graced the center of the floor.

"I was detained, Mother. It could not be helped."

Her thoughts shifted to Mr. Heaton, and the odd warmth washed through her again. Plucking out her fan, she waved it over Hannah's face. "Detained by what, dear?" Her mother came alert. "Did something happen? You do look flushed."

Cassandra reached over and touched her mother's hand. "No. I am quite all right, Mother."

"Well, *I* haven't been quite all right." Her mother dabbed the stiff, perfectly shaped curls framing her face. Her voice emerged as sour as her expression. "While you were out traipsing around town, doing—oh my heavens, I cannot imagine what any proper lady could be doing out at this hour—your sisters have been very naughty."

Cassandra's gaze flashed to Darlene, who slouched into the cushions. Hannah stuck her thumb back into her mouth.

Her mother continued, "Darlene caught a frog. A frog! And she put it in Miss Thain's soup. Of all the things to put into soup! Can you imagine?"

Setting her fan down on the table, Cassandra bit her lip to keep from laughing. Her wayward sisters needed no further encouragement in their mischievous pranks. What they needed was a firm hand, which had disappeared from this house when their father ran off to fight the British in Canada two years ago.

"Needless to say, upon finding the frog, Miss Thain ran screaming from the kitchen and knocked over the meat pies she had prepared for supper. Which that filthy mutt proceeded to eat." Her mother grabbed her ever-ready handkerchief from the table and fluttered it about her face. "Most horrible. Most horrible. All we had to eat were scraps of cold chicken left over from yesterday's meal."

"And some fresh biscuits, Mama," Hannah piped in.

"Yes, dear, but hardly enough for a proper supper."

Darlene lowered her chin. "I'm sorry, Mama." Her loose hair fell in a tangle around her face. "I thought the frog was hungry."

The slight edge of humor in her voice—barely perceptible to most— told Cassandra that her sister was not sorry at all.

Her mother tightened her lips. "Hungry indeed." Her voice sounded so much like the creatures in question that Cassandra once again had to force down a laugh.

"Oh, where is my tea? My poor head." Lifting jeweled fingers to rub her temple, her mother studied Cassandra. "She takes after you, my dear."

Cassandra kissed the top of Hannah's head and tried to shove aside the rebuke. Mainly because it was true. She had always been the difficult child—the rebellious one. Always questioning, investigating, wanting to figure things out on her own, do things on her own. Now, as she looked at Darlene, she saw the same free spirit.

"Perhaps if you punished her more often, Mother?"

"Punish? She doesn't listen to me. She never has. She only listened to her father and he is. . ."

Mrs. Northrop entered with a tray of tea.

"Oh, thank goodness, my tea."

The housekeeper set the tray down on the walnut table that stretched between the sofas and chairs. Brown strands sprang from beneath the servant's white mobcap, which seemed barely able to restrain her thick hair. With her small head, pointed nose, long neck, and round figure, the woman reminded Cassandra of an ostrich she'd once seen in a painting. After she poured tea for Cassandra and her mother, she swung the pot toward the girls' cups.

"No." Cassandra's mother touched the housekeeper's arm, staying her. "Please put the girls to bed, Mrs. Northrop."

"Aye, mum." The woman's smile slipped slightly, but she quickly brought it back into position. Turning, she gestured for the girls to follow her.

After a bout of complaints, Darlene trudged from the room while Hannah scrambled from Cassandra's lap to follow her.

"I'll be up later to kiss you good night," Cassandra said. "Oh, Mrs. Northrop, have the girls clean up the mess they made in the library, if you please."

The housekeeper nodded in reply.

After the girls left, Cassandra leaned back in her chair and sipped her tea.

Her mother pressed down the folds of her silk gown then shot worried blues eyes her way. "Please tell me, Cassandra, that you did not throw away the rest of our money on a privateer?"

"No, I did not, Mother."

"Thank goodness."

"They wouldn't accept a woman investor." Cassandra chafed at the memory.

Her mother dabbed her forehead with her handkerchief. "At least there's some sense left in the world."

Setting down her cup, Cassandra rose and held out her hands to the flames crackling in the fireplace. "Sense? This kind of sense, Mother, will put us in the poorhouse."

"Oh, please do not speak of such gloomy things, dear."

Cassandra spun around. She wanted to be angry at her mother for her nonchalant attitude toward their financial woes, but the look of pain on her aged face stopped her. "I must speak of them, Mother. For I have to find a way to make a living for us."

"No doubt this war will end soon, and your brothers will return." Her mother's forlorn gaze drifted to the window as if searching for her missing offspring.

Outside, darkness gripped the city, much like England gripped America. Cassandra released a heavy sigh. "As much as I'd love for our country to defeat Britain and send those pompous redcoats home in shame, we cannot count on that happening anytime soon."

"But your brothers said they'd return in a year."

"And it's been a year, Mother. We have no idea where they are." An ache formed in Cassandra's heart. Or *if* they are. Yet she wouldn't voice her deepest fears to her mother, knowing how the possibility tormented her.

"Then you must get married, Cassandra. It is our only hope. It's the only way to ensure our survival." The quiver in her mother's voice brought Cassandra around to face her.

"I don't want to get married."

"What about Mr. Crane?" Her mother's cultured brows rose in excitement as if she hadn't heard Cassandra. "He's made his interest known for many months. It's fine time you gave him a little encouragement."

Cassandra shuddered at the thought of the overbearing man.

"And he owns that successful newspaper, the *Baltimore Register*. Why, I imagine he makes over five hundred dollars a year."

"So, I'm to throw my life and my happiness out the door for five hundred dollars a year?"

Tears glistened in her mother's eyes, and she fell back into her chair. "Oh, why did Phillip leave us? And then my boys. Oh, what will befall us?"

Cassandra eased beside her mother on the settee. "Never fear, Mother. We must plan for the worst and expect the best."

"How much money do we have left?"

"One thousand."

"Is that all?" Sitting up straight, her mother waved her handkerchief over her face. "What of the money your brothers got from the sale of our merchant ship?"

"We squandered it this past year, Mother." *You squandered it.* "We can no longer afford luxuries: oriental rugs, the latest hats and gowns from Paris, expensive perfumes. We cannot attend theater each week. We are no longer successful merchants."

A look of confusion, or perhaps shock, claimed her mother's features, though Cassandra had told her mother this same thing a dozen times.

"I fear if I do not find a way to invest our money," Cassandra continued, "it will be gone in just a few years."

"Oh dear, my head." Her mother fell back onto the couch. "You know I cannot bear such burdens."

Cassandra clasped her mother's trembling hands. "Don't overset yourself, Mother. I'll find a way."

"How? We are only women."

"I've a mind equal to any man's."

She flashed Cassandra an incredulous look. "Surely you see that you must get married soon. In fact, I insist on it, Cassandra. Do you want to send us all to the poorhouse?"

Tearing her gaze from the lack of confidence in her mother's eyes, Cassandra turned instead to the portrait of her great-grandfather, Edward Milford Channing, hanging above the fireplace. The man had come to Baltimore in 1747 with barely a coin in his pocket. With nothing but his wit, persistence, and hard work, he'd started his own merchant business, which he had passed on to Cassandra's father. The Channings were survivors. They were strong, independent, and hardworking. And Cassandra was as much a Channing as the men in the family. She rose from her chair and lifted her chin. "It will not come to that, Mother. Mark my words, whatever it takes, I will find a way for this family to survive."

❖ CHAPTER 4 ❖

Crossing the rickety bridge that spanned Jones Falls River, Luke continued down Pratt Street. An odd lightness feathered his steps. Why, he could not fathom. It certainly couldn't be Miss Channing. She'd done nothing but turn her pert little nose up at him. And after he'd saved her life! Luke smiled. What a treasure. What a spitfire! If he'd known it was Miss Channing he was rescuing he would have dispatched the villains sooner—if only to have more time alone with her.

A sea breeze frosted around him as he turned down High Street. Tightening his grip on his overcoat, he hunched against the cold as laughter blared from a cluster of men under the porch overhang of Spears Tavern. Through the windows, an undulating sea of patrons made the small building seem like a living, ghoulish specter. Fiddle music accompanied by strident singing floated with the lantern light onto the street.

"Is that you, Heaton? Come join us!" a man Luke recognized as Ackers, a local merchantman, shouted from the porch.

Jake, a chandler, who stood beside him, lifted his mug toward Luke. "There's a game of Gleek awaiting you, my friend."

"Not tonight, gentlemen," Luke shouted in passing. No. Tonight he had a desire to get home early.

Though he didn't quite know why.

The few coins in his pocket jingled their plea for a chance to reproduce upon the gambling table. But somehow he felt it would taint the lingering memory of his brief time with Miss Channing. Ever since Noah's fateful engagement party two years ago, Luke's eye had oft found its way to the charming red-haired lady. But his gaze was all he would risk offering her. She was far too much a lady to be seen with the likes of him. Too much of a lady to entertain his advances. Luke knew his place. The only women who tolerated his company were tavern wenches, and they only did so for the coin he tossed their way. Up until tonight, Miss Channing had not spoken two words to him. But what a voice she possessed. Like an angel's.

An angel's voice wrapped around a fiery dart!

Lud, such bravery! Where other women would have swooned, she fought against her attackers like a tigress. And when she could have run, she'd chosen to stay and help him. He'd never seen such valor in a woman.

But why had she risked being accosted by strolling about town unescorted? Didn't she have brothers? Two older ones, if he recalled. Another reason why Luke had stayed away.

Besides the fact that she would outright reject any attention on his part.

Which she had definitely done tonight. Then why did his heart feel as full as a sail in high wind instead of as heavy as an anchor? It made no sense at all. But what did it matter? If the lady possessed an astute mind—which it appeared she did—she would no doubt avoid him henceforth and with even more determination.

By the time Luke reached home, his feet dragged as much as his quickly sinking spirits. He still had no money, a rotten bucket of a ship, and his brief time with Miss Cassandra Channing had come to an end.

No sooner had he shut the front door of his small house, however, than a *thump thump thump* sounded, and John hobbled into the room. "You're home early!" The boy, who reached just above Luke's waist, gazed up at him with so much affection, all Luke's problems retreated out the door behind him—at least for the moment.

Luke tousled the lad's hair and returned his embrace as the smells of broiled fish and fresh biscuits enticed his nose. "Nothing can keep me from my favorite brother."

Mrs. Barnes entered the foyer, wiping her hands on her apron. "Apparently many things can. This is the first night this week you've made it home for supper."

John released Luke, a flippant grin on his lips. "And I'm your *only* brother."

Luke clamped John in a headlock and ground his knuckles into his brother's thick brown hair. "You'd still be my favorite if I had a hundred brothers."

Mrs. Barnes clicked her tongue. "Come now, Luke. You're messing up his hair."

"Oh, I would indeed enjoy having so many brothers." John giggled. "Then I wouldn't be so lonely during the day."

Shrugging out of his coat, Luke hung it on a peg as he ignored the guilt sinking in his gut. Gray eyes that reminded him so much of their mother's flashed an admiration toward Luke that he knew he didn't deserve. That, coupled with the look of censure firing from his house-keeper, nearly sent Luke back outside to join his friends at the tavern. Nothing like a drink to drown out the voices constantly berating his conscience.

As if reading his mind, Mrs. Barnes ambled toward him, hooked her arm with his, and led him down the hall and into the dining room. "Now sit and talk with your brother while I bring in supper."

Leaning down, Luke planted a kiss on her wrinkled forehead and gave her a beguiling smile. "What would I do without you?"

A red hue crept up her face as it always did when he kissed her. She slapped his arm and wagged a finger at him. "Your charm doesn't work with me, Luke." Shaking her head, she turned toward the kitchen. "You forget how often I took a strap to your bottom when you were but a child, and I'll do so again if needs be."

Despite her threat, warmth flooded Luke. He had indeed received many a swat from Mrs. Aldora Barnes as he had grown to manhood. Not one of them undeserved. Truth be told, the old housekeeper had been more of a mother to him than his real mother, who had so often been gone on trips with his father to "redeem the dark-hearted savages."

Redeem the savages, indeed.

John stared up at him wide eyed. "I think she means it."

Luke chuckled. "Then I shall have to behave myself, won't I? As you will, as well."

John shrugged. "I always behave."

Pulling out one of the chairs, Luke dropped onto the soft cushion and eyed his brother. Yes, John did always behave. So unlike Luke. John's face twisted as he limped over and struggled to sit in the chair next to Luke's. He stretched out his leg before him, the steel brackets bending the boy's trousers at odd angles. Where one leg was thick and strong and normal, the other was thin and frail and twisted to the right. Luke cringed. He should have been the one with rickets, not his kindhearted brother. "How does your leg fare today?"

"Good." John rubbed his withered thigh.

Always the same response no matter what discomfort the boy was enduring.

"When I get a new brace, I'll be able to walk much faster," John continued. Then casting a glance over his shoulder, he leaned toward Luke and whispered, "Perhaps I can come with you on your ship then?" Excitement sparked in his eyes.

Luke fingered a spoon on the table. "I'm afraid it won't be seaworthy for quite some time." *If ever.* He shifted his gaze from the disappointment tugging on John's face. The boy loved the sea as much as Luke did—had repeatedly begged Luke to take him out on Noah's ship, the *Defender*. But of course that was not possible. A privateer was no place for a lad, especially a crippled one. And with Noah losing his own brother in a ship accident some years ago, he wasn't about to risk Luke's. After a while, John had stopped asking. Until Luke had won his own ship in a game of Piquet two weeks ago, resurrecting the boy's petitions. If John had anything in common with Luke, besides his love of the sea, it was persistence.

"Shall we make a bargain?" Luke said. "If I ever get my ship seaworthy, you may come sailing with me." Luke knew he shouldn't make such a promise, but the chances of acquiring enough money to repair the *Agitation* were less than impossible. And the look of delight now beaming in the boy's eyes was well worth the risk.

"You promise?" John held out his hand. "A gentleman's honor."

Luke chuckled and took John's hand in a firm grip. "Aye, I promise." Though he cringed at pledging upon an honor he did not possess.

Mrs. Barnes swept into the room, her arms loaded with platters of steaming food. "What's this we are pledging to each other?"

"Nothing, Mrs. Barnes." John gazed at the broiled fish, biscuits, rice, and platter of sweet pickles and fried greens that Mrs. Barnes set upon the table. He licked his lips.

Luke's stomach leapt at the succulent smells, reminding him that he'd imbibed nothing but rum all day. While Mrs. Barnes said a prayer over the food, Luke glanced over the dining room, small by comparison with other homes: whitewashed walls devoid of decoration, save three sconces wherein candles flickered; a small brick fireplace with a cloth of painted canvas before it; a chipped wooden buffet that lined the wall beneath a rectangular window framed by dull linen curtains. A silver service tray complete with teapot, china cups, and silverware sat upon it, should company grace their home. Which rarely happened.

Luke clenched his jaw. He'd wanted to do more for his brother. So much more.

"And Father," Mrs. Barnes continued, "thank You for bringing Luke home to us tonight."

Luke flinched. Candlelight flickered off the old woman's face, casting her in a golden glow that made her look much younger than her sixty years.

"Amen," John repeated then eagerly helped himself to a piece of fish.

Their meal passed with laughter and pleasant conversation, during which Luke listened with rapt attention to John's rendition of his visit to the town library that day with Mrs. Barnes. Embellished with mad adventures that involved fighting off a band of gypsies and an encounter with a fire-breathing dragon, the story could match any found in Aesop's fables. The lad had an overactive imagination. And Luke wondered if perhaps he'd be a writer someday. Whatever he did, he'd no doubt be far more successful than Luke.

Then, per John's request, Luke regaled them with one of his adventures at sea, all the while wondering whether he'd ever have any new stories to tell.

Soon after, Luke found himself sitting beside John as he lay in bed.

"You know you don't have to tuck me in. I'm not a baby anymore," John huffed.

"No, you're not." Though he had been just one year old when the responsibility of parenting had fallen solely on Luke. "You're almost a man. I can hardly believe it."

"Will you work on your ship tomorrow?"

"Yes, if you work on your studies with Mrs. Barnes."

John's face soured. "But they are so boring. I want to be with you."

Luke raised his brows. "If you're going to be a sailor, you must be able to read and write and calculate numbers. Every captain I know who is worth his salt has a good education."

"Truly?"

"Indeed." Luke drew the coverlet up to John's chin.

"Will you come home tomorrow for dinner?" The pleading in John's voice stung Luke.

He wiped the hair from John's forehead. "I'll try."

John gave him a placating smile that said he didn't believe him. The boy was growing up too fast. Luke planted a kiss on his forehead then mussed up his hair. "Get some sleep."

Grabbing the lantern, Luke headed for the door.

"I love you, Luke."

Luke halted, emotion clogging his throat. "I love you too, John."

Down in the parlor, Mrs. Barnes filled Luke's mug with coffee then poured herself a cup and sat down in her favorite chair—a Victorian rocking chair—beside the fireplace where simmering coals provided a modicum of heat. A wooden clock sat on the mantel, its time stranded at 9:13. Luke stared at it, willing the hands to move. But they remained frozen in place. Hadn't it been working fine just that morning? *Lud.* That was all Luke needed. Something else broken in his broken-down world.

"I'm glad you came home tonight," Mrs. Barnes said. "That boy adores you."

Luke sipped the hot liquid, enjoying the exotic smell more than its bitter taste. Yet the coffee soothed his throat and settled in a pool of warmth in his belly. "He means the world to me."

"Then come home more often."

"You know I can't."

"Can't? Or won't give up your gambling and drinking?" Mrs. Barnes set down her cup on the table beside her and picked up her knitting as if she hadn't just chastised her employer. A large Bible perched proudly beside her steaming mug. Luke never saw her without it.

"I win more than I lose." Luke shifted his boots over the wool rug, trying to rub away the guilt.

Mrs. Barnes gazed at him from kind brown eyes that seemed far too small for her round face. Gray curls, springing from her mobcap, framed her like a silver halo. "I know a great deal of responsibility was laid upon your shoulders at only seventeen, but—"

"And I have kept us alive since," Luke interrupted, his ire rising.

"I'm not disputing that."

Leaning back in his chair, Luke glanced over the parlor, which boasted of chipped paint, threadbare curtains, and secondhand furniture. "I know this isn't the most comfortable place to live, but it's all I can afford at the moment."

"You know I don't care about that, Luke. I'm concerned for your soul."

"My soul is fine."

"Hmm." She continued her knitting. "If only you'd settle down. Pick an honorable trade."

"I have. A privateer. If this war continues much longer, I can make a fortune."

"You sound as if you wish the war would go on."

"Absurd." Setting his cup down with a clank, Luke rose and began to pace. "I know firsthand what the British are capable of. I hate the blockade. I hate their intrusion onto our land. I want to fight as much as the next man. Only at sea."

Needles flying, Mrs. Barnes joined one strand of white yarn and one strand of black together in a chaotic pattern that made no sense. Much like the pattern of Luke's life.

He stomped about the room, trying to settle his agitation. "When I sailed with Noah, I took great pride in thwarting the British cause by capturing their merchant ships."

"Yet you are no longer with Captain Brenin."

Halting, Luke avoided looking at the censure he knew he would find on Mrs. Barnes's face even as he braced himself for her lecture. Everyone in town knew why Noah had relieved Luke of his duties.

But instead, she gave him a gentle smile. "If privateering is where God is leading you, Luke, then by all means, pursue that course."

Luke warmed at her encouragement. "As soon as I get the funds to fix my ship."

"What happened to the money you had in the bank?"

Luke lowered his chin as silence permeated the room.

"Your parents would not approve of your methods of procuring money. And neither does God."

"My parents followed God and look where it got them." Luke gazed at the rippled, pink skin on the palm of his right hand. "I'm doing things differently. I'm doing things my way. Besides, I'm not hurting anyone with my actions."

"Except John."

"He misses me, that's all." Luke shrugged. "I'll make it up to him when I fix my ship. Teach him to sail. We'll become merchants together after the war."

"That would be nice." Yet her tone held no confidence.

Luke parted the curtains. Aside from a few twinkling lights emanating from nearby homes, nothing but an empty, dark void met his gaze. Empty like his many promises to John. "Why do you stay with us, Mrs. Barnes? Surely your skills and experience could land you a better position in a proper home."

"Why, I wouldn't know what to do in a proper home." Her warm smile reached her eyes in a twinkle. "Besides, I love you boys as if I birthed you myself. And I promised your mother I'd look out after you."

Luke made his way back to his chair, drawn away from the darkness by the love in this precious woman's face. "You are family now, Mrs. Barnes. Which is why I allow you to speak to me with such forthrightness." He winked and slid back onto his chair.

Dropping her knitting into her lap, Mrs. Barnes leaned forward and patted his hand as she always did to comfort him. "Love can only be expressed in truth."

The wise adage drifted through Luke, finally settling on his reason. Love and truth. Two things he didn't know much about.

Mrs. Barnes gazed at the red coals. "The doctor came today."

Leaning forward, Luke planted his elbows on his knees.

"He said there shouldn't be any additional malformation due to the rickets."

"That's great news." Luke nearly leapt from his seat, but Mrs. Barnes's somber expression stifled his enthusiasm. "What else? Will the leg ever heal?"

Mrs. Barnes took a sip of her coffee then wrapped her hands around the cup. "In time, perhaps. The doctor cannot say for sure. But he did say John needs a new brace."

Luke nodded, swallowing down resurging fears for his brother's future. A new brace cost money. Money he didn't have.

"He gave me a bill." Anxiety burned in her eyes. "And the rent is due by the end of the week."

"How much?"

"Including the doctor bill, forty-eight dollars."

Luke ground his teeth together. He had only two silver dollars in his pocket—barely enough to provide food for the week. A sudden yearning for rum instead of coffee screamed from his throat. Picking up his mug, he gazed at the brown liquid swirling in his cup. Around and around it went like a brewing tempest at sea.

A tempest that was surely heading his way.

❖ CHAPTER 5 ❖

"Wake up, miss. Wake up." The sweet voice bade entrance into Cassandra's sleep.

She denied it permission.

It rose again. "Wake up, miss." Followed by the shuffle of curtains, then the clack of shutters. A burst of light flooded Cassandra's eyelids. Her ladies' maid began singing a hymn—something about a fount of blessing and streams of mercy.

Cassandra could not relate. She rolled over. "I'm not feeling well, Margaret."

"But Mr. Crane is here, miss."

Struggling to sit, Cassandra squinted into the sunlight blaring through the window. "Oh bother." She rubbed her eyes. "Mr. Crane?"

"Yes. Remember your mother invited him over for coffee and cakes this morning?"

Tossing her quilt aside, Cassandra swung her legs over the edge of her mattress as her stomach turned to lead. Yes, now she remembered. She had wanted to forget—which was probably why she had forgotten.

Swinging open the armoire, Margaret chose a saffron-colored muslin gown then pulled two petticoats from the chest of drawers in the corner, laying them gently on Cassandra's bed. "Come now, miss, surely the man can't be that distasteful?" She planted her fists atop her rounded waist and smiled at Cassandra. Cheeks that were perpetually rosy adorned her plump, cheery face while strands of black hair escaped from beneath her bonnet.

With a groan, Cassandra hopped to the floor, raised her arms, and allowed Margaret to sweep her night rail over her head. "There's nothing wrong with Mr. Crane. I simply do not wish to marry him."

"Well, miss." Margaret folded her sleeping gown. "Perhaps you should give him a chance. He might improve with time."

Grabbing a stool from the corner, Margaret placed it beside Cassandra and stepped onto it, holding up the first petticoat. Few women were shorter than Cassandra's mere five feet. But dear Margaret, at only four foot eight, made up for her small stature with an enormous heart. Cassandra shrugged into her petticoat. "I doubt I'll find anyone as agreeable as your Mr. Dayle."

Margaret's rosy cheeks turned crimson. "Aye, he's a good man, to be sure. But I suspect the Lord has a kindly gentleman chosen just for you."

Cassandra let out an unladylike snort. "God has better things to do than play matchmaker for me, Margaret. And even if I believed He was involved in my life—which I doubt He is—I would prefer He provide me with a privateer rather than a husband."

"Who says He can't do both, miss?"

Twenty minutes later, Cassandra burst into the breakfast room situated at the back of the house. Silverware and crystal decanters sitting atop the table glittered in the sunlight pouring in through the closed french doors. The aroma of butter, spicy meat, and aromatic coffee whirled about her.

Tossing down his serviette, Mr. Crane rose from his seat and smiled her way. Tall, thin, with neatly combed brown hair, the man was not without some appeal. His attire was fashionable and clean, save for the occasional ink smudge on his skin. In addition, his manners were impeccable and his pedigree spotless. As Cassandra's mother loved to remind her at every turn. Speaking of, her mother, dressed to perfection in a cream-colored gown that was crowned at the neck and sleeves with golden ruffles, sat at the head of the table. Cassandra did not miss the scowl on her face. "Mr. Crane has some urgent business to attend to this morning and could wait no longer for you to join us."

"I am glad you proceeded without me." Cassandra circled the table and helped herself to a cup of coffee from the serving table, passing over the odd-smelling battercakes and blackened sausage. Turning, she found

Mr. Crane's eyes latched on her. "Do have a seat and finish your meal, Mr. Crane." She took a chair across from him. "I hope you'll forgive me. I fear I had a rather hectic day yesterday."

Children's laughter accompanied by the bark of a dog echoed from the back garden.

Mr. Crane flipped out his coattails and sat. "Of course, Miss Channing. I understand women need their rest."

Cassandra tapped her shoe on the floor and scoured him with a pointed gaze. "I was just telling your mother of the happenings down at the *Register*." He chuckled and lifted a piece of battercake to his mouth. After a moment's pause, his lips twisted into an odd shape as he continued chewing.

Cassandra smiled.

Which he must have taken as encouragement to continue his dissertation of the newspaper business.

Searching the table for sugar, Cassandra sighed when she remembered they'd been out for months. She sipped her bitter coffee, trying to drown out the man's incessant babbling.

Thankfully, after a few minutes, Miss Thain, the cook, entered the room. Eyes downcast, she cleared the plates, bobbing and curtseying at every turn.

Mr. Crane stood. "Would you care for a stroll in the garden, Miss Channing?"

"It's a bit cold, isn't it?" Didn't the man say he had an appointment?

"Don't be silly, Cassandra," her mother said. "I'll have Margaret bring down your cloak." She hurried off, returning in a moment with Cassandra's wool cape.

After sweeping it around her shoulders, Cassandra followed Mr. Crane through the french doors into the back garden. Warm sunlight struck her face even as a chilled breeze sent a shiver through her. Though nearly spring, winter seemed unwilling to release its grip on the city. To her left, Mr. Dayle chipped through the hard dirt in preparation for a vegetable garden. Beside him a small stable housed their only horse. To the right, smoke rose from the smokehouse where Miss Thain made the bread and smoked the meat—or where Miss Thain *attempted* to make bread and smoke meat. A small stone path wound among various trees and shrubs whose green buds were just beginning to peek from within gray branches.

Darlene darted across the path in front of them, Dexter on her heels, and leapt into one of the bushes. "I found you!"

With an ear-piercing scream, Hannah leapt out from among the branches, twigs and lace flying through the air. Darlene barreled into her, and the two girls toppled to the ground in a gush of giggles as Dexter stood over them and barked.

Mr. Crane's face scrunched. "Shouldn't the children be attending their studies?"

Cassandra smiled. What an excellent reason to rid herself of this man's company. "Of course, Mr. Crane. I quite agree. Since we were forced to let the nanny go, I'm afraid many of her duties have fallen to me." Ignoring the look of alarm on his face, she continued, "If you'll excuse me, I should get the girls cleaned up and ready for their lessons with Mrs. Northrop." She faced the gardener. "Mr. Dayle, would you please see Mr. Crane to the door?" Then with barely a glance in Mr. Crane's direction, Cassandra started toward her sisters, who were still tumbling on the grass.

"Oh, no, no, no, my dear." Her mother's shrill voice halted her. The older woman dashed into the yard, gathered the children up like a hen escaping a storm, and ushered them inside the house, shouting, "I'll attend to the girls. Carry on, carry on." Dexter followed after them but a closed door barred his passage. The poor sheepdog slumped to the ground and laid his head onto his front paws.

With a huff and a smile so stiff she felt her face would crack, Cassandra turned back toward Mr. Crane.

He cleared his throat. "Very good. Shall we sit?" He gestured toward an iron bench beneath a maple tree.

Reluctantly, Cassandra sat. The cold bars leeched the warmth from her body. Or was it being so close to Mr. Crane—who took the seat beside her—that caused her to shiver? He wasn't such an unpleasant fellow. In fact, he'd always been quite courteous to her. But something in his eyes, in his subtle gestures, pricked at her distrust.

Or maybe she didn't trust anyone anymore.

"Miss Channing." He rubbed at his fingers as if he'd just noticed the ink stains upon them. "Your mother. . .I mean to say, I have asked. . ." His face reddened and he chuckled. "Do forgive me, Miss Channing. I'm usually not this inarticulate."

Oh, bother. He was going to ask if he could court her! "Do not vex your-self, Mr. Crane. Perhaps we can talk some other time." Cassandra stood, her gaze darting about the yard, seeking escape. He grabbed her wrist and stood. "Please, Miss Channing, don't leave. What I am trying to say is, what I'm making a terrible mess of saying is, I have asked your mother's permission to court you and she has said yes."

The sharp smell of ink bit her nose. Cassandra tugged from his grasp and took a step back. Expectation and vulnerability filled his eyes—so different from the confidence and hint of sorrow burning in Mr. Heaton's eyes the night before. "Mr. Crane. I am deeply flattered. But my mother has misspoken. I am in no position to entertain suitors at this time. With my father dead and my brothers missing, surely you can see that I have more pressing matters to contend with."

He wrung his hands once again. "If that is all that concerns you, Miss Channing, I have your solution. I'd be honored if you'd allow me to assist you with your pressing matters. It is too much for a lady to handle alone."

Cassandra stiffened her jaw. "A lady can handle whatever a man can as long as she is given equal opportunity, sir."

He started to chuckle, but when his eyes locked with hers, his laughter withered on his lips.

Mrs. Northrop's head popped out from around the corner then disappeared. Mr. Dayle, still working in the garden, cleared his throat.

Cassandra studied Mr. Crane. For one fleeting moment she considered asking him to invest her money in a privateer. But that idea dissipated when she realized she'd be forced to not only trust him, but she'd be forever bound to him if he agreed. "I am grateful for your concern, sir, but I cannot allow such kindness when I have nothing to offer in return."

"Oh, but you do, my dear." Tugging on his lacy cravat, he lifted pleading brown eyes to hers.

Cassandra nearly shriveled at the look of desire and desperation within them.

He frowned. "At least give me a reason to continue casting my hope in your direction."

"I can give you no such reason, sir. I can only say that my future is yet unknown."

He lowered his chin. "That alone gives me hope."

Truly? Cassandra sighed. Would nothing put the man off?

"I shall bid you *adieu*, then." Taking her hand in his, he placed a gentle kiss upon it, bowed, then headed toward the house. Mr. Dayle leapt to escort him to the door, giving her a sympathetic look in passing.

Shielding her eyes, Cassandra gazed up at the sun halfway to its zenith. A dark cloud that seemed to come out of nowhere drifted over it, swallowing its bright light and sending a shadow over her face and a shiver down her back. An evil foreboding? For once upon a time, Cassandra's future had appeared bright and glorious, but now it seemed nothing but dark and dismal.

It was this war. This horrendous war. And the bedeviled British who had stolen her father, her brothers, her future, and who now wanted her country. But she could not let them. She must invest in a privateer. It was the only way to ensure her family's future and aid in defeating the tyrants who were intent on stealing her freedom.

Making her way to the solarium at the north side of the house, she opened the door to a burst of warm, humid air, perfumed with gardenias. Her precious gardenias. Oh, how she loved gardening—a hobby that she'd often neglected this past year. Though even without daily care, the plants seemed to thrive. Inhaling their sweet fragrance, she fingered the delicate white petals as she made her rounds, examining each bush, before sitting on the wooden chair at the far end. Reaching underneath a workbench, she pulled out a small chest. Inside was a pipe.

Her father's pipe.

Holding it to her nose, she drew in a deep breath of the sweet, smoky scent that always reminded her of Papa. She closed her eyes and pictured him sitting in his leather chair in the library, smoking his pipe while he read one of his two favorite books—John Moore's *The Practical Navigator* or the Bible.

"Oh Papa, I need you."

She could see him glance up from his book and smile at her as he took the pipe from his mouth. "Ah, my little Cassie cherub. Come see your papa." Dashing to him, she would leap into his outstretched arms and crawl into his lap. During those precious moments snuggled within his warm, strong arms, she had felt safe and loved.

Like nothing could ever go wrong.

"Papa." Tears slid down her face, trickling onto the handle of the pipe. "Why did you leave me? I don't know what to do."

No answer came. Just the chirp of birds outside the solarium and the distant sound of her sisters' laughing. Ah, to be young again—too young to be burdened with cares, too young to be forced into a marriage she didn't want. Cassandra dropped her head in her hands. She could not put her mother or Mr. Crane off for long.

The lingering memory of her father disappeared, leaving Cassandra all alone.

Another man's face filled her vision. A man with hair as dark as the night and beguiling blue eyes.

And she knew she had no other choice.

❖ CHAPTER 6 ❖

Luke waded through the muddy bilge in the hold of the *Agitation*. After hours trying to repair the rent in the hull, he should have grown accustomed to the stench, but it still stung his nose and filled his lungs until it seemed to seep from his skin. Setting down his hammer, he shook the sweat from his hair and scanned the chaotic rubble he called his ship. Even if he could afford building materials, without a crew to assist him, it would take him months to get her in sailing shape. Who was he trying to fool? He snorted. Perhaps his time would be better spent investing his last two silver dollars in a game of Piquet.

As if in response, the ship creaked beneath an incoming wave, and a beam fell from the deck head into the squalid muck with a splash. Luke stared at it, benumbed, wondering if he should bother to pick it up. He needed a drink. Grabbing the lantern, he headed for the ladder when a voice calling his name floated down the rungs as if heaven itself were summoning him home.

Which was not possible. If his time on earth was at an end, it wouldn't be heaven's voice he heard.

"Hello! Mr. Heaton." The angelic call trilled again as a slight footstep sounded above.

Slogging toward the hatch, Luke extracted himself from the mire and vaulted up the ladder, finally emerging from the companionway into a burst of sunlight and an icy breeze that caused him to both squint and shiver.

Setting down the lantern, he stared at the elegantly attired figure before him, delight overcoming his confusion when Miss Channing formed in his vision. The fringed parasol she held above her cast a circle of shade over her saffron gown. An emerald sash glimmered from high about her waist while a woolen shawl crowned her shoulders. A breeze sent her auburn curls dancing about her neck as she stood stiff like an unyielding paragon of Baltimore society, casting her gaze about the wreckage as if afraid to be sullied by her surroundings.

"Oh my." She turned her face away from him and took a step back.

He glanced down at his bare chest and smiled at her reaction. Then his eyes landed on the ship's bulwark undulating beside the dock, and he wondered how she'd managed to jump onto the deck without tripping on the flurry of petticoats peeking at him from beneath her gown. Nevertheless, he would not the curse the fortune that gave him another chance to speak with this enchanting lady.

"Welcome to the *Agitation*, Miss Channing," He gave a mock bow. "To what do I owe the pleasure of your visit?"

"If you'll don a shirt, I shall be happy to tell you." The pomposity in her voice deflated his hope that she made a purely social call.

"I am working, and it is hot belowdecks. If you'll state your business, I'll happily relieve you of my unclad presence." He cringed at his curt tone, yet she deserved it. Standing there with her pertinent chin in the air and her shoulders thrown back as if she did him a service by merely speaking to him.

Not to mention that he still felt the sting of her blunt dismissal the night before.

Rum beckoned to him from the capstan. Licking his lips, Luke brushed past her, noting the hesitation, perhaps fear, flickering on her face. Yet she held her ground. Grabbing the bottle, he took a swig and turned to face her. The pungent liquid did nothing to dull the emotions storming through him.

A ship's bell rang, and the scent of roasted pig floated to his nose from one of the taverns across from the docks. A growl churned in his belly, quickly silenced by another gulp of rum.

Miss Channing cocked her head. A breeze fluttered the fringe on her parasol. "Are you always heavy into your cups this early in the day, sir?"

Luke raked a hand through his hair and gazed at the sun high in the sky. "Aye, as often as the occasion permits."

She huffed her disdain, and an odd twinge of regret stung him. "Forgive my manners, Miss Channing. Would you care to sit?" He gestured toward a crate stacked beside the quarterdeck. "However, I fear all I have to offer you to drink is rum."

"No, thank you, sir. I do not intend to stay long." She shifted her parasol and the sunlight angled over her face, setting her skin aglow like ivory pearls he'd once seen in the Caribbean.

Luke swallowed. He knew she was a beauty, but standing here among the squalor of his ship, she stood out like a fresh flower in a dung heap. He lifted the bottle again to his lips, but thinking better of it, he set it down. "What may I do for you, Miss Channing?"

Emerald green eyes met his. Her gaze dipped then sped away as if she couldn't stand the sight of him.

Luke shifted his wet boots over the planks and snapped the hair from his face. Part of him wanted to toss her from his ship for her insolent attitude. Another part of him didn't want her to ever leave.

A pelican landed on the wheel on the quarterdeck. Letting out a squawk, the bird turned his head and gazed at them with one black eye.

Miss Channing smiled. "Your captain, I presume?"

Luke chuckled. "I'd hire him on the spot if he could get this tub out to sea."

The deck tilted and she stumbled. Leaping for her, Luke grabbed her elbow.

"Thank you." She tugged from his grip and shifted her gaze to the stern of the ship, then over the bay where the sunlight set the rippling waters sparkling like diamonds, then at the taverns lining the docks—anywhere, it seemed, but on him.

"I have a proposition for you, Mr. Heaton."

Luke raised his brows as a dozen improper thoughts filled his mind. "Indeed?" He crossed his arms over his chest. "I shall be happy to oblige you."

She faced him now, her eyes widening. "I didn't mean. . . Oh, bother." Lowering her parasol, she snapped it shut, and Luke got the impression she might pummel him with it. No doubt he deserved the beating.

Balancing over the teetering deck, she stepped back from him. "I meant for your *services*, Mr. Heaton."

He grinned again, enjoying the pinkish hue that climbed up her neck and onto her face.

She tapped her right shoe over the planks. "You smell of rum and rot."

"And you smell of gardenias." He eased toward her, drawing in a deep whiff, hoping her sweet scent would chase away the foul air from the hold.

She leveled her parasol at him like a sword, her eyes flashing.

Waves slapped against the hull. A carriage rumbled by on the cobblestone street.

"Are you calling me out, miss?" Luke could barely restrain his laughter. "Parasols at dawn?"

Her eyes narrowed. With a swish of her skirts, she swerved about and headed toward the wharf.

Cursing himself for behaving the cad, Luke started toward her. To apologize, to shower her with flattery, to do anything to keep her from leaving.

She halted and faced him. With a wiggle of her pert little nose, she glanced over the deck. "This is the worst ship I've ever seen."

"Is that what you came to tell me?"

"No, Mr. Heaton, I came here to hire you as a privateer."

❖

Cassandra watched the sardonic gleam in Mr. Heaton's eyes disappear beneath a wave of shock. He ran a hand through the slick black hair hanging to his shoulders and chuckled.

He chuckled.

"I fail to see the humor, Mr. Heaton." She also wished she failed to see his tanned bare chest, gleaming in the sunlight. Though she did her best to avert her eyes, they kept wandering back to his well-shaped biceps, thick chest, and rippled stomach that hinted at his strength beneath. Warmth sped through her as she remembered the ease with which he'd dispatched her assailants the night before.

"My apologies, Miss Channing. I seem to recall how ardently you dismissed my offer last night."

"Things have changed."

"Well, they must have grown quite dire indeed for you to come crawling to the likes of me."

"I never crawl, Mr. Heaton, and my circumstances are none of your affair. Are you or are you not interested in a partnership with me?"

A smile formed on his lips—a disarming smile that no doubt had melted a thousand female hearts. "I am honored that you would ask."

"Save your honor, Mr. Heaton, I had nowhere else to turn."

He held up a hand. "No need to shower me with flattery, miss." His blue eyes gleamed mischief. "But what of your brothers? Have they sent their sister to do a man's work?"

Cassandra ground her teeth together. "I do not need my brothers, nor do I need a man to engage in a business deal any flubberhead could handle."

One side of his mouth curved upward, yet a glimmer of admiration passed through his eyes. "Yes, I can see that."

"As I can see that I'm wasting my time." Grabbing her skirts, she started for the railing.

He clutched her arm. "I agree to your proposal."

Relief sped through her, easing the tight knot between her shoulders. Facing him, she stepped back, putting distance between them. "Very good. I have made arrangements to meet with Mr. Brenin tonight to draw up the necessary papers."

"Lud, such confidence! Were you so sure I would say yes?" He scratched the stubble on his chin and stepped toward her.

She poked him with the tip of her parasol. The man had a way of disregarding propriety's distance, causing her stomach to twitch. "Since you already extended the same offer to me last night, yes, I was. Although I must say, I was unsure whether to accept it."

Even now she wasn't sure she had complete control of her wits.

"What, pray tell, convinced you to accept? My hospitality?" He gripped the bulwark. A chip of rotted wood loosened and fell to the water with a splash. He shrugged. "No doubt it was my fine, seaworthy ship."

Cassandra raised a hand to her mouth to cover her smile even while her insides churned with apprehension. What was she doing? Not only was this man untrustworthy, but this ship would be better off at the bottom of the sea. Yet, hadn't Noah just told her he'd inspected it recently and, aside from some necessary repairs, found it sound?

"Your silence tells all, Miss Channing," he said. "It seems life has cast a cloud of desperation on us both."

"Though I doubt for the same reasons, Mr. Heaton."

His dark, imperious gaze swept over her, making her legs turn to porridge. Confusion spun in her mind. Was she doing the right thing? Should she risk her family's survival on this man?

But what choice did she have?

Yet beyond the roguish facade, a spark of sincerity lingered in his eyes.

"Do you think you can put aside your usual nighttime activities to meet at Mr. Brenin's house tonight? We can sign the papers and I'll see to your payment then."

"I believe I'll have time for both, miss."

"Then I shall see you around seven o'clock."

Stepping up on the bulwarks, he leapt onto the dock then turned to extend his hand.

Against her better judgment, she took it. His strength and warmth seeped though her gloves, sending a jolt up her arm. After he settled her on the wharf, she snagged her hand away, nodded her thanks, and hurried down the dock.

A voice as smooth and as deep as the sea called after her, "Until tonight, Miss Channing."

❖

The teacup rattled on its saucer. Cassandra set it down on the table. Amber liquid sloshed over the rim. "Oh, bother. Please forgive me, Marianne."

Marianne Brenin laid a gentle hand on Cassandra's arm. "Whatever is amiss tonight, Cassandra? You've been a bundle of nerves since you walked in the door."

"Have I?" Cassandra drew a deep breath. Could it be that she was about to give the remainder of her family's money to a man she had no reason to trust? A nervous giggle rose in her throat.

Marianne's brown eyes twinkled from within a face aglow with happiness. Happy indeed. She had a wonderful husband, a beautiful son, and a promising future.

Across the room, Noah tossed seven-month-old Jacob into the air. Giggles bubbled through the Brenin parlor, bouncing off walls and causing all within to grin.

Noah stopped to look at his wife with such deep adoration that Cassandra felt as though she was intruding. She looked away. A yearning tugged at her heart. Would a man ever look at her the way Noah looked at Marianne?

As if lured by her husband's loving gaze, Marianne rose and made her way to him. Swinging an arm over her shoulder, Noah drew her close, swallowing up Jacob between them, and planted a kiss on her forehead.

Marianne ran her fingers over her husband's jaw then suddenly spun around, her face as red as an apple. "Oh, do forgive us, Cassandra. When Noah returns from a long voyage, I often forget when there are other people in the room."

Cassandra couldn't help but smile at her friend's happiness. "I seem to recall you once saying you'd rather boil in oil than marry Noah Brenin."

Noah stared agape at his wife, his lips curving in an incredulous smile. "You don't say?"

Marianne pressed down the folds of her lavender gown. "It was something like that. I truly don't remember."

"Such a thing for Mama to say." Noah tickled Jacob until the boy burst into giggles again.

"We weren't exactly fond of each other back then," Marianne said.

Noah kissed his wife on the cheek and whispered in her ear until her giggles matched their son's.

The loving scene played before Cassandra like a surreal fairy tale. Her mother and father had never expressed such affection, never even offered each other a kind word or loving glance. Until Noah and Marianne had married, Cassandra had not realized that a husband and wife could cherish each other so deeply.

The languid face of Mr. Crane filled her vision and chased her cheery thoughts away. If this investment fell through, she'd be forced to marry him.

Destroying any chance to know the kind of love that filled this home.

Cassandra stood, hoping a turn about the room would settle her nerves, but she bumped into a table, nearly toppling a small carving of a Baltimore clipper. "There I go again." She settled the wooden figure.

Taking Jacob into her arms, Marianne gave Cassandra a curious look as she sat down once again on the settee. "Surely it isn't Mr. Heaton's imminent arrival that has you so. . .hmm. . .so agitated?" She gave a coy smile.

Cassandra clasped her hands together to avoid afflicting further damage. "Don't be absurd, I care not a whit whether Mr. Heaton will be here or not. I simply want this business concluded." Heat flushed her face, and she plucked out her fan. Her eyes took in her reticule lying on the table. "My family's future rests with this investment."

"Are you sure you wish to align yourself with such a man?" Jacob grabbed one of Marianne's curls. Wincing, she extracted it from his chubby fingers.

"Now, love." Noah strode to the service table against the wall and poured himself a sip of Madeira. "Luke is our friend."

"And he is a good friend. But a business partner?" Marianne slid her loose hair behind her ear and clutched Jacob's hands as he reached for it again.

Noah sampled his wine then took a seat beside his wife. "I cannot presume to give you advice in this matter, Cassandra, but I will say that no matter what he may appear to be, Luke is a good man."

Cassandra fanned her face so rapidly, a strand of her hair loosened from its pin. Hadn't she seen some goodness in Mr. Heaton's eyes earlier that day? Something that bade her trust him? "Yet you relieved him of his duty on board your ship?"

"Aye, to teach him a lesson." Noah held his glass of Madeira out of Jacob's reach. "Truth be told, I miss him. He was the best first mate I ever had. But he couldn't control his drinking, and I wanted him to realize how damaging the habit had become."

Cassandra recalled the smell of rum hovering around Mr. Heaton last night and the way he drank on his ship earlier that day. "I fear your plan has not succeeded." Snapping her fan shut, she slid into a chair beside the settee. "Oh, bother. Perhaps I *am* making a mistake."

"Even with his drinking," Noah said, "Luke can handle a ship better than most men I've seen."

Marianne handed Jacob a doll, which he promptly stuffed into his mouth. She lifted her brown eyes, full of concern, to Cassandra. "Have you prayed about this decision?"

"Prayer has never done me much good."

"I used to feel that way." Marianne kissed Jacob's fuzzy head. "I know you've been through a lot. But you must believe God loves you and has all your concerns in His hands."

"Indeed." Noah smiled at his wife. "He's more than proven that to us."

Cassandra was about to say that God seemed to shower some people with blessing while ignoring others, when a knock at the door silenced her.

"Mr. McCulloch," Mr. Sorens, the Brenin butler, announced. Cassandra released a nervous breath as the city customs agent sauntered into the room, wearing a stylish coat of taffeta, a cravat too large for his tiny neck, and brown trousers.

Noah stood to greet him as the butler continued, "And Mr. Luke Heaton."

Dressed in the same black breeches and leather boots he'd been wearing earlier, Mr. Heaton strode into the parlor as if he were the owner of a fleet of ships instead of a lone crumbling heap of wood and tar.

Thank goodness the man had donned a shirt, though the picture of his firm chest was forever imprinted on Cassandra's mind. His eyes locked on hers and remained far too long for her comfort. She shifted her gaze away only to find Marianne and Noah regarding her with suspicion.

Turning, Noah extended his hand. "Good evening, Mr. McCulloch. Thank you for coming."

"My pleasure, sir." Mr. McCulloch's disapproving gaze landed on Cassandra. "I see you have found a captain willing to accept your investment."

"I have, sir." Cassandra thrust out her chin.

"Hmm." He gave Mr. Heaton a cursory glance. "Shall we proceed?"

Jacob looked up from his doll and spotted Mr. Heaton. A huge smile split his mouth as he lifted his chubby hands toward him and strained to be free from his mother's grip. Approaching the child, Mr. Heaton swept him up in his arms and lifted the boy high in the air.

Cassandra stared, dumbfounded, at the sight of their mutual affection.

"Jacob just adores Mr. Heaton," Marianne said with a smile.

Mr. McCulloch cleared his throat. "I have another obligation this evening."

"Absolutely, sir." Noah directed the man to sit then turned to the butler. "Mr. Sorens, will you please take Jacob up to my mother's chamber. She promised to read him a bedtime story."

Mr. Sorens frowned, folding the loose skin beneath his chin, and approached Mr. Heaton, who attempted to untangle the boy's clinging fingers from the collar of his coat. Finally he placed the whining lad into the butler's arms, and with a grunt, the man ambled from the room.

Mr. McCulloch withdrew a stack of papers, a quill pen, and a bottle of ink from his satchel and set them neatly on the table before taking his seat.

Noah sat down once again beside his wife. Mr. Heaton, however, after declining the chair offered him, stood beside Cassandra—so close, she caught his rugged scent of wood, oakum—and rum.

Snapping his attention to one of the documents, Mr. McCulloch rambled through a list of questions directed to Mr. Heaton regarding the tonnage, rig, proposed armament, and number of crew on his vessel. After a bond amount was agreed upon, the customs agent scribbled on the document and gazed at him above the spectacles sliding down his nose. "And the name of the ship, sir?"

"*Agit*—"

"*Destiny*," Cassandra interrupted.

Luke gazed down at her, brow furrowed.

"Well, which is it?" Mr. McCulloch flipped his pocket watch open, glanced at it, then snapped it shut.

Luke made a gesture of deference to her.

"*Destiny*," she stated with finality. She didn't need any further agitation in her life. She needed to create a future, a destiny for her and her family. And to be able to do so on the backs of the British oppressors made it all the sweeter. Opening her reticule, she withdrew the banknote and laid it on the table.

Luke knelt, dipped the pen in ink, and scrawled his signature over the contract then handed the pen to Cassandra.

She poised the pen over the spot awaiting her mark. The quill feathers fluttered beneath her rapid breath. Her heart seized. Jacob's laughter tumbled down from upstairs. Like the countdown to a duel, the grandfather clock in the foyer tick-tocked the final minutes before the deadly shot.

Or the deadly agreement.

Mr. McCulloch sighed.

Cassandra rose to her feet, pen in hand. "Before I sign this contract and hand over my money to you, Mr. Heaton, I have one more condition."

Eyeing her, he folded his arms over his chest. "Which is?"

"That during the time of our partnership, you will cease all drinking and gambling."

❖ CHAPTER 7 ❖

Luke felt his forehead crease. Give up drinking and gambling? Was Miss Channing mad? He didn't know whether to laugh at or berate her foolish request. He chose the former. All eyes shot his way as his chuckle bounced through the parlor—unaccompanied.

Miss Channing's eyes turned to green ice. Luke cleared his throat as Noah arose from his seat. Marianne's brows lifted, and Mr. McCulloch bore his first smile of the evening.

Miss Channing's shoe began a *rat tat tat* on the floor.

"An excellent idea, Miss Channing." Noah tugged on his waistcoat and gave Luke a victorious smile.

Luke growled inside and rubbed his right earlobe. He was tired of people telling him how to live his life. He'd had his fill of that growing up with missionary parents. Their list of oppressive rules still rankled his soul. "Lud, have you lost your senses, miss?"

"No, sir, I have not," Miss Channing retorted. "In fact, I believe I have finally found them. Perhaps you should attempt to find yours."

Luke shifted his gaze over his friends to seek some measure of sympathy, but the satisfied smirk remained on Noah's lips.

"My ability to captain my ship has nothing to do with how I choose to entertain myself." Luke's gaze latched on the banknote on the table. He licked his lips. Thoughts of John and Mrs. Barnes stabbed his conscience. They'd be out on the street within a fortnight if he did not procure the rent. And no one else was foolish enough to invest their money with him. Yes, *foolish* was the word that came to mind when he gazed into those sparkling emerald eyes—foolish and brave and determined.

And exquisitely beautiful.

"Well, what will it be, Mr. Heaton?" the customs agent said. "I don't have all night." Again, he flipped open his pocket watch and stared at it as if wishing it could transport him to another place.

Miss Channing placed one delicate hand on her hip. "I'll not have you besotted while out at sea, Mr. Heaton, putting the crew, the ship, and my investment at risk."

Luke ground his teeth together. "I assure you, miss, besotted or not, I'm the best captain you'll find in Baltimore." He glanced at Noah. "Present company excluded, of course."

Noah nodded with an amused smile.

"Nevertheless, I'll not have my money squandered on rum and ineptitude." Miss Channing snatched the note from the table. Determination glinted in her eyes.

Luke clenched his fists as the decree built an iron cage around his will. But he had no choice. He couldn't let John down again. He owed him a life, a future.

Not a legacy of failure.

All eyes were on him. Miss Channing held the banknote before her like a gold doubloon before a pirate—like a last sip of rum to a man long deprived of drink.

Which was precisely what it meant to Luke. He shifted his stance. "Very well. I promise not to partake of drink while I'm sailing. But when I come ashore, I will do as I please."

Marianne touched Miss Channing's arm and nodded. "That certainly seems fair enough."

Miss Channing pursed her lips. "No rum on board the ship at all."

"My crew will not like that, miss."

"I care not a whit what your crew likes, Mr. Heaton. Those are my terms."

Luke swallowed and stared down at the woven rug beneath his boots, then across the bemused faces of his friends before finally shifting his gaze to Miss Channing. "Very well, you have my word."

Mr. McCulloch cleared his throat. "Do say you'll sign the papers now, Miss Channing?"

But instead of the satisfied smirk Luke expected to see on her face, she turned to Noah and Marianne with a look of apprehension.

Noah nodded. "Mr. Heaton's word is good, Cassandra."

Luke flinched at the compliment even as his heart swelled. Noah had never expressed such faith in him before. A sudden sense of unworthiness struck him. Could he live up to such an affirmation?

With a sigh of resignation, Miss Channing leaned once again over the document. Her hand trembled, sending the pen's feathers quivering. She didn't trust him. But how could he blame her when he didn't trust himself?

Snatching the signed documents, Mr. McCulloch stuffed them inside his satchel and bid them good evening as he charged out of the parlor, yelling over his shoulder that he would see himself out.

Miss Channing held the banknote out to Luke. He tugged on it. She wouldn't let go. Her gaze skittered from him to Noah, then Marianne. Her chest rose and fell beneath the lace trim of her saffron gown. Finally she relinquished it into his hand, following it with her eyes all the way into Luke's waistcoat pocket.

But what was one thousand dollars to the great Channing merchant business? Surely she had plenty more where that came from.

Grabbing her reticule and fan, Cassandra embraced Marianne, thanked Noah, and headed toward the foyer as if she couldn't get away from him fast enough. She halted at the parlor door and turned to address him. "I should like to come see the ship when she's ready to sail."

Luke gave her a mock bow. "I am at your service."

Miss Channing's eyes narrowed.

"I'll walk you out." Marianne broke the tension, moving to her friend's side and weaving her arm through Cassandra's.

After the ladies departed, Noah gave Luke that same look of reprimand he'd often given him as captain aboard the *Defender*.

Ignoring him, as he always had, Luke sauntered toward the service table and lifted the bottle of Madeira. "May I?"

"No sooner do you promise Miss Channing you'll avoid alcohol, than you run straight for a drink."

"I am not at sea." He lifted his goblet. The sweet wine soured as it slid down his throat.

"Perhaps one day you'll learn to handle life's afflictions without numbing your senses."

Luke raised his brows. "Why would I want to do that?"

"It doesn't take away the pain."

"No, but it dulls it enough to bear."

Noah crossed his arms over his chest. "Do right by her, Luke."

Luke met his stern gaze. He had every intention of honoring their agreement. But what he wouldn't tell his friend was that no matter how hard he tried, Luke could not guarantee that he wouldn't fail her as he had everyone else in his life.

"I probably shouldn't inform you of this, but"—Noah nodded toward the note in Luke's pocket—"that's all the money Miss Channing has left in the world."

Luke shrank back. "What of her brothers? The Channing merchant-men?"

"Gone—both her brothers and the ships." Noah sat back down on the settee and stretched his legs out before him. "The brothers to Canada to fight and the ships sold to provide for the family in their absence. You didn't hear?"

Luke shook his head. "No doubt they'll return soon."

"Perhaps." Noah scratched his jaw. "Perhaps not. Who knows with this mad war?"

Luke poured himself another glass. His gut churned. Taking money from a rich merchant was one thing, but taking all the lady had was quite another. Didn't she know he was not dependable? Of course she did. It was why she had hesitated, why she had demanded he refrain from drink. Luke slammed the Madeira toward the back of his throat. He hated responsibility, avoided it as much as possible. Then why did it always seem to find him?

"You are now the only one keeping Miss Channing and her family from poverty." Noah's sobering declaration rang through the room like a ship's beat to quarters before a battle.

"You should have warned her."

"Perhaps. But I have a feeling God has caused this arrangement with Miss Channing. That in some way, the association will lead you both to your destiny."

With a huff of frustration, Luke faced his friend. "Don't include me in your mad prophecies. There is no divine destiny for men like me."

Noah stretched his arm over the back of the settee and smiled. "We shall see."

Luke tore his gaze from the knowing look in his friend's eyes. Despite all of Luke's past mistakes, his shortcomings and blunders, this time he could not fail.

❖

Gripping the shears, Cassandra strolled through the solarium studying each gardenia plant as she went. It had been two weeks since she'd signed over the last of her family's fortune to the town rogue. She nearly laughed at how silly that statement sounded. She *would* laugh at the absurdity of it all if her stomach weren't tied in knots and her blood ringing in her ears. A condition that had started that morning when a messenger from Mr. Heaton had summoned her to inspect the new privateer, *Destiny*, that afternoon.

Surely it was a simple case of nerves brought on by the critical nature of her investment and not the fact that she would see Luke Heaton within an hour. For the sooner the ship set sail, the sooner her chances of catching a prize and the sooner the money would start flowing in. Then Cassandra could pay off her creditors. She didn't know how much longer Mr. Newman would extend her account at the mercantile or Mr. Sikes at the chandlers or Mr. Roberts at the cobblers or if Mr. Kile at the Bank of Baltimore would call in the loan she took out against their property. If any of them demanded payment before her investment with Mr. Heaton paid off, her family would be on the streets.

Stopping, she clipped a dead branch from one of the plants then stooped to cut off a faded flower. She wished she could rid herself of her problems as easily. Drawing a deep whiff of a fresh blossom, she brushed her cheek over its soft petals. The sweet fragrance filled her lungs, luring her eyes closed as she dreamed of happier days when her father was alive and both her brothers were home. Gregory, two years her senior, had inherited their father's flaming red hair and the temper to go with it. But he always came to Cassandra's defense on any issue and never allowed gentlemen callers unless he'd first scrutinized them at length. And Matthew, sweet docile Matthew, who, though only a year older than Cassandra, possessed the wisdom of an ancient scholar and the kindness of a saint. How many evenings had they curled up together in her chamber as children with a candle and a copy of their favorite book, *Keeper's Travels in Search of His Master*, reading late into the night of grand adventures in foreign lands?

The loud clank of the solarium door followed by childish squealing jarred Cassandra from her memories. She opened her eyes to a flash of blond hair and a flutter of petticoats as Darlene darted past her then wove in between a row of plants and disappeared. Hannah barreled in after her,

her wide blue eyes scanning the room.

"Darlene, Hannah!" Margaret's voice flew in from outside.

Setting down the shears, Cassandra fisted her hands at her waist. "Now, you girls know you're not allowed in here."

Giggles burst from the far corner. Ignoring Cassandra, Hannah dashed toward them. Dexter loped into the solarium fast on the girl's heels as she threaded in between two of Cassandra's newly planted sprouts. The clumsy sheepdog bumped into a wooden table. The pot sitting atop it teetered. Cassandra stretched out her hands toward it as a scream stuck in her throat.

Dexter's bark joined screeching laughter from the far end of the solarium as the pot crashed to the floor, sending chips of clay, clods of dirt, and the small plant shooting over the stone tiles.

Cassandra halted. She heard Margaret's gasp behind her. Silence swept the children's laughter away, replaced by the patter of feet and paws as the two girls and Dexter slowly emerged from behind a row of plants, a look of dread on their faces.

"Oh miss, I'm so sorry." Margaret knelt by the broken pot and began to pick up the pieces. "We're sorry, Cassie," Darlene said, her chin lowering.

Hannah stuck her thumb into her mouth and nodded as her eyes filled with tears.

Cassandra laid a hand on Margaret's arm. "Never mind that now. I'll take care of it." She turned to chastise the girls, but Darlene grabbed Hannah and darted out the door, leaving only Dexter to take the brunt of her anger. He gave a rueful whine.

Margaret's pudgy cheeks reddened. "I was trying to collect them for their studies, miss, but they got away from me."

"It's quite all right, Margaret." Cassandra sighed. "I don't believe General Smith himself could corral those girls."

As Margaret's laughter filled the room, Cassandra glanced out the mist-covered windows. "Where is Mrs. Northrop?"

"In the house." Margaret clutched Dexter's collar and led him out the door. "Which reminds me, Mr. Crane arrived just a moment ago and your mother is asking for you." Sympathy deepened her tone.

A sour taste filled Cassandra's mouth, and she doubted it was due to the overcooked oatmeal she'd had for breakfast. "Well, I simply can't stay and socialize. I'm meeting Mr. Heaton at his ship in an hour."

"Indeed? Are you sure it's safe to be alone with him?" Margaret teased.

"Of course. He's my new captain. I must trust him." She had to trust him.

She didn't trust him.

"Besides, we won't be alone. His crew is there." Cassandra stepped out and closed the door.

"I shall pray for your safety, miss, and for God's wisdom," Margaret said.

"Thank you, Margaret. I suppose your prayers couldn't hurt." Though she doubted they'd do much good either.

Back in the house, an odd smell coming from the kitchen curled Cassandra's nose. Waving it away, she drifted past the library on her way up to her chamber. Whispered voices drew her gaze into the room where she spotted Mr. Crane and Mrs. Northrop, their heads bent together in some sort of parley. What on earth would Mr. Crane have to say to the housekeeper? Cassandra halted by the edge of the doorway to listen, but she couldn't make out their words. What did it matter, anyway? She should thank the housekeeper for keeping the man occupied and away from Cassandra. And perhaps giving her a chance to sneak out without speaking to him.

Hurrying up the stairs to her chamber, she checked her reflection in her dressing glass, donned her gloves, grabbed her fur-lined pelisse and parasol, and tried to make a quick exit out the front door before her mother noticed.

"You would simply not believe what this war has done for newspaper sales." Mr. Crane's tone blared like a dissonant trumpet from inside the parlor. "Our sales have increased a hundredfold. Everyone is scrambling for recent news from the battlefronts."

Halfway across the open doors, Cassandra tiptoed onward, not daring to peek inside the room lest she draw attention her way.

A teacup rattled on a saucer. "Oh Cassandra, dear. Where are you going? Mr. Crane has come to call on you."

Cassandra closed her eyes, silently chastising herself for not leaving by the back door. Pasting on a smile, she spun around. "I have an errand to run, Mother." She nodded toward Mr. Crane, who had risen from his seat with a rather baffled look on his face. "Mr. Crane, how nice to see you."

"Alone?" he asked incredulously.

"Yes," Cassandra replied, stepping just inside the room. "Mr. Dayle is otherwise occupied and it is broad daylight. I will be quite safe, I assure you. Now, if you don't mind." Cassandra turned to leave.

"Don't be ridiculous, dear." Her mother's harsh tone turned her back around. "You are being quite rude. Come and sit for a while."

"I fear I cannot, Mother. I have an appointment."

"With whom?"

Cassandra bit her lip. She had not told her mother of her investment yet. Had not wanted to vex her overmuch. But perhaps this would be the best time. With company present, her mother would surely not dive into her usual hysterics, and perhaps Mr. Crane could help allay her fears.

"With Captain Heaton," Cassandra blurted out. "I've invested in his privateer and they are to set sail on the morrow."

Mr. Crane flinched.

Her mother's jaw fell open and appeared to be stuck in that position. Leaning back on her chair, she threw a hand to her forehead. "Tell me you didn't."

Cassandra took a deep breath. "I did. And it will pay off, you'll see. I guarantee we shan't have any further troubles." Yet she heard the uncertainty in her own voice.

"Mr. Luke Heaton?" Mr. Crane seemed to have found his voice, although it came out slow and garbled. "The scoundrel Heaton? The man who drinks and gambles his money away?"

Cassandra lifted her chin. "Yes, that's the one."

Her mother picked up the small bell from the table beside her and rang it profusely. "I need some tonic."

Straightening his gray waistcoat, Mr. Crane approached Cassandra wearing the look of a schoolmaster instructing a foolish child. "This is quite preposterous, Miss Channing. Why would you go to such lengths when the solution to your problems stands before you?"

Cassandra forced a smile. "You are too kind, sir, but as I said before, I cannot in good conscience accept your offer."

"Stubborn girl." Her mother rang the bell again. Its shrill *ding ding ding* hammered on Cassandra's guilt. "Do you see why my nerves are strung tight, Mr. Crane? Perhaps you can talk some sense into her?"

Mrs. Northrop appeared in the doorway. Her eyes locked with Mr. Crane's before she sped to her mistress, bottle of tonic in hand.

As she poured a splash into the elderly woman's tea, Mr. Crane eased his fingers over his neatly combed hair. "Well, the least I can do is escort you to your appointment."

"That isn't necessary." Cassandra moved to her mother and planted a kiss on her cheek. "I shall be back within the hour, Mother."

Picking up her cup, the older woman sipped her tea then waved Mrs. Northrop off, avoiding Cassandra's gaze and instead seeking out Mr. Crane. "Yes, sir. Please do accompany my daughter. With your business sense, perhaps you can assess the terrible risk she has placed on our entire family and determine some way of escape. . . ."

"But, Mother. . ."

"I insist." Her mother slammed down her cup. Some of the golden tea sloshed over the rim and pooled in the saucer.

Cassandra's stomach sank. "Very well."

Grabbing his hat from the sofa, Mr. Crane set it atop his head. "It will be my pleasure."

Cassandra gripped her parasol and followed him out the door. *Oh, bother.* Mr. Crane and Mr. Heaton together in the same place?

It was going to be a very interesting afternoon.

❖ CHAPTER 8 ❖

Spreading the chart over the binnacle, Luke pointed at the spots where various shoals and sandbars transformed the Chesapeake Bay into a dangerous maze.

Biron Abbot shook his head. "It's not the shoals that bother me, Cap'n. It's those bloody British. How are we to slip past twenty of His Majesty's finest ships?"

Luke gazed up at the gray clouds rumbling across the sky. The welcome sting of rain filled his nostrils. "You're the praying man, my friend. Why don't you ask your God to keep this storm up through the night? Or better yet, pray for a fog so thick not even the Royal Navy will dare to stir a wave to chase us." Luke chuckled.

"Aye," young Samuel Rogers interjected from Luke's other side. "And if they should spot us, we can batter them with grapeshot and sail away 'fore they can catch us, eh, Cap'n?"

Luke couldn't help but smile at his new quartermaster. A few golden whiskers on the boy's chin joined his stiff stance as proud evidence of his budding manhood. At only seventeen, the boy had more experience at sea than most of the men Luke had managed to recruit—*bribe* would have been a more fitting word. Yet the lad's experience had not tempered his youthful enthusiasm and courage. Qualities much desired in a successful privateer.

Although at the moment, Samuel behaved more like a midshipman as he stood at attention before Luke. Old habits died hard, Luke supposed, for the lad had served aboard the USS *Syren* for eight years.

"A tempting idea," Luke replied. "Yet I have no desire to engage an enemy warship." No, he'd already attempted that foolhardy feat when he'd been Noah's first mate on board the *Defender*. And they'd barely escaped with their lives. An act of God, Noah had called it. Luke shook his head. More like good fortune that the USS *Constitution* had been there to pick them out of the sea. Good fortune that always seemed to come Noah's way.

But never Luke's.

No, Luke would not count on God or good fortune but on his skill and determination. It was all he had left.

From his spot on the quarterdeck, he surveyed his ship, where most of his crewmen were hard at work putting the finishing touches on the vessel: scrubbing the newly caulked deck, polishing the brass, tarring the lines, greasing the mast. Aside from young Samuel, Luke had been unable to convince any decent sailors to join him. Consequently, he had resorted to hiring criminals, drunks, and gamblers—men just like him. He only hoped they'd perform with bravery and skill when the occasion called for it. But, perhaps like him, they saw privateering as their last chance to turn their life around, to make a fortune and a respectable name for themselves.

To stop a legacy of failure.

A stream of men carried crates and barrels filled with supplies for the journey, from the wharf onto the main deck then down the open hatch into the hold. Luke's gaze landed on two crewmen standing at the prow of the ship, talking—the two men he'd asked to fix the loose railing on the starboard waist.

"Biron, order those men back to work at once."

"Aye, aye, Cap'n." Biron leapt down the quarterdeck ladder with more agility than his fifty-two years should have allowed and began barking orders.

A chilled wind rose from the bay and swirled about Luke, dragging down his spirits. Thunder growled in the distance as the weight of responsibility sank heavy upon his shoulders. Not only was this his first voyage as captain with ultimate authority on board the ship, but it was a voyage in which he must succeed.

For Miss Channing's sake, for John's, and for his own.

Luke folded up the chart and handed it to Samuel. "Take this below to my cabin."

MaryLu Tyndall

"Aye, Cap'n." The boy saluted.

"No need to salute me, Sam. You are no longer in the navy."

He saluted again then laughed at his own mistake before darting away.

Dark clouds stole the remainder of the sun, portending a storm that would bring Luke the cover he so desperately needed to slip past the British blockade. Though his ship had been ready for two days, he and his crew had been forced to wait idly in the bay while a fortune beckoned to him from the sea. So, when Luke had spotted a tempest brewing on the horizon that morning, he thought it best to summon Miss Channing for her requested inspection. Not that he hadn't wished to summon her before. In fact, he'd been unable to get the infernal woman out of his thoughts since that fateful night when he'd saved her from those ruffians. He glanced over at the spot where he'd first seen her across Pratt Street hurrying past the Hanson warehouse. A vision of her pummeling one of the scoundrels with a brick filled his mind, and he couldn't help but smile. Yet as he continued to stare at the spot, his smile sank into a frown as another figure emerged—a tall man dressed in a dark-blue tailcoat with red collar and cuffs and a black crown shako on his head—marching straight toward Luke as if he were marching across a battlefield.

Luke cursed under his breath. Lieutenant Abner Tripp. What did the man want now? Glancing around for a bottle of rum, Luke cursed again when he remembered he hadn't brought any on board. With a groan, he made his way to the main deck just as the lieutenant halted on the wharf beside the ship, his fists stiff by his side, and his narrowed eyes seething at Biron, who was demanding to know his business.

"What is the meaning of this, Heaton?" Lieutenant Tripp shouted.

Luke snapped the hair from his face and approached the port railing. "The meaning of what?" He gave him a cocky smile.

"The meaning of using my ship as a privateer."

"Your ship?" Luke rubbed the stubble on his jaw. "If I recall, I won her from you in a game of Piquet."

Swerving about, Biron shook his head. No doubt as a warning for Luke to stop goading the man.

Which Luke would be happy to do if the rodent would simply leave.

Instead, the lieutenant took up a pace along the wharf, glancing over the ship's masts, sails, rigging, at the crew working, and finally landing on one man in particular who hung over the port side, painting the new name on her bow.

"You called her *Destiny*? Bah!" He ceased his pacing and gripped the pommel of the army saber hanging at his side. "You have no destiny, sir, but to die penniless and alone in your own besotted vomit." Spit flew from his mouth.

Luke's hand twitched beside his cutlass, longing to draw it once again on this buffoon. "I would watch what you say, Lieutenant. My temper has limits. Surely you have not come to receive a twin on your other cheek?"

Chortles burst behind Luke as a spike of white lightning lit up the sky.

Lieutenant Tripp rubbed the pink scar angling over the left side of his face, opened his mouth to say something, then seemed to think better of it.

Luke crossed his arms over his chest. "I would assume you'd be happy to see your former ship put to good use against our common enemy."

"I will only be happy, sir, to see you and it at the bottom of the ocean. You stole my ship and all my money." Wind tore over the lieutenant, fluttering the fringe of the gold epaulette capping his left shoulder.

"Won," Luke corrected him as the ship rose over an incoming wave.

"My fiancée left me."

"I fear I cannot take credit for that, Lieutenant."

More laughter sprang from behind Luke. Even Biron's face cracked into a smile.

Lieutenant Tripp's long, pointy nose seemed to grow in length, and his hand dropped to his saber once again. "I demand satisfaction, sir."

Silence overtook the ship as the crew stopped their work and gazed expectantly at the brewing altercation.

"Now? When I'm ready to set sail?" Luke smiled. He had no desire to further humiliate this man. Why didn't the beef wit simply count his losses and go?

A maroon hue, as red as the plume fluttering atop Lieutenant Tripp's shako, crept across his face. "So, it's true what they say then?"

"And what is that?"

"That without your rum, you are a coward. A miserable sot who preys on innocent women and cheats at cards." His thin lips began to tremble. "A coward who sat back whilst his parents were butchered by savages."

Fury seared through Luke. His vision blurred. In two strides, he flew up on the bulwarks and leapt onto the dock. His crew tossed cheers behind him. All except Biron, who shouted for him to stop.

Fear flooded the lieutenant's eyes. He took a step back. Luke clutched the hilt of his cutlass, intent on teaching the man another lesson, when the flutter of a lacy parasol floating atop a blue muslin gown caught the corner of his eye. Drawn to the vision like a drowning man's glimpse of land, he halted.

Miss Channing strolled down the wharf, a sour-faced dandy at her side.

Relief softened Lieutenant Tripp's features. He glanced over his shoulder at her, then back at Luke, his face as hard as granite once again.

His right eyelid took on an odd twitch before he spun on his heels and marched down the wharf, causing it to wobble beneath his anger. He halted before Miss Channing and her gentleman dandy.

Luke grabbed the hilt of his sword again and started for them. If Tripp dared to lay a hand on her. . .

❖

No sooner had Cassandra turned down the dock where *Destiny* was anchored than she spotted Mr. Heaton and another man in a military uniform engaged in what appeared to be a heated battle. Dressed in black breeches stuffed within tall Hessian boots, a white shirt, and black waistcoat, Mr. Heaton stood before his ship as if he, alone, would defend the vessel to his death. Cassandra's heart jolted at the sight of him then seized when she saw him grip his cutlass and start for the man. But then his eyes locked upon hers and he stopped. A smile curved his lips, and he bowed toward his adversary as if they were the best of friends.

The man, whom Cassandra could now see was a lieutenant in the army, charged her way. Oblivious to all, Mr. Crane continued the incessant chattering he'd smothered her with since they'd left the house, only ceasing when the lieutenant halted before them and cleared his throat.

"Are you Miss Channing?" The lieutenant's face was pink and bloated, and his eyes skittered here and there, unable to focus.

"I am."

"I understand you have invested in this privateer?"

Cassandra's gaze shot behind the man to Mr. Heaton, who stormed toward them as if he'd changed his mind about not killing the lieutenant.

The man glanced over his shoulder. His eyelid twitched. "You have made a grave error, miss."

Mr. Crane chuckled. "As I've been trying to tell her—"

"Mr. Heaton is a failure and his privateer will be a failure as well," the lieutenant interrupted then straightened his coat and marched away before Cassandra could answer him, leaving ill tidings swirling in his wake.

Cassandra shuddered, wondering why he would say such a thing. His words of doom thundered over her, much like the dark clouds churning above, making her feel like a little girl alone in the midst of a storm—a storm that could sweep her and her family out to sea.

A growl bellowed from the sky in confirmation of her fears.

Until she turned to face the confident look on Mr. Heaton's face. Pushing Mr. Crane aside, he took up a stance between her and the departing lieutenant. "Did he harm you, Miss Channing?"

A sense of being protected overcame her—a feeling she hadn't felt in quite some time. It warmed her from head to toe. "Why, no."

"He merely told her the truth." Mr. Crane's chortle spun Mr. Heaton around. He eyed the man as if he were a bothersome gnat. "And you are. . .?"

"Forgive me," Cassandra interjected. "This is Mr. Milton Crane. He is the proprietor of the *Register*."

"Hmm," Mr. Heaton huffed. "You are too early, sir."

"Early?" Mr. Crane's face scrunched.

"To report on *Destiny*'s outlandish success." Luke faced Cassandra and winked. She felt her knees weaken. Then he waved off Mr. Crane, saying, "Come back in a month," before he proffered his elbow to Cassandra.

Shifting her parasol to hide her grin, she accepted Mr. Heaton's arm.

Mr. Crane's footsteps followed them. "You mistake me, sir. I am escorting Miss Channing."

As they approached the ship, Cassandra spotted a man hanging over the bow, putting the finishing touches on the word *Destiny* painted in bright blue on the hull.

"I see you have come armed," Mr. Heaton said.

"Mr. Crane?" Cassandra said. "My mother insisted he accompany me."

"I was referring to your parasol, miss." His dark eyebrows rose above a grin. "Him"—he gestured over his shoulder—"I can handle."

Cassandra's giggle was instantly silenced when she halted and found the eyes of at least two dozen rather shabby-looking men latched upon her from the deck of the *Destiny*. Swallowing down a lump of unease, she threw back her shoulders. These men were in her employ and the sooner she made that clear, the better.

After leaping onto the ship, Mr. Heaton turned to assist her. Ignoring his hand, she closed her parasol, clutched her gown, and stepped onto the teetering deck. She would show this man and his crew that she was not some delicate flower to be plucked and squashed. Yet even as she lifted her chin in victory, the deck tilted and she stumbled. Mr. Heaton gripped her elbow to steady her.

Refusing to look at the grin that was surely on his face, Cassandra turned to inform Mr. Crane that he need not wait for her when he tumbled onto the deck behind her and took his spot at her side.

An older gentleman approached them.

"Mr. Biron, assemble the men, if you please," Mr. Heaton ordered.

"Aye, aye, Cap'n." The man blew a whistle, sending the men on deck and the ones pouring from the hatches scrambling to form a straight line from bow to stern.

While she waited, Cassandra took the opportunity to study the ship. The chips in the bulwarks had been repaired, the wooden deck had been stripped and recaulked, the broken spoke on the capstan was restored, lines were coiled neatly beside belaying pins, and the brass atop the railheads, wheel, and belfry gleamed. She gazed upward to see that one of the sails had been replaced with fresh canvas. The scent of tar and wood filled her lungs.

She dared a glance at Mr. Heaton standing before his men, fists at his waist, dark hair blowing in the breeze, his shoulders stretched with the authority of a captain. She couldn't recall smelling rum on him as he'd escorted her to the ship. Could it be the man intended to keep his promise? For the first time, Cassandra allowed a smidgeon of hope to form within her that Mr. Heaton might prove his reputation wrong and become a great privateer.

As if in defiance of that hope, an icy wind tainted with the sting of rain whirled around her, and Cassandra drew her pelisse tighter about her neck.

"Gentlemen, may I introduce to you Miss Cassandra Channing," Mr. Heaton shouted after all the men had assembled. "She is half owner of this privateering venture."

Crane snorted then coughed into his hand.

"And"—Mr. Heaton's dark gaze snapped to Mr. Crane—"she is here to inspect our fair vessel."

Then leading her to the bow, he proceeded to introduce each crewman. Some barely glanced at her, their faces reddening at the introduction. Others brazenly took her in as if she were a sweet pastry—their salacious scrutiny promptly squelched by one look from Mr. Heaton. The stench of unwashed bodies permeated the air, but she resisted the urge to draw a handkerchief to her nose.

One man dared to spit to the side and say, "Bad luck to have a woman investor."

"Indeed." Mr. Crane's annoying voice buzzed from behind Cassandra.

Ignoring him, Mr. Heaton started for the sailor as if he intended to shove him back, but Cassandra stayed him with a touch to his arm. "Well, I hope to prove you wrong, Mr. Nelson." She smiled, and the sailor seemed befuddled for a moment before he smiled back.

"And this is Biron Abbot, my first mate." Luke stopped before the older gentleman, a rough but kindly looking man who reminded Cassandra of Reverend Drummond. He dipped his gray head. "A pleasure, miss."

The ship lurched over a wave, and she pressed the tip of her parasol onto the deck to keep her balance.

Mr. Heaton moved to the next man. "And Mr. Joseph Keene, my boatswain."

Cassandra nodded at the handsome man who was at least fifteen years her senior. Dressed in colorful silk and lace, he looked more like a pirate than a sailor. His disarming smile, coupled with the mischievous twinkle in his eye, did nothing to dissuade her opinion. He took her hand and placed a kiss upon it as the jewels on his fingers glinted in the daylight.

Mr. Heaton pushed between them, breaking the contact, and moved on to the next man. "Mr. Zachary Ward, my gunner."

Completely bald to the top of his head, yet with a veritable lion's mane flowing down the back, the man presented such an odd sight that Cassandra would have laughed if he wasn't looking at her with hatred burning in his eyes.

She took a deep breath and shifted her parasol into her other hand. She would not let him intimidate her. "Are you familiar with cannons, Mr. Ward?"

"Aye, miss. Was in the American navy, I was."

"Indeed, why are you still not enlisted?"

"Cashiered, miss, for blasphemy and drunkenness." His tone held no remorse.

Cassandra turned to Mr. Heaton. "You seem to be among friends."

A hint of a smile played on his lips.

"Of all the. . . ," Mr. Crane announced with alacrity. "This is pre-posterous. These men are not fit to sail this ship. Surely you can see that, Miss Channing."

Ignoring him, Cassandra studied the gunner. "But I sense you have changed your ways, Mr. Ward?" Her approving tone stripped the defensive wall away.

"That I have, miss." He dipped his head.

She leaned toward him with a smile. "Good for you, sir."

"This is ludicrous," Crane whispered over her shoulder. "These men are wastrels and thieves. Why, they'll do nothing but rob you blind."

Cassandra cringed. Though she tried to prevent Mr. Crane's words from affecting her, they crouched around her budding hope like a pack of wolves around a newborn lamb. Mainly because there was truth in his assessment. Indeed, these men were not the finest gentlemen she'd encountered—probably not the finest sailors either—but Mr. Heaton was the captain and for now she must trust his judgment.

Luke scowled. "The lady has a mind of her own, Mr. Crane. Please allow her to use it."

Cassandra shot him a curious gaze. She had never heard a man declare such a thing. Did he mean it, or was he simply trying to slip into her good graces? Yet when his eyes locked with hers, they held understanding, not insincerity.

Turning his back to Crane, Mr. Heaton took Cassandra's arm and moved her to the next man. "Mr. Samuel Rogers, my quartermaster."

The young boy's wide grin reminded Cassandra of her brother Matthew. Nothing pretentious, no pomposity or hidden meaning lurked in his expression. His long sandy hair was pulled behind him in a tie, and his sparkling blue eyes held a thirst for adventure.

"Aren't you a bit young to be going on such a dangerous journey?" she asked him.

"No, miss. I was born on a ship. Spent me whole life in the navy till I quit last year to become a privateer."

Cassandra couldn't help but admire his enthusiasm—the same she'd seen in her brothers before they'd left to fight in Canada. Did fate have the same thing in store for this young man? "But doesn't war frighten you?"

"No, miss. I love fightin'. I hope to be a pirate someday."

Thunder rumbled in the distance.

"A pirate. Good heavens!" Mr. Crane chortled. "Surely you've heard enough, Miss Channing."

Cassandra spun around. "I have not, sir. If you have, I suggest you leave."

A gust of wind tossed his neatly combed hair into a spin even as his mouth tightened into a thin line. "I am only looking out for your interests."

"Look out for them in silence, if you please." Cassandra turned around to find Mr. Heaton gazing at her with a mixture of ardor and amusement.

He led her onward. "And lastly, Mr. Nyle Sanders, our purser."

With tablet in hand, the small man—who, with his pointy nose and tiny dark eyes hidden behind a pair of spectacles, reminded Cassandra of a rat—greeted her kindly, with nary a glance her way.

"Dismissed!" Mr. Abbot shouted. Cassandra jumped at the abrupt command then watched as the men dispersed as quickly and haphazardly as they had assembled, their bare feet pounding over the wooden deck.

Mr. Crane grabbed Cassandra's arm and drew her to the side. "Miss Channing. Please end this charade. Anyone can see that this is nothing but a ship of villains and reprobates. Do not be so naive to assume you'll see a penny's return on your investment. I urge you to demand your money back and flee this ship of doom at once."

❖

Luke grabbed the hilt of his sword, longing to slice off Mr. Crane's annoying tongue. It was either that or Luke feared he might toss the man overboard. This dandy was nothing but a puffed-up, implacable fribble.

"Too late, Mr. Crane." Miss Channing released a sigh of annoyance. "The money has already been spent. So, you see, your complaints do nothing but cause me discomfort."

"Well, I certainly did not mean. . . ," Mr. Crane stuttered. His cheeks swelled, but before he could finish, Miss Channing swept her pretty face toward Luke, her auburn curls dancing over the fur trim of her pelisse.

And with her sweet smile, all thoughts of murdering Mr. Crane vanished.

In fact, Luke had been amazed at how well she handled herself in front of the motley group of vagrants he called a crew. About as civilized as a band of hungry bears, they were likely to frighten even the most stalwart of women. Yet Miss Channing had greeted each one of them as if they were members of the town council. She neither shrank back from their licentious glances nor took offense at their snide comments. Lud, instead of passing them by with a lift of her nose as he had expected, she'd even asked them questions that went beyond her interest in them as an investment.

"Will you show me the armament you purchased, Mr. Heaton?" Her smile reached her eyes, and at that moment he believed he'd show her anything she wished.

"Armament, ha!" Mr. Crane tugged on his cravat. "I doubt you could have procured anything decent for this waterlogged tub."

Luke gave the man one of his most imperious gazes, the kind that sent men cowering in the taverns. It had the same effect on Mr. Crane. Clearing his throat, he moved to the other side of Miss Channing.

Luke waved at the carronades mounted on the starboard railing. "As you can see, I purchased eight carronades, four on each side." He pointed toward the other group lining the port side of the ship. "And one lone nine at the prow."

"Is that all?" Mr. Crane snorted with disdain. "Hardly enough fire-power to catch a fishing boat, let alone a merchantman."

Enough was enough. Luke's gaze landed on the broken railing, and he found himself suddenly glad the lazy crewmen had not followed his orders to fix it.

"No, Mr. Crane. We also installed two eighteen pounders below-decks. You can see their muzzles jutting out from the gun ports if you look over the starboard railing."

"Eighteen pounders! Preposterous! On a schooner?" Mr. Crane snorted.

"See for yourself." Luke shrugged one shoulder and gestured with his head toward the railing.

Stomping toward the spot, Mr. Crane peered over the edge. "You taunt me, sir. There is nothing there."

Miss Channing's brow furrowed.

"Of course there is." Taking a spot beside the buffoon, Luke pointed over the side. "Can't you see them?"

Mr. Crane leaned on the faulty piece of railing. With an exasperated sigh, he angled the top half of his body over the side. *Crack! Snap!* A chunk of the wood broke from the railing and dropped into the bay.

Mr. Crane's arms flailed before him. His eyes bulged. He let out a broken shriek as he toppled over and splashed into the dark water below.

❖ CHAPTER 9 ❖

Cassandra stepped inside the captain's cabin and took in the masculine furnishings. A sturdy oak desk guarded the stern windows. Charts, a logbook, quill pens, a quadrant, and two lanterns spread across a top that was marred with divots and stains. Rows of books stood at attention on two shelves to the right, a mahogany case filled with weapons lined the opposite wall, and one velvet-upholstered chair stood before the desk. The smell of tar and whale oil and Mr. Heaton filled her nose as he ducked to enter the room behind her. Mr. Abbot followed on his heels, wearing a smirk that had lingered on his lips ever since Mr. Crane had fallen overboard.

And though Cassandra tried to stifle her laughter, another giggle burst from her mouth at the vision of Mr. Crane being pulled from the bay by a fisherman. Afterward, he had simply stood there, dripping like a drowned possum and shaking his fist in the air before he turned and marched away.

"You really should have tossed a rope over for him." Cassandra turned to face Luke.

A mischievous glint flashed in his blue eyes. "Why? He had overstayed his welcome."

"You are incorrigible," she huffed.

"So I am told."

Mr. Abbot chuckled. "I fear you have made another enemy."

"A growing list." Mr. Heaton rubbed his right palm. Pink scars lined the skin, making Cassandra wonder what had happened to cause them.

"The men are asking when we will set sail," Mr. Abbot said, lingering at the open door. Thunder shook the ship as the *tap tap* of rain pounded on the deck above.

"As soon as it's dark." Mr. Heaton stomped toward the shelves as if looking for something then halted and turned back around with a sigh. "I have an errand to run first."

"What errand? We have all our supplies loaded." Mr. Abbot tugged on his red neckerchief and glanced at Cassandra. "Shouldn't we leave while the storm is upon us?"

"I must say good-bye to someone."

Cassandra's gaze shot to Mr. Heaton. The way he'd said the words with such affection, it had to be a woman. She knew of his reputation. Of course a man like Mr. Heaton would have a love interest in town, perhaps many. Then why did her insides burn at the thought?

Sitting on the edge of his desk, Mr. Heaton crossed his arms over his chest. "Biron, order the men to repair that railing at once."

Cassandra flinched. She opened her mouth to ask the elderly man to stay—to not leave her alone with this rake—but he had already slipped into the companionway. The thud of his boots soon faded beneath the caress of the waves against the hull.

She should leave as well. She had seen the entire ship and now the captain's cabin. There was no reason for her to stay.

Except for the pull of Mr. Heaton's eyes as he allowed his gaze to wander over her. Not in a bawdy way as his crew had. But as someone staring at an object of great beauty that he could never possess.

No one had ever looked at her that way before. And it made her feel, all at once, like both a princess and a prig. As if she were precious and yet too pretentious to touch. She approached the chair, putting it between herself and Mr. Heaton, and ran her hand along the carved back. "I suppose Mr. Crane deserved the embarrassment. But do forgive him, Mr. Heaton. I fear it is only jealousy that drives his peevish behavior."

"So, he has some claim on you?"

She pursed her lips, shocked at his bold question. "I don't see how that's any business of yours."

He grinned then gestured for her to sit.

"No, I cannot stay. I should not stay." She glanced at the door, thankful Mr. Abbot had left it open.

Standing, Mr. Heaton approached her until only the chair filled the space between them. A space that instantly heated and crackled beneath some unimaginable force. "Do you fear being alone with me, Miss Channing?" A mischievous glint flashed in his eyes.

Thunder growled. Though he towered over her, she did her best to lift her gaze to meet his. "Should I?" Yet she knew the tremble that coursed through her had nothing to do with fear.

The sheen over his eyes softened, and he raised a hand to touch her face. Cassandra leapt back with a gasp.

He frowned. "I am many things, Miss Channing, but I would never hurt a woman. In fact, I am quite fond of women."

Cassandra tightened her grip on the handle of her parasol. "So I've been told."

He rubbed the back of his neck. "My reputation bothers you."

"Not in the way you might think." *No, in every way possible*. Even in ways she dared not admit. "I only care that you keep your focus on privateering."

"Fortunately for us both, I have the ability to focus on many things at once."

Indeed Cassandra could see many things in his eyes now—sorrow, admiration, yearning. The realization confounded her and set her heart racing. She glanced at the charts spread across his desk. "In what direction do you intend to sail?"

A strand of his black hair slid over his jaw. Glancing over his shoulder at the desk, he eased it behind his ear. "South along the coast and then across the Caribbean trade routes. That should afford us the best chance of crossing hulls with a British merchantman."

Beyond the stern windows, lightning flared across the sky as rain splattered the panes, running down in silver streams.

"And when do you expect to return?" she asked.

"As soon as I catch a prize."

"Soon then, I hope."

A devilish grin curved his lips. "You will miss me?"

A wave of heat flooded Cassandra. "Don't be absurd. My interests lie purely in my investment." She shifted her gaze to the door. "I should be going."

"I'll have Mr. Abbot escort you home."

An odd disappointment settled on Cassandra that Mr. Heaton would not do the honor himself. "It is still light. There is no need."

"There is for me."

"Very well." Cassandra gripped her parasol and made her way to the door. She faced him. "Then I wish you a safe journey, Mr. Heaton."

A touch of sadness softened his eyes. "Never fear, Miss Channing. I will protect your investment with my life."

❖

"Why do you have to go?" John's gray eyes clouded like the storm brewing outside their small house.

Luke drew him near. "Because I must take care of you and Mrs. Barnes."

"Can't I go with you this time?" John gazed up at Luke. "You said if you ever fixed your ship, I could come."

Mrs. Barnes sat in her cushioned rocking chair by the fireplace, sorrow furrowing her brows.

Luke led the boy to the sofa. "Yes, I did. But not on a privateering mission. It's far too dangerous."

John hung his head. "Lots of boys my age work on ships."

The truth of his words stung Luke. Was he being overprotective of his brother? His eyes met Mrs. Barnes's, seeking her advice, but she continued her knitting with a gentle smile on her lips as if she trusted Luke to make the right decision. He huffed. When had he ever made the right decision?

Grabbing John by the back of the neck, he drew him close and stared at the yellow and red flames spewing and crackling like mad demons in the fireplace. A picture of his mother running toward him formed out of the blaze, her face screaming in terror. She handed him a white bundle—a bundle that contained one-year-old John. "Keep him safe!" she shouted above the roar of the fire. "Keep him safe!" Then the inferno swallowed her up.

That was the last thing she had ever said to him.

No, he couldn't risk John.

Luke moved to the sofa and John slumped beside him.

Pain spiked through Luke's right ear. Ignoring it, he gave John his most authoritative look. "Yes, lots of boys your age work on ships, but they don't go out on privateering missions on their first voyage." Yet, perhaps it *was* time to teach John how to sail. To see how he could handle himself on a wobbling ship with his brace. Perhaps, in due time, it would even help strengthen his leg. "I'll tell you what. I'll take you out on the ship when I return."

John lifted his gaze, his eyes sparkling. "When? When will that be?"

"I don't know. But when I do return, it will be with enough money to pay off our debts and buy us all a proper dinner at Queen's Tavern."

John grinned. "Did you hear that, Mrs. Barnes?"

"I did, indeed." The creak of her rocking chair filled the room, but she didn't look up from her knitting. Two balls of thread, one black and one white, sat in her lap.

"What are you making, Mrs. Barnes?" Luke asked.

She gave him a knowing smile. "Oh, I know it doesn't look like much now, but it will be beautiful. You'll see."

Beyond the windows, darkness swallowed up the city. Luke knew he needed to go. He glanced at the clock on the mantle—9:13. Stuck on 9:13 for the past sixteen days—ever since the night he'd first met Miss Channing. It was as if that meeting had stopped time, or perhaps it had set into motion some otherworldly clock, starting a sequence of events that would lead to his destiny, as Noah had said. *Destiny*, the name of his ship. Choking down a bitter chuckle, Luke shook his head. What foolishness had consumed his mind? And he hadn't even had a sip of rum.

❖

Luke stood at the quarter rail, telescope to his eye, scanning the horizon off *Destiny*'s bow. Nothing but the fuzzy blue line dividing sea from sky met his gaze. Lowering his scope, he shielded his eyes against the noon sun and glanced up at the crewman at the crosstrees. "Are you sure, Mr. Kraw?"

"Aye, Cap'n!" The shout returned. "Off the starboard bow."

The announcement of a sail had sparked hope in Luke—hope that had been deflated over the past two months of scanning the Eastern Seaboard for British merchantmen. So far, they had encountered three fishing boats, one whaler on his way north, a French Indiaman, one American privateer, and a British warship of eighty guns. Thankfully, they'd been able to outrun the latter. Now, five long days had passed since they'd seen anything but endless azure sea in every direction.

Beside him, Biron gripped the railing, tufts of gray hair blowing in the wind beneath his hat. "Dear God, let it be the prey we seek."

The ship bucked over a wave. Luke adjusted his stance and lifted the scope once again. A crowd of white sails popped over the horizon. "There she is."

"What do you make of her, Mr. Kraw?" he shouted, noting that his crew had stopped their work to stare at the intruder. He hoped Biron's prayer had been answered, for the men had been none too happy these past months. Their supplies were dwindling as quickly as their spirits, and it had become hard to discipline the unruly lot, especially without any rum for incentive. *Very much appreciated, dear Miss Channing*. The endless days and nights would have passed with much more tranquility and glee with a drink in hand. Luke licked his lips, searching for a hint of the spicy taste he so loved but seemed to have nearly forgotten.

When they'd set out from Baltimore Harbor, Luke's success in sneaking past the British fleet under cover of the storm had sent a huge wave of confidence throughout the crew. The success had not only bolstered Luke's hopes, but had given him confidence to believe that perchance he was not destined to be a failure at privateering as he was at everything else.

The thought encouraged him, for he wanted nothing more than to shower Miss Channing with wealth. To solve all her problems and see admiration and appreciation beaming in her eyes, instead of the mistrust and fear he constantly saw now. Ah, what a treasure she was! Hair the color of burgundy framing glowing skin that housed a pair of fathomless emerald eyes. He would sail around the world and back to possess such a woman.

But what was he thinking? He was so far beneath her in everything that mattered—integrity, honor, education, status, morality—that it still baffled him that she had aligned herself with the likes of him.

"Should I head for them, Cap'n?" Samuel said from his position at the wheel.

"Not yet," Luke said. A blast of hot air tore across the deck, cooling the sweat on his neck and brow. He gazed up at the courses glutted with wind and slapped the scope against his open palm where scars taunted him with a past failure.

His biggest failure of all.

The ship crested another wave and slammed down the other side, sending foam over her bow. The smell of salt and fish stung Luke's nostrils.

"A fair wind today. We should catch them with no problem," Biron stated.

Luke raised the scope again. The ship headed their way. He could make out the square shape of her hull and her three masts reaching for the sky. A good-sized ship. But was she a merchantman? And if so, was she British? For as tempting as it would be to attack any prize that came their way, Luke was no pirate. Though he had begun to think he wasn't beyond such measures if another month passed without satisfaction.

"Steady as she goes, Sam." Luke glanced at Mr. Keene who was standing on the main deck. "Ready the men to go aloft, Mr. Keene, should we need further sail."

"Aye, Cap'n." Mr. Keene shouted orders across the deck, the lace at his sleeves and collar flapping in the breeze. The top men leapt into the shrouds and raced up the ratlines to their posts just as Mr. Ward, the gunner, emerged from below, his eyes sparking with expectation.

Beside Luke, Biron bowed his head in prayer.

"Say an extra one for me, will you?" Luke whispered.

"You can talk to the Almighty just as well as I can," his first mate mumbled.

Luke snorted. "God won't listen to me."

"At least you're admitting He exists." The man continued praying.

Luke didn't know what he believed. If he admitted God existed, then he'd have to admit He was a cruel overlord. A God who cared not a whit for orphans or widows or the poor—or young boys with rickets. Raising his scope, he studied the oncoming ship.

"She's a British frigate!" The call came down on them like hail before Luke could even focus.

His heart stopped.

"And she's bearing down on us fast!"

His crew froze in place.

"Foresheet, jib, and staysail sheet, let go! Helms a-lee!" Luke fired off a string of orders ending with, "Mr. Ward, ready the guns, if you please." Not that they'd do any good against a frigate, but the preparation would keep up the men's spirits. Not Luke's. He knew exactly what he was up against. And unless he could outrun her, he and his men and his ship didn't stand a chance.

"So much for your prayers." He snickered toward Biron.

His first mate shrugged. "I suppose God has other plans."

"Yes, to see me destroyed, no doubt." Luke turned and marched away before Biron responded. Taking the wheel from Sam, he turned the ship about.

"She's picking up speed," Mr. Kraw yelled from the crosstrees.

"And she's got the weather edge," Samuel groaned as he took the wheel back.

Which meant she had the advantage of the wind. Sweat broke on Luke's brow as visions of being impressed into the Royal Navy assailed him. He'd rather die than allow that to happen again.

Releasing the wheel, Luke barreled onto the main deck as Biron barked orders to the men. The ship vaulted over a wave. Salty spray showered him, stinging his eyes. He gripped the port railing until his knuckles whitened as he gazed at the oncoming enemy. Closer now. Even though Luke had brought the ship around and raised every inch of canvas to the wind. The British frigate was a fast bird, indeed. And one that intended to swoop down and gobble up *Destiny* and her crew for supper.

Just as he imagined the fowl carnage in his mind, a plume of orange shot from the enemy's bow. "All hands down!" Luke shouted over his shoulder. His crew toppled to the deck, covering their heads with their arms. All save Luke and Mr. Ward, who exchanged a harried glance. Luke would not cower, and he assumed his gunner had seen too much action in his lifetime to be intimidated by so slight a volley.

An ominous *boom* cracked the sky. The shot struck the sea just twenty yards off their larboard quarter, shooting spray at least five feet into the air. Too close.

Far too close.

Luke's stomach dropped. He swung about, trying to settle his racing heart. His crew scrambled to their feet. Two dozen pairs of fearful eyes settled on him, waiting for him to issue an order.

Waiting for him to save them.

Luke rubbed the scars on his palm and swallowed. With each passing moment, each moment in which he hesitated, the faith in their eyes faded beneath a rising tide of terror. His own terror rose to grip every sinew and fiber of his being. Not a terror of the British, but a terror of failing these men who had put their trust in him.

Biron approached him, concern sharpening his features. "Your orders, Captain?"

Luke's blood pounded in his ears. He glanced at the oncoming frigate then over at his crew.

Another thunderous roar shook the sea, followed by a spray of seawater not ten yards off their stern.

And anger took the place of fear.

Anger and a determination to not fail without giving it all he had. "Lay aloft and loose top foresail!" Luke bellowed then turned to the helmsman. "Hard about, Sam!" He scanned the deck for the gunner. "Mr. Ward, man the starboard guns and be ready to fire on my order." Though he hoped they wouldn't have to.

The bald man grinned, his eyes sparking like embers. "Aye, Cap'n."

Luke faced forward. Biron took a spot beside him. "You'll outrun them." He gave Luke a knowing look that defied their harrowing circumstances. Luke rubbed the wet railing with his thumb then slammed his fist on the hard wood. "Let's hope so. This old bucket of a ship must have some fight in her yet."

Minutes passed like hours. Luke's legs ached from the strain of standing on the heaving planks. Sweat streamed down his back. Tension strung across the deck as tight as the lines that held the sails in place. Aside from his occasional orders in regard to direction and positions of sails, no one spoke. When they weren't adjusting sail, the crew kept their eyes riveted on their pursuer. The frigate fired again. No one bothered to duck this time. The shot plunged into the raging seas. Luke rubbed his aching eyes. Did they deceive him or had the iron ball struck the water farther away this time?

Smiling, Biron grabbed Luke's shoulder and shook him.

"We're outrunning them!" Samuel yelled from the wheel, while Mr. Keene slid down the backstay and nodded his approval to Luke.

The crew shouted "huzzahs" into the air.

Luke's muscles began to unwind. Removing his hat, he ran a hand through his moist hair and studied the frigate. The white foam curling on her bow indicated she still pursued them, but her diminishing size said she was losing the chase.

"Fire a salute to their heroic effort, if you please, Mr. Ward," Luke said with a grin.

Mr. Keene chuckled. "I like the way you think, Captain."

The gunner happily complied by lighting his matchstick to the touch-hole of one of the carronades mounted on the larboard quarter.

The gun roared a proper adieu to the British ship, sending acrid smoke back over the crew and a tremble through the timbers. With his nose still burning from the smell of gunpowder, Luke completed the farewell with a wave of his cocked hat and a mock bow.

The enemy responded with a guttural blast of one of their own guns before veering away.

Minutes later, Luke raised his scope to see the frigate fading against the setting sun. Releasing a deep breath, he stuffed the glass into his belt and addressed Biron standing beside him, "Lower the royals and stays, and tell Sam to set a course three degrees south by southeast."

"Aye, aye, Captain." Biron touched his floppy hat.

His emotions a turbulent whirl of relief, thankfulness, and budding confidence, Luke took the companionway down to his cabin.

He could sure use a drink about now.

❖ CHAPTER 10 ❖

I beg your pardon, Mr. Stokes." Cassandra dropped her gaze to the goods she'd deposited on the mercantile's counter: a one-pound bag of oats, a six-yard bolt of calico to make new dresses for the girls, a tin of coffee beans, a sack of rice, whale oil for the lanterns, and ten fresh apples. All necessities.

Mr. Stokes eased a lock of hair over the bald spot near his temple. "I'm sorry, Miss Channing, but I cannot extend your credit any further until you make a payment." The look in his eyes spoke of genuine sorrow. "With the blockade, the store isn't doing well, and I can't provide for my young ones on credit."

Cassandra closed her eyes for a moment. Just a moment to gather her thoughts and her resolve.

Someone behind her shouted, "If you can't pay, step aside, miss. I don't have all day."

Ignoring him, Cassandra opened her eyes and leaned forward. "Please, Mr. Stokes. Just one more time. I'm expecting a huge return soon on an investment."

Mr. Anderson, one of the dock workers, sidled up beside her. "If you're waitin' for Luke Heaton t' come back wit' your money, you'll be waitin' a long time." He grinned, revealing a single gold-capped tooth. "Why, I'd gamble all my earnings that he took off wit' your money and is right now, piratin' in the Caribbean."

Chuckles shot through the room and pierced her heart with as much

725

pain as if they'd been real darts. Nevertheless, Cassandra straightened her shoulders and faced the man. "Yet word about town is that you're not too good at gambling, Mr. Anderson, so I don't believe I'll take you up on that bet."

Save for a single chortle sounding from the back of the crowd, the room grew silent. A woman in the corner who'd been choosing apples from a bin drew her two children to her skirts.

Mr. Anderson frowned and fumbled with his hat, spearing Cassandra with seething eyes, before he glanced over the crowd and lumbered out the door. Facing Mr. Stokes, Cassandra gave him one last pleading look, but he crossed his arms over his work apron and shook his head.

"Thank you for your time," she mumbled and turned to make her way to the door, avoiding the pitiful gazes that followed her outside. Bursting onto the muddy street, she fought back the burning behind her eyes and lifted her chin to the warm rays of the sun making its descent in the western sky. June's hot, muggy air swamped around her, bringing with it the scent of fish and salt from the bay, luring her to the docks. A group of militiamen dressed in white trousers and dark-blue jackets marched by. The sergeant at their head smiled at her, tipping his hat.

She returned his smile, but her thoughts were on Mr. Heaton. She prayed he hadn't absconded with her money as the man in the store had said.

She pictured him sitting in a tavern somewhere in Barbados, a voluptuous wench on his lap, gambling with the gold doubloons he'd acquired as a pirate. Laughing, as he lifted his glass of rum toward her in a mock toast.

Grinding her teeth together, Cassandra marched onto the street. A horse neighed. She looked up to see the snorting nostrils of the beast just as the rider jerked the reins to avoid her.

"Look out where you're going, miss," the gentleman scolded her as he tried to settle the animal.

"My apologies." Cassandra swung around and nearly bumped into a couple crossing the road. The fashionable lady draped on the gentleman's arm scowled at her.

"Forgive me." Cassandra shook her head, trying to scatter thoughts of Mr. Heaton as she continued to the other side. The bare masts of ships swayed above the roofs of warehouses and taverns like wagging fingers, chastising her for her stupidity, yet luring her toward them nonetheless.

Before long, she found herself standing at the edge of the wharf where *Destiny* had been docked. Of course, there was another ship there now—one of those infamous Baltimore clippers, known for their swift speed.

A bell rang in the distance. A group of fisherman passed, tipping their hats in her direction and leaving the sharp smell of fish in their wake. Sailors working on a ship tied at the next dock stopped to stare at her.

Ignoring them, she closed her eyes.

A warm breeze sent her curls dancing over her neck, tickling her skin. She pictured Mr. Heaton standing tall and confident on the wharf, broad shoulders stretched beneath his shirt, black hair blowing in the breeze. She could still hear his deep voice that reminded her of the soothing sound of a cello. Had she been fooled by his charm like so many others? Had she made a mistake that would cast her and her family onto the streets?

She drew a deep breath of the brackish air. *What am I to do?* Her family couldn't survive much longer on vegetables from the garden and fish Mr. Dayle managed to catch in the bay. And her poor sisters with only tattered clothes to wear. A sob caught in her throat, and she thought of praying. But when had that ever done her any good? After all the prayers and pleading to God to bring her father and brothers home, still they were gone. Her father forever.

She had never felt so alone.

"Miss Channing." The calm voice snapped her eyes open, and she turned to see Reverend Drummond beside her. "I didn't wish to startle you." He smiled and gazed at her with such kindness, Cassandra nearly released the tears pooling in her eyes. Instead, she turned and brushed them away.

"You didn't, Reverend. I was just. . ."

"Praying?"

She shook her head and gazed down at the reticule in her gloved hands. "No."

"Honesty. Very refreshing, Miss Channing, but then I can always count on you for that."

She smiled at him.

He glanced over the multitudes of ships swaying in the bay. "Waiting for someone?"

"No. . . Yes. I await the arrival of the privateer I invested in." A cannon blast thundered from Fort McHenry. Cassandra squinted at the sunlight glinting off the water, searching for an incoming ship. But no sails appeared. No doubt they were only testing the guns.

"Ah yes. Mr. Heaton's ship, *Destiny*." Reverend Drummond gave her an odd look.

Cassandra flinched. "How did you know?"

He chuckled and scratched his gray beard. "There's not much that goes on in this town that doesn't end up being broadcast in the taverns where I minister each night."

Cassandra nodded. "It's been two months. Shouldn't Mr. Heaton be back by now?"

"Not necessarily, Miss Channing. You cannot predict where and when he'll come across a British merchantman." He proffered his arm. "Can I walk you home? It isn't safe for you to be here alone."

Laughter spewed from a tavern down the street, confirming his words. She slid her arm into his. "Perhaps you're right, Reverend."

They strolled down Pratt Street in silence, reminding Cassandra of the times she and her father had walked around town, arm in arm. Happier days, when she had felt loved and secure.

After a while they chatted of Rose, Cassandra's friend and Reverend Drummond's niece, who rarely left their farm at the edge of town. They chatted of the blockade, the British raids on the countryside, battle news from Canada, and the reverend's charity hospital.

Finally, they stopped before Cassandra's house. A splash of maroon and tangerine set the western sky aglow with such peaceful artistry that it seemed as though war and death and struggle could never exist alongside such beauty.

As if reading her mind, Reverend Drummond said, "If you and your family need anything, Miss Channing, please come by the church. Part of my job is to help those in need."

She gazed down at the stain on his waistcoat and knew that though Rose had inherited some wealth from her father, the Drummonds gave most of their earnings away. His forehead folded into lines that were straight and true, just like the man standing before her. Truth be told, she *did* need supplies. Embarrassment heated her face at the thought of accepting charity. But no, they were not that desperate. Not yet.

"Thank you, Reverend, but I will find a way."

"There is no shame in accepting help, lass. God provides in many ways."

A hot wind stirred her mother's garden full of mayflowers, honeysuckles, and roses, wafting their sweet scent over Cassandra. "I have yet to see evidence of that."

"Because you do not believe."

"How can I believe when, despite my prayers, everything has been torn from me?"

"Does that mean that God is not with you?"

Cassandra gazed at him, confused. "What else could it mean?"

"Hmm." Wisdom and genuine concern burned in his eyes.

Cassandra tightened her grip on her reticule and gazed at the house across the street. Through the brightly lit window she caught a glimpse of Mr. Simpson hoisting his young son into the air. Father, family, love, all the things she used to possess. "God has abandoned me just like my father and my brothers. Now, it is up to me to care for my family."

Reverend Drummond laid a hand on her arm. "God never abandons His children, lass. It is we who so often abandon Him."

Cassandra gave a tight smile, tired of the man's empty platitudes. "Thank you for walking me home, Reverend." She turned to leave. "Give my best to Rose."

"I will, lass, and I'll be praying for you."

Cassandra shut the door on the reverend's statement. She didn't want to hear it. Didn't want any prayers lifted on her account. For she didn't want to give God another chance to ignore her.

"Cassandra!" Her mother's shrill voice filled the foyer before her visage appeared around the corner, clutching her gown.

Normally unaffected by her mother's histrionics, Cassandra tightened at the look of terror firing from her eyes. "What is it, Mother?"

"It's Hannah, dear. She's fallen terribly ill with a fever."

❖ CHAPTER 11 ❖

Luke coughed. His lungs filled with smoke. He couldn't breathe. He leapt from his bed. Brilliant ribbons of red and orange fluttered beneath his chamber door. A gray mist slid in through the crack like an unwelcome specter. Jumping into his trousers, he darted for the handle. Pain seared his hand. He leapt back as the stench of burning flesh turned his stomach. Someone screamed. Bracing for the pain, he grabbed the handle again and flung open the door. Flames sprang for him, crackling and chortling. Heat scorched his bare chest.

"Mother! Father!" he yelled, darting into the inferno. Hot coals branded his feet. Pain sizzled up his legs.

"Luke!" He heard his name in the distance. Perhaps they were already outside. Black smoke smothered him. Gasping for air, he dropped to his knees. He crawled into the front parlor, peering into the room. No sign of anyone. Someone bumped into him from behind. He spun about to see the lacy hem of his mother's nightdress.

Jumping to his feet, Luke batted away the smoke and saw her face twisted in horror. She coughed and thrust a white bundle into his arms. "Take John."

She kissed the top of John's head and gripped Luke's arm, a mixture of sorrow and terror etched across her face. "Take care of him, Luke. Promise me." Streaks of gray soot streamed from her eyes. Then she disappeared into the smoke.

"Mother!" Gripping John, Luke barreled over, coughing.

"Your father!" His mother's raspy voice echoed back over him.

Turning, Luke held his breath and rushed toward the front of the house. John began to wail. Shifting him to one arm, Luke darted through a hole in the flames, shouldered the front door, and barreled outside. A blast of crisp night air slapped him and swept the smoke from his face. He tumbled down the porch stairs and onto the dirt. Gasping, he turned to face the house. John's whimpers faded. Poking his head from within the white folds, the child stared, mesmerized by the insidious ballet of yellow and red lights dancing over their small cabin. The fire burst through one of the front windows with a mighty roar, sending a spray of glass over the porch.

Movement caught Luke's gaze, and he turned to see the lithe dark figure of an Indian standing at the edge of the clearing. The native raised his spear in the air and released a war cry that sent chills down Luke. Then he faded into the shadows of the forest.

"Mother! Father!" Luke started for the burning home, but a wall of heat halted him.

John began to cry. Pressing the child tightly to his chest, Luke put his head down and dashed for the house again. He must save his parents.

He would not allow them to burn to death!

Luke jerked upright in bed and struck his head on the bulkhead. Pain shot through his neck. Pressing a hand to the ache, he gasped for air. Sweat dripped off his chin onto his coverlet. The familiar creak and groan of the ship filled his ears.

A nightmare. Just another nightmare.

An odd glow penetrated his closed eyelids even as warmth spread over him. Prying his eyes open, he peered toward the source. The bright figure of a man stood by his cabin door. His entire countenance blazed, yet he did not burn. Luke's heart crashed against his chest. Was he still dreaming? The man's clothing seemed to ripple with life like an ocean of liquid silver under a heavy wind. Luke squinted and held up a hand to block the light, but he couldn't make out the man's face, only the trace of a lingering smile on his lips.

There was something familiar about him.

Luke opened his mouth to ask the man who he was when the vision slowly faded and disappeared. An odd pain throbbed in Luke's right earlobe.

Pound. Pound. Pound. "Cap'n!" The door burst open and Biron dashed inside. "Cap'n."

Luke shifted his gaze from Biron to the place where the luminous man had stood. "Did you see him?"

"See who, Cap'n?" Biron glanced over the cabin.

"Nothing." Luke rubbed his eyes. "I'm just seeing things."

"Well, we aren't seeing things on deck. We spotted what looks to be a merchantman." Biron's eyes flashed. "And she's flying the Union Jack."

Moments later, while shaking the fog of sleep from his head, Luke leapt onto the main deck, marched to the railing, and lifted the scope to his eye. White sails floated like puffs of cotton against the orange glow of dawn. Shifting the glass, he focused it on the ensign flying at her gaff. The red crisscross against a blue background of the Union Jack formed in his vision. He scanned what he could see of the hull. No gun ports, but two brass guns lining her railing on the port side gleamed in the rising sun. From the size of her, she appeared to be a brig. A merchant brig. And she was running fast before the wind.

He lowered the scope. "Make all sail, Biron!" he shouted, turning to seek out his first mate and nearly knocking him over in the process. Biron's aged face crinkled in excited anticipation.

Luke winked. "And clear for action."

Swerving about, Biron bellowed across the deck, "You heard the captain. Make all sail, gentlemen! Up topsails and stays. Clear the deck!"

With an excited gleam in his eye, Mr. Keene, who was standing amidships, piped the crew to quarters. Men swarmed over the ship, some leaping into the shrouds and scrambling aloft to set sail, others clearing away barrels and ropes and anything that wasn't bolted down, while the rest dropped belowdecks.

Destiny rose and plunged over a wave, sending sparkling foam over her bow as her decks buzzed with excitement. Shaking the hair from his face, Luke drew a deep breath, gathering his courage and wit—he'd need every bit to succeed.

Mr. Ward emerged from the companionway and headed straight for Luke, his tiny eyes aglow like the bundle of burning wicks in his hands.

Luke restrained a laugh at the man's enthusiasm. "Ready the larboard guns, if you please, Mr. Ward."

The gunner cracked a smile before turning to shout orders down the hatches. Soon men emerged from the waist hatch carrying round shot, powder bags, langrage, and grape from the magazine. Other sailors grabbed muskets and pikes from the arms chest and ran up the shrouds to take their places at the tops.

Luke gazed aloft. Loosened topsails thundered and flapped hungrily, seeking their airy breakfast as the crew hauled upon the halyards. Suddenly the canvas gave a hearty snap as its belly gorged with wind. *Destiny* sped forward, cresting a massive wave. Balancing his boots on the heaving deck, Luke swung about as sea spray slapped his face. He shook it off and ran a hand through his hair.

Nigh a mile before them and under a full press of sail, the merchant-man fled for her life. Ribbons of foam shot from her stern. Yet *Destiny* gained on her. Luke leapt onto the quarterdeck and nodded toward young Sam. The boy's hands gripped the wheel, his eyes alight with excitement. "Steady as she goes, Sam. Keep us positioned off her larboard quarter."

"Aye, aye, Cap'n."

The wind roared in Luke's ears and tore at the loose strands of his hair. He shoved them into his tie and fisted his hands at his waist. Scanning the deck, he watched as Mr. Ward's men hovered over the guns, loading and priming them while the gunner stood ready with his handful of slow-burning wicks. Above him, the men in the tops, those who weren't trimming sail, held their muskets at the ready should they move in close enough to spray the enemy deck with deadly shot.

Luke shifted his gaze to the brig. She sat low in the water, which meant her hold was full of cargo. Wealth for him and Miss Channing. He had to do this. He could not fail. Wind whipped past him bringing with it familiar taunting voices.

You couldn't even save your parents. How can you win a sea battle?

Shaking them off, Luke swallowed down a burst of dread and clenched his fists. *God, help me,* he breathed more out of impulse than as an actual prayer, but like every request he'd made of God, his words were quickly swept away in the wind.

After two hours of running hard before the wind, *Destiny* came within range of the merchantman. Dark clouds bunched on the horizon, stirring the sea like a witch's cauldron. The sting of rain spiced the hot wind spinning around them. The change in weather did nothing to ease Luke's fears. "Bring in the studding and topsails," he ordered Biron. No sooner did the first mate repeat the orders than a yellow flash followed by a puff of gray smoke shot from the brig's stern. A second later, a thunderous boom cracked the sky.

"Hit the deck!" Mr. Keene yelled. The crew halted and stooped, arms braced over their heads.

The shot splashed impotently off their starboard bow.

Luke gripped the railing. "Bring us athwart her stern, Sam!"

"Aye, aye, Cap'n."

Stomping across the main deck, Biron spouted orders that sent the men aloft to trim the sails to the wind.

"Aim for his rigging, Mr. Ward," Luke shouted.

"Aye." With a crazed look in his sharp eyes, and his hair flailing about in the wind, the gunner looked like the ghost of some ancient sea battle.

The ship tacked to starboard. Sails thundered above. Luke spread his boots on the heaving deck and took up a position behind the guns. He squinted as the sun glinted off the polished brass. Biron came up alongside him, dabbing his neckerchief across his forehead.

As *Destiny* came around, bringing her larboard guns to bear, the stern of the brig rose from the sea like a barnacle-encrusted whale. Crewmen scurried around a stern chaser perched on her railing. But they would be too late. Luke hoped. Though he couldn't be sure. For one well-placed shot could damage his rigging beyond repair. A blast of hot wind struck him even as the low rumble of thunder laughed at him from the horizon.

"On my command, Mr. Ward."

The gunner distributed the burning punks to the men at each gun.

Destiny leveled out keel to stern as she glided past the brig.

"Fire!" Luke yelled.

Smoldering sticks flew to touch holes atop the guns. Four deafening roars shook the ship from stem to stern, flinging a broadside of grape and langrage at the merchantman. A wall of gray smoke crashed over Luke, stinging his eyes and stealing the air from his lungs. Coughing, he spun about, cupped his hands, and shouted aloft, "Unfurl tops!" Then charging onto the quarterdeck, he turned to Sam. "Hard to starboard, Sam."

"Hard to starboard, Cap'n," the boy repeated and the ship jerked, the deck canted, and Luke clutched the quarter rail to keep from falling. White foam hungrily licked the starboard railing. The blocks creaked and groaned from the strain.

Another ominous *boom!* sounded behind them. Luke turned to gaze at the enemy. A spiral of smoke drifted from her stern. The shot struck a rising wave twenty feet off their larboard quarter. Luke's crew cheered.

Raising the scope, Luke studied the brig. Sailors raced frantically across her deck. Her main topmast was shot away. Rigging and sails cluttered the deck below.

"Bring her about, Sam." Luke lowered the glass. "Let's give the British another taste of American hospitality."

Sam's eyes sparkled. "Aye, Cap'n."

Several minutes passed as *Destiny* maneuvered for another round. The ship creaked and complained like an old woman, yet she held tight beneath a full set of sail. Pacing the main deck, Luke gazed at the men in the tops adjusting canvas then down at Mr. Ward's gun crew as they prepared the starboard guns and elevated the quoins beneath the gun breeches to aim once again for the brig's rigging.

The eyes of every crewman shot to Luke, awaiting his next command. This time, not a trace of doubt could be seen within them. *You always fail.* The insidious voice clawed over Luke's soul, tugging on his newfound confidence.

No. Drawing in a deep breath of air tainted with gunpowder, Luke lengthened his stance. No. Not this time.

Destiny swooped athwart the brig's stern once again. Only this time, the enemy was ready. Luke could make out her crew lighting the touchholes of two stern chasers.

"Fire!" Luke bellowed just as two yellow flashes speared out from the brig.

Boom boom boom boom! Destiny's four carronades belched black madness, sending wave after wave of thick smoke back over the deck. The timbers trembled beneath Luke's boots. Coughing, he shouted orders to veer to larboard. The direful swoosh of shot sped past his ears, parting the haze and striking wood with an ominous crunch. More shots screeched past him like hail. The sound of canvas ripping filled the air. A scream of agony. Luke's heart clenched. Fear crowded in his throat.

When the smoke cleared, he marched to the railing and glanced over the main deck. He spotted Biron.

"Damage report."

White eyes, stark against a black-sooted face, stared up at him. "A few tears in the sails and rigging, sir, and the aft bulwark is crushed. Mr. Rockland's arm was nicked. Nothing else of note."

Luke nodded, relieved, then raised his scope and found men dashing over the enemy brig in a state of frenzy. Their entire main mast had cracked and fallen in a tangle of sailcloth cordage and shattered spars, spreading over their deck like a giant spiderweb of confusion.

Luke snapped the hair from his face and smiled. "Bring her about, Sam! Stations for the stays!"

Luke had her. One more broadside and the British merchantman would be his.

Destiny hauled on the wind as the brig began firing once again—the Englishmen shooting wildly and hitting nothing but sea. Which meant they were desperate and frightened. Good. Luke marched across the deck as the ship flew through the heavy seas, plunging into the rollers and shooting spray into the air in brilliant showers. Soon they came within fifty yards alongside the brig.

Mr. Ward's brows raised in anticipation.

"Hold on. Steady now," Luke said.

Mr. Keene crossed his arms over his embroidered waistcoat, a smile of victory on his face.

"But they're preparing to fire on us, Cap'n," Mr. Ward said.

Luke's glance took in the men aboard the brig, frantically buzzing around their guns. But Luke was a gambling man. And he gambled that in their haste, the brig's gun crew wouldn't hit their target. The seas had grown rough and their shot must be timed perfectly with the roll of the waves. They would waste it, and then Luke would have them.

He hoped.

He rubbed the sweat from his scarred palm and gripped the railing.

The thunderous growl of the brig's three guns sliced the darkening sky. But the shots sped overhead and landed in the churning waves off *Destiny's* larboard side.

"Fire!" Luke yelled and the carronades roared, pummeling the brig with yet another broadside of grape shot.

Smoke once again clouded Luke's vision, but distant screams of agony accompanied by the crack and snap of wood told him their shots had hit their mark. When the haze cleared, he smiled at the sight of the Union Jack being lowered in surrender.

The air returned to his lungs. Wiping the sweat from the back of his neck, he felt the tension slip from his body. He had won his first battle. If there was a God, Luke would thank Him for the victory.

If there was a God.

A cheer rose from his crew as all eyes shot to him. "Let's hear it for Captain Heaton!"

"Hip hip hurray. Hip hip hurray!"

Though his insides swelled at their approval, Luke raised his fist in the air. "For America!"

"For America!" they shouted in unison.

"Put the helm down and bring us alongside her, Sam," Luke ordered.

Biron slapped Luke on the back. "That's some fine sailing, Luke. Your first prize."

Luke stared at the brig as she lowered her sails. "I hope there'll be many more."

❖

Luke gazed out the stern windows in his cabin, rising and falling over the moonlit horizon. The *tap tap* of rain struck the glass and slid down in chaotic streams. Though the rough seas had not abated, he and his crew had still managed to board the brig, assess her damage, round up her crew, and inventory the cargo.

Mr. Sanders cleared his throat, and Luke spun around.

The purser adjusted his spectacles and read from a parchment in his hand. "Glass, white lead, coffee, flour, sugar, silk, Holland duck, burgundy wine, and rum, Cap'n." Greed sparkled in the man's oversized blue eyes.

"That should bring us a fair price." Biron commented from his seat in the velvet-upholstered chair. "Not to mention selling the brig itself."

"Aye." Mr. Keene rubbed his jeweled fingers together. "I'm beginning to like this privateering."

"Me too!" Sam punched the air. "You sure took it to those Brits, Cap'n. I never seen anything like it." Admiration beamed in his eyes.

Biron passed a stern look over the three men standing in a line before the captain's desk. "We aren't in this trade just for the money, gentlemen. Our country is at war. And each British merchantman we capture means less money in our enemy's coffers."

Thunder rumbled in the distance as the ship pitched over a wave, swinging the lantern hanging on the deck head and casting shifting shadows over the cabin.

Luke nodded and circled his desk. "I quite agree." Though he needed the money—needed it desperately—he hated the British tyrants even more. "We must do our part to frustrate the plans of the enemy or one day we will wake up and find our liberties stolen from us."

Mr. Sanders continued staring at the list, clearly unmoved by the patriotic speech. "Would you like me to add up the value of the cargo and conjecture on what we can expect to receive?"

"If you wish, Mr. Sanders." Luke leaned back against his desk and crossed his booted feet at the ankle.

The slight man pursed his thin lips. "We may not get what we hoped. The government takes a huge share in custom duties, I'm afraid." He looked up and tugged on his cravat. "Perhaps we should appoint one of the men as prize master and send him and the ship to port while we capture another one."

"Thank you, Mr. Sanders," Luke said. "You are dismissed."

With a scowl, the purser scurried from the cabin.

Mr. Keene cocked his head toward the door. "The man makes a good case, Cap'n. Why not continue the hunt while your luck is high?"

"Not luck, providence, Mr. Keene," Biron interjected in his usual confident tone.

Ignoring him, Luke sighed. "Because I have matters to attend to at home first."

Sam's face twisted into a pout, and Luke raised a hand to silence him. "I promise we will set out again within the month."

"What matters could be more important than money?" Mr. Keene cocked a smile that made him seem more callow than one would expect of a man over forty. "Ah, I know." He pointed a finger toward Luke, flinging his soot-stained sleeve through the air. "A woman?"

Luke flattened his lips. "None of—"

"If it is a woman," Mr. Keene interrupted, "my dear captain, might I remind you that the more money you have, the more women you can attract."

Sam chuckled at the man's display, but Luke studied Mr. Keene as an uncomfortable feeling of familiarity swamped him. "It depends on what type of women you wish to attract." Luke said the words before he even knew from what cultivated corner of his conscience they had hailed, for he certainly had never been meticulous about the sort of female companionship he had kept before.

Biron smiled his approval.

Luke cleared his throat. "Mr. Keene, will you do me the honor of taking command of the British merchantman?"

Mr. Keene's dark eyes flickered. "Of course, Cap'n."

Sam fidgeted in his spot as if he could hardly stand still. Though Luke knew what the boy wanted, he hesitated to send him along with Keene. The man's company could only besmirch Sam's innocence. But Luke couldn't keep the two apart forever. "Sam, you may go with him as his second in command."

"Thank you, Cap'n." The lad grinned. Mr. Keene grabbed him by the neck and fisted a hand playfully over his hair the way Luke often did with John.

A longing to see his brother filled Luke's soul until it ached. A mist covered his eyes, and he turned to gaze at the charts spread across his desk. "Biron, as soon as we are done here, divide the prisoners between the two ships and lock them up below."

Sam's laughter faded. "Where are we heading, Cap'n?"

"We'll sail for Wilmington first thing in the morning and sell the ship and cargo there." Luke faced forward again.

"And then?" Mr. Keene shifted his stance. "The crew is asking."

"We'll find a place to anchor safely. I'll assign a few men to stay with the ship and the rest are free to head over land to Baltimore. Unless the men prefer to stay in Wilmington until I return. It's up to them."

Keene's eyebrows leapt. "To spend our shares on women and wine."

Samuel grinned and threw his shoulders back. "Aye." His voice came out deeper than normal.

Mr. Keene chuckled. "You're too young for such pleasures, boy."

"No, I'm not." Sam shot a glance at Luke. "Am I, Luke? You took up drinking and gambling at my age, didn't you? I heard you tellin' Biron."

Luke shifted uncomfortably on the edge of his desk. Suddenly his vile habits didn't seem so appealing. In fact, they sickened him. Concern rose within him for this young, impressionable lad. Associating with crude sailors would do nothing to produce the qualities esteemed in a true gentleman. And for some reason Luke wanted more for the boy. In truth, he suddenly wanted more for himself.

"Mr. Keene is right, Sam. You'll go home and visit your mother and father. I'm sure they are anxious to hear how you are faring." No, he would not have Sam fritter away his time and money drinking and womanizing, ending up an empty-handed failure in ten years.

Just like Luke.

Sam frowned and scuffed his shoe over the deck. "Yes, sir."

Mr. Keene grabbed the boy by the arm, winked at Luke, and headed out the door.

After they left, Biron opened his mouth to say something when a knock on the door sounded. A sailor entered, bottle of rum in hand.

"Mr. Sanders's compliments, sir. He sent over a crate of rum from the brig." The sailor set the bottle on Luke's desk.

At the sight of the amber liquid, Luke's throat became a desert. "Thank you, Mr. Willis. That will be all," he managed to squeak out.

With a nod, the sailor left and closed the door behind him.

Luke rubbed his stubbled jaw. The rum teetered in the bottle like liquid gold with each movement of the ship. He hadn't had a sip in over two months. During the first week, he'd trembled so badly, he'd thought his brain would shake loose. Didn't he deserve a drink after winning the battle today? After all he'd endured?

Biron quirked a brow. "You promised her."

Luke nodded.

Thunder growled outside the windows. Wind whipped pellets of rain against the glass as if God, aware of his weakening resolve, was warning him to stay away from the tempting liquid.

Or perhaps it was just a portent of coming doom. For the mantle of success that lay temporarily across Luke's shoulders was sure to slip off soon enough.

❖ CHAPTER 12 ❖

Cassandra laid the back of her hand over Hannah's forehead. Heat radiated from the child. Still feverish. Hannah moaned, and Cassandra wrung out a cloth in the basin and dabbed it over the little girl's face and neck before laying it atop her forehead again. Streams of bright sunlight rippled over the bed in defiance of the sickness within, highlighting Hannah's damp red curls as they formed delicate patterns across her neck. The little girl turned her head on the pillow and let out a ragged sigh.

Dexter, lying across the bed at Hannah's feet—where he'd remained since she'd taken ill—lifted his head at the sound but then laid it back down on outstretched paws with a moan.

The tap of Cassandra's mother's slippers as she paced at the foot of the bed joined Hannah's mumbles and Margaret's whispered prayers in a grim melody that only further darkened Cassandra's spirits.

"Oh, what are we to do?" her mother said.

Cassandra turned in her chair to see her mother wringing her hands then spinning about to cross the room again. Fair curls, which were usually strung tight around her face, hung loose over her cheeks. Her blue eyes skittered to and fro from within a pale, droopy face, and though it was nearly midday, she still wore her nightdress and robe.

Cassandra approached her, touching her arm, halting her in her worrisome trek. "She will be all right, Mother. Don't vex yourself so."

Margaret stopped her prayers and looked up from where she knelt on the other side of the bed as if expecting Cassandra to share some profound revelation.

But Cassandra had none. In truth, she didn't know whether Hannah would survive. It had been three weeks since she'd taken ill, and although she had seemed to be recovering the past few days, last night after the medicine ran out, the poor girl had taken a turn for the worse.

Her mother's lip quivered. "How do you know that?" Tears glistened in her eyes. "I have lost my husband and most likely both my sons. I cannot lose my daughter."

Margaret gazed lovingly at Hannah then bowed her head again over her open Bible.

No! Cassandra stomped her foot. There would be no further tragedy in this house. Not if Cassandra had anything to do about it.

She took hold of her mother's shoulders. "You won't lose her, Mother. Hannah is strong. She will recover."

"But Dr. Wilson said there was nothing he could do. She needs the medicines." A tear spilled from her mother's eye. She batted it away. "And we can't afford any more."

Drawing her mother close, Cassandra wrapped her arms around her. The scent of jasmine swept the foul odor of illness from Cassandra's nose—if only for a moment—as her mind spun, seeking an answer. But there was none. She had run out of money weeks ago.

Margaret raised her head. Her misty eyes found Cassandra's and they exchanged a sympathetic glance, making Cassandra wonder how her maid fared reliving a tragedy that must be so fresh to her heart.

"The silverware." Cassandra stepped back from her mother.

The elderly woman wiped her swollen face. "What do you mean, dear?"

"We still have that silver serving set, do we not?"

"No, we sold that last month." Her mother frowned.

"Oh, bother." Cassandra bit her nail and took up her mother's pace. "What of the china oil lamps?"

"Gone."

"The painted plates from France?"

Her mother shook her head.

"All of it?" Cassandra knew her mother had sold some household items last week in order to buy the medicine and some additional food, but she hadn't realized just how much they'd lost.

Hannah groaned and Margaret eased a lock of her hair from her face. Her mother sniffed. "Yes. Everything of value."

Cassandra rubbed her temples. Something tickled her neck. Earrings. Unhooking them, she held them out. "I have these."

Her mother's eyes widened. "And I have my pearl ones. They are all I have left."

"Run up and get them for me, Mother, will you? And any other jewelry you can find."

With a nod, her mother sped out the door, her robe fluttering behind her.

Cassandra knelt by the bed and took Hannah's hand in hers. Placing a kiss on the heated flesh, she glanced at Margaret. "I know this must be hard for you."

Her lady's maid swallowed and lowered her chin. "My sweet baby Grace is in heaven now. A far better place." Though her voice trembled, the conviction within it bespoke of firm belief.

"How did you ever recover?"

"With God's help, one day at a time." Margaret smiled.

Cassandra gazed at Hannah, her ashen skin covered with red blotches, her damp hair clinging to her forehead, her hand limp within Cassandra's. "I would never forgive God if He took Hannah."

Margaret reached over and touched her arm. "Yes, you would. You would come to realize, as I have, that God is good and loving and whatever happens is for our best."

How could a child's death be good for anyone? Cassandra swallowed down her anger. "I'm not like you, Margaret. I don't believe whatever some reverend tells me. I want to find things out for myself. And the more I look for God, the further away He seems."

Margaret closed her Bible and ran her hands over the leather as if the book were the most precious thing in the world. Sunlight rippled over the leather binding, making it glow. "Perhaps you're the one pushing Him away."

Cassandra swallowed. Hadn't Reverend Drummond just said the same thing? Standing, Cassandra waved the thought away. "It doesn't matter!" She exhaled a long breath, noting the worry in Margaret's gaze. "Can you sit with her while I'm gone?"

A putrid smell wafted in through the door. Margaret wrinkled her nose. "What is that?"

Cassandra gave her a wry smile. "I asked Miss Thain to make some soup for Hannah."

"When she gets well enough to partake of some, we'll have to pray it doesn't make her ill again." Margaret's eyes sparkled playfully. "How long will you be?"

"As long as it takes to sell our earrings and get the medicines from the apothecary."

A loud crash sounded from below.

Closing her eyes, Cassandra gathered her resolve. What else could go wrong today? Before she made it to the door, footfalls sounded on the stairs, and Mr. Dayle's harried figure filled the frame. He glanced from his wife to Cassandra, his features twisted in fear.

Cassandra's throat went dry. "What is it, Mr. Dayle?"

"It's Miss Darlene."

Cassandra fisted her hands at her waist. "What did she break now?"

"No." He shook his head, catching his breath. "That was but my clumsiness. I knocked over a vase in my haste."

Cassandra's heart took up a rapid pace. "Then what is it about my sister?"

"Miss Darlene has gone missing."

❖

Luke tossed the stable owner a small pouch of coins and turned to watch the few of his crew who had traveled with them to Baltimore splintering toward the taverns that lined the street. Young Samuel slipped in between two sailors turning left.

"Sam!" Luke called.

The boy halted and turned.

"Isn't your home in the other direction?" Luke jerked a thumb toward his right and raised his brows.

"Ah yes, you're right, Cap'n. My mistake." Sam smiled then turned and darted down the avenue, his chortle bouncing on the wind.

Mr. Keene appeared beside Luke. "You should let the boy do what he wants."

On Luke's other side, Biron scratched his whiskers and stared at Luke as if waiting to see how he would answer.

"He's a good boy." Luke crossed his arms over his chest. "Smart, skilled, and disciplined. He's started on a good path in life, why send him down a wrong one?"

Mr. Keene huffed. "There's nothing wrong with a man enjoying himself after working hard." Then settling his red-plumed hat atop his head, he winked and sauntered away.

Biron tugged at his neckerchief and gestured toward Mr. Keene. "I'd watch out for that one, Captain. He's all charm on the outside but he's got a temper as fierce as any I've seen."

Luke noted the man's arrogant swagger before he disappeared into the crowd. Remorse sank like a brick in his belly. "Reminds you of someone, doesn't he?"

Biron snorted. "I'll admit, he's like you in many ways. Yet, not in others. There's something sinister in his eyes." Biron poked Luke in the chest. "You've got a good heart in there. You just don't know it yet."

"The only thing that keeps my heart the slightest bit good is John." Luke raked a hand through his hair. He gazed over the ships bobbing in the harbor. Nearly the same group of ships that had been there when he'd left nearly three months ago—still landlocked by the British. But one thing had changed. The weather. Though the sun was setting, June's muggy heat refused to release her hold on the city. Luke stretched his neck to a slight breeze flowing in from the bay, but it was barely enough to cool his skin. The smell of horseflesh, fish, and a hint of honeysuckle drifted past his nose. Baltimore. He was home.

"I'm proud of you for keeping your promise to abstain from rum," Biron said.

"I may be a gambler, cheat, and drunken sot, but I'm no liar." Luke grinned but Biron's face remained stoic as he gazed down the street where carriages, horses, and people on foot headed home for the evening.

Luke studied his first mate and saw the dread in his face, the prospect of going home to an empty house. He knew the man's wife had died in childbirth some years ago. "If you'd like to come home with me, I'm sure my housekeeper has a savory dinner prepared."

"No, you go on." He leaned toward Luke. "I think I'll go join the crew and keep them out of trouble."

"A tall order for just one man," Luke called after him with a laugh, resisting the urge to follow his men to the rum he could now smell on the wind.

Biron turned and pointed to the sky. "I have all the help I need."

Lud, God again. Luke started down the street, wincing at the pain spreading down his legs from the long horse ride. He skirted a group of ladies and tipped his hat in their direction, barely noticing them. Their flirtatious giggles brought his gaze around to see them smiling over their shoulders at him. Facing forward, he kept moving. When had he stopped flirting with every lady he saw?

A vision of a petite lady with burgundy hair and emerald eyes filled his mind. His spirits lifted knowing he'd see her soon. He couldn't wait to give her her share of the prize money. And watch the mistrust blossom into appreciation on her face. He had more than proven himself to her—and to himself and his crew. Perhaps his success would engender her trust and, dare he hope, a hint of affection? He shook his head, hoping to dislodge such fanciful notions. Miss Channing deserved a far better man than he would ever be.

Darting between two carriages, he crossed the street and stepped onto the cobblestone walkway. The setting sun spread its golden feathers over the treetops in a final farewell for the day. He had hoped to see Miss Channing tonight, but it would be inappropriate to call on her so late without an invitation.

Besides, a stench he could not describe emanated from his clothes. He needed to wash and don fresh attire before he saw her. And he longed to see John and Mrs. Barnes and tell them of his success.

Success. Luke shifted his shoulders beneath the odd-fitting cloak. Had he truly found something he was good at? A way to redeem his name and help his country?

Even as he mulled over the new sensation, two ladies approached him, children in tow. As soon as they spotted him, they drew their children into their skirts and scurried across the street, as if he would snatch their little girls and turn them into tavern wenches on the spot.

Luke frowned. His mantle of success slipped off one shoulder. Maybe it would never fit at all. Turning, he headed toward his favorite tavern, his lips suddenly parched. It wouldn't hurt to have one small drink before he headed home. His promise to Miss Channing rose to scold him as it had so many times aboard his ship. But he was on land now. Free to do as he pleased.

Entering the open-aired room, he was greeted by several patrons seated at tables or standing at the serving bar. "Hey, Heaton, where you been?"

"Busy," he replied as he headed for the bar. Grant, the owner, set down a glass of rum before Luke, anticipating his request. With a nod of thanks, Luke grabbed it, flipped a coin on the counter, and made his way to one of the open windows. Perching on the ledge, he propped up his boot and gazed outside, ignoring the calls to join various games. The chink of coins and slap of cards beckoned to him from a table in the corner, like the melody of a siren. The same men inhabited each table, each corner, drinking and playing the same games, night after night. Luke took another sip of rum. The pungent liquid warmed his throat and belly as familiar scents of spirits and sweat curled beneath his nose, making him wonder if he'd ever left Baltimore at all. Had he only dreamed of sailing away and capturing a prize? He shifted his back against the hard window frame and patted his waistcoat to ease his harried mind. The thick bulge of dollars reassured him that it had not been a dream. Nevertheless, they pleaded to be freed from his pocket. Yet. . .

He glanced at a circle of men playing a game of Gleek by the bar. He knew each one of them, and none were good at the game. Not like Luke. If the cards went his way, he could double his fortune and give Miss Channing twice her share.

No. He turned away. He could not risk it. He had worked too hard these past few months to risk it. With a sigh, he gazed out upon the street and sipped his rum as a breeze wafted over him, cooling his skin and stirring a loose strand of hair over his cheek.

Across the way, a man emerged from the alleyway beside a brick warehouse, dragging a young girl behind him.

"Let me go! Let me go!"

Luke could barely make out her scream above the fiddle music and the chatter of the men in the tavern.

The man stopped, shouted something at her, and then continued to drag her to a horse tied to a post at the edge of the street.

"Help!"

Perhaps just an unruly child and her father. Yet something pinched Luke's gut. He scanned the surroundings. Though people stared at the altercation, no one made a move to help.

Slamming the rum to the back of his throat, Luke cursed his obnoxious conscience, slid down the other side of the window onto the porch, and charged across the street. He grabbed the man's arm and spun him around. "What are you doing?"

The man, who was taller than Luke's six-foot-one frame, gazed at him as if he were not worthy of an answer. "Taking my daughter to her mama."

"I'm not your daughter!" Light hair the color of wheat tumbled over the girl's shoulders in disarray while green eyes fired his way. She tugged from the man's grasp and stumbled backward. "He's trying to steal me." Tears slid down her cheeks.

The man spat to the side. "Don't listen to her. She's misbehaving." He leaned down to grab the girl again. "Now be gone. This is no business of yours."

The girl kicked the man's shin. He moaned. Tightening his grip on her, he dragged her past Luke, pushing him aside.

Luke grimaced. "I'm making it my business." He drew his sword and pricked the man's back with the tip.

Halting, he slowly faced Luke, rage thundering across his face.

Leveling the blade at the ogre's chest, Luke gestured toward the girl. "Prove she's your daughter and I'll leave you be."

"I don't have to prove nothin' t' you." The man's narrowed eyes fired.

A crowd began to form around them. Men poked their heads out of the windows of the tavern. The music stopped.

The sun absconded with the remaining light, leaving them in shadows.

Luke pressed the tip of his cutlass into the man's chest. A speck of blood blossomed on his stained shirt. "Apparently you do."

"Very well. Have it your way." The ogre released the girl and shoved her aside. She tumbled to the ground in a flurry of lace. He raised his hands in surrender, but his eyes held no compliance. Then leaping backward, he reached inside his coat and pulled out a pistol.

Before he could cock and fire it, Luke barreled forward and knocked it from his hand with the hilt of his sword.

Yelping, the man grabbed his wrist. The shock on his face exploded into fury.

Out of nowhere a rock flew and struck the man's head. A trickle of blood spilled down his cheek. He scoured the surroundings with his maddening gaze, his fierce eyes locking upon the girl. He started for her, but Luke thrust his sword in between them, halting him.

Murmurs spread through the crowd. A man yelled, "Finish him off," from the tavern.

Finally, the ogre grunted, spit to the side, speared Luke with a look of fury, and then dashed away.

Luke turned to find the little girl holding another large rock—at least large for her tiny hands. She dropped it and ran to him, hugging his leg. "Thank you, mister."

Peeling her from his breeches, Luke knelt and examined her from head to toe. Aside from stains and tears in her gown, she appeared unharmed. "Are you all right?"

She nodded. Her lip trembled as if she was trying to keep from crying. The crowd dispersed behind them. The fiddle resumed its off-key ditty.

"What are you doing out here alone?" Luke asked.

"I was trying to find Dr. Wilson's house." She rubbed her eyes.

"By yourself?"

"Yes, my sister is very sick and Mother and Cassie aren't doing anything." She brought her lips into a pout. "I know I've been to his house before. But I got lost."

Something in her green eyes and the sassy tilt of her mouth struck a familiar chord. Luke stepped back to study her. "How long have you been wandering around the city alone?"

She shrugged. "I don't know. But my stomach's making lots of noise."

"Mine too." Luke chuckled. He'd grown tired of shipboard food after the first week and had been looking forward to Mrs. Barnes's cooking again. He glanced down the street, but the villain had disappeared. "Did you know that man?"

The girl shivered. "No. He grabbed me and told me he and his wife were moving far away to the frontier and they needed a daughter."

Luke hugged her. "It's all right now. Tell me where you live and I'll take you home. How does that sound?"

Wiping her eyes with the back of her hands, she nodded. Luke rose to his feet and took her by the hand. "My name is Luke. What is yours?"

"Darlene, Darlene Channing."

❖ CHAPTER 13 ❖

Cassandra dragged her feet up the stairs to her house, numbness overtaking them with each step. How had they lost her? Disappeared without a trace? It seemed impossible to even consider. Taking her arm, Mr. Dayle assisted her up the final step. "We'll look for her first thing in the morning, Miss Channing. Never fear. I'm sure she's somewhere safe."

But where? Halting on the porch, Cassandra turned and gazed over the fading colors of the flower garden, the dirt street before their house, and the city beyond. Buildings of all shapes and sizes wove a haphazard pattern down to the bay where ships rocked limp and useless in the dark waters. Night, like a shadowy bear, hovered over Baltimore, waiting to pounce.

Terror strangled Cassandra's heart. They'd searched all afternoon for Darlene, down every street, every alleyway, in every shop, inquired at all their friends' homes.

The girl had simply disappeared.

"Perhaps the night watchmen will find her." Mr. Dayle's voice lifted in his usual cheery optimism.

"Perhaps." Cassandra breathed a silent prayer that felt more like an inward groan. They had alerted the constable who had consequently alerted each watchman to be on the lookout for Darlene during their nightly shifts.

"To think she's out there alone and frightened." Cassandra wiped

750

away a tear. "I should be helping them search."

At first furious at Darlene for being such a troublesome chit, Cassandra had swept through the town like a storm, determined to punish the girl severely when she found her, Then, after the first hour of searching produced no sign of Darlene, fear had crept over Cassandra like a cold fog.

"You're far too exhausted, miss." Mr. Dayle turned her to face the house. "I'll move much faster without you."

"What am I to tell my mother? I cannot face her." Cassandra stepped toward the door, hesitating.

Mr. Dayle opened his mouth to respond when voices trickled out the parlor window on a shaft of flickering light. Her mother's voice. And a man's. Shaking her head, Cassandra gripped the door handle. She had left her mother nothing but a whimpering, sobbing ball curled up in her bed. Was Darlene home?

Cassandra swung open the door to Mrs. Northrop just reaching for the knob. "I thought I heard you, miss." She smiled and took Cassandra's wrap. "The most marvelous news. Miss Darlene has come back to us!"

Flinging a hand to her throat, Cassandra released a hearty sigh. She shared a smile with Mr. Dayle as he closed the door. A male voice that seemed oddly familiar emanated from the parlor. Confusion took over Cassandra's relief, followed by anger. "Who is here?" she demanded from the housekeeper.

Not waiting for an answer, Cassandra brushed past Mrs. Northrop and stormed into the parlor.

And found Mr. Heaton perched on the sofa across from her mother.

She sat as though a pole had been inserted into her spine. Her expression matched her stiff posture. The air thinned in Cassandra's lungs. She closed her eyes for a second then opened them, expecting a new scene to appear in her vision rather than the one that made no sense at all.

Before she could inquire as to what was going on, Darlene leapt from the chair beside her mother's and flew to Cassandra. "Cassie, Cassie!"

Kneeling, Cassandra pulled the girl into her arms and showered her neck with kisses then nudged her back to examine her. No cuts or bruises and only a few stains and tears on her gown. Cassandra's anger returned. "Where have you been? I was so worried."

Mr. Heaton rose from his seat as if to explain. His presence filled the room and ignited a tempest in her belly.

Ignoring him, Cassandra focused on her sister.

"I'm sorry, Cassie." Darlene thrust out her bottom lip. "I went to get Dr. Wilson for Hannah."

"Can you imagine, all by herself?" Cassandra's mother whined. "Oh, my poor head." She batted the air around her with her handkerchief.

Darlene sniffed and lowered her chin, but Cassandra wasn't buying her sister's penitent act. An act Cassandra had perfected when she was Darlene's age. Standing, she straightened her shoulders. She would have to deal with her sister later.

"Mr. Heaton, what on earth are you doing here?" she asked. "Tell me you didn't lose the ship. I fear I cannot stand any further disasters tonight."

"Quite the contrary." His smile was sincere, lacking its usual sarcasm.

"He saved me, Cassie." Darlene slid her hand in Cassandra's and dragged her to the sofa.

Where Mr. Heaton stood.

Too close. Cassandra could smell the sea on him, along with wood and rum and something else that curled her nose. She retreated a step and laid a hand on the back of a chair for support.

"I was kidnapped! You should have seen him make quick work of that villain." Darlene scrunched her face into an evil twist.

"I had a bit of help." Mr. Heaton chuckled.

Cassandra's brows drew together at the affectionate exchange that passed between them. "What vill—"

"Oh, it truly was quite heroic, Mr. Heaton." Her mother's words did not match the look of suspicion she cast his way. "We are deeply in your debt." She picked up her bell. The strident *ding ding ding* only added to Cassandra's befuddlement.

Mr. Heaton bowed. "My pleasure, madam."

Circling the chair, Cassandra sank into it before her legs gave out. Mrs. Northrop entered with a tray of tea and her mother's tonic.

Darlene inched to stand beside Cassandra's chair. "I got lost, Cassie, and then this evil man grabbed me." She demonstrated by clutching her arm, eyes wide. "He told me he was taking me to be his daughter."

"Oh my." Cassandra leaned forward, hand covering her mouth.

"Then Mr. Heaton fought him off."

"He did?" Cassandra lifted her gaze to Mr. Heaton. A grin quirked his lips.

"Then I threw a rock at him." Darlene flung her hand in the air.

"Such behavior for a young lady," her mother said with scorn as Mrs.

Northrop poured tonic into her tea and handed her the cup.

"Your sister has quite the aim. She struck him square on the head." Luke lowered himself to the sofa. "Reminded me of someone else."

"Oh, to think how close we came to losing you." Cassandra's mother sipped her tea then set the cup down as her eyes misted over. She beckoned to Darlene and the girl dashed into her embrace.

As Mr. Heaton smiled at the scene, Cassandra allowed herself a longer glance his way. Dirt marred his breeches and waistcoat, while black smudges lined his once-white shirt. Gunpowder? Strands of loose hair spilled from his tie, while at least two days' stubble peppered his chin. His rugged masculinity stole the breath from her lungs. Indeed, he looked more like a pirate than a privateer. No wonder her mother was swooning so.

Waving Mrs. Northrop's offer of tea aside with a *No, thank you,* Cassandra attempted an even tone, despite the torrent of emotions spinning within her. "That still doesn't explain what you're doing in town, Mr. Heaton."

He leaned forward, elbows on his knees, his blue eyes sparking. "I have good news."

Cassandra swallowed. She needed good news. Mr. Dayle appeared in the doorway. "Hannah is asking for you, Mrs. Channing."

"Oh, good." Cassandra's mother rose from her chair and took Darlene's hand.

Hannah. Renewed fear swamped Cassandra. She jumped from her seat. "How is she?" Cassandra started for the parlor doors then turned. "Forgive me, Mr. Heaton, but I'm afraid we cannot entertain guests at the moment. My other sister is quite ill."

Her mother gave her a reassuring look. "Never fear, Dr. Wilson is with her now, dear."

Cassandra stared at her in disbelief. "But we can't aff. . . How?"

Her mother waved her handkerchief in Mr. Heaton's direction. "Mr. Heaton brought him along with the medicines she needs."

Cassandra flinched, shifting her gaze between her mother and Mr. Heaton. "I don't understand."

"I'm sure Mr. Heaton will explain it to you." She turned to face him. "Good evening to you, sir. We are very grateful for your kindness. Mr. Dayle will see you out."

Cassandra cringed at her mother's tone—a tone she used to dismiss servants. "In a moment, Mother. I wish to speak to Mr. Heaton before he leaves."

The matron of the house pinched her lips as she raked Mr. Heaton with one of her disapproving glances. "Very well. Mr. Dayle, please stand by. Darlene, come." She tugged upon the girl, who cast a final grin over her shoulder at Mr. Heaton.

Mr. Dayle took up a spot just outside the open parlor doors.

Cassandra spun around to face Mr. Heaton. "I am all astonishment, sir."

"I hear that quite often." His gaze assessed her.

"But rarely as a compliment, I'm sure." Cassandra bit her lip, unsure why she was playing the insolent shrew when this man had saved her sister's life.

But he seemed to take no offense. Instead, he cocked his head and grinned. "Then can I assume your meaning was of the rare kind?"

"Indeed." Cassandra made her way back to her chair. "I cannot thank you enough for saving Darlene."

"Do all the Channing women wander about the streets at night?"

"Not all." Cassandra fingered the mahogany carving on the back of the chair.

He took a step toward her. "When she struck the villain with a rock, I had no doubt she was your relation." Humor rang in his voice.

Cassandra couldn't help but chuckle. "Indeed, I fear Darlene is far too much like me." She gazed up at him and her knees weakened. Weaving around the chair, she quickly slipped onto its soft cushion for fear of falling. "You brought the doctor. How did you know?"

"Darlene told me about her sister. And being familiar with Dr. Wilson, I took the liberty of calling on him. Then together we interrupted the apothecary's evening meal so he could prepare the proper medicines."

"I don't know what to say. I will repay you, of course."

"There is no need."

"I do not take charity, Mr. Heaton."

"You won't have to anymore."

❖

Luke reached inside his waistcoat pocket and pulled out a piece of foolscap. Unfolding it, he pressed it on the table. He watched her, anxious to see her reaction at the numbers scribbled across it and totaled at the bottom.

He couldn't help but watch her.

Her demeanor, her expressions, her words all combined into a fascinating play being acted out before him—a play in which numerous actors skittered across the stage of her eyes. How he longed to see admiration make its debut, perhaps, dare he hope, even ardor.

She examined the paper. Her eyes widened then narrowed in confusion.

Luke could contain himself no longer. "I captured a prize."

She looked up at him. "I see that." She shook her head, sending her red curls dancing. "I don't know what to say."

"You don't have to appear so surprised, Miss Channing." He laughed.

"Forgive me. I meant no offense."

Luke reached inside his waistcoat and pulled out a leather sack. Untying it, he counted out her share and laid it on the table.

Miss Channing's chest began to rise and fall rapidly. She picked up the notes and stared at them as if they were the most beautiful things she'd ever seen. "Ten thousand dollars." Her eyes met his, shimmering emeralds. "I cannot believe it."

Luke swallowed down his own emotion and pointed to the document. "We caught the British merchantman *Hawk* and sold her and her entire cargo in Wilmington for one hundred thousand dollars. US customs took twenty thousand, and I split half of the remainder among the crew. I took my share and that leaves you ten thousand." He pointed to the final number on the document.

"I heard privateering was lucrative, but I had no idea just how lucrative. Do you know what this means to me, Mr. Heaton?" Now, finally, admiration made an appearance in those green eyes. The sight of it set Luke aback, initiating a torrent of feelings he dared not entertain.

He cleared his throat. "I cannot promise you this amount on each voyage. I was lucky. Many privateers sail for months before acquiring a prize."

She smiled, a genuine, unassuming smile that showered him in warmth. "Where is *Destiny* now?"

"In Elizabeth City to the south. We found anchorage there and purchased horses for the two-day ride to Baltimore."

Miss Channing sifted through the bills, shaking her head as if she still didn't believe her eyes. She attempted to speak but her voice choked.

Luke grabbed his hat from the arm of the sofa. "I should allow you to attend to your younger sister. I was sorry to hear of her illness." He didn't want to go—could easily sit here all night staring at Miss

Channing—but remembering her mother's curt invitation to leave, he didn't want to overstay his welcome.

Miss Channing led him to the front door. Opening it, she followed him outside onto the porch. A blast of evening wind gusted over them, enveloping him in her sweet scent of gardenias. He faced her, light from a lantern hanging on the porch sparkling in her eyes.

She smiled again. "You smell like rum." Her tone was playful, yet accusing.

Luke cocked a brow. "Yes, I had one drink, my first in nearly three months."

Disbelief shadowed her face. Then taking a step back, she wrinkled her nose.

He shuffled his boots over the porch, suddenly wishing he'd had time to clean up before seeing her. "My apologies. I just rode into town a few hours ago."

"Quite all right, Mr. Heaton. How long will you be staying?"

"A few weeks. The crew needs a rest. They'll get restless when their pockets are empty again." He glanced over the city, blanketed in darkness, then back at her.

"And you, when will you get restless again?" One side of her lips curved slightly as her gaze probed him.

Which gave him the impetus to toy with her. "That depends."

"On what?"

If you'll allow me to court you, spend time with you, get to know you. "If I have some reason to stay." When concern creased her face, Luke regretted his bold words.

Their footman, still standing in the foyer, glanced his way. "You have saved me and my family, Mr. Heaton." Her tone had regained its metallic formality. "For that I will be eternally grateful. If I can ever help you, please don't hesitate to call." Luke took her hand in his and eased her back toward him, longing to regain a trace of her former tenderness. She trembled and her breath hastened. Was she as affected by him as he was by her? Only one way to find out. He lowered himself to whisper in her ear. "Perhaps a kiss of gratitude?"

Tugging her hand from his, she retreated into the house. "Good evening, Mr. Heaton."

And slammed the door in his face.

❖ CHAPTER 14 ❖

Flinging open the damask curtains, Cassandra rubbed her eyes and squinted at the radiant glow of dawn. Pulling her robe tight about her waist, she studied the morning breeze dancing through the leaves of the maple and birch trees outside her window. She'd hardly slept a wink the past two nights. In fact, with candle in hand, she'd crept down to the solarium more than once to check on the ten thousand dollars she'd hidden in her father's chest. If only to reassure herself that she hadn't dreamt up receiving the fortune from Mr. Heaton.

One thing she knew for sure, however, was that she hadn't dreamt up the rake's inappropriate request for a kiss. Outrage consumed her at the memory. How dare he treat her like one of his common wenches, as if he could purchase her affections with the toss of a coin! She reached up and brushed her fingers over her neck. Then why had her insides melted at the waft of his warm breath over her skin? And her stomach flutter as if a thousand fireflies flew within it?

No doubt it was just the excitement of receiving so much wealth. In one night, her life had gone from poverty, sickness, and shame, to life, health, and a promising future.

All because of the town rogue.

The door opened and Margaret slipped inside humming her favorite hymn. Strands of black hair sprang from her mobcap. "Oh miss, I didn't know you'd arisen." She placed the basin of steaming water on the vanity, then gazed at Cassandra. "Whatever are you thinking, miss? I've never seen such a glorious expression on your face."

Cassandra shook off the uninvited smile. "Nothing."

"Or *who* were you thinking about? I should say."

The heated flush that had begun moments before on Cassandra's neck moved onto her face. She swung about to face the window.

Margaret made her way to the bed and began straightening the sheets. "That Mr. Heaton presents a rather handsome figure, does he not?"

"I hadn't noticed," Cassandra lied.

"Then you must be the only lady in town who hasn't."

Cassandra gave her maid a coy smile. "Well, perhaps I have noticed. But what does it matter? You know his reputation as well as I."

Margaret finished making the bed and shrugged. "I never put much value in town gossip, miss. Besides, he's shown you nothing but kindness."

"Mother disapproves of him."

"And you?" Margaret cocked her head and smiled.

Cassandra moved to the bed and gripped one of the wooden posts. "I haven't made up my mind yet." Her thoughts drifted to the money, and she lifted her hands to her mouth as tears of relief burned behind her eyes. "We are saved, Margaret. I can hardly believe it!" She hadn't allowed the reality to settle firmly in her heart. Not yet. Mainly because her thoughts had been consumed with Hannah. What difference would all the money in the world make if Hannah did not survive? Yet, after sitting by her sister's bedside, spoon-feeding her broth and cooling her forehead with wet rags, Cassandra had watched the little girl finally drift into a peaceful sleep late last night. An hour later, a touch to her forehead indicated her fever had abated.

Margaret took her hands. "Yes, miss. We are saved."

"We have enough money to last us twenty years if need be."

"God has been good to you, miss."

Cassandra pulled away. "I don't know why God would bless me in this way but neglect to save my father." She moved to the chair of her vanity and sat down with a huff.

"He's always been with you, miss. He won't let His children starve. Look what happened to me and Mr. Daley. After our baby died and we had to sell the chandler shop to pay the doctor bills, we would have been living out on the street, begging for food." Margaret stepped behind her and began unraveling Cassandra's long braid.

"I hired you, not God," Cassandra reminded her.

"God can use anyone, miss." Margaret leaned over and smiled at Cassandra in the dressing glass. "Even the town rogue."

Cassandra stared at her reflection, longing to believe Margaret's words, longing to believe that God was still with her and looking out for her—that she wasn't the only one standing between her family and complete ruin.

"I checked on Hannah this morning," Margaret offered as she picked up a brush and began running it through Cassandra's hair. "She is sleeping soundly. Another blessing from God." She began humming once again, and the words Cassandra had often heard accompanying the tune chimed in her head.

Come, thou Fount of every blessing
Tune my heart to sing Thy grace
Streams of mercy, never ceasing
Call for songs of loudest praise. . .

After sweeping up Cassandra's hair and fastening it in place, Margaret stepped toward the armoire and flung open the doors. "What are your plans today, miss?"

"I'm going into town to pay off all our debts and purchase some much-needed food and supplies." The thought pleased her immensely. Finally she'd not have to endure the looks of pity cast her way from proprietors and citizens alike. Finally, she could hold her head up high in the knowledge that she was as capable as any man to provide for her family.

As soon as she finished dressing, Cassandra slipped into the solarium, sat down on her stool, and unlocked her father's chest. Withdrawing the stack of bills, she placed them in her lap and grabbed her father's pipe. Drawing it to her nose, she breathed in the spicy scent that always invoked her father's image with such clarity.

"Papa, I've done it. I've provided for the family!" She caressed the bills and pressed the wad against her chest. "I wish you were here to see this. Wouldn't you be proud of your little girl?"

"Ah, my Cassie girl." She envisioned her father, pipe in hand, looking up from his chair in the library. "I've always been proud of you." He smiled and gestured her forward and Cassandra closed her eyes and imagined his beefy arms engulfing her in strength and warmth. Tears burned in her eyes, but she forced them back. Today was not a day for mourning. Today was a day of celebration.

After counting out enough bills to cover her errands, she tucked the rest into the bottom of the chest beneath the stack of her father's letters. Then after one more whiff of his pipe, she placed it atop the missives, closed the lid, locked it, and slipped the key into her pocket.

❖

Stretching, Luke entered the dining room and tousled John's hair as the boy sat slopping down a bowl of oatmeal. "I smell coffee."

John beamed up at him then spooned more of the creamy cereal into his mouth.

Mrs. Barnes strode into the room from the kitchen, carrying a tray of biscuits, sausage, and cheese, their decadent scents ambling in with her. "Finally you're awake."

Luke yawned. "Never thought I'd miss my lumpy old mattress." Pulling out a chair, he sat and poured himself a cup of coffee.

"It's good to have you back." Mrs. Barnes slid the platters onto the table.

Finishing his oatmeal, John pushed the bowl away and turned to face Luke. "Tell us how you captured that merchantman again."

Luke sipped his coffee. "I already told you, you little scamp." Several times, if he recalled. In fact, Luke had spent the entire day yesterday with John and Mrs. Barnes, regaling them with his adventurous tale. All the while John had sat mesmerized, gazing at Luke with admiration—the same admiration on his face now.

"Quite the story." Mrs. Barnes's eyes crinkled. "Praise God He kept you safe."

"Praise God for the money I gave you, Mrs. Barnes." Luke retorted. "Now you can pay off our debts and buy yourself a new gown."

"Oh my." Mrs. Barnes laid a hand on her wrinkled cheek.

John giggled.

Luke glanced down at John's leg. "And we can afford that new brace for your leg."

"And then I can go with you on your ship," the boy stated as if there would be no argument.

Mrs. Barnes's hawklike gaze scoured Luke from above a pair of wire-rimmed spectacles.

He rubbed the stubble on his chin and looked back into John's expectant gray eyes. John was ten years old. A good age to learn how to sail. It was time Luke stopped babying him.

Take care of him, Luke. His mother's last admonition echoed in Luke's mind. *Take care of him.*

But that didn't mean to hide the boy from the world. Luke wouldn't always be around, and John needed to grow up. Needed to learn how to fend for himself.

Luke sipped his coffee and set the cup down with a clank. "I don't see why not."

John leapt from his seat and stood at attention before Luke, reminding him of Samuel. "I'll be real good, you'll see. I learn things fast."

"I know you will. You're my brother, after all." Luke swallowed a burst of pride.

"You can't be serious?" Mrs. Barnes's red cheeks swelled. "He's just a boy. And we are at war."

"There are many boys his age out at sea. Besides, we encountered relatively little danger on my last trip."

"But you can't be sure that the next trip will go so well."

"I can't be sure of anything in this life." Luke grabbed a biscuit from the pile and took a bite. His parents' murder had taught him that. There were no assurances of safety, no guarantees that people wouldn't get sick—he glanced down at John's deformed leg. That money wouldn't run out. That he wouldn't be dealt another bad hand.

That loved ones wouldn't burn to death.

Pain throbbed in his right ear, and he lifted a hand to rub it. No, life was nothing but a chaotic matrix of haphazard events. And it was only how a man dealt with those events, good or bad, that defined his success. Success that Luke had only just begun to taste.

Mrs. Barnes clasped her hands before her smock. "But that is no license for carelessness, Luke."

"Is it careless or prudent to teach the boy to sail?"

"Sail, yes, but privateer. . . You could be shot at."

John's eyes bounced between Luke and Mrs. Barnes. "Truly?" Excitement raised his voice.

Mrs. Barnes let out an exasperated sigh.

Luke stood. "Never fear, Mrs. Barnes. I have no plans to engage a British warship." He gave her a mischievous smile and leaned to kiss her cheek.

She shook her head.

"Now, if you'll both excuse me," Luke said. "I have business in town."

"Do you have to go?" John slunk back into his chair.

"Yes. You listen to Mrs. Barnes and do your studies. I'm your captain now. If you disobey me"—Luke hunched over and narrowed his eyes, doing his best pirate impression—"I will make ye walk the plank."

John giggled. "Aye, aye, Captain."

Luke headed for the front door, the *slip-tap* of Mrs. Barnes's slippers following him.

"What business do you have?" she demanded.

Luke swept the door open and stepped outside. "I'm not gambling, sweet lady, if that's what you fear. I'm helping Noah bring cannons to the fort." He headed down the pathway. "Although I may attempt my hand at cards this evening," he shouted over his shoulders with a wink.

With an exasperated snort, she waved him off. "You are incorrigible." Then chuckling, she closed the door.

❖

Cassandra stepped out from the mercantile, her mother, Darlene, and Mr. Dayle following behind her. She lifted her face to the hot sun. Summer's warm abundance was at full swing. Not just in the weather, but in Cassandra's family, in her life, in her heart. Until now, Cassandra hadn't believed in fresh starts. She hadn't believed in miracles. But today, anything seemed possible. The scent of sweet ferns drifted by her nose. A bell rang in the distance accompanied by the *clip clop* of horses' hooves over the cobblestones.

"Where are we going now, dear?" her mother asked as Darlene slipped her hand within Cassandra's.

Cassandra glanced down at her list. "Let's see. We've paid the mercantile, the chandler, blacksmith, millinery, cobbler, and the seamstress. Now all we've got to do is pay the butcher and then buy something delicious for dinner. Perhaps a chicken to make some soup for Hannah. And also some cinnamon to settle her stomach."

Turning, she glanced at Mr. Dayle who was already loaded down with packages and sacks. "Just a few more stops, Mr. Dayle."

"No bother, miss."

Her mother patted her tight golden curls. "Oh, I would so love some new fabric for a gown. I haven't had one in months."

"Can we wait on that, Mother?" Cassandra headed down the brick pathway. "I don't want to spend money on luxuries just yet."

"But we have so much money." Her mother tugged at her white gloves with a whine.

For now. But it would be gone in a flash if Cassandra allowed her mother full rein to buy whatever she wished. Why, the entire amount would be gone within the year. And if Cassandra's brothers never returned, and Mr. Heaton never captured another prize. . .

And Cassandra never married—which appeared to be a greater possibility with each passing year.

"We must make it last, Mother. You don't want us to end up destitute again, do you?"

"No, of course not, dear. But we should enjoy our success." She furrowed her brows at Cassandra. "What has happened to you? You used to live life so vivaciously, with reckless abandon."

"I seem to recall that you detest that about me."

"Well, I did. I do," she mumbled. "I simply do not see why you must change now."

Halting, Cassandra gave her mother an incredulous look. "I took on the support of the family, Mother. I had to grow up."

"Oh, pish." Her mother plucked out a handkerchief and began dabbing her neck. "You are so much like your father. He never let me buy anything."

"Father took good care of us." Cassandra proceeded down the walkway.

Friends and acquaintances waved at them as they made their way through the crowds. A few stopped to stare, their heads dipping in conversation as they passed. No doubt discussing Cassandra's recent privateering success. Baltimore kept few secrets. But Cassandra didn't care. Whether they approved of her business venture or of whom she had chosen to align with, she had done what few women had. She had provided for her family. More than provided, in fact.

With her head held high, her list and reticule in one hand, and Darlene holding the other, Cassandra sauntered down Baltimore Street.

"Mr. Heaton!" Darlene slipped away from Cassandra and dashed down the street.

"Darlene, ladies do not run!" her mother yelled after her, but to no avail.

"Oh, bother." Holding her hat down against a blast of hot wind,

Cassandra stormed after the girl, weaving in between people, horses, carriages, and wagons, leaving a trail of angry rebukes in her wake. "Pardon me." Cassandra attempted to placate one angry footman who sat atop a fancy phaeton as he jerked his horse out of her way. She continued onward.

Then she saw him.

Dressed in his usual black breeches, white shirt, and black waistcoat, Mr. Heaton was perched on the seat of a wagon beside Noah and Marianne. Spotting Darlene, he yanked on the reins and leapt to the ground just as the little girl halted before him. He leaned down and laid a finger on her nose, giving her one of those smiles that would melt any female heart. Then straightening his back, his eyes met Cassandra's and an odd moment of understanding stretched between them before he graced her with the same smile. Only this one held a hint of desire that made her stomach spin.

"You're looking lovely today, Miss Channing," he said when she approached.

Cassandra tugged her sister away from him, remembering the ease with which this swaggering rake thought he could procure a kiss from her. "Save your flattery, sir. I am not a woman easily swayed by idle words."

"Then pray tell, miss, what *does* sway you?" He cocked his head with a smile.

Noah cleared his throat.

"Forgive me, Noah." Cassandra gazed up at her friends. "Marianne, so good to see you."

"And you." She dipped her head, a knowing grin on her lips.

"Darlene, how many times have I told you to not run off like that?" Her mother's shrill voice blasted over them from behind. Shielding her eyes from the sun, she greeted Marianne and Noah.

"Good day, Mrs. Channing. Mr. Dayle," Marianne said.

"Congratulations on your privateering success, Cassandra." Noah took the reins and stilled the horse.

"I believe it is Mr. Heaton you should congratulate," Cassandra said.

"Indeed," Noah replied. "But the credit goes to you for choosing a good captain."

Luke rubbed his palms and looked away as if embarrassed by the compliment. Sunlight turned his hair into liquid obsidian.

"Do forgive us for not getting down," Marianne offered, "but we must be on our way."

"Where are you heading?" Cassandra peered in the back of the wagon where thick sheets of canvas covered up whatever they were hauling.

"Naval guns." Mr. Heaton flipped an errant strand of hair from his face and squinted in the sunlight.

Noah tipped his hat up and glanced toward the bay. "Major Armistead and General Smith asked us to strip them from any idle ships in order to reinforce the fort."

Cassandra's mother plucked out her fan. "Oh my, he doesn't expect an attack on Baltimore, does he?"

"Just a precaution, I'm sure, Mrs. Channing," Noah said.

Cassandra turned to Mr. Heaton. "I had no idea you were so patriotic."

His eyes smiled. "There is much you don't know about me."

Darlene tugged on Cassandra's skirt. "Can Mr. Heaton come for dinner?" She looked up at him. "We're having a celebration tonight."

Cassandra's mother groaned. "I'm sure Mr. Heaton has far more"—she scanned him with disdain—"interesting things with which to entertain himself."

Mr. Heaton's shoulders seemed to sag.

Embarrassed by her mother's impudence, Cassandra took a step toward him. She owed him a great deal. Certainly the least she could do was offer him a decent supper. As a bachelor, he no doubt rarely partook of a home-cooked meal. Besides, the prospect of getting to know him better was not completely without appeal.

Though why she dared not ponder overmuch.

"What could be more interesting than a fine meal?" Cassandra asked. "Isn't that right, Mr. Heaton?" Yet even as she said it, Cassandra could not in good conscience apply the description to Miss Thain's cooking. "I insist you join us."

Darlene smiled up at Luke and grabbed his hand.

"That's quite impossible, dear." Cassandra's mother snapped her fan shut. "I've already invited Mr. Crane for supper tonight."

Cassandra's stomach soured. "You did? When?"

"Why yesterday, dear. He came to call on you, but you were busy attending to Hannah."

"Oh, bother." Cassandra tapped her foot. It would never do to have them both to dinner. Especially after Mr. Heaton had all but pushed Mr. Crane into the bay.

By the look of amusement on his face, Mr. Heaton was no doubt enjoying the same memory.

"How is your sister faring?" His tone sobered to one of true concern.

"Much better, thank you." Cassandra eyed him curiously.

Marianne grabbed her husband's arm. "We're very happy to hear it."

A breeze swirled around Cassandra, cooling the perspiration on her neck. Laughter shot from a group of men across the way. Oh, what did it matter if Mr. Crane was coming? It should be up to Mr. Heaton to decide if he wished to endure the man's presence or not. She wished she had the same choice. Besides, Mr. Heaton would offer a pleasant diversion from Mr. Crane's annoying ways. "Do say you'll come to dinner, Mr. Heaton."

His pointed gaze shifted from Cassandra to her mother and back to Cassandra as if considering the genuineness of the invitation. He must have decided the offer was sincere—at least on Cassandra's part—for he dipped his head and said, "I'd be happy to accept."

Ignoring her mother's groan and shrugging off the odd delight that drifted through her, Cassandra gazed up at her friends still seated on the wagon. "And you must come too, Marianne and Noah. We have much to celebrate."

The couple exchanged a loving glance. "Some other time perhaps." A pink hue blossomed on Marianne's cheeks. "This is Noah's last night in town before he sails out again."

"Oh, I see." Cassandra's face heated, and she shifted her gaze, noting a twinkle in Mr. Heaton's eyes.

"Very well, then." Cassandra cleared her throat, suddenly anxious to leave the awkward scene. "I should allow you to attend your business. Good day to you all." Tugging Darlene away from Mr. Heaton, she turned and headed down the street. "Seven o'clock sharp, Mr. Heaton," she shot over her shoulder.

"See you tonight," Darlene shouted as they made their way once again across the street.

Cassandra bit her lip. Mr. Crane, Mr. Heaton, and Cassandra's mother all eating at the same table. Yes, this would be a very interesting evening, indeed.

❖ CHAPTER 15 ❖

Luke waited for the ladies to take their seats before sinking into his chair around the oblong table covered in white linen. Pewter dishes, crystal goblets, and silver platters glowed beneath the light of several candles perched at the center. From her spot at the head of the table, Mrs. Channing glared at him with the same disapproving scowl she'd worn since Luke had first entered the house and been led into the parlor. Where he'd been curtly reintroduced to Mr. Milton Crane, the foppish cur who now took a seat beside him. The man had grunted that he'd already had the pleasure of Luke's acquaintance, but both his spiteful tone, and the way he assessed Luke as if he were a spoiled piece of meat, spoke otherwise. Thankfully, Crane's pride forbade him to mention his swim in Baltimore Bay for Luke doubted he could apologize for something that still brought a smile to his lips.

And though Miss Channing had attempted to include Luke in the pre-dinner conversation—an action that endeared her to him even more—the banter between her mother and Mr. Crane would not permit a word.

Luke cared not a whit that Mrs. Channing did not approve of his presence in her home. It was a chance to see Miss Channing and get to know her better. And for that, he'd happily tuck his pride away for the evening.

As it was, Luke had been content to stand by the hearth and gaze upon Miss Channing seated on the settee, her cream-colored gown spread around her, her delicate curls the color of fine wine lingering about her neck, and her green eyes sparkling as she politely listened to the boorish discourse. Not an ounce of powder or rouge marred her glowing complexion, which always seemed to redden when her eyes met his.

When the housekeeper announced dinner, Luke was fast to Miss Channing's side to offer her his arm. After glancing toward Mr. Crane, she took it and even graced Luke with a small smile in reward. However, Mr. Crane's face twisted in irritation as he spun around and offered his arm to Mrs. Channing while Darlene sped up on Luke's other side and slipped her hand in his.

"Seems you have an admirer." Miss Channing laughed. "One of many, I'm sure."

Darlene gazed up at Luke, and he squeezed her hand. "He's just my friend, Cassie." Her tone of admonishment brought a smile to Luke's lips.

Now, as the housekeeper and another woman of slight figure entered the dining hall and filled the table with steaming platters, Luke dared a glance at Darlene and Miss Channing, who both sat across from him. He promised himself to don his best behavior and prove to them—and to Cassandra's mother—that he was not the cad the town thought he was.

The rumble in his stomach was quickly silenced by a strange smell, emanating from the cuisine, that Luke could not quite place. But he could be sure of one thing—it bore no resemblance to anything edible. Mrs. Channing bowed her head and blessed the dinner with a prayer that, by her tone, sounded more like the recitation of marching orders for God than an offering of thanks.

"Amen." Mr. Crane slapped his hands together and reached for a bowl of boiled potatoes. After shoveling a heap onto his plate, he passed the bowl to the lady of the house and took the liberty of pouring himself a glass of wine from the carafe. "I was most pleased to hear of your good fortune, Miss Channing." He dipped his head toward Cassandra.

Grabbing a plate of what appeared to be fried fish, she handed it to Luke. "Yes, indeed, sir. We have Mr. Heaton to thank for that. As it turns out, he is quite the privateer."

Luke smiled inwardly as he grabbed the platter and slid a portion onto his plate.

Mr. Crane sipped his wine. "Isn't it just a game of luck, Mr. Heaton, this privateering?" he said without looking at Luke. "I mean to say, it's quite a gamble that you'll even encounter a British vessel, let alone one that you can catch and defeat in battle."

Luke opened his mouth to reply but the man continued, "And then she must have a bellyful of cargo to sell to make her worthwhile prey." He plucked a biscuit from a tray and passed the plate to Cassandra. "Yes, indeed, it seems but a game of chance."

"As it turns out, Mr. Crane. I'm quite good at gambling." Luke winked at Darlene as she passed him a bowl of greens. The girl giggled.

"A worthless pastime," Mrs. Channing interjected. "For charlatans and idlers."

"I quite agree." Mr. Crane huffed. "Your reputation, Mr. Heaton, does you no credit. And like all gamblers, I'll wager your luck will run out in time."

"Then you would wish ill luck on me as well, Mr. Crane." Cassandra seethed. "For my success is tied with Mr. Heaton's."

Luke raised a brow at her spiteful tone.

"Not at all, my dear." Alarm rang in Mr. Crane's voice as if he realized his error. "I merely speak in philosophical generalities. No harm done, Mr. Heaton, eh?"

Fury surged through Luke's veins while he forced a calm smile upon his lips. All eyes shot to him as if expecting an angry outburst. "I'm flattered that you have spent so much of your precious time pondering my pastimes and my reputation, sir. Perhaps you should attend to your own."

Cassandra smiled and gazed down at her plate.

Mr. Crane stretched his neck. "I'll have you know, sir, that my reputation is without blemish."

Mrs. Channing helped herself to the meat pie. "Indeed, Mr. Crane. You need not concern yourself in that regard. All of Baltimore can attest to your good name." She gave a nervous chuckle, no doubt anxious to change the topic. Her glance took in the table. "Do forgive the lack of proper dining service. I'm afraid we haven't had time to redeem our china and silverware."

"Ah, no bother. No bother at all, my dear lady." Mr. Crane lifted a spoonful of fish to his mouth then recoiled slightly as he tasted it.

"But, wouldn't you say, Mr. Crane," Cassandra pressed, "that one's reputation is never etched in stone? That it is subject to improvement over time?"

Amazed at her defense of him, Luke sought out her eyes, but she kept them locked upon Crane.

Mr. Crane gazed at her with the patronizing look of a teacher with a child. "A rarity, Miss Channing, for it is my belief that one's character"—he cast a condescending glance at Luke—"or lack thereof, is forged in one's youth."

"I do not agree, sir." Cassandra pursed her pink lips. "And I'll ask you not to further insult Mr. Heaton. He is my guest."

Luke sipped his wine, enjoying the exchange. Enjoying that this fascinating woman stood up for him. Perhaps he should thank Mr. Crane for being such a priggy bumblehead.

Mrs. Channing leaned forward, her pointed gaze landing on her daughter. "Come now, Cassandra, enough of this absurd drivel about reputations." She waved a hand through the air. "Let us enjoy ourselves."

"Nevertheless"—Cassandra flashed Luke a smile that jolted his heart—"you must give credit where credit is due. I, for one, am glad I hired Mr. Heaton as a privateer."

Luke lifted his glass toward her in appreciation of her confidence. Hearing her speak so ardently on his behalf was worth enduring the odious company of Mr. Crane.

"I am, as well," Darlene piped in as she took a bite of biscuit.

Cassandra turned to her mother. "And you, Mother? Are you quite happy to be free of financial worries?"

"Why, of course, dear." The older lady's smile was tighter than a sheet under full wind.

Mr. Crane took a bite of meat pie. His lips twisted in a knot. Grabbing his wine, he poured the remainder down his throat then set his glass down. "Well, it does seem your risky investment has paid off. For now." He poured himself more wine. "However, Miss Channing, you needn't have gone to such extremes. I readily offer you my assistance whenever the need arises."

"So generous, Mr. Crane." Mrs. Channing patted her curls.

Cassandra straightened her shoulders. Candlelight spread a delightful sheen over her burgundy curls. "I do thank you, sir, but I prefer to make my own way."

"Rubbish." Mr. Crane snickered, pushing his food around the plate with a fork. "Women are best at childbearing and managing the home, don't you agree, Mr. Heaton?" He winked at Luke.

"As to childbearing, I agree they are best suited for it." Luke leaned back in his chair, noting that Miss Channing's jaw tightened. "As to managing the home, I do not think they should be forced to limit themselves to only those functions."

A look of shock and appreciation claimed Miss Channing's face.

Mr. Crane snorted his displeasure.

Luke took a bite of fish. A sour taste saturated his mouth. Miss Channing lowered her chin. Longing to bring her gaze back to him, he swallowed the bite and inquired after Miss Hannah.

He was immediately rewarded. "She is much better, Mr. Heaton. Thank you for asking."

Darlene exchanged such a warm glance with her elder sister that a lump formed in the back of Luke's throat, his thoughts flickering to John.

"I cannot wait until she has fully recovered. I miss playing with her," the little girl said.

"In fact, we expect her to be able to leave her bed very soon." Mrs. Channing took a bite of fish then dabbed her lips with her serviette.

Luke sampled the meat pie but found it no better than the fish. Even the cook aboard *Destiny* produced more palatable meals than this. "I am glad to hear of it."

Grabbing his wineglass, Mr. Crane leaned back in his chair. "Ah yes. Miss Hannah. I had quite forgotten she had taken ill."

Cassandra gave the man a look of disdain, which he seemed to miss entirely. Her mother gestured toward Mr. Crane's plate. "You did not find the meal to your liking, Mr. Crane?" Disappointment stung her blue eyes.

"Come now, Mother." Cassandra's delightful giggle lifted the spirit of the room. "I'm sure Mr. Crane is accustomed to finer fare than our humble cook can produce."

"I do not see why you keep her on." Mr. Crane flung his serviette onto the table.

Mrs. Channing's face reddened. "I'm afraid my daughter insists."

"Because, Mr. Crane." Cassandra's voice filled with venom. "She is a war widow and has no family. I'd sooner eat boiled rat every night than put her on the street. Besides, she's improving."

Crane shifted in his seat at her rebuff and refilled his wineglass while Luke allowed this new revelation to find anchor in his mind. He knew Miss Channing was beautiful, feisty, brave, intelligent, and determined.

But he had not realized until now that she also possessed the heart of a saint.

The thought made him as uncomfortable as Crane seemed to be. Yet for a completely different reason. For each new thing he learned about Miss Channing pushed her higher out of the reach of a man like him.

❖

Cassandra eyed Mr. Crane as he downed yet another glass of wine and tugged uncomfortably at his cravat. Her gaze shifted to Mr. Heaton sitting beside him with all the confidence and manners of a titled gentleman. Though she'd been concerned he would overindulge in drink, his wineglass stood half full. Though she'd been concerned he'd ignite a brawl with Mr. Crane, he'd responded with nothing but polite, albeit witty, answers to the man's insulting remarks. And how could she miss the smiles shared between him and Darlene? The young girl adored the man, just as Marianne's son, Jacob, adored him. And though the food tasted like the boiled rat she referred to earlier, Mr. Heaton forced it down with nary a complaint.

Dressed in a suit of black taffeta with silver trim, his dark hair slicked back into a tie, he had nearly stolen her breath when he'd first walked into the parlor. Even the stubble was vacant from his chin. Somehow, Cassandra missed it.

Just then his eyes found hers, a smile lingering at the corners. Flushed, Cassandra looked away.

"May I be excused, Mother?" Darlene asked. "I'd like to go see Hannah."

"By all means." Mrs. Channing lowered her glass to the table as Darlene leaned in to kiss Cassandra on the cheek then flew from the room.

Gazing after her, Mr. Crane sipped more wine. "If I may say so, that girl needs a strong hand. Word has spread through town of her escapade the other day."

"Why, I quite agree, Mr. Crane." Mrs. Channing set down her spoon. "She has been beyond control since my Phillip left. And, my word, but she gave us all such a fright."

Anger pulsed through Cassandra's veins. The audacity of the man. "Though I thank you for your concern, Mr. Crane, we are quite able to handle Darlene. Besides, Mr. Heaton brought her home before any harm came to her."

"Quite the hero, eh, Mr. Heaton?" Mr. Crane's chuckle carried no sincerity.

Mr. Heaton merely smiled in return.

"Indeed," Cassandra said. "He also saved me from thieves a few months past."

Crane gulped his wine. "Odd how you seem to find yourself always in the right place and time to rescue the women of this family."

"A burden I gladly bear, sir," Mr. Heaton said.

"Perhaps you could write a story about him in your paper?" Cassandra couldn't resist toying with Mr. Crane. "He's quite the talk of the town now with his privateering success."

Mr. Crane's forehead twisted. "I'm afraid, Miss Channing, that my paper deals with more, shall we say, matters of higher importance."

"Of course it does." Cassandra's mother gave her a look of censure before she turned to face Mr. Crane. "Oh, do tell us, Mr. Crane, what stories are you working on currently?"

The meat in Cassandra's stomach hardened into a rock as the man, accepting the request with glee, began regaling them with every aspect of running a paper, from rambunctious employees, to secret sources, to the shortage of ink due to the blockade, and to the overwhelming decisions that fell on him each day. With each story, he sat a bit taller in his chair and drank a bit more. And with each sip of wine, his eyes became more glassy and his boasts more emphatic.

Blocking out his incessant drone, Cassandra found her gaze drawn to Mr. Heaton who now sat back in his chair, sipping his wine, while pretending to listen to the babbling man. More than once his eyes met hers and a smile would form on his lips. A smile that sent her heart into a frenzied beat. What was wrong with her? The man was a scoundrel, a gambler, who had more than once tried to steal a kiss from her. True, he had made her a fortune and for that she was grateful, but their relationship must end there. He was not the sort of man a lady entertained thoughts of a future with. Not the sort of man a lady could trust. And trust was of the utmost importance to Cassandra. She would not be abandoned again.

Yet the comparison with Mr. Crane—the respectable, trustworthy businessman—made her head spin. Who was the true gentleman, after all?

Mr. Crane's sharp tone snapped her attention toward him. "Your charity astounds me, Miss Channing. It's one of the many things that endears you so to me."

"Of what charity do you speak?"

"Why, of inviting Mr. Heaton to dine with you." His words slurred as he leaned forward. "In appreciation of his success on your behalf."

"And why do you consider that charity, sir?"

He adjusted his waistcoat and cast a cursory glance toward Luke. "Not to impugn your character further, sir. . ."

"Not that you could, Mr. Crane," Mr. Heaton was quick to respond.

Crane huffed. "But clearly, he is beneath such an invitation. Though I do understand your reasoning, Miss Channing. A bachelor in need of a good meal. Ah, your kind heart astounds me."

"Mr. Crane." Cassandra's blood boiled. "That is not—"

But Mr. Heaton raised a palm, silencing her. Calmly placing his glass on the table, he rose from his seat and bowed toward Cassandra's mother. "Thank you, madam, for having me in your home and for a most interesting meal." He turned to Cassandra, his eyes twinkling with ardor. "Always a pleasure." Then, facing Mr. Crane. "You sir, are a buffoon." And with that, he quietly left the dining hall.

Cassandra's mother gasped. Mr. Crane coughed, his face a bright red. Forcing down a giggle, Cassandra clutched her skirts and darted after Mr. Heaton, catching him just as he'd opened the front door to leave. "Please, Mr. Heaton."

He faced her. Moonlight turned his eyes to silver. He smelled of wood and spice.

"I must apologize for Mr. Crane. He isn't normally so belligerent."

"That's the second time you've apologized for the man."

She lowered her gaze. "He doesn't seem overly fond of you."

Mr. Heaton chuckled. "Indeed. But I believe I can handle the likes of him." Without warning, he brushed a thumb over her jaw.

His touch sent pinpricks over her face and neck. "Yes, I believe you can." Her voice came out breathless.

He leaned toward her. "Thank you, again, for the invitation."

Cassandra tried to release the breath that had crowded in her throat. "It's the least we could do to thank you."

"You owe me nothing." He leaned further and placed a gentle kiss on her cheek before Cassandra could stop him. His warm lips branded her with delight.

She couldn't move.

Then he winked, stepped outside, and closed the door behind him.

The sound of footfalls woke Cassandra from her dream and spun her around to see the back of Mr. Crane stumbling down the hall.

❖ CHAPTER 16 ❖

Luke tossed the last bit of rum into his mouth and gestured toward the barmaid for more. The pungent liquid swirled a rapid trail down his throat before plunging into his belly in a fiery blaze. He nodded at Mr. Sanders and Mr. Keene who were sitting far across the crowded tavern. Luke had seen them when he first entered, but he wasn't in the mood for conversation, especially not with his crew.

"What'll it be, Heaton?" The grimy-toothed man sitting to his left, who smelled no better than the supper Luke had partaken of that night, yelled over the raucous crowd and gestured toward the cards in Luke's hand.

Luke studied them, their images blurring in his vision. He hadn't meant to drink so much. Had intended to go straight home after dining with the Channings. But he could not chase Mr. Crane's insults from his mind. They rose like demons, taunting them with their truth. Crane may be an officious fat wit, but he was right about one thing. Luke had no business dining with such a prestigious family. Further, he had no business entertaining thoughts of calling on Cassandra. He was a drunk, a womanizer, and a gambler. Just because he'd succeeded in capturing a prize didn't mean that the entire voyage hadn't been one huge wager. With no more certainty of success than the game he played now. Simply the luck of the draw. Which, as Luke stared at his cards, he needed at the moment.

Selecting the two of diamonds, he laid it facedown on the table. "Another card, if you please."

A pianoforte chimed from the back of the tavern, overpowering the hum of conversation and occasional curses flung about the shadowy room. A throng of men began belting out a disparaging chorus. Mr. Crenshaw, a shipbuilder, sitting across from him, dealt him another card. Luke picked it up and smiled. The ace of diamonds. This might turn out to be a good night, after all.

Clara, a well-endowed barmaid who enjoyed sharing her voluptuous wealth with others, slapped down another glass of rum in front of Luke then leaned over to capture his approving glance. The sting of tobacco and perfume bit his nose, making him long for Cassandra's sweet scent of gardenias.

"I can offer you much more than rum." The barmaid's salacious slur did not have the same effect on him that it usually had.

Mr. Fairfax chuckled from Luke's right and grabbed the lady, forcing her onto his lap. "How about me?"

Giggling, she struggled to free herself and slapped his arm playfully then planted a hand upon her curvaceous hip and stared at Luke.

"Thank you, Clara, just the rum for now." He swept his gaze from her figure, suddenly finding the unabashed display unappealing.

"Perhaps later then." She pouted and sashayed away, checking over her shoulder to see if he was looking. He was. And yet he wasn't. Something else had caught his eye on the other side of the bar.

A gold epaulette glittered in the lantern light. Along with the brass buttons of a lieutenant's uniform, on top of which perched the squash-shaped head and pointed nose of Abner Tripp.

With a moan, Mr. Fairfax played a card.

Luke watched as the lieutenant stood alone at the bar and ordered a drink. This seedy tavern was not the sort of place Luke would have expected Lieutenant Tripp to frequent. He was more the posh tavern sort, places like Queen's or Grant's Tavern. In fact, it had been at Grant's Tavern that Luke had won his ship from the man in a game of Piquet.

Mr. Crenshaw tossed a coin in the pile and grinned.

Shaking the fog from his head, Luke gazed back at his cards. A breeze swirled in from the window, scattering the stagnant air and flickering the lantern's flame. If he indeed possessed the hand swirling in his vision, then it appeared his luck would hold.

The fishy-smelling man tossed his cards down and let out a belch. "That's it for me, gentlemen."

"And for me, as well." Luke snapped the hair from his face and laid his cards out faceup on the table. Gauging the men for their reactions, he reached inside his coat and fingered his pistol just in case.

Mr. Crenshaw emitted a foul word and scratched his head as if he couldn't fathom how Luke had won. He tossed down his cards. Mr. Fairfax, however, eyed Luke suspiciously. He clung to his hand as if the cards were all he had left in the world. His biting gaze shifted from Luke's cards to his own then across the other players.

Slipping his hand inside his coat, Luke gripped the handle of his pistol. How many men had accused him of cheating? An insult he could never allow to pass without calling for satisfaction. Which was precisely what had happened with Lieutenant Tripp. Normally, Luke would not mind an altercation. It kept his skill with the sword sharp while discouraging others from challenging him. Yet, tonight he found he had no desire to fight.

Finally, Mr. Fairfax tossed down his cards and mopped his sweaty brow. "Your infernal luck, Heaton."

Luck. "It's been a pleasure, gentlemen." Releasing his pistol, he reached to gather his winnings when he spotted Lieutenant Tripp parting the crowd, heading his way.

The annoying man halted before the table. "Heaton," he snorted. "Just where I expected to find you."

"But not where I expected to find you," Luke retorted with a grin.

Tripp straightened his coat and wobbled in place. "I heard of your success with my ship."

"Did you, now?" Luke leaned back in his chair. The man was drunk. It would be no fun taunting him in his condition.

Luke's three companions scooted their chairs back.

"Except it's my ship now, if you recall."

A sneer curled Lieutenant Tripp's lips. "You're nothing but a sot and a wastrel. One day of good fortune at sea cannot change that."

Luke attempted to shrug off the man's words though they sank into his gut, landing atop the ones Mr. Crane had planted there earlier that evening. "Perhaps. But what is that to you?"

"I'll have my ship back."

"So you have said." Luke sipped his rum. "You're drunk, Lieutenant. Go home and sleep it off."

The crowd quieted as eyes shot their way. With the money he'd made,

Luke could almost buy another ship and give *Destiny* back to this moron. If the man ever ceased being such a whining ninny, Luke might do just that.

The lieutenant stumbled again and rubbed the scar on his left cheek. "You will pay, sir."

Luke grew tired of the repetitious threats. He lifted his rum toward the man in a mock salute. "Perhaps. Now if you don't mind. . ." Luke waved his hand toward the door and slammed the rest of the rum to the back of his throat. Yet he had a feeling no amount of alcohol could make the peevish man disappear.

Before Luke could set down his glass, Lieutenant Tripp booted the table over, sending the coins, lantern, and cards flinging through the air, clanging and crashing to the wooden floor. He raised a pistol and pointed it at Luke. Mr. Fairfax doused the lantern flame, while Mr. Crenshaw dropped to his knees, scrambling to retrieve the coins.

The throng of excited onlookers backed away. The pianoforte stopped playing.

Luke released a frustrated sigh, set his glass on the next table, and slowly stood. The man's misty eyes wandered over him. The pistol shook in his hands.

Luke spread out his arms. "Well, shoot me then and get it over with." Certainly a deserving way for him to die. He'd given Mrs. Barnes enough money to last for years, at least until John was old enough to provide for himself. In fact, both she and John might be better off without Luke. Though his heart cramped at the pain the boy would endure at losing his only brother.

Lieutenant Tripp's eyelid began to twitch. He licked his lips. The pistol swung like a pendulum across Luke's chest. Time passed in slow motion. Only the sound of shifting boots, the hiss of lanterns, and the occasional grunt broke through the tense silence. Finally, someone yelled, "Shoot him" from the back of the mob. Others begged Tripp to put the weapon away.

A drop of sweat slid down Lieutenant Tripp's cheek as the pistol teetered in his hand. If Luke didn't stop this madness, the man might shoot an innocent bystander. Growing tired of waiting, Luke charged him, grabbed the gun, and tried to pry it from his fingers. Tripp struggled. He clenched his teeth, growling like a rabid bear. People scattered.

Swinging back his fist, Luke struck the man across the jaw. He let go of the weapon and tumbled backward into the crowd. Uncocking the gun, Luke released a deep breath as the mob broke into a chorus of cheers and chuckles. A man emerged from among them and helped the groaning and red-faced Lieutenant Tripp to his feet.

Luke blinked. *Mr. Crane?* Luke had left him only an hour ago at the Channings'.

"Did Miss Channing toss you out?" Luke chuckled.

Crane led Tripp to a nearby chair then faced Luke. "Don't be daft. I came here to confirm my suspicions of you."

The pianoforte began thrumming again as the throng dispersed back to their depraved revelries.

"Indeed." Luke cocked his head, wondering which suspicions he meant, when Clara sidled up beside him and caressed his arm. "Are you all right, Luke?"

"Yes, thanks, love." He nudged her back.

"Miss Channing thinks you are a man of honor, sir." Mr. Crane's buzz-like voice drew Luke's gaze back to him. "A rather distorted view, I'd say, biased by the fortune you made for her. For I see that the rumors about you are true. You are a drunk." He eyed the cards lying haphazardly across the sticky floor. "A gambler, and a bully who would strike one of the great officers who protects our good nation."

The hypocrite! Fury seared through Luke, pooling in his fist still gripping the pistol, while his other hand wandered dangerously close to the hilt of his cutlass. Could he not escape this man? Only the fact that he was a friend of Miss Channing's kept Luke from drawing his sword.

"Rest assured, sir," the mongrel continued, "Miss Channing will hear of your behavior tonight"—his eyes wandered over Clara standing off to the side—"and I'm sure she will be as horrified as I am to discover just what type of man she has allied herself with."

Setting the pistol down atop a table lest he shoot the bird-witted clod, Luke forced a grin to his lips. "I have no doubt, sir." Then barreling through the throng, he blasted out the front door, only then realizing he'd forgotten his winnings. No matter. He'd have a hard time getting them from Mr. Crenshaw, anyway. Besides, what was a few dollars when he had thousands? A wall of cool night air slapped him, instantly sobering him, and making him thankful he hadn't challenged Mr. Crane. He'd dueled men with far less provocation.

But Miss Channing wouldn't approve.

And he found himself more than anything never wanting to displease her.

Yet this night had established one fact. Luke was not worthy of a treasure like Cassandra. If he continued to shower her with his attentions in the hope of gaining her affection, it would only end up causing her pain. For everything he touched became tainted—sullied. No, for Cassandra's own good, Luke must keep their relationship strictly business. And despite the torrent of feelings she invoked within him, he must do his best to stay away from her.

❖

Milton Crane led the wobbling lieutenant to a table in the far corner, away from the crowd that was still chattering about the altercation.

"That capricious blackguard," the lieutenant cursed as Crane eased him into a chair and asked him if he'd like a drink.

The lieutenant rubbed his forehead. "No, I believe I've had quite enough."

"Milton Crane." Crane held out his hand and took a seat beside the lieutenant.

"Lieutenant Abner Tripp." The man took his hand. "Thank you for your help, sir."

Even in his besotted state, there was no mistaking the pure hatred that burned in the lieutenant's eyes toward Heaton. Such passionate hatred must have its reward. And Crane knew just the thing.

"That was Mr. Heaton who assaulted you, was it not?"

Lieutenant Tripp moaned. "Yes. I should have shot him when I had the chance." He looked up, his gaze drifting back and forth over Crane. "Do you have the misfortune of being acquainted with the villain?"

"Only recently, sir. Though I am quite aware of his reputation."

"Then you've no doubt heard that he stole my ship in a game of cards, took all my money as well, and then had the audacity to call me out to a duel." He rubbed the long purple scar on his cheek.

Crane grinned. This was getting better and better. "I had not heard, sir. But I assure you, I find the man equally repugnant."

The lieutenant's eyes seemed to sober for a moment as he stared at Crane as if he too, could foresee an alliance between them.

Crane gestured with his head toward Mr. Keene and Mr. Sanders who were sitting at the next table. "You see those men. They are part of his crew."

The lieutenant shrugged. "So?"

"So, if they are like Heaton, they have no loyalty to him or anyone else."
Lieutenant Tripp slouched in his chair and shook his head.

"Mr. Heaton stands in the way of something very important to me."
Visions of the scoundrel kissing Miss Channing on the cheek in the foyer
of her home flashed through his mind as well as the dozens of amorous
glances they had shared at dinner. The foolish girl was besotted with him.
And he must put a stop to their growing affection before Miss Channing
was hurt.

"And I perceive," Crane continued, "that you also seek revenge."

"You perceive correctly, sir." Tripp rubbed his long sideburns. "But I
don't see what we can do about it."

"Ah, that's where you are wrong, Lieutenant. If we put our minds
together, I believe we can both get what we want."

"Which is?"

"To destroy Luke Heaton."

❖

"Are you quite sure?" Cassandra turned her back on Mr. Crane and faced
the window of their parlor, not wanting him to see the pain that must
surely be visible on her face.

"Yes, I'm sorry to be the one to inform you, Miss Channing." His
gravelly voice assailed her from behind. "I know how you admire the man.
Not to mention your business arrangement with him."

Yet she doubted Mr. Crane was truly sorry at all, for not a trace of
regret tinged his voice. Cassandra gazed at her mother's roses sparkling
with morning dew in the front garden. "Why should I care if the man was
entertaining a tavern wench?" She kept her voice disinterested, while a
sick feeling clenched her gut and spiked through her heart at Mr. Crane's
description of the buxom woman draped over Luke Heaton's lap last night.

"And I'm afraid he was quite drunk and gambling as well. And he got
into a bit of a scuffle with a military man. Slugged him across the jaw."

Cassandra spun around, suddenly indignant at the man's jealous slurs.
Why had she let him in the house again? She had woken in such high
spirits. Everything in her life appeared to be going well. For once. Then
why did this man's accusations of Mr. Heaton, true or not, squash her joy
like a bug beneath his buckled shoe?

"I fail to see the purpose of telling me this, Mr. Crane. As long as Mr.

Heaton is successful at privateering, I could care less what he does in his free time." Without thinking, she lifted a hand to her cheek where Mr. Heaton's lips had touched her skin.

Mr. Crane must have noticed her sorrow for he gave a sympathetic smile. "I thought you should know the trustworthiness of the man with whom you have invested your wealth."

Trustworthiness. Cassandra sighed. That was the crux of the matter, was it not? Cassandra's trust had been betrayed far too often and by far too many people. Never. Never would she toss her affections upon a man who, for all indications, would betray her, abandon her, and leave her all alone in the world.

❖ CHAPTER 17 ❖

Cassandra entered the Brenin sitting room and dashed into Marianne's outstretched arms. "I came as soon as I got your note. Any word?" She drew back and gazed into her friend's red-rimmed eyes.

Marianne lowered her chin and shook her head. "None so far."

Taking her hand, Cassandra led her to the sofa. "But you don't know which privateer was captured?"

Marianne sniffed and held a handkerchief to her nose. "No, only that it was a brig like Noah's and that it had just set out to sea, as he had done."

"Many of the privateers are brigs." Cassandra squeezed her hand, longing to bring the poor woman some comfort. "And there are hundreds of them out at sea."

Marianne played with the delicate lace on the edge of her handkerchief. "I hate to think of him pressed into the navy again. Or worse, sent to one of those rotting prison hulks." Her shoulders began to quiver.

Slipping an arm over Marianne's shoulders, Cassandra drew her close. "Surely God will take care of Noah." Though she didn't believe the words herself, she knew Marianne would find solace in her faith. A faith Cassandra had always envied and yet found so lacking within herself. Perhaps believing in a God who cared was just a fantasy, after all. The thought oddly weighed upon her heart with a deep sorrow.

Marianne's mother entered the room, young Jacob in her arms. "He's asking for you, dear."

Swiping her tears away, Marianne took the baby and perched him on her lap. Laying her chin atop his head, she inhaled a deep breath as if the scent of her son would bring his father back.

"Good day, Mrs. Denton." Cassandra rose, but the elderly woman waved a hand for her to stay with Marianne.

"Do not get up on my account." She smiled and lowered herself with difficulty into one of the floral-printed chairs beside the hearth.

Cassandra shook her head. Mrs. Denton suffered from far more serious illnesses than Cassandra's mother, yet rarely did a complaint pass through her lips.

Clank clank clank. The front door reverberated with the sound of the brass knocker. Marianne's face paled, and her eyes shot to the foyer. A few seconds passed, and Mr. Sorens announced Reverend Drummond just as the man ambled into the room, fumbling with his hat.

The butler cleared his throat and held out his hand. The reverend stared at him for a moment before handing him his hat. "Ah yes, good fellow. Thank you." He faced Marianne again.

She rose, hoisting Jacob into her arms. "Forgive me, Reverend, but I am quite distressed today. I was not aware you intended to visit."

He bowed toward all three ladies and greeted each one in turn. "My apologies, Mrs. Brenin, for barging in, but I just left Mr. Heaton."

"Mr. Heaton?" Marianne asked.

Luke? Cassandra nearly leapt from her seat. Why did the mere mention of his name cause such a childish reaction? It had been nearly a week since she'd last seen him at her house for dinner. A week since he'd kissed her cheek and run off into the night.

Run off into another woman's arms.

After Mr. Crane's visit, a shroud of gloom had descended on Cassandra, even as she chastised herself for such preposterous feelings. What did it matter how Mr. Heaton conducted himself? He was on land and could do what he wanted. There was no understanding between them that went beyond business. Finally after a few days, she had been able to tuck her confusing emotions away. After which, her senses returned. She needed no man. And she had informed Mr. Crane of that fact in no uncertain terms as she had swept from the parlor.

Had he hoped that after he disparaged Mr. Heaton's character, she would run into his arms and swoon? "Bah!"

All eyes shot to her, bringing her back to the present. She covered her mouth with her hand. "Forgive me. . . . You were saying?"

"Yes," Reverend Drummond continued. "I was saying that Mr. Heaton informed me of your situation, Mrs. Brenin. He is heading to the docks to see if he can uncover any information that will be of help." He took a step closer, his brown eyes brimming with concern. "And I thought I'd come by to see if I could offer you some comfort while you await the news."

"How kind of you, Reverend," Marianne's mother said.

Marianne smiled and sat back down. Jacob waved his hands in the air and grabbed his mother's handkerchief.

"What has Luke to do with this?" Cassandra stood and began to pace.

Marianne collected her son's flailing arms in her hand. "He came by as soon as he heard the news and offered to help."

"Do sit down, Reverend." Marianne's mother gestured toward a chair then asked Mr. Sorens, who had remained at the parlor entrance, to instruct Mrs. Rebbs to serve tea.

Marianne pressed a hand over her belly. "I don't believe I can drink anything right now, Mother."

"You must try, dearest. It will settle your stomach." Her mother folded shriveled hands in her lap and leaned back in her chair, a picture of tranquility, though the nervous blinking of her eyes betrayed her.

"What if it's Noah?" Marianne's voice broke into a sob. "What if he's been captured?"

As Cassandra passed by the sofa, Jacob reached for her. Gathering him in her arms, she extracted the handkerchief from his hands and handed it to Marianne.

"Noah is a competent sailor," Mr. Drummond offered, lowering himself into a chair.

Marianne dabbed at her eyes as another knock rapped through the foyer. The door squeaked open and the thud of heavy boots echoed over the wooden floor. Cassandra's heart froze. She knew the sound of those boots anywhere.

Mr. Heaton's masculine frame filled the doorway. His eyes widened at the sight of her before he greeted Mr. Drummond, Marianne, and her mother.

"Miss Channing," he said, tossing his cocked hat onto a table. "A pleasure as always." Then marching across the room, he planted a kiss on Marianne's cheek.

A kiss. Just like the one he'd given Cassandra. A casual kiss of friendship. That was all it had been. Which would explain the trollop and the fact that Mr. Heaton had not come to call on her in five days. Cassandra felt a hot flush rise up her neck at how silly she had been.

"What news?" Marianne wrung her hands together.

Mr. Heaton gave her a reassuring look. "Nothing yet. But I have an acquaintance looking into it. He'll question them immediately and come here as soon as he discovers anything of note."

Marianne nodded and squeezed his hand. "Thank you, Luke."

"It's the least I can do. Noah has been a good friend. More like a brother to me." Mr. Heaton's jaw tightened, and for a moment Cassandra detected a slight sheen covering his eyes. He cleared his throat. "I see you have family and friends around you."

His gaze brushed over Cassandra as he sat in a chair near the doorway and leaned his elbows on his knees.

Jacob grabbed a lock of Cassandra's hair and pulled it from its pin. The late afternoon sun cut a sharp angle of glittering dust across the room. It spun in a frenzied dance, mimicking Cassandra's insides. Why, when she should be focusing on comforting her friend, did the man's presence affect her so?

After several moments of silence in which everyone fidgeted uncomfortably, Reverend Drummond turned to Marianne. "Would you like me to pray, Mrs. Brenin?"

"Yes, very much." Marianne smiled and she, along with her mother, folded her hands in her lap. The reverend bowed his head. Cassandra did the same, clinging to Jacob, who with thumb in his mouth, now leaned peacefully against her chest.

"Father, we beseech You to protect Noah Brenin. Be with him wherever he is and put a shield of Your warring angels around him. Bring him home safely to his family. And, Father, protect the men who did get captured. We pray it isn't Noah and his crew. But if so, Father, help us to. . . ," he continued, but Cassandra opened her eyes. She wanted to see Mr. Heaton's reaction to the prayer, but his gaze locked onto hers—a gaze burning with such strong yearning and admiration that she dropped her chin again.

"Amens" sounded around the room.

"Thank you, Reverend," Marianne's mother said as Mrs. Rebbs brought in a tray of tea and biscuits and set it on the table.

Reverend Drummond reached over and touched Marianne's arm. "You must trust God."

"I do trust. But I also know that tragedies come our way."

Cassandra nodded. She could well attest to that. What she couldn't fathom was why God allowed such horrible things to happen to His children.

Jacob began to fuss and she wandered to the window, rocking him in her arms. Outside the shadows cast their nets over the street and houses, capturing the last rays of light and dragging them away. She tickled Jacob beneath the chin. He giggled. Kissing him on the forehead, she inhaled his sweet scent as he tried to put his fingers in her mouth. She clutched his tiny hand. No, she would never understand how a Father could hurt His own child.

The clank of spoons on china filled the room, even as the scent of mint tickled her nose.

"Yes, horrible things do happen," Reverend Drummond said. "We live in a fallen world. But if you're God's child, everything serves a purpose—a good purpose. You remember that."

Marianne sighed. "Yes. I learned that lesson well when Noah and I were impressed aboard that British frigate." She gave an embarrassed huff. "You'd think I would never forget."

Cassandra turned around to see Mr. Heaton stretching his booted feet out before him and crossing his arms over his chest. "I beg your pardon, Reverend, but no good came out of my being impressed in the Royal Navy save a sore back and a starving belly."

As if just now noticing Mr. Heaton's presence, Jacob stretched out his arms toward him, nearly leaping from Cassandra's arms.

Rising, Mr. Heaton made his way to her, but his eyes were on the boy.

"Much good came out of that, Luke." Marianne handed a cup of tea to Reverend Drummond. "You were there. We saved the USS *Constitution*."

Luke's blue eyes met Cassandra's—a trace of sorrow in them—before he took Jacob from her arms, flung the boy into the air, and returned to his seat. "Happenstance. The right place at the right time. That's all it was."

Cassandra watched as he set Jacob's feet on the floor and then held onto his hands to help him stand. His faith was even more depleted than hers. But what did she expect from a man who possessed no morals?

"Exactly." The reverend slapped his knee. "The right place at the right time. Hardly feasible unless there's a God controlling things, wouldn't you say, Mr. Heaton?"

Mr. Heaton's face hardened like granite. He placed Jacob's hands on his knees for support then released him. "No, I would not, sir. I cannot believe that. Otherwise it would force me to accept that God is a monster."

"Oh my. How can you say such a thing, Luke?" Marianne's mother gasped.

Marianne stared at him while Reverend Drummond flattened his lips. But the reverend's eyes filled with love, not the anger Cassandra had expected. "You have suffered much, Mr. Heaton. But those who have suffered much are destined for much." He smiled and sipped his tea.

Jacob wobbled and plopped to the ground on his bottom. Before he could whine, Luke swung him into his lap. "Destined for what, Reverend, more suffering?" No bitterness spiked his tone, just a defeat that made Cassandra sad.

"We have all suffered," Marianne's mother said quietly.

Mr. Heaton's gaze shot her way and his expression softened. "Indeed."

Up until now, Cassandra had not considered that Mr. Heaton had suffered overmuch. Yet, she seemed to recall that his parents had been murdered by Indians some years ago.

Marianne passed Cassandra a cup of tea. Her friend's hand trembled. Taking it from her, Cassandra sat beside her, pondering the suffering they all had endured.

Reverend Drummond scratched his beard. "God's destiny is never bad. But it is good and acceptable and perfect just as Paul says in Romans 12:2."

Marianne slid her hand inside Cassandra's as she said, "You speak the truth, Reverend. I have seen God's destiny in action. His plans *are* good." Her glance took in everyone in the room. "They don't always make sense at the time, but in the end they are always good. A very astute young boy said to me once that since I didn't know the end of the story, how could I know if the things that were happening to me were good or bad?"

Reverend Drummond smiled.

Confusion rampaged through Cassandra's mind. How could her father's death and her brothers' disappearance bring anything good to her and her family? When she looked up, she saw that Mr. Heaton seemed to be having an equally difficult time accepting Marianne's statement.

Jacob flung his arms about Luke's neck. The bewilderment slipped from his face. He smiled at the lad and allowed him to pull strands of black hair from his tie.

"It's a lovely thought, Marianne," Cassandra said. "But I have yet to see it played out in my life."

The reverend set down his cup. "You must believe God is good and that He rewards those who diligently seek Him. And you must seek Him, Miss Channing, with your whole heart."

Mr. Heaton snorted and stood.

Cassandra sipped the bitter tea, glancing at the tray for sugar but finding none. She hadn't sought God, yet she'd been rewarded nonetheless with more than enough money to pay off her debts and care for her family. Was life merely just happenstance? Just a thread of chaotic events? Or were there reasons for everything that happened? A plan? A purpose?

Yet another knock on the door brought Marianne once again to her feet. Mr. Sorens ushered in a young man dressed in a checkered shirt, pea jacket, and oiled blue trousers. The scent of fish filled the room. His eyes locked with Mr. Heaton's then glanced over the others. He smoothed down his unruly hair as if suddenly conscious of his appearance.

"William." Reverend Drummond greeted the man as if they were old friends.

Mr. Heaton shifted Jacob to his other arm. "By all means, Mr. Yates, do you have news of Noah Brenin?"

❖ CHAPTER 18 ❖

Luke eyed the sailor, who seemed as out of place in the Brenin parlor as a pirate at a cotillion. Yet his fear for Noah's fate overcame his patience. "Spill it, man, what news?"

"Ah, yes." The sailor grinned. "I have good news. The ship that was caught by the Brits was the *Rover*, not the *Defender*."

"Praise God!" Reverend Drummond shouted, leaping to his feet.

Marianne swayed as if she might faint, and Miss Channing helped her to sit back down on the sofa. Clutching her throat, Marianne released a breath. "God is good."

"Amen," her mother added.

As relief poured through him, Luke thanked the sailor, who dipped his head and spun on his heels as if anxious to leave the cultured surroundings.

"I best be going as well." Reverend Drummond searched for his hat. "I've got business to attend to." Anticipating the request, Mr. Sorens appeared around the corner, Reverend Drummond's hat in hand. Grabbing it with his thanks, the reverend called out after the sailor. "I'll walk with you, lad." Turning, he bid them all adieu, received Marianne's heartfelt thanks, and then left the sitting room. Luke could hear Mr. Drummond slapping the sailor on the back with a chuckle as they closed the front door behind them. Did the reverend hold such close acquaintance with everyone in town?

Marianne's mother rose and crossed the room to sit beside her daughter.

She drew her into an embrace and together they half sobbed, half laughed, while Miss Cassandra gazed on with moist eyes. The tension that had kept the air in the room as stagnant as the doldrums released in a flurry of joy.

"Well, that saves me the trouble of having to go rescue him." Luke winked at Cassandra then knelt and set Jacob on the floor, holding him up by his hands. The boy attempted a step on his own. His wide grin, sporting three teeth and a stream of drool, melted Luke's heart. John was about the same age when Luke had taken over his care. Oh, how he wished he could go back in time and be a better father to the boy.

But God did not give second chances.

Marianne sat up and dabbed her handkerchief beneath her eyes. "He'll be walking before you know it."

"Indeed. They grow up fast." Luke's eyes landed on Miss Channing, who stared at him with an odd mixture of surprise and admiration. He warmed beneath her gaze, which she quickly swept to the window, where encroaching shadows had absconded with the light.

"When do you sail out, Luke?" Marianne asked.

"I leave for Elizabeth City tomorrow. I sent my crew ahead two days ago to prepare the ship."

Marianne's mother gripped the arms of the chair as she struggled to rise. "My goodness, the night has overtaken us unawares. I must bathe Jacob before supper."

"I will help you, Mother." Marianne made her way to Luke. With great reluctance, he relinquished the young boy. And apparently the feeling was mutual as Jacob whimpered and held out his hands toward Luke.

"Please be careful, Luke." Marianne clutched Jacob's hands to settle him. "And if you see Noah"—she looked down with a coy smile—"well, you know what to tell him."

Luke nodded.

"Oh my." Marianne turned to Miss Channing. "However will you get home in the dark?" Yet Luke caught the tiny smile peeking from the corners of her mouth.

Miss Channing stood and lifted her chin. "I am quite capable of finding my own way."

"Nonsense," Marianne's mother scoffed as she moved to her daughter's side.

"I would be happy to escort you, Miss Channing," Luke offered, ignoring the war within him—between his desire to spend time with this captivating woman and his promise to stay away from her.

Cassandra opened her mouth to say something, but Marianne held up a hand. "There, now, it is all settled." She approached Cassandra and touched her arm. "Thank you so much for coming, dear friend. I don't know what I'd do without you."

"I'm so pleased things turned out well." Cassandra clasped her hands together as if suddenly nervous.

"Mr. Sorens will see you out." Then turning, Marianne and her mother, along with a whimpering Jacob, left the room.

Luke raked a hand through his hair and raised his brows at Cassandra. Offering him nothing but a mere flick of her sharp eyes, she swept past him into the foyer, plucked her bonnet and gloves from a table, and waited for Mr. Sorens to open the door. Luke stepped onto the porch after her.

"There really is no need, Mr. Heaton." She tugged on her gloves, despite the muggy air.

"Nevertheless, I would never forgive myself should something happen to you." Luke could not explain her sudden stony demeanor. Last week at her house, she'd been kind, agreeable, and even quite complimentary toward him at the dinner table. She'd even allowed him to plant a kiss on her cheek.

Granted, he'd made himself a promise to avoid her. But now in her presence, he found himself longing to see a spark of ardor beaming from her eyes. Just a glimmer of sentiment would be enough to comfort him on his long sea voyage ahead.

But she kept her eyes from him as she stormed down the steps and out onto the street before he had a chance to offer her his arm. Lud, what an infuriating woman.

With only a quarter moon and a smattering of stars to light his way, Luke marched after her, overtaking her halfway down the street. He offered her his arm. "Unless you don't wish to be seen with me."

"I'm afraid it's too late for that, Mr. Heaton."

"Ah, that's it then, your reputation has been forever tarnished by our association." He chuckled, but she did not join in his amusement.

Instead she shot him a seething glance. "Go back to your trollop, Mr. Heaton."

Luke ground his teeth together, suddenly feeling like the cad everyone believed him to be. So, Mr. Crane had followed through with his threat.

When Luke didn't answer her, she gave an exasperated huff and hurried down the street. Somewhere, a fiddle played and laughter crackled in the air, but otherwise silence reigned on the city as thick as the night. Rubbing his jaw, Luke followed her at a distance, close enough to keep her firmly in his vision. She blazed forward into the darkness like a wild cougar, a tail of lacy petticoats flailing behind her.

No, not a cougar, an angel.

And certainly not one he could ever expect to possess.

She turned down Baltimore Street. The *clip clip* of her shoes over the cobblestones echoed off the brick walls of nearby buildings and local watering holes. Music blared from Payne's Tavern up ahead. Luke knew it well. Why was she traveling this way? Foolish woman. It would be much safer to take the long way around and avoid this section of town.

Yet still she stormed forward as if *she* were the indefatigable town rogue, not him. How the lady survived to be five and twenty defied all logic.

❖

Cassandra charged ahead, only realizing when she'd made it halfway down Baltimore Street that this was not the safest route to take at night. The jangling of a pianoforte, accompanied by a fiddle and raucous discourse, rode upon lantern light bursting from a tavern up ahead. Cursing burned her ears. She glanced over her shoulder, fully expecting to see Mr. Heaton behind her, but he was nowhere to be found. Hadn't she told him to go back to his trollop?

Yet she hadn't expected him to obey her.

Fear prickled her skin. How could he leave her all alone? Facing forward, she lowered her head and crossed the street, hoping the shadows would hide her until she could make it past the tavern, bustling with patrons, up ahead. Most of whom, she was sure, she did not wish to meet.

At least she carried no money with her this time. No banknotes. Nothing anyone would want. A shot echoed in the distance, jerking her gaze in that direction. The British? Or was it just a tavern brawl? Clutching her skirts, she quickened her pace, squinting into the darkness. Moonlight coated the buildings, trees, and cobblestone street in a ghoulish, milky sheen. The sting of alcohol and rain filled her nostrils.

Across the street, clusters of men hovered under the porch of the tavern, their heated conversations jumbled on the wind.

She was nearly past them.

A man barreled down the tavern steps, another on his heels. The first took a swig from a bottle, wiped his mouth on his sleeve, and handed it to his friend.

Cassandra sped to the shadows from a row of buildings up ahead.

"Hey there, missy!"

Her heart seized. She started to run.

"Where ye goin', missy? Come back here." The man's slurred words slinked over her shoulders and slammed into her gut.

Heavy footfalls pounded the road, growing louder and louder.

Not again. Cassandra darted forward. When would she learn her lesson?

"Missy, come join us, eh?" Insidious laughter accompanied the thump of footsteps.

Perspiration dotted her neck. She heaved a breath. One glance behind told her the two men were gaining. Ducking her head, she raced forward.

And ran headfirst into a warm, firm body.

Tar and smoke and wood filled her nostrils. *Mr. Heaton.* She glanced up, but could barely make out his smile in the darkness. He pushed her behind him then faced the villains and crossed his arms over his chest.

She peered around his back, her heartbeat steadying, then stepped beside him, fisting her hands on her hips and pasting a look of defiance on her face.

Her pursuers spotted Mr. Heaton. With wide eyes, they halted, their laughter faltering on their lips.

"Heaton, what ye doin' here?" The man's gaze shifted to Cassandra. She lifted her chin in his direction.

"The lady is with me, gentlemen." Mr. Heaton's stern voice left no room for argument.

A stream of profanity poured from their mouths. "Come on, Heaton. We was just havin' some fun. We weren't goin' t' hurt her none."

"Watch your language in front of the lady, or you'll answer to me," Luke said with authority.

The first man shook his head and scowled, yet he made no move. Instead Cassandra detected fear, dare she say respect emanating from him.

The other man grunted and swayed back and forth like one of the ships in the bay.

Luke waved them off. "Begone with you. There's no fun to be had here."

Turning, the two men shuffled away, passing the bottle between them as if to console themselves on their defeat.

Mr. Heaton faced her, stared at her for a moment, then proffered his elbow. "Now, will you allow me to escort you home?"

"You didn't leave me." Cassandra gaped at him, stunned.

"That is never my desire."

The wind drifted through loose strands of his hair, and for a moment the moonlight offered her a glimpse of something in his eyes that caused her breath to seize. She slid her hand in the crook of his elbow, and he led her forward. "Those men." She glanced over her shoulder to see them join a mob loitering in front of the tavern. "They offered you no resistance."

"They know me." He kept his face forward, his voice deep and resonant.

"In other words, they've seen you use a sword." Her praise brought no reaction. "Such depraved company you keep, Mr. Heaton."

"As you have informed me." He should be mad at her for her foolish behavior. He should be angry at her insults. But instead, a hint of humor spiked his voice.

An awkward silence surrounded them as they turned down Charles Street. Another shot echoed in the distance, followed by baleful laughter, yet Cassandra found no fear within her. As long as she was with Mr. Heaton. The thudding of his boots accompanied the whistle of the wind and the bells of the night watchmen in a whirlwind of emotions that reeled around her like the dust spinning on the street.

Mr. Heaton was a scoundrel, yet she always felt at ease on his arm.

A dark cloud abandoned the moon, showering them in silver light.

He was a drunk, yet he had never behaved improperly in her presence.

They turned down Eutaw Street, lined with quaint homes and decorative flower gardens. The smell of wild bergamot and fresh apple pie drifted over her nose.

He was a gambler, yet she trusted him with her investment.

Turning down the path in front of her house, Mr. Heaton stopped at the bottom of the porch stairs. Cassandra stepped up on the first tread and spun to face him. She was nearly level in height with him—nearly. The lantern light sparkled in his eyes as he placed a boot atop the step and released her arm.

He was a womanizer; then why did she feel her heart yearning for his affection?

He turned to leave.

"Thank you once again for your rescue, Mr. Heaton."

He faced her. A sad grin hovered over his lips. "My pleasure."

"So, you'll be leaving tomorrow?" She longed to keep him here. And hated herself for it.

"Riding out to the ship first thing in the morning."

"How long will you be?" Cassandra asked then realized the absurdity of the question. She laughed. "Of course you don't know that."

He gave her a quizzical look. "Will you miss me?"

"Don't be absurd." Cringing at the dishonest twang in her voice, she stared off toward the bay. "I'm simply anxious for you to catch another prize."

"Ah." He scratched the stubble on his chin and gave her one of his beguiling grins. "Of course."

Cassandra tapped her foot. "Oh, bother, Mr. Heaton. You can wipe that grin off your face. Not every woman in town pines for your affections."

"No." The sorrow in his voice nearly broke through the shield she'd erected around her heart. "Not every woman."

What was she doing? Allowing this rake to charm his way into her graces. Steeling herself against his further attempts, Cassandra pursed her lips. "Mr. Crane informed me of your ignoble activities."

"Which ones?" He jerked the hair from his face and chuckled. Moonlight drifted over a scar on his right earlobe.

"You may make sport of it all you wish, Mr. Heaton, but I hardly consider gambling, drinking, and fighting suitable pursuits for a successful privateer, much less a gentleman."

"Well, Miss Channing, you knew what you were getting when you hired me." One brow cocked, he gave her a pointed gaze. "Besides, I'm hurting no one." His eyes lowered to her lips. He swallowed.

Heat swirled in her belly. "I am not so sure, Mr. Heaton."

"Why are you so interested in what I do at night, Miss Channing? Care to join me?"

"Of course not! I'm sure you have no need of me with all your trollops to entertain you."

Propping his hand on the post, he drew close until she could feel his warm breath on her cheek. "If I were a more astute man, I'd say you were jealous."

Cassandra's heart took up an erratic beat. Lowering her chin, she gathered her resolve to put this man in his place. Then squaring her shoulders, she met his gaze and opened her mouth to give him a tongue lashing. "That's ridicu—"

His lips met hers. Firm, yet gentle. He caressed her mouth ever so briefly like the most delicate flutter of butterfly wings. Then he withdrew, hovering over her, breathing hard. Cassandra's mind swirled. She couldn't think. She couldn't breathe. She just wanted more of him. She inched forward until her lips touched his again. Her feet tingled. The world spun around her. He took control and deepened the kiss, cupping her jaw in his hand and caressing her cheek with his thumb. She drew in the scent of him, never wanting to forget this moment. He tasted of spice and salt.

The trollop barged into her dreamlike state. The one Mr. Crane had described in such detail. Her blond curls, sweet blue eyes, and buxom figure draped over Mr. Heaton.

No! The small part that remained of Cassandra's rational mind screamed. She would not be one of his many conquests. She would not attach her affections to this man, only to be abandoned.

She shoved Mr. Heaton back. Her chest heaved. "How dare you?" Then raising her hand, she slapped him across the cheek.

❖ CHAPTER 19 ❖

Pain lanced across Luke's face. He rubbed his cheek and stared at Cassandra. The woman was indeed an enigma. One minute returning his kiss with surprising intensity and the next, striking his cheek. He would never have made such advances if he'd not seen desire in her eyes. Not to mention an ardor that made his heart soar with hope. Hope that a woman like Cassandra found anything worthy of admiration in a man like him. Then, the way her moist lips shimmered in the moonlight, her puffs of warm breath, inviting him, luring him for a taste. He'd been unable to resist her. And, ah, sweet reward. He hadn't expected so passionate a response. Heat seared through his body while a pleasurable fog had invaded his mind.

What he *had* expected came later—a slap. A worthy punishment for so great a prize.

And now a mixture of horror and ecstasy battled in her eyes as she stood there, red faced with her infernal shoe tapping on the stairs.

He'd never seen a woman so lovely.

Luke rubbed his jaw again. "What, pray tell, was that for?"

"For trying to take liberties with me."

"Trying?" Luke chuckled. "I believe I succeeded. And as for the liberties, they were freely given."

"How dare you!" She lifted her hand again to strike him. He caught it in midair. "Ah, ah, ah, only one slap allowed per kiss." Caressing her hand, he lifted it to his mouth, but she snagged it from his grasp.

"Is everything a joke to you, sir?"

"Not everything." He smiled.

She let out an exasperated sigh and took a step away from him. "This is a business arrangement, Mr. Heaton, and you are nothing but a business partner. I insist you conduct yourself as such in my presence."

Luke could feel the heat coming from her flushed skin. Her chest rose and fell like the bow of a ship upon stormy seas.

"If you're certain that is what you wish." He dipped his head with an unavoidable grin.

"If I'm. . ." She flattened her lips and tore her gaze from him. "Of course I'm certain, you buffoon."

The quiver of desire in her voice belied her statement. Luke offered no response. He simply gazed at her as the moonlight caressed her in sparkling waves. He didn't know how long he'd be gone, and he never wanted to forget how beautiful she was, nor how deeply affected she seemed to be by his kiss.

"Good evening, Mr. Heaton." She met his gaze then turned and opened the door. The voices of children and bark of a dog floated from inside. Halting, she spoke without turning. "Godspeed to you, sir. Have a safe journey."

"Good evening, Miss Channing."

Then, stepping into the foyer, she closed the door behind her.

❖

"This is madness, Luke. I beg you to reconsider." The squeak of Mrs. Barnes's rocking chair increased in tempo.

"I promised John, and I won't go back on my word." Tired of the conversation, Luke set his mug of coffee down on the table and leaned forward with elbows on his knees. Mrs. Barnes's fingers flew, her needles jumping up and down like handles on a bilge pump. He studied the web of black and white threads coming together in a deranged mass. "What is that you're making again?" he asked, mainly to change the subject.

Ceasing her knitting, she glanced down at her creation. "A masterpiece," she announced with assurance. But her brief smile faded into a frown, and she laid her knitting aside. "He's far too young, Luke, and you know it." Her pleading tone reached out to strangle Luke's conviction.

Swimming eyes met his above the glimmer of her spectacles. He pulled his gaze and stared at the cold soot lining the fireplace. "He's as old, if not older, than most boys who go to sea. Besides, with his new brace, he's walking better."

"But on a heaving ship? When you could be attacked? When you probably will attack other ships?" Mrs. Barnes grabbed her cup of tea. Her hands trembled, and the amber liquid sloshed over the sides. She set it down on the saucer with a clank and folded her shriveled hands in her lap.

Luke shot to his feet and took up a pace across the sitting room. He rubbed his jaw where Miss Channing had slapped him earlier that evening. Though the memory brought a smile to his lips, he couldn't help but feel as though he were being slapped all over again by Mrs. Barnes's lack of confidence in him. But what else did he expect? Save for his one success at sea last month, Luke had been a failure at everything else.

But he *had* outsailed a frigate. He had dodged cannon blasts. He had taken a prize. Never once had his crew been in any serious danger. Despite her age, *Destiny* was a swift and agile bird. And Luke a good captain. Surely he had proven that.

"I could not bear to lose him," Mrs. Barnes said.

"And you think I could?"

"No, of course not. But your parents put him in your charge. I beg you to not make such a rash decision."

Trailing a hand through his hair, Luke faced her. "I have thought long and hard about this, Mrs. Barnes. He is ten. Brace or not, we cannot coddle him forever. He must be allowed to face life with all its dangers and heartaches. How else is he to grow up and become a man? How else is he to learn a trade so he can take care of himself someday?"

She opened her mouth to object but Luke raised a hand. "He is going."

A tremble crossed her shoulders. Chastising himself for being so harsh, Luke knelt before her and took her hands in his. "I'll keep him on a long line tied to one of the masts, so there'll be no chance of him falling overboard. When we overtake a prize, I'll send him below. He'll be fine." He kissed her bony fingers.

"I promise you, I'll bring him home safe."

❖

Luke planted his boots firmly on the quarterdeck as *Destiny* rose over yet another swell then plunged down into the murky sea. Waves crashed over the bow, spraying the air with foamy salt and sending a waterfall over the deck. A giggle sounded, and Luke's gaze shot to his brother on the main deck. He was talking with Mr. Ward, the gunner. Feet spread apart, John stumbled only slightly before he righted himself then held out his hands and dipped a bow at Mr. Ward's hearty applause.

Despite his apparent sturdiness, Luke was still glad the boy was tied to the mast with a rope long enough to allow him access to the entire deck. Aside from his initial bout of seasickness, the lad had more than adapted to life aboard the ship during the long weeks at sea. With his positive outlook, cheerful disposition, and strong work ethic, the crew took an immediate liking to John. But it was the odd relationship that had developed between him and the ornery gunner that surprised Luke the most.

Biron crossed the quarterdeck and halted beside Luke. "Courses and mains raised, Cap'n, and the horizon is clear."

Luke shielded his eyes from the setting sun as a hot gust of wind punched him. They'd been running under courses for days now. No need to unfurl the stays and topsails until they gave chase. Or, God forbid, were chased. Either way, they'd not spotted a ship in a week, which was why Luke had ordered *Destiny* on a south-by-southeast course to intercept West Indies trade routes.

Biron chuckled. "Ward's taking a liking to the boy."

"Odd. Yes."

"I wonder if he's the best influence on the lad?" Biron quirked a brow of reprimand at Luke.

"Knowing my brother, it's him who'll be influencing old Ward for the better. Perhaps, the old codger will even stop his swearing and drinking."

"Perhaps you will join him." Biron's voice was etched with sarcasm.

Luke chose to ignore it as the ship crested another wave. Bracing his feet on the moist deck, he breathed in the fresh, salty air. He loved the sea. There was freedom here upon the waves. Freedom and power. For the first time in his life, he felt in control of his own destiny.

Gripping the quarter railing, Luke glanced up at the sails, their white bellies bloated with wind. Mr. Keene stood on the main top, directing the sailors adjusting canvas, lace flapping at his cuffs and collar. His humor was vastly improved from the last voyage. As were several of the sailors. No doubt due to the bottles of rum locked in a crate belowdecks, and the money that still lined their pockets. Bottles Luke had brought aboard, despite Miss Channing's insistence to the contrary, but only on the condition that Luke would dispense the alcohol at his discretion. Which so far had only been two ounces in a cup of lemon water twice a day to each sailor. This seemed to appease the men, but it made Luke's vow to abstain while sailing all the more difficult. He licked his lips. His taut nerves and empty belly yearned for a sip. Just one sip.

Still he had kept to his word. Thus far.

Sam cleared his throat from behind them. "She still feels a bit sluggish, Cap'n."

Luke shrugged off the ill feeling that accompanied Sam's words. He'd already sent Mr. Sanders down twice to check on the hold, and both times the purser had reported nothing amiss. Perhaps it was just Sam's inexperience with such a small ship. "Just keep her south-by-southeast, Sam." Luke squinted at the sun sinking below the horizon as a breeze, bearing a reprieve from the day's scorching heat, cooled the sweat on his neck.

"Aye, aye, Cap'n."

John hobbled up on the quarterdeck with the agility of an experienced seaman.

"When can I take off this silly rope?" He made a face of disgust as the wind tousled his hair.

"When I say you can," Luke replied.

"But I'm steady on my feet now. The sailors make fun of me with this leash on!"

Biron chuckled. "Don't listen to them, boy. One day you'll be their captain and we'll see who's laughing then."

John's face brightened. "You really think so, Mr. Abbot?"

"That I do."

"You have the makings of a great sailor, John. A natural talent"—Luke raised a brow—"but you must still obey your captain."

John saluted. "Aye, sir."

"Sail ho!" The voice brayed from the tops, jerking Luke to attention.

John gripped the railing and scanned the horizon.

"Where away?" Luke shouted, lifting the scope to his eye.

"Two points off our starboard beam!" The shout ricocheted off the deck as Luke spun the glass in that direction. Excited chatter rose from the assembling crew.

Billowing sails, stark against the murky sky, came into view.

"Is she a merchantman, Luke? I mean Captain Luke." John's voice brimmed with enthusiasm.

"Hold steady there, lad," Biron interjected. "It won't matter if she is.

We haven't enough daylight left to take her."

"Ah. . ." John's shoulders lowered.

Luke could relate. Patience had never been one of Luke's finest virtues either. If he possessed any virtues at all. Though he knew privateers could be out for months before seeing any action, the quicker he caught a prize or two, the quicker he could return to Baltimore to see Miss Channing. The quicker he could add another success to outweigh his list of failures. And the quicker he could prove to Mrs. Barnes that he was fully capable of taking care of John at sea.

Several minutes passed as the ship came sharper into view. Waves slapped against the hull. Sails flapped thunderously as his crew awaited orders. Luke studied her armament and the shape of her hull just as a shout from above confirmed his assessment.

"She's a Royal Navy frigate!"

John's eyes widened. "A frigate!" He begged for the glass, nearly plucking it from Luke's hand, then raised it to his eye, looking ever so much like he'd been born to captain a ship. Luke smiled. If Mrs. Barnes could see the boy now, all her worries would blow away in the wind.

Biron tugged at his red neckerchief, his gray brows colliding. "Should we run?"

Luke shook his head as the sun bade its farewell with bands of orange and maroon. "No sense. It will be dark soon." He turned to Sam, manning the wheel with as much seriousness as he had no doubt done in the navy. "Keep her steady, Sam."

John's *oohs* and *aahs* filled the air as he examined the ship through the scope. But soon darkness stole it from their view, and he handed the glass back to Luke.

"Sam, alter course slightly to the east," Luke ordered. "We'll lose them during the night. And Biron, inform the night watch to keep the lanterns cold, if you please. We don't want to give them anything to shoot at, do we?"

"Aye, aye, Cap'n," both men replied.

Untying John, Luke ushered the boy down the companionway to the captain's cabin. After a rather tasteless meal of dried meat and hard biscuits, Luke assisted John with his studies—another thing he'd promised Mrs. Barnes he would do. After going over mathematics, literature, and shipboard navigation, Luke tucked John into the captain's bed. "You're much smarter than I ever was, little brother. I was never very good at my studies."

"I know. Mrs. Barnes told me." John smiled.

Laughing, Luke tapped John on the nose, pride welling up in him. "You're also going to be a great sailor and a good captain."

"I told you I could do it." The young boy nodded.

"And you were right. I should have trusted you."

"I take after you, Luke." John grew serious. "You're a great captain. Mom and Dad would be proud."

Emotion burned in Luke's throat as he pulled the quilt up to John's chin. He doubted that was true. If his parents could see the way Luke lived his life, it would no doubt break their hearts. All the things they had warned him to stay away from, he had run out and done anyway. The gambling, drinking, the womanizing. And all the things they had told him were important, reading his Bible, praying, working hard, and trusting God, he had not done. Why? Rebellion against their rigid rules, he supposed. But it went much deeper than that. Right into the depths of their faith. Where had their devotion to God gotten them? Burned alive in their own house. But Luke didn't blame God for that. How could he blame someone who didn't exist? No, their deaths were on Luke's head. He could have rescued them, but he didn't. Instead, he had stood there like a coward.

A sudden ache sliced through his right ear, and he reached up to rub it.

"Get some sleep, John." Luke stood. "You never know what tomorrow will bring. Perhaps we'll catch a prize!"

John gave him a wide grin then turned on his side and closed his eyes as if obeying Luke would make it come true.

By the time Luke made it to his desk, John's deep breathing filled the cabin. Ah, to be an innocent child again and fall asleep without a care in the world. Sinking down onto the stern window ledge, Luke propped up his boot and gazed out the windows onto the ebony sea beyond. Boisterous laughter and a ribald ballad drifted down from above, reminding Luke that everyone—but him and possibly Biron—was enjoying some rum tonight.

Infernal woman. He leaned his head back on the bulkhead. Infernal, wonderful, beautiful woman. Though it had been weeks, his lips still burned with the passion of her kiss, her taste. The way she had melted at his touch and groaned in pleasure. She had wanted him to kiss her. And he had been unable to stop. Just as he was unable to stop thinking of her now. Did he have a chance to win her affections? He had not thought so until that night. But a seed of hope had wiggled into the hard soil of his heart—albeit a tiny seed—that a woman like Cassandra could love a blackguard like him.

❖

"Captain!" Rough hands gripped Luke's arms. "Get up."

Luke rubbed his eyes and opened them to see a worried look on Biron's lined face.

"What is it?" He sprang from the hammock.

"It's the frigate, Captain." Biron shot a glance out the stern windows where the sun's rays were just intruding into the cabin and then at John, still sound asleep on the bed.

"She's fast on our tail."

❖ CHAPTER 20 ❖

Clutching her gown, Cassandra dragged her tired legs up the stairs to her chamber. She'd been woken far too early that morning when Darlene, Hannah, and Dexter had burst into her room chasing each other in a game of privateer versus British merchantman. With sticks as swords, hairbrushes as pistols, and Dexter's thunderous barks serving as cannon blasts, the trio had pounced on her bed, oblivious to Cassandra's sleeping form. After chastising them, Cassandra had given in to their sobs and gathered them up on her rumpled coverlet where the three of them, and Dexter, had engaged in a renewed battle, only this time using pillows—the likes of which had quickly become casualties of war in a snowstorm of feathers. Cassandra had insisted they all help Mrs. Northrop clean up the mess, but now as Cassandra entered her chamber, she spotted one rebellious feather peeking at her from beneath the bed. Stooping, she picked it up and brushed it over her chin, a smile lifting her lips. Just to see Hannah well again was worth the mayhem.

A scraping sound jerked Cassandra's gaze to her dressing bureau in the far corner where Mrs. Northrop stood gaping at her, a look of terror on her face.

"Mrs. Northrop, whatever are you doing in here?"

The housekeeper waved both hands in the air. "Just searching for more feathers, miss." Her voice quaked and her gaze skittered across the chamber. "Oh, I see you've found one." Dashing toward Cassandra, she plucked it from her hand and rushed out of the room.

Cassandra stared after her. The woman's behavior was becoming more and more peculiar with each passing day.

The shrill *ding ding ding* of a bell shot through the open door, followed by her mother's pathetic howl. Then Darlene's boisterous laughter, accompanied by Hannah's yelp, barreled through the window from outside.

Perhaps the entire house was mad, after all.

Cassandra wandered to her window and sat on the cushioned ledge. Shafts of afternoon sunlight angled across the side of the house and over the top of the solarium below. The leaves of birch and maple trees fluttered in the breeze as pink Virginia creeper circled their trunks. A hot summer breeze caressed her face, swirling the scent of wild mint and thyme beneath her nose. A bell tolled from the docks, and her thoughts drifted to Mr. Heaton. He'd been gone two weeks. Not a day—no, if she were honest—not an hour passed that she did not think of him.

And his kiss. The way her insides had felt like a thousand flickering candles. The look of adoration and desire in his eyes. The shameful way she had responded.

Before she had slapped him.

Yet even her strike had not erased the affection from his gaze or the mischievous smirk from his lips. She missed him. And she hated herself for it. A niggling fear had ignited within her these past days. Privateering was dangerous business. What if something happened to him and his ship? What if she never saw him again?

Cassandra gazed down at the floral pattern on the cushions. She must not think of him. Nor of his kiss. She must not entertain thoughts of any attachment to the man. For he was a blackguard and a philanderer. Not a man to be counted on—trusted. Even if she accepted his courtship, he'd no doubt grow restless and abandon her. No, she could not depend on anyone, not ever again. For everyone had let her down. Even God.

God. Reverend Drummond and Marianne had said that God had a purpose—a good purpose for everything that happened. If that was true, if God was involved in the details of Cassandra's life, would He still listen to her prayers? Even though she had ignored Him for years?

She bowed her head. "God, if You're listening, please protect Mr. Heaton."

The sound of a throat clearing opened Cassandra's eyes. She turned to see Margaret smiling at her from the doorway. Cassandra's face heated.

"Forgive me, miss. I didn't mean to intrude, but your mother requests your presence in the parlor. Mr. Crane has arrived."

Cassandra closed her eyes. "Oh, bother." Lately, the man seemed to appear wherever Cassandra happened to be: at the chandlers, the wheelwright, the seamstress, the butcher. And when she didn't venture out, he showed up at her house. However, his usual dour mood had significantly improved these past few weeks. To the point that he was almost giddy with delight. And for some reason, that annoyed her more than his peevishness. At least he had not brought up the subject of a courtship between them again. Though if that was not his goal, she couldn't imagine why he continued to call on her family. Squaring her shoulders, Cassandra rose from her seat, pressed down the folds of her gown.

"Pardon me for saying so." The maid gave her a coy grin. "But it's good to see you praying again, miss."

Cassandra flung a hand in the air as she brushed past Margaret. "I was just praying for Mr. Heaton's safety."

"Well, if he's the one causing you to talk to God again, I hope he returns to town soon." Margaret's words followed Cassandra downstairs and settled on her heart with equal sentiment.

So did she. So did she.

Before she reached the foyer, whispers slithered over her ears. Peering over the banister, Cassandra spotted Mr. Crane speaking to Mrs. Northrop at the entrance to the long hall that led to the back of the house. Mrs. Northrop nodded and sped away, while Mr. Crane strode to the foot of the stairs, his face aglow with surprise when he saw Cassandra descending.

"Ah, Miss Channing, you look lovely this afternoon."

"Thank you, sir. What on earth were you speaking to my housekeeper about?"

His lips twisted in an odd shape before he answered. "Just ordering some tea for your mother." He proffered his arm and led Cassandra into the sitting room where her mother perched excitedly on the settee.

"Oh, there you are, dear. Isn't it nice that Mr. Crane has taken time away from his duties at the newspaper to call on you?"

Not particularly. Cassandra forced a smile and took a seat beside her mother just as Hannah darted into the room, her eyes red with tears. "Mama, Darlene hit me."

After an embarrassing glance at Mr. Crane, Cassandra's mother placed her fingers atop her temple. "Please, dearest, tell her we do not hit each other in this house."

"I did," Hannah whined.

Darlene tumbled into the room then stopped short when she saw Mr. Crane. "I didn't hit her, Mother."

"Yes, you did." Hannah stomped her foot and folded her arms over her chest.

"No, I didn't."

Cassandra's mother closed her eyes and rang her bell, while Mr. Crane examined the girls with disdain before releasing a huff of impatience.

Seeing an opportunity to relieve herself of Mr. Crane's company, Cassandra rose. "I'll take them upstairs, Mother." She started toward the girls.

"No, dear, I insist you stay and entertain Mr. Crane. I've invited him to stay for supper. Besides, Mrs. Northrop can take care of them." She rang her bell again and the housekeeper appeared, a scowl on her face.

Kneeling beside her sisters, Cassandra gave them both a stern look. "Now go with Mrs. Northrop and attend to your studies. And behave yourselves, both of you."

"I'm sorry, Cassie." Darlene feigned a pout.

"I simply cannot handle them anymore," her mother remarked to Mr. Crane after the girls left.

Cassandra spun around. "You never could handle them, Mother."

Her mother frowned. "I suppose you're right. You were equally as difficult, but at least your father was still here to help."

Cassandra's anger dissipated beneath the look of pain on her mother's face. Taking her seat again, she placed a hand on her mother's arm. "I'm truly sorry, Mother."

Her mother gave a sad smile. "You always did have a mind of your own."

Mr. Crane cleared his throat. "All those girls need is the firm hand of a man's discipline."

"Oh, you are so right, Mr. Crane. You are so right, indeed." Her mother's voice came back to life.

Cassandra leaned back in her chair, desperate to change the subject. "How is the newspaper business, Mr. Crane?"

"Booming." He tugged at the cuffs of his coat and sat on the sofa opposite Cassandra. A breeze stirred the curtains at the windows as the clatter of a horse and carriage ambled by on the street. "War is good for the news business, you know."

Her mother chuckled. "Of course it is."

Cassandra braced herself for another excruciating soliloquy of the happenings down at the *Baltimore Register*. But instead, Mr. Crane brought up a topic that had consumed Cassandra's mind of late. "Have you heard from Mr. Heaton?"

A moment passed in which Cassandra gazed at him in astonishment, then another moment as she wondered at his reasons for asking. He had made his abhorrence of Mr. Heaton quite clear the last time they'd been together.

"Cassandra, you're being rude. Answer Mr. Crane." Her mother laughed nervously.

"No, I have not heard from him, sir. But it's only been a few weeks. It could be months before he returns."

Mr. Crane's lips fell into a frown, and the edges of his nose seemed to droop with them. "So many of Baltimore's privateers have never returned." Leaning forward, he clipped the edge of the table with his forefinger and thumb while he spoke. He did not meet her gaze, though she thought she saw a hint of a smile peeking from the corners of his eyes. "The *Eleanor*, *Phaeton*, *Pioneer*, *Tartar*, all lost at sea. And the *Baltimore*, *Cashier*, *Courier*, *Dolphin*, *Arab*, *Lynx*, and *Falcon* all captured. Ah, the list goes on."

Cassandra shifted uncomfortably on her seat.

"How true, Mr. Crane." Her mother huffed. "But at least our share of Mr. Heaton's first prize should last us a good long while."

Our share? Cassandra eyed her mother. When had it become *their* enterprise and not Cassandra's foolish venture? "Regardless, Mother, there are human lives at stake. Not to mention the fate of our country."

"I'm sure your mother meant no disrespect," Mr. Crane said. "I, for one, can attest to that feeling of security that comes from financial independence." With chin extended, he draped both arms across the back of the settee like a peacock spreading his feathers. "But I do come on another matter."

Her mother nearly jumped from her seat as if she knew of what matter he spoke. Cassandra gazed between them, unsure if she wished to hear it or not.

"Yes, Mr. Crane?" her mother said.

"No doubt you've heard about the upcoming ball at the Fountain Inn."

Cassandra's heart dropped. "I have, sir."

"Please extend me the privilege of escorting you, Miss Channing." His confident smile sent a shiver through her.

"Oh, how kind of you, sir!" Cassandra's mother clapped her hands. "Isn't it, dear?"

"Very kind." Cassandra bit her lip and avoided the man's gaze. Her eyes landed on a tea service on the table, and confusion wracked through her. Mr. Crane had said he ordered Mrs. Northrop to bring tea. With narrowed eyes, she opened her mouth to question him when an ominous crash sounded from the back of the house. Someone screamed, and the pounding of feet echoed down the hallway.

Cassandra's mother moaned. Cassandra shot to her feet and tossed a "pardon me" over her shoulder at Mr. Crane before darting from the room and down the hall as she followed the sound of sobbing coming from the kitchen. She barreled through the swinging door to see Miss Thain on her knees before pieces of broken china and a splattering of red liquid. Dexter sat on his haunches, taller than Miss Thain on her knees, and grinned—if dogs could grin—bloody juice dripping from his furry chin. The smell of pea soup and dog breath assailed her. The door swung open, bumping Cassandra as her mother and Mr. Crane joined her.

Miss Thain wiped the tears from her face. "I'm so sorry, mum. Darlene and Hannah ran through and knocked the tray from my hands. And that beast followed them in and ate the entire roast for dinner."

"Gads!" Mr. Crane said. "Of all the. . ."

Mrs. Northrop entered the room and gasped.

Growling, Dexter charged Mr. Crane and leapt upon him, forcing him back with two enormous paws upon the man's pristine coat. Pristine no longer as blood from the roast, mixed with dog saliva, sprayed over the fabric with each bark.

Mr. Crane's face crumpled in disgust. Cringing, he crossed his arms over his face as Dexter shoved him against the wall. "Get him off of me!"

"Oh dear, Mr. Crane. My apologies, sir." Mrs. Channing hurried toward him. "Dexter, get down this instant!" Her harried gaze swept to Cassandra. "Get that monstrosity of a dog off Mr. Crane and out of here at once!"

Restraining a giggle, Cassandra grabbed Dexter's collar, tugged him from the cowering newspaper man, and led him to the door.

"How many times have I told those girls not to run in the kitchen or to allow that dog in the house!" her mother brayed to no one in particular.

"Be a good boy, now," Cassandra whispered to the dog, closed the door, and turned to see her mother nearly swooning over Mr. Crane, who had somewhat recovered from his display of cowardice. Although to be fair, Cassandra had never seen Dexter behave so violently with anyone before.

"That was to be our supper, Mr. Crane," Cassandra's mother whined. "We had purchased the finest meat we could find in town. Quite expensive, you know. And now we have nothing to offer you."

"Do not vex yourself, Mrs. Channing." Mr. Crane led her to a chair at the preparation table. "I am happy to eat porridge and biscuits if that is all you have to offer me."

"Don't be silly, Mr. Crane." Her mother dropped her forehead into her hand. "We would never think of serving such menial fare to such an important guest."

"How kind of you, madam." Mr. Crane took a step back and examined his soiled coat. He brushed his sleeves in a panicky fashion, as if the pandemonium in the house were infectious.

Miss Thain continued to sob.

"Perhaps you should take Mother to the parlor, Mr. Crane"— Cassandra offered him a sweet smile—"while I straighten this mess out."

"Yes, very well." He tugged at his cravat.

"But what are we to serve for supper?" her mother asked.

Cassandra gazed out the window where bright sunlight lit the garden in a kaleidoscope of greens, browns, and yellows. "Never fear, Mother, it is still early. Margaret and I can go to the market."

Clinging to the table for support, her mother stood and smiled. "Thank you, dear." Then clutching Mr. Crane's arm, she allowed him to lead her from the kitchen.

After they left, Cassandra reassured Miss Thain that she bore no blame for the incident and then instructed Mrs. Northrop to assist the cook in cleaning up the mess. Upstairs, Cassandra retrieved the key to her father's chest from its hiding place in the top drawer of her dressing bureau. If she was to purchase a good cut of fresh meat, she'd need some money.

With key in hand, she ventured out the back door into the garden and made her way around the corner of her house to the solarium. Inside, the warm, moist air saturated her with the smell of gardenias. She drew in a deep breath and shook her head at the madness that seemed to always plague her family. Sitting on her stool, she pulled out the wooden chest from beneath her workbench, inserted the key, and flung it open. Her heart seized.

And shattered into a million pieces.

The money was gone.

❖ CHAPTER 21 ❖

Stuffing a pistol into his baldric and his cutlass into its scabbard, Luke leapt onto the main deck. He plucked the spyglass from his belt and pointed it aft. Mountains of white sails filled his vision—floating atop the hull of a British frigate. The Union Jack flew proudly from her foremast as she bore down on them just a few miles off their stern. They were gaining fast.

Luke's throat closed. "Lud. How did this happen?"

"She appeared out of nowhere as soon as the sun broke the horizon," Biron replied, his tone filled with surprise and something else that Luke had rarely heard from his friend—dread.

Lowering the scope, Luke squinted against the rising sun and scanned the ship where his crew stood gaping at the oncoming enemy. "Get to work, you sluggards!" he barked. "Mr. Keene, make all sail. Up topgallants and stays. Drop every stitch of canvas to the wind."

Standing on the foredeck, Mr. Keene snapped out of a daze and turned to shout orders to the topmen, sending them leaping into the shrouds. Gone was the permanent smirk from his lips, the mischievous glint in his eyes. Instead fear laced his features.

Luke turned his attention to Sam, who stood ever faithful at the wheel. The lad's light hair blew in the breeze. His eyes focused forward as if willing the ship to go faster. "Four points to starboard, Sam. Steady as she goes."

"Steady as she goes, Cap'n," Sam replied in a terse tone.

Luke gazed up at the men unfurling the extra canvas above. When all sails were raised to the wind, *Destiny*'s lighter frame should have no trouble outrunning the much heavier frigate. And on the off chance they couldn't, Luke would bring the ship alongside the coast, where they could slip into a cove that was too shallow for the frigate to follow.

Destiny flew through the water, cresting a rising swell and plummeting down the other side. Churning water leapt over the bow and rolled across the deck. The ship creaked and groaned beneath the strain. Bracing himself for the next wave, Luke raised his scope again. The frigate seemed to have picked up speed. With the wind's advantage, she glided toward them under towering peaks of white canvas, a mustache of milky foam cresting her bow.

Alarm tightened Luke's nerves.

Mr. Ward appeared on deck, followed by Mr. Sanders, the purser's angular face made sharper by fear. The gunner, however, stopped before Luke, determination stiffening his features. "Orders, sir?"

"Prepare the guns, Mr. Ward," Luke said. "And pray we don't need to use them."

As the gunner ambled away, the thunder of sails drew Luke's gaze upward as the topgallants and staysails dropped into the wind. Good. Now perhaps *Destiny* would pick up speed. No sooner had the thought brought him some comfort than a deafening clamor rained down from above.

The main and fore staysails flailed in the breeze like sheets hung out to dry, giant rents splitting them from foot to leech. Luke shook his head, unwilling to believe his eyes. Who would have done such a thing? Hadn't he ordered Mr. Keene to inspect all canvas before they'd set sail? His wary gaze shot to the boatswain as the man slid down the backstay to the main deck. He charged toward Luke.

"Captain, I don't know what happened. I inspected each sail myself before we left." The sincere look in his eyes, coupled with the terror lining his face, convinced Luke that he told the truth. The ship heaved over the rough seas. Balancing himself, Luke charged toward the railing, his mind reeling.

"Furl the damaged ones, Mr. Keene, and get below to retrieve additional canvas."

Mr. Keene nodded, but the brief knowing look they exchanged told Luke they were of the same mind. By the time they got the additional sails hauled up on the stays, it would be too late.

Luke swallowed down a surge of dread. His thoughts drifted to John, still asleep below. Cargo more precious than silver or gold or even the ship itself.

The sun released its grip on the horizon and spread golden wings over the sea. Wings Luke needed at the moment to quicken his ship and fly away.

"Cap'n, she's still sluggish," Sam shouted from the wheel. Luke speared fingers through his hair. Scanning the deck for his first mate, he found Biron assisting the gun crew at one of the larboard carronades. "Biron, get below and check out the hold."

With a nod and a look of concern, Biron jumped down one of the hatches just as Luke turned to see a burst of yellow flame lash out from the bow of the frigate.

Too far away. They were too far away to hit them. Luke stood his ground.

Boom! The gun roared. Luke's crew froze in place and stared toward the advancing enemy.

"Clear the decks. Beat to quarters!" Luke yelled, sending the harried crew buzzing like a hive of agitated bees.

As expected, the shot fell several yards short of their stern. A warning shot. Luke raised his glass to see men scrambling around one of the frigate's bow chasers.

John emerged from the companionway, his eyes widening as he scanned the sea and spotted the British ship.

"Get below, John. Stay in the cabin!" Luke ordered as *Destiny* swooped over another wave. A spray of salty mist showered over him, stinging his eyes.

John approached him. "They shot at us." His soft voice could barely be heard over the roar of the sea.

"Aye, they did. But they are too far away. Go below, John."

"I want to be with you."

Luke gripped his shoulders. "I need you to stay in the cabin." The authority in his voice, tainted with a bit of pleading, left no room for argument from his brother. With a frown, John slipped below and out of sight.

Fear for his brother, for his crew, his ship, consumed Luke, knotting each nerve and muscle. The sailors, who weren't in the tops adjusting sail or assisting Mr. Ward with the guns, congregated on the main deck, shifting their eyes between the oncoming enemy and Luke as if he somehow had the answer to their salvation.

Biron leapt onto the deck from below. His eyes firing the same fear that burned in Luke's gut. "The crates we thought were filled with supplies, well, most of them are filled with iron bars."

Bile filled Luke's mouth. He swallowed. "How. . . ?" But he didn't have time to consider the how or why of such an act. He glanced over his crew. All eyes shot his way.

"Gregson, Rockland, Sikes"—Luke pointed to the first men he saw— "form a line of men leading to the hold. Hoist up the iron bars and toss them overboard."

The men sped off to do his bidding. Above them, sails flapped as the top men attempted to furl them again. Off their stern, the warship plunged over waves, heading straight for them, splitting the sea in a line of noxious foam. At this rate, with no staysails and her hull heavy with iron, *Destiny* would never be able to outrun the frigate. Nor were they close enough to shore to dive into some inland estuary.

They'd be caught. And either pressed into the British navy or sent to prison in England.

And what would happen to John?

To Miss Channing?

"Guns are ready, Cap'n," Mr. Ward shouted.

Luke gripped the hilt of his cutlass. He turned to Biron. "This would be a good time to pray to your God."

The old man nodded and rubbed his gray, stubbled chin. "I've already been doing that. Perchance, He wants to hear from you?"

"I've no time for your sermons," Luke spat. Sweat beaded on his forehead and neck. If God existed, it would indeed take an act of His mighty hand to save them now.

Soon, men emerged from the hold, forming a line that led to the railing. Iron bars passed through the trail of hands, until finally, they were hoisted over the side. Their splashes could barely be heard above the gush of water against the hull.

But it wasn't enough; the frigate still gained. Luke no longer needed the spyglass to see the lines of her hull, the laughing charred mouths of her carronades, and the sparkle of brass in the rising sun.

"They're signaling for us to heave to, Cap'n!" the lookout above shouted.

"Then let's send our reply." Luke turned to the gunner. "Mr. Ward, fire as you bear."

With flashing eyes, the gunner made his way to a carronade at the larboard quarter. Pushing the gun crew aside, he waited for *Destiny* to crest another swell then he lowered the burning wick to the touchhole.

Boom! The air reverberated with the cannon's angry black belch. A tremble coursed through the ship. Her timbers groaned in complaint. Gray smoke drifted back over the deck, stinging Luke's nose. Coughing, he batted it aside and watched the shot fall impotent into the sea several yards before the frigate.

As he'd expected. But the message had been delivered. One that he hoped would deter the frigate from bothering with such small prey.

Yet it seemed to have the opposite effect, for they persisted. "Keep her steady, Sam."

"Aye, Cap'n. They're gaining." The fear in the lad's voice struck Luke in the back like a thousand needles of failure.

Making the next few minutes pass like hours. He couldn't fail. Not this time.

But you always fail, don't you? The voice slithered over Luke. He tried to shake it off, to remember his prior success, but it rooted deep in his soul.

The frigate swept within three hundred yards of *Destiny*, well within range of her guns. At least twenty dark muzzles lining her main and quarterdeck winked at them in the morning sun. Within seconds, the frigate would sweep alongside and fire a broadside that would not only cripple *Destiny*, but probably kill some of Luke's men.

But Luke had a choice. Surrender or die. Gripping the hilt of his cutlass, he scanned the deck, where his crew stood pale faced and tight. The men in the tops clung to the lines, ready with muskets in hand. The gun crews hovered over the guns, ready to hurl deadly cannon shot at their enemy. These men might have been the baseborn, outcasts of society, but they were no cowards. He guessed most of them would rather fight to the death than surrender. But the most precious thing in the world to Luke was below in his cabin.

John deserved a chance at life. A free life.

The frigate swept swiftly upon their larboard quarter. *Caboom!* One of her carronades erupted, sending an ominous echo through the sky. Another warning shot. But this one carried an unspoken message—surrender or be sunk.

British officers formed an imperious line on the quarterdeck, looking down at their sailors standing calmly in position. Even the gun crews, surrounding the twenty guns pointed at *Destiny*, stood at attention, awaiting orders to unleash hell.

"Raise the white flag, Mr. Keene," Luke managed to say through a clenched jaw. "Furl all sail. Put the helm over, Sam."

Shaking his head in disgust, Mr. Keene stomped toward Luke. "We cannot give up!"

"We can and we will."

Biron rubbed the back of his neck with a sigh but said nothing.

Relinquishing his post by the larboard gun, Mr. Ward stormed forward. "Cap'n, I ne'er surrendered wit'out a fight an' I ain't gonna do it now."

Some of the crew grunted their agreement.

"Then we will all die." Luke gazed over the men, raising his voice. "Is that what you want? To sink to the bottom of the sea?"

"Better that than serve the Brits for the rest of me life," one crewmember said.

"Or rot in a prison hulk," another man shot out.

How could Luke tell them that he agreed? That if John weren't on board, he'd be happy to die defending his country. Gripping the quarter rail, he squinted at the sun making its way high in the sky, oblivious to the horror playing out below. Oblivious to the fact that if they didn't surrender they were about to meet a watery grave.

Words, magnified yet muffled, swept over them from the frigate.

On her deck, a man in a lieutenant's uniform held a speaking cone to his lips. "This is the HMS *Audacious* ordering you to stand down and heave to at once or we will fire upon you."

They awaited *Destiny*'s reply. A bitterness born of failure and fear crowded in Luke's throat. He swallowed, hoping to rid himself of it, but it resurged nonetheless. He thought of Mrs. Barnes and the promise he had made. He could not see John die.

"Raise the flag!" Luke shouted.

The men hesitated.

"Now!"

Amidst a flurry of loathing glances, his crew obeyed him, and soon with all canvas furled and all men on deck, *Destiny* slowed to a near standstill.

A cheer of *huzzah*s resounded from the British frigate as *Destiny*'s white flag of surrender replaced the American flag at the gaff. Luke grew numb. He'd served aboard a frigate once before and had the scars to prove it. And he'd become a pious monk before he'd allow his brother to endure the same fate.

As the ship maneuvered to come alongside *Destiny*, Luke sent Biron below to instruct John to stay out of sight no matter what happened. Perhaps Luke could offer himself and his ship to the British on the condition they deposit his crew and John ashore. He hoped the captain was a reasonable man. Not insane as Captain Milford of the HMS *Undefeatable* had been. The memory of the sting of the master mate's switch resurrected across Luke's back. Shifting it away, he leapt to the main deck as Mr. Keene, the topmast men, Samuel, Ward, and even Mr. Sanders formed an arc of men behind him.

"You did your best," Biron said as he stood stoically by his side.

But Luke's best hadn't been good enough. He had failed. He had failed them all. Miss Channing, his brother, Mrs. Barnes, his crew.

His country.

An ache settled in his head and pulsated in his earlobe as he watched the frigate lower a boat, fill it with officers, and head their way. The foreboding thud against the hull signaled their doom and brought back memories of his capture aboard Noah's ship *Fortune*.

Two lieutenants and three marines, resplendent in their red coats, scrambled over the bulwarks, followed by several sailors, all of whom drew pistols and swords and leveled them at Luke and his crew.

The British captain emerged and landed on the deck with a brazen thump. Dressed in white breeches and a brass-buttoned blue coat adorned with emblems of his station, he sauntered toward Luke. Short-cropped, graying hair spilled from beneath his cocked hat, and eyes as hard and penetrating as blades speared into Luke.

"You are the captain, I presume?"

Luke's hopes to appeal to the man's mercy and gain quarter for any of his crew deflated beneath the man's malicious expression of victory. "Captain Heaton, at your service." He gave a caustic smile.

"Captain Raynor of His Britannic Majesty's frigate, the HMS *Audacious*." He held out his hand for the sword hanging at Luke's side.

Pulling it from its sheath, Luke held it toward him, hilt first, wondering why the captain had not stayed on his ship as was the usual practice.

MaryLu Tyndall

Raynor took it and passed it to a man behind him then snapped his fingers. "Search every inch of the ship." All but the two lieutenants and three marines separated from the group and dispersed.

"You men"—Captain Raynor waved a hand over Luke's crew—"toss your weapons in a pile." He gestured to an open spot on the deck beneath the fore rail.

A gust of wind, plump with the sting of gunpowder and fear, tore across the ship and formed into tiny whirlwinds—whirlwinds of possibility. Mr. Keene seemed of the same mind as he inched beside Luke and cast him a knowing look. The hard metal of Luke's hidden pistol pressed against his belly. He had forty armed crewmen against only fifteen Brits—only six of which stood before them now. And the HMS *Audacious* would never fire upon their own captain.

Clearing his throat, Luke glanced over his shoulder at his men, hoping his eyes portrayed his intent.

"I said, drop your weapons, sir!" the captain barked.

Swords drawn, the marines advanced. Luke drew his pistol. Behind him, the click of pistols cocking and the chime of swords rang like sweet music through the air.

Captain Raynor's eyes turned to steel. "You are outnumbered, sir. Do you all wish to die?"

"Do you?" Luke pointed his pistol at the captain's head. "For you will be the first to go."

Rays from the sun, high above them, reflected off the drawn blades and radiated in waves of heat off the deck. *Destiny's* aged timbers creaked and moaned in protest.

A British sailor emerged from below, dragging John by the collar. He halted. John's wide eyes took in the proceedings. A metallic taste filled Luke's mouth. Captain Raynor noted the change in Luke's demeanor. "And whom do we have here?"

"I found this boy hiding in the master cabin."

"Indeed?" Captain Raynor grinned and waved a hand through the air. "Shoot him."

"No!" Luke charged toward John, his only thought to save him. In a vision blurred by terror, he saw the sailor draw a pistol and hold it to John's head.

Shouts and screams muffled in a mass of confusion in Luke's ears. Something sharp pierced his neck. Pain shot into his head and through his shoulders. He froze. The tip of a lieutenant's sword jabbed him below his chin. The man's face bunched like a knot of gunpowder ready to explode. Luke knew he wouldn't hesitate to run him through.

Behind him swords clanged and a moan sounded. Then silence.

"Hold," the captain ordered. The sailor lifted the gun from John's head. Captain Raynor sauntered toward Luke. "Now hear me and hear me good, Captain Heaton. You will order your men to stand down and relieve themselves of their weapons, or I *will* shoot the lad. Are we clear?"

From the look in his eyes, Luke had no doubt the man would do just that. He nodded, and the captain ordered the lieutenant to withdraw his sword from Luke.

Turning, Luke motioned for his crew to comply, noting that Mr. Keene pressed a hand over a bloody wound on his shoulder. With groans, the men tossed their weapons onto a pile. Clanks and clinks of metal sounded like the incessant hammering of nails into a coffin. Luke's coffin.

"A noble effort." Captain Raynor clasped his hands together as if pleased at the exciting interruption. "I would expect no less from a privateer, eh?"

Rubbing his neck, Luke raised his brows. "We are but an innocent merchant ship from Baltimore on our way to pick up spices and sugar from Jamaica."

"Baltimore? That nest of pirates!" Captain Raynor grunted in disgust. "No, I think not, Captain. A privateer sailing under the same name captured one of our merchantmen off the Carolinas last month."

"A mere coincidence." Luke doubted the man would agree, especially when Mr. Keene chuckled.

"Ah, you have jesters on board." The captain's cutting eyes skewered Mr. Keene. "How nice. My men can use some diversion."

"Sir, if you please." Biron stepped forward. "We are but simple merchantmen. And we mean no harm to you or your country."

"Balderdash!" Captain Raynor's bark was as loud as a cannon's. "You are Americans and privateers. And now, you are prisoners of war."

"Blasted Brits," young Sam spat under his breath.

One of the lieutenants flashed his sword toward Sam.

Nudging the boy aside, Luke held up a hand. "No need for that, Lieutenant."

Captain Raynor cocked his head. "There is fight in you, Captain. I see it in your eyes." His glance took in the men standing behind Luke. "And

MaryLu Tyndall

loyalty in your crew. I take it you are a good captain, though perhaps not a good sailor."

The British sailors chuckled. Luke fisted his hands.

"I shall take you as a prize," the captain continued as he glanced over the ship. "Though this tub is hardly worth the effort." He gestured toward John. "Bring the lad here."

The sailor pushed John, sending him tumbling to the deck. Luke charged him, raising his fist to put the man in his place. Shouts assailed him from behind. Clawlike hands gripped Luke's shoulders and pulled him back.

"It's all right, Luke." John struggled to his feet and brushed off his shirt. The bravery in his eyes sent a wave of pride through Luke.

"Your son?" The captain's eyes traveled between them. He put a finger on his chin. "No. Your brother, I believe."

Luke struggled against the pinched grip of two British marines. "What does it matter?"

The captain turned and whispered something to a man behind him, sending him over the railing and back to the British frigate.

"It changes things a great deal." Captain Raynor took up a pace across the deck. The sun gleamed off his brass buttons and set the gold-fringed epaulettes on his shoulders glimmering as they flapped in the breeze. "You see, I'm in need of fresh supplies. And you're in a position to get them for me."

"You'll get nothing but bilge water from me."

The captain smiled. "Ah, but I will. Because, you see, I will have this boy, this relation of yours."

Luke's heart stopped beating.

"We shall make an accord, you and I," the captain continued, his voice laced with pompous humor. "You will bring me supplies every few weeks, and I'll let the boy live. And when the war is over and we've won, you may have him back."

John trembled but stood his ground.

Biron tugged on his neckerchief. "Kidnapping a boy is beyond all decency, sir. Even in time of war."

"Ah, that is where you are wrong." Captain Raynor grinned. "There are no dictums of decency in war."

"He's just a boy." Ward charged forward. "Let him be."

Mr. Keene tossed up his good arm to hold the gunner back.

Jerking free from the marines, Luke thrust himself in front of John. "Take me instead."

Captain Raynor held up a hand to stop the advancing marines from grabbing Luke again. "Ah, but would your crew commit treason for *you*?" He scoured Luke with a gaze from head to toe. "I think not, sir. But I do sense you would do so for this lad."

The deck teetered over a wave. John eased from behind Luke and stood by his side.

"I'm no thief." Captain Raynor withdrew his hat and dabbed at his forehead with a handkerchief. "I'll pay you for the supplies. You'll make money. Your crew will be happy. Your brother, or whoever he is, will live. And you'll be helping to shorten the war."

Luke's mind reeled with the ultimatum he knew he must accept. "I am no traitor."

"You already are, Captain. You and all the American rebels are traitors to England."

"And if I refuse?"

"I will confiscate your ship as prize and all of you will join the British Navy." Captain Raynor's gaze landed on John. "At least those of you strong enough to serve. The rest? We have prisons where they can await the war's end."

The man returned from the frigate and handed the captain a scrap of foolscap. "Betraying your rebel country. Or slavery for all of you—including the lad. Which do you choose?"

Luke searched his mind for some way out. "Your scheme will not work. The people in Baltimore will grow suspicious."

"You'll think of some explanation, I have no doubt, Captain Heaton. Here are the coordinates." He handed Luke the paper. "You'll meet us here in two weeks with as much food, water, gunpowder, and shot as you can carry."

"Then you'll give me the boy?"

"We shall see."

"How will I slip past the blockade?"

"Don't you anchor in other ports?"

"If I am to meet you in a fortnight at this location, Baltimore is the closest port with enough supplies to meet your needs." Not really. But, stationed at home, Luke could possibly elicit help to rescue John.

"Very well." Captain Raynor shrugged. "Raise the following ensigns in this order. Red, blue, yellow, and green striped, then white. That will identify you to our fleet as a supplier. You won't be harmed." He glanced up at the sky as if bored. "If I see any other ship but yours approaching, I'll kill the boy. If you do not show up within a day of our appointed time, I'll kill the boy." His eyes met Luke's. "Is that understood?"

"You bedeviled mongrel," one of Luke's men whispered from behind. Thankfully, the captain didn't seem to hear it.

Luke knelt before John and gripped his shoulders.

John swallowed. "Don't do it, Luke. Don't betray our country." His voice faltered, but his expression was sincere. "If I die, I'll go to heaven and be with Mother and Father. I'll be all right."

Amazed at the boy's courage and faith, Luke shook his head. "I promised Mother I'd take care of you, and I will. Be strong for me."

John nodded.

Luke leaned in to kiss him on the cheek. "I'll come back for you. I promise."

"How touching." The captain's voice was sickly sweet. He waved a hand. "Take him away."

A lieutenant grabbed John and shoved him toward the bulwarks. He disappeared over the side. Luke's fingers twitched. He could grab the captain's sword and thrust it into his depraved heart before anyone could stop him. But what would that do but get them all killed?

With a contemptuous snort, Raynor dipped his head. "Until we meet again, Captain Heaton. A pleasure doing business with you." The British sailors laughed. Then turning, he marched across the deck and lowered himself over the side, his men following behind him. Luke started after him, but Biron and Mr. Keene held him back.

"Not now, Captain. We'll figure out a way," Biron said.

But Luke knew there was no way.

❖ CHAPTER 22 ❖

Luke stabbed a hand through his hair and yanked on the strands until his head hurt. Spinning around, he retraced his steps across his cabin. A cascade of foul words spilled from his mouth, joining the thud of his boots.

"We'll get him back, Luke." Biron's voice held an anger Luke had never heard before.

"How?" Luke shot fiery eyes his way then scanned the line of men standing before his desk. Mr. Sanders twitched nervously and did not meet his gaze. Beside him, Sam kept repeating "Blasted British, blasted British" under his breath. Mr. Keene's jaw knotted as he leaned against the bulkhead, and Mr. Ward perched on the barrel of the twelve-pounder guarding the foot of Luke's bed, his meaty arms folded over his chest, and a look as if he could kill the devil himself storming across his face.

Destiny rolled over a wave. Her timbers creaked and groaned as the lantern hanging from the deck head cast shifting shadows over the men, creating menacing specters over the painted canvas beneath their boots.

"We'll think of something. We'll put our heads together and think of something." Biron's voice pummeled Luke's back as he continued his nervous trek. Swerving yet again, he retraced his steps and finally halted before his desk. He leaned on the oak top and gripped the edges until his fingers burned. How could this have happened? How could he have failed so miserably? His promise to his mother—his promise to Mrs. Barnes—to protect John slapped him in the face.

"Rescue a boy from a British frigate?" His laugh came out bitter. "Impossible."

"Nothing is impossible with God," Biron said.

Luke lifted a hand to his friend. "Not now, Biron. Not now." If God existed, then He had allowed this to happen. And despite what Reverend Drummond had said, Luke could not see how anything but heartache and death could come of it.

Mr. Keene shook his head. "What I can't understand is how the stay-sails got torn."

"Or the iron got into our supply crates," Mr. Ward growled.

Luke eyed his crew. What reason would any of them have to sabotage the ship? Even if they harbored some animosity toward him, why would they risk their own lives?

Mr. Sanders raised his oversized blue eyes to Luke. His nose twitched. "My apologies, Captain. I didn't see the iron when you sent me below."

"Not your fault." Luke rubbed the scars on his right hand. "The perpetrators hid it well. I'm the captain. I should have gone below myself." He should have done many things. The odor of whale oil and body sweat rose to join the stench of his own inadequacy.

"There was that new sailor you hired." Mr. Keene lifted a jeweled finger in the air.

"Yes, Mr. Flanders," Samuel shot out.

Dread sucked the breath from Luke's lungs. "What new sailor?"

"The man who joined us when you sent us ahead to prepare the ship." Mr. Keene's brow furrowed.

"I sent no such man."

Biron scratched his head. "You didn't hire a Mr. Flanders?"

Luke shook his head, his mouth suddenly parched. He could use a drink. "Is he still on board?"

"I ain't laid eyes on him since," Mr. Ward spoke up.

"Ward, Sanders." Luke gestured toward the two men. "Go search for him and report back to me at once."

"Aye, aye, Cap'n." They sped off, ducking beneath the frame of the open cabin door.

The deck tilted, and the men braced their boots firmly to keep from stumbling. Wind sped past the stern windows in a sinister whistle.

"What did this man have access to, Mr. Keene?" Luke asked.

"He helped load supplies, checked the lines and the canvas. . . ." Mr. Keene froze.

"Blast!" Luke struck his desk. Pain spiked into his arms. He spun around. Darkness as thick as molasses seeped through the stern windows, held back only by the occasional flash of lantern light.

"No doubt he was hired by someone else," Biron said.

"Someone who hates me." Someone like Lieutenant Abner Tripp. Hadn't the man sworn to get his revenge? Luke gazed down at the burn scars on his hand. How could he have been so foolish? He should have been on his guard. This was all his fault.

"Who?" Sam said.

Luke swerved around. "It doesn't matter."

Mr. Ward and Mr. Sanders returned, shaking their heads. Mr. Keene's face twisted with rage. "If Flanders were still here, I'd keelhaul him."

Mr. Sanders shivered, no doubt at his friend's cruel suggestion. "What will you do, Captain?"

Luke eyed his men. Misfits all of them. Would they stay with him now that his privateering career was over? How far did their loyalty extend, especially to a man like Luke? "I'm going to sell Captain Raynor his supplies."

Biron nodded. "It's the right course, Captain. For the boy."

The older man's approval settled well on Luke. "But I can't ask you all to join me. If we are caught, we'll be hanged for treason."

The only answer came from the thunder of sails above and the ravenous purl of the sea against the hull. Lantern light flickered over the men as their gazes dropped to the floor. All except Sam and Biron.

"Of course we'll join you, Captain." The boy's enthusiastic smile sent a sliver of warmth through Luke's frozen heart.

A devilish glint overtook Mr. Keene's eyes. "I'm in. Treason or not, it's a way to make money."

Luke cringed at the man's lack of scruples.

Mr. Ward scratched his bald head. "What other ship is going to hire a drunken cur like me?"

Mr. Sanders's eyes widened, and he glanced around at his fellow crewman then back at Luke. "For how long? I don't fancy a rope about my neck."

"Until we rescue John," Biron said.

"Yes." Luke crossed his arms over his chest, seeking the faith he saw so frequently in Biron's eyes. "And that won't take long if I have my way."

"That's the spirit, sir!" Sam nearly leapt. And the men chuckled at the boy's enthusiasm.

Emotion burned in Luke's throat at his crew's loyalty. "I thank you, gentlemen."

"What about the rest of the crew?" Sanders's mouth twitched.

"Biron, choose the men you believe will be comfortable with our mission and ask them to join us," Luke said, even as the fear of discovery began to gnaw at him.

"In other words, Captain, the blackguards. Those with loyalty to nothing but coin?" Biron arched his brow.

"Yes, those are the ones." Luke huffed. "The rest we'll inform that our privateering days are over and excuse them from duty when we reach Baltimore. Now, off with you." He tilted his head toward the door. "Grab your supper from the galley and then back to your posts, men."

One by one they left the cabin, leaving only Biron behind. The first mate shut the door and approached Luke, concern written on his face. "How are you holding up?"

"Not well." Luke spun around to face the stern windows, not wanting Biron to see the moisture in his eyes. "I can't imagine what John is enduring right now."

"He's a strong lad, Luke. He's got your blood flowing through him."

"But he's just a boy." Luke rubbed his ear. "And you forget I know what happens aboard a British warship."

"I haven't forgotten."

"I need a drink."

"That won't help anything right now."

Luke sighed and turned around. "How are we going to get him off that ship?"

Biron flattened his lips and released a sigh. "I don't know. With God's help, we'll find a way."

Luke huffed. God again. Lowering himself into a chair, he dropped his head into his hands. "I've lost him, Biron. I failed him and everyone else."

The ship tilted, sending lantern light spinning in circles over the painted canvas rug.

"When my wife and babe died in childbirth," Biron said, "I thought I'd failed them both, too."

"How could you not blame God for that?" Luke didn't look up.

"For a time I did," Biron said. "But what good does that do? God has His reasons for things, and they're good reasons. For the ultimate good. I'll find out someday."

"I don't have the patience to wait that long." Luke looked up. Nor could he wait to repay Lieutenant Tripp for his part in this. "First thing I'm going to do when I get home is accept Lieutenant Tripp's challenge to a duel and send him to the depths of hell where he belongs."

"You can't do that."

"Quite the contrary." Luke snorted. "I believe I can."

"No, think, man. If you get your revenge, he'll know his plan worked. But he'll see you still have your ship, your crew. He's no dull wit. He'll figure out what you're up to."

"Not if he's dead."

Biron arched his brow.

Luke lowered his gaze beneath the look of reprimand on his friend's face. "So, I can't kill him and neither can I take pleasure in beating him to shreds?"

"No. Besides, there's far grander pleasure in being kind to the man. God's Word says that if your enemy is hungry, give him bread, if he be thirsty give him water. For thou shalt heap coals of fire upon his head, and the Lord shall reward thee."

Luke chuckled. "Why don't I just skip to dumping the hot coals on his head?"

Biron smiled. "Kindness will kill him more slowly."

"Kindness? You're crazy, old man."

"Perhaps. But hear me, Luke. If you arrive in Baltimore a successful privateer, it will drive the lieutenant mad, I assure you."

Luke studied his friend, allowing his words to form sense in his mind. Yes, perhaps the old man was wiser than Luke gave him credit. Or, this God of his was.

Biron headed for the door. "We'll be in Baltimore in a few days. Get some rest, Captain. We will think of a way to rescue John."

Luke heard him leave as the door shut again. Rest, how could he rest knowing what his brother was enduring on that frigate? Rising, he opened a drawer of his desk and pulled out a bottle of rum. He held it up to the lantern light. Mr. Sanders had brought it to him a few nights ago. Luke had not taken a sip. Not a single sip. Wanting to honor his promise to

Miss Channing. But what did it matter now? What did anything matter now? Uncorking it, he took a long draft, hoping the burning liquid would warm his gut and numb his senses. But after several swigs, he felt nothing but grief—deep seated, clawing into his soul. Lifting the bottle, he tossed it against the bulkhead. It shattered, spraying rum over his bookshelves and onto the deck. Shards of glass clanked to the floor in a glittering shower, dripping with the vile liquid.

Sinking back onto his chair, he dropped his head in his hands once more. "Oh God, what am I to do?"

Sometime in the night, he must have dozed off beneath exhaustion and grief. He dreamed of cannon blasts and smoke and men being lashed by a cat-o'-nine-tails and John crying Luke's name in echoed ripples over the sea. And in the middle of the mayhem, a glowing figure appeared. Tall and muscular, shining like bronze, with a sword hanging at his side. He said, "Never fear."

❖

Marianne shoved a roll of dollars into Cassandra's hands. "Here, take this."

"How can I thank you?" Cassandra's eyes burned. "I am so ashamed to have to ask you for help. I know you and Noah don't have a great deal of wealth." She slipped the wad into her reticule and set it down on the table.

Marianne cupped Cassandra's hands with her own. "God has blessed us. I'm happy to help you. So, not another word about it." Releasing her, she skirted the table in her sitting room and poured two cups of tea, handing one to Cassandra.

"Thank you." Cassandra warmed her hands on the cup then took a sip. She gazed out the window, where afternoon sunlight splintered the room in glittering swords.

"Now, tell me what happened." Marianne patted the sofa beside her.

"I don't really know." The cup shook in Cassandra's hands. The soothing mint turned to ash in her mouth. She lowered the cup to her lap. "No one knew where I hid the money. The chest wasn't broken so they must have used my key, which I keep in the desk in my chamber."

Marianne frowned. "It must be someone in the house, then. But who?"

Cassandra had driven herself mad the past two days trying to figure out the answer to that question. All her servants had been with her for years, and she had never seen a spark of disloyalty among any of them. Visions of Mrs. Northrop standing in her chamber a few days ago sped across her mind. But no. The housekeeper had always been a bit of a snoop. Nothing unusual about that. "I fear my mother has taken to her bed with a case of headaches and hysterics, which has left my sisters to run amok through the house."

"Why didn't you put the money in the bank?" Marianne asked.

"I was careless. I had been without funds for so long, I didn't trust anyone, not even the bank." Cassandra's hands trembled, and she set the cup on the saucer with a clank lest she spilled the tea on her gown. "I've gone and ruined everything. I've put my family at great risk again."

Marianne touched her hand. "It's only money."

"It would have lasted us years."

"Luke will return soon with more, you'll see."

Mr. Heaton's name sent a spark of joy through Cassandra. "I'll pay you back upon his return, I promise. Until then, this will help me buy some much-needed food."

Marianne's brown eyes sparkled. "Word about town is that Mr. Crane is bringing your family food. A goose one night, two chickens the next, and fresh cod and crab last evening?"

Cassandra couldn't help but laugh at how quickly rumors spread in the town. "Is nothing secret?"

"Well, not when the man tells everyone that you and he are courting."

"Courting?" Cassandra frowned. "Oh, bother. We are doing no such thing. How dare he spread such tales!"

"I wouldn't be so hard on him. No doubt he considers the courtship firm since you have accepted his charity."

"Which is precisely why I needed to borrow this money. Good grief, the man keeps insisting he take me to the Fountain Inn Ball."

"Why not go with him?" Marianne waved a hand through the air, then she stopped and gazed at Cassandra as if she could see into her thoughts. "Unless you are waiting for someone else to ask you. . .someone who is perhaps out to sea at the moment?"

"Don't be absurd." Cassandra looked away. "*If* I marry it will be to a man I can depend on. A man who is stable and grounded. Someone I can trust."

"Odd. That sounds precisely like Mr. Crane." Marianne sipped her tea, a grin playing on her lips.

Cassandra made a face at her friend, though she supposed Marianne was right. Why, then, didn't Cassandra long for Mr. Crane's attention?

Why didn't her heart bounce when he walked into the room? Perhaps marriage was not meant to be based on such foolish sentiments, but on mutual respect and financial and familial practicality.

If so, Cassandra would be better off alone.

"I wouldn't disqualify Mr. Heaton just yet on those counts," Marianne said.

"Who said anything about Mr. Heaton?"

"Oh, I don't know. . . . You just had that dreamy look in your eye again." A child's laughter filtered down from above, and Marianne glanced out the parlor door before she faced Cassandra with a smile. "I've seen the way he looks at you."

Why did her statement send a thrill through Cassandra?

"Mr. Heaton is my business partner, nothing more." Cassandra folded her hands in her lap.

"God doesn't always choose the men we think are best for us. Take Noah and me. For years, I couldn't stand the sight of him."

"God doesn't choose for me. If He does, I can hardly trust Him, given the bad choices He's made so far."

Marianne set down her cup. "You'll see that He is looking out only for your good in the end."

Uncomfortable talking about a God who obviously paid her no mind, Cassandra stood and made her way to the window. "Noah is not yet returned?"

"No. I do miss him so." Marianne joined her and gazed out onto the carriages and pedestrians strolling down the street. "And so does Jacob. I pray this war will be over soon and we can get back to a normal life."

"Only if we win."

"Indeed." Marianne offered her a sad smile.

And only after Mr. Heaton has caught another prize. Cassandra cringed at her selfish thought.

After finishing her tea and thanking Marianne for the money, Cassandra began her trek home. Casting a glance toward the west at the setting sun, she guessed she had enough time to visit the harbor before dark. Pulling the pelisse tight around her chest, she turned down Pratt Street. For some reason, seeing all the ships made her feel close to Mr. Heaton. And feeling close to Mr. Heaton brought her more comfort than she cared to admit. She shrugged the sentiment away, reasoning that it was only her need for the money he would bring home. But deep down, she knew it was more than that.

She greeted several people as she made her way down the cobblestone walkway then darted across the street between a phaeton and a wagon— avoiding the horses' deposits—to the dock side of the street. Halting, she scanned the bay, its dark waters rustling against the pilings of the wharves. Salt and fish and tar filled her nostrils. A fisherman hawked his fresh catch. A bell rang and a burst of wind tore at her straw bonnet. A few dockworkers turned to look at her. Her eyes landed on a schooner anchored off Spears Wharf. It seemed familiar. She headed in that direction then crept out on the wobbling dock just far enough to see the name painted on the ship's bow.

Destiny.

❖ CHAPTER 23 ❖

Vague shapes formed behind Luke's eyelids, like shadowy specters of light and dark drifting over his eyes. A clank sounded from somewhere in the distance. The scent of coffee spiraled beneath his nose and thrummed on his rousing senses. No. He tried to push his mind back into the abyss of apathy, back into the soothing comfort of unconsciousness.

But another clank jarred him. Then the pain struck. Like a grappling hook clawing through his brain. He moaned and waved a hand around his head to see if someone was hammering on it. He touched his face. Nothing but damp flesh met his fingers. Cold and damp. And what was that stench that infiltrated the sweet smell of coffee?

Footfalls sounded, and he pried open one eye to see the blurry shape of Mrs. Barnes enter the sitting room with a tray. Setting it on the table, she sank into her favorite rocking chair with a heavy sigh. "I made you breakfast." Her voice was thick and choppy, devoid of its usual cheerfulness.

Luke wanted to say thank you. Wanted to tell her to leave him alone. But he felt as though someone had stuffed a rag in his mouth. He opened his other eye to peer at the wooden ceiling and waited until the room stopped swirling.

"I see you drank yourself into unconsciousness." Mrs. Barnes began to rock in her chair, the *creak creak* scraping holes in his wall of alcohol-induced narcosis.

Allowing memories to barge into his mind. The image of John being stolen by the British captain struck Luke first like a broadside in the gut, jarring him fully awake. Then the vision of Mrs. Barnes when he'd told her the news. The horror in her eyes, her ragged breathing, trembling lips, and the white sheen that had covered her face. Luke had grabbed her before she'd fallen and led her to a chair where she had sobbed for nearly an hour. Fighting wave after wave of guilt and battling his own tears, Luke had fumbled in the kitchen, attempting to make her some tea to soothe her nerves.

But no amount of tea or apologies or promises had been able to assuage the grief-stricken woman.

Closing his eyes, Luke struggled to sit. He felt as though a twenty-pound cannonball sat on his neck. He leaned on his knees, hoping the room would stop spinning. An empty bottle of brandy leaned on its side atop the hearth. The brandy he'd found in the kitchen. The brandy he'd intended to take only a few sips of to settle his raging soul.

Hair hanging in his face, he dared a glance at Mrs. Barnes. Her skin was even paler than last night. The lines etched across it deeper. Dark circles tugged on eyes that were red and puffy. A look of pity crossed them, and she poured him a cup of coffee that she passed his way.

Luke set it on the table, his stomach rebelling at the sight. "You serve me coffee after what I've done?" he moaned.

"You're a son to me, Luke. I love you no less than I love John."

The sound of his brother's name pierced Luke's heart. He hung his head. Not once after Luke had told her the news had Mrs. Barnes scolded him. Not once had she shouted or screamed or cursed him for what he'd done. No. She'd simply sat in her rocking chair, with her Bible in her lap, alternating between bouts of tears and gazing numbly into the burning logs of the fire.

Rebuke, shouting, even hatred, Luke could bear. But not her silence. Not her agony. So he had taken to drink to numb the pain.

"What happened, happened," Mrs. Barnes said. "Maybe John was too young to go to sea. Maybe he wasn't. You did what you thought best."

"He was good out there, Mrs. Barnes," Luke said, pride swelling within him, even now. "You should have seen him. He took to sailing as if he'd been born on a ship."

"Why wouldn't he?" The hint of a smile twitched one side of her mouth before it faded. "He's got your blood running through him."

Luke didn't want to hear that. John was nothing like Luke. John was kind and pure and good. He would make something of his life.

If Luke hadn't already sent him to his grave.

Mrs. Barnes drew her Bible to her chest and gripped it as if it held the answer to their dilemma. She stared once again at the coals in the fireplace, now black and cold. "I've been up all night praying, you see. And God has told me there is a reason this happened."

Luke shot to his feet and instantly regretted it. His head spun and his stomach lurched. "I grow tired of hearing that God has a reason for every bad thing that happens." Bile rose in his throat, but the desert raging in his mouth forbade him to swallow it down. "Bad things happen because there are bad people in the world, nothing more." Bad people, of whom he was one. "John is. . . John is. . ." He ran a hand through his hair, unable to even say the words out loud. "This is all my fault. I should have known Tripp would try something. I should have checked the sails and supplies myself." Luke sank back down onto the couch and dropped his head in his hands.

He heard the rocking chair squeak and felt Mrs. Barnes's wrinkled hand on his arm. "This isn't your fault, Luke."

He raised a shocked gaze to her. "How can you say that?"

"Not everything is your fault, Luke. Not your parents' death and not John's kidnapping." A peace Luke envied glowed from her glassy eyes. "Your pounding head is your fault. The gambling, the drinking, those are your fault." She shook her head. "Not John's kidnapping."

❖

Sitting on the stool, Cassandra unlocked the small wooden chest, replaced the key in the pocket of her gown, and opened the lid. Hope sparked in some small part of her that still believed in miracles—hope that the money would be there. But of course, it wasn't. Though she refused to believe any of her family or servants could have stolen it, that seemed the only logical conclusion. But who? It pained her to even think of it. Removing her father's pipe, she raised it to her nose and drew a whiff of the fragrant, spicy smell.

"Oh Papa, what am I to do?" Toying with the pipe, she glanced over her leafy-green gardenia bushes, the fading sunlight spilling from their leaves, replaced by the golden glow from the lantern overhead.

After purchasing enough food for a week with the money Marianne had loaned her, Cassandra had headed home, still baffled by the sight of Luke's ship anchored in the bay.

"He must not have caught a prize, Papa, for that is the only reason I can think of that he would have returned and not come to see me."

The wind whistled over the panes of glass in the solarium, and Cassandra released a heavy sigh. "And if that is true, I fear, Papa, that we are done for." She certainly couldn't borrow any more money from Marianne and Noah. And what were they to do when the food ran out in a week's time?

Her gaze landed on her father's Bible tucked within the chest. Closing her eyes, she pictured him sitting in his chair in the library, the Holy Book opened in his lap, his blue eyes, so full of life, glancing up at her as she entered the room.

"Come here, my darling Cassie," he would say as he set the book aside. And Cassandra would crawl into his lap—her favorite place in all the world. Then he would stroke her arm and kiss the top of her head and tell her how much he loved her.

The Bible seemed to glow from within the chest. Cassandra rubbed her eyes. She was seeing things. Memories of what Marianne, Reverend Drummond, and even Margaret had told her of God's love, purpose, and provision flooded her mind. But none of it could be true, could it? Not when He had taken so much from them.

A tear slipped down her cheek. "Papa, I don't know how to take care of Mother and my sisters. We have no money. Soon, no food. I haven't paid the servants in weeks. Why would someone steal from me?" She fisted her hands and pounded her lap. "Why was I so foolish to keep the money here? Oh Papa, why did you leave me all alone?"

Nothing but the rustle of the wind answered her as the last traces of sunlight slipped from sight. Cassandra drew a deep breath and straightened her shoulders. There was only one thing left to be done. If Mr. Heaton had indeed returned without a prize, then Cassandra would have no choice but to accept Mr. Crane's courtship. She would not allow her family to starve or end up on the street because of her own selfishness.

The crank of the door latch drew her gaze to the front of the solarium. Those unruly urchins. Couldn't they leave her alone for one minute? But then heavy footsteps thumped on the hard dirt, giving her pause. Her heart hammered against her chest. Cassandra peered between the leaves of a bush just as a deep voice said, "Hello."

Mr. Heaton stood just inside the door, cocked hat in hand, gazing over her bushes. Her heart took on a different sort of thump. She slowly rose.

His eyes met hers. A smile lifted his lips. "Good evening, Miss Channing. I hope I didn't startle you."

Cassandra could not find her voice. Perhaps it had been swept away in the tide of hot waves that flooded her at the sight of him standing there in his black boots, brown breeches, and white shirt. Absent the neckerchief and waistcoat propriety dictated. Aside from a few loose strands, his black hair was tied behind him, and there, peppering his chin was the ever-present stubble, as if his beard were as stubborn as he.

An imposing figure so out of place among her flowers. Yet she found no fear within her. Quite the opposite, in fact.

"Why, no, Mr. Heaton," she said. "I'm surprised to see you is all."

"Your maid." He gestured toward the front of the house. "She said I might find you here."

Margaret. Cassandra flattened her lips. She would speak to her later.

He took a step toward her. "So, this is why you always smell like gardenias."

Cassandra smiled. "I love these flowers." She caressed one of the leaves. "I come here to think."

"And I have disturbed you. I hope you'll forgive me, but I come on an important matter."

It occurred to her she'd been so happy to see him that she'd not even considered that he'd come with news of a prize. "I saw your ship at anchor earlier in the day." Cassandra approached him.

"Yes, I sailed in late last night."

"How did you get past the blockade?"

She thought she saw a flicker of unease pass over his blue eyes. "*Destiny* is swift and hard to see in the dark." He would not meet her gaze.

"Did you capture a prize?"

He shook his head, and her hopes tumbled. "Not this time, miss."

Cassandra's throat burned. She fought back a flood of tears. Even if Mr. Heaton caught twenty prizes in the next six months, it would be too late to keep the house and provide food for her family. She pressed a hand over her stomach.

Mr. Heaton grabbed her elbow and leaned toward her, his face full of concern. "Are you unwell, Miss Channing?"

"Yes. . . No." Warmth spiraled up her arm at his touch, and she pulled away from him. "I had hoped"—she waved a hand in the air—"oh, what does it matter?" She eyed him. "You smell like a tavern, sir."

He frowned. "I'm on land again, miss."

"Why are you back so soon?"

"I needed supplies."

The statement made no sense to her, but she didn't inquire further.

Shifting his stance, Luke gazed out the windows onto the back garden. "I went to see Marianne today."

The odd statement jarred Cassandra, and she dared a glance into his eyes—so close she could see the lantern light flicker in their depths.

At her inquisitive look, he scratched the stubble on his chin and gave her one of his roguish grins. "Well, in truth, I hoped to see Noah, but the blasted man is still out scouring the seas for British prey." He chuckled.

"Why are you telling me this, Mr. Heaton?"

He reached inside his waistcoat and pulled out a leather billfold and handed it to her.

Cassandra shook her head. "What is this?"

"Take it, Miss Channing."

Grabbing it, she unhooked the clip and opened it to find several dollar bills—at least eighty. Confusion left her stunned. "What? I can't take this."

"I assure you, you can."

"How? I don't. . ."

"Marianne told me of your plight."

The solarium began to spin. Cassandra lifted a hand to her forehead. "But this is from your share of the last prize."

He said nothing. He just looked at her as if she were as precious as one of the gardenias blossoming beside her.

"I cannot accept this." She shoved the billfold back toward him.

He held out a hand. "I have no need of it at the moment." Sorrow crossed his face. He looked away.

"Still, Mr. Heaton, it is most inappropriate."

"If you wish it not to be a gift, you can repay me out of our next prize earnings. This should last you a few months until then."

She shifted her eyes between his but found no insincerity within them. Could this be true? Her legs transformed into noodles and she staggered.

Mr. Heaton reached out to steady her. She fell against him. "Are you all right, miss?" His warmth and strength surrounded her, and an odd sense of well-being invaded her turbulent soul. A feeling she'd not had since her father had been alive. Was it possible this rogue, this blackguard, could be trusted?

"Forgive me, Mr. Heaton, It's just that"—she stepped out of his embrace—"it's just that you have no idea how much I needed this money. I fear I had decided to take drastic measures."

His eyes wandered down to the pipe in her hand.

"Smoke a pipe?" He chuckled.

She joined him. "No! I was about to accept the proposal of a certain gentleman. . . ."

"Ah." Mr. Heaton's dark brows rose. "Mr. Crane, I presume?"

Cassandra looked down. "Yes, I fear he's become quite persistent, insisting I accompany him to some ball happening at the Fountain Inn."

He studied her with that look that held possibilities she dare not entertain. "I can see why."

Her face heated. She took a step back.

"Forgive me," he said, but the flirtatious look remained. "Perhaps you could inform him that you're attending the ball with me?"

Cassandra blinked even as a thrill sped through her. "Why would I say that?"

"Because it will give you an excuse to turn him down. And because attending with me will be far more adventurous, I assure you."

Of that, Cassandra had no doubt. She brushed a finger over one of her gardenias, trying to settle her rampant emotions. Why was she all aquiver over this rake's invitation and so repulsed by Mr. Crane's? "Then, shall I presume you are extending an invitation to escort me, sir?"

❖

Luke smiled at the coy look on her face, both thrilled and shocked that she seemed at all interested in attending the ball with him. "I am."

"But how long will you be in town?" she asked.

He shrugged and pushed an errant strand of hair behind his ear. "I will make sure I'm here for the event."

"Then I accept your kind invitation, sir," Cassandra said.

Luke gave her a befuddled look, wondering if he were dreaming. Never in a thousand years would he have ever hoped to escort a lady like Cassandra Channing to a ball.

She lowered her gaze to the billfold in her hand. "You don't know how grateful I am for this money, Mr. Heaton. I will accept it, but only as a loan."

Then it hit Luke. Like a stone sinking in his stomach. "I hope you didn't agree to my invitation because of the money."

"No, not at all." Setting down the pipe and money on a nearby stool, she laid a hand on his arm.

"Because there are no obligations attached to the gif—loan." But when he raised his eyes to hers, Luke could see his fears were unfounded, for nothing but candor flashed in their depths.

"Of course," she said. "We are partners, after all."

His gaze dropped to her lips. He licked his own and swallowed an urgent desire to kiss her. Shifting both his thoughts and his gaze away, he gestured toward the billfold on the stool. "Might I suggest you put it in the bank this time?"

"I deserved that." Her lips slanted.

He cocked his head. "And if I might make one small request?"

She hesitated, eyeing him, but saying nothing.

"Please make no mention of the money to anyone or from whence it came. We don't wish to alert the thief a second time. Even for so small an amount."

"Indeed."

Luke's heart soared at the appreciation beaming from Miss Channing's face. If only for the moment, at least in her eyes, he was no failure. At least in her eyes, he was a champion. He had failed everyone else, even himself, but he never wanted to fail her. The trust and confidence in her gaze made him want to be a better man—to become a man she could trust, a man she could love.

The way the lantern light glittered in her burgundy hair and caressed her soft cheek, sliding down her neck. . .

Luke caught hold of his wayward thoughts and took a step back, fumbling with his hat. For the first time in his life, a woman had him befuddled—unsure of himself.

Against his will, his gaze landed once again on her lips. He remembered the soft feel of them, their moist response to his kiss weeks ago. His throat grew parched, longing for just one sip. But she would think him presumptuous after she'd accepted the money. It wouldn't be right.

For once, he withdrew.

"I should leave you, miss." He started to turn away when the press of her hand on his arm stayed him. He faced her again.

She gazed at him mystified, mesmerized before her lips met his.

❖ CHAPTER 24 ❖

Cassandra had no idea what she was doing. In fact, she was absolutely sure that she could, here and henceforth, be classified as a witless hussy. Why did she force her kiss on Mr. Heaton? After he had turned away from her as a true gentleman should? Dash it all, she had thrown herself into his arms as if she were one of his tavern wenches. Yet, as soon as her lips met his and he responded by engulfing her in his embrace, she no longer cared. Reputation and propriety tossed to the wind, she drank him in as if she could never assuage her thirst. He tasted of smoke and spice. His breath tickled her cheek while his stubble scratched her skin. A plethora of delights soared through her until every ounce of her sizzled like hot coals. He cupped her face in his warm hands and kissed her deeply then placed light gentle kisses over her face and neck.

Cassandra moaned and fell against him. He stroked her hair, his chest rising and falling rapidly beneath her cheek.

She felt warm and safe and loved. And she never wanted him to leave.

"Aren't you going to slap me again?"

Cassandra shook her head, regaining some of her senses. She pushed back from him, horrified that she'd kissed him. "I don't know what came over me. Please forgive me." She lowered her chin.

His finger raised it, until their eyes met. "I fear I cannot." He looked at her as if she were a rare treasure—something to protect and cherish.

But then it struck her. How many other women had he graced with that adoring look? Kissed with such hungry fervor? He was skilled in the art of *l'amour*. As evidenced by the wake of broken hearts he left behind.

And she was a fool.

Cassandra took a step back. "This means nothing."

The smile slipped from his mouth. "To you, perhaps."

"I lost my head. It was the money, your charity." Cassandra tore her gaze from him and hugged herself against a sudden chill. "We are nothing but business partners."

"Indeed?" He cocked his head and studied her. A sigh, laden with sorrow, blew from his lips.

Cassandra fingered a gardenia petal. Her body still tingled from his kiss. Confusion galloped unbridled through her thoughts, pounding them into dust before she could make sense of them. Could she actually be falling in love with this rogue?

"You don't trust me," he said.

"I trust no one, Mr. Heaton."

"I hope to remedy that, Miss Channing." Before she could stop him, he leaned down and brushed his lips over her cheek then placed his hat on his head, opened the door, and left.

Caressing the spot on her face where his lips last touched, Cassandra watched as the shadows stole him from view.

❖

Luke stood on the teetering deck of the HMS *Audacious* as the British purser, a rather stubby fellow with a pointed chin, checked items off a list. Luke's men, aided by British sailors, hauled aboard crates, barrels, and sacks from *Destiny*'s hold, dropping them on deck for inspection before additional British sailors carried them below. Flanked by his lieutenants, Captain Raynor gazed down upon the proceedings from the quarter rail in a pompous display of dark-blue coats and cocked hats that made Luke sick to his stomach. He glanced over at the lines strung taut on belaying pins off the larboard quarter, and renewed pain etched down his back. Not two years ago, he stood in that very spot on a different British frigate, hauling lines while the master's mate whipped his back repeatedly with the rattan.

The thought shot renewed terror through his veins like shards of ice. Terror for John. Where was he? Since Luke had boarded, he'd scanned every inch of the deck. But his brother was nowhere to be seen.

And Luke had to get close to John in order for his plan to work. Close enough to pass him a scrap of foolscap containing important instructions.

The scrap that now seemed to be shouting from within Luke's pocket.

"That's it, Captain." The purser lifted his gaze. Four sacks of rice, six sacks of flour, one crate of fresh fish, two pigs, five sacks of coal, ten barrels of water, twenty chickens, one crate of apples, two barrels of rum, and twenty-five pounds of gunpowder.

Gunpowder that might kill Luke's own countrymen.

The ship canted over a swell. Bracing his boots on the deck, Luke ground his teeth together and reached for his sword by instinct. Of course, it wasn't there. Nor was his pistol. He and his men standing behind him had been searched before they'd boarded the frigate. Even if his entire crew were armed, what could twenty men do against hundreds? Thunder charged through the broiling, gray sky that hung low enough to touch. A vile wind whipped across the deck, stinging Luke's nose with the scent of brine and rain.

"Very good, Mr. Garrison," Captain Raynor said. "Pay the man his due."

The purser tossed a bag of coins to Luke. He caught it and turned his attention to the captain. "I demand to see my brother."

"Demand, is it now?" The man chuckled and glanced at his lieutenants, who joined him in laughter. Lightning flashed, casting a silver glow over his maniacal expression and transforming the gray and black streaks of his hair into eerie shades of blue.

"I am, Captain, or I'll bring one of our navy's warships to our next meeting." Luke knew his threat was empty. The American Navy would never risk a ship to rescue the brother of a traitor.

"The American Navy, you say?" Captain Raynor grinned. "Last I heard you had less than ten frigates and a couple of sloops against our hundreds of warships." He shook his head. "Ah, you Americans. Entertaining at best. At the least, full of impotent threats and boasts. But alas, you may see the lad if you wish." He turned and said something to one of the midshipmen standing behind him and the man dropped below, returning in moments with John.

The instant the boy saw Luke, he broke into a huge smile that helped settle Luke's taut nerves. The man released him, and John dashed toward his brother, barreling into his embrace. Luke swallowed him up, wishing he'd never have to let go. After a moment, however, John pushed back as if embarrassed at the affectionate exchange. He glanced over Luke's shoulder. "Mr. Abbot, Mr. Keene, Mr. Ward."

"Hi there, lad," Mr. Ward said. "How are you faring?"

"I'm well." His gaze returned to Luke. "They make me work hard, but they feed me too."

Luke knelt and slipped his hand into his pocket for the foolscap. "How is your brace holding up?"

The boy nodded. "Good." He eyed Luke for a moment and cocked his head. "Don't worry about me. God is here with me."

Luke huffed. If God was here, He would have freed his brother already. But he would let the lad have his fantasy if it brought him comfort. Luke's eyes dropped to the blisters on his brother's hands and his torn trousers. He gripped the boy's shoulders. He felt bonier than before, and Luke wondered if he'd lost weight. "I'm going to get you out of here," he whispered. Sliding the note to the inside of his palm, Luke eased his hands to John's waist. "Do what the note says. I'll be waiting." He shoved it inside John's trousers.

John's eyes nodded but he said nothing. Good boy. So brave.

"Enough!" The captain's voice ricocheted over the deck. Two marines grabbed John and drew him back before Luke could embrace him once more.

Rising, Luke branded the captain with a fiery gaze. What he wouldn't give to challenge the man to a duel right now. Just the two of them. To the death, for John's freedom. Rain started to fall, bouncing on the deck in large drops as if heaven itself were sad at the proceedings below.

Plop plop plop, like the beating of a war drum. The frigate heaved over the agitated sea. Salty spray lashed across Luke's face. He shook it away.

"We shall see you in a fortnight, Captain Heaton." Raynor dismissed them with a wave of his hand. "Escort these men from the ship, if you please, Mr. Leonard."

John cast Luke one final glance before the sailor shoved him down the companionway ladder. Jerking from the marine's grasp, Luke followed his men over the bulwarks, down the rope, and onto the deck of *Destiny*.

Thunder bellowed as the lines tying the two ships together were released and the hulls slipped apart.

"Do you think it'll work, Captain?" Biron said from beside him.

"It has to. I can think of no other way to get him off that ship." Luke shook the rain from his hair then slicked back the wet strands. "Let's be on our way, Biron."

"Aye, Captain." Biron turned and shot a string of orders across the ship. "Stand by to make sail! Lay aloft, topmen! Man the halyards and sheets!"

Sam approached. "Where should I point her, Cap'n?"

"West, as if we're sailing back to Baltimore." Luke winked.

The boy saluted and raced up on the quarterdeck to take the wheel.

As Biron's and Mr. Keene's orders filled the air, Luke heard his crew scrambling over the deck. He heard their grunts as they leapt into the shrouds to raise sail, their moans as they hauled on lines. And within minutes *Destiny's* canvas caught the wind in a thundering snap and sped on her way over the rising swells of the sea.

A burst of salty wind struck Luke as he watched the frigate fade behind a curtain of rain.

Biron appeared by his side. "He's a brave lad, I'll give him that. If he reads the note and can slip away during the night watch as you told him, he should have no trouble making it over the side."

"Unless they're keeping him locked up below at night." Mr. Ward approached the railing.

Luke shook his head. "They didn't keep me in irons, why would they keep a boy?"

"Will he jump, though? That's the question." Mr. Keene joined them.

"He'll jump," Luke said. "He's my brother." Shielding his eyes from the rain, he glanced up. "It will be dark in an hour. And with this weather, most of the night watch will be hunched under their coats. Maybe God is looking out for us tonight, after all."

"He's always looking out for you," Biron said. "You heard your brother."

"Ah, it's best to count on wit, might, and money, Mr. Abbot," Mr. Keene said. "Those are the things that will never let you down."

Yet Luke wished above all else that there *was* a God to whom he could appeal tonight—that there was an almighty, all-powerful God who could swoop down and close the eyes of the British watch so Luke and his crew could rescue John.

As his men dispersed to their duties, Luke stood at the starboard railing, gazing at the turbulent, dark sea. Lightning etched a white fork across the clouds. When he was sure no one was looking his way, Luke bowed his head. On the off chance there *was* a God, Luke uttered a silent appeal for His help—for John's sake, not Luke's.

But instead of the peace Biron so often spoke of, heavy rain pelted Luke as if God spat on him in reply.

Seven hours later, Luke knew his appeal had fallen on deaf ears. After darkness had transformed the sea into liquid onyx and hidden them from their enemy, *Destiny* had crept to within a half mile of the HMS *Audacious's* larboard quarter. The frigate had furled all sail, drifting through the darkness under top gallants alone on a southern tack. Luke leveled his scope at the quarterdeck, desperately seeking a glimpse of his brother crawling over the side. A jolly boat rocked alongside *Destiny*, manned by four of Luke's crew, ready to pluck the boy from the water.

The note had told John to jump over the side at that exact spot between one and two in the morning. Luke's eyes strained from the intense focus he had maintained for over an hour. Now, at ten minutes past two, and with still no sign of his brother, Luke's hopes began to sink beneath the murky waters.

"We should be going, Captain." Biron's voice was heavy with sorrow yet held a tenderness not often heard from the man. "They'll spot us if we linger here much longer."

"He could still come." Luke gripped the railing, not wanting to let go. Not wanting to give up. He could not allow his brother to be enslaved for one more minute, not allow himself to be a traitor to his country one more time. His knuckles ached as he peered into the darkness, searching for the one thing his heart yearned to see. But all that met his gaze was the shadowy outline of the frigate's hull, lit by the fluttering glow of a lantern mounted at her stern.

Biron tugged at his neckerchief. "You told him not to come after two in the morning. He's a good lad. He'll obey you."

"I guess he couldn't get away," Sam added.

Luke sighed, knowing they were right. If his brother had the opportunity to come above deck, he would have. "Raise topsails, Mr. Keene, and move us out of sight of this dastardly ship. Then head back to Baltimore at first light, Sam." Back to a town of patriots ravaged by British troops on all sides. Back to being a traitor to everyone he knew and everything he believed in. Back to Mrs. Barnes, once again without his brother. Back to Miss Channing.

If she ever discovered his traitorous activities, she would have nothing to do with him. And he wouldn't blame her in the least.

❖

"Cassandra, dear. Mr. Crane asked you a question." Her mother's shrill voice snapped Cassandra from her musings.

Musings about Mr. Heaton. A topic that seemed to occupy much of her thoughts of late. Wondering how he fared out at sea, wondering if he caught another prize, wondering if he was well, wondering if he thought of her as much as she thought of him.

"Oh, do forgive me, Mr. Crane. I fear my mind was elsewhere." Picking up her glass, she sipped the cool mint tea then set it down and glanced at the man across the dining table. She'd had a week's reprieve from enduring his company—a peaceful, glorious week. Well, if she didn't count the ongoing antics of Darlene and Hannah. But, at her mother's invitation, Mr. Crane had joined them once again for supper.

He dabbed the serviette over his lips. "I asked you—*yet again*—if you would honor me by allowing me to escort you to the Fountain Inn Ball?"

Cassandra dropped her fork onto the plate with a loud *clank.* "I had no idea the ball was so fast upon us."

"Cassandra, whatever is wrong with you?" Her mother's forehead wrinkled.

"Nothing." Nothing except the man sitting across from her. Everything else was going well. They had paid this month's mortgage, had food for a month, and had given the servants their back pay. Her mother had even purchased a new hat. But Luke had only just set out to sea last week. Would he catch a prize and return before her money ran out? Cassandra tried to settle her agitated nerves. Whimpering, followed by the scrape of claws on glass drew Cassandra's gaze to poor Dexter, banished to the back garden while Mr. Crane was visiting.

At the sight of the dog, Mr. Crane's nose wrinkled. His impatient gaze shot to Cassandra. "Your answer, miss?"

Thankfully, Miss Thain entered the dining room and began clearing plates, providing the diversion Cassandra needed to avoid answering the question, as she wondered how she would tell Mr. Crane that she had already accepted Mr. Heaton's invitation to the Fountain Inn Ball. Regardless of her feelings about the newspaper man, she didn't wish to wound Mr. Crane's pride. Nor his heart. Nor crush her mother's expectations. But lately it seemed, she did nothing but disappoint everyone around her. Especially herself.

Never making eye contact, Miss Thain swept through the room, gathering up utensils and platters, finally ending with Mr. Crane's half-full plate of boiled wild geese, fried potatoes, and baked beets from the garden. The fact that it neither resembled nor tasted like any of those things was no longer a shock to Cassandra.

"Thank you, Miss Thain," she said as the woman darted from the room, plates stacked up her arms.

"Now that you can afford a good cook, perhaps you should hire one?" Mr. Crane leaned back in his chair and cocked one brow.

Cassandra's jaw tightened.

"Though where you obtained additional funds is beyond me," he said. Cassandra's mother fluttered her napkin about her face. "Dreadful, simply dreadful business the way our money was stolen. And without your help those few days afterward, we would have starved."

Mr. Crane returned her smile with a forced one of his own before he faced Cassandra. "A distant, wealthy relative die and leave you a fortune?"

"I fail to see how that is any of your affair, Mr. Crane." Cassandra thought she saw a flicker of turmoil cross his eyes before he swept them away.

"Wealthy relative die?" Her mother laughed nervously. "Wouldn't that be a turn of fortune?"

Cassandra gave her mother a pointed gaze, reminding her that she'd instructed her not to say anything about where the additional money had come from.

Her mother coughed and set her serviette on the table. "Shall we have coffee in the parlor?"

Mr. Crane extended his chin. "As I said, I'm more than happy to provide whatever you need, Miss Channing."

"And as I have said, you are too kind, sir." Cassandra stood as a playful scream sounded from above stairs, followed by giggling, the stomp of tiny footsteps, and Mrs. Northrop's harsh voice.

"Oh dear." Cassandra's mother rose. "I had hoped Mrs. Northrop would have gotten the girls abed by now."

Frowning his disapproval, Mr. Crane stood and proffered his arm to Cassandra's mother, leading her down the hall to the parlor.

Cassandra dipped her head in the kitchen door to ask Miss Thain to bring coffee before she followed them.

No sooner had she sat down on the sofa and spread her skirts about her than Mr. Crane, standing at the hearth, one arm draped over the mantel as if he owned the home, brought up the Fountain Inn Ball once again.

A warm breeze swept into the room, fluttering the curtains. Cassandra gazed into the darkness creeping in from outside.

Mr. Crane cleared his throat. "The ball is in ten days, Miss Channing.

Surely you have not made other arrangements?"

"But I'm afraid I have, sir." Cassandra smiled sweetly, hoping her demeanor would soften the blow. "I have agreed to be escorted by Mr. Heaton."

Her mother gasped. Grabbing her bell, she shook it vigorously.

Mr. Crane's bushy brows bunched together. His mouth dropped open. "Mr. *Luke* Heaton?"

As if there could be any other.

Miss Thain entered with a tray of coffee and set it on the table, seemingly oblivious to the incessant chiming bouncing off the walls.

"One and the same." Cassandra reached over and stayed the bell in her mother's hands.

Miss Thain's oversized eyes met Cassandra's before she lowered them and began to pour the coffee.

Cassandra's mother raised a hand to her forehead. "Oh, never mind that, Miss Thain. Please have Mrs. Northrop bring my tonic immediately."

After the cook left the parlor, Cassandra's mother glared at Cassandra. "You cannot be serious, dear. This is unheard of!"

"Isn't the man out to sea?" Mr. Crane's normally calm voice cracked.

Cassandra poured a cup of coffee and handed it to her mother, but the woman merely stared at her as if she'd lost her mind. Setting the cup back down with a *clank*, she swallowed. "He assured me he would be in town for the occasion."

"How can he assure you of such a thing? Of all the. . ." Mr. Crane gazed up at the picture of Cassandra's great-grandfather as if trying to garner some wisdom from the aged man.

"Mr. Heaton cannot predict when he is in town and when he isn't." Suspicion twisted his features.

"Dear." Her mother touched her arm. "I know you feel you owe Mr. Heaton for his success at sea, but this type of charity is simply beyond the pale."

Cassandra tapped her shoe over the ornate rug. "Yet I have given him my word, and I intend to abide by it."

Mrs. Northrop entered the room with tonic in hand. Crossing to the table, she poured a splash of the magical elixir into Cassandra's mother's coffee and left without saying a word or speaking to any of them.

Mr. Crane tugged on his embroidered waistcoat, crossed to the table, and poured himself a cup of coffee. The sharp scent of ink followed him.

From his terse expression Cassandra knew she had hurt him, but there was nothing to be done about it. The sooner he realized she could not possibly accept his hand, the freer he would be to find some other lady upon whom to shower his affections.

He tossed the coffee to the back of his throat then grimaced, no doubt from the scalding liquid. Setting the cup down, he dipped his head toward them. "I thank you for supper, Mrs. Channing, but I fear important matters draw me away early this evening." Cassandra's mother rose. She pressed her trembling hands together, a wild, pleading look in her eyes. "So soon, sir?"

"I'm afraid so." He shot a gaze so filled with outrage toward Cassandra it sent a chill down her.

As he made his way to the door, her mother eased beside him. "Forgive her, Mr. Crane. I will speak to her." Though she whispered, her words found their way to Cassandra's ears. "Rest assured, she will attend the ball with you."

❖

After Mrs. Channing saw him out, Mr. Crane made his way down the flagstone path to the street, anger tossing the putrid contents of his supper into a tempest. How dare the young tart refuse him? And for that swaggering miscreant? After all Crane had done for this family. He clenched his jaw until it hurt then turned toward the shrubbery that marked the corner of the Channing property. There as expected, the housekeeper, Mrs. Northrop, emerged from the shadows.

"What do you have for me?" he asked, settling his hat atop his head.

A breeze, ripe with the scents of honeysuckle and roses, tousled wisps of the elderly woman's hair from beneath her mobcap. She puckered her lips and gazed back at the house. "I thought you should know, sir, that it was Mr. Heaton who gave Miss Channing the money."

"Mr. Heaton again!" he shouted then slammed his mouth shut with a groan. He closed his eyes as a horse and rider walked past. "Why does she take his money and not mine?"

Mrs. Northrop stretched her already elongated neck. "She says it is only a loan until he catches another prize."

The news rankled over Crane's already agitated nerves. Catch another prize, indeed. Not if he could help it. "Anything else?"

"No, sir. But I'll keep my eyes and ears open for anything unusual like you said." She held out her hand.

Mr. Crane huffed. "I gave you five dollars last time."

"It's not easy sneaking around listening in on conversations. Mrs. Channing is getting suspicious. Besides, I took a big risk for you stealing Miss Channing's money."

"And you were handsomely paid for that."

Yet the servant's hand would not retreat. Mr. Crane plucked a couple of coins from his waistcoat pocket and deposited them atop her greedy palm—if only to buy her continued silence.

"Thank you, sir." Turning, she snuck away into the darkness.

Mr. Crane stormed down the dirt street, his mood as dark as the evening shadows around him and as turbulent as the skies above. He cursed Luke Heaton. How did the man keep succeeding at sea? Lieutenant Tripp had assured him that he'd sufficiently sabotaged Mr. Heaton's ship. Yet five days ago, the scoundrel had sailed into Baltimore harbor a victor. His ship none the worse for wear and his pockets full of coins. "To the devil with him!" Mr. Crane shouted as he turned down Lombard Street. The man was up to something. No privateer could capture a prize and return to port in that short amount of time. Nor would luck allow him to slip undetected past the British blockade more than once.

One thing Crane knew. Mr. Heaton must be dealt with. Without him in the way, Miss Channing would have no choice but to accept Crane's courtship. No, the rake was up to something.

And Crane intended to find out just what that something was.

❖ CHAPTER 25 ❖

Cassandra exited the drapers, wrapped package in hand. Margaret followed her outside onto the street bustling with people, horses, and carriages. From his spot leaning against a wooden post, Margaret's husband, Mr. Dayle, lengthened his stance, picked up two empty buckets from the ground, and greeted them, his gentle smile ever present.

"Success, ladies?"

"Yes, thank you, Mr. Dayle." Cassandra tilted her head into the hot August sun.

"The gown looks glorious on you, miss." Margaret's eyes twinkled. "Mr. Heaton will no doubt be speechless at your beauty."

Warmth flooded Cassandra's face as she turned and proceeded down the walkway—warmth that had nothing to do with the sultry afternoon. "I care not what effect my beauty has on Mr. Heaton. I simply needed a new gown and the ball provided me with an excuse." Though she could ill afford the extra expense.

Margaret's giggle reminded Cassandra that she'd forgotten to chastise her maid for telling Mr. Heaton she was in her solarium alone those. . . how many nights ago? It seemed an eternity since she'd seen the man.

Felt his strong arms surround her.

His lips on hers.

More heat swamped her.

"Miss, are you all right? Your face is as red as a beet," Margaret said.

Cassandra glanced at her maid, expecting to see a look of concern. Instead she saw a mischievous grin. Opening her parasol with a snap, Cassandra stopped to cross the street. "You are incorrigible, Margaret."

"Indeed," Mr. Dayle agreed as his eyes took in his wife with affection. "My wife fancies herself a matchmaker."

"It's just that I wish everyone could be as happy as we are, my love." Margaret smiled up at him, her cheeks as rosy as her lips.

A twinge of jealousy pinched Cassandra at the adoring affection that stretched between the couple. "Well, I assure you, you are wasting your matchmaking skills with me. I have enough of that with my mother. Besides, I cannot hope for such a fortuitous match as yours. Most marriages occur out of necessity and are merely contracts of convenience by reason of wealth or pedigree."

Mr. Dayle stepped into the road, leading the way between a passing landau—overflowing with passengers donned in lace and exotic feathers—and a wagon filled with children dressed in rags sitting amongst barrels. Cassandra smiled at one of wee ones, and the little girl waved.

Margaret weaved her arm through Cassandra's. "Contracts such as the one between you and Mr. Heaton?"

Cassandra shook her head and laughed. "I surrender, Margaret." A breeze blew in from the harbor, cooling the perspiration on her neck and dancing through the lace that fringed her parasol. "Now, let's go fetch water from the spring and get home before this heat becomes unbearable. And I'll have no further talk of Mr. Heaton or any other man for that matter."

Yet, as they headed down the crowded street, Cassandra could think of nothing but Mr. Heaton. She had spotted *Destiny* anchored at bay when they passed by the harbor that morning. Odd that only he had successfully slipped past the blockade yet again. Ignoring the nip of suspicion, Cassandra settled on the fact that he was a better captain than she or the entire town had given him credit for.

He was in town! Which meant she would soon see him. Which also meant he had kept his promise to be home in time to escort her to the ball.

A group of militiamen marched by, muskets propped on their shoulders, their boots stirring a dust cloud in the street, reminding Cassandra that they were at war. But how could she forget that with the British fleet sitting just miles off their coast, repeatedly threatening to sail toward Baltimore? Not to mention the musket shots that peppered the sky many a night, waking Cassandra from a deep sleep. Perhaps she shouldn't allow herself such flighty thoughts of balls and gowns and romance during such a time as this.

She was still pondering these things when they turned the corner onto the city square, where a natural spring provided not only fresh water, but the perfect meeting place for the inhabitants of Baltimore. Several groups of people mulled about the area. Feathered bonnets and cocked hats huddled in deep conversation. Children darted here and there. Giggles and the thrum of chatter accompanied the *clip-clop* of horses' hooves and the slosh of water being collected from the spring. As Cassandra scanned the crowd, her eyes latched onto a tall man with dark hair standing with his back to her.

Her heart vaulted into her throat.

"Cassandra!" Marianne waved at her from her spot beside Mr. Heaton. Noah and another powerfully built man with brown hair and a regal bearing lifted their gazes in her direction.

Trying to avoid looking at Mr. Heaton, lest she give away her excitement at seeing him, Cassandra approached the group and gave her friend a hug.

Margaret joined her husband at the well where they waited their turn to fill the buckets.

"Noah, so good to see you. When did you get home?" Cassandra asked, avoiding Mr. Heaton's gaze.

"Two days ago." He gave his wife an endearing look. "I had a very successful voyage."

"I'm happy to hear it." She turned to Mr. Heaton. "I saw your ship in the bay."

"Indeed. I sailed in last night." He drank her in with his eyes.

Marianne turned to the other gentleman. "Oh, forgive my bad manners. This is Lieu. . .Mr. Reed. He is a friend of Rose's."

Tearing her gaze from the trance Luke placed on her, Cassandra faced the newcomer. "Rose McGuire?"

He dipped his head. "The same." Sorrow crossed his deep brown eyes. Then taking Cassandra's gloved hand, he placed a kiss upon it. "A pleasure to meet you, miss." His voice reeked of British nobility.

"How do you do, Mr. Reed. Pray tell, how do you know Rose?"

Luke snorted and lowered his chin.

Noah waved a hand through the air. "It is a long story, I'm afraid. For another time, perhaps."

The alarm firing over Marianne's face sent a prickle of unease through Cassandra, but she shrugged it off. It was none of her business.

Against her will, her gaze found its way back to Luke. "So your voyage was met with success?"

A perpetual grin sat on his mouth as his eyes kept wandering to her lips.

Sending her stomach into a whirl. *Cad.*

"Quite," he said. "In fact, I was on my way to see you about the prize money."

A burst of wind tugged at her parasol, drawing Luke's glance. A playful smirk lifted his lips as a loose strand of his hair brushed over his jaw. "Why not come for supper, Mr. Heaton? We can settle accounts then." The invitation flew from her mouth before she could ponder the wisdom of it. Yet, perhaps, if her mother spent more time with him, she would see that he was a gentleman. And one who possessed just as much charm, intelligence, and dependability as Mr. Crane.

She shocked herself with her confidence in the man.

Mr. Heaton's gaze shifted to Noah, who smiled toward Cassandra. "I'm afraid I have need of Luke tonight, Cassandra. He's assisting me and Mr. Reed with an important task."

A look of understanding passed between the men, causing her uneasiness to grow. But when she looked to Marianne for understanding, her friend gazed at her husband with concern.

"Very well, then"—Cassandra smiled—"perhaps we can discuss business when you come to call on Saturday."

Mr. Heaton's brow furrowed. "Saturday?"

"The ball?" Cassandra tamped her foot on the mud.

He flinched. "Yes, of course."

"You forgot?" She snapped her parasol shut.

Eyeing it, he backed away. And she resisted the urge to poke him with it.

The prattle of the crowd seemed to rise up around her as if, with wagging tongues and looks of pity, everyone in the square witnessed Cassandra's humiliation.

"Forgive me, Miss Channing. I've had much on my mind." An unusual sadness tugged on Luke's features.

But she would not fall for his act. All the happiness she'd allowed herself to feel these past weeks dissolved into a single drop of despair. "We only forget things that are not of import to us. I shall relieve you of your obligation to escort me." She faced her friends. Sympathy filled Marianne's eyes. Noah gave Luke a caustic look, and Mr. Reed glanced off to the side.

"Good day to you all." Then turning, Cassandra stomped away.

She heard the thud of his boots following her. He grabbed her arm and spun her around. "Miss Channing, I truly wish to escort you to the ball."

"You have an odd way of showing it, Mr. Heaton." She headed down the street.

And again he stopped her. Desperation crinkled the corners of his blue eyes. "I'm a cad, Miss Channing." He gestured toward the bundle in her arms. "I see that you've had a new gown made for the occasion. How can I make it up to you?"

"Don't flatter yourself, Mr. Heaton. This gown is not for the ball. If you'll please deduct what I owe you from my share of your most recent prize and send the paperwork and any additional funds to me by courier, I'd be obliged." Then turning, she stormed away.

Only this time, she did not hear him following.

Margaret fell in step beside her, while Mr. Dayle, with full buckets in hand, followed behind. A hundred unflattering names for Mr. Heaton sped through Cassandra's mind, empowering her steps. Reprobate, scoundrel, villain, blackguard, libertine. Clutching her closed parasol in one hand, she pressed the gown to her chest, if only to prevent herself from tossing it to the dirt as she wished.

She had no need of it now.

But she wouldn't give the insolent rake the satisfaction. She would keep the new gown for another occasion—when a true gentleman came to escort her for the evening.

Someone who would not use his charm to worm his way into her trust—to gain kisses she had given to no one else. Then, once he had obtained them, once he was satisfied with her desire for him and his insatiable vanity was fed, he abandoned her like the string of broken women before her.

How could she have allowed him to woo her? She knew what type of man he was. Fighting back tears, she turned the corner onto Market Street. Just when she had finally begun to trust him—finally begun to think he was noble and honorable. Someone she could depend on.

"I'm sorry, miss," Margaret said as they weaved their way down the busy street. "It's only a silly ball."

"It's not the ball, Margaret. It's that I counted on him. For the first time in a long time, I counted on someone. And he let me down."

Instead of uttering one of her platitudes, Margaret took Cassandra's arm in a consoling grip and walked silently beside her.

Hearing the slosh of the water as Mr. Dayle struggled to maintain their harried pace, Cassandra slowed. Besides, people were beginning to stare. She drew in a deep breath and raised her chin. "What does it matter anyway?"

Yet the tears pooling in her eyes belied her words. Why, oh why, had she done the very thing she had forbidden herself to do?

Why had she fallen in love with the town rogue?

❖

"Good evening to you, Miss Addington, always a pleasure. And Mr. Snyder." Luke shoved his hat back onto his head and backed out of the humble cottage. "I'll trouble you no further tonight."

Before Miss Addington had shut the door, Mr. Snyder, the city councilman, shouted from within his house, "What is that noise?" The sound of his buckled shoes clipped over the wooden floor. Hurrying down the front steps, Luke waited in the shadow of a tree for his friends to appear from behind the house. If the councilman caught them in his chamber, he would no doubt implicate Luke in the crime. More trouble Luke did not need. But how could he refuse Noah's help? The man was his best friend and he had saved his life on more than one occasion. Mr. Reed was another story. Luke was yet unconvinced that the British Royal Navy lieutenant meant them no harm—that his actions were in the best interest of Rose McGuire, as he professed. But Noah believed him. And that was all Luke needed to go along with the nefarious deed.

Seconds passed like long minutes as Luke peered into the darkness. Finally, the duo appeared, darting from the left side of the house, Mr. Snyder's shout following them like cannon shot. Mr. Reed pressed a bundle to his chest. Moonlight glimmered off a sword in his hand as the three men sprinted down the street without saying a word. Once they turned the corner, Noah slowed to a walk, his chest heaving. Then his and Mr. Reed's chuckles filled the air.

"I take it you got what you came for?" Luke asked.

"I did." Mr. Reed's tone lifted in excitement. "Thank you for your help, Mr. Heaton, especially considering our past."

The past he referred to, as well as his British accent, still grated over Luke. The past in which Luke had been enslaved aboard the HMS *Undefeatable* where Mr. Reed was second lieutenant. "I did it for Miss McGuire, not for you."

"I thank you nonetheless, sir." Though Luke could not make out Mr. Reed's expression in the darkness, his voice was sincere.

A fleeting thought drifted through Luke's mind. Perhaps Mr. Reed could aid him in rescuing his brother. But no. That would mean confessing Luke's traitorous activities to Noah. Noah was an honorable man. A patriot. Friendship or not, Luke doubted that Noah's irreproachable conscience would allow him to do anything but turn Luke in.

"If that's all you need tonight, gentlemen," Luke said as they approached the street that led to his favorite tavern. After his meeting today with Miss Channing, he needed a drink. He knew he had crushed the bud of their relationship beneath his stupidity. He knew she would probably never forgive him. His flickering hope for any courtship between them was sufficiently doused. It was for the best. She deserved much better than him.

"I would impose on you one more time, Luke," Noah said, stopping him. "Mr. Reed and I need your help at the ball in three days."

"I'm not attending."

Noah halted and touched Luke's arm, stopping him. "Will you attend for me? Mr. Reed wishes to bid Miss McGuire one last adieu and pass along some good news."

"Why do you need me?" Luke huffed. "Another lady to distract?"

"No. A man. Mr. Snyder, to be exact."

Fisting his hands at his waist, Luke chuckled. Truth be told, he was no friend to the slimy councilman and would love to see the man put in his place. Besides, he had several days before his next rendezvous with the frigate. Since he'd already devised a new plan to rescue John, he had naught else to do but sulk about and drown his sorrows with rum. Now that he was not attending the ball with Miss Channing, what would it matter if he aided Noah and Mr. Reed?

"You can count on me."

❖ CHAPTER 26 ❖

Struggling for a breath, Luke tugged upon the silk neckerchief Mrs. Barnes had elegantly tied around his neck. How did men continually wear these infernal things? He gazed down at the suit of black lute string trimmed in velvet that he'd borrowed from Noah. Though it fit him perfectly, he felt like an overprimped fop. Lifting the glass to his lips, he sipped the wine punch and gazed at the display of pomposity spread across the dance floor and hovering in cackling clusters about the room. Baltimore's finest citizens attired like peacocks, men in their silk-embroidered waistcoats, ladies in the latest gowns, adorned with colorful sashes and glittering jewels. Their hair alone, twined with pearls and golden pins, must have taken hours to fashion.

Biron appeared beside him. "Cheer up, Captain. You look as though your ship just sank."

"You know I despise these functions." Luke snorted as a malodorous cloud of perfumes stung his nose. His first mate adjusted his velvet waistcoat and smiled at a passing lady. Luke had never seen the old man in anything but his dirty breeches, gray shirt, and red neckerchief. Nor had he ever seen him so chipper. In fact, he'd been completely surprised to discover that Biron was attending the ball at all.

"You wouldn't despise such grand affairs if you were escorting Miss Channing." Censure rang in Biron's voice.

Just the sound of her name sent pain sprawling across Luke. "Certain things are worth enduring for women like her."

"And for friends who need your help," Biron added, a twinkle in his eye.

"Aye, which is why I'm here dressed like a stuffed pig and feeling like a fool." Luke sipped his drink again, noting the wine was getting quite low. He would need a refill soon if he was going to endure this night.

"It feels indecent to be here amongst all this luxury," he said. "Enjoying my wine, when John is no doubt huddling belowdecks, lonely and hungry, aboard that frigate."

"Aye, Captain, but there's naught to be done about it now. It's better to be here helping your friends than sitting in some tavern, flooding your belly with rum and losing what's left of your money." Biron's eyes lit up. "Besides, the scenery here is much more appealing."

Luke huffed. Perhaps his friend was right.

The quadrille ended, and the couples bowed and curtseyed to each other as they moved from the dance floor. Several ladies peered at him above silk fans.

"Ah, to be young and as handsome as you are, Captain." Biron dipped his head toward the giggling ladies, shocking Luke.

"I've never known you to desire the company of the softer gender."

"In truth, after my wife died, I had no interest, but the older I get, the more I'm findin' the need for companionship. God said it isn't good for man to be alone. And I do believe He was right."

"So, *that* explains why you came tonight."

"Aye, look at all the sweet angels floating about the room."

Luke chuckled as his eyes landed on Mr. Keene, dressed in his usual pomp, at the edge of the dance floor, kissing the hand of a young lady who seemed barely old enough to be out in society. She tugged her hand from his grip, her eyes pools of pain and betrayal, before she clutched her gown and flew away like a wounded bird.

Instead of following her to make amends for whatever caused her distress, Mr. Keene immediately veered his gaze to another lady standing off to his side and shrugged. The woman laughed and gave him a coy come-hither glance. Which the man immediately obliged. After a few seconds, in which it appeared the lady scribbled Mr. Keene's name on her dance card, he turned, spotted Luke and Biron, and headed their way.

"What was all that about?" Luke asked.

Mr. Keene raised his eyebrows in innocence. Luke pointed with his drink to the door on the far side of the room where he'd seen the troubled lady exit. "That young woman. She seemed vexed."

Mr. Keene clasped his hands behind his back. "Ah yes, Miss Melody. She was under the mistaken impression that we were courting." He chuckled.

Biron scratched his head. "Hmm. I wonder how she came to that conclusion."

"I have no idea. You know how women can be." Mr. Keene gave a sensuous smile to a passing lady, who returned it with a wave of her fan. "I suppose I called on her on a few occasions."

"Just called on her?" Luke asked.

"I suppose I may have kissed her once or twice." Mr. Keene rubbed his jaw. The jewel on his finger winked at Luke from within the lacy folds of his cuff.

Luke shook his head, finding it difficult to contain his anger. "To a proper lady, a kiss is nearly equal to a proposal of marriage." But guilt tightened his gut at the thought of the kisses he'd shared with Miss Channing. How was he any different from Mr. Keene?

Mr. Keene looked incredulous. "You can't possibly think I could limit myself to a single lady when there are so many delectably ripe fruits from which to pick?" He waved a hand over the crowd, and his gaze froze on a particularly succulent fruit smiling at him from the corner. "If you'll excuse me, gentlemen." And off he went in a flourish of satin.

Luke followed him with an angry gaze, remembering the look of agony in the woman's eyes moments ago.

Biron crossed his arms over his chest. "A dangerous man, that one. At least to the ladies. And he's a mite old to be playing such games."

Luke nodded. At one and forty, the man still presented a handsome figure. Yet his age gave the incorrect impression of maturity and stability. "He should take care with the sentiments of others."

"In truth, he reminds me a bit of you, Captain."

"Me?" Luke said. "Bite your tongue, man."

"How many hearts have you broken in this town?"

Biron's words struck Luke like a frigid wind. He could always count on the blunt assessment of his friend. Yet, in truth, Luke had never actually considered it. Hadn't he spent his life flitting from woman to woman, never landing on one long enough to form an attachment? Suddenly, dozens of tear-filled eyes—just like the eyes he'd seen on that young lady—paraded across his vision.

At the time he had brushed them off as overemotional females. Now, he understood their pain—felt it himself down to his core. Shame soured in his stomach. In fifteen years, would Luke end up like Mr. Keene, a flashy, pretentious philanderer whose only skills included cards, drink, and meaningless trysts with wanton women? At six and twenty, he was well on his way. Or he *had* been until Miss Channing had given him a chance to better himself. Until she had given him the desire to be a better man.

"I'm not like that anymore," he announced, raising his empty glass with a frown.

"I'm glad to hear it." Biron gave him a knowing look before his eyes latched onto an elderly woman standing beside a much younger one at the edge of the dance floor. "Now, if you'll excuse me. I see the lady I've been looking for."

Luke watched as his old friend wove his way through the crowd to stand before the older woman as the younger wandered off to dance. She smiled and dipped her head in agreement to whatever he was saying. The scene brought a glimmer of joy to Luke's otherwise dour mood. Turning, he started for the refreshment table in the next room when the shimmer of an emerald gown hooked his gaze, drawing it toward a red-haired beauty across the dance floor.

*Cassandra. . .*Miss Channing.

What was she doing here? Had she found someone else to escort her? Jealousy twisted in his gut. She stood beside Marianne and Miss Rose, the trio of heads drawn together in some covert feminine scheme. Her burgundy-colored hair fell in ringlets around her neck and sparkled like garnets when she moved. Mesmerized by the sight of her, Luke forgot where he'd been going. Then she turned and glanced across the room as if looking for someone. Her eyes met his and her smile faded. He lifted his empty glass toward her in a salute as Miss Rose leaned and whispered something in her ear. Marianne grinned, and Miss Channing turned her back to Luke once again.

What was he thinking? Of course she'd found another escort. She was a beautiful woman who possessed manners and charm and intelligence and courage.

And the kindest heart he'd ever known.

With a huff, he turned and slipped through the door into the next room in search of two things: Noah and a drink. The sooner he aided his friend in getting rid of Mr. Snyder, the sooner Luke could leave this ostentatious ball and head toward the tavern where he belonged. So much for his promise to Biron. He found Noah standing next to the man in question—Mr. Snyder—who was relaying some lavish tale to the mayor, General Smith, and two other councilmen. Noah gave Luke a nod to carry out the plan they'd spoken of earlier.

Selecting a glass of wine from the oblong refreshment table set against the wall, Luke reached for the bottle of laudanum inside his coat pocket and poured a hefty amount into the glass. He handed it to Noah, who handed it to Mr. Snyder. Three glasses later, the man had not slowed a breath in his fervent speech. Finally, the mayor made some excuse to leave, and the party broke up. Mr. Snyder, with a barely perceivable stumble, made his way to Miss Rose across the room. Cassandra stood beside her.

Much to her apparent dismay, Mr. Snyder grabbed Miss Rose's arm and dragged her into the other room toward the dance floor where a Virginia reel was just beginning. Noah and the ladies followed, leaving Luke with no recourse but to join them. Not that he minded. Though Miss Channing would not grace him with even a glance, Luke relished their close proximity.

Taking his wife's arm, Noah swung about and faced Miss Channing. "If you would honor Mr. Heaton with a dance, Cassandra, it will help us keep an eye on Snyder."

Luke started to protest, not wanting the woman to be forced to taint herself with his touch, but she agreed before he could utter a word.

"For Rose," she said and lifted her gloved hand.

An unavoidable grin on his face, Luke placed it within the crook of his elbow. He must thank Noah later.

Her hand was stiff on his arm as he led her to a spot in the line of women and took his position across from her. The music began and the couples bowed toward each other then stepped together. "I can see how it pains you to be close to me." Looping his elbow through hers, he swung her about.

"I will endure it for my friend's sake." Her voice was as sharp as glass.

They retreated and waited as the head couple sashayed down the middle of the line. "How noble." He gave her a spurious grin.

She pursed her lips and lifted her chin. "What would you know of nobility?"

The couples surrounding them began to stare.

Infernal woman. They came together again at the head of the line. Luke lifted his hand, but she hovered hers atop his as if she loathed to touch him. He escorted her down the line of dancers. "About as much as you know of forgiveness, miss."

Her eyes narrowed into shards of emerald. She opened her mouth to say something when beside them, Mr. Snyder emitted an odd giggle and began to sway. All eyes shot toward Rose as she attempted to keep the man from falling.

Disappointment weighted Luke's shoulders. The laudanum had worked too soon. Yet what did it matter? His conversation with Miss Channing had been nothing but an exchange of insults. She turned to her friend, her rigid features of only a moment ago softening as she helped Rose and Mr. Snyder from the floor. Noah gave an approving nod to Luke.

Mr. Snyder took up a harried pace through the press of people, nudging them aside as he went and sputtering words in some sort of tirade. Finally, collapsing into a chair, he lowered his head into his hands.

Critical whispers collected behind fans, riding upon looks of repugnance. Finally the butler at the front door announced the entrance of a new actor to this mad play. "Mr. Alexander Reed."

Everyone's heads swerved.

Including Miss Rose, who stumbled backward in shock. Mr. Snyder slumped to the ground. Luke dashed to him, pulling him up by one arm while Noah grabbed the other.

Miss Rose, her brow lined with concern, leaned over her unconscious escort.

"He'll be all right, Miss Rose." Luke winked. "He just needs to sleep it off." Then, with great difficulty, he and Noah dragged the councilman through the parting crowd, out into the gardens, up the stairs, and into a room they'd previously purchased.

"Heavy old bugger." Noah chuckled as they deposited Mr. Snyder on the bed and swung his feet up on the coverlet. "That should hold him for a couple hours." Noah slapped his hands together.

"I still don't see why you're doing this for that British lieutenant." Luke stared at the drooling councilman.

"Miss Rose seems to find favor in the man. Besides, he's going back to his ship tonight."

"To terrorize and murder more Americans?" Luke growled. "We could be hanged for allowing him to escape." Even as he said it, he realized his own hypocrisy.

"Aye, I realize that." Noah crossed his arms over his chest. "But there's nothing to be done for it. It would break Rose's heart. Besides, Mr. Reed is an honorable man who regrets his part in this war."

Luke gazed at Mr. Snyder. "Honor. A quality sorely lacking in the councilman."

The two men left the room, closing the door tight, and returned to the ballroom. Upon seeing Marianne, Noah excused himself, leaving Luke alone once again. He scanned the room but saw no sign of Cassandra. It was just as well. He had no desire to see her in another man's arms.

Turning to leave, Luke nearly ran into Mr. Crane, his face an expanding mass of red angst.

"How dare you, sir?"

"How dare I, what?" Luke huffed and raised a brow.

Mr. Crane's lips twisted in disgust. "How dare you escort Miss Channing to this ball and then abandon her." He jerked his head to the left, and Luke glanced over to see the object of their discussion, standing along the back wall, forlornly watching the dancers float across the floor. Oddly, Biron stood beside her.

Luke longed for a drink. "I neither escorted her, sir, nor abandoned her."

Mr. Crane's face crumbled. "Then, why is she here? Why are *you* here?"

"As to the first, you may ask her yourself. As to the second, I shall remedy that immediately." Luke dipped his head to the shorter man and brushed past him and out the door.

❖

Cassandra eyed the weathered seaman beside her. As soon as he had approached, she recognized him as Mr. Heaton's first mate. "Are you enjoying yourself, Mr. Abbot?"

"Aye, I am, miss," he said. "I don't attend functions like this very often, but I was finally able to purchase a suit to wear from my earnings aboard *Destiny*."

"Well, you look very handsome, sir." She smiled and glanced at the dancers twirling and gliding over the floor like lilies on a swirling pond, happy to see Noah and Marianne enjoying themselves.

Mr. Abbot shuffled his shoes and shifted his glance between her and the crowd.

"Did you wish to speak to me about something, Mr. Abbot?"

He sighed. "Aye, it's about Luke. . .Mr. Heaton."

"Did he send you?" Just then she spotted him across the room talking with Mr. Crane. Odd.

"I thought you should know," Mr. Abbot said, "how terrible he feels about not remembering the ball."

"I'm quite sure." *Sure that he's an unfeeling sot.*

"He thinks quite highly of you, miss. He's got much on his mind lately."

His many other lady friends, no doubt. "Just not me, apparently."

"Beggin' your pardon, that's where you're wrong, miss."

Cassandra could hear no more. "I know you must think me some vain shrew, Mr. Abbot." Actually, she wasn't sure why she was behaving in such a way. "I know privateering is not easy business, and I imagine it's quite harrowing and dangerous at times, but a gentleman's word is a gentleman's word." And she had been so excited, so hopeful that she could depend on the word of that particular gentleman, if she could refer to him by that title. Even so, when Luke had shown up at the ball anyway, she thought perhaps she might give him another chance. Then she realized he'd only come to help Noah, not to see her. And she'd been crushed all over again.

"He hurt you." Mr. Abbot cocked his head.

She lifted her chin. "Don't be silly. It would take much more than the broken word of a cad to distress me."

"He has more than privateering on his mind," he said. "A private matter that eats away at him. I thought you should know."

Cassandra's traitorous gaze swept back to Mr. Heaton, still speaking with Mr. Crane. What problems could the man possibly have that surpassed her own? He had only himself to care for. And only his drinking and gambling habits to fund. Yet, she had sensed a hint of sorrow about him in the solarium that night.

Finally, Mr. Heaton and Mr. Crane separated, and the latter headed toward her. "Oh, bother."

"And I thought you should also know"—Mr. Abbot dipped his head at a passing elderly lady—"that he kept his word to you about not partakin' of rum out at sea."

Cassandra studied the old sailor. A wisdom she had not expected to see intensified his eyes, while his words about Luke befuddled her mind. Why would he honor such a difficult promise and yet forget all about the ball? "Mr. Abbot, you are a loyal friend to Mr. Heaton. He doesn't deserve you."

As Mr. Crane approached, his frown transformed into a sickly smile. "Miss Channing"—he bowed—"how lovely to see you. I have just heard from Mr. Heaton that you are here without an escort."

Mr. Abbot groaned, excused himself, and walked away, Mr. Crane's glare following him through the mob.

"That is true, sir." Her voice snapped his attention back to her.

"May I have the pleasure of the next dance?"

Cassandra eyed the man—the slight quiver of his bottom lip, the anticipation in his eyes. But her mind swam with what Mr. Abbot had said, and her heart was drawn out the door where Mr. Heaton had disappeared.

"I thank you, Mr. Crane, but I'm afraid I only came to help a friend. I am not in the mood to dance tonight."

His face fell and fury filled his eyes. "I see your privateer has returned." He gestured toward the door where Luke had exited.

"Indeed."

"With more prize money?"

"That is none of your concern."

A frown folded his lips. "But what is my concern, Miss Channing"—with raised brows, he leaned toward her, his cologne unable to mask his inky smell—"is how the man manages to slip past the British blockade. At least three times now, is it? When men of far greater nautical skill either do not attempt it or get caught in the process."

"What are you saying, sir?" Although Cassandra knew precisely what he implied—had entertained similar questions herself.

"I'm not saying anything, miss." He brushed dust from his shoulder. "Just speculating."

Cassandra's jaw tightened. "Well, I'll thank you, sir, to keep your speculations to yourself until you have evidence to back them." The hypocrisy of her defense of Mr. Heaton, when only moments before she accused him of being dishonorable, was not lost on her.

Mr. Crane's eyes narrowed. He appeared to be having trouble breathing. And frankly, Cassandra found her tolerance of his company waxing thin.

"If you'll excuse me, Mr. Crane. . ." Clutching her gown, she hurried away, weaving a spiraled path amongst the crowd. All she could think of was catching up to Mr. Heaton. Had she misjudged him? Had she even given him a chance to explain? Cursing her selfishness, she dashed from the room into the garden. Stopping only long enough to ensure he was not there, she pushed her way through the throng that mobbed the front stairs and dashed out onto the street. Muggy air, filled with the fragrance of sweet magnolia, stole the odor of tawdry perfume and tobacco smoke from her nostrils. Taking a deep breath, she scanned the street in both directions. Thank goodness they had lit the lanterns on Light Street or she'd not be able to see very far. As it was, she spotted a lone man, dressed in black, walking toward the harbor. She knew that confident gait.

Ignoring the myriad eyes staring her way, she darted down the street, her slippers clacking over the cobblestones and her heart racing in her chest.

"Mr. Heaton!" she shouted when she thought he might be able to hear her.

He didn't turn around.

"Luke!"

Still, he continued on his way.

Her chest heaving, she halted, tears forming in her eyes.

Then as if sensing her distress, he stopped.

And slowly turned to face her.

❖ CHAPTER 27 ❖

Sensing, rather than hearing, someone following him, Luke turned around. He shook his head at the vision that met his eyes—Miss Channing floating on a cloud of green satin, haloed in golden light from the street lantern above her. He rubbed his eyes. Surely, he hadn't consumed *that* much alcohol. Yet instead of vanishing like all the good things in his life, she moved toward him, growing more real and lovely with each passing moment.

Only when her scent of gardenias tickled his nose did he truly believe she had followed him.

"You shouldn't be out here alone."

"I'm not alone now, Mr. Heaton."

He could not fathom why she had chased after him. She'd been nothing but churlish all evening. He gazed into her eyes and swallowed at the yearning and affection he saw within them. "Come to whip me with more angry retorts?"

She lowered her chin. Her creamy chest rose and fell beneath the gold trim of her gown. "I spoke with your first mate, Mr. Abbot."

A landau clattered past, laughter spilling from within onto the cobblestones.

"Indeed. I saw you together," Luke said, uneasy at what the foolish old duff might have told her. Yet she wouldn't be standing here now—adorable, shy, inviting—if he'd told her the truth of his actions.

A gentle smile graced her lips. "You inspire loyalty among your crew."

Luke huffed and pushed a strand of hair behind his ear. "A fact that shocks me as much as I'm sure it does you."

She gazed past him as a breeze from the harbor frolicked in her delicate curls. Luke longed to do the same, but instead he locked his hands together behind his back.

"Perhaps I was a bit hasty in my anger, Mr. Heaton."

He cocked his head. Had the poor woman taken to drink as well? "I was a cad to forget the ball. I deserved your anger."

She searched his eyes as if looking for something. "Something troubles you, some travesty."

A bell rang from the harbor. Hot, muggy air moistened his neck and forehead. "Is that what Mr. Abbot told you?" Luke untied his cravat, allowing the white silk to hang down upon his coat.

"I fear my thoughts have been only for my own hurt pride." She swallowed and looked away but then met his gaze once again. "So what troubles you, Mr. Heaton? Is there something I can do to help?" The concern pouring from her eyes set him back. It took all his strength to keep from taking her in his arms.

"It is a private matter, Miss Channing. One I must deal with on my own."

Music and laughter bubbled out onto the street from the Fountain Inn. A horse with a rider clip-clopped past.

"Very well." She bit her lip.

Luke shifted his stance. He wanted more than anything for her to stay. But he did not want her pity. "Was there something else?"

She smiled. "Only that I formally accept your apology."

Luke chuckled, drawing fire from her eyes.

She placed a gloved hand on her hip. "Did you or did you not beg my forgiveness, Mr. Heaton?"

"It would please me greatly if you'd call me Luke." He grinned.

"That would hardly be prop—"

Luke lowered his lips to hers. He could stand it no further. He delighted in her fervid response. . .her scent of gardenias. Her taste. And the way her curves molded against him. No other woman had affected him so. His world spun and he wanted nothing but her in his arms. Forever.

Withdrawing, she pushed back, her chest heaving. Glancing over her shoulder at the ladies and gentlemen clustered around the inn, she raised a hand to her lips. "We shouldn't."

Luke brushed his thumb over her jaw. Soft, delicate, like the petal of one of her gardenias. She closed her eyes. He eased his hand down her neck, finally fingering her silky hair as he had so often longed to do. He drew her close to him once again.

"I love you, Cassandra," Luke whispered in her ear, no longer caring what she thought, what her reaction would be. He could no longer contain the secret—a secret so important, so wonderful, it could never be kept within the heart of a man.

She gazed up at him, her breath heavy and ragged. A moist sheen covered her eyes.

Then hardened into glass. "How many other women have you said that to?"

Luke frowned. "None." He spoke the truth.

She lowered her gaze.

Lifting her chin with his finger, he leaned toward her and stared into her eyes. "None, Cassandra. I do not speak those words lightly."

The glass in her eyes dissolved into liquid emeralds. She pressed down the folds of her gown and stared into the darkness.

Luke fingered the scars on his hand. Baffling woman. He had no idea what she was thinking. Feeling. Or why she even remained. "I've offended you with my bold affections. Forgive me."

"No."

"You will not forgive me?"

"No, you have not offended me."

Luke flinched as hope began to rise within him. "Then what troubles you?"

She gave him a coy smile, even as her eyes took on a mischievous sparkle. "That I have fallen in love with the town rogue."

Heart bursting, Luke engulfed her in his arms. He kissed her forehead as she snuggled against him. "You make me not want to be a rogue anymore. You make me want to be honorable and good and dependable."

She pushed away from him. Her gaze shifted across his. "Can you be those things, Luke? If not, I fear you will break my heart."

At the thought of his traitorous activities, guilt trampled Luke's joy. "I would never wish to hurt you, Cassandra. As long as I live, all I want is to protect and cherish you."

A tear slipped down her cheek. She fell against him again.

Yet, as Luke held her, a battle waged within him. Now that he had won the love of such an exquisite, wonderful woman, how could he expect to keep it when he was betraying his city, his country, and most of all her?

❖

Crane stormed back into the Fountain Inn, his jaw clenched so tight it hurt. Shoving his way through the crowd, he entered the side room, grabbed a glass of punch wine, and tossed it to the back of his throat, ignoring the gasps of a few ladies nearby. When he lowered his glass, it was to the curious gaze of Lieutenant Abner Tripp.

"Something vexing you, Mr. Crane?"

"Yes, indeed." He tugged the lieutenant to the side, out of the hearing of curious ears. "You told me that if I confiscated Miss Channing's prize winnings, you'd take care of Mr. Heaton for me." Setting his empty glass on the tray of a passing butler, he grabbed another full one. "And I just saw him in a rather passionate embrace with the lady outside."

The lieutenant's eyes narrowed. "Yes, it seems my initial plan failed." He gazed across the chattering crowd. "Though I cannot imagine why. The man should have been caught by a British warship or sunk."

Crane sipped his drink. "But instead, he sails into town on that heap of wood and tar with more earnings. How am I to impress upon Miss Channing her need to marry me when that tavern mongrel"—he growled—"continually feeds her money and charm. And the woman soaks it up like the gullible hussy she is."

"Indeed, I quite agree." Lieutenant Tripp rubbed the scar on his face. "It is inconceivable that the man continues to have so much success at sea. And in such a short amount of time. And I daresay, I find his avoidance of the blockade quite baffling."

Crane drained the remaining wine from his glass. "So, we have established that the man is a good privateer. How does that work in our favor?"

"Because, kind sir, I do not believe he is as skilled as he pretends. No"—the lieutenant leaned closer to Crane, lowering his voice—"I suspect foul play."

"I am of the same mind, sir!" Crane shouted, happy to find a partner in his suspicions, but quickly slammed his mouth shut at the lieutenant's look of censure.

Tripp smiled at a passing couple then shifted his slitted eyes around the crowd. They halted on a man hovering over the refreshment table.

"Ah, and there is the solution to our problem, sir."

Crane's muddled vision found the dandy in question, a man the lieutenant had pointed out before as Mr. Keene, the boatswain aboard Mr. Heaton's ship. "What does it matter, sir? All Heaton's vermin are loyal to him."

"Perhaps, yes. But I've heard Mr. Keene likes his drink. And I've also heard his tongue loosens considerably the deeper into his cups he becomes."

Crane smiled. "What do you say we set up a meeting at a nearby tavern with the man?"

❖

Stretching, Cassandra pushed aside the curtains and sat in the window seat, peering down at her solarium. Laughter shifted her gaze to the back garden where Hannah and Darlene held hands and twirled in a circle, singing "Ring around the Rosie." She smiled. Sunlight coated her in warmth, and she drew a deep breath of the fresh dewy morning. An odd sensation over came her. One she hadn't felt in years.

Happiness.

After Mr. Heaton's. . .*Luke's* declaration of love two nights past, she'd hardly slept a second. Closing her eyes, she pictured him standing in the moonlight, a loose strand of his black hair grazing the stubble on his jaw. The look of adoration in his eyes. The tender love in his kiss. The feel of his strong arms around her. He loved her! And he had vowed to change.

Perhaps she was a fool to trust him. But she couldn't help it. She'd never been more sure of anything or anyone in her life.

Opening her eyes, she hugged herself and smiled. She had enough money to provide for her family and was being courted by the most fascinating, strong, capable man.

"You're in love, miss." Margaret's voice jerked Cassandra from her daze, tossing her heart into her throat.

"Sorry to startle you. I knocked but there was no answer." The perky maid flitted into the room, carrying a pitcher of water and a grin on her rosy face.

Cassandra slid off the seat. "What did you say?"

"You are positively glowing this morning, miss. You must be thinking of him."

"Why, whoever are you referring to?" Cassandra gave her a coy look.

"Why"—Margaret lifted her brows—"Mr. Heaton, of course."

Cassandra moved to her bed and grabbed the post. "Yes. I admit it. I do love him." She touched Margaret's arm, stopping her. "Have I gone mad?"

"Love is never madness, miss." Margaret continued to the dressing table and poured water into a china basin. She began humming a hymn.

Cassandra clutched the folds of her white nightdress. "But his reputation. . ."

"We have all made mistakes. People change, miss."

"I hope you're right." Cassandra settled onto her bed. "But what will Mother think?"

"Your mother will accept him, in time."

Cassandra wished she harbored the same confidence.

Her maid's eyes flashed. "Perhaps God has not abandoned you after all?"

"Perhaps." Cassandra flipped her long braid over her shoulder. Yet she was not quite ready to concede on that point. "We shall see. But do help me get dressed, Margaret. Luke is coming to call, and I want to look my best."

Two hours later, a knock on the front door sent Cassandra's heart spinning as she sat in the parlor reading a storybook to Hannah and Darlene.

Her mother looked up from her crocheting. "Whoever could that be? We aren't expecting anyone."

Before Cassandra could answer, Mr. Dayle, with a smirk on his face, announced Mr. Heaton. The handsome privateer stepped into the room. He had combed his hair and tied it neatly back and even shaved for the occasion. Cassandra lifted a hand to her cheek, remembering the scratch of his stubble on her skin.

An unavoidable smile flirted on her lips, no doubt noticed by her mother.

Frowning, she tossed aside her crocheting and rose from her seat. "Mr. Heaton. This is most unexpected."

But his eyes were on Cassandra. His smile warmed her. Turning, he dipped his head toward her mother. "Your daughter invited me to call, Mrs. Channing."

Her mother's incredulous gaze sped to Cassandra.

"Do sit down, Luke." Cassandra gestured toward the sofa. "Forgive me, Mother, I forgot to mention it," she lied. In truth, she didn't know how to tell her mother that she and Mr. Heaton were courting.

Leaping from the sofa, Darlene barreled into Luke. He swept her up into his arms. "There's my little runaway." Darlene giggled and gestured for Hannah to join her.

"Hannah, this is Mr. Heaton," Cassandra said. "He's the captain of the privateer I've hired."

The little girl inched toward him, thumb in her mouth. She curtseyed and mumbled something that resembled, "Pleased to meet you, sir."

"I'm happy to see you well, Miss Hannah." Luke smiled down at the little girl. "I heard you were ill."

Hannah plucked her thumb from her mouth. "Miss Margaret says God healed me."

Bending over, Luke set Darlene down and held out his hand to Hannah. Much to Cassandra's surprise, the little girl didn't hesitate to reach for him. He placed a kiss upon her hand. "You are both as beautiful as your older sister."

They giggled, and Hannah gave him a wide grin.

Cassandra shook her head. His charm on women held no boundaries.

Luke faced her mother, who stood staring at the display as if the devil himself had just charmed her daughters into selling their souls to him. "Mrs. Channing, a vision of loveliness as always." He gave her that beguiling grin that had melted a thousand hearts.

It softened the look of horror on her mother's face. "You flatter me, sir." She looked away. And for the first time, Cassandra saw a blush rise on her mother's cheeks. Had she ever seen such a reaction to her father's attention? Luke's blue eyes found Cassandra again, and a look of affection stretched between them. Her heart fluttered like a thousand birds in flight.

Out of the corner of her vision, Cassandra could see her mother pick up her handkerchief and wave it about her flushed face, eyeing them with suspicion.

"Didn't you say, dear, that you need to go to the chandler for some more candles? You should gather Margaret and go before the heat becomes unbearable."

"Mother, we have a guest. I can go anytime."

Resigned, her mother sank back onto her chair.

Mrs. Northrop entered with a service tray and slid it onto the table. "Mr. Dayle suggested you'd be wanting tea for your guest, miss." She poured three cups and scurried away.

Luke lowered himself onto the sofa.

Darlene slid beside him, but Hannah squeezed in between them and gazed up at him curiously. "Are you a pirate?"

Luke smiled and a chuckle escaped his lips. Twisting his face, he hunched over and growled. "Arg, ye be right about that." Sending both girls into a fit of giggles.

"Oh my." Her mother heaved a sigh. But Cassandra blinked at the sight, unable to reconcile the town ruffian with this man who appeared so at ease with children.

"Do you ever fire your cannons?" Darlene battled Hannah for a spot beside him then finally moved to sit on his other side.

"Girls, this is hardly appropriate conversation." Mrs. Channing's sharp tone pierced the joy that had infiltrated the room.

"Fire my guns? Why, all the time." Luke's eyes beamed as he picked up his tea. The china cup appeared ill placed in his large, tanned hands. "Perhaps I'll let you come aboard and fire one sometime."

Darlene's face lit in excitement. "I'd like that very much."

"Me too! Me too!" Hannah jumped up and down, nearly spilling the tea in Luke's cup. He set it down on the table.

A loud bark preceded Dexter, who romped into the room on all fours. The massive dog charged toward Luke and tossed his front paws onto Luke's lap before he could move out of the way. Not that he would have done so, for he seemed to welcome the dog as he chuckled and ran his fingers through the animal's fur—even allowing Dexter to lick his face.

Shocked, Cassandra stood. "Get down, Dexter." She dashed toward them. "Luke, please forgive him. He's not normally so affectionate with strangers."

"Oh, my head." Grabbing her bell, Mrs. Channing, shook it, sending a *ding ding ding* bouncing over the walls.

Luke rose to his feet, shifting the animal from his lap. "It's no bother."

Dexter barked and leapt onto the spot on the sofa that Luke had just vacated. Darlene and Hannah began wrestling with the animal.

Ignoring the mayhem, Cassandra stared at Luke, longing to be alone with him. "When are you setting sail?"

"In two days."

"So soon?"

"I'm afraid so." His blue eyes adored her. "The war takes no respite."

Mrs. Northrop stomped into the room and turned expectant eyes to Cassandra's mother, who stopped ringing her bell and waved toward the cyclonic havoc occupying the sofa. "Please take that unruly beast out to the garden," she ordered.

Clutching Dexter by the collar, Mrs. Northrop led him away with a huff.

"Hannah, Darlene," her mother barked. "Both of you settle down as well or you'll be joining Dexter."

Much to Cassandra's surprise, both girls sat back and folded their hands in their laps.

"Did you hear the musket shots last night?" Her mother's attempt at breaking the spell that kept Cassandra's and Luke's gazes locked on each other was obvious.

Severing the connection, Luke faced the elder woman. "I've heard rumors of British troop movements to the south. Some say they are heading for Washington." He lowered himself to sit between Hannah and Darlene, stretching his booted feet out before him.

"Surely they won't attempt to capture our capital?" Cassandra took her seat again, envious of her sisters' close proximity to Luke.

"Who can know?" He shrugged. A strand of hair that had loosened during the chaos slid over his jaw. "But General Smith has the fort on alert and has ordered the entire militia to be on the ready."

"What is militia, Cassie?" Darlene asked.

"They are citizen soldiers, sweetheart."

An unsettled silence permeated the room.

Her mother eyed Luke as if she wished she could summon Mrs. Northrop to take him out back as well. She took a sip of tea. "What is the purpose of your call, Mr. Heaton?"

Cassandra squeezed her hands together and cleared her throat. She had best just blurt it out. "Mother, you should know that Mr. Heaton and I are courting."

Mrs. Channing dropped her cup with a clank on its side, spilling her remaining tea into the saucer. "Oh my." Closing her eyes, she raised a hand to her brow. "What of Mr. Crane?"

"What *of* Mr. Crane, Mother?" Anger overcame Cassandra's concern for her mother's nerves.

"He's made his interest in you quite clear, my dear."

"That he has," Cassandra said. "But I hardly think that mentioning it in front of Mr. Heaton is appropriate."

"But Mr. Crane is. . ." Her mother opened her eyes and shook her head as if trying to shake off the words she'd just heard. "He's. . ."

"Much more respectable than I? Much more stable? Honorable?"

Luke leaned forward on his knees and cocked his head. "Is that what you intended to say, Mrs. Channing?"

"Since we're being forthright, sir. Yes. That is precisely what I was going to say."

"Really, Mother!" Shame burned Cassandra's neck, followed by an apprehension of how Luke would respond to such an affront.

"But, Mama." Darlene thrust out her chin. "Mr. Heaton saved my life. He is a hero."

Hannah's uneasy gaze swept over all of them before she plunged her thumb into her mouth.

"I agree with you completely, madam." Luke's statement jolted Cassandra and folded her mother's brow.

"I am in no way deserving of a woman like your daughter." His eyes flitted to Cassandra. "But I promise I shall make every endeavor to alter that fact, as well as your opinion of me."

Disdain burned in her mother's eyes. "We shall see, Mr. Heaton. However, let me be clear. I do not approve of you calling on Cassandra. But she's never listened to me or taken my advice, so it would be pointless for me to protest."

"Come now, Mother." Cassandra sighed. "Surely you understand why I wish to choose whose courtship I accept."

"No, I do not understand, Cassandra." Anger tightened the lines around her mouth. "Not when our family's future is at stake." She slowly rose. "I fear I do not feel well. If you'll excuse me, Mr. Heaton." She faced Cassandra. "Do not forget to purchase candles."

"Can we go with you?" Darlene's face lit in expectation.

"Yes, take the girls, dear. I could use some quiet," her mother said as she left the room.

Cassandra started to chase after her. To apologize. To console her. But what good would it do? Cassandra would never be able to make her understand.

Luke approached and laid a hand on her arm. He gave her a sympathetic look, but then his eyes filled with a yearning that sent an odd swirl through her belly.

"I'd be happy to escort you as far as the chandler." He eased a lock of her hair behind her ear. Her breath caught.

She stepped back. "We would love that, Mr. Heaton." Tearing her gaze from his, Cassandra glanced at her sisters, astounded to find them still sitting politely on the sofa. "Wouldn't we, girls?"

Their calm facade faded beneath happy yelps of agreement.

As soon as Margaret and Mr. Dayle joined them, Cassandra grabbed her reticule and followed Luke and the girls out the door. Squinting at the glare of the sun off the stone walkway, she tugged on her gloves. Ahead of her, Luke scooped Hannah into his arms, and then he reached down to grab Darlene's hand.

Emotion clogged Cassandra's throat. Would this man never cease to surprise her? The last thing she would have expected was that he would be so tender, so caring with children. How could Cassandra have so misjudged him from the start?

Hot air blasted over her. Dark clouds bunched on the horizon, churning and broiling as they made their way up to steal the light of the sun.

Misjudged, indeed. Yet as she stepped out from her porch, she couldn't help the niggling feeling that things were not as they seemed.

❖ CHAPTER 28 ❖

Luke allowed the hot August sun to melt the chill of Mrs. Channing's icy reception. He had expected her disdain. Always expected it from polite society, but that never seemed to dull its sting. Now, as he strolled down the street, Cassandra and her sisters by his side, it seemed as though they were a family. A happy family. And suddenly—if he could only rescue John—life held the possibility of a hope and joy he'd never thought possible.

Until he remembered that he was a traitor.

And if Cassandra ever discovered his nefarious activities, this happy moment would dissipate along with all his dreams. Even if she could excuse his behavior given his brother's abduction, how could she ever forgive him for allowing her to spend money dripping with the blood of Americans?

Luke shifted his shoulders, hoping to shrug off the morbid fear settling on him as thick as the storm clouds roiling across the horizon. If his next plan to rescue John worked, no one need know of his treachery at all.

He bent his arm toward Cassandra and was pleased when she slipped her hand within the crook of his elbow and smiled, a sweet smile, full of possibilities. It sent a thrill through him. On his right, Darlene gripped tightly to his other hand, while Hannah clung to Cassandra's on her other side. Together they strolled down South Street, drawing the critical gazes of the town's gossips.

"I fear your reputation is at stake, Miss Channing." Luke gestured toward a cluster of elderly ladies across the way, heads bent together, tongues clacking.

"Your company is worth the risk." She lifted her pert nose.

Enamored by her words and by the gleam of ardor in her eye, Luke fought the urge to take her in his arms and kiss her right there.

But Mr. Dayle's and Margaret's footfalls behind them reminded Luke that Cassandra's chaperones would never allow him to take such liberties. Besides, there were children present. Adorable creatures so full of life. Just like their sister.

Darlene pranced beside him as if she were actually proud to be seen with him. Amazing. She smiled up at him, and he gave her hand a squeeze.

A breeze, ripe with the sting of rain and salt, wafted over them. Somewhere fiddle music played, floating atop the hum of conversation, the *clip-clop* of horses' hooves, and a bell chiming in the distance.

Lifting his face to the warm sun, Luke could never remember feeling such joy. Such hope for the future. *God, if You're there and responsible for this, thank You.* He shocked himself at the prayer, but since he had opened up the conversation, he might as well add, *And please help me rescue John.*

He heard Cassandra groan, and he lowered his gaze just as she bumped into a man exiting the butcher's with a wrapped package of meat in his hand.

"Oh, Mr. McCulloch, pardon me," she said. "Good day to you, sir."

The customs agent tipped his hat as his eyes shifted from her to Luke. "Good day, Miss Channing, Mr. Heaton. How fares the privateering business these days?"

Margaret and Mr. Dayle stopped behind them.

A curious look twisted Cassandra's expression. "Surely you know, sir, since Mr. Heaton has no doubt declared his prizes in your office."

The agent's face seemed to fold in on itself. "Miss Channing, I fear you are mistaken, for I've never done business with Mr. Heaton."

Ice coursed through Luke's veins.

Cassandra's emerald eyes bore into him. "Pray tell how, Luke, do you declare the cargo you confiscate? And the ships?" She released her hold on his arm.

The air chilled. Luke shifted his stance, feeling the loss of her touch like an anchor in his gut. "At other ports," he explained.

Dark clouds captured the sun, casting the street in gray shadows.

Cassandra cocked her head. "Yet since you've been able to slip past the blockade, why not sell them here?"

"I certainly cannot sail a prize British ship through the blockade." Luke forced a smile, not meeting her gaze. The anchor clawed his insides.

No doubt bored with the conversation, Hannah released Cassandra's hand and poked Darlene from behind, giggling.

"Stop it!" Darlene shouted. "Cassie, Hannah hit me."

Grabbing Hannah, Cassandra handed her off to Margaret.

Mr. McCulloch's brows scrunched. "How *do you* slip your ship past the blockade, Mr. Heaton? I, for one, am enamored at the skill of those few privateers able to accomplish such a feat."

"He's the best captain in the world," Darlene exclaimed, still clinging to his hand. "That's how he does it."

Luke smiled at the girl. Would that her elder sister believed the same. He faced the customs agent. "That's all it is, sir, I assure you. Skill with a bit of luck mixed in."

"Hmm." Mr. McCulloch did not seem satisfied. "Well, I must be going. I need to get this pork home to the cook." He tipped his hat again and ambled away.

Thunder rumbled across the sky, portending Luke's doom. He tried to shake it off but the look of suspicion glazing Cassandra's eyes confirmed his fears.

"I should be going as well," Luke said, anything to avoid the censure pouring from Cassandra. "I have much to do to ready the ship to sail."

"Of course." She smiled, but the light was gone from her eyes.

Darlene tugged on his hand. "May I come and help?"

Luke knelt and Hannah stormed into his embrace. "Not this time."

Darlene pouted. Luke hugged both girls and stood, risking a glance at Cassandra. "May I call on you when I return to port?"

"You may."

Seizing the flicker of affection in her eyes, Luke kissed her on the cheek then nodded toward Margaret and Mr. Dayle and marched down the street. He hated lying to Cassandra. The sooner he put an end to this deceit, the better. He would appeal to Captain Raynor's honor. He would load up his ship with as many goods as he could carry, offer to give them as a gift to the British captain in return for his brother and Luke's vow to never again attack British ships.

Any man possessing an ounce of decency would agree to it.

Trouble was, Luke wasn't sure the British captain possessed an ounce of decency.

❖

Hoping to escape for a few moments' peace, Cassandra slipped down the stairway and headed toward the back door. Hannah's and Darlene's screams shot through the house like deviant trumpets, accompanied by the incessant clanging of her mother's bell. How could anyone think in the midst of such clamor? And thinking was precisely what Cassandra needed.

The nagging feeling she'd had yesterday as Luke escorted them into town had burst into a suspicion as hot and dense as the muggy air that suffocated the city. Though it was certainly possible for Luke to sail his prizes and goods into other ports, it left him precious little time to spend here in Baltimore. And how did he slip past the blockade unscathed on so many occasions? Mr. McCulloch's questions had awakened doubts that had been squashed beneath her rising infatuation of the handsome privateer. To make matters worse, Mr. Crane's prior accusations reappeared above the waters of her denial, reeking more of truth than jealousy. In fact, the more she thought about it, the more impossible it seemed that Luke could sail out of Baltimore, capture a prize, sail into another port, sell the goods, deal with customs, and sail home in the short duration of his recent voyages.

But how else could he be making money? He'd sent her a fair amount in the post before the ball, along with the paperwork. Though not as much as before, the funds would last Cassandra and her family almost a year. Opening the back door, she braced herself against the sizzling heat, grabbed her skirts, and made her way around the corner of the house. Each strike of the hot sun jarred her reason awake and plunged her heart into fear.

By the time she entered the solarium, her spirits were as heavy as the air that surrounded her.

A yelp brought her heart into her throat and her gaze up to see Mrs. Northrop standing with Cassandra's open chest in hand.

Terror streaked across the housekeeper's wide eyes. "I thought you were in town, miss."

Marching toward the woman, Cassandra tore the chest from her grasp then grabbed the key from her hand. "What on earth are you doing with my personal belongings? How dare you?"

Mrs. Northrop's swallow ran down her long neck. "I'll be going now, miss." She started toward the door.

Cassandra grabbed her arm and spun her around. "You will do no such thing. I demand to know what you were doing looking through my father's chest!"

"Nothing." She stared at the ground.

Closing the lid, Cassandra set the chest down on the bench and fingered the key in her hand. Her mind swam in the confusing horror of betrayal. Then the realization hit her.

"You." She gaped at the woman. "You stole my money."

Mrs. Northrop backed away, wringing her hands. She bumped into a gardenia bush. "It was Mr. Crane. He made me do it, miss."

"Mr. Crane?" Cassandra shook her head. Why would the man do such a thing? Her legs weakened, and she sank onto the stool. "He wanted my family to be beholden to his charity," she spoke her thoughts aloud. "He wanted me." Cassandra stared at the trembling housekeeper. "Why would you agree to this?"

"He paid me a good sum, miss. An' I wasn't getting my due from you."

"You should have come to me."

Mrs. Northrop's eyes misted. "What are you going to do, miss?"

Drawing a deep breath, Cassandra squared her shoulders and stood. "You are dismissed at once. Gather your things and leave this house by nightfall. Is that clear?"

Tears wove crooked trails down Mrs. Northrop's cheeks.

"Where is the money?" Cassandra demanded.

"I gave it to Mr. Crane. I didn't keep any of it, miss. I swear."

"Very well." Cassandra gestured toward the door. "Get out."

Mrs. Northrop's bottom lip quivered. Clutching her skirts, she tore from the solarium.

An hour later, with the sun's hot rays forming beads of perspiration on her brow and neck, Cassandra hurried down Liberty Street on her way to the *Baltimore Register* to confront Mr. Crane. Fortunately, for him, he was not there when she arrived. "But I expect him to return in a few hours, miss," his clerk had declared. "May I give him a message?"

"Indeed." Cassandra waved her fan about her face. "You may inform Mr. Crane that I know he stole my money, and he will return it or face charges of thievery."

The poor clerk's face had blanched considerably at her statement, but she hadn't stayed to witness any further effects. Now, hurrying down Pratt Street, Cassandra was exhausted and overheated, but too angry to care. Darkness cruised the city, absconding with the light. She needed to get home.

Unable to resist, she stole a glance at the wharf where *Destiny* was docked, hoping for a glimpse of Luke. She wasn't ready to talk to him. Wasn't entirely sure what he was up to. But certainly a glimpse would do her no harm. It might even help her recall how much she cared for him. Though, in that regard, her heart needed no reminder.

What she saw halted her on the spot. There on the wharf, which sagged beneath its weight, were dozens and dozens of barrels, crates, and sacks ready to be loaded onto Luke's ship. And still more came, carried by workers trudging down the dock. Luke's crew scrambled across the ship as Mr. Abbot stood atop the bulwarks, directing the men in bringing the supplies aboard, whilst Mr. Sanders—if she remembered his name correctly—stood by his side, scribbling on a paper in his hand. Luke was nowhere in sight.

Why would a privateer need that many supplies? Enough to feed dozens of privateers for a month, by her estimation. Though they did not know how long they'd be at sea, certainly stuffing the hold would allow no room for the goods they'd confiscate from the British.

It made no sense.

A surge of torrid wind clawed at her bonnet and stole the breath from her mouth. She gripped the brim of her hat, standing her ground.

What was Luke up to? If she confronted him, she couldn't be sure he would answer her. She'd accepted that he was a private man. She'd accepted that something heavy weighed upon him as Mr. Abbot had told her. What she couldn't accept was him doing anything subversive with her money.

Since he was to set sail on the morrow, there was only one way to find out the truth. And that was to stow away on his ship and see for herself.

❖

But Luke did not set sail the next day. Or at least Cassandra hoped he hadn't. By the time she had arrived home that night, rumors rampaged through the city that British troops were marching into Washington, DC. Warning bells rang incessantly as terror held the city in its tight grip through the long hours of the night. And although some citizens bravely stood on Federal Hill to watch the distant glow of fires raging through the capital, Cassandra had stayed home to comfort her mother, who was enduring a fit of nerves at the unhappy tidings.

Then, the following day, before anyone could recover from the tragedy and discover the fate of their great nation, the storm hit. Winds as fierce as any Cassandra had experienced stampeded over the house, seeking entrance into their shelter and flinging spears of rain at their windows. In the glow of candles, Cassandra, her sisters, mother, servants, and Dexter had huddled at the center of the house, waiting to be blown away.

But after a few hours, the winds abated, the rain ceased, and the clouds withdrew, leaving behind toppled trees, torn-down fences, and the joyous news that the British had retreated from Washington. Margaret, who had been appealing to God all through the afternoon, gave praise for His mighty deliverance.

Cassandra was not so sure.

Nor was she sure why Mr. Crane had not been by to answer her accusation. Nor why Luke had not come calling to see if she and her family had suffered any injuries from the storm.

After spending the rest of that day and most of the next one cleaning up the wreckage and helping neighbors do the same, Cassandra now stood before her dressing glass in her chamber as evening tossed shadows upon the unusually quiet town.

"Miss, I don't think this is a good idea." Margaret's reflection behind Cassandra was one of anxiety. Her normally rosy cheeks had gone pale, and her eyes sparked with fear. Cassandra gazed at her visage in the mirror. Baggy gray breeches stuffed in oversized boots, a white cotton shirt covered in a gray waistcoat and black overcoat. A red neckerchief rode high upon her neck. Atop her head a cocked hat perched. Noting a rebellious curl peeking out from the side, she stuffed it back in place, giggling at the sight.

"Even with the bandages around your chest and the dirt on your jaw and chin, you still look like a woman, miss." Margaret touched Cassandra's arm. "Please don't do this. It's far too dangerous."

"Oh, bother, Margaret. You fret too much," Cassandra said. "I'm far safer wandering about town looking like this, than dressed as a lady."

"What if he has already set sail?"

"Then I shall come home." Though she knew Luke hadn't left yet—had heard just today from Mr. Dayle, who had ventured out for supplies, that *Destiny* had survived the storm unscathed and was preparing to leave that night.

"I'll sneak on board Mr. Heaton's ship before anyone sees me. No one will know I'm there."

Margaret shook her head, the normal luster gone from her eyes. "But what if you are at sea for weeks, months even, before you discover what you wish to know?"

"You mean that the man I love might be a traitor to our country?" Cassandra tugged her hat farther down on her head as the last rays of sunlight withdrew from her chamber. "I'll find out the truth soon enough. Mr. Heaton doesn't seem to be gone for more than a week or so at a time." Which also didn't speak well for his innocence. "If too much time passes, that will prove my suspicions wrong. Then I shall reveal myself and beg his forgiveness. I'm sure he'll bring me home immediately."

"What will you eat and drink?"

"I have enough food and water to last four days in my knapsack. Plus, I imagine there's plenty of stored food belowdecks."

"What of the rats?" Margaret shivered.

Cassandra's belly gurgled in queasiness. "I shall have to endure them."

"I do not see why you cannot just ask Luke."

Cassandra swung around. "Do you think if he's betraying his country—and me—that he'll tell me the truth?" She walked to the window, nearly stumbling in the awkward boots. "No, I must find out for myself. This is the only way. I cannot"—she swallowed down a lump of heart-ache—"I cannot give my heart to a man who is a liar and a traitor." She plopped down on the window seat. "All my life, I only wanted someone to depend on."

"You can depend on God, miss."

Cassandra smiled. "Such a saint you are, Margaret." Rising, she grabbed a piece of foolscap from her dresser. "If I do not return tonight, give this letter to Mother tomorrow. It will explain everything." At the look of horror on her maid's face, Cassandra took Margaret's hands in hers. "Never fear, I shall return soon. Tell the girls to behave. And do watch over them now that Mrs. Northrop is gone, will you?"

"Of course." Margaret nodded. "What if you discover Luke *is* a traitor and he. . ." Margaret looked away. "He. . ."

"Luke wouldn't hurt me. I don't believe that. Fear spiraled through Cassandra, pricking at her resolve. Perhaps she should just call off the courtship and let it be. But if her suspicions were true, how could she go on spending money gained by the blood of her countrymen? No, she must find out for sure.

"Now, go make sure no one is below so I can make my escape."

Margaret stopped at the door. "God go with you, miss. I shall pray for you every day."

Twenty minutes later, with head lowered and a knapsack strung over her shoulder, Cassandra did her best to march like a man down the muddy street. In her trek to the wharves, not a single person stopped her, most barely gazed at her: ladies with children hurrying home; groups of merchantmen; the chandler, Mr. Sikes, who didn't seem to recognize her. One gentleman had even bumped into her and offered no apology. Cassandra smiled beneath the shadow of her hat, even as an odd feeling of being ignored settled on her. Odd because wherever she went she usually drew quite a bit of attention. It had never occurred to her that some people drifted through life like shadows, their presence rarely acknowledged. Pondering this, she hastened to the wharf where *Destiny* was anchored. She knew Luke usually set sail close to midnight and since it was no later than eight, she hoped only a few crewmen were on board.

What she didn't expect was the swarm of workers and sailors hauling all manner of crates and barrels onto the ship. Again. Perhaps they'd been forced to unload everything during the storm. Halting near the dock's entrance, she searched for Luke, but he was nowhere in sight. However, in the light of several lanterns hanging from the main and fore masts, she spotted Mr. Abbot and Mr. Keene marching across the deck, bellowing orders.

Now, how to get on board?

Across the bay, the retreating glow of sunlight quivered over frolicking dark waters. Bare masts rose like spires of defeat into the bowl of night descending upon the city. Only Luke's ship was a plethora of activity.

Cassandra's heart thundered against her ribs. It wasn't too late to turn around and go home, sleep in her own warm bed. But if she did, she would be more fool than coward. And she would not be made a fool of, nor abandoned by some man who was even better at lying than charming the opposite sex. Or perhaps the two went together.

Taking a deep breath as if she could inhale courage, she picked up a box that was sitting atop a barrel and hefted it onto her left shoulder. Though it wasn't too heavy for her, the sharp edges bit through her coat as she eased into the line of men heading toward the ship. Keeping her head behind the box, she followed the man in front of her, hoping she didn't trip on her way onto the ship. Already her boots—borrowed from Mr. Dayle—rubbed the skin on her ankles to soreness. Ignoring the pain and the fear screaming in her head, she stepped onto the teetering plank, watched it bow beneath the weight of the large man before her, then leapt onto the deck with a thud. Pain shot up her legs, and she stumbled for a second as the ship rocked.

"Hurry up, there, boy!" the man behind her yelled, shoving her forward. Thankfully before Mr. Abbot saw her. Navigating down the companionway ladder was no easy task, especially with one's hands full. Alone, she may have toppled into the darkness below, but the burly men before and after her cushioned her against a fall.

Following the men down another level, Cassandra squinted into the darkness of the hold where only a single lantern swayed from a hook on the deck head. Across a vast expanse of muck and crates, empty-handed men ascended another ladder above. A putrid stench rose up from the depths like some viper to strike her, filling her nostrils and lungs with the smell of mold and waste and something else indescribable. She coughed. Some of the men looked her way. She lowered her head. A man she recognized as one of Luke's crew, Mr. Sanders, directed the men where to deposit their loads. Cassandra scanned the shadowy hold. Toward her left, beneath a low beam, was a section where the light did not reach. If she could slip away undetected, she could find a place to hide.

Mr. Sanders stopped two of the workers and demanded they lower the crate they carried. "Open it. I want to see what it contains." His squeaky voice echoed over the waterlogged hull.

Cursing, the men slammed down the container. The screech of the lid being pried off sent a tremble through Cassandra.

While the rest of the men stopped to watch, Cassandra inched backward into the shadows.

"What is this? Bolts of fabric! We did not purchase this, nor have we need of it. Take it away." Mr. Sanders waved his hand then made a mark on his document.

Cassandra continued backing up. Fear prickled her skin. Her boot struck something hard, sending a thud through the air and an ache through her feet. She halted. But no one looked her way. Setting down her box, she retreated into the darkness at the rear of the ship and ducked behind a large crate.

Hours later, after the men had left and the hold groaned with a full load of supplies, Mr. Sanders grabbed the lantern and ascended the ladder, leaving Cassandra in a darkness so thick it seemed to ooze over her. Two questions began to weigh heavy on her mind. Had she lost a grasp on all good sense and reason? And what was she going to do about the pattering of little feet advancing toward her?

❖ CHAPTER 29 ❖

Light from the lantern high up on the foremast flickered over the signal flags flapping from *Destiny*'s gaff. Signal flags that gave Luke and his crew free passage through the British blockade.

Flags that marked him as a traitor.

He gripped the quarter railing. Frustration and anger bunched a tight knot in his jaw. Hot wind sped past his ears, tainted with the fury of yesterday's storm. He gazed upward. No stars dared to peek at them from behind the black curtain that hung over a sea transformed into molten coal.

"We've brought enough supplies for near the entire fleet," Biron commented as he leapt onto the deck beside Luke. "Let's pray we find Captain Raynor in a good humor."

Luke tightened his lips. "If not, I can think of no other way to rescue John without putting him in danger."

"You can't blame yourself for this, Luke." Biron placed a hand on Luke's back.

"Who can I blame for it, God?" But no, Luke wasn't the sort to blame God or anyone else for his failings. It was his own fault.

Biron frowned. "It was God who saved our grand capital yesterday."

"Lud. You refer to the sudden storm?" Luke snorted. "Not that unusual of an occurrence."

"But one that just so happened upon Washington when she was being burnt to the ground." Biron chuckled.

Luke rubbed his ear. "A mere coincidence." He thought of Cassandra and wondered how she had fared through the tempest. It had taken all his strength to keep from calling on her. But Luke didn't want to face her again as a traitor. No, the next time he faced her, he wanted to be the man of honor he saw reflected in her eyes.

"I've discovered"—Biron lifted his hat to scratch his head—"that many of what we call coincidences are actually God's mighty intervention."

The hull of a ship loomed several yards off their port bow. Part of the British fleet. Despite having passed through the blockade several times, Luke could not shake his uneasiness at the sight. "Coincidence or not, at least the Almighty spared *Destiny* in the storm." He couldn't say the same for many of the ships anchored in Baltimore Harbor.

"Quick thinking on your part, Captain, to move her away from the other ships and tie her to multiple pilings with lines long enough to handle the surge."

Luke nodded. He'd learned from the best, Noah Brenin.

"God spared us, indeed." Biron sighed.

Luke gave his friend a disbelieving glance. "If God spared us, then why did He allow the storm to destroy many of Washington's buildings?"

Biron shrugged. "Still, the British were sent packing. And Washington is in American hands again."

"Indeed." Luke folded his hands across his chest. "And now they are more angry than ever. Which gives me little hope for my negotiations with the infamous Captain Raynor."

Whom he would see within four days at their normal rendezvous spot two miles off the coast of Virginia. *Destiny*'s sails thundered as they caught the windy remnants of the harrowing storm, sending the ship careening over a wave. Bracing his boots on the deck, Luke snapped the hair from his face and took a deep breath of salty air. Somehow, he knew deep in his soul that this was his last chance. His last chance to end his traitorous activities.

His last chance to rescue John.

❖

Cassandra had lost track of time. And days. Her world had morphed into nothing but undulating darkness, creaks and groans of madness, a stench that made her toes curl, and the constant assault of rats. The fresh water in her knapsack had run out yesterday, along with the dried beef and bread she'd brought. Willing to risk getting caught rather than dying, she had finally ventured out of the hold late last night when the cessation of foot-falls and voices told her that most of the crew was abed.

She hadn't realized how much she missed the wind and the air and the sky until she stepped onto the upper deck and made her way to the port railing, sinking behind the small boat latched to its moorings on the deck. There, she had gorged on a dried biscuit she'd found in the galley. It sank like a brick into the stale water mixed with beer she'd previously poured down her throat. Regardless of her pathetic meal, she wished she could have stayed on deck all night, but it was too risky. After a few hours of breathing in the fresh sea air, she had slumped below to her putrid abode.

Now, as she crawled to sit atop the highest crate she could find, she wondered at the sanity of her decision. What if they were to get into a real sea battle and cannon shot pierced the hold, flooding the ship and sending her to a watery grave?

The thunder of footsteps above, along with the peal of a bell, told her that another day had dawned. Another day of hunger clawing at her belly, thirst scraping her throat. Another day of kicking away rats while she sat on her hellish throne. Another day in which her mind dove deeper into madness.

Luke's authoritative timbre drifted down from above, sending a traitor-ous leap through her heart. She longed to go to him, feel his arms around her, and hear him reassure her of his innocence. But she couldn't. She couldn't allow her affections to take root until she knew the truth. Bringing her legs to her chest, she laid her head on top of her knees and prepared for the heat that accompanied the rising sun. Already perspiration formed on her brow. She wiped it away and tried to concentrate on the *whoosh* of water against the hull, a soothing sound in its constancy and bland melody.

But suddenly the sound lessened. The purl of water transformed into jarring splashes. And the plod of feet and the shout of men increased above her. Cassandra sat up, tilting her ear toward the deck. More shouts. Luke's powerful voice filled the dank air, and the ship slowed even more. Why were they stopping? Shouldn't they speed up at the sight of a poten-tial prize? Or perhaps they sailed back into Baltimore. She wished it were so. Because that would mean Luke was no traitor and she would soon be home! Finally, after several minutes, the ship came to a near stop. Only the gentle rise and fall of the deck and the sound of waves lapping against the hull told Cassandra they were still at sea. She was about to descend from the crate when something thumped against the ship, nearly toppling her to the floor. Something massive. A groan echoed through the hold. The timbers creaked in complaint.

Men's voices grew louder as dozens of footfalls thundered down from above. Cassandra leapt from her perch and dove into the shadows just as light filled the hold and a group of sailors descended, one of whom hooked a lantern on the deck head. Peering from her hiding place, Cassandra watched as the men hefted crates, barrels, and sacks onto their backs and climbed back up the ladder.

Confusion twirled her crazed mind into a frenzy, unwilling to land on the only possible explanation. Blood pounded in her ears. Her heart refused to settle. Just as well. Because if it did, Cassandra was sure it would break in half. An hour passed as she waited and watched while the crew carried all the cargo up the ladder. Men's voices, including Luke's, crowded the air above her. She had to know what was going on. She had to make sure her suspicions were true.

On shaky legs, she ascended the ladder, nearly falling twice in her weakened condition. Continuing past the sailors' berth, which was empty, she made her way up the companionway ladder onto the main deck. Bright light brought her hand up to shield her eyes as she scanned the scene. *Destiny* floated hull-to-hull alongside a larger ship, grappled together with tight lines. Lifting her gaze, Cassandra saw the Union Jack flying from the head of the larger ship's main mast. A British frigate. The air escaped her lungs, and she leaned on a nearby barrel to keep from toppling to the deck.

"What is all this?" A distinguished-looking man standing at the frigate's railing waved a hand over the barrels and crates crowding *Destiny's* decks. His British accent grated over Cassandra's ears.

"I propose a new bargain, Captain." Luke's voice responded from somewhere atop the frigate's deck. Confirming Cassandra's fears. Anger scoured through her—searing, thrashing, all-encompassing anger. Anger at Luke's betrayal. Anger that she had fallen in love with a traitor. Anger that he had made her an accomplice in such a despicable deed.

She barreled forward, weaving through the maze of cargo and shoving aside sailors who stood in her way.

❖

"A bargain?" Captain Raynor laughed. "I don't bargain with rebels."

Luke grimaced and glanced at John, who stood just below the quarterdeck ladder. He looked well, tired and thinner, but well. Facing the captain again, Luke resisted the urge to punch the supercilious smirk off his face. "Yet you have already bargained with this particular rebel, sir. Hear me out, I beg you."

The captain glanced at his first and second lieutenants, flanking him on the main deck of the frigate, and huffed his impatience. He gave Luke a look of boredom. "Make it quick."

"All of these supplies, which are enough to feed you and at least five ships like yours for more than a month, including several hundred bottles of rum, I offer you entirely without cost." Waves, slapping the hull, laughed at Luke's offer.

Captain Raynor studied him. "Unless you have come to your senses and wish to throw your lot in with the victors of this war, I cannot see why you would make such an offer, sir."

"I make it on the following conditions." Luke tried to steady his voice, tried to drown out the urgency screaming in his head. "That you return my brother to me, and I give you my word I will quit privateering."

Captain Raynor gave a scoff of surprise as if Luke had asked for a chest of gold. "Your word, sir?" This time the lieutenants as well as some of the crew standing nearby chuckled. "What is the word of an American worth?"

The frigate rose over a swell. Luke adjusted his footing, refusing to answer the man's absurd question.

Captain Raynor grimaced and tipped his cocked hat against the rays of the rising sun. "Besides, what is to stop me from absconding with all of these supplies and keeping your brother as well?"

"Nothing but your honor, sir." Luke hoped that Captain Raynor held his honor in high esteem, or at least his pride. For the captain certainly wouldn't want to be seen breaking a gentleman's oath in front of his entire crew.

Captain Raynor narrowed his eyes.

Hope began to stir within Luke. He was about to restate his terms when a familiar female voice sprang over the frigate's bulwarks like a grappling hook.

"You are a traitor, Luke Heaton! A traitor and a cad. How dare you sell supplies to our enemies?"

Luke closed his eyes, wishing the voice away, hoping it came from his tortured conscience and not from the source that frightened him the most.

Scuffling sounded from below on *Destiny*'s deck. Then Biron's disbelieving groan confirmed Luke's worst fears. Opening his eyes, he approached the railing and peered over the side. There, struggling in Biron's and Mr. Keene's grasp, stood Cassandra—in breeches and shirt, of all things—her auburn hair flailing in the breeze, and her eyes pointed at Luke like two loaded cannons.

Captain Raynor grinned. "Friend of yours, sir?"

Shock stiffened Luke, followed by terror. How did she get on board? Why was she dressed like a man? But there was no time to find out.

"Yes. . . No," Luke mumbled, facing Raynor. "She's the ship's cook. Ignore her. She's quite mad." He leaned over the railing. "Mr. Keene, if you would escort Miss Channing below."

The boatswain nodded and headed toward the companionway with Cassandra in tow when she tore from his grasp and shoved her way toward the rope ladder.

"Bring the woman up here. I'd like to meet her." Captain Raynor's words fired into Luke's gut.

Luke waved a hand through the air. "She's nobody, Captain, ignore her." He cringed at his own pleading tone.

A tone not missed by the captain of the HMS *Audacious*—he grinned. "Yet she seems to be quite surprised at your nefarious activities, no?"

Luke saw Cassandra's red hair pop above the bulwarks as she hoisted herself over the railing. She landed on the deck with a determined thump. Catcalls rang across the ship before the master's mate silenced the men. Ignoring them, Cassandra approached Luke, her icy stare lancing him before she scanned the assembly of British officers, sailors, and marines crowding the deck.

Did the woman fear nothing?

Spotting the captain, she charged toward him. Two midshipmen grabbed her arms before she got too close.

"Is this man selling you goods, Captain?"

Luke's throat closed. Heated wind slapped him in the face.

"Why, yes, madam, he is." The captain seemed to be enjoying himself immensely.

Tearing free from the midshipmen's grip, Cassandra marched toward Luke. Raising her fists, she pounded on his chest. He allowed her. He deserved it. Each blow caused his heart to shrink a bit more until he wondered if there was anything left.

The crew of the *Audacious*, however, found the scene much to their amusement, as laughter bounced through the air.

Finally, after her anger was spent, Cassandra bent over in a sob.

Luke grabbed her arms and drew her close, whispering in her ear. "This isn't as it seems, Cassandra. Go back to the ship." But she jerked from him, too disgusted to even meet his gaze.

"Very good. Very good." Captain Raynor clapped his hands together as if applauding a performance. "And who, may I ask, are you, miss?"

Sweat slid down Luke's back. *Do not tell him. Keep your mouth shut.* His gaze found John, still standing by the quarterdeck, and looking as frightened as Luke felt.

Drawing a breath, she lifted her shoulders and faced the captain. "I am Cassandra Channing from Baltimore."

Luke shook his head. The ship groaned over a swell, mimicking his silent moan within.

"Ah," the captain said. "And might I assume you weren't aware of this man's. . .activities?"

"You assume correctly, sir." She grimaced and pointed a finger his way. "For I would have shot him myself rather than allowed him to trade with the likes of you."

"Gentlemen"—the captain gestured toward Cassandra—"behold the ill-tempered shrews these colonies breed."

The men seemed more than happy to obey the order as all eyes took Cassandra in as if she were the feast at a royal ball. Only then did Luke notice that the breeches she wore revealed far too much of her feminine curves.

Captain Raynor smiled. "As it happens, I've been in dire need of a decent cook for quite some time. Mr. Milner over there"—he flicked a hand toward a man on his right—"can't boil a chicken without making it taste like tar."

The grimy cook lifted one shoulder and smiled.

A metallic taste filled Luke's mouth. The sun beat down on him, lashing him for failing once again.

For the first time, fear took residence on Cassandra's features, as if she'd only just awakened from a dream. "I am no cook, Captain."

"Indeed? Regardless, you would make a lovely addition to our ship." Pompous victory rang in the captain's tone. "And from the look in Captain Heaton's eyes, you are much more than a cook to him."

"She is nothing to me," Luke growled, desperate to say anything to save her.

Cassandra shot him a pained glance as Biron eased over the railing to join them.

"Then you won't mind if I borrow her?" Removing his hat, the captain dabbed a handkerchief over his forehead. "All the more incentive for you to return with more supplies. I do say, my men and I are becoming quite accustomed to eating fresh food."

Grumbles of assent thundered through the crowd.

Luke clenched his fists. His fingernails dug into his skin. "John is more than enough incentive."

Cassandra backed toward the railing. "You cannot kidnap me, sir. I am neither a privateer nor in the military. I am but an innocent citizen of Baltimore."

"There are no innocents in that haven of pirates!" Captain Raynor barked then stuffed his handkerchief inside his coat. "I can take whatever I wish to take. When the subjects of our great and glorious king defy his laws and resist his rule, they lose all rights."

"She's just a lady, sir." Biron shared a harried glance with Luke.

Luke reached for the hilt of his sword out of habit, meeting dead air. He stepped in front of Cassandra. "Take me instead. My crew will still do as you say."

"I don't quite agree, Captain. The woman ensures your return. Besides, it's been a long time since I've had female companionship." Raynor smiled at the lieutenant standing to his right, who returned his grin with a chuckle.

Loose sails flapped above them.

Cassandra's eyes took on a haunted look. Gone was the anger, the hatred, replaced by sheer terror.

Luke's blood pulsed in his head. He must do something. But what? He was outmanned, outgunned, outwitted.

"No. I will not allow it!" He charged toward the captain, no longer caring what happened to him. The metallic chime of a sword screeched over his ears before the tip landed on his chest, halting him.

Cassandra gasped. John screamed, "No!"

The captain grinned.

Luke stared at the marine holding the sword. The hatred in the man's eyes sent a chill through Luke. Settling his breath, he took a step back. He couldn't help Cassandra and John if he were dead.

"Oh, and by the by," Captain Raynor added with a smirk. "We found the note you gave the lad, so I wouldn't be trying that pathetic ploy again if I were you." He gazed up at the sun and frowned. "Infernal heat of these colonies!" Then with a flick of his finger, he gestured for the purser to step forward. "I wish to purchase only what we agreed upon, Captain Heaton. Take the rest home. We shall see you two weeks hence."

And with that, he swung about to speak to his first lieutenant. Two sailors grabbed Cassandra's arms and led her away. The last thing Luke saw was her pleading gaze before she dropped belowdecks.

❖

Cassandra couldn't feel her feet. Couldn't feel her hands as the men led her below. Was her heart still beating?

"Put her in the warrant officer's cabin, Mr. Windor." The marine on her left released her to the other man, who then ushered her down a narrow hall, lit by intermittent lanterns swaying with the movement of the ship. Halting before a door, he opened it and shoved Cassandra into a cabin not much bigger than a coffin. A wooden plank attached to the bulkhead and covered with a straw tick formed the bed. Beside it, a tiny desk and chair filled the rest of the space. Uniforms hung from hooks on the opposite wall. The sailor lit the lantern then backed out of the room, his eyes hungrily roving over her. He shut the door, and the lock clicked.

Cassandra stood there, numb and empty and alone. She heard the cargo being loaded on board, the shouts of men, the boatswain's pipe, the thunder of sails flapping to catch the wind. But not until the ship jerked and began to move, did she fall to the bed in a heap.

What have I done? She began to sob as stories Marianne had told of her impressment aboard the HMS *Undefeatable* rose in Cassandra's memory to torture her. Stories of endless days cleaning and polishing and scrubbing and catering to the every whim of a mad British captain with no rescue or end in sight.

The ship yawed to starboard, and Cassandra clung to the bed frame to keep from falling. Every inch they sailed over the sea sped her farther away from her home, her family.

Why had she been so foolish? Fury had dulled her reason. She slammed her fist against the bulkhead. Pain burned up her wrist. She should have known better. She should have contained her rage.

Even now, despite her terrifying predicament, that rage stirred to life within her. Or maybe because of it. It was Luke's fault she was here. If he hadn't been a traitor, hadn't lied to her, hadn't broken her heart, she would never have snuck on board his ship.

Drawing her boots up on the bed, she curled into a ball and hugged herself, trembling. Fear battled heartache for preeminence as tears poured down her cheeks onto the burlap coverlet. An hour or two passed. Or maybe more. The sun, like an apathetic actor, passed over the stage of her porthole until it disappeared beyond.

Finally the latch lifted, and the door creaked open to reveal a boy around nine or ten years of age, holding a tray of food. Unkempt dark brown hair fell around his face and nearly reached his shoulders. Gray eyes twinkled above a smile that reminded Cassandra of Luke. She looked away. She didn't want to be reminded of Luke. The boy slipped inside and set the tray on the desk.

"Captain sends his regards, miss. He thought you might be hungry."

Cassandra eyed the steaming tea and plateful of apple slices and cheese, but her stomach lurched at the sight. "You may inform the captain I've lost my appetite."

The boy gave an understanding nod. "It's not so bad here, miss. You'll get used to it."

"I don't want to—" Cassandra stared at the boy. "Are you a prisoner too?"

He nodded. "For a month now, as well as I can guess. At first, I was real scared like you are now, but"—he shrugged—"most everyone's been nice to me, though they do make me work all the time."

The ship bucked, and he stumbled, favoring one of his legs.

"I'm John." His kind smile eased over Cassandra's nerves.

"A pleasure, John." She nodded. "I'm Cassandra." She studied him. "How did you get here?"

"Same as you, miss. I was taken from Luke's ship."

Frowning, Cassandra rubbed her forehead. Nothing made sense anymore. "What were you doing aboard Luke's ship?"

The boy beamed with pride. "Why, miss, don't you know? I'm his brother."

❖ CHAPTER 30 ❖

Luke paced across Noah's library, the thump of his boots on the oak floor hammering his guilt deeper and deeper into his gut until he felt he would implode.

"You did what?" Noah leapt from his chair behind his desk, his eyes blazing, his hand reaching for the sword strapped to his hip. "Are you drunk?"

Luke shook his head. He wished he was. He wished all that had transpired was merely a rum-induced nightmare.

Mr. Reed, standing by the cold hearth, turned with a groan, his dark brow furrowed.

Luke halted, still not believing he'd finally said it out loud. He'd admitted to being a traitor to his country. Yet instead of feeling relieved, all remaining hope dissipated beneath the look of disgust and disappointment on Noah's face. "They captured John."

"John," Noah repeated, his voice spiked with shock. "Your brother?"

Clawing a hand through his hair, Luke took up a pace again. "Yes."

"Upon my word, how did the British get ahold of your brother?" The enemy's accent throbbed in Mr. Reed's voice.

Grinding his teeth together, Luke faced Noah. "Does *he* have to be here?"

One brow of censure rose over Noah's sharp eyes. "He is my houseguest and engaged to Miss Rose. And you will treat him accordingly." His captain's voice gave no room for argument.

"Engaged?" Luke stared at the British lieutenant. "I thought you were reporting back to your ship."

"God had other ideas." Mr. Reed gave a slight chuckle then grew serious and took a step toward Luke. "I've joined the Americans."

Before Luke could process the information, Noah's harsh voice blasted over his ears. "And exactly *whose* side are you on, Luke?" His friend circled the desk, sliding his hand over the walnut top and landing inches from his pistol.

Pain seared Luke's heart at the thought that his friend would ever use the weapon against him. But how could he blame him? "Shoot me if you wish. Turn me in if you want. But I had no choice. They would have killed John."

The tight lines around Noah's eyes softened. A hint of relief freed the breath in Luke's throat. But it caught again when he remembered he had yet to inform them about Cassandra.

"How long has the boy been there?" Mr. Reed asked.

"A month." Luke shook his head. Fury fisted his hands, and he fought the urge to punch something, anything, if only to release the rage within him.

Noah sat on the edge of his desk and crossed his arms over his chest. "And you've been supplying them ever since?"

"What other choice did I have?"

Mr. Reed's mouth quirked in disgust. "The choice to not be so rash, sir. To seek aid instead of putting others at risk with your own self-pitying stubbornness."

Enough from this pompous Brit! Luke charged the man, raising a fist in the air. Taking a step back, Mr. Reed raised his own, preparing to fight. But Noah darted between them, grabbed Luke's wrist in midair, and shoved him back.

"Confound it all! Fighting is not the answer. Mr. Reed is right. You should have come to me sooner." Noah's face flamed. "We could have figured something out."

Seething, Luke retreated. He should leave. If Noah would even allow him to, now. Unclenching his fist, he rubbed the scars on his palm. "Yes, of course," Luke said with a smirk. "We could have sent my schooner and your brig against a Royal Navy frigate. Even if we managed to fire a broadside at them, my only brother is on board." *Not to mention the woman I love.*

"Instead, you chose to suffer alone and betray your country," Noah growled. "Blast your pride, man!"

"Don't you think I've been trying to get him back?" Luke snapped.

Noah's eyes narrowed. He shook his head in disdain.

Perhaps, Luke had made a mistake in coming here. Perhaps, friend or not, Noah would summon General Smith immediately and have Luke hauled off for treason.

Tugging on his coat, Mr. Reed took a stance of authority as he'd often done when they'd been his slaves aboard the HMS *Undefeatable*. "So, why now? What has humbled you enough to seek help?"

Luke backed away and sank into a leather chair. "Something else happened. I met the frigate four days ago to offer the captain my entire hold full of supplies for free if he'd release my brother."

Mr. Reed frowned. "Unlikely any British captain would agree to that."

Luke swallowed. "As I discovered. But it was my last hope."

"And?" Noah studied him, apprehension on his face.

"Turns out I had an unexpected stowaway." Luke prepared himself for the pain it would cause him to simply say her name. To admit what he'd done. "Miss Channing. They took her."

Mr. Reed released a moan that—based on his intimate knowledge of the happenings aboard a British warship—did not bode well for Cassandra's future.

"Cassandra?" Noah winced. Eyes wide, he stumbled backward. "What was she doing on board your ship?"

Luke grimaced. "I imagine she suspected my activities."

"I cannot believe it." Noah pinched the bridge of his nose and closed his eyes. "We must not tell Marianne. It would vex her overmuch."

Luke dropped his head into his hands. "This is my fault. I don't know what to do." He raised his gaze to see Mr. Reed, hands fisted at his waist, staring into space as if in deep concentration.

"Do you know this Captain Raynor?" Luke asked.

"Only by reputation." Mr. Reed rubbed his chin. "If it helps, he isn't the erratic ogre Captain Milford is."

Luke drew in a deep breath. "You offer me little consolation, sir. Now, offer me a way to get Cassandra and John back. These treacherous mongrels are your people. You know how they think. I beg you"—Luke hesitated, wondering if Reed would help him after Luke had nearly assaulted him—"tell me you have an idea."

"I do." The Brit's eyes sparkled.

"Egad, Alex! Let's hear it." Noah's tone was anxious.

"I still have my uniform." Mr. Reed grinned. "All we need is a small ship, a British ensign, and forged papers ordering Captain Raynor to release the prisoners into my custody."

"Will that work?" Luke asked, afraid to entertain the hope sparking within him.

"With courage, wit, and God's help, it just might," Mr. Reed replied.

Luke shook his head. Though warmed by the Brit's offer to help, it was too much to ask. "No, I cannot allow it. You risk too much." He glanced at Noah. "Both of you."

"You risked the same for me," Alex said. "When you arranged for me to see Rose at the ball."

Noah gripped Luke's arm. "Allow me to choose my own risks."

"But if we are caught, we'll quite possibly all be hanged as traitors."

"Perhaps." Noah's brow rose. "Or perhaps we'll be hailed heroes for rescuing an innocent American woman and child."

"And I'll be hanged when the story is revealed of how they came to be captured." Luke released a ragged sigh. "But that is no more than I deserve."

"God will decide such things, Luke. Will you take the risk? Will you trust Him?" Noah asked.

Luke's eyes burned at his friend's loyalty. "Trusting God, I cannot promise. But laying my life down to save my brother and Cassandra, that's a risk I'll gladly take."

❖

Lieutenant Abner Tripp poured more brandy into Mr. Keene's mug. "I daresay, I do admire a man who can hold his liquor."

Mr. Keene laughed and lifted the mug to his lips. "And I, sir, admire any man who buys me a drink."

The door to the tavern opened and three rugged-looking fellows entered. Wind snaked in behind them and stirred the flame of the candle on the table. It flickered in Mr. Keene's glassy eyes as he took another sip.

"To what do I owe the pleasure of such a distinguished officer's company?" Mr. Keene's words finally began to garble.

Finally. Tripp had been buying him drinks and telling him jokes for nearly an hour. The stench of tallow, sweat, and alcohol burned in Tripp's nose. He doubted he'd ever get the smell out. Yet still the fop avoided answering questions about Mr. Heaton. Unable to converse with Mr. Keene at the Fountain Inn Ball before he'd left, Tripp's search of the city's taverns the past two weeks had finally paid off when he happened upon the ostentatious fat wit here at Payne's Tavern engaged in a game of Gleek.

Now, the bumbling fool insisted on flirting with every doxy who passed by while drinking away Tripp's meager wages without giving him a scrap of information in return.

"Another one, Mr. Keene?" Tripp grabbed the bottle and poured another swig into the glass. "I find privateering absolutely fascinating. What exactly is it that you do aboard *Destiny*?"

"I'm a boatswain. Directing the sails and such." He sipped his drink, slumped back in his chair, and waved a jeweled hand, framed in lace, through the air.

"Indeed? I assumed a man of your years and intelligence would be the captain or at least the first mate."

Mr. Keene smiled then hiccupped. "Kind of you to say, sir."

"Privateering agrees with you and your captain, I'd say. Word is you've had plenty of coin to spend on every gentleman's pleasure available in the city."

"Indeed I have, sir. Easiest coin I ever made." A tavern wench sashayed toward the table and deposited another bottle of brandy in the middle. Though it was Tripp who dropped coins in her outstretched palm, her eyes swam over Mr. Keene.

"Still meeting me later tonight?" she asked, her painted lips forming a red bow.

Grabbing the edge of the table, Keene struggled to his feet, swayed for a moment, then leaned over to whisper something in the woman's ear. Giggling, she darted off, blowing a kiss at him over her shoulder.

He plopped down into his chair with such force, it nearly tipped. Waving his arms through the air like a demented bird, he steadied himself.

Tripp restrained a groan of disgust. *Ah, the vermin Mr. Heaton surrounds himself with!* But what did Tripp expect? He leaned in with a wink. "I admire any man with enough business sense to make money during wartime."

"I quite agree, sir!" Keene's expression grew serious. "If we must fight a war, let the wisest and shrewdest of us profit."

Now Tripp was getting somewhere. After glancing around them for prying ears, he gave Keene a sly look. "I, for one, intend to use this blasted war to line my pockets with gold."

"Aye, we are of the same mind." Keene tossed the remaining brandy to the back of his throat. His eyes shifted over the dark tavern but seemed unable to focus.

"Here's to ill-gotten gains!" Tripp lifted his mug.

Mr. Keene blinked in slow motion. Grabbing his drink, he managed to strike empty air three times before finding Tripp's mug. "To ill-gotten gains."

Disgust bittered Tripp's mouth.

Nearly dropping his cup, Keene settled it on the table and leaned forward on his elbows. His gaze wavered over Tripp as if he couldn't determine which one of him to focus on. "Let me tell you about ill-gotten gains, sir."

❖

Pressing down the folds of the oversized silk gown that the captain insisted she wear, Cassandra made her way down the companionway to the stern of the ship. Flickering lanterns perched at intervals afforded the only light in the otherwise gloomy narrow hall, making Cassandra feel like a mouse trapped in a maze. Raucous male laugher blaring from behind the door halted her, but the marine behind her nudged her forward with the barrel of his pistol. Why the man thought he needed the weapon was beyond Cassandra. Standing at just over five feet, she couldn't do much damage to anyone—well, unless she had a brick in hand.

Or her parasol, of course. She smiled.

The marine brushed past her, their bodies touching. A lecherous smirk lifted his lips before he knocked and opened the door at the gruff "enter" that came from within. Then all but shoving her inside, he closed the door behind her. The smell of roasted duck and sweet butter instantly filled her nose as the flickering of a dozen candle flames struck her eyes. An oblong wooden table centered the captain's quarters, upon which perched two silver candelabras, platters of steaming food, pewter mugs and plates, silverware, and glittering goblets filled with some type of drink that contained nutmeg. The eyes of seven men lighted on her above smiles, some salacious in nature, others filled with hate, while a few held nothing but casual admiration.

"Do come in, Miss Channing. I hope you don't mind dining with a bunch of old crotchety sailors." Captain Raynor stood and gestured toward a chair at the far end of the table.

"Do I have a choice?" She took her seat, surprised to see a clean serviette beside her plate. Taking it, she slipped it into her lap, threw back her shoulders, and met their gazes with a boldness she did not feel within. If she had to endure imprisonment aboard this ship, she would endure it with grace and courage and show these sanctimonious, ill-bred Brits the real spirit of America.

That her countrymen weren't backward, ignorant ruffians cowering beneath their beds. That Americans were strong and smart and courageous and boasted of more honor than any British could lay claim to.

"You have a choice to eat or to starve, Miss Channing," the captain said, shifting his jaw. "But if you choose the former, I'm afraid you'll have to endure our company."

Cassandra gave him a tight smile. Better to eat and maintain her strength, not to mention have a chance to overhear some valuable information. "Gentlemen," the captain gestured to her with his hand. "May I present Miss Cassandra Channing, American rebel from Baltimore."

Cassandra poured herself some of the peach-colored liquid. "I prefer *patriot*, Captain."

"I suppose it all depends on your perspective," a chubby man, sitting on her left, said.

Nodding to him, she took a sip of the rum-laced tea and coughed.

"Perhaps you'd prefer the fresh water your. . .your. . ." A look of feigned consternation claimed the captain's face. "Now what shall we call Mr. Heaton, your paramour?"

Heat sped up Cassandra's neck. The men chuckled.

Captain Raynor cocked his head. "Your beau? Your friend? Your—"

"He is none of those things." Cassandra cut him off, longing for a fan to wave back the blush that was surely evident on her face. "And yes, I would prefer water."

The captain snapped his fingers to a steward who stood against the bulkhead, sending the boy out of the cabin. The men, three lieutenants and two midshipmen, if Cassandra's assessment of the buttons and epaulettes adorning their uniforms was correct, began piling food onto their plates. A platter of roasted duck, bowl of rice, corn, boiled potatoes in sweet cream, and biscuits passed by her.

She took a small portion of each, though her appetite had abandoned her—just as Luke had done.

But dare she admit that the revelation of Luke's reasons for his traitorous activities—in the form of the sweet, young boy she'd met earlier—had softened her anger considerably? For she knew, without a doubt, that if Hannah or Darlene had been thus kidnapped, she wouldn't hesitate to do whatever it took to rescue them unscathed.

The steward returned, pitcher of water in hand, and poured some into her mug. She thanked him. Smiling, he returned to his post. So young. Not much older than John. She wondered if he had chosen to be on this ship, in the Royal Navy. Had his parents arranged the position for him, proud to send their son off to a grand career at sea, or was he impressed as they were?

The men proceeded to eat with more civility than Cassandra expected, but then again they were officers. Talk of the sea, the operation of the ship, and longing for loved ones back home dominated the conversation, but their words blended into a nonsensical drone as Cassandra nibbled at her food and gazed out the stern windows into the darkness beyond. From the slight rock of the ship, she'd guessed they'd all but stopped for the night. Barely perceptible stars winked at her like devilish sprites, reminding Cassandra of her desperate situation.

Not that she needed reminding. A massive cannon guarding the captain's berth, a sentinel of the strength and superiority of the British navy, along with a row of glistening swords, knives, and axes, hanging on the bulkhead, did a sufficient job of scrambling the contents of her stomach.

"Do tell us how life is in Baltimore these days, Miss Channing?" The captain's grating voice brought her gaze forward. Candlelight blazed a mischievous glint in his eyes.

Stirring Cassandra's anger.

"As you have heard, Captain, Baltimore is the largest thorn in your side. Its people are brave, determined, and well armed. Our fort is impenetrable, and we have sent out more privateers to nip your heels than any other American port city." She regretted the words instantly as anger contorted the captain's face. Yet the chuckles of two of his lieutenants seemed to soften his expression.

"She is goading you, Captain," one of them said. "What do women know of such things?"

Captain Raynor dabbed his lips with his serviette then tossed it onto the table. "And what, pray tell, are the defenses of this impenetrable fort?"

He snorted, sharing a look of annoyance with his officers. "Stones and sticks, no doubt?"

"Why, as you know, I can hardly divulge such secrets, Captain. Besides, what do women know of such things?" She gave the lieutenant a smirk.

The captain sipped his drink and leaned back in his chair, lacing his hands over his belly. "We shall see what the good citizens of Baltimore think when our ships sail into her harbor and reinstate British rule."

The food soured in Cassandra's stomach.

One of the lieutenants, a gruff man with more hair on his eyebrows than on top of his head, slammed his mug onto the table—giving Cassandra a start. He gazed at his comrades as excitement filled his tone. "If the task is to be as easy as the taking of the rebel capital, we should place British boots on Baltimore's streets within a fortnight!"

The men raised their glasses in a toast of impending success.

Cassandra's throat felt as though it had been stuffed with sand. "Are you to burn Baltimore down as well?" What would become of her sisters? Her mother?

The captain plopped a piece of duck meat into his mouth. "If need be, I suppose."

Her empty spoon fell to her plate with a *clank*. "What need could there be, Captain, to destroy shops, homes, and libraries and force people onto the street? I see no honor in that."

"Honor!" Spittle flew from Captain Raynor's lips. "You speak to me of honor when it is you and your rebels who have turned against our sovereign king."

Cassandra stood, her anger squashing what was left of her fear and her reason. "Whenever a government becomes abusive and destructive, it is the right of the people to alter or to abolish it. To institute a new government—a government where man rules himself, where his rights—which are life, liberty, and the pursuit of happiness—come from God and not from man, not from some pompous, uncaring monarch."

The captain's brows scrunched together. "What sort of gibberish is this? And here I thought you would provide my men and me with a pleasant diversion. I tire of your company, Miss Channing."

"Let her stay, Captain. I find her zeal exhilarating," the hairy-browed lieutenant said with a wink in her direction.

"And quite comical." One of the midshipmen chomped on a biscuit.

"Are all American women so brash?" The chubby man to her left did not direct the question to her, but rather addressed his bumbling friends.

"I dare say, sadly, I've heard it is the case," a midshipman across from him answered.

"Then 'tis no wonder the American men prefer war. It keeps them away from the shrews at home."

The officers broke into a fit of laughter.

"How dare you!" Cassandra's voice faltered in the boisterous revelry.

When the laughter subsided, the captain's hard eyes latched on her. "Nevertheless, Miss Channing, you have depleted my patience." He waved her off. "Mr. Olsen!" His shout brought a marine back into the room. "Take Miss Channing back to her cabin."

"Captain." Cassandra tried to steady her voice. "If I displease you so, send me and the boy home. You have no use for us here."

"On the contrary, I have every use for you. To procure supplies." He gave her a sordid smirk. "And after we've won, perhaps I'll keep you as an example to all shrewish women in the colonies that they should submit not only to their husbands, but to their new rulers."

❖ CHAPTER 31 ❖

Cassandra wrung her hands together and took two steps across her tiny cabin before the bulkhead barred her way. She swung around. Two steps fore and two steps aft. That was the extent of freedom left to her. Instead of granting her more independence, every decision she had made in the past six months had limited it. Investing all her money in a dubious venture had put her family at great risk and restricted her options. Not storing her prize winnings at the bank had left them near destitute. And now, stowing aboard Luke's ship had made her a prisoner, possibly for life. How would her family manage without her? Instead of helping them, she had only put them in more danger.

Instead of aiding her country, she had unwittingly been aiding the enemy.

The ship bucked, tossing her against the frame of her bed. Pain radiated through her knee. She no longer cared. She'd grown used to the bumps and bruises that marred her arms and legs from constantly being thrashed about. It had been six days since her altercation with the captain in his cabin. And he'd not summoned her since. Not that she wanted to spend another moment with the implacable blackguard, but neither did she wish to remain entombed in her cabin.

Twice a day, a marine escorted her on deck for an hour, during which time dozens of piercing gazes and vulgar comments assailed her, making her feel like a dancer on stage in a bawdy saloon. Even so, as she stood at the railing and stared at the sea, the hour went by far too quickly before she was given access to the captain's private privy and then locked in her cabin once again. Meals, consisting of biscuits, fish, water, and an orange or lemon, were brought to her twice a day by a man with a permanent stoop and a pungent body odor that would ruin anyone's appetite. Nevertheless, she thanked him and tried to eat the food as best she could, even remembering now and then to ask God's blessing on it. She smiled, knowing her mother would be pleased, but more than that, in her present predicament, Cassandra was thankful for anything she received.

For she knew her life and her future rested in the hands of this British crew.

When asked why they kept her locked up, the marine mumbled something about another lady prisoner who had been able to do much damage to a British ship. Smiling, Cassandra wondered if they referred to Marianne.

A knock on the door froze her in place. The jingle of keys and clank of the latch reverberated through the room, and the door opened to reveal young John with a smile on his face and his hands behind his back.

"Only a minute, boy." The marine behind John shoved him inside and slammed the door. Sweeping his arms out, the boy presented her with a leather-bound book.

Upon further inspection, a rather holy book. "A Bible?" Cassandra didn't take it.

"One of the sailors gave it to me, miss. I thought you could use it about now." He stretched it toward her.

She waved it off. "I thank you, John, but keep it. It has never done me much good."

Sadness tore the smile from his face. "Then you need it much more than I thought, miss." He shoved it toward her again. She took it this time, if only to be polite, then sank onto her bed and gazed at the frayed pages and weathered leather binding. "Unless this will sprout wings and fly me back to shore, I don't see how it will help."

"Perhaps it *will* sprout wings." John's eyes danced. "God can do anything He wants. He is with us, Miss Channing. I've felt His presence ever since I boarded."

Cassandra flattened her lips. "I believe what you're feeling is dread."

He chuckled, and the curve of his mouth reminded Cassandra of Luke. Heaviness settled on her chest. Would she ever see him again?

"Fear doesn't bring hope, miss. Only faith and love do."

Cassandra lifted a skeptical brow. "And you have hope we'll get off this ship?"

"Yes, I do."

Envious of the joy and assurance in his eyes, Cassandra lowered her chin. "God abandoned me long ago."

The deck canted. Stumbling, John gripped the door frame and adjusted one of his legs. He winced.

Cassandra reached out for him. "Are you all right? Have they harmed you?"

"No, miss." He lifted one side of his breeches. An odd metal contraption hooked around his ankle, extending to a brace that disappeared up his leg.

At her look of astonishment, he said, "I have rickets."

Concern for this poor boy flooded Cassandra. She stared at him, unsure of what to say. All this time, Luke not only had a brother he cared for, but an ill child.

"It's not serious, miss. Besides, Luke was able to purchase this new brace with his prize money." He released the pant leg, once again hiding his withered leg.

Just as the outward appearance of man often hides the evil intentions of the heart. Cassandra's thoughts sped to Luke—a loving heart loyal to family yet hidden beneath a rough exterior. And what of Mr. Crane? A black heart hidden beneath the prim polish of a wealthy newspaper owner.

Rays from the setting sun peered in through the porthole and bounced over the back of the door with each move of the ship. Up down, up down, as if the light were restricted from going beyond certain boundaries.

"Luke sounds like a good brother."

"He's the best, miss. Been taking care of me since I was a baby."

"Yes, I heard your parents were killed. I'm sorry."

John's eyes grew vacant as he glanced out the porthole. "I don't remember them." Then his face brightened. "But I'm sure I'll see them in heaven."

Cassandra smiled. "I would have never known you wore a brace."

"Not everything is as it seems." John snapped his hair from his face, reminding her once again of Luke. "Which is why we must believe God has a plan."

She studied him. "How can you say that when you've been trapped here for a month?"

He shrugged. "God doesn't want me to leave yet. When He does, I will." A whistle sounded from above, followed by the *clang clang* of a bell.

John nodded toward her, his eyes widening. "And God has something for you to do as well."

"Me?" Cassandra nearly laughed. Such childlike faith. But Cassandra wasn't a child. She was a grown woman who had experienced enough of life to know that faith in God was for pastors and children and the simpleminded.

A knock pounded on the door. "Boy!"

John frowned, but then his eyes took on a sparkle. "Oh, I nearly forgot." He reached into a pocket in his oversized breeches and brought out a piece of foolscap, a tiny bottle of ink, and a quill pen.

"What are these for?" Cassandra asked.

"If you want to write a note to Luke or someone back home, I can try to slip it to him next time he comes. I thought it would help pass the time."

"Thank you, John." Cassandra took them and set them aside. Then grasping his hands, she squeezed them. "Be careful, John. These men are our enemies."

"I know." Stepping toward her, John embraced her. "Be careful as well, miss."

Startled by his affection, Cassandra wrapped her arms around him as her memories drifted to Hannah and Darlene. Sorrow threatened to overwhelm her.

"Hurry up, boy!" The shout sent John reaching for the door handle.

"You remind me of your brother," Cassandra said. "Though smaller and kinder and not so angry."

The statement brought a huge smile to the boy's face. "You're the woman he talked about, aren't you?"

"One of many, I am sure."

"No. He told me you were special. One of a kind. A true lady."

Initial elation gave way to sorrow as Cassandra realized that, just like everyone else in town, she had not believed that Luke was anything but a rogue. If she had, if she had shown faith in him, maybe he would have trusted her and told her the truth. Then maybe she could have helped him think of a way to rescue John.

"I'll come back as soon as I can." John opened the door, and the marine tugged him out before Cassandra could say good-bye. Gathering the pen and ink, she lifted her skirt and tucked them inside the pocket she'd sown in her petticoat. No doubt if that stiff marine saw them in her cabin, he'd take them from her. The boy's infectious faith remained in the cabin long after he left, giving rise to a yearning within Cassandra—a yearning to believe she was not alone, that everything that had happened was part of a plan, for a purpose, and that her life and the world were not spinning chaotically out of control toward some final destruction.

With the Bible snug in her lap, Cassandra sat for hours and watched as the sun's rays withdrew from the door and slid over the deck head until finally disappearing out the porthole, taking with them the last trace of hope left by John's presence.

Despair took its place. It crowded in her throat and threatened to fill her eyes with tears. Unless she could figure out a way for her and John to escape—or by some miracle Luke rescued them—she'd be stuck on this ship forever. In this cabin all alone, or worse. . .

What would become of her mother and sisters? They had only enough money to last a year. Would her mother be frugal enough to stretch the funds beyond that? And what of Darlene and Hannah's upbringing? Aside from Margaret and Mr. Dayle, they had no decent instructors in life. Without a firm hand, Darlene would only grow more unruly with each passing year. Who knew what trouble she would become entangled in with her rebellious, carefree spirit?

Like you.

Me? Cassandra glanced over the shadows burgeoning from the corners of the cabin as memories assailed her of all the times she'd disobeyed her mother and father. All the times she'd left home without permission, snuck food into her bedchamber, put spiders in Mrs. Northrop's bed, garden snakes in the stew, ink on her brother Gregory's teeth while he slept. The list went on endlessly, bringing a smile to her lips. Her rising shame quickly transformed it into a frown. Each time she'd been caught for one of her seditious deeds her father had coddled her, rescuing her from her mother's wrath. Yet now, Cassandra wondered if he had done her more of a disservice.

"I'm different now. I've grown up," she said out loud to the creaking timbers of the ship.

But visions assaulted her: how she traipsed about town at night with a large-summed banknote in her reticule, invested in a privateer against her mother's wishes, and dressed like a man and sneaked aboard Luke's ship.

All reckless acts that had led her to her current dire situation.

"Oh, bother." She hung her head as her eyes filled with tears. She had never really changed, had she? She had always done exactly what she wanted, went her own way, caused her parents grief. And not trusted anyone. In particular, God. And where had it gotten her?

Doomed to a life of slavery.

"But I wouldn't have done those things if You hadn't left me, God. I had to take care of my family."

I never left you.

A chill struck Cassandra. Hugging herself, she sent a wary gaze about the tiny cabin. No doubt the many hours she'd spent alone were causing her to hear things. She set the Bible on the desk and stood to light the lantern hanging from the deck head. Its glow chased the shadows back into hiding as the room filled with the smell of whale oil.

Yet if God was speaking to her, if He was listening, she had some things to tell Him. Her jaw hardened. "But You took my father, my brothers."

Silence.

As she thought. God wasn't there.

Sails thundered above and the bell rang again, followed by the pounding of feet. The change of a watch, no doubt. The smells of some kind of stew permeated the thin walls, making her stomach growl. She rubbed it, regretting that she'd stubbornly turned down her noon meal. It would be at least an hour before the sailor brought her supper.

Stubborn pride. She knew it well. Had seen it mirrored in Darlene. It was the kind of pride that made Cassandra refuse to rely on anyone else— forced her to accomplish everything herself. For if she did not trust, she would never be hurt, abandoned, or disappointed. Would she?

Distant thunder hammered the evening sky. Or was it cannon fire? Standing on her tiptoes, Cassandra peered out the porthole at the undulating sea. Coral and crimson fingers stretched over the indigo waters in one final caress of the sun. The ship jolted. Staggering, she fell back on her bed. The lantern flung shifting silhouettes of shadow and light across the bulkheads. Dark and light, good and evil, faith and unbelief. Life was full of choices.

Cassandra hadn't realized until now how important those choices were.

She opened the Bible. She didn't know why. She'd heard plenty of passages read in church, hundreds of sermons. Flipping through the pages, she landed on James. Her eyes idly scanned the text until the word *proud* seemed to magnify on the paper.

"God resisteth the proud, but giveth grace unto the humble. Submit your-selves therefore to God. Resist the devil, and he will flee from you. Draw nigh to God, and he will draw nigh to you."

Had God resisted her because of her pride? And her unbelief? Was it too late to draw near to Him? Would He still answer her prayers? Or had her arrogant rebellion formed an impenetrable wall between them?

Releasing a heavy sigh, she sifted through the pages, seeking answers, stopping in Hebrews.

"But without faith it is impossible to please him: for he that cometh to God must believe that he is, and that he is a rewarder of them that diligently seek him."

Instead of seeking God, Cassandra had been running from Him, thinking He was not worthy of her trust. That He, like everyone else, had abandoned her. Hope peeked out from her despair. If she diligently sought God now as His Word said, would He reward her? Would He come to her aid?

Hadn't Reverend Drummond told her that God would never leave her and would always provide? And what of Margaret? Still loving God. Still trusting Him after He took her only child.

Confusion sent Cassandra's convictions into a whirl. Bad things, terrible things still happened. And God could have prevented all of them. She glanced over the shadowy room.

"Why didn't You? Why did You let Papa die and my brothers leave us?"

They chose.

"But You could have stopped them."

Silence, save for the creaks and groans of the timbers.

Seek Me. Trust Me.

The ship rose and crashed over a swell, and somewhere a fiddle began to play.

Closing the Bible, Cassandra pressed it against her chest. This time it felt as though she held holy words in her hands. For she knew without a doubt that God had spoken to her.

"I want to trust You." To know she was never alone. To know that Almighty God would always be there to help her, protect her, love her. It was too much to hope for. Too good to be true. Too much to believe. Wasn't it?

I Am.

Wiping the tears from her face, she glanced over the room. An explosion of joy and peace filled the air, permeating every crack and crevice. Gooseflesh ran from her head down to her toes.

And she knew God was there.

"I'm so sorry, Lord." Dropping to her knees, she set the Bible on her bed and leaned her head on top of it. "I'm sorry I've been proud, resisting You, not believing You loved me. I'm sorry I've been running from You." Tears trickled down her cheeks, dropping onto the leather. "I've been a fool."

I love you, precious daughter.

Several minutes passed. When she opened her eyes, moonlight spilled through the porthole, forming milky arms that curled around her in a warm embrace. And for the first time since she arrived on this abominable ship, Cassandra curled up on the bed and fell into a deep sleep.

❖

Laying his coat, sword, and pistol onto the table in the foyer, Luke entered the sitting room. Mrs. Barnes sat in her chair by the fireplace, knitting. Where she'd been nearly every minute since John had been kidnapped. Luke had even caught her sleeping there many a night.

She glanced up, and a sad smile lifted the corner of her lips. "Do you think your plan will work?"

"It has to." Luke huffed and glanced out the window at the darkening sky. All was in place. They'd spent the past two days disguising *Destiny*: removing her name, painting her hull, changing the position of her cannons. Noah had managed to garner two British naval uniforms from the fort—discards from prisoners of war—and Mr. Reed was putting the final touches on forged orders for the transfer of prisoners.

Mrs. Barnes returned to her knitting, and Luke's gaze drifted to her open Bible on the table beside her. "We could use your prayers." He could hardly believe he was asking such a thing. *Creak, creak, creak.* The rhythmic rock of her chair echoed through the room. Though the sound usually soothed Luke's nerves, tonight it raked over them with claws of guilt and failure.

"I *have* been praying," she said. "We'll have John back soon. I know it."

Marching to the window, Luke peered at the tumble of clouds forming on the horizon. "I wish I had your confidence." He snorted. "Both in myself and in your God."

"Two things that must be remedied before you can truly succeed," she said. "The latter before the former."

Her words stirred an odd desire within Luke for both.

"You have good friends," she said. "Mr. Brenin and Mr. Reed. They risk much for you."

"Not for me. For Cassandra and John."

Turning around, he strode to the sofa and took a seat across from her. Her hands dipped and shifted over needle and yarn like a conductor before an orchestra.

"I don't think I've seen you stop knitting for weeks now."

She laughed. "Better to work than to fret." She spread the product of her efforts over her lap. A beautiful tapestry of white and black thread formed delicate patterns in graceful symmetry.

"Did you intend for it to turn out so beautifully?"

"Why yes, of course." She stroked it lovingly. "I planned it from the beginning. It's a blanket for John when he returns." Her eyes sparkled assurance.

Luke shook his head. He had not expected to see such an exquisite coverlet come from Mrs. Barnes's harried movements. Order from chaos, beauty from simplicity, dark and light molded together in a meaningful pattern.

Could God do the same? Luke wondered.

Could God use chaos and darkness to create beauty and light?

Shaking the silly musings from his head, he rose.

Mrs. Barnes's sharp eyes found him. "I've smelled no rum on you lately."

"I need a clear mind." He glanced at the clock, ever stuck at 9:13. "We should get that fixed someday."

"When John returns. But perhaps God is telling us something. Perhaps it's not a time, but a date? It is September thirteenth in three days. . ."

Stifling a chuckle at the woman's delusions, Luke knelt before her. She set down her knitting, and he took her hands in his. "I'll do my best to get him back, Mrs. Barnes." He fell short of promising something he had no reason to believe he could do. Maybe he should appeal to God, after all, for it would take Almighty intervention for their plan to work.

The prayer sat idle on his lips when a *pound pound pound* drew his gaze to the front door. Mrs. Barnes's face knotted in concern. Luke stood, wondering who it could be. He'd told Noah and Reed to meet him at the ship by ten, but that was at least an hour from now.

Stomping to the door, he swung it open to a cold chill and the sight of Lieutenant Tripp, a bombastic smirk on his face and two armed privates by his side.

Luke had no time for his theatrics. "What do you want?"

"I have come to arrest you, sir."

Mrs. Barnes gasped.

"On what charge?"

"On the charge of treason."

❖ CHAPTER 32 ❖

A loud *clank* barged into Cassandra's sweet sleep, stirring her to consciousness. Ignoring the sound, she drew her wool blanket up around her neck and sank back into the oblivion of her dreams.

Until firm hands gripped her arms and shook her.

With a scream, she jerked to a sitting position, forcing her eyes open to see the red coat of a marine standing over her. "Captain's orders, miss. He wants to see you immediately." The shiny brass hilt of his sword winked at her in the first rays of dawn angling through the porthole.

Of all the times for the captain to summon her, he had to choose the first time she'd been able to sleep in days.

Yet even as she started to grumble, terror gripped her at what the man could possibly want.

"Now." The marine stood erect. The urgency of his tone threatened to dissolve Cassandra's newfound faith.

Tossing the blanket aside, she scrambled to her feet, rubbed her eyes, patted down the wrinkles of her gown, and lifted her chin. "Very well."

As she followed the marine onto the main deck, Cassandra couldn't help but notice that a mood of apprehension, even excitement, had settled over the ship. Squinting at the sun rising on the horizon, she spotted the yards overhead, full of men unfurling sail. Shouted orders from lieutenants on the quarterdeck sent the remainder of the sailors scampering over the decks.

Something was happening. Something important.

Whatever it was did not bode well for her—or for America. As she made her way down the companionway to the captain's cabin, dismal thoughts tortured her. Were they setting sail for England, where she'd be forever separated from her country and her family—and Luke? Or were they about to attack some American ship or worse, America itself?

On trembling legs, she entered the main cabin. Captain Raynor, sitting behind his desk, barely peeked at her from above the document he was reading. But it was John who drew Cassandra's gaze. Turning from his position standing before the captain, he smiled at her, sending a wave of relief over her tight nerves.

The marine stood to attention just inside the door.

"Miss Channing, you and the lad are being moved to an American truce ship." The captain tore the spectacles from his nose.

Hope jolted her heart, though she didn't dare allow it to grow. "Truce ship?"

"Aye." Tossing down the papers, Captain Raynor rose to his full ominous height.

"Then"—she gulped—"we are free?"

"Hardly, madam. You will be guarded well. And when we succeed in our plans, you and all the citizens of your fair city will once again be subjects of the Crown."

Cassandra grimaced at the man's arrogance. She squared her shoulders. "And just what *are* your plans, Captain?"

He grinned, his eyes lighting up with malicious glee. "Why, my dear, we are attacking Baltimore from both land and sea. You and your city don't stand a chance."

❖

Bands of light coursed over Luke's eyelids, like slow-moving waves at sea, passing in swells of warmth and cold. Shouts beckoned to him, jarring his memories. He moved his hand. Moist stones scraped his fingers. Something bit his neck. He swatted it. A bugle sounded. The pounding of drums thundered in his head. Snapping his eyes open, he struggled to rise, ignoring the ache in his back from sitting all night against the wall of his cell in the guardhouse. Making his way to the tiny window, he gripped the iron bars and peered into the inner courtyard of Fort McHenry.

Soldiers from various Maryland regiments, muskets in hand and haversacks tossed over their shoulders, darted across the dirt and out the entrance of the fort. One soldier dropped his canteen and stopped to pick it up.

"What's happening?" Luke shouted.

The man, who could be no older than eighteen, flung his canteen strap over his shoulder and stared at Luke. "It's the British. They've landed at North Point and are marching toward the city." His voice held a fear that registered on his face before he sped away as if it occurred to him that perhaps he shouldn't be speaking to a prisoner.

Which was exactly what Luke was. A prisoner. A traitor.

Sinking back into his dank cell, he took up his daily pace. He hadn't seen Lieutenant Tripp since the man had tossed him in here two nights ago. Last night after spending a sleepless night and an entire day listening to the pounding of soldiers' boots and the harried shouts of officers outside his window, Luke grew desperate for news. So when a young boy brought him a crusty piece of stale bread and a mug of putrid water, Luke had begged him for information. Hesitant at first, the lad finally told Luke that some fifty British warships had sailed up the Patapsco River and anchored just three miles from the fort.

The news had driven a knife into Luke's gut. He'd been unable to sleep yet again, unable to do anything but pace his cell until exhaustion had pulled him to the ground in a heap. Now, the additional news of a land invasion sealed the tomb on Luke's hope. The British were making their move. A full assault by land and sea. And although General Smith had made extensive enhancements to the fort, how could Baltimore survive against the greatest military and naval power in the world?

Luke's thoughts drifted to John and Cassandra. Had Noah and Mr. Reed carried out their plans to rescue them without Luke? He hoped so. It was the only thing that had kept his heart from sinking into despair—believing that they were both safe at home. The first rays of the sun made a courageous effort to shine but were soon subdued by thick, ominous clouds broiling across the sky. Stifling air, heavy with moisture and the smell of gunpowder and fear, settled, rather than swept into his cell. Thunder roared as if God was angry at the invasion. Luke hoped that was the case. For maybe the Almighty would finally intervene. Soon, rain began to fall, offering some reprieve from the torturous heat of the day. It slashed at the roof and battered the mud, mimicking the march of boots. Muffled shouts drifted to his ears, but Luke could no longer make out the words.

Minutes stretched into hours, and hours stretched into the early evening. Luke felt like a caged animal, rage and fury churning within him. Fury at Mr. Keene for his betrayal. Though at first Luke hadn't wanted to believe Tripp's revelation of the man's disloyalty, he knew there was no other explanation. How could Mr. Keene have been so careless? Drunkenness was no excuse for a loose tongue, especially when lives were at stake.

He slapped another mosquito on his arm. Yet how often had Luke done foolish things when he'd been deep into his cups? He halted and rubbed the sweat from the back of his neck. In truth, Mr. Keene and Luke had more in common than Luke cared to admit. And watching his faults play out before him sickened Luke to the core. But no doubt, Mr. Keene was already paying dearly for his betrayal. He, along with Luke's entire crew, had most likely been rounded up and tossed in prison as well. Luke longed to talk to Biron. His old friend always had a wise word of comfort. And Sam. Poor Sam. So young. With so much promise. The foolish lad had longed to emulate Luke in every way. Now, tossed in prison as a traitor, his wish had come true.

Luke moaned. Was there no one in his life who had not been harmed by his foolhardy actions?

Lightning lit his cell in bursts of eerie gray. Gripping the iron bars, Luke peered across the yard. Rain slammed against the stone window ledge and sprayed his face. He shook the water off as a band of soldiers marched by. Mud oozed down their once-white trousers, and the *squish squish* of their boots filled the muggy air with a determination that could be seen on their expressions. A hint of fear quaked in their voices as they waited for the first bombs to strike. Across the way, Luke spotted Major Armistead speaking to a group of officers. Earlier, Luke had overheard the man's urgent orders to transport his pregnant wife out of Baltimore. The general probably feared he'd never see her again.

Just like Luke would never see Cassandra. Thunder rattled the bars. Daylight retreated beneath the encroaching darkness. He stepped away from the window, wondering where she was and what horrors she must be enduring. Was she still angry at him for what he had done? Or, upon meeting his brother, did she understand his actions? Were she and John allowed to speak? A smile, the first one in days, taunted his tight lips. John would lift her spirits and encourage her. It was his way. Small consolation though it was, Luke was pleased to think that the two people he loved more than anything in the world were together.

A cannon boomed in the distance, followed by a spray of musket shot. Luke wondered how the troops had fared that day. He wondered why the British fleet had not attacked the fort. He wondered where Lieutenant Tripp had gone.

Most of all, Luke wondered if he'd ever get out of this cell.

He thought of Noah's and Reverend Drummond's words that God had a plan. He snorted and ran a hand through his hair. Not a plan for Luke. No, there was no divine purpose for his life. Luke was a failure. And he infected everyone he touched with his disease.

He spun around and barreled the other way, striking the wall with his fist. Pain lanced up his arm. He rubbed it as he stared at the rainwater pooling on the stones by his feet. Storming toward the door, he pounded on the thick wood. "Let me out!" But no one came.

Thunder shook the timber and stone. Sweat streamed down his back. This cage was as fitting a place as any to die, he supposed. For he felt as though he'd been in a cage his entire life—a cage of emptiness and failure. A cage he'd built from each bad decision and wayward deed, a prison that kept him trapped in an empty existence.

Darkness as thick as tar rose from the corners and slithered on the floor. Luke watched it with detached curiosity. He was either going mad or dying. He preferred the latter.

Failure, failure.

Worthless, worthless.

The voices stabbed him like a thousand devilish prods. A cold mist enveloped him. He sank to the floor. Rainwater seeped into his breeches.

And he knew.

He knew that if he gave in to the darkness he would die.

He closed his eyes. "God, help me." But thunder muted his voice. Exhaustion tugged at him, and he felt himself falling into an empty void.

God, if You're there, help me.

Seconds passed, minutes maybe, as rain pounded above and wind whistled past his window, laughing at him. But then, a warm glow illuminated his eyelids. Luke looked up. A man—no, some otherworldly being—stood just inside the door. White light rippled out from him in glittering waves. Luke's blood turned cold. Holding up a hand to shield his eyes, he tried to make out his face, but the glow was too bright. Yet. . . recognition struck him. "I know you."

The man nodded.

"Who. . .who are you?"

The being drew a massive sword from a scabbard at his hip, sending a chime ringing through the air that was instantly set aglow.

Luke shrank back against the cold stones. His ear began to throb. He rubbed it as flashes of memories filled his mind.

One in particular—the shining man with his sword drawn, standing in front of a burning house.

Luke stared at the man aghast. "You were there."

Again the man nodded. And sheathed his sword with a resounding scrape of metal.

Gripping the stone wall behind him, Luke inched his way to standing. Flames filled his cell, devouring his family home. Little John in his arms. His mother's scream and. . . "You stopped me. You cut me!" Luke grabbed his ear.

"You were persistent." The man's voice sounded like the rush of a waterfall, drowning out the sound of the storm.

Luke's skin grew clammy. His breath escaped him. He had not failed to save his parents! Their deaths were not his fault. The revelation gripped him, breathing life into his soul. Yet anger took the place of fear. "Why?" he cried out. "Why did you stop me?"

"To save you and John. It was not your time."

"And it was my parents' time?" Luke fisted the wall.

The being nodded. "Their task was complete. Yours and John's were not."

"What task?"

"Good works which the Father predestined for you to do before you were born."

Now Luke knew he had surely gone mad. "Me? Good works? You got the wrong man."

The glowing being said nothing, but Luke thought he saw a smile on his blinding visage. "The Father wants you to know you are greatly loved."

Thunder bellowed. The stones quaked, and Luke closed his eyes. The glow dissipated. Jerking alert, Luke glanced over his cell. All was dark again. A dream. Just a dream.

Greatly loved.

The words shot through the hard crust around Luke's heart, dissolving it.

No, not a dream.

"You're real, God." Luke swallowed. "All this time, You've protected me and John. You stayed with me through all my wanderings. All this time, I thought I failed my parents. But it was meant to be. Everything was meant to be." Clenching his fists, he hung his head. "I'm sorry for not believing, for not seeing."

Dawn's glow showered in through the tiny window and surrounded Luke in glittering light. Where had the night gone? What seemed only minutes must have taken hours. A presence filled the cell. A strong sense of peace and love.

The squeaking of a rusty hinge met his ears. He looked up to see the door of his cell ajar. Thunder bellowed. No, not thunder. He knew that sound. It was a cannon blast. The menacing whine of an incoming shell flew overhead.

Before an explosion rocked the fort.

❖ CHAPTER 33 ❖

Clutching her skirts, Cassandra followed John up the ladder and emerged onto the main deck of the sloop *Minden*. Ever since they'd boarded the American truce ship the morning before, heavy rains had kept them cooped up below. Cassandra hadn't minded. Together, she and John had read the Holy Scriptures and talked about the things of God and Cassandra's newfound faith. They'd also talked of Luke, how John and he had lost their parents in a savage fire, and how Luke had been forced to care for John since he was but a babe. Every story John told Cassandra about Luke, about his love for John, the way he'd provided for him and their housekeeper all these years, flew in the face of her initial impressions of the man. Though she didn't completely understand why Luke had taken to drinking, gambling, and womanizing, John's obvious admiration and love for his brother spoke volumes as to the man's heart. Though lately, she needed no aid in attesting to the same.

Heavens, she had no idea he even had a brother. Neither Marianne nor Noah had mentioned it. If they had even known. And a crippled brother at that. Though now as she watched the lad ascend the ladder, hobbling slightly, she realized his physical impediment had not limited him nearly as much as her spiritual one of rebellion had limited her.

She stepped onto the main deck to a burst of rain-laden wind and drew a deep breath, hoping to rid her lungs of the musky air below. Black clouds churned above them, mimicking the dark waters of the Patapsco River that slammed against the hull of the tiny ship. Throwing out her arms to catch her balance on the teetering deck, she peered into the gloom. Surrounding them, dark hulls rose like dragons from the deep, the sharp teeth of their masts stabbing the low-hanging clouds.

The British fleet in all its majestic and terrifying glory wound tight like a pack of ravenous wolves ready to spring on innocent Baltimore.

John took her hand and led her portside, where her fellow prisoners huddled in deep conversation. She gripped the wet railing. A chill seeped through the moist wood into her hands and up her arms. In the distance, the massive stars and stripes billowed proudly above Fort McHenry, daring the British onward. Daring them to try to steal the freedom represented in that grandiose flag.

Sorrow burned in her throat, her eyes, her gut. She could not bear to see her country fall. And would she ever see Luke again? Would she ever be able to tell him she understood why he'd betrayed his country? And that she loved him more than anything? She sighed. That was in God's hands now. She was no longer alone. Her life and the lives of her loved ones were in the capable hands of Almighty God. Ah, such sweet comfort even in the midst of troubling times.

Troubling indeed—and harrowing—confirmed by the British marines, resplendent in their red coats and white breeches, with long muskets in their hands as they lined the deck of the *Minden*. Though an American ship originally, the sloop had been seized by the British and all those upon it were now prisoners of this horrid war. As their punishment, they were being forced to watch the British attack their country, their city. Helpless to do anything.

Terror seized Cassandra's throat. Bowing her head, she whispered a plea to God to spare her city and her country.

A man eased beside her. "I see we are of the same mind, madam. Only divine intervention can save us now."

Opening her eyes, Cassandra stared at the modishly attired man. "How did you know I was praying?"

"The look on your face, pleading yet peaceful, reflecting heaven's glow." He smiled.

Cassandra felt a blush rising.

"Forgive me, I've embarrassed you. Allow me to introduce myself. I am Sir Francis Scott Key." He bowed elegantly. "At your service, madam. I had heard a woman prisoner had come aboard."

"A pleasure, sir." Cassandra put a protective arm around John. "I am Cassandra Channing of Baltimore."

He dipped his head, and his eyes lowered to John. "Your son?" He gazed up at Cassandra. "No, you are far too young. Brother?"

John giggled. "No, sir, I am John Heaton, brother to the great privateer Luke Heaton."

"Ah, a privateer! Courageous fellows, all! We owe them the highest gratitude."

Distant musket fire splintered the air, drawing Cassandra's gaze to the stretch of land alongside the Patapsco River.

Mr. Key followed her gaze, worry twisting his features. "Word is our American troops have retreated from North Point."

"God be with them," Cassandra said.

"Indeed." He faced her again. "Pray tell, how is it you and John find yourselves prisoners of the British navy?"

Cassandra proceeded to relay their harrowing tale, with John piping in now and then filling in the more colorful details.

"Fascinating, indeed." Mr. Key rubbed his chin. "A most daunting position. I cannot say I wouldn't have done the same thing in Mr. Heaton's shoes."

Lightning flashed silver over his somber expression.

"And how did you come to be here, Mr. Key?"

"Ah, not so adventurous a tale as yours, miss, I'm afraid." He took a step back and motioned for two men, who had been conversing to his left, to come forward. He introduced them as Dr. William Beanes and Colonel John Skinner, an American agent for prisoners.

"Colonel Skinner and I boarded this ship, raised a white flag of truce, and went in search of our dear friend Dr. Beanes, who had been taken prisoner," Mr. Key explained. "As it turns out we found him on board Admiral Cockrane's eighty-gun flagship, the HMS *Tonnant.*"

"Indeed?" Cassandra turned to Dr. Beanes, a humble-looking man of small stature. "You are not a military man, sir. May I ask why the British kept you prisoner?"

He cocked his head. "For the crime of tossing some rather unruly British soldiers in jail." His gentle smile gave no indication of the hardship he had no doubt endured.

Thunder quivered the gray sky. The ship canted. Clinging to John, Cassandra gripped the railing as a foam-capped wave slapped the hull, showering them both with salty spray. Wiping the moisture from her face, she turned to Mr. Key. "I see your mission was somewhat successful." She wondered what magic they wielded to achieve such a feat when Luke had tried everything in his power to free a boy who had done nothing.

"At first not," Mr. Key said. "But we were finally able to persuade General Ross, a rather reasonable fellow as far as the British go." His features sank. "I heard the poor man was killed at North Point." He sighed. "Nevertheless, we seem to have managed only to move Dr. Beanes from one prison to another. And got ourselves captured as well."

Colonel Skinner gazed toward Baltimore. "And now we're forced to witness the invasion of our country."

Musket fire popped in the distance. Thunder shook the tiny ship as she rode upon another swell. Cassandra glanced over the morbid scene.

"I wonder where Luke is," John said.

She drew the boy close. "Pray for him, John. And pray for our country."

Shouts echoed through the gloom from the British ships. Cassandra could make out the shapes of sailors scampering about the deck, hovering over cannons like bees over nectar—deadly nectar.

They were preparing to fire on Baltimore.

❖

Luke stared at the open cell door, too shocked to move. Had the angel opened it or had the explosion jarred the lock? Either way, Luke knew he had not been dreaming. He had seen the angel, heard his words, and through them, God had released Luke from a different kind of prison—one Luke had created for himself out of unbelief and failure.

Another thunderous explosion shook the building, and dust showered him from above. Darting from his cell, down the gloomy hall, he emerged into the empty guardhouse then out into the courtyard of the fort. Officers brayed orders. Soldiers stomped across the ground, mud flinging from their boots, their faces masks of fear and torment. Militiamen and citizens stormed in and out of the open front gate.

Open, with no guard in sight.

In the mayhem Luke would have no trouble slipping out unseen. Ducking into the shadows beneath the building's overhang, he lowered his head and started toward the entrance. Yet with each thud of his boots, something tugged at his heart, urging him to stay. To fight. Even if it meant his death.

Hadn't the angel said Luke had important works, good works to do? Perhaps this was one of them. Perhaps everything that had happened was meant to bring him to this spot.

At this time.

He halted. He was tired of running. Tired of running from God, tired of running from himself. And tired of failing. Anger stormed through his veins. The British had impressed him into their navy, whipped his back, stolen his brother, made Luke into a traitor, kidnapped the woman he loved, and now they were intent on stealing his freedom.

And he was not going to let them succeed without a fight.

Searching the yard for someone in authority, he spotted a colonel standing by the bunkhouse directing a band of militiamen. Fear surged through Luke. Would the man recognize him? Yet, some invisible force nudged him forward even as peace registered in his heart. He must do this. He couldn't explain it, but he knew he was supposed to help defend the fort. Regardless of whether they tossed him back in his cell, he had to try. Snapping the hair from his face, Luke dashed into the rain and halted before him.

"What can I do to help, Colonel?"

The man's eyes narrowed as another explosion split the sky. "Who are you, sir?"

"Luke Heaton, privateer."

"Very good, Mr. Heaton." The man dismissed the militiamen. "Can you handle an eighteen-pounder?"

"Aye, sir." Relief brought a smile to Luke's lips.

"Then report to Captain Nicholson and the Baltimore Fencibles on the shore battery."

Luke hesitated, thinking of the incoming British fleet. "Have you sunk any ships in the bay to bar their passage?"

The colonel huffed. "Where have you been, man? We sunk several merchant ships yesterday. I assure you, the Brits will get no farther than they are, at least not by ship."

With a nod, Luke started off, glad to be helping, glad he had not been thrown back in his cell. As he marched out of the fort, over the moat, and around to the battery, rain stung his face. White-hot lightning etched across the gray sky.

Please, God, give me strength and wisdom and protect this fort and this city. Though his whispered prayer felt odd on his lips, peace as he'd never known washed over him. Approaching the man he assumed to be Nicholson, he glanced at the ominous barricade of British warships perched in the dark waters just three miles from the fort—like a line of soldiers, well armed, their faces like flint, their determination unyielding. He wondered if Cassandra and John were among them. Sorrow crushed his heart as an orange flash shot out from the lead ship, followed by a thunderous boom. Soldiers across the field froze. Some ducked. A splash of water flung toward the sky where the shot fell short of land.

Luke reported to Nicholson and was immediately put to work loading and priming an eighteen-pound messenger of death. At least he hoped it would deliver that resounding message to the Brits. The next several hours passed in a melee of commands, screams, and explosions. Giving up on its single shots, the British fleet began firing several bombs into the air at once, raining deadly hail upon the fort and the men defending it. Fortunately, most of the shots missed the fort. Yet their impact on land and sea did not fail to shake the ground as well as Luke's nerves. And though he and his crew returned fire as rapidly as they could, their shots always fell short of the row of ships.

British mortar bombs continued to pound them even as the wind and rain assailed them from all sides. Hours passed as Luke, sweat laden and sore muscled, went through the methodical motions of working the gun. Bending over to catch his breath, he inhaled a gulp of smoke-laden air. It stung his nose and throat. He backed up, coughing, and bumped into a passing soldier.

"Luke." The man's incredulous voice spun Luke around. Noah stared at him, eyes brimming with shock from within a soot-encrusted face. Blackthorn stood by his side.

"What in the blazes are you doing here?" Noah asked.

"I could ask you the same," Luke said, gripping his friend's arm. "Did you rescue John and Cassandra?"

A group of militiamen stormed past. Shouts filled the air.

Noah shook his head, sorrow filling his eyes. "Without you, we had no idea where to meet the frigate."

Of course. Luke released his friend. He hadn't thought of that.

"Blackthorn and I came to help the fort." Noah scanned Luke as if he expected him to disappear at any moment. "I'm very glad to see you alive, my friend."

Blackthorn ducked beneath another explosion. "We heard you were arrested."

"You heard correctly," Luke shouted and ran a sleeve over his forehead, marring the white cotton with soot. He leaned toward them. "Do not worry, neither of you were implicated."

Noah's brow folded. "How did you get free?"

"God set me free, my friend." Luke gestured above.

The eerie whine of a bomb sailed overhead.

"It's a long tale." Luke ducked as the explosion shook the ground. "For another time."

A passing corporal pointed toward Noah. "Brenin, Blackthorn, with me!"

Noah clasped Luke's arm. "Take care, my friend."

"You too." Luke returned his grip.

After Noah and Blackthorn rushed off, Luke faced the British fleet. More shots fired from the ships in rapid succession, pummeling both land and sea, like an angry giant pounding on a door. Behind him, one of the bombs met their mark on one of the fort's buildings. The ground trembled. Luke crouched as a shower of stone stung his back and screams of agony battered his ears. When nothing but raindrops struck him, Luke rose, swiped off the debris, and returned to his duties.

The sergeant in charge of the gun Luke was assigned to lowered his scope. "They have rocket launchers on board their sloop. How are we to withstand such a force?" His eyes grew vacant with terror.

"We keep fighting, sir." Luke hefted another iron ball into the mouth of the cannon. He faced him with a look of defiance. "We do not give up."

The sergeant nodded and released a ragged sigh. "Indeed." He glanced down at an empty bucket. "Mr. Heaton, go fetch some more powder bags."

Grabbing the container, Luke headed toward the fort when a firm hand on his shoulder flung him around.

Lieutenant Tripp. With black smudges on his face, rain dripping from his chin, his uniform torn, and a look of shocked abhorrence twisting his features. "What are you doing here, Heaton?" he shouted over the noise.

Luke's stomach folded in on itself. "I'm helping to fight, Lieutenant."

Explosions thundered the sky. Rain slammed down on the mud, skipping over the puddles. "How did you get out of your cell?" The lieutenant's eyes seethed hatred. "It doesn't matter, you will come with me now!" he barked.

An eerie whine coiled around Luke's ears. He glanced up to see the flame of an incoming shell. Too close. Far too close.

"Get down!" He shoved Tripp. Eyes wide, the lieutenant's arms flailed as he tumbled backward several feet before toppling to the ground.

Leaping, Luke dove and covered his head with his hands.

The bomb landed on one of the battery guns. Mud and pebbles quivered against Luke's cheek. A scream of torment rent the air. Scraps of iron and flesh lashed his back.

After a few seconds, Luke raised his head. Two men lay dead, another severely injured, and the gun they'd been using was nothing but a smoking pile of sheared metal. Men swamped the scene, attending to the dead and injured. The shouts, the blasts, the pounding rain—every sound seemed to drift into the distance beneath the thumping of Luke's heart and the ringing in his ears. He shook his head.

Three yards to his right, Tripp struggled to his knees, brushing mud from his shirt. Their eyes met. Blood sliced a red line on his right sleeve. Gripping his arm, the lieutenant nodded begrudging thanks to Luke and then ambled back to his post.

❖ CHAPTER 34 ❖

Staring at the same spot she'd been looking at since the shelling began, Cassandra gripped the railing of the sloop until her knuckles whitened. Though the sun had long since set, darkness could not hide the constant bursts of orange and scarlet flaming from the British fleet, nor the arc of glittering fire that spanned the sky and exploded in showers of red-hot sparks above Fort McHenry.

Her legs ached from balancing so long on the heaving deck. Her head throbbed from the endless roar of cannons. Her throat and nose stung from the incessant smoke that filled the air. But most of all her heart broke for the lost lives of the brave soldiers at the fort.

John slipped his hand into hers. "It will be all right, miss." His comforting tone did nothing to assuage her fears.

"I don't see how."

Beside her, Mr. Key and his companions' shouts of defiance and victory had long since faded into shocked silence, broken only by groans of defeat.

It didn't help that every time it appeared that a British bomb had hit its mark, the marines guarding them shouted "huzzahs!" of victory, making Cassandra feel attacked from both front and rear.

"Egad, how much can the fort take?" Mr. Key exclaimed. "They've been firing rockets at them for nigh on twenty-three hours!"

"I didn't realize the British could house so many bombs aboard their ships," Dr. Beanes added.

The third man, Colonel Skinner, grabbed a backstay and slunk down to sit on the railing with a moan.

Cassandra took up a pace. "It is unbearable to sit idly by and watch our city, our country under attack." A blast of wind engulfed the ship in smoke. Gunpowder stung her nose. Coughing, she batted away the fumes.

"I quite agree, miss." Mr. Key propped one boot on the railing and held a handkerchief to his nose. "But we must not give up hope."

Boom boom boom caboom.

Another barrage thundered the air. Violent flames surged from the fleet, flashing a sinister glow upon the British ships before darkness swallowed them up again. Bombs riding on streams of fire sped toward the fort. Explosions, barely distinguishable from the thunder growling its displeasure from above, rocked the peninsula.

"What is to become of us?" The deck tilted, and Cassandra hugged John, drawing him close. He trembled, and she knew he was thinking of Luke. As was she. "Never fear. You know how resilient your brother is. I'm sure he is all right."

She hoped he was. Prayed he was. John said nothing.

Cassandra could not imagine living under British rule. Though her grandparents had suffered during the Revolution, and her mother was but a child during the fighting, Cassandra had been born into freedom. The freedom to elect those who would represent her in government, the freedom to speak out in defiance of injustice, the freedom to choose her own way. She sighed. Perhaps she had taken that freedom for granted too long.

Another round of rockets roared through the air. One crashed onto the ground—either near or on the fort, she couldn't tell which. The deafening explosion plunged a dagger into her heart. She hugged John tighter as Mr. Key offered her his hand. "Shall we pray for our country, Miss Channing?"

Wiping her tears, she slid her hand into his and bowed her head.

Hours later, Cassandra leaned back on a barrel one of the men had rolled over for her to sit on. John stood by her side, while Mr. Key and his friends lined the starboard railing, frozen in shock. Each bomb bursting over the fort reflected the red glow of horror on their faces. Cassandra's hope had long since given way to despair. She placed a hand on her aching back. There was no way Fort McHenry could survive such an onslaught of rockets. So many she'd lost count. Hundreds, even thousands. Yet neither the darkness nor the distance allowed them to determine how much of the fort had been destroyed.

Or how many men had lost their lives.

Fierce wind whipped around her, tearing her hair from its pins and thrashing the wet strands against her neck. She didn't have the strength to brush them away. The sloop rose over a wave. Gripping John, Cassandra clung to the barrel as she dropped her sodden shawl into her lap. She no longer noticed the chill that iced her bones.

Only the chill that penetrated her heart.

"I wonder about the land invasion," she said absently.

Mr. Key turned toward her. Lantern light oscillated over his haggard features. "I've heard no musket shot for some time."

"What if the Brits are ravaging Baltimore as we speak?" Cassandra's voice cracked. She fought back tears. What of her mother and sisters? And Marianne and Rose and poor little Jacob? What would the monsters do to them?

Approaching her, Mr. Key took her hands. "We do not know that. We must trust God and not speculate on the worst."

"I agree, Miss Channing," John said. "God is in control. Besides, Luke is in town. He won't let those nasty Brits come anywhere near his friends."

Cassandra smiled at the boy's trust. "But what can one man do?"

"One man and God can change the world, Miss Channing," Mr. Key said as another volley of cannon fire drew their gazes to a fiery glare arching over the black sky. He shifted his shoulders beneath his coat, dripping with rain. "Besides, the fact that the ships are still firing is a good sign."

"How so?"

"It means they have not taken the fort."

"Of course." Cassandra hadn't thought of that.

"It's when the bombing stops that we need to be concerned." He rubbed the back of his neck.

Cassandra peered into the thick darkness. Though the storm had subsided, a light mist settled in the air, cloaking the scene in a surreal gray mirage. Above them, the heavens revealed a sparkling serenity of stars that defied the proceedings below. Even so, the night dragged on interminably, and Cassandra began to wonder if she'd ever see the light of day again.

Another broadside from the fleet released its fury.

The ship teetered, creaking and groaning as if it were just as tired as they of the nightlong onslaught.

"Look." John pointed east. "Dawn is coming."

Cassandra lifted her chin to see a brushstroke of golden light paint the horizon.

Dr. Beanes approached the railing. "We shall know soon enough, then."

Slowly rising, her eyes locked upon where she knew the fort stood, though she still couldn't make it out.

Several minutes passed. Cannon fire punched the air. All coming from the British fleet. Silence hung over the fort. But what did that mean? Were all the Americans dead? The guns destroyed? Had the British landed and stormed through the town?

Nothing but the creak of the ship and the chuckles of marines playing cards answered Cassandra's frenzied questions.

Grabbing a halyard, Mr. Key leapt up on the bulwarks, straining to see in the distance. "Look for which flag flies above the fort. If the Union Jack, we are doomed."

Cassandra swallowed. Her breath crowded in her throat. She drew John to her and together, they focused their gazes into the darkness.

A darkness that soon transformed to gray. Shadowy objects formed in the distance. The warble of birds greeted the dawn as if no slaughter had taken place overnight.

Boom! The British ships fired again.

Cassandra's heart seized. She felt John tense beside her.

Then the sun burst over the horizon in all its glory, chasing away the darkness. All eyes peered toward the fort, whose buildings now formed before them.

Mr. Key laughed. Then he chuckled, ecstatic joy bursting in his throat. "I see her! She's sodden and limp, but yes, 'tis the stars and stripes!"

He leapt down and grabbed Cassandra's shoulders. "We've held them off!"

Stunned, Cassandra could only stare at him. The air thinned in her lungs as tears of joy filled her eyes.

Mr. Key embraced his friends.

"I told you, Miss Channing." John looked up at her and smiled.

She brushed wet strands of hair from his forehead. "Yes, you did, John. Yes, you did."

"Colonel Skinner," Mr. Key said. "Go below, if you please, and find me a pen and something to write on."

"Of course. Whatever for?"

Mr. Key gazed at the fort. "I must write about this. A poem, a song, explodes in my head, I can hardly contain it."

Within minutes, the colonel returned. "There is no pen to be found, sir. I did find this envelope, but no pen."

"No pen?" Mr. Key looked stricken.

The colonel shook his head and frowned.

"Blast it all!" Grabbing the envelope, Mr. Key spun around.

A faint remembrance jarred Cassandra. Turning her back to them, she lifted her skirt and reached into the pocket of her petticoat for the quill pen and ink jar John had given her. Amazed, she smiled at John and handed them to Mr. Key.

"Where did you get these?" he asked.

Cassandra swallowed as the realization struck her. "God provides, Mr. Key."

"Indeed, He does." He kissed her on the cheek then laid the envelope on top of the bulwarks, dipped his pen in ink, and began to write.

❖

Luke sank to his knees as the first rays of light shot over the horizon, scattering the gloom and stirring the mist hovering over the water. Wet mud seeped into his breeches. He wiped the grime and sweat from his brow with his torn sleeve as he noticed the splatters of blood on the fabric. Not his. But the blood of the injured he had carried to the infirmary. How many, he had lost count. Wind slapped strands of his hair against his cheek. He jerked them away and glanced up at the American flag hanging proudly over the fort.

They had won!

They had repelled an invasion from the greatest naval power in the world. And Luke had been a part of it. As the sun crested the horizon, he bowed his head and thanked God for the victory and the privilege.

"Luke Heaton praying?" Noah chuckled as he and Blackthorn came up on either side of him.

Struggling to his feet, Luke smiled, despite the fact that every muscle and bone in his body screamed in agony. "Miracles do happen."

Noah raised his brows. "War brings many men to their knees."

"It was long overdue." They exchanged a knowing glance.

Before Luke could stop him, Noah clutched him in a manly embrace. "I'm glad to hear it."

"An' me as well," Blackthorn growled. Removing his hat, he slapped it against his leg.

"They are sailing away!" A shout came from the tower, and one by one, the men who had sunk, exhausted, to the ground where they stood, rose to their feet and inched toward the shore.

White sails, gleaming in the sunlight, appeared on the yards of the British ships like snowy clouds. And within minutes, the ships grew smaller in size.

The fort's morning gun fired, sounding rather dull compared to the onslaught that had met Luke's ears throughout the night. Above them, men lowered the storm flag and raised the massive American ensign above the fort. A band began playing "Yankee Doodle."

Luke glanced at his friends covered in mud and ashes, their shirts and breeches torn and sopping wet. "Aren't you both a sore sight?"

Tossing his arms over both Luke's and Blackthorn's shoulders, Noah drew the trio together. "Aye, but we are alive. And God is good to give me such friends."

Uncomfortable with the emotional exchange, Luke backed away as "hip hip hurrays" trumpeted from the exhausted troops. Hats flew into the air and congratulations abounded over the shore battery.

Luke glanced at the departing British fleet. Even amid the triumph and gaiety that surrounded him, his heart collapsed in pain. What of Cassandra and John? Were they still on the HMS *Audacious,* and if so, where was the ship? He had failed to rescue them, and they were lost to him forever.

Noah laid a hand on his shoulder. The joy on his face faded to sympathy, and something else. Determination. "We'll find them."

Luke nodded, though he saw no possibility of that now. Especially if he was locked up and tried for treason. He scanned the crowd. No sign of Lieutenant Tripp. But he would have to face the man sooner or later. And be tossed in his cell once again. No less than Luke deserved. He should be grateful to God he'd been allowed to help defend his great city. To pay a small recompense for his traitorous deeds.

"What of my crew?" he asked Noah. "Were they rounded up?"

"No." His friend shook his head. "I'm told your Mr. Keene made a deal with Tripp. Only you were to be charged."

Another thing to thank God for. Though Keene's betrayal stung Luke hard.

The sun shot ribbons of golden light over the murky waters of the Patapsco River, dividing the mist like the Red Sea. Luke squinted. *Oh God, please save Cassandra and John. And, whether locked up or free, have Your will in my life.* He could hardly believe he prayed such a prayer. That he could submit his future to a distant God. No, not distant. He rubbed the scars on his hand. Always with Luke.

Blackthorn shifted his stance. "I've never seen so many shots. I thought it would never end."

"I spoke with Major Armistead." Noah tugged his muddy cravat from his neck. "Last count, near eighteen hundred bombs were fired our way. Four hundred landing within the fort."

"How many dead?" Luke was afraid to ask. "Only four." Noah blew out a sigh. "Can you believe it? Several wounded, but only four dead."

Blackthorn shook his head. The brawny man touched a wound on his forehead and winced. "It's a miracle."

"Indeed," Noah said, squinting into the rising sun. "Against such overwhelming forces, only God Almighty could have prevailed."

Shifting his boots in the mud, Luke followed Noah's gaze, though he was blinded by the light. He thought of the angel. He thought of destiny. Of freedom and God's love. And he realized that he'd been living in the darkness for far too long.

Noah gestured beyond the fort. "Let's go home, shall we?"

Luke swallowed as his old familiar friend—failure—begged entrance into his soul. "I don't know if I can."

Noah flattened his lips. "Let us find out."

They made their way around the side of the fort where Major Armistead and several of his officers stood together looking like a pack of sopping stray dogs. Yet despite their disheveled appearance, relief softened the taut lines on their faces. At the edge of the group stood Lieutenant Tripp, mud streaked over his uniform, one boot missing and the epaulette on his left shoulder hanging in tatters.

Bile churned in Luke's empty belly.

Noah swung an arm over his shoulders. "Better to face him now."

Luke knew his friend was right. He must face the consequences of his actions and allow God to decide his fate. Time to stop running. Flanked by his friends, he threw back his aching shoulders and pressed on. They halted before the officers, drawing the gaze of Major Armistead.

"Well done, men. I owe you all a debt of gratitude for coming to fight alongside my troops." The major's voice brimmed with sincere appreciation. "Have we been introduced?"

Luke studied Tripp, expecting him to draw his sword and drag Luke back to his cell, but the infernal man would not meet his gaze.

Noah cleared his throat. "No, sir. Forgive me. I am Noah Brenin, privateer." He gestured toward Blackthorn and introduced him as his first mate. Then the major turned to Luke.

"Heaton, sir. Luke Heaton." Would the major recognize his name as the traitor who had been locked in the fort's guardhouse? Lieutenant Tripp's eyes finally landed on Luke. Surely he would say something now. But the man's mud-strewn expression carried no trace of the arrogance and anger that usually simmered in it.

"Very good, Mr. Heaton." Major Armistead clasped the hilt of the sword hanging at his hip as confusion claimed his face. "Ah, Heaton. Wait a minute. That name *does* sound familiar."

❖ CHAPTER 35 ❖

Luke's gut twisted in a knot as Major Armistead's unyielding gaze fixed on him. "Yes, I have heard your name before. But where?"

The major gripped the hilt of his sword even tighter, and Luke braced himself for the inevitable arrest.

Instead, the major's eyebrows rose. "Ah yes." He dipped his head toward Tripp. "I understand you saved the lieutenant's life?"

Luke blinked. An odd look of surrender settled on Tripp's expression.

Major Armistead chuckled. "Come now, don't be modest, Mr. Heaton. The lieutenant regaled me with the tale himself."

Tripp lifted his chin. "I owe you my life, sir." He tugged Luke aside and leaned toward his ear. "Mr. Brenin told me of your brother," he whispered. "And the paperwork of your arrest seems to have disappeared in the mayhem." Then stepping back, he winked at Luke before he rejoined the group. Luke numbly followed him.

"Shall we call our accounts settled then?" Tripp cleared his throat.

Luke stared dumbfounded at the man for a moment before he nodded. Yet surely this was some cruel joke. He braced himself for the laughter that was sure to come before they hauled him away.

"And we have just received word"—Major Armistead glanced over his men with glee—"that the British advance was halted at North Point as well. So, off with you, men. Go home. Kiss your wives, your sweethearts. Your country thanks you for your service and your courage."

Luke shared a look of shock with Noah. He hesitated. They weren't going to arrest him? He was free?

Grabbing his arm, Noah dragged Luke away as the major's final words penetrated his heart. *Service and courage.* Reverend Drummond had said Luke had a destiny. But Luke had never considered it would be such an important one.

❖

Cassandra hugged herself. Morning mist hovered over the river, slipping over the sides of the small boat and swirling about her feet. John leaned his head against her shoulder and she looped an arm around him and drew him near.

"Where are they taking us?" he whispered.

She kissed the top of his head. "I don't know." Recognizing the fear icing her voice, she added in a more cheerful tone, "Perhaps home."

His shoulders loosened and he smiled.

The splash of paddles and squeak of oarlocks echoed through the fog, scraping over Cassandra's nerves. She and John had been ushered off the truce ship in such haste, they'd been unable to say good-bye to Mr. Key and his friends. A dozen terrifying possibilities crowded her thoughts. Though they'd seen the American flag over the fort, perhaps their celebration had been premature. Perhaps Baltimore had been taken by the British. Perhaps she and John were being escorted to a city she would not recognize. A town occupied by the enemy. Or worse, perhaps she and John were to be executed

For treason against the Crown.

But surely the British would have done the nefarious deed aboard their fleet? Why head into town?

And what would happen to Mr. Key, Dr. Beanes, and Colonel Skinner? Why had they not been brought along?

Cassandra rubbed her head. Too many questions. And none of them had answers that helped settle her nerves.

Sunlight angled through distant trees, chasing away the mist and revealing land up ahead. Her heart tight and her mind reeling, she hugged John tighter and lowered her head to pray.

Please protect us, Father. Please protect Baltimore and our country. And whatever Your will is, please give me the grace to accept it.

No sooner had she raised her gaze than the tiny craft struck the shore, nearly tossing her from the thwarts. Birds chirped a cheerful melody while the smell of cedar and pine wafted over her. The marines leapt into the shallow water and tugged the boat farther onto the sand.

One of them held his hand out for her, his unyielding expression offering no indication of her fate.

Staggering to her feet, she took his hand, noticing her that her own were trembling. Thankfully, John took her other hand then splashed into the water beside the marine.

Cassandra's oversized boots sank into the sand as she and John plodded onto dry land.

A splash and creak of wood turned her around. Both marines hopped back into the boat and made ready to leave.

"What is happening, sir?" she demanded.

One of them looked up as he swung the oar backward and plunged it into the water.

"You and the boy are free to go."

❖

Luke wove his way through the throng of cheerful citizens, singing and dancing in celebration of their victory. Boys dashed between adults, sticks in hands, playing mock battle. Little girls, in flurries of lace, whirled to the sound of fiddles and pianofortes chiming from taverns. Church bells rang. Men slapped each other on the back while women embraced. Luke plowed through them, unaffected by their giddiness. How could he join in the celebration when every passing moment sent Cassandra and John farther away?

Not that he wasn't grateful God had freed him from the noose. Luke rubbed his neck at the thought. *Yes, Father, more grateful than I can say.* Only newly committed to God, and already the Almighty had performed a miracle. Several this day, in fact.

But now, if Luke was to rescue Cassandra and John, he needed another one. And fast.

"What do you intend to do?" Noah caught up to him, breathless.

"I intend to go after them."

"The entire Royal fleet?" Clutching his arm, Noah spun him around. "Are you mad?"

Luke clenched his jaw. "Go home to your wife, Noah." Blackthorn had done as much as soon as they'd entered the city.

Turning down Pratt Street, Luke ducked and dove between clusters of revelry makers and passing carriages. He spotted *Destiny*'s bare masts jutting into the morning sky at the end of the long wharf and breathed a sigh of relief. She hadn't been sunk in the effort to keep the British from advancing.

Noah kept pace at his side. "Think, man. Even if you could navigate past the sunken merchant ships, what do you intend to do? Sail up to the British fleet in your small schooner and beg their leave?"

Luke ground his teeth together as he forged ahead.

Noah groaned. "Do you expect them to be in a generous mood after their humiliating defeat?"

"All the more reason why I must rescue John and Cassandra as soon as possible." Luke continued, slower this time, as he searched his mind for a solution.

Noah stopped him. "Haven't we missed your last rendezvous?"

"Yes, but what does it matter? I am sure he has no further interest in making our appointments." A gust of wind blasted over them, sending a chill through Luke's wet clothes.

"The captain knows he still holds something of extreme value to you." Noah's calm tone held a wisdom Luke envied. "Perhaps he is greedy enough to seek an exchange."

Luke huffed. He rubbed his eyes, thankful for his friend's level thinking.

"Let's go home," Noah said. "Get a good night's sleep and something warm in our bellies. Then tomorrow at dawn, we'll head out to my ship at Elizabeth City and sail to the rendezvous spot. Perhaps this Captain Raynor will show up."

Luke was about to agree when a female voice shouted Noah's name. Spinning around, Noah rushed to Marianne who held Jacob in her arms. Behind them, Miss Rose and Mr. Reed approached. Noah showered his wife and son with kisses in such a display of exuberant affection that Luke tore his gaze away at the intimacy. His eyes landed on Miss Rose. She smiled in return before gazing up at Mr. Reed. Luke could not help but see the affection that strung between them. Raking a hand through his damp hair, he approached his friends.

"We simply could not wait another minute to see you, Noah." Marianne brushed tears from her face. "I was so frightened you'd been injured. We were on our way to the fort when we saw you standing here."

She scanned him. "Are you injured?"

"No, just tired and"—he gazed down at his torn filthy attire—"and quite dirty, I'm afraid." Noah pointed toward her gown, where evidence of their embrace smudged over the cotton fabric. "I've ruined your gown."

"Do you think I care about that?" Marianne handed Jacob to Noah and fell into his arms again. The baby flung his hands up and down, giggling.

Rose stepped toward Luke. "We heard you were arrested. We were so frightened."

"Indeed," Luke said. "But God worked all that out."

"God?" Miss Rose cocked her head, studying him.

Luke nodded toward Mr. Reed. "Congratulations on your engagement."

Red blossomed on Rose's face as she slid her arm through Mr. Reed's. "Thank you. We are very blessed."

The Brit leaned down and planted a kiss on her forehead.

Though happy for his friends, Luke turned away from viewing yet more affection he would never experience. Sunlight cast a smattering of glittering diamonds over the bay. Without Cassandra, the beautiful sight seemed empty. Exhaustion tugged on him as agony weighed his heart. Noah was right. There was nothing to be done at the moment to find John and Cassandra. Nothing but pray. Yet, hadn't he proved, of all the things he could do, prayer was the most powerful?

Please help them, Lord. Bring them home to me.

Bells of jubilee rang through the streets.

An odd sensation traversed his back, as if someone was looking at him. A sensation of delightful foreboding that sent pinpricks down his spine. Shaking it off to his exhausted state, Luke turned and scanned the crowd nonetheless. Nothing unusual.

A soldier led a weary horse down the center of the street. Behind him, on the saddle perched a woman and a young boy, their faces hidden in the folds of the soldier's cloak. The man pulled his horse to a stop then reached behind to help his passengers dismount.

A crush of people passed in front of Luke, blocking his view.

His heart thrashed against his chest. Why, he couldn't say. But there was something. . .

He forged toward them, gently nudging people aside, peering through the throng, desperate, yearning, hoping.

Then he saw her.

Cassandra, hand in hand with John, craned her neck over the mob. Their eyes met. She stopped. Her chest rose and fell. A tiny smile crept over her lips.

The throng of people parted, their movements slowing. The clamor of voices and music faded, and all Luke could hear was the wild *thump thump thump* of his heart.

"Luke!" Breaking free from Cassandra, John flew into Luke's arms. Bending over, Luke swallowed him up and spun him around and around, laughing. His heart felt as though it would burst. He set the lad down. "How did you get here?"

"The British released us early this morning, and that nice soldier gave us a ride on his horse." Gripping his brother's arms, Luke shook him, if only to make sure he was real, uninjured, whole. "You look well."

"I am. Miss Channing took good care of me."

"More like the other way around." Her sweet voice eased over Luke's ears like a soothing ballad. Rising to his full height, he gazed into emerald eyes, glistening with tears.

But before he could utter a word, Marianne and Rose crowded around Cassandra, taking turns hugging her.

"You'll never believe what your mother told me." Marianne pulled away and smiled. "Apparently Mr. Crane found the money that was stolen from you. And he has returned it all!" She squeezed Cassandra's hands. "She came to tell me two days ago before the fighting began, and also to see if there was any word about you or Luke. She's been out of her mind with worry."

Cassandra exchanged a smile with Luke. "That is good news, indeed. I will go see her soon."

"John." Noah drew the boy away. "Come tell us of your adventures." He took his wife's hand, pulling her from Cassandra. Rose followed them.

But Luke hardly noticed, so mesmerized was he by the love beaming from Cassandra's face.

He took a tentative step toward her. Wind danced through her auburn hair, half-torn from her pins and hanging down her back. Her petite curves were swallowed up in an oversized pink gown that dipped too low in the front. Sunlight glistened over her skin. Muddy boots covered her feet and dark shadows curved beneath her eyes.

Luke thought she was the most beautiful woman he had ever seen.

He reached to touch her. Worried she was only a dream. Worried she would not welcome his caress, but needing to touch her anyway, needing it more than anything. He brushed a thumb over her cheek.

Leaning into his hand, she smiled. "John told me everything, Luke. I'm so sorry I doubted you."

"Sorry?" Luke snorted. "Lud, woman. I'm the one who should be sorry."

She swallowed. "You did what you had to. I should have trusted you." A tear spilled down her cheek.

Luke brushed it away. "I gave you no cause." He reached for her hand, hoping it wasn't too late to win her heart. "But if you'll give me a chance. . ."

❖

A chance? Cassandra nearly laughed. She would give anything to own the heart of this honorable, courageous man. In fact, her own heart had not ceased to dance wildly in her chest since she'd spotted him, standing by the docks: dark hair hanging in his face, open shirt flapping in the breeze over his muscled chest, the sharp cut of his stubbled jaw, his flashing blue eyes the color of the sea he loved so much, and stains of blood and dirt smudging his clothes.

Earlier today, she thought she'd never see him again. And now she knew she could never live without him.

Blood! Alarm snapped her gaze to his arm. She touched the stains on his sleeve. "Are you injured?"

He cupped his hand over hers and drew it to his lips. "No. It's not my blood. I was at the fort."

"During the bombing?" Cassandra could hardly believe anyone could survive what she had witnessed all night.

He nodded, kissing her hand. Warmth spread up her arm. He entwined his fingers with hers and stared at her, caressing her with his eyes, drinking her in as if she were a deep pool after crossing a desert.

Flustered and overjoyed at his perusal, she lowered her gaze. "Thank God you weren't kill—"

His lips touched hers. Moist, warm, gently caressing. He drew her close. Pressed her against him. She felt the heat through his damp clothes. A tempest swirled in her belly, a pleasurable tempest she hoped never to dissipate. Then he withdrew slightly and leaned toward her ear. "Marry me, Cassandra." His whispered breath caressed her neck, sending shivers down her back. Delightful, glorious shivers.

Air escaped her lungs. She couldn't speak. Couldn't move. Didn't want this moment to end. But then he backed away. A breeze filled the space between them. She wanted him back. Wanted to dwell in his arms.

But uncertainty clouded his face.

"Marry the town rogue?" She gave him a coy smile, hoping to brighten his mood. "Surely, you jest."

Lowering his chin, he stepped back. "Forgive my presump—"

She placed a finger on his lips. "Yes."

A devilish glint sparked in his eyes. "Yes, you'll forgive my presumptuous behavior?"

"No, you fool. Yes, I will marry you."

One side of his lips cocked in that beguiling grin of his, before he hoisted her into his arms and flung her around. Their laughter mingled in the air above them.

Soon, clinging to Luke's arm, Cassandra led him to their friends. As they approached, wide grins and knowing looks met them as congratulations were passed all around. John could hardly contain his glee.

Another boom of victory sounded from the fort, drawing Cassandra's gaze. Throwing one arm around her and his other around John, Luke drew them both close. Overcome with thankfulness at what God had done, Cassandra glanced at her friends: Marianne and Noah stood arm in arm, Jacob perched on Noah's shoulders; Rose leaned back on Mr. Reed's chest, his hands folded protectively in front of her.

All of them gazed with pride at the massive flag flapping in the wind over Fort McHenry.

"God had a great destiny for us all in this war," Marianne said.

"Destiny and love," Rose added, exchanging a glance with Mr. Reed.

Cassandra gazed up at Luke then lifted her face to the light of the sun. "He did indeed. And I don't think He's done with us yet."

❖ HISTORICAL NOTE ❖

At noon on September 11, 1814, the British fleet sailed to the mouth of the Patapsco River and anchored off North Point, just fourteen miles from Baltimore. Arrogantly spurred on by their successful march into Washington, DC, three weeks earlier, the British planned to attack the "Nest of Pirates," as they called the city, from both land and sea. Early in the morning on September 13, while British troops advanced on land from North Point toward Baltimore, five bomb ships and several other warships maneuvered into a semicircle two miles from Fort McHenry. Just after dawn, the bombing commenced.

Major Armistead, commander of the fort, would later estimate that in the next twenty-five hours, the British would hurl between 1,500 and 1,800 exploding shells at them. A few never hit their mark, but most exploded directly over the fort, showering destruction on the defenders. One bomb exploded on the southwest bastion, destroying a twenty-four-pounder, killing Lieutenant Levi Claggett, and wounding several men. Soon after, another shell crashed through the roof of the gunpowder magazine. By the grace of God, it did not ignite. Major Armistead soon ordered the barrels of powder removed and stored elsewhere.

While the British land invasion was failing due to the courage and preparation of Baltimore's militia, the bombardment of Fort McHenry continued throughout the long night. Finally at 7:00 a.m. on September

14, the shelling ceased, and the British fleet withdrew. Major Armistead immediately brought down the dripping storm flag that flew over the fort and hoisted in its place the forty-two-by-thirty-foot flag sewn by Mary Pickersgill, the action accompanied by the fort's band playing "Yankee Doodle."

Eight miles away, aboard an American truce ship, Sir Francis Scott Key, overcome with emotion at the sight of the flag, penned what would become our national anthem, "The Star-Spangled Banner." Miraculously, Baltimore successfully defended itself against an attack by the greatest military and naval power on earth. The humiliating defeat suffered by the British changed the course of the war, and three months later, on Christmas Eve, Britain made peace with the United States at Ghent. In Baltimore, the *Niles Weekly Register* announced the news with the headline: "Long live the Republic! All hail! Last asylum of oppressed humanity!"

May it ever be so!

"The Star-Spangled Banner" Lyrics
By Francis Scott Key 1814

Oh, say can you see by the dawn's early light
 What so proudly we hailed at the twilight's last gleaming?
Whose broad stripes and bright stars through the perilous fight,
 O'er the ramparts we watched were so gallantly streaming?
And the rockets' red glare, the bombs bursting in air,
 Gave proof through the night that our flag was still there.
Oh, say does that star-spangled banner yet wave
 O'er the land of the free and the home of the brave?

On the shore, dimly seen through the mists of the deep,
 Where the foe's haughty host in dread silence reposes,
What is that which the breeze, o'er the towering steep,
 As it fitfully blows, half conceals, half discloses?
Now it catches the gleam of the morning's first beam,
 In full glory reflected now shines in the stream:
'Tis the star-spangled banner! Oh long may it wave
 O'er the land of the free and the home of the brave!

And where is that band who so vauntingly swore
 That the havoc of war and the battle's confusion,
A home and a country should leave us no more!
 Their blood has washed out their foul footsteps' pollution.
No refuge could save the hireling and slave
 From the terror of flight, or the gloom of the grave:
And the star-spangled banner in triumph doth wave
 O'er the land of the free and the home of the brave!

Oh! thus be it ever, when freemen shall stand
 Between their loved home and the war's desolation!
Blest with victory and peace, may the heav'n rescued land
 Praise the Power that hath made and preserved us a nation.
Then conquer we must, when our cause it is just,
 And this be our motto: "In God is our trust."
And the star-spangled banner in triumph shall wave
 O'er the land of the free and the home of the brave!

Dexter

ABOUT THE AUTHOR

MaryLu Tyndall

MaryLu Tyndall, a Christy Award finalist and bestselling author of the Legacy of the King's Pirates series, is known for her adventurous historical romances filled with deep spiritual themes. She holds a degree in math and worked as a software engineer for fifteen years before testing the waters as a writer. MaryLu currently writes full time and makes her home on the California coast with her husband, six kids, and four cats. Her passion is to write page-turning, romantic adventures that not only entertain but open people's eyes to their God-given potential. MaryLu is a member of American Christian Fiction Writers and Romance Writers of America.